To be made w... ...
the Palo Duro... ...
head and be willing to share his loot with the
mayor. If he did, he would be safe from the law.
By arrangement with their chief, the
Kweharehnuh Comanches protected Hell and
kept away unwanted visitors.

Being determined to wipe out the outlaws'
stronghold, but wishing to avoid starting an
Indian war, the Governor of Texas asked a
friend for help. So Ole Devil Hardin's floating
outfit set off on another dangerous assignment.
Not only did Dusty Fog, the Ysabel Kid and
Waco have to get by the Kweharehnuh, they had
to try to stay alive once they reached the town
called Hell.

Also available from Corgi Books

J.T. EDSON OMNIBUS 1
J.T. EDSON OMNIBUS 2
J.T. EDSON OMNIBUS 3
J.T. EDSON OMNIBUS 4
J.T. EDSON OMNIBUS 5
J.T. EDSON OMNIBUS 6
J.T. EDSON OMNIBUS 7
J.T. EDSON OMNIBUS 8
J.T. EDSON OMNIBUS 9
J.T. EDSON OMNIBUS 10
J.T. EDSON OMNIBUS 12

Revised list of J.T. EDSON titles in chronological and categorical sequence:

Ole Devil Hardin series

YOUNG OLE DEVIL
OLE DEVIL AND THE CAPLOCKS
OLE DEVIL AND THE MULE TRAIN
OLE DEVIL AT SAN JACINTO
GET URREA

The Civil War Series

COMANCHE
THE START OF THE LEGEND }*
How Belle Boyd Became The Rebel Spy
YOU'RE IN COMMAND NOW, MR. FOG
THE BIG GUN
UNDER THE STARS AND BARS
THE FASTEST GUN IN TEXAS
A MATTER OF HONOUR
KILL DUSTY FOG!
THE DEVIL GUN
THE COLT AND THE SABRE
THE REBEL SPY
THE BLOODY BORDER
BACK TO THE BLOODY BORDER

The Floating Outfit series

THE YSABEL KID
.44 CALIBRE MAN
A HORSE CALLED MOGOLLON
GOODNIGHT'S DREAM
FROM HIDE AND HORN
SET TEXAS BACK ON HER FEET
THE HIDE AND TALLOW MEN
THE HOODED RIDERS
QUIET TOWN
TRAIL BOSS
WAGONS TO BACKSIGHT
TROUBLED RANGE
SIDEWINDER
RANGELAND HERCULES
McGRAW'S INHERITANCE
THE HALF BREED
WHITE INDIANS
THE WILDCATS
THE BAD BUNCH
THE FAST GUN
CUCHILO
A TOWN CALLED YELLOWDOG
TRIGGER FAST
THE MAKING OF A LAWMAN
THE TROUBLE BUSTERS
DECISION FOR DUSTY FOG
DIAMONDS, EMERALDS, CARDS AND COLTS
THE CODE OF DUSTY FOG
THE GENTLE GIANT
SET A-FOOT
THE LAW OF THE GUN
THE PEACEMAKERS
TO ARMS! TO ARMS! IN DIXIE
HELL IN THE PALO DURO
GO BACK TO HELL
THE SOUTH WILL RISE AGAIN
THE QUEST FOR BOWIE'S BLADE
BEGUINAGE
BEGUINAGE IS DEAD
MASTER OF TRIGGERNOMETRY
THE RUSHERS
BUFFALO ARE COMING
THE FORTUNE HUNTERS
RIO GUNS
GUN WIZARD
THE TEXAN
OLD MOCCASINS ON THE TRAIL
MARK COUNTER'S KIN
THE RIO HONDO KID
OLE DEVIL'S HANDS AND FEET
WACO'S DEBT

The Floating Outfit series cont'd

THE HARD RIDERS
THE FLOATING OUTFIT
APACHE RAMPAGE
THE RIO HONDO WAR
THE MAN FROM TEXAS
GUNSMOKE THUNDER
THE SMALL TEXAN
THE TOWN TAMERS
RETURN TO BACKSIGHT
TERROR VALLEY
GUNS IN THE NIGHT

Waco series

WACO'S BADGE
SAGEBRUSH SLEUTH
ARIZONA RANGER
WACO RIDES IN
THE DRIFTER
DOC LEROY, M.D.
HOUND DOG MAN

Calamity Jane series

CALAMITY, MARK AND BELLE
COLD DECK, HOT LEAD
THE BULL WHIP BREED
TROUBLE TRAIL
THE COW THIEVES
THE HIDE AND HORN SALOON
CUT ONE, THEY ALL BLEED
CALAMITY SPELLS TROUBLE
WHITE STALLION, RED MARE
THE REMITTANCE KID
THE WHIP AND THE WAR LANCE
THE BIG HUNT

Waxahachie Smith series

NO FINGER ON THE TRIGGER
SLIP GUN
CURE THE TEXAS FEVER*

Alvin Dustine 'Cap' Fog series

YOU'RE A TEXAS RANGER, ALVIN FOG
RAPIDO CLINT
THE JUSTICE OF COMPANY 'Z'
'CAP' FOG, TEXAS RANGER, MEET MR. J.G. REEDER
THE RETURN OF RAPIDO CLINT AND MR. J.G. REEDER

The Rockabye County series

THE SIXTEEN DOLLAR SHOOTER
THE LAWMEN OF ROCKABYE COUNTY
THE SHERIFF OF ROCKABYE COUNTY
THE PROFESSIONAL KILLERS
THE ¼ SECOND DRAW
THE DEPUTIES
POINT OF CONTACT
THE OWLHOOT
RUN FOR THE BORDER
BAD HOMBRE

Bunduki series

BUNDUKI
BUNDUKI AND DAWN
SACRIFICE FOR THE QUAGGA GOD
FEARLESS MASTER OF THE JUNGLE

Miscellaneous titles

J.T.'S HUNDREDTH
J.T.'S LADIES
J.T.'S LADIES RIDE AGAIN
MORE J.T.'S LADIES
IS-A-MAN

WANTED! BELLE STARR
SLAUGHTER'S WAY
TWO MILES TO THE BORDER
BLONDE GENIUS (*Written in collaboration with Peter Clawson*)

**Title awaiting publication*

J.T. EDSON OMNIBUS
Volume 11

HELL IN THE PALO DURO
GO BACK TO HELL
THE SOUTH WILL RISE AGAIN

CORGI BOOKS

J.T. EDSON OMNIBUS VOLUME 11
A CORGI BOOK 0 552 13865 7

HELL IN THE PALO DURO, GO BACK TO HELL and
THE SOUTH WILL RISE AGAIN originally published in
Great Britain by Corgi Books, a division of Transworld
Publishers Ltd

PRINTING HISTORY – HELL IN THE PALO DURO
Corgi edition published 1971
Corgi edition reprinted 1975

PRINTING HISTORY – GO BACK TO HELL
Corgi edition published 1972
Corgi edition reprinted 1978

PRINTING HISTORY – THE SOUTH WILL RISE AGAIN
Corgi edition published 1972
Corgi edition reprinted 1978

Corgi Omnibus edition published 1992

HELL IN THE PALO DURO Copyright © J.T. Edson 1971
GO BACK TO HELL Copyright © J.T. Edson 1972
THE SOUTH WILL RISE AGAIN Copyright © J.T. Edson 1972

The right of J.T. Edson to be identified as the author of this work
has been asserted in accordance with sections 77 and 78 of the
Copyright Designs and Patents Act 1988.

Conditions of sale
1. This book is sold subject to the condition that it shall not, by
way of trade *or otherwise*, be lent, re-sold, hired out or otherwise
circulated in any form of binding or cover other than that in which
it is published *and without a similar condition including this
condition being imposed on the subsequent purchaser.*

2. This book is sold subject to the Standard Conditions of Sale of
Net Books and may not be re-sold in the UK below the net price
fixed by the publishers for the book.

Corgi Books are published by Transworld Publishers Ltd.,
61–63 Uxbridge Road, Ealing, London W5 5SA, in Australia by
Transworld Publishers (Australia) Pty. Ltd., 15–23 Helles
Avenue, Moorebank, NSW 2170, and in New Zealand by
Transworld Publishers (N.Z.) Ltd., 3 William Pickering Drive,
Albany, Auckland.

Printed and bound in Great Britain by
Cox & Wyman Ltd., Reading, Berks.

HELL IN THE PALO DURO

For everybody who attended the 1970 Corgi Books Salesman of the Year dinner. In the sincere hope that your hangovers were as bad as mine.

CHAPTER ONE

DON'T COME AFTER ME

THE Ysabel Kid, Waco and Sheriff Ian Laurie agreed that there were several puzzling aspects about the way in which the Glover gang had been acting since robbing the bank in Wichita Falls.

It was not so much the fact that Andy Glover had quit his normal hunting grounds in Eastern Texas. Having received orders from Governor Stanton Howard, the Texas Rangers had launched a vigorous campaign to stamp out the lawlessness which was flourishing in the Lone Star State. Naturally the owlhoots in the more civilized eastern counties were the first to feel the pressure.

Nor was there too much of a surprise in discovering that, having brought off a successful robbery for the loss of one man, the gang did not cover the twenty or so miles to the Red River to cross into the Indian Nations. Working in conjunction with the Texas Rangers, the Army and U.S. marshals planned to run out the outlaws who had settled in that territory.

Having learned of that policy, which had not been kept a secret, Andy Glover might have decided that Indian Nations no longer afforded a safe refuge. Yet, on the face of it, neither did the route he and his men had been following for the past three days.

During the gang's flight from Wichita Falls, the Kid had shot and wounded one of them. Questioned about his companions' destination, the dying outlaw had replied to the effect that they were going to hell in the Palo Duro. He had died before he could clarify the statement. At first, the sheriff of Wichita County had regarded the words as a lie designed to send his posse off in the wrong direction, or the deranged utterings of a man in mortal pain. All the evidence now pointed to Billy Robinson having told the truth.

There had been some debate on the first afternoon of the hunt about whether the posse should make camp on the gang's trail at sun-down, or head for the Red River and search out Glover's crossing point in the morning. Accepting the Ysabel Kid's suggestion, Laurie had decided to make camp. It had proved to be the correct decision.

Soon after moving off the next morning, the posse had found that the gang's tracks veered sharply to the west. Using the old cavalry technique of riding for an hour at a fast trot, then halting, removing the saddles and allowing the horses to roll, graze and relax for fifteen minutes, they were able to make better time than the outlaws. Slowly, but surely, they were closing the distance between them and the Glover gang.

Continuing the process of riding and halting until some of the horses were too tired to roll, the posse had reached the Pease River about twenty miles above its junction with the Red by nightfall. They had been in the vicinity of the Box V ranch house and Laurie had sent men in search of information and fresh horses to keep up their rapid pace.

The gang had swung well clear of the ranch, but returned to the river and kept going upstream. On reaching the point where the North Pease – as it had become – swung sharply to the south-west, the gang had gone north.

Making good time, the posse had tracked their quarry across what would one day become Hall and Briscoe Counties to the Red River's Prairie Dog Town Fork. On crossing over, they had discovered that the gang had once more headed west. That appeared to rule out the possibility of Glover returning to the Indian Nations after having laid a long, false trail. It could also mean that he had selected his route in the hope of bluffing the posse into turning back.

On coming to the junction of the Swisher Creek and the Prairie Dog Town Fork, Laurie had once more sought information and fresh mounts. Each had been found at Dan Torrant's Lazy T ranch. According to Torrant, there had been no sign of the outlaws near his house. However, one of his men had claimed to have seen signal smoke to the west. Torrant was of the opinion that the gang would turn back once they had become aware of it.

Sheriff Laurie had faced a difficult decision. Although he wanted to take back the gang and its loot, he felt himself responsible for the lives of his posse. In addition to the Ysabel Kid and Waco, he had along his brash, hot-headed young deputy, Eric Narrow, and four citizens. Skilled fighting men, the latter quartet each had a family in Wichita Falls. So Laurie had wondered if he was justified in taking them into the Palo Duro country.

While the other Comanche bands had made peace a few years earlier, due in some part to the Ysabel Kid's efforts,* the *Kweharehnuh*, Antelope, band had refused to do so. Returning to the wild, virtually unexplored canyons, draws and hillocks of the Tule and Palo Duro country, they had continued to live in the traditional *Nemenuh*† manner and were known strenuously to resent trespass on their domain.

After long, deep thought, Laurie had concluded that Glover knew he was being hunted and intended to bluff them into quitting. Believing that the gang would turn away before reaching the area from which the signal smoke had been seen, he had told the Kid to keep following their tracks.

Now the sheriff wondered if he had guessed wrongly.

Instead of turning away, the gang's trail had led the posse straight towards the location of the smoke. Then the Kid had made an interesting – and puzzling – discovery. A man had met Glover's party. Telling the sheriff to let the horses rest, the Kid had back-tracked the newcomer. Returning thirty minutes later, the Kid had said the man had sent up the smoke signal from the top of a hill which offered an excellent view of the surrounding terrain. He had also claimed that the man walked like an Indian, but rode a shod horse; hinting at mixed blood. Whoever he might be, he had accompanied the gang westward after the meeting.

Much to Deputy Narrow's undisguised annoyance, Laurie had consulted the Kid on what the posse ought to do next. They had closed the distance separating them from the gang to slightly over a mile. Given reasonable luck, they would catch up and capture the outlaws during the night. Against that was the danger of coming across a *Kweharehnuh* hunt-

* Told in *Sidewinder*.
†*Nemenuh*: 'The People', the Comanches' name for their nation.

ing party. If it should happen, the Kid believed that he could avert trouble and might even be granted permission to keep going after the gang.

On Laurie putting the situation to the posse, they had agreed to stay with him. Apart from Narrow, they had faith in the judgment of the Ysabel Kid. Possibly the deputy shared it, but he had no intention of letting it be known. To someone who did not know the facts, that faith might have seemed strange, or even misplaced.

Around six foot in height, the Kid had a wiry frame suggestive of untiring and whipcord-tough strength. Every item of his clothing, from the low-crowned, wide-brimmed J.B. Stetson hat, through bandana, vest, shirt, Levi's pants to the flat-heeled boots, was black in colour. On a gunbelt of the same sober hue, he carried a walnut-handled Dragoon Colt butt forward in a low cavaltry-twist holster at the right and an ivory-hilted James Black bowie knife sheathed at the left. Across the crook of his left arm, encased in a fringed buckskin pouch of Indian manufacture, rested a Winchester Model '66 rifle.

The armament appeared out of keeping, taken with the handsome, almost babyishly-innocent aspect of his Indian-dark face. Or might if one discounted his red-hazel eyes. They implied that a savage, untrammelled wildness lay behind the black-haired Texan's youthful exterior.

Slouching apparently at ease on a horse borrowed from the Lazy T, with his magnificent white stallion – which looked as untamed as its master – loping bare-backed at his side, he exuded a sense of being more Indian than white. People who knew him were aware of how close that came to being true.

Although his mother had died giving birth to him, Loncey Dalton Ysabel had survived to be raised as a member of the *Pehnane* – Wasp, Quick-Stinger, Raider – Comanches. His maternal grandfather, Long Walker, was war chief of the Dog Soldier lodge. From that source, his father – an Irish Kentuckian called Sam Ysabel – being away much of the time on the family's business of smuggling, the child had learned all the subjects a brave-heart warrior was expected to know.*

* Told in *Comanche*.

By his fourteenth year, when he had ridden off on his first war trail, the boy had already gained the man-name *Cuchilo* by virtue of his skill in using a bowie knife. To the Mexicans along the Rio Grande, where he had helped his father on contraband-running expeditions, he became known as *Cabrito*, the Kid. The Texans with whom he had come into contact called him first Sam Ysabel's Kid, then changed it to the Ysabel Kid. Members of all three races were unanimous in their opinion that he would become a fighting man second to none and he had fulfilled the predictions. Maybe he was not *real* fast with his old Dragoon, but he could claim few peers when it came to accuracy in using a rifle.

At the outbreak of the War Between The States, the Kid and his father had joined Mosby's Raiders. The Confederate States' Government had soon found an even more useful purpose in which their specialized talents could serve the South. So they had spent the remainder of the hostilities collecting shipments of essential materials from Matamoros and delivering the goods across the Rio Grande to the authorities in Texas. Whilst doing so, the Kid had increased his reputation of being a bad man to cross.

Bushwhack lead had cut down Sam Ysabel soon after the War had ended. While searching for his father's killers, the Kid had met a man who changed the whole course of his life. The Rio Hondo gun wizard, Dusty Fog, had been conducting a mission on which the peace between the United States and Mexico hung balanced and the Kid had helped him bring it to a successful conclusion.* At the same time, the Kid had also avenged his father's murder. That had left him with the problem of what to do next. Smuggling was unprofitable in the War-impoverished Lone Star State and, without his father along, it had no longer appealed to him. So he had accepted Dusty Fog's offer and joined the OD Connected ranch's floating outfit.

In that way, a potentially dangerous young man had been transformed into a useful member of the community. The people of Texas could be grateful that he had. His Comanche-trained skills – silent movement, locating hidden enemies and remaining concealed from keen-eyed searchers,

* Told in *The Ysabel Kid*.

how to follow a track or hide his own trail, exceptional ability with a variety of weapons and at horse-handling – would have made him a formidable outlaw with no exaggerated notions about the sanctity of human life. However, since joining the elite of General Ole Devil Hardin's ranch crew, he had used his talents solely for the cause of law and order.

On resuming the hunt, the Kid had told Waco to handle the tracking. Instead of studying the marks on the ground, the Kid concentrated his efforts on scouring the terrain ahead. Having seen the youngster, whose only name was Waco, read sign during the hunt, Laurie raised no objections. The sheriff knew that the Kid was acting in a correct manner and was better occupied in locating an ambush should one be attempted.

Maybe two inches taller than the Kid, Waco had a spread to his shoulders that hinted at a powerful frame fast developing to full manhood. In dress and appearance, he was a typical Texas cowhand. Blond, blue-eyed and handsome, he wore two staghorn-butted 1860 Army Colts in the carefully-designed holsters of a well-made gunbelt. He too sat a borrowed horse and led his big, powerful paint stallion. A Winchester Model of 1873 rifle dangled from his right hand.

Like the Kid, Waco had once teetered on the verge of the owlhoot trail. Where smuggling might have brought the Indian-dark young man into conflict with the law, Waco could easily have turned into a wanted, desperate killer.

Left an orphan almost from birth by a Waco Indian raid, the blond youngster had been raised as part of a North Texas rancher's sizeable family. Guns had always been a part of his life and his sixteenth birthday had seen him employed by Clay Allison. In that tough wild-onion crew, noted for their boisterous ways and generally dangerous behaviour, Waco had perfected his ability to draw fast and shoot accurately. Living constantly in the company of older men, he had grown sullen, quick to temper and ever ready to take offence. It had seemed only a matter of time before he would become involved in that one shoot-out too many which would have seen him branded as a killer, with a price on his head.

Fortunately for Waco, that day did not come. From the

moment that Dusty Fog had saved his life – at considerable risk to his own– the youngster had started to change for the better.* Leaving Allison, with the Washita curly-wolf's blessing, he had found himself accepted as a member of the floating outfit. From the other members, who treated him like a favourite younger brother, he had learned many useful lessons. His skill in handling revolvers had not diminished, but he now knew *when* as well as *how* to shoot.

Six miles had fallen behind the posse since the Kid had relinquished his post as tracker. Suddenly he brought his horses to a halt.

'Stay put, boy!' he ordered as Waco's head swung in his direction.

'Yo!' the youngster answered.

'Hold it back there, sheriff,' the Kid went on, looking over his shoulder. 'I'm going to make some talk to them *Kweharehnuh* bucks up ahead.'

'*Kweh*—!' Laurie began, motioning to Narrow and the townsmen to stop and advancing to join the cowhands. 'I don't see 'em!'

'They're there,' the Kid assured him. 'So stay put. No matter what happens don't start shooting and don't come after me.'

'We won't,' promised Laurie.

'That goes for you more than any of them, boy,' the Kid said, eyeing his companion coldly.

'I hear you,' Waco drawled.

'Mind you do it then!' growled the Kid.

'You'd reckon he didn't trust me to do it,' Waco commented to the tall wiry peace officer, as the Kid transferred to the white stallion's bare back without setting foot on the ground.

'Maybe he knows you,' Laurie replied.

'I'll fix his wagon,' threatened the young blond, without denying the allegation. 'When we get down to home, I'll lay all the blame on him for us being late back.'

On their way home after a successful and profitable trail drive to Mulrooney, Kansas, the floating outfit had called at Bent's Ford in the Indian Nations. Dusty had found a telegraph message from Ole Devil awaiting his arrival, telling

* Told in *Trigger Fast*.

him to call and see the Governor of Texas at Austin. Doing so had created something of a problem. Part of the trail herd had belonged to a friend who ranched near Throckmorton and had been unable to make the drive. After some discussion, it had been decided that the Kid should deliver the friend's share of the money brought in by the cattle.

Sharing the Indian-dark cowhand's aversion to wearing formal clothes and a neck-tie – which would most likely be expected of him when visiting the Governor – Waco had volunteered to accompany the Kid. They had been in Wichita Falls during the bank robbery and offered their services to the sheriff. Before setting out with the posse, the Kid had notified Dusty of their actions by telegraph. Neither of them felt any qualms at turning aside from their duty, knowing that Dusty and Ole Devil would approve of them doing so under the circumstances.

'What's up, Ian?' Narrow demanded as he and the four townsmen gathered around the sheriff.

'The Kid's seen some *Kweharehnuh* and's going to talk to them,' Laurie replied. 'Keep your rifles on your saddles and don't nobody shoot unless I give you the word.'

A low rumbled mutter of surprise rose from the men. They all tried, without success, to locate the Indians which the Kid had claimed he was going to interview. Ahead, the range was little different to the kind of terrain through which they had travelled all day. Rolling, broken by folds, mounds and draws, it hardly seemed capable of offering hiding places for a large body of men. Apart from the solitary, black-clad figure on the huge white stallion, there was no sign of human life in front of them. As usual, Narrow was inclined to scoff.

'They must be a hell of a long ways off,' the deputy declared. 'I can't see hide nor hair of them.'

'Which's likely why the sheriff had Lon and not you riding the point,' drawled Waco.

Although Narrow let out a hiss of annoyance, he made no reply. Early in the hunt, he had found out that his assumption of tough superiority did not impress Waco. So he sat back in his saddle and watched the Kid with an air of disbelief. At the moment, Narrow found himself torn between two desires. While he looked forward to a fight with the

Indians, he also hoped the Kid would prove to be wrong. Then the sheriff would stop listening to the cowhand and pay more attention to his deputy's opinions.

'Reckon he's joshing us about them *Kweharehnuh*, Waco?' asked a posseman called Bretton.

'He wouldn't know how at a time like this,' the young blond replied.

With each sequence of hoof-beats in the stallion's walking gait carrying him deeper into danger, the Kid maintained his ceaseless vigilance. Detecting the whole of the Antelope party might spell the difference between life and death. So, although he slouched casually as if a part of the horse, he had never been more alert.

Give them their full due, the *Kweharehnuh* braves sure knew how to keep out of a man's sight. Like the Kid, they must have taken seriously their childhood games of *nanip'ka*, 'guess over the hill', in which the players had to hide so that the one who was 'it' could not locate them. It offered mighty good training in concealment as well as for the discovery of hidden men.

That is, all but one of them remembered the lessons of *nanip'ka*.

Flattened on a slope behind a fair-sized rock, the solitary transgressor had allowed the single eagle's feather of his head-dress to rise into view. He must be a *tuivitsi** fresh from horse-herding and on his first man's chore. Happen he did not improve his technique, he would never make a *tehnap*,† much less reach the honoured state of *tsukup*.‡ The feather's movement in the breeze had been sufficient to attract the Kid's attention and so spoiled what would have been an effective ambush.

The nearer the Kid rode, the more uneasy he became. So far, he had picked out twenty braves and feared that there might be others still hidden from him. A gentle touch on the reins of the stallion's hackmore ended its forward motion about sixty yards from the nearest located Indian. That ought to leave him sufficient distance to turn and get the hell back to the posse happen things should go wrong.

---

* *Tuivitsi*: an adolescent youth.
† *Tehnap*: an experienced warrior.
‡ *Tsukup*: old man.

Gripping the rifle at the wrist of the butt and end of the barrel, he elevated it above his head. That allowed the *Kweharehnuh* to see the red, white and blue patterns on the buckskin container. With such a well-planned ambush, there must be a *tehnap* present who would be able to identify the medicine symbols. If so, they would know the container to be a Dog Soldier's medicine boot; given to each member of that hardy, savage lodge on his initiation.

Three times the Kid raised and lowered the rifle. Then, taking his right hand from the butt, he turned the rifle so it pointed forward with the barrel still in his left fist. After that, it was just a matter of waiting. He had let them see the medicine boot and made a sign identifying himself as a Dog Soldier who asked to make talk. That put the play into the *Kweharehnuh's* hands. The next move must come from them.

It came!

Rearing to kneel on the rock, the *tuivitsi* who had betrayed the ambush flipped the butt of his rifle to his shoulder and pressed its trigger.

CHAPTER TWO

YOU'RE NOT ABOUT TO BE COMING BACK

'THEY'RE attacking him!' screeched Bretton as the young *Kweharehnuh* brave appeared and fired in the Kid's direction.

'Come on!' Narrow shouted, starting his horse moving. 'Let's go—!'

Remembering the Kid's orders and seeing that his *amigo* had not been hit, Waco jumped his horses to swing into the other men's path.

'Stay put!' the youngster snapped and the foregrip of his Winchester slapped into his left palm as he prepared to enforce the demand should it become necessary. 'Lon's all right and he's not high-tailing it back here.'

'Do like Waco says!' the sheriff commanded. 'Form a line, just in case, but hold your fire unless I tell you different.'

When the bullet flung up dirt less than a yard in front of his horse, the Kid uttered a silent prayer that the posse would not attempt to intervene. He stiffened just a trifle, alert to pivot the stallion around and go like a bat out of hell should the need become apparent. So far, only the *tuivitsi* had thrown lead. Other *Kweharehnuh* came popping out of their hiding places, many of which hardly appeared to offer enough cover to conceal a jack-rabbit. However, they made no hostile gestures.

With a sensation of relief, the Kid noticed that a few obvious *tehnap* and a war bonnet chief were present. The latter barked an order for the *tuivitsi* to refrain from further shooting. That indicated a willingness to talk. On the other hand, to add to the Kid's concern, he observed that every man – even the youngest *tuivitsi* – carried a rifle.

And not just *a* rifle!

The weapons they held were all *repeaters*!

Looking closer, the Kid saw the big side-hammers and distinctive trigger-guards of Spencer carbines. In addition to brass-framed Winchester Model of 1866 'yellow boys', there were a few all-steel Model '73's. What was more, from the raw *tuivitsi* to the war bonnet chief, each warrior had at least one belt with bullet-loaded loops on his person.

'Who are you, white man?' called the chief in the quick-tongued dialect of the *Kweharehnuh*. 'You wear the clothes of a ride-plenty, but signal that you are a *Pehnane* Dog Soldier.'

'My name is *Cuchilo*, the Knife,' replied the Kid, using the slower-spoken *Pehnane* accent fluently. 'My grandfather is Long Walker. I come to make peace talk with my *Kweharehnuh* brothers.'

'I have heard of Long Walker, and of *Cuchilo*,' the chief admitted as the Kid rode up to him. 'But it is said that you are now a white man. And all men know that Long Walker eats the beef on the reservation.'

'Long Walker has made peace with the white men, as did chiefs of other bands,' answered the Kid, watching the braves coming closer to hear what might be said. 'Just as I now live with them. But if any man doubts that I am still one of the *Nemenuh*—'

While addressing the chief, the Kid had eased the boot from his rifle and draped it across the stallion's neck. Giving no hint of what he planned to do, he let the one-piece reins fall, swung his left leg forward and up, jumping to the ground on the horse's Indian side.* As he landed, he snapped the Winchester to his shoulder. Now his left hand held the foregrip, while the right inserted its forefinger into the triggerguard and curled the other three through the ring of the lever. Almost as soon as his feet touched the ground, he had the sights laid. Three times in a second and a half, blurring the lever through its reloading cycle, he sent .44 calibre bullets spinning from the muzzle.

Once again Waco displayed his quick grasp of the situation. Realizing from the Kid's apparently passive acceptance that the *tuivitsi's* shot had been no more than a test of courage, the blond cowhand had been waiting for his

* Unlike the white man, the Indian mounted and dismounted on the right side.

amigo's response. Knowing him, Waco had expected the answer to the challenge to be something sudden and dramatic.

'Keep the guns down!' Waco warned, even before the Kid's Winchester had started to crack. 'He's all right.'

Shock twisted at the *tuivitsi's* face as he realized that the black-dressed ride-plenty, cowhand, was lining a rifle at him. Before he could make a move to counter the threat, bullets started slamming between his spread-apart knees and spattering his bare legs with flying chips of rock. Letting out a startled yelp, he bounded into the air. Coming down, he slipped from his perch and landed rump-first on the ground. Although the descent and arrival proved painful, he retained his grip on the Spencer carbine. Spitting out furious words, he tried to raise it and avenge his deflated ego.

Having expected such a reaction, the Kid was already bounding forward. Giving the *tuivitsi* no opportunity to point the Spencer his way, he lashed up with his left foot and kicked it from the other's hands. In a continuation of the attack, the Kid elevated his Winchester and propelled its metal-shod butt against the side of the brave's head. Down went the *tuivitsi*, flopping limply on to his side. Without sparing his victim as much as a glance, the Kid returned and vaulted afork the stallion's seventeen hand back as if it stood no higher than a newly born foal.

Hoots of laughter burst from the stocky, thick-bodied warriors in the antelope-hide clothing. Like most Indians, the Comanches had a lively sense of humour when amongst their own kind. They had appreciated the manner in which the Kid had handled their companion. That had been the way of a *tehnap* dealing with a *tuivitsi* who had forgotten his proper station in the band's social structure. Fast, painful and very effective.

No matter how the Kid might be dressed, the *Kwehareh-nuh* braves now accepted that he was a Comanche. Every action he had made since being fired at by the *tuivitsi* had been that of an experienced name-warrior.

'Well, chief,' challenged the Kid. 'Am I still *Nemenuh*?'

'You are still *Nemenuh, Cuchilo*,' confirmed the chief. 'I am called Kills Something.'

'The fame of *Pakawa* has reached my ears,' the Kid said

conventionally, using the other's Comanche name.

'Why do you bring white men into the land of the *Kweharehnuh, Cuchilo*?'

That had an ominous ring to it. Normally there would have been more talk; a lengthy delivery of compliments, or an exchange of tribal gossip. So the Kid felt puzzled by its omission. Something else was wrong, too. With Glover's gang so near, the warriors must have seen them. Yet there had not been time for the *Kweharehnuh* to have killed the five men silently and then taken up their ambush positions. It seemed unlikely that *Pakawa* would permit the smaller party to pass and go for the larger.

'We are hunting for thieves,' the Kid answered frankly, knowing that stealing from one's own people rated as a serious crime amongst the Comanches. 'The men who went by here not long ago.'

'What is it you want from us?' Kills Something inquired, but his voice held no hint of making an amiable request for information.

'To go after them and take them back to their people.'

'No!'

'They are like mad wolves, *Pakawa*,' the Kid pointed out 'As long as such live, nobody, red or white, is safe fror them.'

'I must still say no,' the chief stated.

'Can I ask why?'

'It is the order of *Paruwa Semehno* and the medicine woman *Pohawe*. They say that no white men, except the chosen, may enter our land.'

'And the four white men and the half-breed are th(chosen?'

'Yes. The man of no people has the medicine, so we let them pass. Tell the men with you to turn back, *Cuchilo*.'

'What if they won't do it?'

'You are a *tehnap, Cuchilo*,' Kills Something replied. 'So you will know when it is time to fight and when to ride away. There are three of us, each with a repeating rifle, for every one of you. If you come, there will be dead men in the Land of Good Hunting. I do not think they will be *Nemenuh*. And tell the one with the star to think well on what he orders. There are young braves with me who want to count coups.

20

Let them taste blood, and they will go looking for more. If they do, many will die.'

'All this I will remember, *Pakawa*,' promised the Kid. 'May your squaws give you many children.'

With that, the Kid turned his stallion and rode towards his companions. He did not look back. To do so would be discourteous in that it would imply a lack of trust in the warriors he was leaving.

'When do we take out after 'em, Kid?' demanded Narrow, before any of the others could speak.

'I don't reckon we can,' the Kid replied flatly.

'But we're not more'n a mile behind 'em,' the deputy protested.

'And there's twenty or more *Kweharehnuh* brave-hearts less'n half a mile ahead of us,' warned the Kid.

'So?' grunted Narrow. 'They was talking peaceable enough to you.'

'Why sure,' the Kid agreed. 'Only they'll stop acting peaceable happen we try to go by 'em.'

'I'll be damned if I've rid' this far to be turned back by a handful of tail-dragging Injuns!' Narrow bellowed, still refusing to let the others get a word in. 'I say we go on and the hell with what they figure to do about it.'

'You try it, deputy,' drawled the Kid, 'and you're not about to be coming back.'

'It's as bad as that, huh Kid?' the sheriff put in, silencing his deputy with a scowl.

'It's that bad,' the Kid confirmed. 'Every one of them, down to the youngest *tuivitsi*'s toting a repeater and enough bullets to start *two* wars. And they've been told by old Chief Ten Bears 'n' their medicine woman to keep white folk out of the Palo Duro. Unless that 'breed who met Glover's with 'em.'

'We could go 'round em—' Narrow began.

'There's not even part of a hope of doing it,' the Kid declared. 'They'll have a couple of scouts trail us and, happen we're *loco* enough to try, the rest'll be on hand so fast you'll think the hawgs've jumped us.'

'Damn it all, Kid!' growled the sheriff. 'Why should they let owlhoots go through and stop us?'

'I don't know, sheriff. It's medicine business and, rightly, they don't talk about *that* even to a feller from another *Nemenuh* band.'

'So you're saying we should go back, Kid?' asked posseman Hobart.

'That's what I'd say, was I trail bossing this posse,' the Kid answered. 'If we push on and get wiped out, those young bucks'll think they've got real strong war medicine and set off to try it out. Folks'll die then. But I'll go along with whatever the sheriff says we do.'

'Couldn't we set up camp here and wait 'em out?' asked Bretton.

'Happen they got short on patience, they're more likely to jump us than head for home,' the Kid replied. 'I could maybe get through alone and talk to old *Paruwa Semehno*. Only, way *Pakawa* spoke, I reckon I'd be wasting my time. For some reason, he's shielding them owlhoots and a whole lot farther east than I'd've figured on. Fact being, I was counting on taking Glover tonight and well clear of the *Kweharehnuh's* range. Those bucks won't let it happen.'

'So was I,' Laurie admitted.

By bringing only a small, hand-picked posse, the sheriff had hoped to catch up with the gang before they penetrated too deeply into the Palo Duro country. Faced with the present situation, he could see only one answer. To go on meant fighting, probably getting killed. Given a victory to whet their appetite, the young bucks would sweep off on a rampage of looting and slaughter.

'What'll we do, Ian?' Bretton wanted to know.

'We go back,' the sheriff replied quietly and bitterly.

Although the townsmen, the Kid and Waco nodded their agreement, Narrow registered his disapproval.

'So we're going back with our tails dragging 'tween our legs?' the deputy snarled. 'That'll look good comes next election.'

'So'd going on and stirring up an Injun war, *hombre*,' drawled Waco.

'It's easy enough for you to talk about pulling out,' Narrow answered. 'You didn't have money in our bank.'

'I did!' Poplar, the third member of the posse, injected coldly. 'Likely more than you did, Eric. But I'm still ready to go along with whatever Ian says we should do.'

'There's no way out, Kid?' Laurie asked.

'It's turn back, or go all the way and likely stay permanent. You want me to, I can maybe sneak by the *Kweharehnuh* in the dark and go after Glover. Only there'll be none of them coming back with me and, way I'll have to travel after it's done, I'll not be able to fetch back your money.'

'I want justice, not that kind of revenge,' Laurie answered. 'No. We'll all go back.'

Guiding their horses around, the dejected posse began to ride in the direction from which they had come. Without making it obvious, the Kid kept a watch to the rear. As he had expected, they were followed at a distance by two braves. After they had covered about three miles, the sheriff joined the Kid and Waco behind the party.

'You said *all* them bucks had repeaters, Kid?' Laurie asked.

'Every last blasted one.'

'That's not usual, is it?'

'It's damned *unusual*, sheriff. You'll mostly find a few repeaters in each village. But it's near on always the chiefs and name-warriors who own 'em. And bullets're mostly in short supply.'

'Then somebody must've been selling them to the *Kweharehnuh*,' Laurie said.

'What'd the *tuivitsi* have to buy them with?' countered the Kid. 'It'd take a whole heap of trade goods to buy a repeater. More than a *tuivitsi*'d be likely to own.'

'Couldn't the *tuivitsi*'ve had the rifles give' 'em?' Waco inquired. 'You told me a warrior often gives his loot away.'

'Not a repeater, especially if there's so much ammunition around for it,' corrected the Kid. 'And, happen a war party'd pulled a raid that brought in so many rifles, we'd've heard about it.'

'It could've happened a fair time back,' the sheriff pointed out.

'Not all that long,' objected the Kid. 'Some of them were toting Model 73's and they've not been around a year yet.'

'What worries me as a peace officer,' Laurie said soberly, 'is why they let a bunch of owlhoots through.'

'And me,' admitted the Kid. 'Comanches don't cotton to thieves.'

'How about when they're wide-looping hosses?' challenged Waco.

'That's not stealing, it's raiding,' the Kid explained. 'And they don't do it again' another *Nemenuh*.'

'Do you think that old Ten Bears's been paid, either with money to buy them or the rifles and ammunition, to let Glover and his men through?'

'You mean that Glover'd fixed it up, through the 'breed they met, sheriff?' Waco asked. 'It could be, Lon. If Glover was getting hard-pushed by the Rangers and figured the Nations to be unhealthy for white owlhoots, he might've decided to come this way.'

'And sent the 'breed on ahead to dicker the way by the *Kweharehnuh* for them?' asked Laurie.

'Something like that,' agreed the blond youngster.

'Would Glover've made enough money to be able to pay for that many rep—,' the Kid began, then his head swivelled around and he pointed. 'Hey. Look there!'

Following the direction indicated by the Kid, Waco and Laurie found that a cavalry patrol was coming towards them. Fanned out in line abreast, ten privates flanked a first lieutenant, sergeant and civilian scout. Unlike the posse, who had returned their rifles to the saddleboots, the soldiers carried their Springfield carbines in their hands.

'Halt!' yelled the officer, apparently addressing the posse, for his own men kept moving. 'Halt in the name of the United States Government.'

'Means us, I'd say,' drawled the Kid.

'Best do it,' Waco commented, studying the officer's non-regulation white planter's hat, shoulder-long brown hair, the buckskin jacket over an official blue shirt and Western-style gunbelt. 'He reckons he's ole Yellow Hair Custer.'

Stopping their horses, Laurie's party watched the patrol advancing in what looked suspiciously like a skirmishing line. Instead of riding straight up, the lieutenant brought his men to a halt about fifty yards away. The soldiers did not boot their carbines. Rather they shifted the weapons to a position of greater readiness which the Kid, for one, found disconcerting and annoying.

'Who are you men?' demanded the officer in a harsh, challenging tone.

'The sheriff of Wichita County and his posse,' Laurie called back, moving slowly around so that his badge of office would be visible. 'Don't you remember me, Sergeant Gamba?'

'It's him all right, sir,' declared the stocky Italian noncom.

Not until he had received the assurance did the officer show any sign of relaxing. Ordering his men to sling their carbines, he rode forward. Asking the Kid to accompany him, Laurie went to meet the patrol.

'What brings you out this way, sheriff?' asked the officer, without the formality of an introduction.

'I was after the Glover gang,' Laurie replied. 'They robbed the bank at Wichita Falls.'

'Did you catch them?'

'Nope. The *Kweharehnuh* turned us back.'

'*Kweharehnuh!*' repeated the officer eagerly. 'Did they attack you?'

'Just told us to turn back,' corrected the sheriff.

'And, of course, you obeyed,' the lieutenant said dryly.

'Seeing's how there was twenty or more of 'em, all toting Winchesters or Spencers,' the Kid put in, 'it seemed like a right smart thing to do.'

'There were only twenty of them?'

'Maybe twenty-four, or -six. I didn't stop to take no careful trail count on them, mister. 'Specially when they could right soon get more to help out should they need 'em.'

'Where do I find them?' the officer demanded and a light of battle glowed in his eyes.

'Was you *loco* enough to go looking, they're maybe four, five miles back,' the Kid replied. 'All 'cepting two scouts who're watching us talking to you.'

'I don't see any scouts,' announced the lieutenant, after taking a cursory glance at the surrounding country.

'That figures,' the Kid sniffed. 'They're not fixing to be seen.'

Although the officer, his name was Raynor, heard the words, he ignored both them and the speaker. An ardent admirer of General George Armstrong Custer and a disciple of his policy towards Indians, Raynor saw the chance of coming to the notice of his superiors. Oblivious of the fact that he commanded a mere ten men, and they barely beyond the recruit stage, he was prepared to take on whatever force the *Kwehareknuh* might have at hand. If there was honour and distinction to be gained, however, he did not intend to share it with an obscure civilian peace officer.

'Wait here for an hour, sheriff,' Raynor ordered. 'Then we'll accompany you after the outlaws.'

'But—!' Laurie gasped, realizing what the officer meant to do.

'Handling Indians comes under the jurisdiction of the United States Army,' Raynor interrupted pompously. 'And this is far beyond the boundaries of Wichita County.'

'You mean you're fixing to lock horns with them *Kweharehnuh*,' growled the Kid, 'knowing they're all toting repeaters?'

'I shall do my duty as I see it, cowboy,' Raynor replied. 'If you'll wait here, sheriff, I'll send back word when it's safe for you to join me.'

CHAPTER THREE

YOU'RE LETTING THEM GET KILLED

RIDING westwards once more at a slow walk, the posse heard the crashing of many shots from where the cavalry patrol had disappeared into a valley. It could not be said that the sound came as any great surprise to Sheriff Laurie and his companions.

Stubbornly refusing to listen to the Kid's warning, and overriding the sheriff's offers of assistance, 1st Lieutenant Raynor had insisted on taking his small body of men in search of the *Kweharehnuh*. Nothing anybody had said came close to persuading him that he was acting in a foolishly dangerous manner. The two scouts had either concealed themselves exceptionally well, or withdrawn at the sight of the posse meeting the patrol. So, on his own scout failing to locate them, Raynor had made it clear that he doubted if they had ever existed.

When the Kid had tried to pass his warning to Sergeant Gamba, Raynor had flown into a rage and threatened to arrest him for trying to seduce members of the United States Army from their duty. Laurie's intervention had saved the officer from paying the penalty for such incautious, ill-advised behaviour. Unfortunately, the damage had been done. Filled with an over-inflated sense of his own importance, Raynor had taken the Kid's words as a personal affront and refused to discuss the matter further. Repeating his order for the posse to remain at that spot until his men had cleared a way through the Indians, Raynor had set off to meet his destiny.

If it had not been for the very real danger of Raynor stirring up an Indian war, Laurie might have left the officer to his fate. As things stood, the civilians knew that they must back up the military. Allowing the patrol to cover about three-quarters of a mile, the sheriff had followed with his men.

Absorbed in daydreams of the acclaim his victory over the *Kweharehnuh* would bring, Raynor had remained in ignorance of the flagrant disobedience shown by the civilians. Concentrating on the range ahead, for they had taken the Kid's warning seriously, Gamba and the scout had evidently decided that they could forget the danger of an attack from the rear. None of the other soldiers had seen sufficient service to take the precaution of maintaining an all round watch in such a situation.

'Come up careful!' snapped the Kid, making another of his spectacular changes from the borrowed horse – remounted on his return from the interview with Kills Something – to his stallion and sending it leaping forward.

Before starting to follow the soldiers, the members of the posse had drawn their rifles. Armed and ready for battle, they set off after the Kid. Their horses might still have been walking, the way the big white – unburdened by a saddle and other equipment – drew ahead of them.

Despite the urgency of the situation, the Kid did not forget his lessons in the art of making war *Nemenuh*-fashion. He scanned the rim of the valley, searching for any scouts the *Kweharehnuh* might have placed there. Not that he really expected to find them. Acting as scouts was work for the younger braves, but not at such a moment. No properly raised *Nemenuh* warrior would be willing to take such a passive role when there was honour to be won, coups available to be counted and loot for the gathering. So the whole bunch he had met earlier would be involved in the ambush.

Given just a smidgin of good Texas luck, the posse's arrival might not be detected until it was too late for the *Kweharehnuh* to deal with them.

Approaching the rim, the Kid signalled for his horse to stop. Even before its forward momentum had ceased, he quit its back and ran on. Dropping to his stomach, he wriggled to the edge of the valley and looked over. He had expected to find the patrol in difficulties; but not in that deep.

Below the Kid, the slope descended at an easy angle and was covered with a coating of rocks and bushes. It formed one side of a narrow, winding valley through which the posse had earlier followed the Glover gang. At the time, it had struck the Kid as a good place for an ambush. Studying what lay before him, he found that his judgment had been very accurate.

Raynor sprawled motionless on his back halfway across the bottom. Close by lay his scout, his skull a hideous mess where a heavy-calibre Spencer's bullet had torn through it. One private and four dead horses completed the toll taken by the *Kweharehnuh's* opening volley.

Hunched behind a rock at the foot of the slope, his right arm dangling limp and bloody from where a .44 Winchester ball had struck it, Sergeant Gamba held a long-barrelled Peacemaker in his left hand and yelled encouragement to his remaining men. They had lost all their horses, the Kid observed, and apparently most of their ammunition. Crouching in whatever cover they could find, they still returned the hail of lead which came hurling their way from various points on the other slope. So far, the *Kweharehnuh* remained concealed except for brief appearances to rise and throw shots at the soldiers.

Nearer rumbled the hooves of the posse's horses. The sound slammed the Kid back to reality. There was only one way in which his party could hope to save the remnants of the patrol. Done properly, it would inflict such a defeat on the *Kweharehnuh* as to chill their desire for further riding of the war trail.

Swiftly the Kid backed away from the rim and rose. Turning, he sprinted towards his companions, waving for them to halt. While uncertain of what he wanted, the sheriff was willing to back him up. Reining in his own horse, Laurie yelled for the others to stop. All but Narrow obeyed. Every bit as hot-headed and reckless as the late Lieutenant Raynor, the deputy was too excited by the prospect of a fight to take notice of what went on around him.

The Kid spat out a curse. All too well he knew the way of the Comanche braves in that kind of a fight. Only by acting as he wanted could the posse hope to be effective in their rescue bid. So he did not mean to let the deputy spoil the plan he had in mind.

Flinging himself forward, the Kid shot out his left hand to

grab the reins of Narrow's horse close to the bridle's curb chain. With a jerk, he caused the animal to turn so abruptly that it nearly fell and almost unseated its rider. By dropping his rifle and clutching the horn in both hands, Narrow saved himself from being dislodged. Rage flared in his eyes as he glared down at the Kid's unsmiling, Comanche-savage face. At that moment, the Indian-dark cowhand looked anything but young and innocent.

'What the hell—?' the deputy snarled.

'Get down, *pronto*!' answered the Kid, still holding the reins. 'If you don't, I'll gut this critter and you for making me do it!' Then he swung his gaze to the other men. 'Get off them hosses and head for the rim. Be careful. Don't let the Injuns see you and don't start shooting until I give the word.'

'Do it!' Waco advised, leaping to the ground. The fact that the Kid had said 'Injuns' instead of '*Kweharehnuh*' gave the youngster some notion of how urgently and seriously he regarded the situation.

'Come on, boys!' Laurie went on and set the townsmen an example by dismounting to dart after Waco on foot.

Leaving their horses ground-hitched by the trailing reins, the four men headed towards the rim. Retaining his grip on Narrow's reins, the Kid watched them. He nodded in satisfaction when he saw that his orders were being carried out to the letter. Then he turned his eyes to meet the deputy's.

'On your feet, or not at all, *hombre*,' the Kid warned. 'And make up your mind fast.'

'All right,' Narrow answered and swung from his saddle.

While the deputy checked his rifle, the Kid joined their companions on the rim. Still the steady rain of bullets flew from the opposite slope, being answered by an ever-decreasing response from the soldiers. So far, fortunately, the *Kweharehnuh* did not appear to have realized that a new factor had entered the game.

'No shooting!' the Kid gritted, hearing Hobart's low-spoken exclamation of anger and seeing him lining his rifle.

'You're letting them get killed!' Narrow raged, having arrived and flattened himself alongside Waco. 'And I'm damned if I'll stand by—'

'You shoot and so do I,' the blond threatened, twisting to thrust the muzzle of his rifle into the deputy's side. 'Lon knows what he's doing.'

'Get set!' ordered the Kid, moving his rifle into position and watching the way in which the *Kweharehnuh* braves exposed themselves for longer periods when rising to shoot at the soldiers. 'They'll be charging – *Now*!'

Suddenly, bringing the final word of the Kid's warning in a sharp, loud crack, stocky warriors seemed to spout from their places of concealment.

'Brave up, brothers!' roared a young *tehnap* who wore as his war-medicine a head-dress with a pair of pronghorn antelope horns large enough to turn a white trophy hunter wild with envy. 'This is a good day to die!'

With their repeaters cracking as fast as the levers could be worked – and, in the case of the Spencers, the hammers cocked manually – the warriors hurled themselves eagerly towards the soldiers.

It was an awe-inspiring sight and made more so by the ear-splitting war-whoops which burst from each brave's lips as he charged. No bunch of unblooded soldiers, especially after having been so badly mauled, could be expected to remain unaffected in the face of such an assault. Their heads having been filled with old soldiers' stories of the consequences of defeat when Indian-fighting, the remnants of the patrol showed signs of panic. Desperately Sergeant Gamba tried to rally them.

Everything seemed to be going exactly as the *Kweharehnuh* wanted.

All but for one small, yet very significant detail.

In their excitement, the Antelopes had either overlooked or discounted the posse. Even worse for them, they had forgotten the presence of the black-dressed ride-plenty who had been educated as a Comanche and won himself the man-name *Cuchilo*.

The Kid had known that, no matter how advantageous it might be, the younger braves would not content themselves with a long-distance fight against an all but beaten enemy. Coups counted by personal contact rated too highly for that. So he had been determined to keep his party's presence unsuspected until the moment when their intervention would carry the greatest weight.

'Fire!' snapped the sheriff, at last understanding why the Kid had insisted upon waiting.

Seven rifles crashed in a ragged volley, followed by the eighth as Waco swung his Winchester away from Narrow. Down went the young *tehnap*, hit by three bullets. His antelope horn medicine had proved ineffective. Death took two more of the braves at almost the same moment. A fourth screamed and crumpled forward as red hot lead drilled through his thigh; and a fifth's 'yellow boy' was sent spinning from his grasp.

'Pour it into them!' Laurie roared, his sights swinging away from the *tehnap* who had led the charge.

Even as he worked the lever of his Winchester, the Kid knew that he had not been the only one to send a bullet into the *tehnap*. Waco would have selected another warrior, knowing how the Kid's mind worked. Probably the sheriff and that loud-mouthed deputy had gone for the buck as the most profitable – or in Narrow's case, the most impressive – target. Not that the Kid devoted much attention to the matter, being more concerned with saving what was left of the patrol.

Caught in the withering blast of fire, the braves' assault wavered. Another two warriors tumbled to the ground and the rest came to an uncertain halt.

'Get at them!' bellowed the Kid, leaping to his feet.

Giving the ringing war-yell of the *Pehnane*, the dark cowhand bounded down the incline with the agility of a bighorn ram in a hurry. He knew that the posse must press home its advantage and avoid permitting the braves to recover. There was no sign of Kills Something, or the three oldest *tehnaps*. That figured. Warriors of their standing had earned sufficient honours and would be more respected if they stayed in the background and increased the chances of the younger brave-hearts to count coup. Seeing the attack brought to a halt, they would either rush up to give their support, or remain concealed ready to cover the other braves' retreat. In either event, they would be a force to be reckoned with. So, as he ran and cut loose with his rifle, the Kid kept a careful watch for the quartet of experienced fighters.

Waco was the first to follow the Kid's lead, beating Laurie

to it by a fraction of a second. Not that the four townsmen lagged behind. Thrusting themselves to their feet, they rushed after the sheriff and cowhands. Only Narrow remained on the rim. Already his Winchester had accounted for the buck with the pronghorn head-dress and, he felt sure, cut down another *Kweharehnuh*. He wanted to increase his tally and, shooting on the run being notoriously inaccurate, he doubted if he could do it by leaving his present position.

Twisting around ready to run away, a soldier saw the approaching figures. For a moment he seemed to be on the verge of raising the revolver which dangled in his right hand. Then, recognizing that help was on hand, he turned to use the weapon against the Comanches. By his actions, he spurred his companions into continuing their resistance. They resumed their firing, adding to the *Kweharehnuhs'* confusion.

An uneasy sensation of having missed something began to eat at the Kid as he passed the soldiers. Another two strides brought him almost to the foot of the slope and produced a realization of what he had missed. While Kills Something and the older *tehnaps* would have allowed their less experienced companions to carry out the ambush, they ought to be taking a hand now things had gone wrong.

So where in hell might they be?

The outcome of the affair could easily hang upon the answer to that vitally important question.

Catching a slight hint of movement from the corner of his left eye, the Kid swung his head in that direction. What he saw handed him a shock. Instead of remaining behind the men laying the ambush, at least one of the *tehnaps* had crossed the valley. Rising from behind a large rock, the brave lined his Winchester '73 at the black-dressed cause of his companions' misfortunes. Instantly, showing the superb coordination of mind and muscles developed in his formative years, the Kid hurled himself down in a rolling dive. While his speedy response saved him from the *tehnap's* first bullet – the wind of which stirred the back of his shirt – he felt sure the next would be better aimed. So he landed expecting to feel the flat-nosed .44.40 bullet strike his body.

As he followed the Kid, Waco saw a shape rising from

amongst a clump of buffalo-berry bushes to his right. Behind the blond, the sheriff found a greater need to notice the warrior. Cradled at his shoulder, the brave's rifle was pointing at Laurie's chest. Like Waco, the sheriff held his Winchester so its barrel was pointing to the left. He doubted if he could turn it quickly enough to save his life. Waco's thoughts paralleled the sheriff's, but he came up with a different answer. Instead of trying to use the rifle, the blond held its foregrip in his left hand. Leaving the wrist of the butt, his right flashed to the staghorn butt of his off-side Army Colt.

To Waco's rear, Laurie watched everything. In his time as a peace officer, he had seen a number of real fast men in action. That tall, blond youngster, in his opinion, could have matched the best. All in a single, incredibly swift motion, Waco produced and fired the revolver. Its bullet took the *tehnap* in the centre of the torso. The breast-bone cracked, mingling with his cry of pain. He staggered and disappeared as suddenly as he had come into view.

On the rim, Narrow had found the rapidly departing braves an elusive and hard-to-hit target. Six times his rifle had spoken, without the sight of an Indian falling to delight him. So he decided that he might as well join the other members of the posse. Standing up, he observed the *tehnap* rising at the Kid's left. Presented with a stationary target, Narrow hurriedly revised his plans. Taking aim as the warrior sent the shot at the Kid, Narrow fired in echo to it.

'That's another!' the deputy enthused as the *tehnap* collapsed.

Completing his roll by springing to his feet, the Kid turned to the left and wondered why he had not been shot. He saw the *tehnap* going down and commenced a silent vote of thanks to whoever had saved his life. Even as he did so, a savage war screech caused him to forget all thoughts of gratitude.

The young *tuivitsi* was not among those making good their escape. Although he had fallen, he was unharmed. Since his humiliation at the Kid's hands, he had suffered from the mockery of his companions. So he had decided to perform a deed which would retrieve his lost honour. It had been his intention to let the newcomers join the soldiers, then rise and open fire on them – without having given any thought to how he might escape after doing it.

Seeing that his humiliator led the rescuers, the *tuivitsi* had hastily revised his scheme. There would be greater honour if he killed the man who had been responsible for his shame. Looking up, he found that the *Pehnane* was facing to the left and unaware of his presence. Thrusting himself erect with a wild yell, the inexperienced *Kweharehnuh* called attention to himself.

Snapping up his rifle, Laurie took aim and fired. Four more weapons hurled lead at the *tuivitsi*. Two of the bullets missed, but any one of the others would have been fatal and he was thrown backwards by their impact.

The Kid spun around. With the *tuivitsi* and the *tehnap* no longer menacing his existence, he looked for Kills Something. Although he figured that the chief would also be on his side of the valley, the Kid was just a shade too late in locating him.

Having positioned himself closer to the rim than the two *tehnaps*, Kills Something had found himself cut off from his companions. There was, however, a way in which the loss of honour could be lessened if not entirely removed. Already Old Man and two of the *tuivitsi* had gathered and driven off the soldiers' horses. So *Pakawa* would take the mounts of the *Pehnane* and the other white men.

Approaching the top of the slope, Kills Something had seen Narrow. Unfortunately for him, the deputy had not been equally observant. Standing erect and in plain sight, thinking of the story he would be able to tell to his cronies on returning to Wichita Falls, Narrow paid the price for his carelessness. Raising his rifle, the chief laid his sights and squeezed the trigger. Puncturing Narrow's left temple, the bullet shattered through the other side of his head. He died without knowing what had hit him.

While turning in search of the chief, the Kid had cradled the butt of the old 'yellow boy' against his right shoulder. On detecting Kills Something, he made a rough alignment of the barrel rather than the sights and started shooting. Five times, as fast as he could operate the mechanism, lead spurted from the rifle's barrel. As he fired, the Kid moved the muzzle in a horizontal arc. Fast though he acted, he failed to prevent Narrow being killed. An instant before the first of the Kid's bullets struck him, the chief had made wolf-bait of the deputy. Three of the Kid's shots found their mark and Kills Something fell out of sight beyond the rim.

Lowering his rifle, the Kid snarled out a curse at Raynor's stupidity. Then he swung back to the bottom of the valley and his companions. They showed every sign of continuing to pursue the fleeing braves and he understood the danger of doing it. Chasing surprised, dismounted Comanches was one thing. Going after them once they had reached and boarded their war ponies was a horse of a very different colour.

By the time the posse reached the top of the other slope, the braves would be in what had become a Comanche's natural state; on the back of a horse. They would then be ideally suited to escape – or to launch a counter-attack. If they selected the latter course, the posse might find them a vastly different and more dangerous proposition.

'Hold it, sheriff!' the Kid yelled. 'Let them go!'

Having reached much the same conclusions, Laurie needed only to hear the Kid's words to respond. Nor did any of the other members of the posse raise objections when Laurie called for them to stop.

'Looks like we can get after Glover's bunch again, Ian,' Poplar suggested as the men gathered about the sheriff.

'Like hell we can,' answered the Kid. 'This neck of the woods'll be all aswarm with *Kweharehnuh* once word of the fight gets around. And that'll not be long. We're going to need luck to hit Torrant's afore they jump us, with all the wounded soldiers along. The sooner we get headed that way, the better our chances of doing it.'

CHAPTER FOUR

THERE'LL BE A PRICE ON YOUR HEADS

'WE got back to Torrant's without any more trouble from the *Kweharehnuh*, borrowed some hosses from him and got the wounded to Wichita Falls,' the Ysabel Kid concluded, after describing the hunt for the Glover gang and its consequences. 'Found your telegraph message waiting for us, Dusty, and come down here as fast as we could make it.'

Dirty, unshaven, showing signs of having travelled hard and at speed over a long distance, the Kid and Waco sat at the dining-room table in the log cabin maintained as a base for hunting by the Governor of Texas. Situated on the banks of the Colorado River, the building was sufficiently far from Austin to ensure Stanton Howard's privacy, yet close enough for him to be reached in an emergency.

Three more men shared the table. Big, handsome, impressive even in his hunting clothes, Governor Howard sat drumming his fingers on the wood. To his right, tall and slim in his undress uniform, Colonel Edge of the U.S. Army's Adjutant General's Department frowned at the roof. However, the Kid and Waco gave most of their attention to the third of their audience. He was the segundo of their ranch, a man for whom either of them would have given his life without hesitation. His name, Dusty Fog.

Ask almost anybody in Texas about Dusty Fog and they would have plenty to tell. How, at seventeen, he had commanded Company 'C' of the Texas Light Cavalry and earned a reputation as a military raider equal to that of John Singleton Mosby and Turner Ashby. In adition to harassing the Yankee forces in Arkansas,* he had prevented a plot by Union fanatics to start an Indian uprising which would have decimated the Lone Star State.† It was whis-

* Told in *Kill Dusty Fog!* and *Under the Stars and Bars*.
† Told in *The Devil Gun*.

37

pered that he had assisted Belle Boyd,* the Rebel Spy, on two successful missions.†

With the War over and Ole Devil Hardin crippled in a riding accident,‡ Dusty had handled much business on his behalf. He had become known as a cowhand of considerable ability, trail boss equal to the best and the man who had brought law and order to two wild, wide open towns.§ He was said to be the fastest and most accurate revolver-toter in Texas. According to all reports, he topped off his talents by being exceptionally capable at defending himself with his bare hands.

By popular conception, such a man ought to be a veritable giant in stature and handsome to boot.

Dustine Edward Marsden Fog stood no more than five foot six in his high heeled, fancy-stitched boots. Small, insignificant almost, the dusty blond Texan might appear, but he possessed a muscular development that went beyond his inches. There was a strength of will about his good-looking face and a glint in his grey eyes which hinted that he was no man to trifle with. Although his range clothing had cost good money, he gave it an air of being somebody's cast-offs.

Studying Dusty, the Kid and Waco felt puzzled. Like them, he was unshaven and untidy. Nobody expected members of a hunting party to dress as neatly as if they were going to a Sunday afternoon prayer-meeting, but Dusty's appearance went beyond the usual bounds. Taken with the pair having seen their work mounts∥ in the coral, guarded by the OD Connected's wrangler, Dusty's appearance suggested that something unusual was in the air.

'Why didn't the *Kweharehnuh* come after you?' asked Colonel Edge.

'We'd dropped their war bonnet chief and spoiled their medicine,' the Kid explained. 'A scout trailed us to Torrant's, watched us pull out again and turned back.'

* Some of Belle Boyd's history is told in: *The Bloody Border, Back to the Bloody Border, The Bad Bunch* and *The Hooded Riders*.

† Told in: *The Colt and the Sabre* and *The Rebel Spy*.

‡ Told in the 'The Paint' episode of *The Fastest Gun in Texas*.

§ Told in: *Quiet Town, The Making of a Lawman, The Trouble Busters*.

∥ A Texan used the word 'mount' and not 'string' for his work horses.

'We wasn't a lil bit sorry to see him go,' Waco drawled.

'They wouldn't let you go after Glover's gang then?' Dusty asked.

'Nope,' confirmed the Kid. 'I'm damned if I can figure out why not. 'Less that 'breed had bought a way through for 'em by handing out repeaters.'

'You say that they *all* had repeaters, Lon?' Howard inquired.

'Every last son-of-a-bitching one, Governor,' replied the Kid. 'And plenty of shells to use in 'em.'

'Then it's true, Dusty!' Howard ejaculated.

'It's starting to look that way, sir,' the small Texan agreed. 'We know now what the *Kweharehnuh's* price was for their part in it. A repeater and ammunition for every man'd go a long way to making them act friendly to the right sort of folk.'

'What's it all about, Dusty?' Waco asked.

'There may be a town in the Palo Duro where men on the dodge can go and hide out safe from the law,' Dusty answered.

'Hey, Lon!' Waco said. 'Maybe that's what the feller you shot meant when he said the gang was going to hell in the Palo Duro.'

'According to Jules Murat,' Dusty put in. 'That's the name of the town.'

'What?' asked Waco.

'Hell,' Dusty elaborated. 'Jules says that the town's called "Hell".'

With his two *amigos* listening and taking in every word, Dusty went on with the explanation. Captain Jules Murat of the Texas Rangers had been trying to locate the notorious Siddons gang, without any success. Then an informer had claimed that they had gone to a town called Hell in the Palo Duro. At first Murat had been inclined to scoff at the idea. Not for long. Checking with the heads of other Ranger Companies, he had learned that several badly wanted gangs had formed the habit of disappearing as if the ground had swallowed them when things grew too hot. So he had done some more investigating and believed that the town did exist.

'From what I saw of the *Kweharehnuh* at the Fort Sorrel

peace meeting, I'd've said it wasn't possible,' Dusty finished. 'Only what you'd told us is making me change my mind.'

'Jules isn't an alarmist,' Howard continued soberly. 'Such a place would be a blessing for outlaws. If I discarded the idea, it was only because I couldn't see how they could reach it in the heart of the Antelope's country.'

'You've given us the answer,' Dusty told his friends. 'According to Jules' informers, the folk who run Hell have done a deal with the *Kweharehnuh*. On top of that, they put out scouts to watch for white folks coming. Said scouts check on who they are and, if they're all right, take them past the Antelopes.'

'What's your opinion, Kid?' Edge wanted to know.

'It's possible,' the Kid admitted. 'We saw the repeaters and shells that bunch was toting. 'n' Kills Something allowed he'd had orders from old Ten Bears to keep most white folk out.'

'That 'breed was a scout for the town,' Waco declared. 'He saw Glover's bunch coming and sent up the smoke. Anybody's didn't know about it would steer clear of smoke signals. When they headed towards 'em, he knowed they was on the dodge.' He nodded. 'I like that better'n Glover having sent the 'breed on ahead with either the repeaters or the money to buy 'em. Even if Glover could trust the feller that much, it'd've cost him one hell of a pile of money.'

'Between thirty and sixty dollars apiece, depending on which kind of rifle they handed out,' Dusty agreed. 'One gang couldn't afford an outlay like that, but a town drawing money from a lot of outlaws could.'

'Thing I don't see is how these folks at the town got friendly enough with Ten Bears to make the deal,' drawled the Kid. 'He's always been one for counting coup on the white brother first and talking a long second.'

'You're saying they couldn't have done it?' Edge queried.

'Not after what I saw out there,' corrected the Kid. 'I'm only wondering how it was done.'

'The U.S. Army's thinking of going to learn the answer to that,' Edge remarked, watching the Kid as he spoke.

'Happen you try, Colonel,' drawled the dark-faced cowhand. 'The *Kweharehnuh*'ll make whoever goes wish they hadn't.'

'The column would be adequately supported,' Edge pointed out. 'I think the Indians would find cannon and Gatling guns a match for their repeaters.'

'You don't reckon they'd be *loco* enough to lock horns with your column head on, now do you, Colonel?' the Kid countered. 'Those fellers'll be crossing Ten Bears' home range, which he knows like they'll not get the chance to learn. Maybe you'd get the *Kweharehnuh* in the end, but it'd cost you plenty of lives. And that's not counting how the news'd go with the folks on the reservations.'

'How do you mean?' Edge wanted to know.

'You take after the *Kweharehnuh* 'n' get licked, which could happen with them toting repeaters, and every bad-hat or restless buck on the reservation'll be headed for the Palo Duro to take cards. Them folks might even hand out guns to 'em to hold the Army out of the town. That happens, and we might's well never had the peace talks at Fort Sorrel. Because, Colonel, you're likely to get the whole blasted Comanche Nation cutting in.'

Going by the glance Howard darted at Edge, the Kid had been confirming points already made. For his part, the officer was surprised to hear such logic from one so young. Edge decided that the stories of the Ysabel Kid's Indian-savvy he had heard might be true. Certainly the Kid had just expressed the arguments set out by several experienced Indian-fighters who had been consulted by the Governor.

'What's the answer, would you say, Lon?' Howard inquired.

'Send somebody in to see if the town's there and find out just how far they could go to support the *Kweharehnuh*,' the Kid answered without hesitation.

'When would be the best time to move against the *Kweharehnuh*, discounting the town and its supply of weapons?'

'Middle of autumn, Colonel. When the braves're back from the winter-food gathering and've started to make medicine. Sent in good men then, and you might get the band without too much fighting. I figure you've got to fetch them in. 's long's they're out, it'll always tempt bucks on the reservations to go and join them.'

'That's how the Army sees it, Kid,' Edge admitted. 'So we want to know in time to get things set up ready.'

'Whoever you send in there's not going to have an easy time,' Waco commented. 'If it's a peace officer, he's likely to get recognized. There's maybe owlhoots from all over Texas there.'

'That's why I won't let Jules or the other Ranger captains send in their men,' Howard said grimly. 'I don't have to explain. We can all remember what happened in Prairiedog.'

For a moment, Dusty's face clouded at the painful memory produced by the Governor's words. Sent to investigate complaints from the citizens of the town that had been called Prairiedog — but now bore another, less complimentary name — his younger brother, Danny, had been exposed as a member of the Texas Rangers and murdered.*

'We could go,' Waco offered eagerly. 'Ain't none of us's held a law badge in Texas. Faking up reward posters'd be easy enough done.'

'*Too* easy, boy,' Dusty drawled. 'It'd take a whole heap more than just sticking made-up names on wanted dodgers to get us accepted. Whoever's running the town's no fool. And I don't reckon he's a soft-shell do-gooder trying to prove that all every owlhoot's needing is a second chance to turn him into a honest man. Which means him, and the folks in it with him, are doing it for money. Jules's heard they take a cut of the loot from everybody who arrives.'

'So we're not going?' said the Kid, sounding disappointed.

'*We*'re not,' Dusty answered and stood up. Crossing to the side-piece, he returned and laid a copy of the *Texas State Gazette* on the table before the cowhands. Tapping an item with his forefinger, he went on, 'These *hombres* are.'

Looking down, the Kid and Waco read the article indicated by Dusty.

'U.S. ARMY PAYMASTER ROBBED
$100,000.00 *HAUL FOR GANG*

Two weeks ago, three men robbed U.S. Army Paymaster, Colonel Stafford J. Klegg, of one hundred thousand dollars in bills and gold. The money, payment for remounts and the

* Told in *A Town Called Yellowdog.*

Fort Sorrel garrison, was taken following an ambush in which Colonel Klegg, Sergeant Magoon and the six man escort had been shot and killed.

Questioned by our correspondent regarding the small size of the escort, Colonel Edge of the Adjutant General's Department replied, "The delivery had been kept a secret, even from the escort. It was decided that sending more men might arouse unwanted suspicions. Other deliveries have been made in the same manner. All the escort were veterans with considerable line service."

Colonel Edge also stated that news of the robbery had not been released earlier so as to increase the chances of apprehending the culprits.

Captain Jules Murat, commanding Company "G", Texas Rangers, has been working in conjunction with the Adjutant General's Department in the investigation. Displaying the kind of efficiency we have come to expect of this officer, Captain Murat has already uncovered details of the evil plot behind the robbery. According to a woman of ill-repute with whom he had been associating, Sergeant Magoon had discovered the true nature of his assignment and formed an alliance with the robbers. If so, it appears that he received his just deserts when his companions-in-crime double-crossed him and murdered him along with the rest of the escort.

Captain Murat says that the men concerned have been identified as:

EDWARD JASON CAXTON; in his mid-twenties, around five foot six in height, sturdily-built, blond-haired, grey-eyed, reasonably handsome, may be wearing cowhand clothes and carries matched white-handled Colt Civilian Model Peacemakers in cross-draw holsters. Is said to be exceptionally fast with them.

MATTHEW "BOY" CAXTON; half-brother to the above. Six foot two, blue-eyed, blond, well-built, not more than eighteen years of age. Wears cowhand clothes, and two staghorn handled 1860 Army Colts in tied-down holsters. Can draw and shoot very fast.

ALVIN "COMANCHE" BLOOD: six foot tall, lean, black-haired, with reddish-brown eyes, dark-faced. Wears buckskin shirt, Levi's and Comanche moccasins, is usually armed with a Colt Dragoon, in a low cavalry twist-hand draw holster and an ivory hilted bowie knife. Is very dangerous when roused.

A reward of $10,000.00 has been offered by the Army for the apprehension of each of the above-named men. Captain Murat warns that they are armed, desperate and should be approached with caution. He hopes to make an early arrest.'

'So that's how we're going to—' Waco began, having read the story.

'Try this one first,' Dusty suggested and indicated another item of news.

'*PROTESTS OVER ARMY BEEF CONTRACT*

Already vigorous protests are being lodged against a contract to deliver beef to the Army and Navy in New Orleans having been awarded to General "Ole Devil" Hardin's OD Connected ranch. Captain Miffin Kennedy, Captain Dick King and Shangai Pierce each claims that his ranch would be better situated to make the deliveries.

Tempers were high at a recent meeting between Captain Dusty Fog of the OD Connected and the opposing ranchers. Governor Stanton Howard has intervened and is gathering the affected parties in San Antonio de Bexar for a conference to work out an equitable solution.

As the first consignment of cattle is required for shipment at Brownsville, Captain Fog will be sending his ranch's floating outfit to deliver it. He says his men will accompany the cattle to New Orleans in order to study the problems of delivery by sea.'

'Damn it!' Waco yelped, looking up from the newspaper. 'I thought I'd got what was happening, but now—'

'I didn't know we was dickering for a beef contract from the Army, Dusty,' the Kid remarked as the youngster's words trailed off. 'But you sure's hell don't get me going on no boat. They're trouble. It was boats that brought you blasted white folks to our country.'

'What do you reckon now, boy?' Dusty inquired, watching Waco.

'You, Lon 'n' me're them three miscreants who robbed the

Paymaster and made wolf-bait out of poor ole Paddy Magoon,' Waco replied. 'It'll be Mark who goes as "Dusty Fog" to meet them riled-up ranchers in San Antone, while the rest of the floating outfit're hard to work driving cattle along to Brownsville and riding the boat some folks's so scared of to New Orleans.'

Surprise flickered on Edge's face at the rapid way in which the blond youngster had reached the correct conclusion. When the idea of sending in the floating outfit had been suggested, Dusty had wisely insisted on careful preparations and precautions. In addition to providing a covering story in the newspaper, he had thought up the scheme to divert attention from the trio of 'wanted men's' similarity to himself, the Kid and Waco. There had been numerous occasions in the past when people had mistaken Mark Counter for Dusty. The handsome blond giant looked like the kind of man people expected Dusty to be.* So, with the backing of the three 'protesting' ranchers, he would pose as Dusty in San Antonio. Clearly Waco understood all that.

'Anybody talks about the way you tote your guns, you can say you're copying Dusty Fog,' the Kid remarked. 'Folks mostly think about a rifle, not my hand-gun. But it's sure lucky we haven't given the boy his— Ow!'

A sharp kick to the Kid's shin, delivered by Dusty, prevented him from finishing his reference to a pair of staghorn handled, engraved Colt Artillery Peacemakers which the floating outfit had purchased as a birthday present for the youngster.

'What haven't you given me?' demanded Waco suspiciously.

'A rawhiding for leading Lon astray,' Dusty lied. 'What do you pair reckon to the notion of being owlhoots?'

'It could be dangerous,' warned the Governor. 'There'll be a price on your heads and it's high enough to arouse plenty of interest.'

'Damned if you look worth ten thousand simoleons, boy,' the Kid scoffed. 'Happen I shoot him, Governor, can I have the reward money in gold? I don't trust that paper stuff.'

* Mark Counter's part in the floating outfit is recorded in their other stories.

'Now *me*,' countered the young blond. 'I never figured *you* was worth ten *cents*. It'll be a sure-enough pleasure not to have that blasted white goat of your'n tromping on my heels.'

In their work, which sometimes consisted of helping friends of Old Devil Hardin out of difficulties, the floating outfit occasionally needed to keep secret their connection with the ranch. So each of them had one well-trained horse in his mount which did not bear the spread's brand. While the Kid's stallion carried no brand, it was such a distinguishable animal that he would be unable to use it. Having seen the OD Connected's wrangler – one of the few people who could handle the white with reasonable safety – at the corral, the youngster had deduced that the trio would be riding their unmarked animals.

'We'll need some money to tote along, Dusty,' the Kid said, acting as if Waco was beneath the dignity of a reply.

'And we'll have it,' Dusty answered. 'Near on a hundred thousand dollars, in new bills and gold shared between us.'

'That much?' Waco ejaculated.

'We're not playing for penny-ante stakes, boy,' Dusty warned. 'The town boss'll expect us to show him a fair sum. And, remember this, from the moment we leave here, we're the Caxton brothers and Alvin "Comanche" Blood. We'll have to fix up our story and all tell it the same way. A feller smart enough to organize that town'll not be easy to fool. We make mistakes and we'll be staying there permanent.'

'There's a rider coming at a fair lick, Dusty,' the Kid remarked. 'You gents expecting company?'

'Not that I know of,' Howard replied.

Ten minutes later, a tall, gangling man stood at the table. He was dressed like a cowhand and was a sergeant in Murat's Ranger Company. From all the signs, he had ridden hard and he wasted no time in getting down to business.

'Cap'n Jules figured you should know, Cap'n Dusty. Toby Siddons and all five of his gang've been brought in dead for the reward, up to Paducah, Cottle County. Sheriff up there's telegraphed and asked if he can pay on 'em.'

'Did Jules agree?' asked Howard.

'Not straight off,' Sergeant Sid Jethcup admitted. 'He thought Sheriff Butterfield's name sounded a mite familiar and checked. That's the third bunch of dead owlhoots that's been brought in to him for the bounty on 'em. So Cap'n Jules sent off word that he'd have to be sure it was the Siddons gang, seeing's how he'd got told they was down in San Luis Potosi.'

'What'd the sheriff say to that, Sid?' Dusty inquired, guessing there must be something more for Jules Murat to send his sergeant. Going by Jethcup's attitude, it was of a sensational nature.

'Damned if Butterfield didn't wire straight back and say we could send a man along to identify them if we was so minded,' the sergeant replied. 'Allowed the bodies'd keep a while, seeing's the feller who brought them in'd had them embalmed.'

'Whee-dogie!' breathed Waco. 'It sounds like them fellers in Hell don't just take a share of the loot, they go the whole hawg, grab the lot and whatever bounty's on the owlhoot's head. I'm starting to think this chore could be a mite dangerous, Dusty.'

CHAPTER FIVE

WE'VE GOT TO GET OUT OF SIGHT

DRESSED and armed as described in the *Texas State Gazette*, their faces bearing a ten days old growth of whiskers, Dusty Fog, the Ysabel Kid and Waco sat their unbranded horses – a *grulla*, a blue roan and a black and white *tobiano*, each a gelding – studying the terrain that lay beyond the distant Tierra Blanca Creek. They were selecting the places from which scouts employed by the citizens of Hell might be keeping watch.

In view of the news brought by Sergeant Jethcup, Dusty had insisted upon a slight variation to their plans. The trio had visited the town of Paducah to see what could be learned. While there, they had acted in a manner which had established their characters in the eyes of the customers of the Anvil Saloon. Then, as Dusty had arranged, they had escaped 'arrest' by Sheriff Butterfield, Jethcup and another Ranger. The latter had been sent along, ostensibly to identify the dead outlaws, but really to help establish Dusty's party and to check up on the local peace officers.

At the saloon, before being compelled to take a hurried departure, the trio had seen the burly, sombre-looking man who had brought in the embalmed bodies of the Siddons gang. They had also discovered that the sheriff kept pigeons, which had struck them as an unusual hobby unless the birds served another purpose.

Although a posse had been formed and set out from Paducah after them, it had not carried out its duties with any great show of determination. When night had fallen, in accordance with Dusty's plan for such a contingency, the Kid had contacted Jethcup secretly and been informed of the latest developments.

Doing so had not been difficult for a man trained as a

Pehnane brave. Finding a place of concealment at sundown, the Kid had watched the posse, following the trio's tracks, halt and make camp. Later, he had moved closer on foot. When Jethcup had left the camp – under the pretence of going to answer the call of nature – the Kid had joined him. Hidden by bushes, holding their voices down to whispers, they had been able to talk unheard and unseen by the rest of the posse.

According to the sergeant, Butterfield had done all he could to delay the pursuit. Which suggested that the overweight sheriff was in cahoots with the people of Hell. Before Jethcup had gone to meet the Kid, Butterfield had been warning him that the 'Caxtons' and 'Comanche Blood' would soon be outside Cottle County and hinting that the posse had no legal right to keep after them once that happened. Jethcup had gone on to state that, going by the way they acted, the sheriff and the bounty hunter – who went by the name of Orville Hatchet – had not been fooled by hints the trio had dropped at the saloon about heading for the Rio Grande. Being satisfied as to their ultimate destination, the two men had been determined that they should escape to reach it.*

To provide the posse – and the Rangers – with an excuse to turn back, the Kid had stampeded their horses during the night. As Jethcup and his companion had been riding horses borrowed from the livery barn in Paducah, they suffered no loss through his action. Later, they could come out without the posse and 'lose' the trio's trail in a way that would arouse no suspicion.

Although the pursuit had been effectively halted, the trio had known they would face other difficulties before they reached Hell. If their suspicions should prove correct, Sheriff Butterfield would dispatch a pigeon carrying a message about them on his return to Paducah. As the bird could travel faster than their horses, the people who ran Hell would learn of their coming long before they could hope to arrive.

* That had puzzled the Kid, until Dusty had explained why the following day. If the trio had been arrested by the posse, their loot would have to be returned to the Army and the reward shared with the other men involved in their capture. By letting them get through to Hell, Butterfield and Hatchet could expect to make far more money.

By riding west along the White River for two days, then swinging to the north, Dusty, the Kid and Waco hoped to slip past the watchers who would be sent to locate them and reach the town unescorted. Doing so might annoy the men behind the outlaws' town, but it would also impress them.

'What do you reckon, boy?' asked the Kid, as he completed his examination of the land ahead.

'I'd say up on that hill's looks like a gal's tit, alongside the nipple,' Waco replied. 'Or over to the east, top of that peak's stands higher than the rest of 'em. Them scouts could see a hell of a ways from either.'

'They're the most likely looking places, Brother Matt,' Dusty agreed, it having been decided that they would use their assumed names at all times to lessen the danger of a mistake. 'Let's hear from the heathen, though.'

'Can't be me he's meaning,' grunted the Kid when Waco look at him expectantly. 'I ain't no heathen, no matter what low company I keep.'

'Don't you never go taking no vote on that,' Waco warned. 'And quit hedging. If you can't see that far, come on out and say so like a man.'

'There's another hill, back of them two a couple of miles's they could be using,' the Kid said, after telling Waco what he thought of him. 'Can't say to anywhere else right now, though.'

'I'd seen it,' Waco declared. 'Didn't say nothing, 'cause I was testing you-all.'

'How much farther can we go, you reckon, without them seeing us?' Dusty wanted to know, giving Waco a glare that silenced him.

'Maybe's far as the Tierra Blanca,' estimated the Kid. 'To make sure, we'll keep off the sky-line as much's we can. Once we're over, though, we'll have to do most of our travelling by night.'

'How do we find the town happen we do that, Comanch'?' Waco inquired.

'In the day, while we're hid up, we'll look for the chimney-smoke,' the Kid explained. 'What do you reckon, Ed?'

'Seems about right to me,' Dusty admitted. 'Let's get moving.'

Sundown found them on the edge of the Tierra Blanca

Creek. Crossing it, they halted on the northern bank. Being in wooded country, the Kid announced that they could light a fire without the risk of its smoke or flames being seen. Doing so, they made coffee and cooked the last of the raw food they had brought with them. Then they pushed on through the darkness.

When the first grey light of dawn crept into the eastern sky-line, the Kid selected a draw in which they could camp through the hours of daylight. They tended to their horses before making a meal on some pemmican and jerked meat carried as emergency rations. As a precaution against being located and surprised, one of them kept watch while the other two relaxed and slept near the horses.

All through the day, with the help of a pair of field glasses acquired by Dusty from a Yankee officer during the War, the man on guard searched for *Kweharehnuh* warriors, the scouts put out by the people of Hell, or any hint of the town's position. Night fell without them having been disturbed, but neither had they seen anything to help guide them to their destination.

Another night's riding commenced as the sun disappeared beyond the western rims. It proved fortunate that night that Waco had accompanied the rest of the floating outfit in their campaign to prevent General Marcus and his accomplices provoking a war between the United States and Mexico.* During those wild days south of the Rio Grande, he had developed considerable skill in the art of silent horse movement. It was put to good use when the Kid, returning from scouting ahead, announced that they must go within half a mile of a bunch of resting *Kweharehnuh* braves. The nature of the surrounding terrain precluded their making a longer detour.

There followed a very tense fifteen minutes or so as the Kid, Waco and Dusty, moving in single file, had slipped by the sleeping warriors. They passed down-wind of the camp, to prevent the Indians' horses catching their scent and raising the alarm. Doing so meant that they had to remain constantly alert, ready to stop their own mounts smelling the *Kweharehnuhs'* animals and betraying their presence.

Walking with each foot testing the nature of the ground

* Told in *The Peacemakers*.

before coming down upon it, leading and keeping one's horse quiet, with at least twenty hostile *Kweharehnuh* bravehearts close enough to detect any undue amount of sound, was a testing experience for the blond youngster. He felt sweat soaking the back of his shirt and wondered if his companions were experiencing similar emotions. Despite his normally exuberant nature and unquestionable courage, Waco was unable to hold down a sigh of relief when the Kid finally declared that they could mount up and ride.

Although he never mentioned the subject, Waco felt sure that he heard a matching response by Dusty to the Kid's words.

On travelled the trio, alert for any warning sounds and carrying their Winchesters ready for use. As dawn drew near, the Kid ranged ahead once more. He returned with disquieting news.

'From what I can see, there's no place around for us to hide in,' the dark-featured cowhand said grimly. 'Not close enough for us to reach afore it's full light, anyways.'

'Except—?' Dusty queried, having detected an inflexion in the other's voice that hinted at a not-too-palatable possibility.

'Except down at the bottom of a dry-wash we should hit afore it gets light enough to be seen from them high places.'

'So what's up with us using it?' demanded Waco.

'The sides're's steep as hell,' explained the Kid. 'Not straight down, but close enough to it.'

'Let's take a look at it, Comanch',' Dusty drawled. 'We've got to get out of sight. If the feller sees us, he'll let those bucks know that we're here.'

Advancing across the gradually lightening range, the three young men came to the edge of a deep, wide dry-wash. One glance was all any of them needed to tell that there was no easy point of descent within visual distance. Nor did they have sufficient time to conduct an extensive search. It would only be a matter of five minutes at most before the high points came into view. When that happened, any lookout who was there would be able to see them.

'Hell's fire!' growled the Kid, pointing to the edge of the wash. 'A grizzly come along this way late on yesterday afternoon.'

While Dusty could not detect the tracks which had led the Kid to draw that conclusion, he felt certain that the other had made no mistake. Which only added to their difficulties. A thick coating of trees and bushes at the bottom of the wash would offer the trio all the shelter and concealment they required, if they could get down. Unfortunately, it would present the same qualities to any predatory, dangerous animal seeking for a place to den up.

There were, Dusty knew, few more dangerous creatures in the Lone Star State than a Texas flat-headed grizzly bear. More than that, *Ursus Texensis Texensis*, like the other subdivisions of its species, was known to favour such locations as a resting place after a night's roaming in search of food.

Going down into the wash, if the bear should be in occupation, would almost certainly provoke an attack. Neither the Winchester Model '66 or '73, with respectively weak and inadequate twenty-eight and forty grain powder loads, rated as an ideal tool to stop a charging grizzly at close quarters.

'Well,' said Waco, having reached similar conclusions to Dusty and being aware of the need to take cover quickly. 'Ain't but the one way to find out if he's down there.' He paused briefly and raised his eyes to the sky. 'Lord, happen there's a bear down there and you can't help a miserable sinner like me, don't you go helping him.'

Before the other two could object, the youngster had guided his horse to the edge. For a moment, the *tobiano* hesitated, but Waco's capable handling had won its trust and confidence. So, in response to his signals, it went over. Thrusting out its front legs and tucking the hind limbs under its body, the gelding started to slide down the incline.

With the threat of an attack being made by a grizzly bear when he reached the bottom, Waco had not booted his rifle. Gripping it at the wrist of the butt in his right hand, he did his best to help the horse make the descent. Shoving his feet forward until they were level with the *tobiano*'s shoulders, he tilted his torso to the rear so that the small of his back rested on the bed-roll lashed to his cantle. He held out the rifle and raised his reins-filled left hand as an aid to maintaining his and the gelding's balance.

On completing the descent, amidst a swirl of dust and a

miniature avalanche of dislodged rocks, Waco kicked up with his right leg. Allowing the reins to fall, he sprang clear of the gelding. Landing with his left hand closing upon the Winchester's foregrip, he started to throw the butt to his shoulder. There was a sudden rustling amongst the bushes, then a covey of prairie chickens burst out and winged hurriedly along the wash. Making an effort of will, the youngster refrained from shooting at them. He grinned sheepishly and hoped that his *amigos* had not noticed his involuntary action in aiming at the birds' position. Lowering the rifle, he turned and waved a cheery hand at them.

Knowing that the birds would not have been in the wash if a bear, or other dangerous animal was present, Dusty and the Kid made their descent. Each of them hoped that Waco had not seen him whip up his Winchester as the birds made their noisy appearance. Deciding that attack was the best form of defence, the small Texan gave the youngster no opportunity to comment if he had observed their hasty, unnecessary actions.

'Blasted young fool!' Dusty growled as he reined in his *grulla* and glared at the unabashed blond. 'You could've got into a bad fix coming down thataways.'

'Which's why I did it,' Waco replied. 'You pair're getting too old 'n' stiff in the joints for fancy foot-stepping should you've got jumped.'

'Boy!' Dusty ejaculated. 'There's the blister-end of a shovel just waiting to be ridden when we get back to the OD Connected.'

'Matt Caxton's not likely to be going there,' Waco pointed out. 'Anyways, we're down here safe 'n' all our buttons fastened.'

That was the essential and vital point. They were now safely hidden from any lookouts who might have been posted. After some more good-natured abuse, which Waco regarded as being high praise and complete approval of his behaviour, the trio set about what had become their usual routine. Saddles and bridles were removed, hobbles fixed and the horses allowed to drink at the small stream that trickled along the centre of the wash. Leaving the animals to graze, Dusty, the Kid and Waco studied their surroundings.

Finding a place up which they could climb when night

fell, they settled down to rest. Once again the man on guard searched for a concentration of smoke columns to guide them to the town, without doing so. That night, they passed unchallenged between the nearest pair of high points they had selected as lookout places. Dawn found them secure in the cover offered by an extensive clump of post oaks, on a slope that allowed them a good view of the land ahead, to the east or the west.

Hoping that they would locate the town that day, Waco volunteered to take the first spell on watch. He had only just reached his position when he gave a low whistle that caused the other two to join him.

'Smoke,' the youngster said laconically. 'Up on top of that knob there.'

'Just the one fire and made for signalling,' decided the Kid, studying the density of the column which rose from the most distant of the points he had picked back beyond the Tierra Blanca Creek. 'Only I can't see anybody for him to be signalling.'

'Keep watching, boy,' Dusty ordered. 'I don't reckon it's us he's seen and's sending up the smoke for. So I want to know who it is.'

Although Waco continued his vigil for two hours, constantly sweeping from east to west and back with the field glasses, he saw no reason for the smoke signal. Then, just as the Kid came to relieve him, he halted the movement of the glasses and stared hard at the knob.

'There's a feller coming down, L – Comanch'!' the blond announced.

'Try looking off to the east,' suggested the Kid and returned to wake Dusty.

'We've hit pay-dirt!' Waco enthused as his companions came up. 'There's four fellers coming to meet that *hombre* from the knob.'

Taking the glasses from the youngster, Dusty watched the meeting which took place. The lookout – assuming that was his purpose for being in the area – was a tall, lean, plainly-dressed Mexican and the others, four unshaven North Americans. Although they were a long way from the trio's hiding place, Dusty could make out a few details. Whatever the Mexican was saying apparently did not meet with the quartet's approval. After some talk and gesticulation, they yielded to his demands.

'Well what do you know about that?' Dusty breathed. 'The Mexican's making them hand over their gunbelts.'

'And rifles,' the Kid went on. 'Them folk who run Hell don't take chances. Their man pulls the owlhoots' teeth afore he takes them in.'

Having disarmed the four men, the Mexican led them off in a westerly direction. They went by the post oaks at a distance of around a mile and were clearly unaware of being observed by the three young Texans.

'That settles one thing,' Dusty stated. 'We're going to have to find the town instead of meeting one of their scouts. I'll be damned if I'll go there with my guns across another man's saddle.'

Going by their expressions, the Kid and Waco were in complete agreement with Dusty. The day before, they had discussed changing their arrangements if they did not find the town in the next twenty-four hours. Having witnessed the scene which had just taken place, they no longer intended to let themselves be seen by a scout and guided to Hell, if doing it meant being deprived of their weapons.

'We should be able to get a notion of where the town lies by watching 'em,' Waco suggested. 'It must be a fair ways off, though, if we still can't see their smoke.'

'They'd likely not want to meet the owlhoots too close to town,' the Kid pointed out. 'Give me the glasses, Dusty. I'll—'

'Try watching that you get the names right'd be a good thing,' Waco interrupted, delighted that the Kid had for once fallen into error.

'Go grab some sleep, you blasted paleface!' snorted the Kid.

'It'd be best, Brother Matt,' Dusty agreed. 'Watch 'em as far as you can, Comanch'. Only mind that there's likely to be another of the scouts on the knob.'

'I'll mind it,' promised the Kid.

Keeping the possibility of a second lookout in mind, the Kid remained in the trees as he watched the departing men. He picked out landmarks which would allow him to follow their route even in the dark. After they had disappeared, he concentrated on a fruitless search for the town's smoke.

In the middle of the afternoon, the scout returned. He was riding a different horse, which suggested that he had delivered the four men to Hell and obtained a fresh mount. It also implied that the town could not be too far away. Yet the Texans still could not detect any hint of it.

'I'm damned if I know what to make of it,' Dusty declared as they left the post oaks in the darkness. 'We'll go after those fellers as far as we can. Then we'll stop until it's light enough to let you follow their trail, Comanch'. It'll mean moving by daylight, but that's a chance we'll have to take.'

'We've not seen any sign of the *Kweharehnuh* for the last two days,' the Kid replied. 'Could be we're by them and the town's scouts. We ought to make it.'

Shortly after midnight, the Kid brought his roan to a halt and his signal caused the other two to do the same. Peering through the darkness, Dusty and Waco could see him sitting with his head cocked to one side as if he was straining his ears to catch some very faint sound.

'What's up, Comanch'?' Waco inquired, when the Kid allowed them to come to his side.

'I'm damned if this chore's not sending me into a tizz,' the Kid answered. 'I could've sworn I just heard a piano.'

'Where?' Dusty demanded.

'Down wind, some place. A long ways off.'

'Lordy lord!' Dusty groaned, slapping his thigh in exasperation. What've we been using for brains these last couple of days?'

'Huh?' grunted the Kid.

'We've not been making a fire during the day so's there'd be no smoke rising to give us away,' Dusty elaborated. 'And the folks at Hell do the same. Keep moving down into the wind, Comanch', and I'll bet you'll hear that piano again. Then we go to wherever it's being played and we'll be in Hell.'

CHAPTER SIX

I'LL START BY TAKING YOUR GUNS

'By order of the Civic Council, the lighting of fires in the vicinity of the city limits is strictly prohibited during the hours of daylight.
ANY PERSON FAILING TO COMPLY WITH THIS WILL BE SHOT
Signed: Simeon B. Rampart, Mayor.'

'Right friendly way to greet folks,' commented the Ysabel Kid dryly, indicating the sign. It was one of many similar warnings they had seen since their arrival at Hell.

With the Kid lounging afork the roan to his left and Waco astride the *tobiano* on his right, Dusty Fog rode at a leisurely pace along the town's main – in fact only – street towards the large, plank-built livery barn. No smoke rose from any chimney, which was not surprising if the penalty for disobeying the notices was enforced.

'Makes a feller wonder if it was worthwhile coming,' Waco went on and favoured the dark cowhand with a scowl. 'You and your blasted piano.'

'Them signs show you was right about why we didn't see the smoke during the day, Ed,' the Kid remarked, ignoring the blond. 'How do we play it now we've got here?'

'Any way the cards fall,' Dusty decided. 'And we'll start by letting them come to us.'

Finding the town had not been too difficult, although not quite so easy as Dusty had suggested the previous night. Riding into the wind, the Kid and, soon after, his companions had heard the faint jangling of a piano. There had been others sounds to tell them that people – and not Indians – were ahead. At first the trio had been puzzled by the absence of glowing lights to go with the sounds of revelry. Passing through an area of dense woodland, they had learned the reason. Surrounded by the trees and errected in the bottom of an enormous basin-like crater, Hell was effectively concealed until one was almost on top of it.

Although there had been considerable activity — in fact the place had the atmosphere of a Kansas railroad town at the height of the trail drive season — Dusty had decided that they would put off their arrival until morning. He had wanted to form a better idea of what they were riding into. It had also struck the trio as making good sense to conduct their entrance when they had rested and were fully alert.

Seen from the edge of the trees and by daylight, Hell had looked much the same as any other small cow-country town. Maybe a mite more prosperous than most, but giving no hint of its true nature and purpose. There did not appear to be a church or school. On the slope down which the Texans had made their entrance was a graveyard that seemed too large for the size of the town. To the rear of the livery barn, situated at the extreme western end of the street, four large, adobe-walled corrals held a number of horses.

While approaching, the trio had noticed that, apart from those along the street, all the town's buildings had been constructed of adobe many years before and more recently repaired. Wooden planks appeared to be *de rigueur* for the premises flanking the main thoroughfare. It offered much the usual selection of businesses and trades to be found in any town of comparable size. Two of the learned professions were represented by shingles advertising respectively a doctor and a lawyer. Noticeable omissions were the normally ubiquitous stagecoach depot, law enforcement offices, jail-house and bank.

The largest building in town — as might have been expected — with a size even exceeding that of the livery barn, was the two-storey high Honest Man Saloon. On its upper front verandah rail, it had a bullet-pocked name-board which was devoid of the usual descriptive illustration favoured by similar establishments.

Flanking the saloon, if somewhat overhadowed by it, were the premises of Doctor Ludwig Connolly and Simeon Lampart, attorney-at-law. The latter was a good-sized, one-floor building of sturdy construction, with thick iron bars at the left front window that bore the inscription, 'MAYOR'S

OFFICE'. Facing the Honest Man, almost matching it in length if not height, the undertaker's establishment must have had a sobering effect upon revellers with a price on their heads, or a hangman's rope awaiting them if they should be captured. Only a town with a high mortality rate could support such a large concern.

On reaching the double doors of the barn without being challenged, or even addressed, by such of the citizens as they had seen, the trio dismounted. Leading their horses inside, Dusty read the words, 'Ivan Basmanov, Prop.' painted above the front doors. Entering they found only four stalls empty and none of them adjacent to the others. Overhead, a hayloft stretched half-way across the stable portion of the building, being reached by a ladder in the centre of the frontal supports. The cooing of pigeons in the loft came to their ears as they continued to examine their surroundings. Two doors in each side wall gave access to an office, tack-, fodder- and storerooms. Opposite the front entrance, an equally large pair of doors were open to show two of the adobe corrals' gates.

Hinges creaked and a big, bulky man came from what appeared to be the barn's business office. Sullen-featured, with a heavy, drooping moustache, he wore a good quality grey shirt, Levi's pants and low-heeled Wellington-leg boots. Slanting down to his right thigh hung a gunbelt carrying an ivory-handled Remington 1861 Army revolver. It was the rig of a fast man with a gun. A flicker of surprise showed on his face as he looked from the newcomers to the otherwise deserted barn.

'Who brought you in?' demanded the man in a hard, guttural voice.

'Our hosses,' Dusty replied. 'So now we'd like to bed them down comfortable and let them rest.'

'But – But—!' the man spluttered.

'Are you that Ivan Basmanov prop. *hombre,* who's got his name on the wall outside?' Dusty asked.

'I am.'

'Then you're the feller's can say whether we can leave them or not.'

'I am also the head of the Civic Regulators,' Basmanov growled. 'Which of our guides brought you into town?'

Letting the reins slip from his fingers, Dusty moved away from the *grulla* and faced Basmanov. Releasing their horses, the Kid and Waco fanned out on either side of the small Texan.

'Can't rightly say any of them did, mister,' Dusty answered. 'We come in together and without help.'

'You reached here without being stopped by the *Kweharehnuh*, or seen by our lookouts?' The barn's proprietor almost yelped out the words.

'Is it supposed to be difficult?' Dusty countered and let a harder note creep into his voice. 'Can we put up our horses or not?'

For a moment Basmanov made no reply. He seemed to be weighing up his chances of taking a firm line against the trio. If so, he must have concluded that the odds were not in his favour. The three young men had positioned themselves in a manner that made it impossible for even the fastest hand with a gun to deal with them simultaneously.

Not only that, but Bosmanov noticed a coolly confident attitude about the small Texan, except that Dusty no longer gave an impression of being small. There stood a *big* man and one fully competent in all matters *pistolero*; or the barn's owner missed his guess. In all probability, he would not even require the backing of his watchful, proddy-looking companions to deal with Basmanov.

'Put your horses up, if you want to,' the owner muttered, darting a glance at the hay-loft. Then he sucked in a breath as if steeling himself to continue. 'The price is ten dollars a night, or fifty the week, for a stall. It's seven or thirty if you want to put them in the corrals.'

'Each, or for the lot?' asked Waco coldly.

'Each!' Basmanov answered.

'That's sort of high, ain't it?' Waco challenged.

'This's no ordinary town, Brother Matt,' Dusty pointed out, concealing his pleasure at the way in which the youngster had made the correct response to permit his answer.

'Fellers like us have to pay high for what we'll get here.'

'That's true,' affirmed Basmanov, with an air of relief.

'We'll take a stall each for a week as starters, mister,' Dusty went on, returning to the *grulla*, opening his saddlebag and extracting payment for the three animals' accommodation.

'My men aren't around yet,' Bosmanov commented, slightly louder than was necessary, as he accepted the money. 'If you don't mind making a start on your horses, I'll go and fetch them.'

'For what we're paying—!' Waco began, bristling with indignation.

'We can do the gent a lil favour,' Dusty interrupted. 'Let's make a start.'

Although he had taken no part in the conversation, the Kid had not been idle. His eyes and ears had continued to work, the latter gathering information that might prove of use later. Bosmanov returned to his office and closed the door. Looking pointedly at the hay-loft, the Kid raised his right forefinger in a quick point and then vertically as if indicating the number 'one'. Nodding to show they understood, Dusty and the youngster selected stalls and led in their horses. While taking care of the animals, the trio discussed their plans for celebrating and Dusty warned the other two about taking too many drinks.

Basmanov still had not returned by the time the trio had off-saddled and attended to the feeding of their horses. While they did not mention the matter, each of them assumed that he had left through another door in his office and was reporting their arrival to the mayor. Each of them stood outside his horse's stall, waiting for it to finish eating. The sound of approaching footsteps and voices, one a woman's, reached their ears. It seemed unlikely that the proprietor's 'Regulators' would announce their coming in such a manner; but, instead of taking chances, the trio turned towards the front doors.

Accompanied by four young men, a small, petite, shapely and beautiful brunette entered. Dressed in a top hat, with a long, flowing silk securing band, riding habit and boots, she looked to be in her early twenties and seemed to enjoy being the centre of the quartet's attention. The riding gloves she wore concealed her marital status. Whatever it might be, going by her companions, she showed mighty poor judgment of character or a misplaced faith in human nature.

All the quartet dressed well, like cowhands after being

paid off from a trail drive. Their guns hung in fast-draw holsters and they exhibited a kind of wolf-cautious meanness that screamed a warning to eyes which knew the West. Even more than his companions, that applied to the tallest newcomer.

The swarthily-handsome features of Ben Columbo had been displayed prominently on wanted posters outside most Texas law enforcement offices. He had committed a number of robberies, always killing his male victims and doing much worse to any woman unfortunate enough to fall into his hands.

Although Dusty could not place them, two of Columbo's companions probably had prices on their heads. He harboured no such doubts about the third. The last time they had met, Joey Pinter was a member of Smoky Hill Thompson's gang and Dusty had been the marshal of Mulrooney, Kansas. Luckily for the success of the trio's mission, rumour claimed that Pinter had branched out on his own recently. Dusty hoped it was true. He had no wish for Thompson, an old friend, to be in Hell, as that might complicate matters. Recalling how he had rough-handled Pinter at their last meeting, Dusty knew that the other would neither have forgotten nor forgiven him.

Everything depended on how effectively the beard served to disguise Dusty.

Becoming aware of the trio's presence, the new arrivals stopped talking. All of them looked hard at Dusty, Waco and the Kid. As yet, Pinter showed no hint of recognition.

'You are strangers,' the brunette challenged, her voice holding just a touch of a foreign accent that tended to enhance her obvious charms. 'Has my husband seen you?'

'Depends on which of these gents he is, ma'am,' Dusty replied.

'None of them. He is the mayor of Hell,' the woman explained. 'But, if he has not seen you, why are you wearing those guns?'

'I didn't know we was supposed to check them in, ma'am,' Dusty said, watching the quartet studying his party. 'Anyways, these gents're wearing their'n.'

'But yes,' agreed the brunette. 'My husband has given them permission to do so. It is the ruling of the Civic

Council that no visitor may wear a gun without being given permission. Surely your guide explained that to you?'

'No, ma'am,' Dusty drawled, growing increasingly aware of the scrutiny to which Pinter was subjecting him. 'We didn't bother with no guide to get here. Still, if them's the rules, we'll play along. Let's go and see the mayor, Brother Matt, Comanch'.'

A sensation of cold annoyance bit at Columbo as he thought back to how he had been compelled, by the threat of lurking *Kweharehnuh* warriors, to hand over his weapons. That he had submitted to such an indignity and the small, insignificant stranger had avoided it aroused his anger. He knew how Giselle Lampart regarded such matters and suspected a threat to his position as her favourite escort.

'It's not that easy, *hombre*,' Columbo declared, stepping away from the woman. 'You don't walk around heeled until *after* Mayor Lampart says so.'

'Is that the for-real legal law?' Waco inquired, lounging with his left shoulder against the gate-post of the *tobiano*'s stall.

'It is here in Hell,' Columbo confirmed and, attracting one of his companions' attention, gave a nod which sent him moving towards the young blond.

'Are you the town's duly-sworn and appointed peace officers?' Dusty asked.

'You might say that,' answered Columbo. 'Which being so, I'll start by taking your guns.'

'Ma'am,' Dusty said, addressing the brunette but keeping his gaze on the men. 'Would you mind waiting outside?'

'But why?' smiled Giselle Lampart.

'If Columbo tries to take my guns, I'm going to stop him,' Dusty explained in a matter-of-fact tone. 'And I'd hate to shed his blood before a beautiful and gracious lady.'

'Gallantly said, sir!' Giselle applauded, knowing her actions would act as a goad to Columbo.

'Just go wait by your hoss, Giselle,' Columbo ordered, cheeks turning red. 'This won't take but a minute.'

'My!' the brunette sighed. 'I feel just like a lady from the days of King Arthur, with the knights jousting for my favours.'

With that, Giselle strolled to where a dainty palomino

gelding stood in a stall. Her whole attitude was one of complete unconcern and suggested that such incidents had become commonplace in her daily life. Reaching the gate, she turned to watch the men with an air of eager anticipation.

'All right, short-stuff,' Columbo snarled menacingly. 'Hand over the guns and nobody'll get hurt.'

'If you want 'em, you'll have to come and take 'em,' Dusty warned. 'Only, happen that's your notion, fill your hand before you start. Because if you try, I'll see you don't get the chance to rape another girl.'

'You've just got yourself killed, you short-growed son-of-a-bitch!' Columbo spat out and flickered a glance to his right. 'Watch the 'breed, Joey. You keep the kid out of it, Heck. Leave short-stuff to me, Topple.'

About to obey, Pinter became aware of the change which had apparently come over Dusty. In some way, the small Texan appeared to have gained size, bulk – and an identity which showed through the beard and the trail dirt.

Like most men who had locked horns with and been bested by Dusty Fog, Pinter had ceased to think of him in mere feet and inches. Instead, he regarded the small Texan as a *very* big, tough and capable fighting man. A man such like the bearded blond giant who loomed so menacingly before them.

Exactly like him, in fact!

'Watch him, Ben!' Pinter barked, commencing his draw. 'He's—!'

Due to his surprise and haste to deliver the warning, Pinter had made an unfortunate selection of words. Catching the urgency in his voice as he said, 'Watch him,' Columbo did not wait to hear the rest of the message. Already as tense as a spring under compression, Columbo needed little stimulation to trigger him into action. Even as Pinter tried to identify Dusty, Columbo's right hand started to grab for its gun's fancy pearl butt.

Since coming to Hell, Giselle Lampart had witnessed a number of gun fights and even provoked a few of them. So she considered herself to be a connoisseur of such matters. In her opinion – and it was the reason why she had shown him so much attention – Ben Columbo was the fastest man with a gun she had ever seen. It seemed most unlikely that his small adversary could hope to survive the encounter.

Crossing so fast that the eye could barely follow their movements, Dusty's hands closed on the bone handles of his Colts. Half a second later, the guns had left their holsters, been cocked, turned outwards, had the triggers depressed and roared so close together that the two detonations could not be detected as separate sounds. At almost the same instant, a .45 of an inch hole opened in the centre of Pinter's forehead and a second bullet caught Columbo in the centre of the chest.

Having come to a halt some twenty feet from Waco, Heck heard Pinter's shout and started his draw. Thrusting himself away from the gate, the young blond sent his right hand dipping to the off side Army Colt. Flowing swiftly from its contour-fitting holster, the gun lined and bellowed. Hit over the left eye, Heck went down with his weapon still not clear of the holster.

Having decided that his help would not be needed, Topple stood with his thumbs hooked into his gunbelt. At the sight of Columbo reeling backwards and Pinter's lifeless body spinning around, he snatched free his right hand with the intention of rectifying his mistake. Alert for such a possibility, Dusty also realized that the young outlaw possessed sufficient skill to pose a very real threat to his existence.

Cocking his Colts as they rose on the recoils' kick, Dusty swung their barrels to the right. Even as Topple's revolver started to lift in the small Texan's direction, two 250-grain bullets passed over it and into the outlaw's torso. Flung from his feet, Topple dropped his gun and crashed to the floor.

Although he had taken a serious wound, Columbo neither fell nor dropped his Colt. Bringing his bullet-propelled retreat to a halt, he tried to lift and aim his weapon. Almost of its own volition, Dusty's right hand Colt cocked, passed beneath his extended left arm and turned towards the vicious young killer. Again flame spurted from the muzzle and lead struck Columbo; still without knocking him down. Turning his left hand Colt and elevating it to eye level, Dusty took the split second needed for a rough alignment of the sights. He squeezed the trigger and the hammer fell. The top of Columbo's head seemed to burst open as the bullet drove up through the handsome face and out of his skull. Stumbling backwards, he struck the wall by the door and collapsed.

Once again Dusty thumb-cocked the Colts as their barrels lifted to the thrust of the recoil. Spinning to the left, he pointed his guns at the men who appeared through the door of the tack-room.

'Stay put until I know who you are and where you stand!' Dusty commanded.

'Which's my sentiments all along the trail,' Waco went on, turning right to cover another pair of townsmen who came out of Basmanov's office.

Satisfied that his *amigos* could attend to the new arrivals, the Kid let them get on with it. Twisting out his old Colt, he tilted its barrel towards the floor of the hay-loft.

'And tell that feller's was stamping around up there to come down, *pronto*,' the Kid continued. 'Else I'll send something up's'll make him wish he'd been more fairy-footed.'

'You are right, Ivan,' boomed the man who stood behind the barn's owner at the tack-room's door. Stepping by Basmanov, he walked towards Dusty. 'They *are* remarkable young men. Gentlemen, please put up your guns. I'm Mayor Lampart and I extend you a cordial welcome to the town of Hell.'

CHAPTER SEVEN

ONE TENTH OF YOUR LOOT

THE mayor of Hell was a rubbery, blocky man of middle height, jovial-faced and with a pencil-line moustache over full lips. Clad in a well-cut grey Eastern suit, a diamond stick-pin glowing on his silk cravat, he exuded an air of disarming amiability like a professional politician.

At a word from Lampart, Basmanov ordered the man to come down from the hay-loft. The other new arrivals crowded forward to look at the four bodies. As a sign of his good faith, Dusty holstered his Colts.

'I'm right sorry I had to do that in front of your good lady, sir,' the small Texan stated, indicating the dead outlaws. 'Only you can't let that kind push you around.'

'I suppose not,' Lampart replied and gave his wife a glance. It was the first sign he had made of being aware of her presence. 'Giselle will survive it. Won't you, my dove?'

'I will,' agreed the brunette, displaying neither distress nor concern over having seen her four companions shot down. 'But I don't think Ben will be so lucky.'

'His death was only a matter of time,' Lampart said philosophically. 'A most unstable young man, with a number of objectionable traits, I always found him. And whom, may I ask, do I have the pleasure of addressing?'

'Didn't ole Lard-Guts Butterfield's pigeon get here to say we was coming?' Waco inquired, having holstered his Colt and strolled to Dusty's side.

'You know about *that*?' Lampart demanded and Basmanov let out a low exclamation in a barbaric-sounding foreign language.

'Brother Ed figured it out,' Waco explained, in a tone which implied that, with his 'brother' doing the figuring, it must be so. 'He allowed ole Lard-Guts'd send word's soon's he got back to Paducah and'd soaked his aching feet-bones in hot water.'

'Huh?' grunted the mayor, looking puzzled.'

'They do reckon doing it's good for aching feet-bones like he'd have,' Waco grinned.

'I – I'm afraid I don't understand,' Lampart told Dusty in his pompous East-Coast accent.

'Two Rangers tried to jump us in Paducah, but we got the drop on them,' Dusty elaborated. 'Sheriff had to get up a posse and come after us. We figured he'd take kind to having an excuse to stop afore he caught us, so Comanch' here went back the first night out and give him one.'

'How?' Giselle asked, staring at Dusty with considerable interest.

'He ran off all their hosses, ma'am,' Waco answered. 'Serves 'em right, for shame, fetching along that undertaker when they was chasing us.'

'Undertaker?' the brunette gasped, swivelling her gaze at her husband.

'If he warn't, he sure dressed like one,' Waco told her. 'Big, hungry-looking jasper. That gun he toted, though, he could maybe drum up some business if there wasn't any.'

While Dusty had said that the trio should try to impress the people of Hell by deducing Butterfield's connection with the town, he had also decided that they should pretend that they did not tie Hatchet in with it.

'You ran off Orv Hatchet's horse?' Giselle gurgled delightedly. 'Oh dear. What I would give to have seen his face.'

'You know the gent, ma'am?' Dusty asked.

'You made a shrewd assumption about the sheriff, Mr. Caxton,' Lampart interrupted, silencing his wife with a glare. 'Now, if you gentlemen will accompany me to my office, I will acquaint you with certain matters pertaining to the running of our community.'

'How about those four?' Dusty asked, nodding to the corpses.

'How about them?' Basmanov challenged.

'There's ten thousand dollars on Columbo's head,' Dusty replied. 'Pinter's worth another five and I'd say there's a reward on the other two.'

'So?' growled Basmanov.

'So it's a right pity we're out here and got no way of toting them someplace's we could turn 'em in,' Dusty drawled. 'Only they'd not keep above ground long enough in this heat.'

'That's true,' Lampart agreed. 'So we will accommodate them in our boothill. Leave these gentlemen of the Regulators to attend to that.'

'It's your town, Mr. Mayor,' Dusty answered. 'Get your gear, boys. We're ready when you are, sir.'

A small crowd had gathered at the front doors, being kept outside by the man from the hay-loft and some of the Regulators. These latter had the appearance of prosperous businessmen. All wore guns, but did not give the impression of being experts in their use.

Taking his wife's arm, Lampart glanced at the front doors and suggested that they leave by the side entrance. With their saddles and bridles slung over a shoulder and saddle-bags dangling over the other arm, Dusty, the Kid and Waco accompanied the couple from the building. While leaving, Lampart acted as if he were watching for somebody. If that was so, the expected parties did not make an appearance. Looking relieved, Lampart led the way along the rear of the buildings.

As the party was passing the Honest Man Saloon, the centre of its rear doors opened. A statuesque, beautiful blonde woman stepped out to confront them. From the looks of her, she had not long been out of bed. Her face had no make-up and the hair was held back with a blue ribbon. One naked, shapely leg emerged provocatively through the front of her blue satin robe and it was open sufficiently low to suggest that it came close to being her only garment.

'Who was it, Simmy?' the blonde asked, in a relaxed, comradely manner that implied she made her living entertaining men.

'Ben Columbo, Joey Pinter, Heck Smith and Topple,' the mayor replied.

'I figured somebody'd get around to them,' the blonde said calmly, looking at Dusty. 'Did you take Columbo out?'

'He sure did, ma'am,' Waco enthused. 'Along of Pinter 'n'

Topple. Getting a regular hawg that ways, Brother Ed is. Didn't leave but that Smith *hombre* to lil me.'

'If you burned down Heck Smith, you'd best watch out for his brothers. One of them's a limping, scar-faced runt,' the blonde warned. 'The other two look like Heck, only older, dirtier and meaner.'

'I'll mind it, ma'am,' Waco promised, ogling the woman's richly endowed frame with frank, juvenile admiration.

'You're new here,' the blonde hinted, ignoring the youngster and directing the words to Dusty.

'This is Edward and Matthew Caxton, and Alvin Blood, Emma,' the mayor introduced. 'Gentlemen, may I present Miss Emma Nene, the owner of the Honest Man.'

'Right pleased to know you, ma'am,' Dusty said.

'We've been expecting you,' Emma Nene declared. 'Hey! Seeing how you boys made wolf-bait of them four hame-headed yacks, the drinks are on me tonight.'

'Then we'll be in there, a-drinking free, regular 'n' plentiful, ma'am,' Waco assured her. ' 'Cause we done got every last blasted one of 'em.'

'Shall we take these gentlemen to your office, Simeon?' Giselle suggested, her voice and attitude showing that she did not like the blonde.

'Of course,' Lampart agreed. 'If you'll excuse us, Emma—?'

'Why not,' the blonde answered. 'The shooting woke me up, but I reckon I can get to sleep again. Don't you boys forget to come around tonight, mind.'

'Ma'am,' Waco declared fervently, keeping his gaze fixed on the valley between the hillocks of her breasts. 'You just couldn't keep us away.'

Walking on. Dusty was conscious of the blonde's eyes following him. The party turned along the alley separating the saloon from what was apparently the Lamparts' home as well as his place of business. The front door opened into a pleasantly-decorated hall. To the left, a sign of the door in the centre of the wall announced 'Mayor's Office' and at the right was the entrance to Lampart's second room in which, apparently, he carried out his duties as attorney-at-law. Excusing herself, with a dazzling smile at Dusty, Giselle disappeared through a curtain-draped opening leading to the rear half of the building. Lampart opened up the mayor's chambers and waved the Texans to enter.

As Dusty passed through the doorway, he noticed the thickness of the interior wall. He concluded that, if those on the outside were equally sturdy, the room would be secure from unwanted visitors. That view was increased by the stout timbers of the door and heavily barred windows. The room itself proved to be a comfortable, but functional, place of business. In its centre, a large desk faced the door. On its otherwise empty top, an ivory-handled Colt Civilian Peacemaker lay conveniently placed for the right hand of anybody who sat behind the desk. The reason for the cocked revolver and sturdy fittings might be found in the steel-bound oak boxes which formed a line along two of the walls.

While his guests were setting down their saddles and freeing the money-bags, Lampart drew three chairs to the front of the desk. He waved the trio to sit down and went to occupy the chair behind the desk, but kept his right hand well away from the revolver.

'Now, gentlemen,' Lampart said, producing a box of cigars from the right side drawer and offering it to Dusty. 'You will understand that, as mayor of this somewhat special community, I must ask questions which might sound impolite.'

'Ask ahead,' Dusty authorized, accepting a cigar. He opened the left bag and took a copy of the *Texas State Gazette* from it. 'This'll tell you the parts Sheriff Butterfield couldn't get on his message.'

While Lampart examined the paper, Dusty, the Kid and Waco lit up their cigars. After a short time, the mayor raised his eyes and nodded.

'This clears up some of the details, but there are others which require further clarification.'

'Fire them at us,' offered Dusty.

'Since bringing Hell into being, I have, naturally, gained considerable knowledge of outlaws in Texas, New Mexico and the Indian Nations. Yet I have never heard any of your names mentioned.'

'That figures, Matt, Comanch' and I've never pulled a robbery afore this one. But it was too good a chance to miss.'

'You must have been fortunate to have met this Sergeant Magoon,' Lampart remarked, tapping the paper with his forefinger.

'Not all the way,' Dusty objected. 'Sure, it was lucky meeting him at the right time. But we'd knowed him afore when we joined the Cavalry. Fact being, we'd done one of those payroll deliveries, afore they got wise to the boy's real age and talked about heaving him out. We all quit afore they could do it. Then one night we met Magoon in a saloon. He was drunk and talking mean about the Army, 'cause they'd passed him over for top-sergeant. While he was belly-aching about it, he let enough slip for me to figure he was on one of the escorts. We got him more liquor and talked him 'round to our way of thinking. After that, it was easy. We knew where, when and how to hit.'

'And Magoon?'

'Once a talker, allus a talker's how I see it. Happen we'd given him a share, he'd've got stinking drunk and bawled it to the world what he'd done. So we dropped him.'

'Only the bastard'd already done some lip-flapping,' Waco put in indignantly. 'That's how the Rangers got on to us so quick.'

'It's possible,' Lampart said non-committally. 'How did you know about Hell?'

'Man learns more than soldiering in the Army,' Dusty replied. 'Was a feller who'd been on the dodge and he told us about it. So, soon's we heard the Rangers knowed us, we came on up here.'

'But how did you avoid the Indians and our scouts, and find the town?'

'Comanch' was raised Injun,' Waco answered. 'He brought us through's easy 's falling off a log.'

'Not all that easy, boy,' Dusty objected. 'Fact being, we had some luck in doing it. We travelled by night all the time until we found the tracks of shod horses. Allowed they must be coming here and followed them in.'

'What made you suspect Butterfield?' Lampart wanted to know.

'He dresses a heap too well for a John Law in a one-hoss county,' Dusty replied. 'Saw the pigeons on the way in and found out who they belonged to. The rest was easy.

Somebody was paying him good, and it wasn't the citizens of Cottle County. So it near on had to be you folks in Hell, having him pass the word about anything's happened or owlhoots headed your way.'

'That's shrewd thinking,' Lampart praised.

'Are you satisfied with us now?' Dusty inquired.

'I am, although I may ask you to supply further details or to clear up a few points later.'

'That's all right with us,' Dusty declared.

'Then there is only one thing more to be settled,' Lampart announced. 'The matter of payment for the benefits we offer you.'

'How much'd that come to?' Waco asked suspiciously.

'One tenth of your loot,' Lampart said, with the air of expecting to hear protests.

'A *tenth*!' Waco yelped, acting his part with customary skill.

'That's a fair price,' Dusty drawled.

'Fair!' Waco spat back. 'Hell, Brother Ed, that's—'

'Your brother is aware of the advantages, young man,' Lampart said calmly. 'If I know the Army, much of the paper money is in new, easily-traced bills.'

'Yeah,' the youngster mumbled. 'It is!'

'So there is nowhere in Texas, or even in the whole country, where you can chance spending it for some considerable time to come,' Lampart enlarged. 'If you tried, you'd bring the law down on your heads. One tenth is a small price to pay for your safety, and that is what you get for your money. Not only safety. Here, you can find girls, gambling, drinking, clothing. Everything in fact that you committed the robbery to get. And without needing to watch over your shoulder while you're enjoying them.'

'And when the money's gone?' Dusty asked.

'You will be faced with the same solution to that as would await you anywhere else,' Lampart replied. 'Work for, or steal, some more. Our guides will take you out by the *Kweharehnuh* so that you can do it. Occasionally, we are in a position to suggest further – employment – to men we can trust to come back.'

'You're saying we can stay here, whooping it up, as long's

our money lasts out,' drawled the Kid. 'Then we get told to leave?'

'Of course we don't tell you to leave,' objected Lampart. 'Unfortunately, supplies cost us more than they would in an ordinary town. So the chances of obtaining charity are correspondingly smaller. And no man of spirit likes to live on hand-outs, does he?'

'Way you put it, the deal sounds reasonable to me,' commented the Kid. 'Do we go in on the pot, Ed?'

'We go in,' Dusty confirmed. 'Count out ten thousand dollars and give it to his honour, Brother Matt.'

'You say so, Brother Ed,' Waco muttered. 'Lend me a hand, Comanch'.'

'Where can we bed down, sir?' Dusty said as his companions started to count out pads of new bills.

'At the hotel,' the mayor suggested. 'You'll find it at the other end of the street to the livery barn. There's sure to be at least two empty rooms. But the prices are high—'

'Same's at the barn!' grunted Waco, stopping counting.

'And for the same reason,' Dusty pointed out. 'These folks here have a whole slew of expenses other towns don't.'

'That's true,' agreed Lampart, eyeing Dusty in a calculating manner. 'If you wish, gentlemen, you may leave the bulk of your money here. In one of those boxes, to which you alone will have the keys. You can, of course, draw it out as and when you need it.'

'That's a smart notion,' Dusty declared, silencing Waco's protest before it could be made. With the youngster scowling in a convincingly suspicious manner, he went on, 'Hold back five hundred for each of us, Comanch', and put the rest in one of the boxes.'

'You trust me?' Lampart smiled.

'Why shouldn't I?' countered Dusty. 'You don't need to bother robbing us. Sooner or later, you or one of the other folks'll get most of our money without going to that much trouble.'

'How do you mean?' Waco growled.

'Who else do we spend it with while we're here?' Dusty asked. ' 'Sides which, setting up this place cost too much and running it's too profitable for the folks to want it spoiling that way.'

'As I have said before, Mr. Caxton,' Lampart declared. 'You are a most perceptive young man. Taken with your gun-savvy, that makes a formidable combination.'

'Comes in handy to have it on your side, sir,' Dusty remarked. 'Which box do we use?'

With the payment made, the remainder of the money was placed in one of the boxes. Dusty pocketed his five hundred dollars and the keys. Going to the door, Lampart opened it and his wife entered carrying a tray.

'Mr. Caxton and his friends will be staying, my dove,' the mayor said.

'Good,' Giselle answered, pouring out cups of coffee.

While drinking and making idle conversation, they heard the front door open. Going to investigate, Lampart returned with two of the men who had been in the barn. He introduced them as Manny Goldberg, the owner of the hotel, and Jean le Blanc, the barber. Middle-sized and Gallic-looking, le Blanc started to talk.

'I have seen Pinter's gang and they are not concerned with avenging his death. Money is short with them and they are considering leaving; have been wanting to for the past few days, but he wouldn't go. Topple's leader is more relieved than angry as he was getting ambitious and, with Columbo's backing, might have taken over the gang.'

'That leaves Columbo's bunch,' Dusty drawled.

'They are the Smith brothers,' le Blanc replied. 'At the moment, all three are at Dolly's whore-house and too drunk to cause you any trouble. But you must walk warily in their presence, *mes braves.*'

'They can walk warily 'round us,' Waco snorted truculently.

'How does the town stand on it, happen we have to take their toes up, Mr. Lampart?' Dusty wanted to know.

'We let our visitors settle such matters amongst themselves,' the mayor replied. 'Beyond the city limits for preference. There's a hollow in which duels can be fought without endangering civic property or innocent bystanders.'

'Happen they want it that way, we'll go there with them,' Dusty said. 'But the first move'll come from them. You hear me, Comanch', Brother Matt?'

'I hear,' grunted the Kid.

'You, Brother Matt?' Dusty demanded, a grimmer timbre creeping into his voice.

'All right,' Waco answered in a grudgingly resigned tone. 'I hear you.'

Interested eyes studied the trio as they left the mayor's house and walked along the street to the hotel, but nobody interfered with them in any way. They had been told by Goldberg to go and ask for rooms, while le Blanc had put the facilities of his shop and bath-house at their services. Walking along the centre of the street, a logical precaution considering what had happened at the livery barn and the presence of Heck Smith's brothers in town, they were able to talk without the risk of being overheard.

'Lampart's interested in you-all, Brother Ed,' Waco drawled.

'Let's hope he stays that way,' the Kid went on, for the plan was that they should gain the confidence of the town's boss.

'Happen he does,' Dusty warned, 'you pair might have to watch how you go.'

'Why?' Waco asked.

'He could figure I'll be more use to him – and safe – with you both dead,' Dusty explained.

CHAPTER EIGHT

IT WAS ME HE WANTED SAVING

'I saw a big-pig Yankee marshal a-coming down the street,
Got two big sixguns in his hands 'n' looks fierce enough to eat.'

Sitting in a cubicle of the barber's bath-house, the Ysabel Kid raised his pleasant tenor voice in a song guaranteed to start a fight with peace officers anywhere north of the Mason–Dixon line. As he sang, he soaped his lean brown torso with lather raised on a wash-cloth and let the heat of a tub full of water soothe him after the long journey. Close by, his gunbelt lay across the seat of the chair which also held a towel and his newly-bought clothes. His old garments lay on the floor where he had dropped them as he undressed.

On their arrival at the hotel, Dusty, the Kid and Waco had been allocated quarters. Dusty would occupy a small single room and his companions share another with two double beds. The building had offered a good standard of comfort and cleanliness, which was not surprising considering that the management charged three times the normal tariff.

With their saddles and rifles locked away, the trio had set off to buy new clothes and freshen up their appearances. The bathroom section of the barber's premises had only two cubicles, so the Kid had allowed his companions to make use of them first. With Dusty and Waco finished and gone into the front half of the building, the Kid had taken his turn in a hot bath.

'Now big-pig Yankee stay away, stay right away from me,
I'm just one lil Texas boy 'n' scared as I can be.'

Having rendered the chorus, the Kid prepared to give out the second verse. He heard a soft, stealthy foot-fall outside the cubicle and its door began to inch open. Even as he opened his mouth to call out that it was occupied, shots thundered from the front section of the building.

Like the hotel, the barber's shop had furnishings and fittings worthy of any city's high-rent district. It offered two comfortable, well-padded leather swivel chairs, white towels and cloths. On a shelf in front of a large mirror stood bottles of lotions, hair-tonics, patent medicines and other products of the tonsorial arts.

Lounging at ease in the right hand chair, Dusty allowed le Blanc to work on his head with combs and scissors. The barber carried out his task with a deft touch. Incompetence at his trade had not been the reason why he had settled and gone into business in Hell. Waco was in the second chair, with le Blanc's tall, lean young assistant trimming his hair.

Although Dusty was seated with his back to the door, the big mirror allowed him to keep watch on it. With the type of customer he catered for, le Blanc must have been compelled to have such a fitting installed. No man with a price on his head took to the notion of having people come up behind him, unless he had the means to keep an eye on them.

All the time the scissors were clicking, Dusty kept the door under observation. That was partly caution, but also because of the interest le Blanc and the assistant showed in what was going on outside. Ever since Dusty and Waco had taken their seats, the two barbers had repeatedly glanced through the window at the far side of the street.

'You wish the beard removed. *M'sieur* Caxton?' le Blanc inquired as he was putting the finishing touches to Dusty's hair.

'Trim it up a mite is all,' the small Texan replied. 'I've always found the gals go for a feller with hair on his face. They want to know if it tickles when he kisses them.'

'That is a very good reason,' le Blanc smiled, throwing another look at the window and stiffening slightly. He laid his left hand on the back of the chair. 'I will make it so that the ladies fall in love with you at first sight.'

At that moment, two men walked into the shop. Tall, lean, the first looked like an older, dirtier and meaner version of the late Heck Smith; he moved to his left. The other was smaller, with a long scar twisting his right cheek. As he stepped to his right, he exhibited a noticeable limp. Even without seeing their hands dropping towards holstered revolvers, Dusty had decided that they must be the dead man's brothers. Nor did it call for any deep thought to realize that they had come to take revenge for the killing of their kinsman and gang's leader.

The man who entered the Kid's cubicle had a sufficiently strong family resemblance to Heck Smith for there to be need to swap introductions. Tall, young, hard-eyed, he was already drawing his Army Colt. Glancing first at the dirty buckskins on the floor, he swivelled his eyes to the figure in the bath. Indignant at the invasion of his privacy, the Kid knew who the man must be and why he had come. Things looked desperate for the Indian-dark cowhand, but that brief interval while the intruder checked his identity gave him all the respite he needed.

Before the man could slant the revolver his way, the Kid acted with typical *Pehnane* speed. Swinging up the soapy wash-cloth, he flung it so that it hit and wrapped wetly around Smith's face. Letting out a startled, muffled yelp, the man grabbed at the cloth with his empty left hand in an attempt to restore his obliterated vision.

Bringing down the hand that had flung the cloth, the Kid used it to help him rise and drop over the edge of the bath. Landing on the floor, he rolled across his old clothes to the chair. Gripping the front leg with his left hand to hold the chair steady, he folded the fingers of his right fist about the ivory hilt of the bowie knife. Looking over his shoulder, he took aim and plucked the great knife from its sheath. Then he swung his right arm parallel to the floor, releasing his hold on the weapon at the appropriate moment.

The knife hissed through the air as the would-be killer tore the soaking cloth from his features. Vision returned too late to save him. Flying on a horizontal plane, the clip point spiked between two of his ribs. The weight, balance and design of the weapon – brought to perfection at the instigation of a master knife-fighter – caused it to drive on until it impaled his heart. Letting his gun fall, he clutched ineffectively at where the hilt rose from his torso. Then he stumbled and blundered helplessly out of the cubicle.

Coming to his feet, as naked as the day he was born, the Kid jerked the Dragoon Colt from its holster. Cocking it, he made for the door. He heard voices from the front of the building. Realizing that he could not go there in his current state of undress, he returned and draped a towel about his waist.

Bad though the position might appear, Dusty knew that it was not entirely hopeless for Waco or himself. Their gunbelts were hanging with their hats on the sets of wapiti horns fixed to the wall for that purpose. If the Smith brothers had been more observant, they might have noticed that both the belts had something missing. Each of their prospective victims, did the brothers but know it, was nursing his right hand Colt under the long cloth which the barber had draped around his neck to protect his new clothing. All that remained for the OD Connected men to do was spring from the chairs, turn and face their respective assailants – if they could do it before the outlaws' guns came out and threw lead into them.

About to shove himself from his seat, Dusty felt it starting to move. Gripping the back of the chair, le Blanc tugged sharply at it. Instead of trying to jump, Dusty gambled on a hunch and allowed himself to be carried around. Sure enough, the barber halted the chair as its occupant faced Smith.

Shock twisted briefly at the tall outlaw's face as he took in the sight. He opened his mouth to speak. Then the cloth covering Dusty from the neck down formed a pyramid. Flame burst from its apex and a bullet twirled across the room into the man's head. All expression left his face and his mouth dangled open without words leaving it. Reeling backwards, he collided with the wall and slid down it until he sat in a heap on the floor.

If anything, Waco had been slightly better prepared than Dusty for the pair's arrival. From his seat, he had been able to see the door and out of the left-hand window. With his attention drawn that way by the assistant barber's behaviour, he had observed two men crossing the street at an angle that would bring them to the door of the shop. At least, he had assumed that to be their destination when he had noticed the taller's resemblance to Heck Smith and the other's scarred face.

There had not been time for Waco to warn Dusty of the danger. However, the youngster assumed that his 'brother' was equally alert to its possibility. So, like Dusty, Waco was preparing to leap from his seat when the assistant barber started to swing it around.

Seeing that le Blanc had treated Dusty the same way, Waco formed rapid conclusions from the actions of the barbers. It seemed that the two townsmen intended to help their customers escape from the gun-trap. Yet in his eagerness to do so, the assistant had put too much force into his pull on the back of Waco's chair. The youngster knew that it was turning too fast to halt when he faced Heck Smith's limping brother.

With Waco, to think was to act. Ramming his shoulders against the back of the chair, he used them to thrust himself sideways and roll off it. The smallest Smith proved to be faster than any of his brothers. Out flashed his revolver and lined at the blond cowhand's chair. Smith was still trying to correct his aim in the light of Waco's actions when the gun crashed. Lead winged above Waco and embedded itself in the back of the seat he had just deserted.

Tearing off the barber's cloth as he fell, Waco landed on his left side and continued to roll. As his back came to rest on the floor, he stabbed forward the long-barrelled Army Colt. Already cocked, it roared and missed. Across lashed his left hand, its heel catching the spur of the Colt's hammer and carrying the mechanism to fully cocked, while his forefinger held back the trigger. On being released, the hammer flew forward and set off another load. Three times Waco repeated the process.

Fanning the hammer offered the fastest known method of emptying the cylinder of a single-action revolver, but had never been noted for accuracy. During the one and a half seconds taken by Waco to get off the shots, the method proved accurate enough. Although scattered about his body, all four bullets struck Smith. Dropping his smoking gun, so that it fired and sent a bullet into the floor, he pitched headlong across the room and crumpled lifeless in a corner.

Snatching off the smouldering white cloth, which had been ignited by the Peacemaker's muzzle-blast, Dusty tossed it aside and stepped from the chair. While treading on it to put out the fire, he looked to where Waco was rising, 'Are you all right, boy?' Dusty asked.

'He missed,' the youngster replied. 'Hey! There's three of 'em. Maybe the other's gone—'

'Hell, yes!' Dusty spat out and darted to the door which gave access to the bathroom.

Going through, with Waco on his heels, Dusty almost tripped over the body of the Kid's victim. Dragoon in hand, the Indian-dark cowhand stepped cautiously out of the cubicle. The weapon lined at them, then lowered.

'Figured you'd be all right,' the Kid remarked calmly. 'Only I didn't aim to take no chances was I wrong.'

'Damned if he ain't gone back to the war-whoops, Brother Ed,' Waco grinned, eyeing the towel which formed the Kid's only item of clothing. 'That sure is one fancy lil breech cloth.'

'He'll send all them sweet lil *naivis** into a tizz happen he wears it at a Give-Away dance,' Dusty agreed, watching the Kid retrieve his bowie knife.

'I *allus* did,' declared the Kid and stalked with what dignity he could muster into the cubicle. 'Why'n't you blasted palefaces go leave a man to take his bath in peace?'

Returning to the barber's shop portion of the building, the Texans found le Blanc and his assistant examining the bodies.

'They cashed in?' Dusty inquired.

'I've never seen anybody more cashed in,' le Blanc answered cheerfully.

'Toby Siddons ought to be grateful to you, Mr. Caxton,' the assistant went on, looking at Waco in a worried manner. 'Limpy Smith shot him in the back two weeks ago.'

'It's nice to know we've shot somebody and won't have another bunch coming after us,' Waco replied. 'Wonder if Toby'll set up the drinks for us, Brother Ed?'

'It's not likely,' the assistant warned. 'Toby's dead and buried in our boothill. His gang left just after the funeral to see if they could raise some more money.'

* *Naivi:* an adolescent Comanche girl.

From the way in which he spoke, the assistant was acting like a man trying to stop another thinking about a mistake he had recently made. Despite having certain suspicions, Waco wanted to convince le Blanc that he suspected nothing about having been treated in a different manner to Dusty.

'Anyways, *gracias, amigo*,' the youngster said to the assistant. 'You sure saved my hide. Only, should it happen again, don't shove the chair so hard. You near on spun me all the way 'round instead of towards him.'

'I – I'm sorry,' the assistant said, exhibiting signs of alarm.

'Shuckens. You've got no call to be, seeing's you saved my life,' Waco assured him. 'Likely you was's surprised's Brother Ed 'n' me when they come busting in. But you acted for the best and I'm right grateful.'

Several people, including Lampart and Basmanov, had heard the shooting and come to investigate. As at the livery barn, a couple of townsmen stood at the door and kept the curious onlookers outside the shop.

'There's another of them,' the mayor announced, glancing at the bodies. 'He might have gone after Mr. Blood.'

'He did,' Waco admitted. 'Had he asked, I could've told him not to. Ole Comanch's a mite touchy who he shares his bath with.'

'Mr. Blood isn't injured?' Lampart inquired.

'Nope,' grinned Waco. 'But he's sure a sight to see, with that lil ole towel wrapped around him.'

While the mayor was talking with Waco, Dusty watched Basmanov examine the two corpses. To the small Texan, it seemed that the owner of the livery barn looked a mite relieved at discovering that both had been killed almost instantaneously and so would have been unable to do any talking before they died.

'I never thought they'd come after you so soon, Mr. Caxton,' Lampart remarked to Dusty.

'Or me,' growled Waco. 'After we was told about them being stinking drunk.'

'Easy, boy,' Dusty ordered. 'They must've got sobered up when they heard what had happened—'

'They didn't hear about it from Manny and me!' le Blanc declared.

'If they had, you wouldn't've saved us the way you did, sir,' Dusty replied soothingly and saw Basmanov dart a scowling glance at the barber. 'Or they maybe wasn't's drunk as they made out. Would there be anybody else likely to take this up for them, Mr. Lampart?'

'I shouldn't think so,' the mayor answered. 'They weren't the most popular or likeable of our visitors. And, in view of what's happened since you came, there'll be second thoughts before *anybody* decides to go up against you gentlemen. By the way, Ed – if I may dispense with formality—?'

'Feel free, sir. It's your town.'

'It's remiss of me not to have done so earlier, but my wife and I are giving a dinner-party for the gang leaders tonight at the hotel and we would like to offer you an invitation to attend.'

'Just me?'

'Meaning no disprespect to your brother and Mr. Blood, it is only for the gang's *leaders*,' Lampart apologized. 'Much as I would enjoy your company, gentlemen, I can't invite you without asking along all the other visitors.'

'Well,' Dusty began hesitantly. 'That being the case, I don't—'

'Aw. You go on and go to it, Brother Ed,' Waco suggested, his attitude hinting that he would not be averse to being away from his 'elder brother' with a celebration in the offing. 'Comanch' and me's not much for them fancy, sitting-down polite dinners. And, anyways, that blonde gal's setting up free drinks for us tonight at the saloon.'

'Mind you don't have too many of them,' Dusty ordered bluntly. Then he turned to Lampart and continued, 'I'd be right honoured to come, sir. Only I'd maybe best get these whiskers trimmed decent first.'

'No sooner said than done, *mon ami*,' le Blanc announced, darting a triumphant grin at the scowling Basmanov. Swinging on his heel, the barn's owner stalked from the room and the barber went on, waving to his chairs, 'If you and your brother will sit down, we'll attend to you. This time there shouldn't be any interruptions.'

'How do you read the sign on what happened in there, D – Ed?' the Kid asked half an hour later as he, Dusty and Waco strolled towards the hotel. 'Way I see it, the barber and his louse figured the Smiths'd be coming and saved your lives when they did.'

'Likely that's what Lampart told them to do,' Dusty replied. 'Only, was I you pair, I'd not count on it happening while I'm not with you tonight. It was me he wanted saving.'

'But le Blanc's boy twirled "Brother Matt" there around—' the Kid objected, recalling the conversation which had taken place, while he was having his hair cut and beard trimmed, discussing the shooting at length.

'And damned near twirled me too far,' Waco interrupted. 'Way I see it, there's not much goes on in Hell that Lampart doesn't get to hear about. You can bet he knowed the Smiths was sober enough to be figuring on coming after us. If he'd wanted us all dead, he'd've passed the word to let them get us. And he'd've warned us happen he'd wanted all three of us alive.'

'I'm with you so far,' admitted the Kid.

'Instead, he must've told le Blanc to keep watch and save just Brother Ed. They figured to let you take your chance, Comanch'; and to let Smith get me, but make it look like they'd tried to save me. If I'd've took lead, you'd likely've reckoned it was through the young feller spooking and turning the chair too hard.'

'That's about the size of it,' Dusty conceded.

'Just leave us have that young yahoo off somewheres quiet for a spell,' suggested the Kid, sounding as mild and innocent as was humanly possible. 'We'll soon know if your figuring's right or not.'

'Leave it be,' Dusty advised. 'We'll let them believe we're thinking the way they want us to. I reckon that Lampart's looking for backing against that Basmanov *hombre*. If so, given a mite of luck, I'll get him thinking that three of us're better than one. If we can get close to him, we can learn all there is to know about this town and how to bust it wide open.'

'We know one thing now,' Waco said soberly. 'They kill off fellers with rewards on their heads and get the bodies out to towns where they can collect the bounties.'

'We'd figured that much afore we got to Paducah,' commented the Kid.

'And we know for sure now,' Waco insisted. 'Toby Siddons was back-shot in town and buried here, 'cording to the barber's louse. It'd be mighty interesting to try opening up some more of those graves in boothill.'

'Don't try doing it tonight,' Dusty ordered. 'And watch how you go, boys. Basmanov might get somebody else to try and make wolf-bait of us, to stop us tying in with Lampart.'

CHAPTER NINE

I WAS SAWING MY WIFE IN HALF

WEARING his freshly-cleaned black Stetson, a frilly-bosomed white silk shirt, black string tie, grey town-fashion trousers tucked neatly into shining Wellington-leg boots and a Colt-ladened gunbelt, Dusty Fog strolled into the hotel's dining-room. The time was just after ten o'clock in the evening of his first day at Hell. As the mayor had explained in a note which had been delivered to the small Texan, due to the rule prohibiting the lighting of fires during the hours of daylight, the dinner could not be prepared and served any earlier.

That afternoon, Dusty, the Ysabel Kid and Waco had made an extensive examination of the town and its surroundings. To avoid arousing suspicions as to their motives – cowhands being notorious for their dislike of walking – Dusty had given a reason publicly for their perambulations. While enjoying an excellent cold lunch at the hotel, he had announced in loud tones that he and his *amigos* would be taking a stroll that afternoon. So, happen any of Columbo's, Pinter's, Topple's or the Smith brothers' friends had the notion, the trio would be ready and available to accept objections.

The challenge had not been taken up. So Dusty, the Kid and Waco had conducted an enlightening survey of the area. Passing through the graveyard, they had located Toby Siddons' 'grave' and studied head-boards bearing the names of other outlaws. Half a dozen Mexicans and Chinese coolies had been digging holes to accommodate Columbo, Pinter, Topple and the Smith brothers. Walking on, Dusty had wondered if the men killed by himself and his *amigos* would occupy the graves. Or if the other corpses whose names appeared on the head-boards were really buried there.

Sixty or more adobe buildings were scattered around the wooden establishments on the street. Some were used by outlaws who probably objected to paying the hotel's high prices, or had been unable to obtain rooms in it. Others housed the Chinese and Mexicans who were employed to carry out various menial tasks in the town. The Kid had guessed that the latter were once slaves owned by the *Kweharehnuh* and traded, or given, to the citizens of Hell.

The discovery of six large wagons parked in three of the buildings had led the trio to make a closer scrutiny of the livery barn's corrals. They had found that a number of the horses were of a type bred for heavy haulage work. That had helped to explain how the town obtained its supplies.

One building in particular had aroused Dusty's interest. Situated about two hundred yards to the rear of the mayor's residence, it conveyed a similar impression of sturdiness. Small, cubic in shape, in an exceptional state of repair, its adobe walls had a single stoutly-made oak door, secured, like the heavily shuttered window, with double padlocks. Although Dusty had noticed the building while accompanying the Lamparts from the livery barn, he had not been aware of the full implications. The door and window were at the rear and on a bench under a shady porch, two Mexicans armed with shotguns kept watch on them. All the trio had wondered why the place should require a guard and Dusty had resolved to find out as soon as possible.

Ever curious, Waco had asked why the original settlers had selected such an inhospitable region for their home. The Kid had suggested that they were Spanish colonists. Adobe was a building material with lasting qualities and, apart from various repairs which had been carried out recently, the houses looked to be of considerable age. Going by the absence of a church, normally the first thing erected by the priest-ridden Spanish colonists, Dusty had concluded that the settlers had been non-believers driven by religious persecution to take refuge in the Palo Duro country.

Returning to the hotel at the conclusion of their inspection, the trio had exchanged gossip with le Blanc in the bar-room. Then they had gone to their rooms where they had rested and tidied up ready for the night's celebrations.

Before coming downstairs, Dusty had given Waco and the Kid instructions as to how they were to act when they arrived at the saloon. By doing so, they would help him to convince Lampart that they too would be of the greatest use to him.

Like his equally duded-up companions, Dusty now sported a neatly-trimmed chin beard and moustache which he hoped would continue to serve as a disguise. Looking around the crowd of guests, he saw nobody whom he recognized from other towns and wondered if it would be mutual. Some of the male faces appeared to be familiar, but only because he had seen them on wanted posters. Others belonged to townsmen who had been at the livery barn that morning.

To Dusty, it was obvious that the citizens had started to form into two factions. Those who supported Lampart stood slightly apart from Basmanov's group. Although the mayor seemed to have the largest number on his side, Dusty guessed that some of them would be fence-sitting and waiting for a definite show of strength before declaring on his behalf. Having the backing of the acknowledged fastest gun in town would be tremendously in Lampart's favour. Which probably accounted for the way the mayor left his companion on seeing the small Texan arrive in the dining-room.

Although Dusty had devised an excuse for wearing his guns, he soon discovered that there would be no need for him to make it. Every man in the room, with the exception of Lampart, carried at least one revolver on his person.

'Ah, Edward!' the mayor greeted, coming over and extending his right hand. 'Let me introduce you to the other guests before my wife gets here.' He indicated a tall, handsome Mexican in an excellently tailored charro costume and wearing a low-hanging 1860 Army Colt with a set of decorative Tiffany grips. 'This is Don Miguel Santiago. You already know Jean here. These are Doctor Connolly, our medical practitioner, and our undertaker, Emmet Youseman.'

'I hope you can guess which of us is which,' boomed the big, red-faced, cheerful man in the loud check suit. 'In case you can't, I'm *not* the doctor.'

There was, Dusty decided, good cause for the comment.

Tall, cadaverous and dressed in sober black, Doctor Connolly fitted the popular conception of an undertaker far better than the hearty, extroverted Youseman.

'It's looking the way I do that made me settle here,' the undertaker went on jovially, shaking hands with the small Texan. 'Fellers I get here don't have kin-folks to object. I reckon Doc helps my business. When a wounded feller sees him, he figures he's so close to the grave that he might's well go the whole hog and get into it.'

'It's no matter for levity,' Connolly declared in a high, dry voice and turned to walk away without acknowledging Lampart's introduction.

'Don't pay him no never-mind, Ed,' Youseman advised. 'He's riled because you boys gave me all the trade instead of him.'

'I'll mind it, happen I have to shoot anybody else,' Dusty promised. 'Only I've always been taught that any man who's acting bad enough for me to draw down on him is acting bad enough to be killed for it.'

Even as he finished speaking, Dusty realized that his words had come during a lull in the general conversation. Not that he regretted them for he realized that such a flat statement might do some good.

With the casual ease of an experienced host, Lampart steered Dusty onwards and rattled off other introductions. Nine of the men, like Santiago, could be found prominently – if not honourably – mentioned in the 'Bible Two', the Texas Rangers' annually published list of fugitives and wanted persons, which most peace officers in the Lone Star State read far more regularly than the original bible. Wary eyes studied Dusty, but the greetings and handshakes were cordial until he reached the man who stood by Basmanov. Tall, handsome, well-dressed, he had a pearl handled Colt Artillery Peacemaker in a fast-draw holster tied to his right thigh.

'And Andy Glover,' Lampart concluded.

'You're the *hombre* who dropped Ben Columbo, huh?' Glover growled, keeping his right hand at his side. 'Ben was real fast.'

'Sure,' Dusty conceded. 'There was only one thing wrong. Just the once, he wasn't fast enough.'

'Can't say I've heard your name,' Glover said sullenly, conscious that every eye had turned towards him and the small Texan.

'I've heard yours,' Dusty answered. 'Seen it on wanted posters, too. That's the difference between us, *Mr.* Glover. I've been too smart to get myself wanted until the stakes were worth it.'

'They say you robbed an Army Paymaster,' Glover gritted, not caring for the chuckles which greeted 'Caxton's' response. 'I've never known the blue-bellies sent their money about thataways.'

'Happen a secret gets known to too many folks, it stops being a secret,' Dusty countered. 'I just happened to have been in a position to get to know. That's how me and the boys managed to pull it off, *mister*. We knew where, when and how to do it.'

'And you're still on the dodge.'

'So're you, *mister*. Only I'm willing to bet that I brought in more money with that one robbery than you and your bunch were toting when you hit Hell.'

More laughter rose from the majority of the guests. It was common knowledge that, due to the Rangers' continual harassment, Glover's gang had been compelled to leave behind most of their loot. The bank robbery at Wichita Falls had been their last throw of the dice and had failed to come anywhere near their expectations in the amount of money it had produced. Dull red flooded into Glover's cheeks, but he had noted 'Caxton's' repeated use of the word 'mister'. No Texan said it after being introduced, unless he wished to show that he did not like the person he addressed it to.

'I see that you prefer the cross-draw, *senor*,' Santiago remarked. 'The same as Dusty Fog.'

'Why sure,' Dusty agreed, wondering if there might be some hidden meaning behind the Mexican's words. 'Fog's real fast, they do tell. So I figured the way he totes his guns must be something to do with it. That's why I wear them like I do.'

'Makes you fast, huh?' Glover muttered sullenly.

'Ben Columbo, Joey Pinter and Topple likely wondered that self same thing, *mister*,' Dusty drawled, looking straight at the big outlaw. 'They learned. If *anybody* feels so inclined to find out, I'm willing to step out on to the street and accommodate them.'

Gently spoken the words had been, but everybody present knew that they put the gauntlet straight into Glover's teeth. The remainder of the guests began to draw farther away, waiting silently to see what developed. Despite being the host, Lampart made no attempt to intervene. Nor did Basmanov, in his capacity as head of the Civic Regulators, do anything to try to keep the peace.

Almost thirty seconds ticked away, although they seemed to drag by for Glover. Much as he wanted to, the tall gang leader could not look away from his challenger. The *big* blond Texan's grey eyes held his own and appeared to be boring through and reading his innermost thoughts.

One thought beat at Glover. Before him stood the man who had simultaneously out-drawn and -shot Columbo and Joey Pinter, killing Topple an instant later. That put him into a class of *pistolero*-skill to which Glover could not hope to aspire. Yet if Glover backed down, he was finished in Hell. The story would be all around the town by morning and might even lose him the control he had previously exerted over the men in his gang.

Although determined to stand up against any man who tried to ride him, a good way to stay alive in such company, Dusty did not particularly want to kill Glover. So, having asserted himself, he sought for a way in which he might avoid taking the affair to a fatal conclusion. Sensing that Glover wanted to back off, Dusty saw an opportunity to let him do so. It had a certain amount of risk to the small Texan, but he felt sure that other issues swayed it in his favour.

Giselle Lampart stood at the open door, looking into the room. Jewellery sparkled at her fingers, wrists and neck, while the dress she wore leaned more to daring than decorous. Turning his back on Glover, Dusty swept off his Stetson with his left hand and walked towards the brunette.

'Good evening, ma'am.' the small Texan greeted. his whole attitude suggesting that he regarded the incident with Glover closed. 'My thanks for your kind invitation.'

Sucking in a deep breath of mingled anger and relief, Glover glared after the departing Texan. The outlaw's right hand hooked talon-like over its revolver's butt, almost quivering with anticipation as he tried to decide whether to draw or not. Commonsense, and a knowledge of the other guests' feelings, supplied him with the answer. If he started to pull the gun, one of his rivals might warn 'Caxton'. In fact, somebody was certain to do it for Glover's action would endanger Giselle Lampart. Given the slightest hint of what Glover was planning, 'Caxton' would turn to deal with the situation. Glover could not forget the *big* Texan's earlier comment on how he would treat any man who made him draw.

'Come and sit down, Andy,' Basmanov said in a loud voice. 'We don't want any unpleasantness.'

Never had the Russian barn owner's voice sounded so delightful to Glover. Yet the outlaw could sense a tinge of disappointment in it. Refusing to let that disturb him, he swung on his heel and walked with Basmanov to the long table which had been laid for the dinner.

'It looks as if nobody feels inclined to find out, Edward,' Giselle remarked with a mischievous smile. 'You may escort me to the table. I've had you placed next to Simmy and myself so that I will have a handsome man on each side of me.'

The tension had oozed away with the entrance of the brunette and Glover's retreat. Talk rose again and there was a general movement in the direction of the table. Guided by Giselle, Dusty went to the end of the table presided over by her husband. On the other end, Basmanov stood scowling from Dusty to the mayor. Going by the knowing looks thrown at him from various gang leaders, Dusty sensed that he was being awarded a place of honour. Perhaps the last time the Lamparts had given a dinner, Ben Columbo had occupied it. Dusty refused to let that thought worry him. To his left were Giselle and her husband, with Santiago on his right and le Blanc facing him across the table.

Moving with well-trained precision, Goldberg's Mexican waiters started to serve the meal. The food and wine proved to be of excellent quality, which did not surprise Dusty in the light of what he had already seen around the hotel. Soon conversations were being carried on and laughter rolled out. Although apparently at ease, Dusty remained constantly alert. Carefully he guided the talk in his group to the presence of the town in the Palo Duro.

'That was Simeon's doing,' le Blanc declared. 'Why not tell Ed how it happened, Simmy?'

'There's not much to tell,' the mayor replied, in a mock depreciatory tone and went on in a matter-of-fact manner. 'The first time the *Kweharehnuh* saw me, I was sawing my wife in half.'

'Huh?' Dusty grunted, genuinely startled.

'That's right, Ed,' Giselle confirmed. 'And it wasn't the first time. He'd done it to me twice a night for years.'

'You're a magician!' Dusty ejaculated, staring at Lampart with a growing understanding.

'One of the best, if I do say so myself,' the mayor agreed. 'A most useful talent, I've always found it. And never more so than that night. We, the present citizens of Hell, were on a wagon train making its way down from the railroad in Kansas to Santa Fe. Our scout rode in to say that we were surrounded by Indians and they would attack our camp at dawn. We wouldn't have stood a chance in a fight, so I decided to try something else. Luckily I had all my props along. So Giselle and I put on our entire performance by fire- and lamplight. Of all my extensive repertoire, sawing Giselle in half went down the best. Ten Bears had never seen anything like it—'

'Or me, the way I dressed for the act,' Giselle put in, eyeing Dusty in a teasing manner.

'The whole band came down to watch,' Lampart continued. 'Next day, instead of attacking, they brought the medicine woman to see and, I suspect, explain the miracle. When she couldn't, Ten Bears decided that I must have extra powerful medicine and made me his blood-brother. After that, getting permission for us to make our homes here was easy.'

'Don't you want to know *why* we chose to settle here, Ed?' asked Youseman, sitting between the mayor and the barber.

'I figure that, happen he reckons it's my business, Mr. Lampart'll tell me about it,' Dusty replied, guessing that no further information would be forthcoming right then.

'I always feel so immodest when I talk about it,' Lampart remarked, placing a hand over his glass as the wine-waiter offered to fill it. 'No more for me, thank you.'

'If a man's done something as smart as starting this town, I don't see why he needs be that way about telling it,' Dusty praised. 'Fact is, the only modest fellers I've ever met are that way because they've never done anything and don't have any other choice.' He looked up and shook his head at the wine-waiter. 'I'll pass this deal, *amigo*.'

'You don't drink much, Edward,' Giselle commented. 'Aren't you enjoying yourself with us?'

'I'm having a right fine time, ma'am,' Dusty answered. 'Only I figure a man who has to pour liquor down his throat to enjoy himself doesn't have much to enjoy.'

'You object to people drinking, *senor*?' Santiago inquired, but in a polite and friendly manner.

'I object to *me* drinking,' Dusty corrected, hoping that somebody would take the bait. 'What other fellers do is none of my never-mind.'

'From the way your brother talks,' Lampart put in, just as Dusty had hoped. 'I don't think he shares your views.'

'Matt talks better than he drinks,' Dusty replied, taking the chance to impress the mayor with the Kid's and Waco's sterling qualities and the fact that they would be of use to him. 'They're good kids, him and Comanch' both. As loyal as they come and they always do just what I tell them. Tell you what, gents, I said they should stay sober tonight. And I'll bet a thousand dollars they're that way if we go along to the saloon when we're through here.'

'With Emma handing out the free drinks?' le Blanc laughed. 'You have much faith in them, *mon ami*.'

'Enough to make it five thousand dollars they'll still be sober,' Dusty offered, watching Lampart out of the corner of his eye and seeing him give a quick confirmatory nod to the barber.

'You are on, *mon brave*,' le Blanc declared, thrusting his right hand across the table. 'Who will hold the stakes?'

'Anybody who suits you,' Dusty said indifferently. 'I don't care who I get the money off.'

'You are so sure of winning then, Edward? Giselle asked.

'So sure that I'd go up to ten thousand simoleons on it,' Dusty declared, apparently addressing le Blanc, but actually watching the mayor's reaction.

'Not with me,' le Blanc chuckled, as he received a negative head-shake from Lampart. 'Against such confidence, I almost wish I had not made the wager.'

'Call it off, you feel that way,' offered Dusty. 'I know those boys and you-all don't.'

'No,' the barber decided, after another glance in the mayor's direction had told him what to do. 'We shook hands on it, so the bet is on. Besides, I too have faith. In Emma's hospitality and persuasive powers. We will see what happens when we get to the Happy Man. But who holds the stakes?'

'Mr. Lampart'll suit me fine,' Dusty stated. 'That way, he can put your money straight into my box in his office after I've won.'

CHAPTER TEN

IF YOU WASN'T WEARING THEM GUNS

'ED CAXTON!' Emma Nene said accusingly, bearing down on Dusty as he entered the Honest Man Saloon with Lampart, le Blanc and Santiago. 'What have you told those two boys of yours?'

With the dinner at an end, the party had started to split up and go their separate ways. First to leave had been Basmanov's faction, including the scowling, still angry Glover. Dusty had noticed that two of the men who had been with the Russian earlier stayed behind. Others, whom the small Texan had marked down as fence-sitters, showed a more open friendship towards Lampart. Already, it seemed, the fact that the mayor was apparently winning the support of 'Ed Caxton' was bringing its rewards.

There had been some after-dinner talk, then the men had decided to make their way to the saloon. Clearly Lampart had no intention of allowing his rival to make friendly advances towards Dusty and intended to reduce the chances of a succesful attempt to assassinate the small Texan. The mayor had asked Dusty, along with le Blanc and Santiago, to be his guests at the saloon after they all had escorted Giselle home.

For all the deficiencies of its sign-board, the Honest Man Saloon came up to the high standard set by the rest of the town. On a dais at the left side of the room, the piano which had guided Dusty, the Kid and Waco to Hell combined with three guitars, two violins and a trumpet to beat out a lively dance rhythm. Before the dais was a space left clear for dancing. At the moment of Dusty's arrival, it was hidden behind a wall of laughing, cheering Mexicans, members of Santiago's gang. Several pretty, shapely girls, white, Mexican and Chinese, in no more scanty attire than would be seen at a saloon in a normal town, mingled with the sixty or so male customers. Behind the bar counter, two Mexicans and a burly, heavily moustached white man served drinks from the extensive range of bottles gracing the shelves of the rear wall. Mexican waiters glided about carrying trays. Two tiger-decorated faro layouts, a chuck-a-luck table, a wheel-of-fortune and three poker games catered for the visitors who wished to gamble. At each end of the bar, a flight of stairs led up to the first floor.

Clearly Emma Nene did not apply the almost sedate clothing standards to herself. She wore a flame-coloured dress with an extreme décolleté which left no doubt that all under it was flesh and blood, and which clung to her magnificently feminine body like a second skin. Its hem extended to her feet, but was slit up the left side to the level of her hip. One leg, made more sensual by a covering of black silk, showed through the slit in a tantalizing manner. Her eyes held a puzzled, yet admiring, expression as she addressed the small Texan.

'How do you mean, ma'am?' Dusty answered, although he could guess.

'I thought they'd be drinking me dry, seeing that I offered to pay and going by the way they talked,' Emma elaborated. 'Instead, they've only had a couple of whiskies apiece and won't take any more.'

'Oh no!' le Blanc groaned.

'Something wrong, Jean?' the blonde asked.

'It would seem that I have lost five thousand dollars,' the barber replied. 'Ed bet me that his friends would still be sober when we arrived.'

'They're that, sure enough,' Emma admitted. 'Are you fellers going to stand here all night, or come over and buy a girl a drink?'

'It'll be my pleasure to buy one for you, ma'am,' Dusty declared.

'Hey, Brother Ed!' Waco whooped, coming up with his left arm hooked around the waist of a pretty, red-haired girl. 'This here's Red and she reckons I'm the best-looking feller she knows.'

'She shows right good taste, boy,' Dusty grinned. 'Where's Comanch'?'

'Whooping up a storm over there with a right sweet lil *senorita*,' the youngster replied, waving a hand to the dance-floor. 'And me all this time thinking all he knowed was war-dances 'n' hoedowns.'

As the party made their way to the bar, Dusty looked through the gap in the Mexican crowd. Beyond them, the Kid and a vivacious girl of Latin blood were giving a spirited rendering of a *paso doble*. From the sounds let out by the onlookers, even Santiago's gang were impressed by the Indian-dark Texan's part in the performance.

'He sure dances pretty,' Dusty drawled. 'How're things going, boy?'

'Couldn't be better,' Waco enthused and nodded to the blonde. 'Soon's Miss Emma seed we wasn't wanting to drink, she called up Red and Juanita to see after us. This's sure one friendly lil town.'

'Looks that way,' Dusty admitted. 'Go have your fun, boy. Only keep minding what I told you.'

'Don't I always?' Waco grinned. 'Come on, Red gal. Let's go buck the tiger for a whirl.'

'You were right, Ed,' Lampart said, watching Waco depart with an air of calculating appraisal. 'It's fortunate that they survived the Smiths' treacherous attack.'

'Right fortunate,' Dusty agreed. 'Three sets of guns're better than one comes a fuss.'

'Do they *always* do as you tell them, Ed?' Emma inquired, signalling to the white bartender.

'They've found life's a whole heap easier if they do,' Dusty answered.

'Mr. Caxton's money is no good tonight, Hubert,' Emma informed her employee. 'Set the drinks up over at my table.' She smiled at the men. 'It's not ladylike to stand guzzling at the bar. Do you insist on other people doing everything you tell them, Ed?'

'Depends on who they are,' Dusty declared. 'I can take orders just as easy as giving them, provided I think the man doing the giving's smarter than me.'

Although Dusty spoke to the blonde, his words had been directed at Lampart and he knew that the mayor was taking them in.

'Such as who for instance, *mon ami*?' le Blanc challenged.

'Like I said, *anybody* who's smarter than me,' Dusty countered and looked around. 'This's some place you've got here, ma'am.'

'Why thank you, kind sir,' Emma smiled and led the way to a table on the right side of the room.

'Yes sir,' Dusty said, as if half to himself. 'I'd surely admire to be the man who made this whole town possible.'

'You'll be making me blush next,' Lampart warned, but he could not hide the pleasure he felt at the praise. 'Sit down. This is Emma's private table and reserved for the guests she says can share it with her.'

'Take the end seat, Ed,' the blonde offered. 'You're our guest of honour tonight, and deserve to be for ridding Hell of a bunch of murderous rats.'

Sitting down, Dusty watched the other men take their places. Emma seated herself around the corner from him and Lampart sat opposite to her with his back to the wall.

'Pup-Tent Dorset's bucking the tiger, Miss Emma,' the bartender said *sotto voce* as he set down a tray of drinks. 'He's losing heavy and getting riled.'

'Is Glover here?' the blonde asked, turning to glance around the room.

'Come in with Basmanov,' Hubert answered. 'They got a bunch up in one of the rooms for a game of poker.'

'Did Dorset talk to Glover before they went up?' Lampart put in.

'Him and Styles Homburg went over to ask for some money, what I could see of it,' Hubert replied. 'They talked for a spell over by the stairs. Funny thing though, Glover made 'em hand over their guns afore he gave them a stake.'

'Dorset and Homburg are always poor losers,' Emma commented, after the bartender had returned to his duties. 'Oh ho! They're coming over here now.'

Turning his head, Dusty studied the two men who were approaching from the faro layout to which Waco had taken the saloon-girl. Pup-Tent Dorset was slightly over medium height, moustached, with a stocky, powerful build. Dressed in plain range clothes, his gunbelt's holster was empty. Bigger, bulkier, Styles Homburg looked like a sedate travelling salesman in a brown town suit. He too appeared to be unarmed.

After studying Dorset and Homburg, Dusty darted a quick glance around the room. The dance had ended and the Kid was taking Juanita through the laughing, applauding Mexicans to join Waco at the faro table. From his friends, the small Texans turned his attention to locating possible enemies. At the bar, standing clear of the other customers, he located the remainder of the Glover gang. Tommy Eel, tall, slim and tough-looking, leaned by the shorter, heavier, surly-featured Saw Cowper. Each of them had a revolver holstered at his right side.

'Hi, boys,' Emma greeted, in her professionally cordial manner, as the two outlaws came to a halt at her table. 'Can I help you?'

'Not you,' Dorset replied and pointed at Lampart. 'Him. We want some money from you, *hombre*.'

'In that case, I would suggest you go and ask Mr. Glover,' the mayor advised. 'He holds the only keys to your gang's box.'

'And you know just how little's in it,' Homburg growled. 'Not enough for us to have another week here. So we reckon you should ought to do something about it.'

'You can hardly blame me for your extravagances,' Lampart pointed out. 'I warned you on the day you arrived that this was an expensive town.'

'And took a tenth of our loot,' Dorset spat out. 'So we figure we're entitled to some of it back.'

'I don't, in fact can't, see it that way,' Lampart protested, aware that he was the focal point of much attention.

Silence had fallen on the room. The band had stopped playing, conversations ceased and various games of chance were temporarily forgotten as the customers and employees turned their gaze to Emma's table.

'What's that mean?' demanded Dorset.

'I told you when you first arrived that it was a donation to the Civic Improvement Fund,' Lampart explained. 'If I hand some of your donation back, I'll be expected to do the same with everybody who asks.'

'We said we wanted to borrow—' Dorset began.

'And meant you wanted a gift,' the mayor interrupted. 'Where could you get money to repay me?'

'We'd maybe win it, was the games in here straight,'

Dorset answered, seeing that the crowd sympathized with Lampart's point and hoping to turn them in his and Homburg's favour.

'Are you sore-losers trying to say my games aren't honest?' Emma challenged indignantly.

'*Your* games?' Dorset sneered. 'Word has it you don't but run this place all cosy and loving for Lampart. And him with a nice, sweet lil wife, for shame.'

Wood squeaked against wood as Dusty sent his chair skidding back. Coming to his feet, he faced the two men.

'Was you wanting to stay healthy,' the small Texan drawled. 'You'd best say "Sorry we lied about you, ma'am." and then get the hell out of here.'

'Wha—?' Dorset began.

'You got business with Mr. Lampart, that's fine,' Dusty continued. 'Only some'd say you've picked a poor time to come doing it. It stops being fine when you start mean-mouthing and lie-spouting about a for-real lady. So I'm telling you to wear out some boot-leather walking away.'

'Lampart's hired your gun, huh?' Homburg almost shouted, recollecting the orders Glover had given regarding the pair's behaviour.

'If Glover told you that, he's as big a liar as you pair,' Dusty countered. 'And I'm getting quick-sick of seeing your faces.'

'You're the feller who dropped Ben Columbo, ain't you?' said Dorset. 'That makes you a real big man.'

'Talking pretty won't make me like you,' Dusty warned.

'Could be you wouldn't be so big,' Dorset declared, 'if you wasn't wearing them guns.'

'Now there's an interesting thought,' Dusty answered, starting to unfasten the pigging thongs which held the tips of his holsters to his legs. 'You figure happen I was to take them off, you could make me eat crow?'

For a moment, Dorset stood dumbfounded by the unexpected turn of events. He was uncertain of what he should do next. Then he realized what a chance was being presented to him and he nodded eagerly.

'That's just what I think!'

'And now you got all these good folks wondering if it be

true,' Dusty continued as he unbuckled and laid his gunbelt on the table. 'So we're just natural' going to have to find out.'

'You fixing to take on me or Styles?' Dorset grinned.

'You, him – or both,' Dusty confirmed. 'Call it any way you've a mind.'

'I reckon I'll be enough,' Dorset declared, the grin fading away. 'Come ahead, short-stuff. This I'm going to enjoy.'

Clenching his fists, Dusty adopted the kind of stance favoured by the professional pugilists of the day. At least, he positioned his hands and arms in the conventional manner. His feet formed a 'T' position, the right pointing to the front and, a shoulders' width away, the left directed outwards. By bending his knees slightly, he distributed his weight evenly on the balls of his feet.

Throwing a grin at Homburg, Dorset moved towards Dusty. An experienced fist fighter, the outlaw watched Dusty's hands for a hint of how he planned to attack. At the same time, Dorset stabbed his right at the blond's face. Weaving his torso aside and letting the blow hiss by his head, Dusty swung his left foot around and up.

Concentrating on Dusty's hands, the kick took Dorset by surprise. Caught in the groin, he might have counted himself fortunate in that Dusty had not been able to build up full power while making the attack. As it was, pain caused him to double over and retreat. Gliding closer, Dusty hooked his knotted left fist into the outlaw's descending face. Lifted upright, Dorset was wide open for the continuation of his small assailant's assault. Hearing footsteps approaching from his rear, Dusty hurled across his right hand. Hard knuckles landed on the side of Dorset's jaw, sending him spinning and reeling back to the faro table he had recently quit. Landing on it, he scattered markers, coppers, money and cards in all directions.*

Even as Dusty knocked Dorset away, he felt himself gripped by the shoulders from behind. Giving a lifting heave, Homburg hurled the small Texan towards the bar. At first Dusty could do nothing to halt himself as the savage propulsion caused him to turn in Homburg's direction and

* A more detailed description of a faro game is given in *Rangeland Hercules*.

run backwards. So far, the big outlaw had not followed him; which proved to be a foolish omission. Waiting until he had regained control of his equilibrium, Dusty seemed to tumble backwards. A concerted gasp rose as he went down, mingling with Homburg's yell of triumph. Then the man started to rush forward, with the intention of stomping Dusty into the floorboards.

Spitting out a mouthful of blood, Dorset sank until his left knee touched the floor. His right hand went to and started to draw a knife from its sheath in the top of his right boot. The blade came clear, but its owner was given no chance to use it. Powerful fingers clamped on to his right wrist and the scruff of his neck. Then his trapped arm was twisted behind his back and he felt himself being dragged until he leaned face-down on the table once more.

Unlike the majority of the crowd, the Kid felt no concern over the sight of Dusty toppling backwards. He was aware that the small Texan possessed considerable acrobatic agility. In part, it had been developed as a precaution against injury if he should be thrown when taking the bed-springs out of bad horses' bellies. It had also served him well while receiving instruction in the fighting skills which did so much to offset his lack of inches when dealing with larger, heavier men. Down in the Rio Hondo, working as Ole Devil Hardin's personal servant, lived a small man thought by many to be Chinese. While undeniably Oriental, Tommy Okasi insisted that he came from some place called Nippon. To Dusty, he had handed on the secrets – all but unknown at that period outside Japan – of *ju-jitsu* and *karate*. Learning how to fall had been an important and vital lesson. So the Kid expected Dusty to avert the danger of the stomping, probably in a spectacular manner. He was not disappointed.

Breaking his fall on his shoulders as Tommy Okasi had taught him, Dusty rolled into a ball. Then, with a surging thrust, he uncoiled and catapulted back to his feet. The action took Homburg by surprise, just as the kick had Dorset, and he was granted as little opportunity to recover. Ducking under Homburg's belatedly grabbing hands, Dusty wrapped his arms around the outlaw's thighs, just above the knees. Drawing the legs together, Dusty exerted all his not inconsiderable strength and straightened up. He lifted Homburg from the floor, heaving the man backwards. Coming down flat-footed and with his legs still not parted, the impact against the floor-boards knocked him breathless and witless.

Bounding after the man, Dusty sprang into the air. Tilting back until his body was horizontal, he hurled the soles of his boots full into the centre of Homburg's chest. Hurtling across the room, the outlaw crashed through the bat-wing doors. He barely touched the sidewalk while crossing it and sprawled face down on to the hard-packed surface of the street.

Maintaining his twin grips, Waco kept up the pressure on Dorset's trapped arm until the hand opened and released the knife. With that accomplished, the youngster transferred his other hand to the outlaw's collar, jerked him erect and thrust him away.

'Go pick on Broth—' the youngster began.

Catching his balance, Dorset spun around and hurled a punch to the side of Waco's head. Twirling on his heels, the youngster landed back-down on the table. Instead of turning to Dusty, the outlaw leapt closer to the young blond. Grabbing hold of Waco's throat, Dorset hauled him up and started to choke him.

At the bar, Eel and Cowper had been watching the developments with a growing sense of alarm. When they saw Dusty leap up and kick Homburg backwards, while Waco was disarming Dorset, the pair knew that they must help carry out their boss's orders. They also decided that barehanded tactics were not for them. Moving away from the bar, they started to reach for their guns.

Instantly a menacing figure seemed to just appear in front of them. It wore a grey shirt, string tie, town trousers and Indian moccasins; the white man's attire being topped by the savage features of a Comanche warrior on the look-out for a coup-counting.

Having been certain that Dusty could deal with Homburg, the Kid had kept the other two members of the Glover gang under observation. When they made their move, he stepped in fully ready to counter it.

'I ain't like Ed 'n' Matt, so I don't waste time with fool

fist-fighting,' the Kid warned and the Dragoon in his right hand seemed to vibrate with homicidal eagerness. 'You want to side your *amigos*, shed your guns and go to it. But, happen your pleasure's shooting, I'll be right willing to oblige.'

Although partially dazed by the blow, Waco threw off its effects fast. Placing his palms together, he thrust them up between Dorset's arms. Snapping the hands apart, he knocked the fingers from his throat. Then he bunched his left fist, dropped his shoulder behind it and ripped a straight-arm punch to the centre of Dorset's face. Nostrils spurting blood, the outlaw blundered backwards across the room.

Landing from his leaping high kick, Dusty turned and saw Waco's predicament. Before the small Texan could go to his *amigo*'s assistance, Waco escaped and put Dorset into retreat. As Dorset came towards him, still going backwards, Dusty interlaced his fingers. Looking like a baseball batter swinging for a home run, Dusty pivoted and smashed his hands into the man's kidney region. Agony contorted Dorset's features as the blow arrived. He arched his back and stumbled helplessly in the direction from which he had come. Leaping to meet him, Waco hurled a power-packed right cross. With a solid 'whap!', the youngster's knuckles struck Dorset's temple. The outlaw pitched sideways and slid several feet before coming to a stop.

'How do you want it?' the Kid demanded as Dorset's limp body came to a halt. 'Now's the time to say.'

'Pup-Tent and Styles called the play,' Eel replied. 'It's none of our fuss, feller.'

Glover stood with Basmanov and others of the poker game on the right side set of stairs. Glaring furiously at the scene, the gang leader advanced a couple of steps below his companions. Drawing his revolver, he started to line it at the small Texan.

CHAPTER ELEVEN

HE'S GOT A FORTUNE STASHED AWAY

THE crash of a shot sounded over the excited chatter which had followed the unexpected ending of the fight. On the stairs, Glover heard the eerie sound of a close-passing bullet, felt its wind on his face and gave a startled yelp. Jerking back in an involuntary motion, he sat down hard. Across the room, at Emma Nene's private table, smoke curled from the barrel of Santiago's Colt.

'What is the betting that I won't miss a second time?' asked the *bandido*, taking a more deliberate aim as he cocked the revolver's hammer.

Fright flickered on Glover's face, for he knew that his life had never been in greater danger. If anybody offered to bet, the Mexican would not hesitate to shoot. For a moment, Glover thought of trying to turn his weapon on Santiago. Yet doing so would avail him but little. Even if he should be successful, the *bandido*'s men would kill him. Covered by 'Comanche Blood's' Dragoon, Eel and Cowper would be unable to back his play. Nor could he count on help from Basmanov's party. That had been made plain to him during the poker game. As the Russian had warned, Glover's future in Hell depended upon how the plan worked that had been hatched between them after leaving the hotel. From what Glover had seen since coming downstairs, it had been a miserable failure.

'Easy there, Mig!' Glover said, trying to keep his voice firm and friendly. He dropped his gun. 'What was I to think when I come down and see the Caxtons beating up one of my boys and Blood there holding the others back with a gun.'

'Put up your gun, *amigo*,' Dusty agreed, going to the table and picking up his belt. 'Man's right about the way it looked.

Trouble being, things aren't always how they look.' Once more silence had come to the room and its occupants listened to his words with rapt attention. 'No sir. Take when them two yacks of his came over. Way they talked and acted, it could've looked like I'd been hired by Mr. Lampart to stop folks getting their right and fair money out of his office.'

'That was the impression they tried to give,' Santiago confirmed.

'Some's say they was lucky, them two, that their boss'd taken their guns away—' Dusty went on.

'I could see they was getting riled over losing at faro,' Glover interrupted, standing up. 'So I did it for the best.'

'Why sure,' Dusty agreed. 'It looks that way. Only you could've got them both killed, doing it.'

'How?' Glover growled.

'Would Ben Columbo or Joey Pinter've taken off their guns to deal with them?' Dusty challenged. 'And if I hadn't, when I concluded to stop them mean-mouthing Miss Emma with their lies about her and her games, folks might've seen it wrong. They might start to figure – 'specially was somebody to put it into their heads—' his eyes flickered briefly at Basmanov, 'that I was working for Mr. Lampart and the other gents with money in his care could wind up dead when they wanted it back.'

A startled exclamation in his native tongue broke from Basmanov as he heard Dusty exposing his plot. Not only exposing it, but doing so in such a manner that nothing could be salvaged from it.

Glover had been willing to sacrifice Dorset and Homburg in the interests of raising mistrust against the mayor. Far from the most intelligent of men, the pair had been persuaded to hand over their guns and then provoke a fight with 'Ed Caxton'. There had been a chance that he would grandstand, to impress Lampart and Emma Nene, by agreeing to fight bare-handed. The conspirators, however, had felt it more likely that he would shoot his challengers down regardless of them being unarmed. If Eel and Cowper had been able to avenge their companions by killing 'Caxton', all well and good. If not, Basmanov would be able to circulate the kind of rumour that the small Texan had suggested.

Instead of achieving their ends, the whole affair had gone

wrong. Worse than that. Basmanov sensed that the *big* dangerous newcomer suspected his part in the scheme.

'Put that blasted hand-cannon away, Comanch',' Dusty commanded, having completed the buckling on of his belt and secured its holsters to his legs while apparently addressing Glover but really speaking to the crowd, 'Those two fellers only want to tend to their *amigos*' hurts.'

'Yo!' answered the Kid and obeyed.

'Do it,' Glover said as Eel and Cowper glanced at him. 'You'd best have Doc Connolly see to them, they could be hurt bad.'

'Hank,' Dusty called, to a gang leader who wore the clothes favoured by professional gamblers. 'Just to straighten out any doubts them two yacks might have stirred up, will you check over that faro lay-out.'

'I've done it every night,' the man replied. 'It's like all the games in here, as straight as Emma's beautiful.'

'You saying things like that about the lady, I reckon I'd best ask you to show Mr. Glover and his boys what to look for in a crooked game,' Dusty grinned. 'Fancy-talking competition like yours, I can do without. 'Course, they might not want to take your word on it.'

'Hank knows what he's talking about and what he's said's good enough for us,' Glover growled, picking up and holstering his revolver. 'Pup-Tent and Styles was allus poor losers. So I took their guns off 'em, to stop them making trouble if their luck stayed bad.'

'Like I said, they was lucky you did it,' Dusty drawled. 'Only, happen they come mean-mouthing or spreading lies about Emma again, I'll not waste effort fist fighting. And that goes whether *they're* wearing guns or not.'

'That Dorset *hombre*'s got a real hard head,' Waco went on, alternately rubbing his right hand's knuckles and working its fingers. 'Happen we lock horns again, I'll be inclined to hit him with a teensy bit of lead 'stead of my dainty lil fist.'

'We'll mind it,' Glover promised sullenly. 'Come on, Tommy, Saw. Let's get the boys to the doctor's.'

'Hey, you musicians!' Emma called. 'Earn your pay. Come on, fellers, you'll put me in the poor-house, sitting on your hands instead of buying or playing.'

Taking their cue from the blonde, the band started to play a lively tune. Girls and waiters set about stimulating the activities which had been brought to a halt by the trouble. By the time Glover, Eel and Cowper had carried Dorset from the room, it reverberated with the sound of revelry.

'Where-at's Emmet Youseman?' Dusty inquired. 'Don't tell me he's undertaking at this hour of the night?'

'I shouldn't think so,' Lampart answered looking a touch furtive.

'He didn't strike me as a feller who'd miss the chance to bend an elbow in good company,' Dusty remarked, flickering a glance at Waco.

'Most likely he's doing some undertaking at the cat-house,' le Blanc remarked. 'Only with live customers.'

'Where's Red got to?' Waco whooped and the girl ran up. Scooping her in his left arm, he kissed her. 'I thought you'd backed out, gal.'

'What on?' Emma demanded.

'Why, I've bet her that I've got more hair on my chest than she has,' the youngster explained. 'And, happen it's all right with you, Miss Emma, I was figuring on taking her out for a whiles to show for most.'

'I told you that Red was your gal,' Emma reminded him. 'Run along and get your bet settled.'

'You heard the boss-lady, Red gal,' Waco grinned. 'Let's go.'

'What it is to be young,' Emma smiled, almost wistfully, watching Waco and the girl making for a side door.

'Aren't you going to fix Ed up with a girl, Emma?' le Blanc asked.

'I already have,' the blonde stated. 'Come on, let's set the paying customers a good example. Sit down and get happy.'

'Let's do that,' Dusty agreed. 'I sure hope that gal of mine's a blonde.'

'You know,' Emma replied. 'She just might be at that.'

Although the party sat down and resumed their conversation, the subject of the motives behind the fight received no discussion. In fact, to Dusty it seemed that Lampart was trying to avoid it. The mayor kept the others laughing with a flow of rude stories. When he ran out, he offered to demonstrate a few of the tricks he had learned as a stage magician.

'You're not sawing me in half,' Emma warned.

'Spoil-sport,' Lampart chuckled. 'Get me a couple of decks of cards, I may be able to baffle you.'

Dusty had to admit that Lampart was a skilled performer. Handling the cards with deft professionalism, he kept his audience baffled. Emma had been asked to sing a song and was on her way to oblige, while Lampart concluded his show by demonstrating how to shuffle a deck of cards in each hand, when Glover returned.

'Look, Simmy, I don't want to bother you,' the outlaw said as he came to the table. 'But I need some money to pay Doc Connolly. The boys aren't the only ones who lost tonight.'

'Very well,' Lampart replied.

'I wasn't fixing to ask,' Dusty drawled, 'but seeing's you've got to open your office, I'll come and get myself a stake. There's a diamond bracelet down to the jewellery store that'd just do fine for a birthday present.'

'Who for?' le Blanc smiled.

'Not my mother, you can count on that,' Dusty grinned back.

'You know the rules, Andy,' Lampart said. 'I have to have a member of the Civic Regulators with me if I open the office after dark.'

'Mr. Basmanov's upstairs,' Dusty hinted.

'So he is,' agreed Lampart. 'Why should he sit gambling and carousing when I've got to work. Ask him if he'll come with us, will you please, Jean?'

'With the greatest of pleasure,' Le Blanc responded and went to do so.

By the time a scowling Basmanov had arrived, Emma was coming to the end of her somewhat ribald song. Acknowledging the applause, she left the dais and walked back to her table. On being told that Dusty would be leaving, she extracted his promise to return as soon as possible.

'Tommy'll have to come along,' Glover said, indicating Eel standing on the sidewalk as the men emerged from the saloon. 'He's got the other key to our box.'

'That's all right with me,' Lampart confirmed, but he

caught Dusty's eye and shook his head briefly. 'Where's Mr. Cowper?'

'Down to the doctor's,' Glover replied. 'You stove in three of Styles Homburg's ribs when you jumped up and kicked him, Ed.'

'Feller who taught me to do it allowed that could happen,' Dusty answered disinterestedly. 'How's the other one?'

'Still unconscious,' Eel put in. 'His head's broke, the doctor says.'

'They called the play,' Dusty reminded the outlaws.

'Nobody's gainsaying it,' Glover grunted.

Approaching the mayor's house, Dusty saw a glint of light showing through a crack in the curtains at the window of the mayor's office. He recollected his host having mentioned that the room was kept illuminated all night as a precaution against attempted thefts.

Unlocking the front door, Lampart allowed the other men to precede him into the hall. A lamp hung in the centre of the ceiling, throwing its light over the party. Closing the door, the mayor went to his office.

'Come in, Andy,' he said, turning another key. 'You'll have to wait until I've dealt with these gentlemen, Ed.'

'That's all right with me, sir,' Dusty drawled. 'Just so long as I can get to the jewellery shop before it closes.'

'You'll do that easy enough,' Basmanov said, in a more friendly voice than he had previously employed. 'He stays open until daybreak. Fellers get generous to Emma and her girls late on. You don't need me in there, do you, Simmy?'

'No,' the mayor replied, but Dusty thought he detected an undercurrent of worry in the one word. 'I'll handle things.'

'What do you think of Simmy?' the Russian inquired as he and Dusty stood in the hall after the other three had disappeared behind the door of the office.

'I like him fine,' Dusty replied. 'He's a good man. Smart, too.'

'What with his cut from you fellers' loot and the saloon's takings – he owns it, not Emma, you know,' Basmanov went on, 'he's got a fortune stashed away.'

'It says right in the Good Book that the labourer's worthy of his hire,' Dusty pointed out. 'Which I don't reckon any of you fellers who live here's wives need to take in washing to help buy your bacon and beans.'

'I admit it's profitable,' the Russian replied. 'But some are making more than the others.'

'Drop those guns!'

Muffled by the thickness of the walls and door, Lampart's shouted words came to Dusty's ears. They were followed by four shots which sounded as a very rapid roll of detonations.

'What the hell!' Basmanov spat out in Russian, leaping towards the door.

About to follow him, Dusty became aware of another factor entering the game. The front door flew open and Cowper burst in with a revolver held ready for use. At the sight of Basmanov, he seemed to hesitate. That cost him his life. Dusty's left hand had already commenced its movement towards his right side. Steel rasped on leather, being all but drowned as the off side Colt came from its holster, lined and crashed.

With his mouth opening to yell something, Cowper received a bullet between his eyes. Back snapped his head, while his feet continued to advance. The latter left the floor and the former struck it with a shattering thud which the outlaw did not feel.

'Watch that one!' Dusty barked, springing by Basmanov.

On trying the office's door, Dusty found it to be locked. Although he had kicked an entrance into a room on occasion, he doubted if he could do so with that sturdy door. Bare feet slapped on the floor at the rear of the passage. Clad in a robe donned hurriedly after leaving her bed, Giselle darted in. Skidding to a halt, she stared from the smoking Colt in Dusty's hand to the body lying half in and half out of the front door.

'What's—?' the brunette began.

'Do you have a key for this door?' Dusty demanded.

'No,' Giselle answered, with surprising calm under the circumstances. 'But why should—?'

'There's no other way out of it?' Dusty interrupted.

'Of course not!' Giselle declared. 'What is happening, Edward?'

'There's been some shooting in the office,' Basmanov explained. 'We want to get in to investigate.'

'You could try breaking down the door,' Giselle suggested, still not displaying any concern for her husband's safety.

'You'd best get some of the Regulators at the windows before we try it,' Dusty told the Russian. 'But if they've got Mr. Lampart alive, we're in trouble.'

At that moment, the lock clicked and the door opened. Instantly Dusty pushed Giselle along the passage with his right hand and lined the Colt with his left. Holding the revolver from his desk, Lampart stood in the doorway. Fear showed on his face as he found himself staring down the barrel of Dusty's gun.

'Hey!' Lampart yelped feebly.

'Are you all right, Mr. Lampart?' Dusty asked, lowering the revolver.

'Yes,' the mayor confirmed and looked relieved. He stepped back, pointing with his empty hand. 'I'm afraid I had to kill them both.'

Entering the office and holstering his Colt, Dusty looked around. Gripping a revolver in his right fist, Glover sprawled on his back. Blood oozed from the two holes in his chest. Eel hung face down along the line of boxes to the left of his boss, his gun on the floor and his back a gory mess where two bullets had burst out. Going closer, Dusty noticed that the hammer of each dead man's revolver was still at the down position and Glover's forefinger extended along the outside of the triggerguard. Two padlock keys lay in front of a box.

Allowing Basmanov and Dusty to make their examination of the office, Lampart went to his desk. He flopped into his chair and laid the revolver in its usual place. Walking over, Dusty leaned on the desk to place a hand upon the mayor's shoulder. At the same time, his other hand rested on the cold metal of Lampart's Colt.

'Are you all right, sir?' Dusty asked gently.

'Y – Yes,' Lampart answered. 'I had to do it, Ivan, Ed.'

'Likely you did, sir,' Dusty drawled. 'Best tell us all that happened.'

'We came in and I did as I always do when somebody is drawing out money, sat behind the desk here. They went to their box, then turned and drew their guns. I had to start shooting. It was them or me.'

'You did the right thing, sir,' Dusty declared. 'Don't you reckon so, Mr. Basmanov?'

'Yes!' grunted the Russian. 'But why would they try it?'

'They were almost out of money, 'ccording to what was said at the saloon,' Dusty pointed out. 'Taken with their *amigo* coming busting in at the front door, when he was supposed to be along at the doctor's place with them hurt fellers, I'd say it all points to them figuring on robbing Mr. Lampart.'

'I suppose so,' Basmanov admitted sullenly, aware that several people had arrived and were listening.

So was Dusty. Figuring that some of the arrivals would be outlaws, he went on. 'And not just Mr. Lampart. Had they got away with it, they'd've emptied all our boxes to take with them.'

'Without the keys?' Basmanov asked, trying to salvage something from the death of Glover.

'Why not?' challenged Dusty. 'They likely aimed to keep Mr. Lampart quiet while they bust the locks. It could be done without too much noise. Quietly enough not to be heard outside, anyways.'

Seeing that, for the time being at any rate, he could not use the incident in his campaign to unseat the mayor, Basmanov raised no further objections. Instead, he set about his duty as head of the Regulators and attended to the removal of the bodies.

Waco and the Kid had both been among the crowd, but, having satisfied themselves that Dusty was safe, they returned to the waiting girls. Listening to Red warning the young blond that she 'wouldn't go walking 'round no more creepy ole graveyards', Dusty grinned. Clearly Waco had been trying to solve one of the mysteries which puzzled the trio. Then, seeing the possessive manner in which the girls clung to his companions' arms, he realized what was happening. Lampart was keeping 'Matt Caxton' and 'Comanche Blood' under observation in a way which would be unlikely to arouse their suspicion.

Having taken some money from his party's box, Dusty called at the jeweller's store and purchased the best diamond bracelet in his extensive stock. Then he went back to the saloon. Although Emma came straight over to ask what had happened and if he was hurt, Dusty did not find the opportunity to hand over his present until just before the place closed.

'For your birthday,' Dusty whispered, slipping the bracelet into her hand as they watched the other customers leaving.

'My—?' Emma gasped.

'This year's, or last's, whichever's closest,' Dusty explained.

'Why thank you, Ed!' the blonde purred. 'My, you did dirty your shirt in the fight. You can't wear it until it's been washed.'

'You want for me to change it down here?'

'Of course not. Come upstairs and I'll show you where you can do it.'

Going upstairs and to the rear of the building, Emma escorted him into the bedroom section of her quarters.

'Take it off and I'll have my maid wash it,' the blonde offered.

Removing his tie, Dusty peeled off the shirt. Emma took it from him and left the room. She returned empty handed and her eyes roamed over his powerfully developed bare torso.

'Oh my!' she said, reaching behind her and unhooking her dress. 'Haven't I made a mistake? You can't walk out of here without a shirt.'

'What'll I do then?' Dusty inquired.

The dress slid away. All Emma wore under it was a pair of black silk tights.

'Can't you think of anything?' she asked.

'You know,' Dusty replied. 'I just might be able to at that.'

CHAPTER TWELVE

THEY WON'T TOUCH THAT BUILDING

'Whooee!' enthused the Kid as he and his companions exercised their horses on the fringe of the wooded country which surrounded the vast hollow that held the town of Hell. 'Ole Mark'd sure enjoy being here. Who won that bet, boy?'

'You mind your own blasted business!' the youngster ordered indignantly. 'Way your bed was a-creaking and a-groaning last night Red and me didn't hardly get any sleep.'

'What Juanita and me heard through the wall, you pair wasn't doing much of that sleeping anyways,' countered the Kid. 'Which I'm right grateful to you for the loan of your room, Ed.'

'Emma and me figured you might's well use it, seeing I'd paid for it and wouldn't be,' Dusty answered. 'So she sent her maid along with the key. Did you pair learn anything from the gals?'

'Only that I've got more hair on my chest than she has,' Waco grinned, then became more serious. 'They don't know anything much. Only that some gangs go and come back and others just come the once.'

'We already had that figured out,' Dusty said.

'I was fixing to take a *pasear* round the back of the undertaker's afore I went to bed,' the Kid stated. 'But those gals wouldn't go leave us long enough and I didn't take to the notion of climbing that fence back of the shop with Juanita hanging on my shirt-tail.'

'It can't be helped,' Dusty said philosophically. 'They didn't leave me on my lonesome, either.'

'I talked to a couple of fellers who saw Columbo's bunch being planted,' Waco remarked. 'Can't say's I claim to know sic 'em about undertakering, but I don't reckon there'd've been time for ole Happy Youseman to've embalmed them afore he put them under.'

'I wonder if anybody saw them in the coffins?' Dusty replied.

'Maybe they've planted those *hombres* and don't aim to claim the bounty,' the Kid suggested. 'Just to still the talk.' He shook his head. 'If there's been any talk, I haven't heard it. And Columbo 'n' Pinter both're worth a damned sight more in reward money than Toby Siddons was.'

'When I asked, they reckoned Youseman was at the hawg-ranch,' Dusty pointed out. 'It could be.'

'Did Glover try to stick the mayor up, you reckon, Brother Matt?' Waco inquired, changing the subject.

'Could be,' Dusty replied. 'Couple of the Regulators found their horses, saddled and ready for travelling, around the back of the houses.'

'Was Basmanov in on it?' the Kid wanted to know.

'He may have known they planned something like it, suggested that they tried it even,' Dusty answered. 'But I don't reckon he was expecting it last night, or he wouldn't've come with us.'

'Maybe Glover just meant to collect his money from the box, then rob one of the other townsmen afore they lit out,' Waco suggested, selecting the true reason although he would never know it. 'With that cocked Colt on Lampart's desk, they'd know better than try it against him.'

'You'd figure they would,' Dusty agreed. Then he gave his companions a warning about that particular weapon, concluding. 'It's just a notion I've got, but keep it in mind. It could help keep you alive.'

'We'll not forget,' the Kid promised. 'Did you learn anything from Emma?'

'Nothing to help us,' Dusty admitted. 'But I got the feeling she wanted to tell me something. Could be she's got notions of how she'd rate around town with us three backing her play, only she's not sure how I stand with Lampart.'

'Talking about him,' Waco drawled. 'His missus's headed this way.'

'I'd a notion she might,' Dusty replied. 'They made sure we couldn't get together and talk in private last night and it looks like they figure to keep on doing it.'

Giselle's arrival, riding her dainty *palomino*, brought the trio's discussion to an end. However, they had managed to exchange some information – mostly negative – and, more important, Dusty had had the opportunity to warn his *amigos* about the revolver which always lay cocked and ready for use on Lampart's desk.

'I wish I'd known you meant to come riding, Edward,' Giselle said. 'I do enjoy taking Goldie here out, but Simmy prefers I have an escort.'

'We'll keep it in mind, ma'am,' Dusty declared.

Clearly Lampart did not intend letting Basmanov make an attempt to win 'Ed Caxton's' friendship. On returning from their ride, the trio found the mayor and le Blanc waiting at the stable with an invitation for them to go to lunch. The Russian watched them go, scowling and brooding, but made no comment and did not try to interfere.

Playing on Lampart's eagerness to impress him and his companions, and win their approbation, Dusty led him to talk about the town. The mayor had great pride in the community, or rather in his part in founding it. So he needed little prompting to divulge details of its history.

From what Lampart told them, Dusty, the Kid and Waco began to realize that the wagon train had been of a somewhat unusual nature. With the exception of the Lamparts and Orville Hatchet, their scout, every person on it had been a fugitive from justice. It had been Lampart who gathered them and arranged what should have been a safe passage to Mexico. Wishing to avoid coming into contact with peace officers, they had swung east of the regular route and so found themselves in danger of being massacred by the *Kweharehnuh*. The trio had already heard how that peril was averted and turned to Lampart's advantage. Beyond mentioning how he had possessed contacts who put him in touch with a prime selection of fugitives, Lampart had refused to give further information in le Blanc's presence.

The rest of the day passed quietly. In the afternoon, Hatchet, returned from 'buying supplies' in Paducah. Showing a lack of tact, Giselle told him that 'Comanche Blood' was responsible for the loss of his horse when he had been riding with the posse. No trouble came from the remark, for Hatchet claimed he knew who had done it and why.

Dusty and his *amigos* found no opportunity to hold a private discussion that day. The Lamparts kept them occupied until sundown, then Emma and the girls took over. Once again Dusty shared the blonde's bed. While she made passionate love to him, he sensed she wanted to take him into her confidence on some matter. However, they separated next morning without her doing so. He wondered if he should encourage her, or if he would be better employed in keeping Lampart satisfied with his loyalty. There was a chance that Emma had been told to learn his real feelings and report them to the mayor.

Due to the ruling about fires, the town tended to do most of its business at night. Consequently most of its residents and visitors slept late in the mornings. Dusty, the Kid and Waco were no exception to the rule.

Picking Giselle up at noon, the trio escorted her on a ride around the area. They were repaid by information when she mentioned that Hatchet had already left town to collect more supplies; and did not need an explanation of what that meant. On their return, they were invited to take a belated lunch with the Lamparts. As they were alone, the mayor expanded on the histories of the people who inhabited Hell.

Youseman had been a surgeon and Connolly's partner carrying out experimental research on the subject of longevity. Needing corpses to work on, they had dealt with New York body-snatchers. Then they had graduated to killing healthy people to obtain fresh blood, tissues and organs for their experiments. The law had got wind of their activities, causing them to flee for their lives. They had been able to produce sufficient money to buy places on Lampart's wagon train.

Le Blanc had been a fashionable barber in New York until he had fallen in love with the beautiful wife of an elderly millionaire. Not until he had killed her husband did he discover that she loved another man and had merely been using him. He had murdered the couple in jealous rage, but was cool enough to carry off a large sum of money and a valuable collection of jewellery they had obtained to use as a start to their new life. With no other avenue of escape open to him, le Blanc had been willing to accept Lampart's offer of transportation.

Goldberg and the jeweller had been prominent Wall Street brokers, manipulating the stock market for their mutual advantage. After they had organized a slump which ruined thousands of investors, they had been exposed by a Pinkerton agent planted in their office. Needing a safe haven for themselves and their ill-gotten gains, they had snapped up Lampart's offer of providing it.

Driven from Russia because of his political activities, Basmanov had soon been up to his old tricks in the United States. Along with other anarchist agitators, he had formed a society whose aims had been to overthrow the government and take control in the 'interests' of the people. They had extorted money from immigrants and their funds had been further swelled by donations from various 'liberal' associations. Unfortunately, one of their number had planted a bomb on a bridge, wrecking a train with a heavy loss of lives and drawing unwanted attention to their activities. Sensing the net tightening about him, Basmanov had betrayed his companions and absconded with their not-inconsiderable funds. He too had been drawn into Lampart's band of escaping criminals.

None of the other citizens had more savoury backgrounds, their activities covering everything from white-slaving to drug smuggling and mass murder. One thing they all had in common: they were rich enough to pay their way and live in comfort–providing the forces of law and order did not find them.

From acquainting his audience with the unworthy natures of his fellow citizens, Lampart went on to impress them with his own brilliance. On winning the confidence of the *Kweharehnuh* and hearing about the ruined village deep in the Palo Duro country, he had seen its possibilities. After some argument, he had brought the other travellers around to his way of thinking. They had become persuaded that not only would they be safer than in Mexico, but they could also make their accumulated money earn more while awaiting the day when it would be safe for them to show their faces in public again.

Between them, the travellers had possessed the finances needed to rebuild the town. Owing to his part in a bloody racial conflict, the owner of the Chinese laundry was wanted by the law. However, he was an influential member of his Tong and brought in coolies to help with the work of building. As the Kid had guessed, the Mexican peons were slaves purchased from the *Kweharehnuh*. When all was ready,

Hatchet had passed the word around the outlaw trails of what the town had to offer. The news could not have been better timed. It had come just after the Rangers were reformed and they were striking hard, closing down many hide-outs used by the gangs.

From the beginning, Lampart had insisted on offering the visitors a high standard of service. Not only were the food and drinks of top quality, but the gambling games at the saloon were scrupulously honest. Considering that some of the players would be crooked gamblers capable of detecting any cheating method or device, the latter had been a wise precaution.

The high standard served a dual purpose, Lampart told the Texans. Scouts were posted to meet and check on the men who came to Hell, disarming them before guiding them in. That was to safeguard against protests when the outlaws learned they must hand over one tenth of their total loot if they wanted to stay. Lampart could point out the excellent amenities, and explain how much they cost, as an excuse for taking the money. Secondly, the quality went towards justifying the increased prices charged in the town. He stated that, after their first visit, none of the outlaws had raised objections to paying to the Civic Improvements Fund when they came again.

That, apparently, was as far as the mayor intended to go on the subject of the visitors. Guessing that they would not hear about the fate of the dead outlaws, the Kid had asked about Ten Bears' reaction to having white men passing through his territory. Lampart admitted that, at first, the chief had not been keen on the idea. A further display of magic, backed by the offer of a repeating rifle and ammunition for every brave in the band, had brought him to a more amenable frame of mind.

'Could be a mite risky giving all them bucks rifles and shells,' Waco warned. 'They might figure, having 'em, their medicine's stronger than your'n.'

'I made sure they know they'll only have luck as long as they use the guns to help me,' Lampart replied. 'And I only hand out fifty rounds a month to each man. I had one bit of good fortune. A war bonnet chief called Kills Something was getting restless. He borrowed bullets from other men to arm a war party. They ambushed a patrol, but something went wrong and he was killed. His party had used up a whole lot of ammunition, with precious little but dead and wounded to show for it. That's quietened the others down. They know there's no more bullets for them until the next new moon.'

'That's fine as long as you don't disappoint them when the time comes,' Waco said, catching the Kid's eye and wondering what he thought about having, inadvertently, helped Lampart to keep control of the *Kweharehnuh*.

'I can,' Lampart claimed. 'The shack behind the house is filled with ammunition, and they know it.'

'Maybe they'll figure on helping themselves afore the new moon,' Waco went on. '"Comanch" allows that *Nemenuh* brave-hearts can sneak a man's hoss from under him on a dark night, and him not know until he tries to ride off on it. Be they close to that good, they'd get by them fellers you've got guarding it.'

'They won't touch that building,' Lampart declared, with an air of self-satisfied confidence. 'I've made sure of that.'

'How?' asked the Kid.

'In two ways. I've had photographs of Ten Bears and the medicine woman taken. They think I've captured their souls and they'll be damned if I destroy the pictures. So they use their influence to keep the braves in hand.'

'Which's only one way,' Dusty hinted.

'When the first of the guns and ammunition arrived, I called a meeting with Ten Bears and his men,' Lampart obliged. 'I warned them that I'd put a curse on the whole consignment which would kill any man who tried to steal from me or harm my friends. Then I gave them a practical demonstration. I placed a keg of powder out in the centre of a large, bare patch of sand, stood fifty yards from it and told any brave who thought I was lying to try to fetch it back. Two took the challenge and the keg blew up when they reached it.' He paused and finished, 'Before they had even touched it at that.'

'You had a feller hid out and he put a bullet into it,' Waco guessed, knowing that the mayor wanted them to try to explain how he had worked the trick.

'Unless it had been fired from so far away that the man

could barely see the keg, much less hit it,' Lampart replied, 'they would have heard the shot.'

'You couldn't've run a fuse out to the keg,' the Kid decided. 'The braves'd've known what you was up to when you lit it.'

'True enough, Comanche,' Lampart grinned. 'What do you think, Ed?'

'You used a wire fuse and a "magnetic" battery to set the keg off,' the small Texan stated, watching the mayor's face register mingled annoyance and admiration at his summation. 'I've heard tell of such, but never seen one used.'

'The Indians hadn't even heard tell of it,' Lampart announced. 'On the night before the meeting, I'd buried the wire and smoothed away all traces of it. Next day, while Giselle performed a special "medicine" dance around the box holding the battery, I carried the keg out to the wire.'

'The Indians were all watching me,' the brunette remarked. 'And, if you'd seen what I was wearing, you'd know why.'

'It distracted them all right,' Lampart agreed. 'None of them saw me find the wire and connect it to the detonator in the bottom of the keg. Then I came back, joined Giselle and we both made some "medicine" while I coupled up the other end to the battery. Misdirecting the audience is the basic part of a magician's trade. I got the braves to take up my challenge and set off the keg when they reached it. You can imagine what kind of effect that made.'

'Near enough,' Dusty agreed. 'But there's more to it, isn't there?'

'A little. I had Giselle do another dance around a second keg and let the Indians see me take it into the shack. Ten Bears and his braves believe it will explode if anybody tries to take it. And it will.'

'Now you've lost me,' Dusty admitted, guessing what was implied but hoping to gain more information.

'I've got that keg wired up to a battery in my desk,' Lampart explained, indicating the left side drawer. 'The moment one of my guards raises the alarm, Giselle or I come in here and touch it off.'

'You've sure got it all worked out slicker'n a hawg greased down for cooking,' the Kid praised inelegantly.

'Yes, sir,' Waco agreed, then grinned. 'No offence, sir, and with all respect, ma'am, I'd sure admire to see you do that medicine dance.'

'You'll have your chance in six days,' Giselle promised. 'I do it every time the braves come in to draw their ammunition. We have to take the medicine off and put it back on again. And Ten Bears likes to see me do it.'

'He's not alone in that,' Waco declared, playing 'Matt Caxton' to the limit.

'Aren't you interested in how Emma comes to be here, Ed?' Giselle inquired, making it plain that she wanted the subject changing.

'I figure she'd tell me, was I to ask,' Dusty replied.

'Don't let my wife worry you, Edward,' Lampart said soothingly. 'There's not much to tell. We knew Emma from our theatre days and when I decided to open the saloon, I sent for her to come and run it. She agreed and has proved capable and efficient. There are no wanted posters out on her, or any murky secrets.'

'I never thought there was,' Dusty stated. 'But she's sure one hell of a woman, if you'll pardon the word, ma'am, and we get along just fine.'

'Lord!' Lampart barked, looking at the clock on the dining-room wall. 'Is that the time? I've got to go to a meeting of the Civic Council. Basmanov's trying to get the "no fires" rule cancelled again. Do you think it would be a good thing to let him, Ed?'

'Nope,' Dusty declared, aware of that answer being expected. 'You get all this town's smoke rising and somebody might figure out its here. Somebody we none of us want to see, like a cavalry patrol.'

'They're likely to be out in strength, seeing's one of their patrols got jumped,' the Kid went on. 'Maybe even strong enough to push through this far. Was I you, I'd stand firm against having fires during the day.'

'Rest assured that I will,' the mayor promised. 'I must go now.'

'We better drift down the barn, boys,' Dusty remarked. 'Time we've bedded the horses down, it'll be coming up towards dinner. Juanita and Red won't like it happen you pair's late to the Honest Man.'

CHAPTER THIRTEEN

IT'S OUR TOWN NOW, ED

'Nice neighbourly sort of folks hereabouts, Ed,' the Kid commented as the trio walked behind the street's buildings towards the livery barn. 'One or another of them, they've done just about every meanness 'cept hoss-stealing.'

'Bet some of them's even done that, but they're ashamed to admit it,' Waco went on. 'Not even their mothers could like 'em.'

'That's the way Lampart wants us to think,' Dusty admitted. 'Then we'll not be likely to throw in our hands with anybody else.'

'He made Emma out clean enough, though,' Waco remarked. 'You reckon it's the truth he told, Brother Ed?'

'I reckon so,' Dusty decided. 'He allows I've got a fond feeling for her and doesn't want to chance lying 'case I learn the truth.'

'He's one smart son-of-a-bitch,' drawled the Kid. 'Way he's played things, I can see how he's got Ten Bears and the medicine woman eating out of his hand.'

'We'll either have to bust up his medicine, or get rid of that ammunition before we pull out,' Dusty declared. 'Only, right now, I don't see how we're going to do either. So we'll keep playing along with him and watch our chance.'

'You reckon he trusts us all along the line now, Ed?' the Kid inquired.

'I'd say he's close to it,' Dusty replied. 'At least, he's letting us walk around without anybody hanging on to our shirt tails.'

When the trio reached the barn, they found it deserted except for Pigeons, the custodian of the town's winged messengers. Apparently Basmanov had already left to attend the meeting of the Civic Council. Being one of the Russian's supporters, Pigeons exhibited a distinct lack of cordiality and did not offer to help them with their work.

Having fed and done everything necessary for their horses' well-being, Dusty and his companions returned to the hotel. There they found Red and Juanita waiting, demanding the dinner treat which had been promised to them. Leaving the Kid and Waco to deal with the girls, Dusty went to his own room. Unlocking the door, he went in and slammed to a halt.

'What the hell—?' he growled, hurriedly closing the door.

Smiling at his surprise, Giselle rose from his bed. A long cloak was draped over a chair and Dusty could understand why she had worn it. All she had on was a most abbreviated white doeskin copy of an Indian girl's costume. In two pieces, it covered so little of her that its use on a stage would have resulted in the authorities closing down the theatre. Dusty had to admit that the brunette, small though she might be, had a body perfectly developed to complement the outfit. Looking at her, he could see that she had not been boasting when she claimed that she had held the Indian's attention while her husband had made his preparations to fool them.

'With Simmy at the Council meeting,' Giselle remarked, gliding towards Dusty in an undulating, sensual manner, 'I thought I'd come and show you my medicine dance costume.'

'You made a poor thought, ma'am,' Dusty answered, noticing that she halted well clear of his arms' reach.

'Don't you like me?' Giselle challenged, placing her hands on her head and rotating slowly to let him study her gorgeously moulded little body from all sides. 'I am beautiful, aren't I? Don't you think so?'

'You'll get no argument from me on that, ma'am,' Dusty admitted. 'Any man would, *Mrs.* Lampart.'

'But the fact that I am married bothers you.'

'What bothers me most is you're married to a man I admire and respect. Which being so, I reckon you'd best get covered over and head for home.'

'After I picked your lock to get in to see you?' Giselle pouted, but still kept her distance. 'You're sure that's what you want?'

'I've never been surer,' Dusty stated. 'I'm going to see the boys, ma'am, and I'd be truly grateful if you'll be gone when I get back.'

Leaving the room, Dusty shut the door. He went to his companions' quarters and found them getting ready, helped by the girls, for the evening's round of entertainment. With Red and Juanita present, he could not discuss Giselle's visit. When he returned to his room, he found that the brunette had gone.

That evening, on entering the saloon, Dusty went to where Lampart was sitting in solitary state at Emma's private table.

'I don't know whether to be riled or flattered,' the small Texan announced as he sat down.

'That went straight by me,' Lampart smiled.

'You sent your wife along to my room to try me out,' Dusty elaborated. 'That could've riled me up some, except that I reckoned you must trust me enough to know she'd be safe.'

'And you fully justified my faith in you,' the mayor praised, then the arrival of Youseman and le Blanc brought the conversation to an end.

During the evening, Dusty noticed an increased air of hostility between Basmanov's supporters and Lampart's clique. That told the small Texan why the mayor had been so loquacious at lunch and had sent Giselle to test his loyalty. Unless Dusty missed his guess, Lampart intended to lock horns with the Russian and settle who would control the town; so wanted to be sure of having 'Ed Caxton's' backing in the showdown.

Nothing was said on the subject until Emma mentioned it indirectly. It was after the saloon had closed for the night and she lay in bed with Dusty's arms around her.

'That was one stormy Council meeting this afternoon, Ed,' the blonde remarked as they separated from a kiss.

'Was, huh?' Dusty replied, feeling her snuggling closer to him. 'Is Basmanov still pushing to get that "no fires" ruling changed?'

'That's only part of it,' Emma answered and kissed him with fiery passion. Drawing back her face, she went on, 'Mostly he's trying to make Simmy share out the Civic Improvement Fund instead of holding it all at his place.'

'Does Simmy do that?'

'He does. Even some of his own crowd aren't too happy about it.'

Having delivered the information, Emma started to make love. Dusty had never known her so insistent, or eager to give herself to him. After a time, they lay side by side on their backs and the blonde spoke again.

'I bet Simmy's got well over half a million dollars stashed away, Ed, what with the Fund, the profits from the saloon and his share in the other—'

'What other?' Dusty demanded as the words trailed off.

'Connolly and Youseman have found a way of embalming bodies so they'll keep long enough to be sent out of the Palo Duro and the bounty collected on them.'

'The hell you say!' Dusty growled, simulating surprise as he sat up and stared at the blonde through the darkness.

'It's true,' Emma insisted. 'That's why Youseman wasn't in the saloon the night you first came in. They were treating the bodies of those fellers you'd shot. I got the story from Youseman one night when he was drunk. What they do, I mean; it was before you got here. Him and Connolly found out how to do it at Simmy's suggestion. He fixed up the rest. Hatchet takes the bodies out to one of the towns where the sheriff's in cahoots with them. They had to take Basmanov in with them when he found out about it. None of them care much for that.'

'And nobody else knows?'

'Nobody. Youseman was so drunk that he's forgotten he told me. They put the bodies in trick coffins, so anybody who wants can see them. Then, when the lid's screwed on, the bottom opens to drop the corpse into the basement, the empty box is buried and the body sent out.'

'That's the sort of neat planning I'd expect from Simmy,' Dusty drawled.

'Is that all it means to you?' Emma asked, sitting up.

'What else should it mean?' Dusty countered.

'There's ten thousand dollars on each of your heads,' the blonde reminded him and slid closer to wrap her arms around him.

'Simmy's my friend,' Dusty pointed out.

'He was Ben Columbo's friend too,' Emma warned, sagging back to the pillow and drawing him with her. 'There's still an empty coffin in his grave.'

'Simmy needs me and the boys' guns,' Dusty began, being stopped by her lips crushing against his mouth and tongue slipping between his teeth.

'The time will come when he doesn't,' the blonde cautioned at the completion of the kiss. Her hands roamed over Dusty's body. 'What a waste it would be, Ed. Embalming you, I mean.'

'I'll have something to say afore they get the chance to do it,' Dusty threatened.

'So will I,' Emma promised and pressed her lips lightly to his. Then she whispered, 'Ed. Over half a million is a lot of money.'

There the matter came to an end. Clearly waiting for Dusty to make a comment, Emma said no more. He made no response, other than returning her caresses, until sleep claimed them both. The exertions of their love-making caused them to be late out of bed next morning. In fact, it was way past noon before they had eaten breakfast and dressed to go downstairs. They found Waco and the Kid in the bar room, although Red and Juanita were no longer in evidence.

'You pair expecting a war?' Dusty inquired, nodding to the Winchester in the Kid's right hand.

'Nope,' Waco replied. 'Last night my Red gal got saying how she just loves turkey. So Comanch's fixing to go out and shoot one for her.'

'There's a gentleman for you,' Emma praised. 'The boys take after you, Ed.'

'They couldn't pick a better ex—' Dusty began, then stopped to stare as the side door opened and Giselle ran in. 'What's up, Mrs. Lampart?'

'It's Basmanov,' the brunette replied. She was wearing her usual style of clothing and looked concerned. 'He's lit the fire in his office stove and Simmy's going down there to make him put it out.'

'Could be he'll need help,' Dusty barked. 'Let's go, boys.'

'I'll see to Mrs. Lampart,' Emma remarked, catching hold of the brunette's right arm in a firm rather than gentle grip. 'Leave her to me, Ed.'

'*Gracias, querida,*' Dusty drawled. 'Don't you fret none, ma'am, we'll see Simmy comes back safe.'

Giselle had obviously wasted no time in bringing the news. Leaving the saloon by the rear door, the three Texans saw Lampart half-way along the back of Doctor Connolly's premises. Hearing their footsteps, he turned to face them.

'What – How—?' the mayor gasped, showing surprise and relief.

'Your lady told us what's happening,' Dusty explained. 'We concluded that you'd need some help.'

'I do,' Lampart admitted and indicated the white-handled revolver thrust into his waistband. 'After the way Basmanov took on at yesterday's meeting, I'm sure this is his way of calling me out for a showdown.'

'He'll have friends along,' Dusty declared, not offering to walk on.

'It's possible,' the mayor admitted. 'Pigeons will be there. Probably Diebitch, the blacksmith, Rossi, his usual clique.'

'Then we're going to play it smart,' Dusty decided. 'I don't reckon they've seen us yet. So you and me'll go along the street, bold as all get out, right through the front door.'

'Just the two of us?'

'Matt and Comanch'll be around when we need them.'

Leaving his companions, Dusty accompanied the mayor at a leisurely pace through an alley to the street. Already the smoke rising from the barn's chimney had attracted considerable attention. Men and women pointed it out to each other. Then they turned their gaze to Dusty and Lampart. Only le Blanc offered to help. Carrying a twin-barrelled shotgun, he ran from his shop.

'It's come then, Simmy?' the barber greeted.

'As you say, Jean,' Lampart confirmed. 'It's come.'

'Don't walk so fast,' Dusty advised. 'Diebitch's watching us from the front door, so we'll be expected. Leave them sweat it out a whiles – And let my boys get into place before we go in.'

'I don't see Matt or Comanche,' Lampart reported worriedly, glancing in passing along the alley which separated the barn from its next-door neighbour.

'It's lucky Diebitch's ducked back in,' Dusty growled. 'You'd've give the whole snap away. They're around. You can count on it.'

Walking on, the three men stepped through the open front doors of the barn. With le Blanc to his left and Lampart at the right, Dusty studied his surroundings. Basmanov and the slim, vicious-looking Diebitch confronted the trio, but there was no sign of any other members of the Russian's faction.

'You know the penalty for lighting a fire between dawn and sundown, Ivan?' Lampart challenged.

'I do,' Basmanov admitted. 'And you'll pay it. You and one of your magic tricks lit the stove.'

'Now who'll believe that?' Lampart asked.

'I reckon they'll believe whichever of us comes out of it alive,' Basmanov grinned. 'Only you wouldn't have the guts to face me man to man.'

'Wouldn't I?' countered Lampart.

'You've brought le Blanc and Caxton along,' the Russian pointed out.

'Only to see fair doings,' Dusty drawled. 'If Mr. Diebitch'll back off, me and Jean'll leave you gents settle this between you.'

'That suits me,' Diebitch stated fervently and moved aside.

'And me,' Lampart declared. 'Go and wait by the doors, gentlemen.'

'To show I don't want no edge,' Basmanov said, when Dusty and le Blanc had obeyed. 'I'll ask you to count to five, Mr. Caxton. We'll draw when you get there.'

'Go ahead, Ed,' Lampart commanded.

'One!' Dusty said. 'Two!'

Down drove Basmanov's right hand, closing about the butt of his gun. At the same moment, he saw a mocking smile playing on Lampart's lips. It was the expression of a man who had out-bluffed a bluffer.

As soon as Basmanov moved, the mayor whipped out his own revolver. Although it had an ivory handle, it proved to be a snub-nosed British Webley Bulldog and not the Colt Peacemaker from the top of his desk. Twice the weapon crashed, with a speed that was only possible by trigger pressure – as opposed to fanning the hammer – when using a self-cocking, double-action mechanism. Although he had started his draw slightly after the Russian, Lampart had about six inches less barrel to get clear. That made all the difference. His bullets tore into Basmanov's chest before the other's gun could point at him.

'Get them!' Diebitch screamed, grabbing for the revolver he wore.

Throwing up his shotgun, le Blanc cut loose from waist level. Seven of the nine buckshot balls which belched from the right hand tube found their mark and flung Diebitch lifeless from his feet.

While Dusty had agreed to take a passive role, he had been under no delusions regarding Basmanov's sense of fair play. So he had been prepared for treachery and knew instinctively where it would come from. Sure enough, Pigeons loomed into sight from behind the hay-bales at the front of the loft and started to swing a shotgun to his shoulder. Even as Lampart's Webley spoke, Dusty's hands crossed with their usual speed. The small Texan took the extra split-second needed to raise his right hand weapon to eye-level and take aim. He shot the only way he dared in the circumstances, for an instant kill. Passing Pigeons' rising shotgun, the .45 bullet winged into his head.

Big and bulky, the blacksmith had also risen from concealment in the loft. The ambush had been planned. That was obvious from the way the men took aim at and shot le Blanc, although he did so too late to save Diebitch. In echo to the blacksmith's revolver, Dusty's left hand Colt lined and barked. Hit in the body, Pigeons' companion screamed, spun around, toppled over the bales and crashed to the floor below.

In the tack-room, Rossi and another man gripped their revolvers and waited to cut in on the fight which would determine who ran Hell. So interested were they in what was going on between Basmanov and Lampart that they failed to notice the face which peered in through the window. On seeing the Russian's bid fail, Rossi prepared to throw open the door leading into the stable.

Having reached the barn undetected, Waco saw enough through the window to know that he must act fast. Kicking open the outside door as he had learned to do from Dusty, he plunged into the tack-room. The two men heard the crash and spun around with their weapons thrusting in the youngster's direction. Left, right, left, right, flame erupted from the muzzles of Waco's Army Colts. Rossi died instantly, a bullet severing his jugular vein. Hit in the shoulder, the second man dropped his gun and stumbled into the stable. Being unarmed did not save him. Turning fast, Lampart shot him in the head.

While that was happening, the Kid raced in through the back doors. Bounding along the gap between two lots of stalls, he appeared before another pair of Basmanov's supporters as they came from one of the storerooms. Seeing the dark-faced savage, they forgot their intention of shooting Lampart and tried to turn their guns on the Kid. Lead hissed by him, calling for an immediate response. Working his Winchester's lever at its fastest possible speed, he poured out eight bullets in an arc that encompassed the two men's torsos. Both went down, torn to doll-rags by the tempest of flying lead.

No more men appeared. The bloody battle for mastery of the town had come to an end. Horses squealed, snorted, reared and kicked at their stalls in fright as the acrid powder smoke wafted away.

'See to the horses – Comanch', Matt,' Dusty ordered, having to make an effort to prevent himself using their real names. Looking at le Blanc, he went on, 'Jean's cashed in.'

'He's been avenged,' Lampart answered and started to go around Basmanov's party to check on their condition. 'And he'll have plenty of company; they're all dead too.'

People came pouring into the barn. Outlaws went to help the Kid and Waco calm down the horses. Townsmen studied the bodies and exchanged glances. Those who had supported Lampart showed their satisfaction. On other faces, anxiety and concern left their marks. Those were the emotions of Basmanov's less active partisans, who wondered what the future held for them on account of it. Already the fence-sitters were beaming their approval at the mayor. However, Lampart ignored all of them. After ordering the jeweller to put out the fire in the office's stove and directing Youseman to give le Blanc the best possible funeral, he apologized to such outlaws as were present for disturbing their horses. Then he called the three Texans to him, thanked them for their support and asked them to accompany him to his home.

On the street, the men found Giselle, Red, Juanita and Emma waiting. The blonde held a bottle of champagne and declared that the victory called for a celebration. Giving his agreement, Lampart took them to his house and established them comfortably in the sitting-room. With the drinks served and toasts to their continued success drunk, Dusty decided to obtain some information.

'How did you know when to set the fire off, Simmy?' the small Texan asked. 'If you'd done it too early, we might none of us been around to back your play.'

'I waited until I saw Comanche and Matt taking the young ladies back to the saloon. Emma's maid had already drawn the curtains in her bedroom, which meant you and she were up and about. So I made my arrangements, knowing your brother and Comanche would be waiting for you.'

'How'd you get in and light the fire?' Waco inquired. 'You couldn't've just touched her off and got out, somebody'd likely've seen you.'

'It's a trick I learned, making a fire start at a given moment. I won't say more than that, a magician is under oath not to divulge the nature of his secrets. I went there, picked the office because it was empty, made my arrangements and came back to await results.'

'You knew Basmanov'd see the smoke and guess what your game was,' Dusty drawled. 'But you counted on him wanting a showdown, gathering his stoutest side-kicks and waiting for you to come.'

'That's true,' Lampart admitted. 'I also knew that, with you helping me, I had the edge. None of them could even come close to matching your gun skill.'

'That's for sure,' Waco put in. 'They didn't have the sense to watch the outside windows.'

'All went off perfectly,' Lampart declared, showing no hint of regret over le Blanc's death. 'It's my town now.'

'*Your* town, Simmy?' Dusty queried, seeing Emma throw him a glance pregnant with meaning.

'That wasn't what I meant,' Lampart amended. 'It's *our* town now, Ed.'

'I said you could count on Simmy to do the right thing, Ed,' Emma remarked.

CHAPTER FOURTEEN

TAKE YOUR CLAWS OFF MY MAN

In all his eventful young life, Dusty Fog had never received a shock to equal that which greeted him as he entered the mayor's office towards sundown on the day after the gun battle. Fortunately, Lampart had his back to the door and did not see the small Texan's reaction to the sight of the woman who was placing a bulky set of saddlebags into one of the deposit boxes. Straightening up and closing the lid, she stared in Dusty's direction. At first surprise played on her strikingly beautiful features, to be replaced almost immediately by an expression which denoted understanding.

Black hair flowed from beneath the brim of a grey Stetson hat with a band decorated by silver conchas. She wore a fringed buckskin jacket, open down its front to exhibit a dark grey shirt tucked into figure-hugging black riding breeches. High-heeled boots with spurs attached graced her feet. The clothes served to display a body every bit as voluptuously curvaceous as Emma Nene's. Emphasizing the full contours of her hips, a gunbelt slanted down with the tip of its holster tied to her magnificently moulded right thigh. In the holster, carefully positioned to facilitate a fast draw, rode what looked like a wooden-handled Colt Model 1851 Navy revolver.

Without the need for closer examination, Dusty knew the woman's gun to be a five shot copy of the Navy Colt manufactured by the now-defunct Manhattan Firearms Company. Going by her display of emotion on his arrival, she could identify him despite his clothes, the beard and moustache. She had been a blonde on their two previous meetings, but Dusty found no difficulty in recognizing the famous lady outlaw, Belle Starr.

'Ed!' Belle greeted, her voice a pleasant, warmly-inviting Southern drawl. 'I just might have known I'd find you here, after all the things I've been reading about you-all in the *Texas State Gazette*.'

'You know each other?' Lampart inquired, bringing his gaze from its contemplation of Belle's physique.

There was a hint of suspicion in the mayor's voice and Dusty could figure out what had caused it. Lampart had not forgotten how 'Ed Caxton' had claimed to have led a law-abiding life, until committing the robbery which had resulted in him fleeing for safety to Hell. So Lampart was wondering how he could have made the acquaintance of such a prominent member of outlaw society.

'Why sure,' Dusty agreed, thinking fast. 'It was while we were with the Army up in the Indian Nations. Me and the boys got sent with a patrol to search for Miss Belle at her pappy's place.'

'Why they just did me the biggest favour in my whole life,' Belle went on. 'The three of them were sent to search the barn and Comanche found my hiding place. But Ed said for me to be covered up again and they never let on where I was to that mean old officer.'

In view of her close relationship with Mark Counter,* Dusty had not expected Belle to betray him. She had recognized him immediately, recollected the story of the robbery in the newspapers and guessed what was happening. No matter why she had come to Hell, it seemed that she was willing to play along with the small Texan's game.

'You paid us back in Dallas,' Dusty pointed out, feeling that so short an acquaintance would not account for her recognizing him. 'If you hadn't loaned me that five hundred dollars, I might've had to kill some of the gambling man's side-kicks to stop them pestering me for it.'

'I had my money's worth,' Belle claimed, darting an arch smile at Lampart. She too felt that the situation needed a little expanding. 'Ed's quite a man, you know, Simmy. Although I don't suppose you *could* know, not that way.'

---

* How that relationship began, developed and finally ended is told in the 'The Bounty On Belle Starr's Scalp' episode of *Troubled Range*, *The Bad Bunch*, *Rangeland Hercules*, the 'A Lady Known as Belle' episode of *The Hard Riders* and *Guns in the Night*.

'I suppose not,' Lampart agreed stiffly and looked at Dusty, 'Miss Starr—'

'I've already said you can call me "Belle",' the girl interrupted.

'Belle has just arrived, Ed,' the mayor went on. 'I've explained the rules of the town and she agrees to them.'

'That figures,' Dusty drawled, glancing at the girl's gunbelt. 'Did you have trouble getting here, Belle?'

'None. But I was just a teensy mite worried when the guide said I'd have to hand over my guns. He was telling the truth about me getting them back after I'd talked to the mayor.'

'Why'd you need to come?' Dusty challenged, knowing some such comment would be expected by Lampart.

'Belle had heard of our community,' the mayor injected, just a shade too quickly. 'And, with the Indian Nations being somewhat disturbed—'

'*Disturbed!*' Belle ejaculated. 'Land-sakes a-mercy, Ed, it's hotter than a two dollar pistol up there right now. So I concluded I'd better stay away from home for a spell. Of course I'd heard of Hell and decided to take a look at it.'

'Seeing's how Belle's such an old friend of mine,' Dusty remarked to the mayor, 'I reckon we can forget her contribution to the Civic Improvement Fund.'

'Well, I admit a twentieth of my money does seem a lot,' Belle purred, glancing at the stack of bills which lay alongside the white-handled Peacemaker on the desk. 'But I shouldn't have any special favours. It just wouldn't be fitting, Ed.'

'A *twentieth's* a whole heap of money,' Dusty said coldly. 'Has Simmy introduced you to his wife, Belle?'

'I was going to, after we'd concluded our business,' the mayor declared, with an annoyed glare at the small Texan.

'If she's busy, it can wait her convenience, Simmy,' Belle smiled. 'Why don't you show me to the hotel, Ed. I'm just dying to hear all about that robbery you and the boys pulled.'

Although he threw a scowl at Dusty, Lampart raised no objections. Belle locked her box and dropped the keys into a jacket pocket. Then she and Dusty left the office. Giselle peered around the curtain at the back end of the hall, but withdrew without coming to be introduced. On emerging from the mayor's house, Dusty became aware of somebody watching him. Looking at the saloon, he saw two of the girls standing on the first floor's verandah. They were displaying considerable interest in Belle and himself. Even as he watched, one of them darted into the building. Dusty did not need much thought to figure out where she was going. So he concluded that he had better get Belle off the street before Emma came to investigate.

'What's the game, Dusty?' Belle asked as he started her moving away from the saloon. 'I nearly had a fit when you walked in. Luckily I remembered that story in the paper and came up with the right answer – or some of it.'

'Thanks for not saying who I am,' Dusty replied. 'I hoped you wouldn't.'

'Now play fair with me,' Belle suggested. 'I'm here on business and I'd like to know where I—'

'Mr. Caxton,' called a voice and Dusty saw the jeweller waddling across the street in his direction. 'I was hoping to see you. I've had the clasp on that necklace repaired and it's ready for you.'

'*Gracias*,' Dusty answered. 'I'll come around later and—'

'Now who would you be buying a necklace for, Ed?' Belle challenged, a merry gleam dancing in her eyes. 'Come on. I'm dying to see it.'

'Maybe you should go and get a room at the hotel,' Dusty told her.

'There's time for that later,' Belle insisted. 'Come on.'

So far, Dusty observed as he made for the jeweller's shop, Emma had not made an appearance. The delay would allow her time to do so before he could get Belle inside the hotel. So, in the interests of peace and quiet, he figured he had best take the lady outlaw out of the blonde's sight. They entered the shop without Emma having emerged from the Honest Man. Passing around the end of the counter, the owner disappeared into a back room. He seemed to take an exceptionally long time before he returned carrying a magnificent diamond necklace. Dusty could hear significant sounds from the street, but hoped he might be wrong about their meaning. From what he could see through the window, he doubted if he was.

'My!' Belle breathed, laying a hand on Dusty's sleeve. 'Now isn't that the sweetest lil ole trinket you ever did see?'

The front door flew open and a furious feminine voice hissed, 'Take your claws off my man!'

Turning with the speed of a wildcat preparing to defend itself, Belle confronted Emma. The blonde was dressed ready for her night's work and a couple of rings with sizeable stones flashed on her fingers. Ignoring the people who gathered behind her, Emma looked Belle over from head to toe. The saloongirls had spread the word and a number of men and women waited to see what would develop.

'Easy, Emma,' Dusty said soothingly. 'I was just taking Miss Starr down to the hotel.'

'Why, Ed,' Belle purred. 'You've never called me "Miss Starr" before.'

Annoyance bit at Dusty. Instead of Belle letting him handle things, she seemed set on provoking trouble. Dull red flooded into Emma's cheeks and she bunched her right hand to form a capable-looking fist.

'He won't do it ag—!' the blonde began, drawing back her arm.

Out flashed Belle's Manhattan, its hammer clicking back and muzzle pointing at Emma's heaving bosom. Poised to attack, the protruding stone of a ring glinting evilly on her clenched fist, the blonde stood very still.

'You try to ram that blazer into my face,' Belle threatened, 'and I'll put a window in your apples.'

'I can soon enough take the rings off!' Emma spat back, making a move as if to do so.

'Please ladies,' the jeweller implored. 'No fighting in here.'

'Let it drop, both of you!' Dusty ordered.

'If *you* say so, Ed,' Belle replied. 'What do folks do for entertainment around here, Mr. Jewellery-Man?'

'G – Go to the Honest Man Saloon,' the shop's owner replied.

'You put your face inside it,' Emma promised grimly, 'and I'll throw you right back out.'

'Will you be there tonight, Ed?' Belle inquired.

'That won't matter to you,' Emma declared before Dusty could reply. 'What I said goes. If you show your face in my place tonight, gun or no gun, I'll make you wish you'd hid in some other brothel instead of coming here.'

'That's big talk for a fat old harridan,' Belle jeered, conscious that the exchange had an audience. 'I'll be there tonight. Without my gun and, to give you a chance, wearing moccasins. That'll make us even, for all your blazers and long talons.'

With that, Belle holstered the Manhattan and pushed by Emma to leave the building. For a moment, the blonde appeared to be on the verge of hurling herself after the lady outlaw. Then, glancing at her rings and finger-nails, Emma stalked out of the door. She did not even look at Dusty before departing.

'Whoo!' ejaculated the jeweller and ran the tip of his tongue across his lips. 'It should be something to see at the Honest Man tonight, Mr. Caxton.'

'Likely,' Dusty admitted absently, wondering why Belle had taken such an attitude.

'How about the necklace?' the man asked as Dusty turned from the counter.

'I reckon I'd best take it with me,' the small Texan decided, thinking that it might prove useful as a peace offering to Emma.

Apparently practically everybody in town shared the jeweller's summation. Dusty had never seen such a crowd as he found in the Honest Man Saloon on his arrival at nine o'clock. There were people present he would never have expected to find in a saloon. Giselle sat with Lampart at Emma's table. Other townsmen had also brought their wives. The madam of the brothel was there, accompanied by her whole staff. So far, neither Emma nor Belle had made an appearance. Dusty figured that they soon would.

Despite his efforts, Dusty had failed to change either of their minds. Although delighted with the necklace, Emma had stated the only way she would forget the incident was if Belle made a public apology and never entered the saloon. Due to the interest her arrival had aroused, Dusty could not manage to get Belle alone for more than a few seconds.

Asked to let the matter drop, she had declared herself willing to do so; if Emma invited her into the Honest Man.

Consulting the Kid and Waco, Dusty had finally decided to leave the women to settle the issue themselves. From what Mark had told them, Belle could take care of herself. She had also fixed it so that Emma would be unable to wear the dangerous rings and most likely had to cut short her nails. So both should escape serious damage. Waco had warned that the town would deeply resent any interference which halted the fight. Already, the trio suspected, Lampart was seeking a way to remove them. There was no point in giving him a weapon with which to turn the population against them.

'Mig Santiago will be annoyed to have missed this,' Giselle remarked, after Dusty had sat down and exchanged greetings.

Any comment the small Texan might have considered making on the subject of the Mexican's departure, under pressure from his financially-embarrassed gang, went unsaid. The low hum of conversation died away around the room. Every head swung to stare at Belle as she strolled through the batwing doors.

True to her promise, the lady outlaw had left off her gun-belt and boots. Missing too were the Stetson and her jacket. She made an attractive picture in her moccasins, riding breeches as tight as a second skin, shirt with its sleeves rolled up and hands covered by thin black leather gloves.

Posted to keep watch for Belle, a girl on the balcony darted away. When Emma came slinking gracefully down the stairs, the way in which she was clothed threatened to overshadow the black-haired beauty's appearance. The blonde wore nothing but a brief, lace-trimmed white bodice, black silk tights and high heeled slippers with pompons on the toes. Showing her unadorned hands, she drew on a pair of white gloves. Then, in a silence that could almost be felt, she advanced to the centre of the area in front of the bar which had been cleared of tables and chairs to make room for the anticipated battle.

'I'll set up drinks all round after I've handed her her needings, folks,' Belle announced, moving towards Emma like a great cat stalking its prey.

'*If* she licks me,' the blonde countered. 'I'll give drinks to the house all night.'

That was all the conversation carried out. Warily the two gorgeous creatures circled each other. Suddenly Belle whipped her arm right back and swung her open palm in a round-house slap to Emma's left cheek. It cracked with a sharp, vicious sound, snapping the blonde's head around and bringing an involuntary squeak of pain. For all that, Emma responded almost immediately by whipping out first one hand, then the other. The explosive smacks of her palms against Belle's face rang out loud. Eager to follow up her advantage, the blonde crowded forward with arms flailing. Bewildered by the onslaught, Belle was forced to retreat. Excited yells rose from the crowd. Men and women came to their feet, moving to form a wall of humanity around the open space in which the girls were tangling.

Desperate to halt the stinging punishment, Belle suddenly entwined her fingers into Emma's blonde tresses. She backed off a long stride, hauling the saloonkeeper's head down and throwing up her knee. An experienced bar room brawler, Emma had known what to expect. Swiftly she folded her arms in front of her face and Belle's knee struck them. Although the blonde had saved herself from serious damage, the impact snapped her erect. Belle had retained her hold on Emma's hair, so the pain caused by the halting of her head's upwards movement ripped into the blonde. Letting out a screech, Emma sank both hands deep into Belle's free-flowing black hair. She jerked and twisted at the ensnared locks with deliberate fury, only to have Belle reply in a similar manner.

Lurching from side to side, their heads bobbing and shaking with the violence they put into the hair-yanking, the girls also staggered back and forwards a few steps at a time. They clung determinedly to each other's hair, looking as if they desired to hand-scalp each other. Forehead to forehead, they panted and grunted, striving all the time to retain their balance on wide spread legs.

It could not last. With a final wrench bringing squeaks of agony, almost as if by mutual consent, they jerked free their hands and went into a clinch. For a few seconds they tussled on their feet. Then Belle managed to twist away and drag

Emma over her buttocks. Turning a somersault, the blonde went to the floor. However, she had clung on to Belle and the outlaw followed her. Curling over in mid-air, Belle lit down on her back.

Rolling over swiftly, Emma writhed until her open thighs made an arch over Belle's head and her knees held the outlaw's arms pinned to the floor. Bending forward, the blonde thrust her fingers on to the trapped girl's bust. With the pain knifing into her, Belle supported herself on her bent left leg, and, lifting her rump from the unyielding planks, jerked her right knee hard against the top of the blonde's forward tilted skull. The blow caused Emma to remove her fingers from the sensitive region and lurch away.

Snatching her arms from beneath Emma's knees, Belle rolled into a sitting position. She turned just in time to meet the blonde's diving attack. Bust to bust, fingers again ripping at hair, they pitched full length on the floor. Belle's legs were doubled under her, but she managed to writhe them free. A sudden heave brought the outlaw on top, both hands tugging outwards at hanks of blonde hair. Shrieking in torment, Emma tried to bow her body upwards. Her left hand lost its grip on Belle's hair. Scrabbling for a fresh hold, she grasped the open neck of Belle's shirt. A fresh surge of pain from the tortured locks of hair caused Emma to wrench savagely at the garment. Buttons popped and, dragged out of Belle's breeches, the shirt split open down its front.

Angered by the damage to her clothing, Belle released the hair. Wriggling until her right knee rammed against Emma's abdomen, she sought for revenge. Drawn down around her right bicep, the shirt did not entangle her arms sufficiently to inconvenience her. Laying her right hand on Emma's face, she pressed the blonde's head to the floor. Greedily the outlaw's left fist clamped on the front of the bodice, tugging and pulling until the flimsy material came apart from décolleté to waist.

Almost unseated by Emma's furious struggles, Belle advanced to sit astride her shoulders. Transferring her hand to the side of the blonde's head, she drew back the other fist ready to pound Emma's face. At the table, Dusty wondered if he should intervene. To do so might bring about his death, for the wildly excited crowd would expect to see the fight through to a decisive victory for one or the other girl. Yet, held down in such a way, Emma might suffer serious damage at the hands of her enraged rival. Before he could reach a decision, Dusty saw Emma was shouting something. Although the noisy acclaim of the spectators prevented the small Texan from catching the words, Belle obviously heard them.

Instead of pummelling the blonde's face to a bloody ruin, the outlaw's fist held back. Like a flash, Emma braced her feet and head against the floor. Up curved her body, with a force that flung Belle forward and away from her. Rolling on to her stomach as Belle landed face down, Emma plunged on to the outlaw's back. For several seconds, the blonde remained on top. With her thighs squirming to hold down Belle's legs, the blonde hooked her left arm under and around the other's throat while her right alternately punched the trapped head and tore away the remains of the shirt.

Screeching and struggling with the strength of rage-filled desperation, Belle contrived to roll on to her right side. The arm was still about her neck and the blonde's legs, the knees showing whitely through the ruptured silk of the tights, straddled her hips. While Belle's right arm attempted to drag Emma away by the hair, her left fingers raked ineffectively at the blonde's ribs to complete the destruction and removal of the bodice.

Oblivious of her naked torso, Emma fought on. So did Belle. Losing her choke-hold, the blonde allowed the outlaw to reach a sitting position. Then, sitting up herself, she wrapped her legs in a scissor grip about Belle's bare midsection. Gasping as the crushing pressure bit at her, Belle clawed at Emma's upper leg in a futile effort at escaping. Tilting sideways and resting on her left elbow, the saloon-keeper slammed her clenched right hand into the centre of the outlaw's face. Blood trickled from Belle's nostrils. Mouthing croaks of pain, Belle took her hands from Emma's right leg. She put them to better use by grabbing hold of and crushing at the blonde's jutting bare right breast. Emma's scream rang out loud. Lifting her right leg, she shoved up with the left to try to dislodge her tormentress. Such was

Belle's relief at the end of the scissors that she released her own hold and rolled away.

Dragging themselves to their feet, the girls stood for a moment to regain something of their energy. Then they rushed at each other with fists flying. Wildly propelled knuckles impacted on faces, busts, stomachs, or missed as chance dictated. Coming in close to try to minimize the punishment being inflicted, they went into a mindless tangle of primitive, unscientific wrestling. Arms, legs, elbows, hands and feet were used indiscriminately and teeth brought into play. Emma was bare-footed, her tights in ribbons, while Belle had lost one moccasin and her other leg showed where the breeches' seam had split. Six times they made their feet and went down, while the crowds screamed itself hoarse, encouraging them to further efforts.

On the seventh time of rising, the girls clutched at one another's throats and held on with a choking grip. Reddish blotches showed around their fingers as the digits gouged into sweat-soddened flesh. Guttural sounds broke from them. Although fairly evenly matched, Emma had a slight weight advantage. Not much, but enough in their present condition. Slowly she bore Belle backwards, but without causing the other to let go.

In an attempt to free herself, Belle slid her legs between Emma's spread-apart feet and lowered her rump to the floor. And found she had made a serious mistake. She was sitting with the back almost touching the dais on which, at other times, the band played. Before she could rectify the situation, Belle was trapped. Spreading open her thighs, Emma lunged to kneel on the dais and crush Belle against it.

Realizing the consequences of failure, Belle put all her strength into a desperate effort. Bracing her shoulders against the dais, she thrust forward. Finding herself being tilted off balance, the blonde tried to spring to the rear. Landing awkwardly, she sat down hard. Lurching upright, Belle swung around her right leg. The sole of the bare foot slammed against the side of Emma's jaw. As she fell backwards, Belle stumbled away.

Sobbing with exhaustion, the outlaw turned to defend herself. She saw Emma lying supine, right leg bent, right hand clasped on her forehead and left arm stretched out limply. Calling on her last dregs of energy, Belle returned to the blonde's side. Standing astride the motionless figure, Belle folded her legs until her rump came to rest on Emma's bosom. She had the blonde at her mercy, arms trapped beneath her knees, but waited to regather her strength. Then she felt two hands beneath her arm-pits, lifting her. For a moment, she tried to struggle and twisted her head to see who was holding her.

'For God's sake, Belle,' Dusty Fog said, dragging her from the unconscious blonde. 'Leave Emma be. She's licked.'

'T-Take-me-hotel!' Belle croaked back. 'D-Damn it. Take me. I've won and it's due to me.'

CHAPTER FIFTEEN

WE HAD TO KNOW WHO'S BOSS

'I HOPE you haven't got the wrong idea, Dusty,' Belle Starr remarked as she stood with her back to him and, wincing a little, donned a flimsy nightgown. 'Because only one man has ever shared my bed.'

'So Mark told me,' Dusty replied. 'What the hell did you fight Emma for?'

As soon as Dusty had seen Emma was beaten, he had left the table and prevented Belle from inflicting further punishment. Nobody had objected, being more concerned with reaping the full benefits of the blonde's defeat. Deeply puzzled by the lady outlaw's behaviour, he had escorted her to the hotel. She had clearly made arrangements for her return. A hip bath, filled with warm water, stood in the corner of her room and she had used it to wash away the dirt, sawdust and sweat of the fight. Powdered witch-hazel leaves had stopped the bleeding from her nose and other minor abrasions. Although she had a mouse under her left eye and a mottling of bruises, she did not appear to have suffered any serious damage.

'For two reasons,' Belle said, sitting on the edge of the bed. 'I don't take to blonde calico-cats mean-mouthing me. And I wanted a chance for a long, private talk with you.' She gingerly touched her swollen, discoloured left eye. 'If I'd known how tough that girl of yours was, I'd've picked an easier way of doing it.'

'She's not my gal,' Dusty corrected. 'Except that she figures "Ed Caxton" might be able to help her against Mayor Lampart.'

'Does she?' Belle said, with some interest. 'And why is "Ed Caxton" here?'

'I could ask you the same thing. Day comes when the

149

Indian Nations gets so "disturbed" Belle Starr has to run out, I'll start voting Republican.'

'Considering what I went through tonight, just to be all on our lonesome with you, *Ed* honey, I think *you* should answer me first.'

'All right,' Dusty drawled, not offering to leave the chair he had occupied since entering the room. 'Me and the boys came here to find out all we could about this town, so that the Governor can figure out a way to close it down.'

'I thought that's about what it would be,' Belle admitted. 'From all I've heard, you've been busy since you got here. Word has it that you're Lampart's right hand gun.'

'I've made myself useful,' Dusty said, with an expression of distaste. 'So far, everybody I've had to kill've been fellers who deserved it.'

'You're going to break Lampart before you leave,' Belle commented, as a statement and not a question.

'If I can,' Dusty agreed and told her all he had learned since coming to Hell.

Belle sat and listened without interruption all through Dusty's lengthy recital of the town's history. Relying on Mark Counter's assessment of her character, the small Texan held back no aspect of the citizens' and the mayor's infamy. Revulsion flickered on her bruised features as she heard of how men had been murdered for the bounty on their heads. Then he mentioned one last thing; an item which he figured would seal her hatred of Lampart.

'Lordy lord!' the lady outlaw ejaculated. 'You mean he's actually given repeaters and ammunition to the *Kwehareh-nuh*?'

'I wouldn't lie to you, Belle,' Dusty declared.

'Lands-sakes-a-mercy!' the girl gasped, shutting her eyes and visualizing what could result from the mayor's actions. 'They're a prime set of scum, the people here. But I do declare that Lampart's the worst of them all.'

'Out and away the worst,' Dusty confirmed.

'I'm right pleased that I was asked to come here and help rob him,' Belle announced.

Almost ten seconds ticked by before Dusty spoke. From along the street came the sounds of celebration. If the noise was anything to go by, the crowd were enjoying to the full the free liquor brought to them by Belle's victory over Emma.

'So that's why you're here,' Dusty breathed. 'Who sent for you?'

'I didn't have time to find out before your sweet-honey called me for a showdown,' Belle replied, a faint smile playing on her lips.

'You don't know?'

'I had this offer, through a man I can trust, to come here for the job. I was given a thousand dollars travelling money and half a hundred dollar bill. Whoever wanted me here would show me the other half and we could make our deal. It seemed worth looking into, so I came along. I'd heard about having to hand over a tenth of the loot, so I fetched along around fifteen thousand dollars.'

'That's a heap of cash money—'

'I'm not a two-bit thief,' Belle pointed out. 'So I'd be expected to have plenty. Anyways, all but three thousand of it's Confederate States' currency. And I did get a reduction from Simmy.'

'So I noticed,' Dusty grinned. 'Mark always said you could charm a bird down off a tree, had you a mind to.'

'It saves waving a gun ar—' Belle began.

'What's up?' Dusty whispered as the girl stopped speaking and adopted an attitude of listening.

'Somebody's just come and's listening outside the door!' Belle answered, just as quietly. 'Quick. Strip to the waist, Stay sat and lift your legs so's I can pull your boots off.'

Swiftly, Dusty unbuckled and removed his gunbelt. Then, while Belle drew off first one boot and the other, he divested himself of tie, shirt and undershirt. Having completed her part of the undressing, Belle rose, threw back the covers and climbed into bed. Drawing his right hand Colt, Dusty tiptoed across the room. Looking at what should have been a continuous strip of lamplight glowing between the floor and the bottom of the door, he made out the dark blobs caused by the listener's feet. Turning the key, he unlocked and threw open the door in practically one motion.

'What the—?' Dusty spat out as a figure clad in a hooded cape almost fell through the door into his arms.

'Let me in, Ed!' Emma Nene begged, *sotto voce* but urgently. 'Quick. I'm not here to make trouble.'

Having already seen the thing she gripped in her right hand, Dusty knew that the blonde was speaking the truth. So he withdrew and allowed her to dart by. Glancing along the lamp-illuminated passage to make sure they had not been observed, Dusty closed and relocked the door.

'I didn't think you could make it before morning, after the licking I handed you,' Belle smiled, sitting up and swinging her legs from the bed. 'Do you have the other half of the bill?'

Thrusting back the hood, Emma allowed her cloak to fall open. Under it, she wore the nightgown which Dusty had come to know so well during his stay in Hell. Like Belle, the blonde had bathed and attended to her injuries. Emma's top lip was swollen and her right eye resembled a Blue Point oyster peeping out of its shell. Walking to the bed as if Dusty did not exist, she held out the half of a hundred dollar bill which had told him that she had come on a peaceful visit. It had also given him food for speculation, in view of what Belle had said.

'Here's mine,' the blonde said. 'Where's yours?'

Taking down her gunbelt, from where it hung around the post at the head of the bed, Belle produced the other half of the bill from a secret pocket. She handed it to Dusty and told Emma to do the same.

'They match,' the small Texan affirmed, placing the edges together. 'Now will somebody tell me what the hell it's all about?'

'Your sweet-honey had me come here to help rob the mayor, Ed,' Belle replied and repeated what she had already told him so that Emma would not suspect they had discussed the matter.

'How do *you* stand on it, Ed?' the blonde inquired, having scanned his face worriedly all through the story.

'You-all gave me half a million good reasons for not trusting Simmy, Emma gal,' Dusty drawled and saw relief replace the anxiety on her face. 'But, knowing who she was and why she'd come, why in hell did you pick that fight with Belle?'

'I didn't know for sure, until it was too late,' Emma insisted. 'By the time I did, there were folks listening. What would they have thought, knowing *me*, if I'd done nothing after coming on some stray tail-peddler pawing at my man? And, what's more important, Simmy would have got suspicious if he'd heard I let her get away with it, even knowing she was Belle Starr. He's smart enough to starting guessing I'd got a reason for keeping friendly with her.'

'You could've let Belle know—' Dusty began.

'She did,' the lady outlaw commented dryly. 'Just as soon as I got her held down and primed for plucking, she squealed out that she'd got the other half of the bill. Then, when I held back from whomping her even uglier than she is, she cut a rusty and bucked me off.'

'You could've broke it off easy enough,' Dusty pointed out, recollecting the incident. 'All one of you had to do was make out she was licked.'

'Which one?' Emma countered. 'I didn't aim to and she sure as hell wouldn't.'

'She's right, Ed,' Belle went on. 'After it'd got that far, we had to know who's boss.'

'It was your fault!' the blonde hissed, glaring at Belle. 'You didn't have to come to my place. I'd've come and seen you later.'

'Not that it would have stopped me coming, but I still didn't know how you tied in with me,' the lady outlaw answered. 'How would it have looked to whoever had sent for me if I'd shown as such a fraidy-cat that I let a fat, blowsy calico queen back me down?'

'Just because you got lucky—!' the blonde spat, clenching her hands.

'Are you pair going to quit mean-mouthing each other and get down to horse-trading?' Dusty growled, sounding his most savage. 'Because, happen you start hair-yanking again, I'm going to chill both of your milk *pronto*, and I won't do it gentle. I'm not missing my chance of a cut in a half-million dollar pot because two blasted she-males don't like each other.'

'Don't get riled, Ed!' Belle yelped, in well-simulated anxiety, knowing that his outburst was directed mainly at the blonde. 'I'm sorry for what I said, Emma. If you'll say the same, we'll forget our quarrels.'

'You're no tail-peddler,' Emma apologized and sat down on the end of the bed. 'It's over as far as I'm concerned.'

'Let's hope you both mean it,' Dusty said, swinging his left leg over the back of the chair and settling astride its seat.

'Now I like you pair fine, and it's sure pleasing to a man's ego to have you fighting over him. But there's a time and a place for it. You can snatch each other bald-headed, or bite off your apples so you're both flat-chested once this chore's over. Until then, you'll stay peaceable.'

'We'll mind it, Ed,' Belle promised, seeing that the blonde was taking the warning very much to heart. 'Now I'd like to hear what kind of game I'm getting dealt into.'

'Simmy keeps all his money, packed in flour sacks in case he has to load up and get out in a hurry, in a cellar under his office,' the blonde explained. 'It's got a secret, trick door that only two people know how to open.'

'You're one of them?'

'No, Belle.'

'Forcing Simmy to open up won't be easy,' Dusty warned, thinking furiously of how he could turn the unexpected situation to his advantage. 'He's one tough *hombre* no matter how he acts and talks.'

'We won't have to force him,' Emma corrected. 'Giselle's going to open up for us.'

'His *wife*?' Belle ejaculated.

'And *my* half-sister,' the blonde elaborated. 'She doesn't like the way he uses her and she's sick to the guts of being buried alive in this God-forsaken hell-hole. Only she's like me, she hates going hungry. That's why we've figured this deal out.'

'Why send for me?' Belle wanted to know. 'There're dozens of men in and out here all the time who could have helped you.'

'Do you know why I don't have a picture on my sign board?' Emma countered. 'Because you can't get a painting of something that doesn't exist.'

'*Gracias,*' Dusty drawled.

'Somehow, the Lord knows how, I get the feeling I can trust you, Ed. But you hadn't come when I sent for Belle. I needed somebody with brains enough to help me set things up, and with enough knowledge to get us away after we'd pulled the robbery. I'd always heard you're a square-shooter, Belle, so I got in touch with you.'

'Then why make the big play for me?' Dusty asked.

'We decided we could use a few **real good** guns to back us up if things went wrong,' Emma admitted frankly. 'Giselle was set on bringing in Ben Columbo and his riff-raff. I was sure relieved when you boys made wolf-bait of them all, Ed. And, after I'd watched you for a spell, I believed we could count on you, Matt and Comanche.'

'I get a notion this's *not* going to work out as easy as it looks from the top,' Belle remarked. 'Way I see it, we'll need a wagon to tote away all that much money—'

'The saloon could use some supplies,' Emma told her. 'And Ed owns the livery barn. Its last owner left it to him in his will.'

'It was Simmy's idea I should have the place,' Dusty explained. 'For helping him gun down its old owner and his side-kicks.'

'And, if I know Simmy,' Emma went on. 'He's already figuring out ways to get you boys killed and take it back. That's the wagon, and a reason for wanting it, fixed up, Belle.'

'There's a right good way we could pull it off tomorrow, happen you girls're up to it,' Dusty drawled.

'Tom—!' Emma gasped, darting an inquiring glance at the lady outlaw.

'I'm up to it, if you are, Emma,' Belle declared and the blonde nodded.

'How many of your crowd can you trust, Emma?' Dusty inquired. 'I mean trust all the way. With your life, because that's what's at stake if you're wrong about any one of them.'

'Hubert's the only man of 'em. Simmy hired all the others. Then there's Red, Juanita and four more of the girls. But—'

'That'll be enough, way I plan it,' Dusty insisted and went on with a comment in keeping with the character he was playing in Hell. 'We don't want to have to cut the pot too many ways, now do we?'

'If we use them,' Emma announced grimly. 'They're in for their share.'

'Why not? It's big enough,' Dusty smiled, sensing that the blonde was sincere and liking her for it.

'What's this idea of yours, Ed?' Belle inquired.

Instead of answering, the small Texan cocked his head in

the direction of the window. The sounds of revelry still rolled unabated from the Honest Man Saloon.

'You sure packed them in tonight, Emma gal,' Dusty finally said.

'Just about everybody in town. I've never drawn such a crowd,' the blonde answered and threw a grin at the lady outlaw. 'If we wasn't figuring to be gone by night, I'd near on suggest that you and I lock horns again tomorrow, Belle.'

'Now it's funny you-all coming out and saying that,' Dusty put in and something about the way in which he spoke drew the girls' eyes to his face. 'I was just going to say you should do it.'

Silence followed the small Texan's words, lasting for several seconds as Belle and Emma digested the implication behind the soft-spoken, but significant words. Involuntarily, two sets of female fingers fluttered to bruised faces. Then the girls looked at each other and Dusty could see the speculation in both sets of features.

'You mean you want us to put on another cat-fight to get everybody in my place watching us,' Emma guessed. 'Then your boys, Hubert and my girls go with Giselle, load up the wagon with Simmy's money and pull out?'

'Something like that,' Dusty agreed.

'And what happens to us when he finds out the money's gone?' the blonde demanded. 'He'll figure who must have taken it and how.'

'I've got a way around *that*,' Dusty assured her. 'Time he knows about it, we'll have a good head start on him. Only the fight's not going to take place at the saloon. You're going to have it out at that hollow on the other side of town from Simmy's place.'

'I think I noticed it on the way in,' Belle remarked, nodding in satisfaction. 'Anybody out there won't be able to see Simmy's house for the other buildings in between. You've hit it, Ed.'

Emma did not join in the lady outlaw's paean of congratulation. Having been longer than Belle in Hell, the blonde knew that the hollow in question was the area set aside beyond the town limits, so that visitors could settle disagreements without endangering lives or civic property – using guns.

CHAPTER SIXTEEN

I'LL BRING 'EM BACK TAMED

LEAVING his saddled *grulla* standing ground hitched by its dangling reins, Dusty Fog looked around. With the time wanting ten minutes before four in the afternoon, almost everybody in the town had already gathered at the hollow. They were all eagerly awaiting a continuation of the events which had so excited them in the Honest Man Saloon the night before. A glance towards Hell told Dusty that he had been correct about the invisibility of the mayor's house from the hollow. If careful planning and attention to detail could command success, the small Texan hoped that his work in the town called Hell would soon be at an end.

At first, on learning where he wished the clash to take place, Emma had vehemently refused to take part in it. Even Belle had been startled on being told of the purpose to which the hollow was usually put. Patiently, Dusty had elaborated on his plan and the girls had admitted that it could work. So they had discussed it at length, amending and improving, until all had felt sure that it stood a better than average chance of succeeding. Despite facing the prospect of another confrontation, the girls had parted on friendly terms. So much so that Emma had not raised a single objection to 'Ed' remaining in Belle's room for the rest of the night.

'I don't want to be a hog, Belle,' the blonde had claimed cheerfully. 'And if you feel like love-making tonight, I'll near on be willing to admit you're a tougher gal than me.'

Not that Emma had needed to worry about such an eventuality; although the reason for Belle abstaining from 'love-making' had nothing to do with her current physical condition. As the lady outlaw had told Dusty earlier, only one man had shared her bed – and Mark Counter was the small Texan's *amigo*. So Dusty had slept on the floor, which had been his intention all along.

Rising somewhat earlier in the morning than had become his habit since arriving in Hell, Dusty had left Belle and gone to find his companions. On wakening the Kid and Juanita, he discovered that Emma had wasted no time the previous night.

On her return to the saloon, slipping in by a rear entrance as unnoticed as she had left, Emma had waited until the place was closing and sent her maid to collect the Kid, Waco and the trusted members of her staff. After satisfying herself that they were all sober enough to understand what she was saying, she had told them of 'Ed Caxton's' plan. Sharing Giselle's antipathy towards the town, Hubert and the girls had stated their eagerness to leave; especially as they would do so with a sizeable stake for their futures. Before they had gone to their respective beds, they had all known the parts they would play in the robbery. Always something of a madcap, Red had been particularly pleased with the role she was selected to play.

Leaving his *amigos* to dress, Dusty had visited the livery barn and given orders for a wagon to be prepared. To lull any suspicions the bleary-eyed hostlers might have felt, Dusty had explained that the previous night's celebrations had depleted the saloon's stocks to such an extent that there was some urgency in obtaining a fresh supply of liquor.

That had paved the way for the next stage of the operation. Returning to the hotel, Dusty had escorted Belle to lunch in the crowded dining-room. Before the meal had ended, Emma stormed in. Give the girls their due, they had put on quite a performance. Screaming insults at each other, they had seemed on the verge of coming to blows. When Dusty had intervened, Belle had warned Emma that she intended to settle the matter permanently. Instantly the blonde had flung out a challenge to meet Belle at the hollow. Amidst a low mutter of excited comment from the eavesdropping occupants of the room, the lady outlaw had taken up the challenge. Mockingly saying that Emma would need time to settle her affairs, Belle had suggested they met at four o'clock. Agreeing, Emma had stalked away.

So, at ten minutes to four, the scene was set, the audience

assembled and waiting for the arrival of the principal performers in the drama. Soon after lunch, the Kid had brought word that Emma had contacted Giselle and the little brunette was ready to play her part. On visiting the barn, Dusty had found the wagon provisioned for the journey, its team hitched up, but the whole staff already on their way to the hollow so as to make sure of a good view of the proceedings. When Dusty had left in the wake of the crowd, Hell had had the appearance of a ghost town.

Elbowing his way arrogantly through the crowd, Dusty found Lampart in the forefront. The small Texan now had a part to play, one which would make a tremendous difference to the success of the plan. Glancing around and seeing a couple of the Honest Man's gamblers taking bets amongst the crowd, he believed he knew how to handle things.

'Hey, Simmy,' Dusty greeted. 'Where's Giselle?'

'She's decided not to come,' the mayor replied. 'Had too much to drink last night and's feeling the effects.'

'Sounded like you sure had a time,' Dusty grinned.

'Yes,' said Lampart coldly. 'And all free.'

'Why worry? You'll get it back and more, way they'll be drinking and talking after this. It's a pity we can't get some betting on it.'

'Can't we?' Lampart asked.

'Hell. Who's going to bet against Belle in a shoot-out?'

'You're sure she'll win?'

'I'd say it's a foregone conclusion.'

'I wouldn't,' Lampart answered. 'Emma's a damned good shot.'

'You tricky ole son,' Dusty drawled admiringly. 'Hell, though, you've made one lil mistake. Emma might be able to shoot, but I'm betting she can't lick Belle to the draw.'

'Damn it!' the mayor ejaculated. 'You're right. If—There's a way out.'

'There'd best be,' Dusty drawled. ''Cause Belle's coming now.'

Carrying her coat and hat, Belle walked through the crowd. She was dressed in a shirt, Levi's pants and moccasins, with her gunbelt strapped on. Behind her, ground hitched by Dusty's *grulla*, stood her powerful bay gelding. Hooves drummed and Emma, clothed in the same way as Belle but with a Navy Colt thrust into her waistband, rode up. Dismounting, she dropped her reins and followed the lady outlaw through the gap which had opened in the crowd.

'Hi Ed, honey,' Belle greeted, then jerked her head in the blonde's direction. 'Your fat slack-puller's not backed out.

'I sure hope you got all you wanted last night, tail-peddler!' Emma replied. 'Because it was your last night in this world.'

'Yeah?' Belle hissed, crouching slightly and hooking her right hand over the Manhattan. 'Well—'

'Ladies!' Lampart barked and the girls looked at him. 'I thought this was supposed to be a fair fight?'

Concealing his grin of elation, Dusty watched the mayor do just what the plan called for. When Belle insisted that she would not have it any other way than fair, Lampart pointed out her advantage in a draw-and-shoot affair. Then he suggested that they fought as in a formal duel.

'You'll stand back to back, each holding her gun,' Lampart enlarged. 'Then I'll give the word. You each step off six strides, turn and start shooting.'

'That's all right with me!' Belle declared.

'Anyway'll do me just so I can get a bead on her,' Emma went on.

Going into the centre of the hollow, the girls stood back to back. Looking around, Dusty was satisfied that none of the crowd had eyes for anything other than Emma and Bella. Across at the other side of the circle, Waco stood between Red and a Chinese girl from the brothel. The size of the crowd caused the girl to press against his side. That too was what Dusty wanted to happen.

'If you're ready, ladies,' Lampart said, from the rim of the hollow and on receiving answers in the affirmative, continued, 'Start when I reach three. One! Two!—'

Having made a circle of the town to make sure that all was clear, the Ysabel Kid returned to the livery barn. Hubert sat on the box of the wagon and, at the Kid's nod, started the team moving. By the time they had reached Lampart's house, Juanita and the other girls were already inside.

'Move it, all of you!' the Kid ordered, looking in at the rear door.

'We already have,' Giselle answered, indicating the pile of bulging flour sacks on the floor. 'Get them loaded while I pick the locks on the deposit boxes. There's no sense in leaving their contents behind.'

'Nope,' grinned the Kid, thinking of how the losses would affect the town and its citizens. 'There sure ain't.'

'What about the guards at the shack there, Comanche?' Hubert inquired, darting a worried glance at the adobe building and remembering the men who usually stood watch over it.

'They've gone to see the fight like everybody else,' drawled the Kid. 'Go help the gals. I'll make sure nobody comes around asking what we're at.'

Sweating girls, unused to strenuous activity, darted to and fro, fetching and dumping sacks of money into the wagon. While they did so, Giselle put to use her ability as a lock-picker to unfasten the boxes in which various gang leaders had left their loot for safe keeping. Working swiftly, the girls emptied each box in turn and the brunette locked it up again. All the time, the Kid's party were conscious of a continuous rumble of noise reminiscent of the crowd's reaction to the previous night's fight at the saloon.

'We've got it all,' Giselle announced at last, hurrying out of the house.

'Don't forget that key,' warned the Kid.

'I won't,' the brunette replied. She closed the door and left the key on the outside but did not lock it. 'I've left a note telling Simmy that I'll be down at the saloon until dinner time.'

'Will he figure anything suspicious about that?' the Kid demanded, watching the girls boarding the wagon. 'You and Emma never acted friendly.'

'It's all right,' Giselle insisted. 'Before Simmy left for the hollow, I told him that I meant to take over the saloon if Emma was killed. He'll think that's what I'm doing.'

'It'll maybe buy us some more time then,' drawled the Kid. 'Get aboard, ma'am, so's we can be going.'

With all the women in the rear of the wagon and its canopy's flaps closed, the Kid leapt astride his roan. Hubert set the team into motion, swinging them away from the street. As they reached the top of the slope, the Kid looked back to make sure they had not been observed and followed.

'Three!' Lampart finished and the crowd waited in silent expectation.

Instead of stepping straight off, Belle addressed Emma over her shoulder. Her words carried to the spectators' ears.

'Hey, slack-puller. You're lucky I'm going to kill you. After last night, Ed wouldn't waste his time bedding with a fat old whore like you.'

Letting out a shrill shriek of what sounded like genuine rage, Emma hurled her revolver aside. She twirled around, left hand shooting forward to catch hold of Belle's right shoulder. With a jerk, the blonde swung the lady outlaw to face her and delivered a slap with the other hand. There was no faking with the blow. It impacted on Belle's cheek, sending her reeling and, in part, causing her to drop the Manhattan.

Landing on one knee, Belle saw Emma rushing at her. With a yell, the lady outlaw plunged upwards, diving to tackle the blonde about the waist. Down they went, rolling and thrashing on the ground in a brawl every bit as wild as the one they had put up the previous night.

Although the crowd had come to witness a gun fight, none of them raised objections at the way things had turned out. Prudence and caution had caused them to stay on the edge of the hollow when lead might start flying. Once Belle and Emma discarded their firearms and resumed the kind of fighting which had entertained the onlookers at the Honest Man, the crowd began to move forward. Throwing a grin at Red, Waco contrived to keep the Chinese prostitute at his other side.

Walking to the waiting horses, Dusty watched the people moving down into the hollow. Lampart was going with them. Despite his gamblers having money wagered on the result, he could not resist the temptation to sample once more the erotic delight of watching two beautiful women embroiled in primitive conflict. Everything was still going as the small Texan had planned.

Dusty had realized from the beginning that a gun fight,

even if its result could be faked, would not last for long enough to let the robbery be carried out and the wagon disappear over the rim of the crater. So he had told the two girls how to act. Belle's reference to Emma as a slack-puller – which, like tail-peddler, meant a whore of the cheapest variety – and comment about the previous night had been sufficient to bring the blonde's reaction without arousing the spectators' suspicions.

'Come on, Lon!' Dusty thought. 'Get things moving!'

If the Kid and his party had set to work as soon as possible, they ought to be coming into view soon. The longer the delay, the greater chance of something going wrong. Lamp-art might become aware of the ammunition guards' presence in the crowd and order them to return to their post.

There was the wagon now!

Good for Lon and Hubert. They had remembered their orders and hidden the girls in the back of the wagon. Trust Lon to restrain any urge the bartender might show towards making the team go faster. If anybody should happen to see the wagon ascending the slope, there was nothing about it to hint at a hurried, illicit departure. However, the leisurely pace also had its disadvantages.

While Belle and Emma were aware that they must keep their fight going for long enough to let the wagon's party escape undetected, things could go wrong. In the heat and excitement of the tangle, tempers might easily be lost and one or the other knock her opponent unconscious. So far, from all Dusty could see and hear, they were carrying out their assignment in a satisfactory manner.

At last, after what seemed a far longer period than it had actually taken, the wagon disappeared amongst the trees. With a long exhalation of relief, Dusty hung Belle's jacket and hat – handed into his keeping by the lady outlaw before going out to take up the duelling position – on her saddle. Vaulting afork his *grulla*, he gathered up the other horses' reins and set the three animals into motion. Riding on to the slope, he caused a hurried scattering of spectators anxious to avoid being ridden down. On reaching the front of the crowd, he saw that he had not come too soon.

With fingers interlaced in matted, sodden, dishevelled hair, Belle and Emma knelt clinging weakly to each other.

Their shirts had gone and they looked to be close to collapsing through sheer exhaustion. Leaping from his saddle, Dusty stalked forward. Silence fell over the crowd as they watched and wondered what the small Texan planned to do. Reaching the girls, he bent and gripped their back hair in his hands. Drawing the heads apart, he snapped them together with a hard, crisp click.

'What the hell?' Lampart barked as Dusty released the girls' hair and they crumpled in a heap at his feet.

'If these two bitches wanted to shoot it out, it was fine with me,' Dusty replied, bending again and lifting Belle from Emma. Holding the lady outlaw in his arms, he continued his explanation while walking towards the horses. 'That way, I'd've been shut of one or the other. I'll be damned if I'm going to have them keep cat-clawing each other over me. Neither's fit to bed with when she's through fighting.'

'But what are you planning to do with them?' Lampart insisted, watching Dusty heave Belle belly down across her saddle.

'I'm going to take 'em off aways, just me and them,' Dusty explained and went to collect Emma. With the blonde draped limply over her horse's back, he went on. 'Comes night, I'll bring 'em back tamed.'

'But – But—!' Lampart spluttered, wondering how he could turn the small Texan's actions to his own advantage.

Slowly Dusty walked over and retrieved Belle's Manhattan. A low mutter rose from the crowd, querulous in its timbre if not out-and-out hostile. Straightening up, he stuck the revolver into his waistband. Hooking his thumbs into the gunbelt, he swung around and left a descent of silence where his eyes had passed over.

'Anybody who objects can step right out and say so,' Dusty declared. 'Only he'd best come to do it with a gun in his hand.'

There was no reply. Everybody present knew 'Ed Caxton' as the feller who had simultaneously out-drawn two of the fastest gun hands Hell had ever seen, then made wolf bait of a slew of other bad *hombres* who had crossed his trail. If any member of the crowd should accept the challenge, that man would die almost as soon as he mentioned his intentions. In every male mind – except possibly Lampart's – lurked the same summation. They had seen a mighty enjoyable cat-fight. One which, way the contestants had been looking during the last few seconds, would have tamely ended in a draw through them both fainting from exhaustion.

So why get killed over it having been stopped?

'Ed Caxton' sounded like he aimed to keep both girls around. One thing was for sure if he did, they would be unlikely to grow friendlier. So, for all his proposed 'taming', there was always the chance that they would lock horns again. In which case, the wisest thing for every man present to do was let that big Texan tote them off – stay alive himself, and wait to see what the future held.

Seeing that he had made his point, Dusty mounted his *grulla*. He rode up the slope, leading the two horses and their inert burdens. Lampert watched him go, thinking fast.

'Didn't some of you fellers have money bet on who won?' the mayor inquired as Dusty rode over the edge of the top of the hollow.

At the words, Waco gave Red a nudge with his hip to warn her that she must play her part. Excitement glinted in her eyes. Springing by the youngster, she confronted the Chinese girl.

'You quit a-pawing my feller, you slit-eyed whore!' Red shrieked.

'What you speak, round-eye calico?' the Chinese girl spat back, for there was no love lost between the prostitutes and Emma's employees.

'I'll show you what I speak!' Red promised, conscious of being watched by both factions.

Ducking her head, Red leapt at and butted the Oriental in the chest. Reeling backwards, the girl sat down. Another of the brothel's contingent made as if to attack Red. That did it. Already brought to a pitch of wild excitement by the fight between Belle and Emma, the two factions needed no more urging. Squeals and yells rose, then that section of the crowd exploded into a multiple tangle of hair-pulling, fist-swinging, screeching females.

'You started th—!' the brothel's bouncer began, moving towards Waco.

Before the words ended, the blond youngster's fist took the

165

man under the jaw and knocked him from his feet. Like the ripples spread by throwing a stone into a pond, the fight developed until it engulfed every member of the crowd. Even Goldberg's plump, pompous wife joined in, mixing it as gamely as any saloon-girl with her husband's partner's younger, prettier spouse.

A good ten minutes went by before Waco found himself close to Red. In that period, the fight had become general and a matter of attacking the nearest person of the same sex. Red sat astride Mrs. Goldberg and the jeweller's wife, pounding indiscriminately at both while they continued to settle old scores. Grabbing the girl by the hair, Waco hauled her bodily clear of the mêlée. When she tried to turn on him, he first slapped, then shook her into a more pacific frame of mind.

'That's better,' Waco growled, carrying her up the slope. 'I'll take you back to the saloon and you can get into something you can travel in.'

'Wh – When do we g–go?' Red gasped, brushing away her tears.

'After I've done a lil job for Du – Ed,' Waco replied.

Fortunately, Red's exertions had left her in no state to think clearly. So she did not notice the blond youngster's mistake. Clinging to him, she pressed her bruised, scratched face against his shoulder.

'What's the lil job?' the girl asked. 'Is it important?'

'Enough,' Waco answered.

The blond did not explain how if he succeeded in his 'lil job' he would most likely save the lives of many people – or that the penalty for failure was even more likely to be death.

CHAPTER SEVENTEEN

MISS NENE, MEET CAPTAIN DUSTY FOG

'Howdy, Simmy,' Waco greeted, strolling along the sidewalk to where the mayor was unlocking his front door in a decidedly furtive manner.

Lampart looked anything but his usual, neat, immaculate self. Unable to slip away before the general brawl had entrapped him, he had been compelled to fight back until he had dropped to the ground and feigned unconsciousness. By the time he had finally escaped, leaving the battle still raging, he had lost his hat, jacket and cravat. His torn shirt looked as if it had been walked on – and had. It had been his hope to reach his home without anybody seeing him, for he knew there would be those who wanted to know why he had done nothing to end the conflict. Although the street was clear, that blasted blond youngster had come through the alley and surprised him.

'How did you get here?' the mayor demanded ungraciously.

'Same's you. I got out soon's I could.'

'So it seems,' Lampart growled, glaring at Waco's unmarked features and all too aware of his own injuries. 'What do you want?'

'Some money out of our box.'

'Can't it wait?'

'Sure. Happen you don't mind the chance of the saloon getting damaged.'

'Huh?' grunted the mayor.

'I sure's hell don't aim to stay away from it,' Waco explained. 'And there could be them's reckons Red 'n' me's to blame for that ruckus at the hollow. So I conclude buying drinks good 'n' regular ought to change their minds. Talked to your lady down there, and she claims I've got a right smart notion.'

'My wife's at the saloon?'

'Why sure. Taking on like she owns it.'

That figured to anybody who knew Giselle, the mayor mused. From what she had been saying when she had heard about the gun fight, his wife had expected her half-sister to be killed. So she had not waited to hear the result before going to assert her control of the saloon. One thing was for sure. No matter who ran the Honest Man, its profits – and losses – descended on Lampart. What young 'Caxton' said was true, too. After a night without a drink being sold – although many were consumed – due to that blonde bitch's boastful stupidity, Lampart had no desire to incur further losses.

'Come in and get what you need,' the mayor ordered, wanting to get off the street as quickly as he could.

With which sentiment Waco heartily concurred. Nobody had seen him meet the mayor. Even Red was unaware that he had, having gone to her room to change ready for their departure. That made the blond youngster's task just that much safer.

'I allus got the notion Ma Goldberg and that fancy young wife of the jeweller's didn't cotton to each other,' Waco commented cheerily as Lampart took him inside and locked the front door. 'They sure was whomping each other all ways when I lit out.'

'She always blamed Melissa for Goldberg getting caught out,' the mayor answered, opening up his office. 'I should have one of the Regulators here—'

'You've got one,' Waco pointed out. 'Me. You made me one after we'd got rid of ole Basmanov's bunch for you.'

'Of course,' Lampart grunted and waved his hand towards the boxes. 'Help yourself.'

'*Gracias*,' the youngster drawled, walking by the desk. Scooping the Colt from it, he turned and threw down on the mayor. 'Only I've changed my mind.'

'You've done what?' Lampart spat, staring at the Peacemaker as it lined on his chest.

'Changed my mind,' Waco repeated, thumb-cocking the revolver. 'So, if you'll open up that drawer with the "magnetic" battery in it, I'll touch off your ammunition supply and head for home.'

'Home? With a price on your head!'

'Shuckens, that's not worrying me one lil bit.'

'Do you reckon that the Army will forget what you've done just because you've got rid of my ammunition?' Lampart sneered.

'Just what have I done?' Waco countered.

'Helped to kill a colonel, sergeant and six men,' the mayor reminded him.

'You shouldn't believe all you read in the newspapers, Mr. Mayor,' the blond youngster drawled. 'Those fellers're no closer to heaven – or hell, I'd say in Paddy Magoon's case – than down to the OD Connected.'

'The—?' Lampart gulped.

'The OD Connected. That's our spread. Me, the Ysabel Kid – and Dusty Fog's.'

'Dusty Fog?' croaked Lampart.

'Yes sir, Mr. Mayor,' Waco confirmed. 'My "Brother Ed's" Dusty Fog. Now open that drawer, or I'll do it myself.'

'Can you?' Lampart challenged.

'I can give it a whirl. This room's pretty thick-walled. I could burst the desk open without making enough noise to be heard outside of 'em.'

'You've a point,' Lampart admitted sullenly, hanging his head in dejected fashion. He walked around and sat behind his desk. Without looking at Waco, he opened the required drawer with his left hand. 'Here you are.'

For all his beaten aspect, Lampart was grinning inwardly. In addition to having been a successful stage illusionist, he was also a skilled maker of magical tricks and gadgets. Being aware of the type of people with whom he would be dealing, he had put his inventive genius to work in Hell. Not only had he fitted a secret door to the cellar which held his wealth, but he had equipped the desk with a protective mechanism. The latter had already proved its worth.

On their last night alive, Glover and Eel had not meant to return to Hell. So their use as a future source of revenue had ended. They had not attempted to draw their guns until he had shouted the unnecessary warning – and by that time it was too late. In fact, he had even been compelled to pull out Eel's weapon to make his story ring true. Fortunately, Cowper had been close enough to the building to hear the shots. Rushing in to investigate, holding his gun, naturally, he had died at 'Ed Caxton's' hand.

Except that the *big* Texan was not 'Ed Caxton', if the blond youngster was telling the truth. He was Dusty Fog and he had come with his two companions to destroy Hell.

Which raised the question of why Fog had sent the young blond to handle the dangerous task of blowing up the *Kweharehnuh's* reserve ammunition supply.

Most likely the blond had asked to do so, as a means of winning acclaim and, probably, higher financial rewards. Judging the Rio Hondo gun wizard by his own standards, Lampart decided that Dusty Fog would be only too pleased to let another man take the risk. Whatever had happened, the blond was going to pay for the rash, impetuous offer with his life.

Still keeping his head bowed, so that no hint of his true feelings would flash a warning to his victim, Lampart rubbed his left foot against the inner support leg of his desk. A click sounded and a section of the desk's top hinged up close to his left hand. Out of the hole exposed by the section rose a block of wood. On top of the block rested the ivory-handled Webley Bulldog which had taken Basmanov's, Glover's and Eel's lives. Scooping up the weapon, he lifted his eyes to Waco's face and a mocking smile twisted at his lips.

Ever since organizing the escape of so many badly wanted criminals, Lampart had felt a growing sense of his own brilliance. He had brought Hell into being, arranging for it to become the lucrative proposition which it now was. With each achievement, he had grown more certain that no lesser man could equal his superlative genius, or defeat him in a match of wits.

Fog and his companions might think they were clever, but Lampart would teach them differently. There was no need for haste, not even in dealing with that impetuous young fool who stood before him. He wanted to see the other's expression on pulling the Peacemaker's trigger when only a dull, dry click rewarded the gesture. The appearance of the Bulldog would have been a severe shock, but the failure of the Colt would be even worse.

So Lampart moved in an almost leisurely manner – and paid the penalty.

Instead of trying to fire the useless Peacemaker, Waco had drawn his left hand Army Colt as soon as the section of the desk began to move. Flame ripped from the eight inch barrel as the Webley was lifted from its resting place. Hit in the head, Lampart slammed back. Tipping over under his weight, the chair deposited him on the floor. The Webley slid unfired from his lifeless left hand.

'Dusty was right,' the youngster breathed, placing the Peacemaker on the desk and darting to the window which overlooked the street. 'Knowing about that old plough-handle did help to save my life.'

Even before Dusty had touched the revolver and found it was too cold to have been fired, he had suspected that some other weapon was responsible for Glover's and Eel's deaths. The shots had been fired too quickly for a single action even being fanned. Which meant that the mayor had another firearm. It was not on his person, so it must have been concealed in the desk. Confirmation for the suspicion had come from the examination of the bodies. If Glover had been pointing his revolver at Lampart, his forefinger would have been in the triggerguard. A man with the outlaw's experience, however, would have known better than to place his finger on the trigger until the barrel had left the holster and was pointing away from him.*

Having heard Dusty's warning, Waco had turned his own thoughts to the matter and come up with further conclusions. One clue had come from Dusty's description of Lampart's ambidextrous card manipulation. Considering that, the youngster had decided the mayor had used his left hand when firing the hide-away gun. The cocked Peacemaker would be there to distract his victim. Carried a stage further, Waco had decided it was unlikely that the Colt would fire. It would be too easily available to an enemy – as his own actions had proved – for a *hombre* as smart and tricky as the mayor to chance having it capable of being turned on him with live ammunition in the cylinders.

So Waco had never intended trying to defend himself with the borrowed Colt. Instead, he had gambled on his own ambidextrous ability and had won.

Looking along the street, the youngster decided that the

* Why is told in *The Fast Gun*.

shot had not been heard. He returned his Colt to its holster as he went to the desk. Taking hold of Lampart's body, he dragged it to a corner so that it could not be seen from either window. With that done, he went to examine the contents of the open drawer. A sigh of relief burst unbidden from his lips. The 'magnetic' battery was there, coupled up and ready for operation. It was one of the portable variety designed to supply an electric current for use with a mobile telegraph station. Bent had one just like it at his place in the Indian Nations and, ever curious about unusual things, Waco had learned how it was worked.

On Waco throwing the activating switch, there was a deep roaring bellow from behind the house. The adobe shack disintegrated in a sheet of flame and billowing black smoke. Even in the mayor's office, Waco could feel the blast and concussion of the explosion shake the house. Glass shattered as windows broke and he heard shouts of alarm rising. Darting from the office, he locked its door and pocketed the key. Then he sprinted through the living quarters. Giselle had followed Dusty's orders to the letter – trust ole Lon to see to that. Going out he found the key in place in the rear door. He turned, removed and pocketed it. Then, as the first of the people attracted by the commotion appeared, he began to shake at the door.

'What happened, Matt?' demanded an outlaw whose face carried marks from the battle at the hollow.

'I'm damned if I know,' the youngster replied. 'That blasted bullet-shack just son-of-a-bitching went up.'

'Where's Lampart?' the jeweller demanded, looking around. 'I've warned him that this might happen, keeping that blasted fuse wired up.'

'Door's locked,' Waco replied. 'Sombody'd best go around the front.'

Men dashed to do so, returning with the news – which did not surprise Waco – that there was no sign of the mayor or his wife.

'I'll tell you one thing,' Waco yelled. 'I'm not waiting around to find out where he is. When the *Kweharehnuh* hear there's no bullets coming to 'em, they're going to get mean. Comes that happening, I figure to be long gone.'

With that, he pushed through the crowd and headed for

the livery barn. Red was waiting, dressed in Levi's pants, a blouse and dainty hat.

'What hap—?' the girl began.

'Don't talk, mount up and ride,' Waco interrupted, indicating the horses which stood saddled and ready. 'We've got some miles to cover afore we catch up with the others.'

Three days later, the united party made camp a few miles north of the Swisher Creek's junction with the Prairiedog Fork of the Red River. They had come that far without difficulty, other than that suffered by Belle and Emma. Although each claimed that she had held herself in check all through the second fight, both now had two blackened eyes and so many additional bruises that they could not ride their horses.

On being questioned about the explosion, Waco had told the truth without revealing his companions' true identity. He had said that he considered his actions were for the best. Destroying the ammunition would cause even the outlaws whose boxes had been looted to be more concerned with fleeing from the Palo Duro than in pursuing their party. Giselle had taken the news of her widowhood calmly, declaring that she was relieved to know that she need never worry about Simmy tracking her down.

Waco's summation had proved correct, for nobody had come after them. They had seen one group of *Kweharehnuh* warriors, who had ridden by without stopping. Indicating a distant column of smoke, the Kid had guessed that it rose from the Antelopes' village and was calling the various parties of braves in for a conference about the destruction of their ammunition.

A couple of the town's guides had approached the party. On hearing what had happened in Hell and discovering that their presence was unwelcome, they had ridden away. When last seen, they had been heading east as fast as their horses would carry them.

After supper, while Waco was hoorawing the Kid for having forgotten the excuse which it had been arranged that Giselle would use to prevent her husband suspecting she had left town, Dusty asked Belle and Emma to join him for a stroll. They were in safe country at last and the time had come for certain matters to be settled. Once out of earshot of the others, the blonde raised the very subject which Dusty had meant to introduce.

'When do we share out the loot, Ed?' Emma asked.

'That's what I asked you both out here to talk about,' Dusty admitted.

'What's to talk about?' Emma demanded. 'We just sit around the fire and go, "One for you". "One for you". "One for you", until it's all split up even.'

'Not quite,' Dusty objected. 'You stop going "one for you" when you, Belle and Giselle have fifty thousand apiece and the girls and Hubert have ten thousand each.'

'There's well over half a million in the pot, Ed,' Emma said coldly. 'I'd say you and your boys're taking a kind of selfish split.'

'Not when you consider we've got to share it with all the banks it came from,' Dusty countered.

'B–Banks—' Emma spluttered and swung to the lady outlaw. 'Do you know what the hell he's talking about?'

'Yes,' Belle replied. 'I think I do. He's giving us a reward for helping him finish off a chore.'

'Now I don't know what the hell *you*'re talking about,' Emma groaned. 'Unless you're in cahoots—'

'You might say we are,' Belle smiled. 'And before you start something we'll both of us regret, I reckon I should introduce you to this feller you've been fighting me for.'

'Intro—!' Emma yelped. 'I know who he i—'

'Miss Nene, meet Captain Dusty Fog,' Belle interrupted.

'Is—' the blonde finished, then her mouth trailed open and she stared at the *big* Texan. 'D–Did she say *Dusty Fog?*'

'That's what she said,' Dusty confirmed.

'Then you're not Ed – You've been using me!'

'No more than you were willing to use me,' Dusty pointed out, studying the play of emotions on the blonde's face. 'I was sent by the Governor to close Hell down and, with you folks' help, I've done it. Now this's my deal. You-all take the cut I've just offered and go with Belle. She'll see you safe through the Indian Nations to Kansas. And you've got my word that I'll not say a thing about you being part of the town.'

'It's a good offer, Emma,' Belle remarked. 'And seeing that we've no other choice, I reckon we'd best take it.'

'You're not Ed Caxton!' the blonde breathed, eyes fixed on Dusty and showing no sign that she had heard the lady outlaw. 'You're— I've slept with Dusty Fog!'

'Stop your bragging just because you've done something I haven't,' Belle suggested with a smile.

'You mean that you and E-D – nothing happened last night?' Emma gasped, showing she had heard Belle's last comment.

'Dusty slept on the floor like a perfect gentleman,' Belle declared. 'How about it, Emma, do we take Dusty's offer? If not, I took a lot of lumps for nothing.'

'I reckon fifty thousand dollars ought to make up for them,' Emma replied. 'You're calling the play, E-D – Captain Fog.'

GO BACK TO HELL

For Mrs Kate Elizabeth Hill of Westcliff-On-Sea, who has taught her family to say, 'Thank you 'most to death'.

AUTHOR'S NOTE

Whilst complete in itself, this book continues with the events recorded in HELL IN THE PALO DURO.

CHAPTER ONE

YOU'RE ALL HONEST MEN

'There's a bank down to Corsicana we could take,' Dick Shalupka remarked, lounging at ease by the fire. 'Ain't but an itty-bitty one-hoss town. We could go in and wouldn't have no trouble in coming out rich.'

'You're talking wild, Dick,' protested Bernie Stoll. 'There ain't but the three of us left.'

'So what'd you have us do, Bernie?' demanded Henny Shalupka, indignant at the implied criticism of his elder brother. 'Go back to working cattle at thirty a month and found?'

None of the trio had ever worked cattle, even at less than thirty dollars a month, or performed any other task that was demanding in terms of effort and sweat. Until adopting what had struck them as the easier and more genteel occupation of outlaw, they had worked – when driven by dire necessity and for as short a period as possible – at various menial tasks around the Kansas trail end towns.

However, even if it only deluded themselves, the pretence of having once been cowhands implied a higher social standing than any one of them had attained.

The fire's light threw an eerie red glow across a clearing amongst a grove of post oaks on the banks of Lake Kemp in Baylor County, Texas. It illuminated a camp, set up in a slovenly, haphazard manner, for a night under the bright stars and quarter moon. Four horses, hobbled by the forelegs, grazed restlessly on the edge of the lake. Around the fire lay a quartet of saddles. Standing on their skirts, three of them would have told any West-wise observer that their owners were not connected with the cattle industry. No cowhand would ever risk causing damage to his most important item of equipment by setting it down in such a manner. A bed roll was spread by each saddle and a rifle rested on every seat.

There was an almost family likeness about the three young men, although Stoll was not related to the Shalupkas. All were tall and lean, their faces hinting at sly, dissipated natures. They wore clothes of the style favoured by trail hands who had been paid off at the end of a cattle drive, just a shade too loud and ornate for everyday usage. The garments were dirty and showed traces of voluntary neglect. White handled Colt 1860 Army revolvers hung, in what were sold to the unwary or inexperienced as fast-draw holsters, at their sides.

'Ain't no call for talk like that, Henny,' Dick grunted. 'Hell, Bernie-boy, we know how to take a bank, or a stagecoach. Damn it, we've rid with Joey Pinter long enough to handle things without him.'

'A three-way split licks sharing 'tween four or five any ole day,' Henny chortled.

'Hold your voice down!' Dick ordered, darting a pointed glance to the southern edge of the clearing.

'Who cares if he hears us?' Henny asked; but apparently he did, for he had pitched his tones to a much lower level. 'I ain't sure's I wants him to go on bossing the gang.'

'You reckon we can take that old bank in Corsicana?' Stoll inquired, wishing to avoid being brought into a discussion on the leadership of their gang.

'It'll be easier'n falling off a log,' Dick promised. 'All we have to do is go in—'

'Good evening, gentlemen.'

The voice, polite in its inflexion, came from the shadows beyond the northern fringe of the fire-light. At the first word, the trio let out mutually startled gasps and tried to rise hurriedly with hands grabbing towards the butts of guns. They stared at the shape, looming up darker than the surrounding blackness, which came towards them.

Holding out his hands at shoulder height, to show their empty palms, a tall man approached the fire. All in all, he made a somewhat unusual and almost theatrical figure to be emerging out of a Texas post oak grove. A black stovepipe hat tilted at a jaunty angle on a thatch of long, flaming red hair. With almost V-shaped rufus brows over deep-set eyes, a hook nose and tight lips above a sharp chin, he had a Mephistophelian cast of features. A black opera cloak with a red satin lining was draped over his shoulders. He wore a black broadcloth coat and matching vest. His dress shirt had one of those new-fangled celluloid collars, with a black silk cravat knotted bow-tie fashion, and wide, hard-starched detachable cuffs. More suited to Western travelling conditions, his yellowish-brown nankeen trousers were tucked into low-heeled black Wellington-leg boots. Looking out of place against his other attire, a wide brown leather gunbelt, with a large, ornate brass buckle, slanted down to his right thigh. In a contoured holster reposed an ivory-handled Colt Cavalry Model Peacemaker.

'I hope that my coming up just now did not startle you,' the newcomer said, in a friendly voice that belied his sardonic expression.

'Wha – Who—?' Dick spluttered, first of his party to regain even a semblance of speech.

'I saw your fire and came over to ask if I might share it for the night,' the man announced calmly.

'Huh?' croaked Dick, too surprised by the stranger's arrival to make any more useful contribution to the conversation.

'I've never been much for bedding down alone,' the man continued, coming to a halt alongside the unoccupied bed roll and looking across the fire at the trio. 'Maybe I'd best introduce myself. The name's O'Day. My friends call me "Break".'

Lowering his hands to his sides, but keeping them outside the cloak, the newcomer had the attitude of one who had cracked a joke and was waiting for a response to it.

' "Break"?' Dick repeated, while his companions looked equally uncomprehending. Then he cut loose with a guffaw of understanding. 'Break O'Day. Hey! Do you fellers cotton on to it?'

'Oh sure,' Henny agreed and squatted on his heels.

Clearly sharing the younger brother's opinion that the newcomer was harmless, Dick and Stoll also settled down on their bed rolls.

'Help yourself to the coffee, happen you're so minded,'

Dick offered, indicating the pot which bubbled and steamed on the edge of the fire. 'We don't have any food.'

'The coffee'll be all I need,' the man assured him, but made no move to help himself. 'And I've always found that it helps to know who I'm addressing.'

Coldly avaricious eyes studied the man, taking note of his expensive clothing, the gold cuff-links and well-tooled gunbelt. That was one of the new, metallic cartridge Colt revolvers and looked to be of the Best Citizen's blued finish. Undoubtedly he would have money on him, while his horse, saddle and rigging – wherever they might be – would offer even more loot. To three young outlaws in serious financial straits, he had the appearance of manna from heaven.

If the man felt any anxiety over the trio's scrutiny, he gave no sign of it. Standing by the fire, he might have been safe in the bar of an exclusive dude sporting club for all the concern he showed. In fact, he displayed an air of calm superiority as if satisfied that he had inadvertently blundered into the society of his social inferiors.

'I'm Tom Smith and this's my brother, Bill,' Dick introduced, wanting to learn more about their visitor before deciding upon a line of action. 'This here's Jack Brown.'

'You took a big chance coming up on us like that, mister,' Henny went on, annoyed by the man's attitude and wanting to throw a scare into him. 'We might've been owlhoots.'

'Anybody can see you're all honest men,' the stranger protested. 'You're not the sort to go robbing stagecoaches, nor even a bank in some one-horse town like Corsicana. Now if you'd been somebody like Joey Pinter—'

None of the trio could have been termed quick-witted, so the inference behind the man's words did not strike them straight away. Slowly the feeling crept into their skulls that he had just mentioned a subject which they had been discussing before his arrival. Yet he claimed to have come directly through the grove and to the fire. He should not have known about their professional interest in stagecoaches and the bank at Corsicana. There had also been his reference to Joey Pinter. That had hardly been inspired by coincidence, not when he was addressing leading members of the selfsame outlaw's gang. Several unpleasant reasons for his eavesdropping upon what should have been a strictly private conversation sprang – or crawled slowly – into their minds.

For all his outlandish dude clothing, Break O'Day must be a peace officer of some kind. Or, even worse, a bounty hunter who tracked down and killed wanted men for the price on their heads. Neither the Shalupka brothers nor Stoll paused to consider that their activities had failed to bring down such a penalty as having a reward offered for their capture. To their way of thinking, O'Day had located them for his own financial gain.

Well, the trio figured there was a right smart answer to *that*.

'Now there's some's'd say you know a heap too much,' Dick warned, starting to straighten his knees and lift himself erect.

'A hell of a lot too much!' Dick's brother confirmed, also beginning to rise and grabbing for his holstered Colt.

'I fail to see what you mean, gentlemen,' O'Day replied mildly, resting his elbows lightly against the sides of the cloak and holding his upturned, open hands towards the brothers.

Stoll made their meaning even plainer as he came to his feet with a lurching thrust and joined his companions in reaching hip-wards for guns.

'Kill the son-of-a-bitch!' was his contribution.

Through all the signs of consternation and aggression, O'Day continued to stand like a statue. Although his gunbelt and holster had really been designed to facilitate a rapid withdrawal of the seven-and-a-half inch barrelled Colt – not as a cheaply-made imitation for purchase by would-be *pistoleros* who knew no better than entrust their lives to shoddy workmanship – he seemed to be badly positioned to make the most of his advantages. The broadcloth coat was unbuttoned, but it and the cloak would both be in the way as his right hand tried to reach the Colt's butt. Nor were his hands held anything like ready for making a draw.

Having observed the extended, empty, upturned palms, the three young men were confident that they could give O'Day an unforgettable, permanent lesson in manners. By the time they were through, that blasted dude would know better than to sneak up on experienced desperadoes and listen to their private conversations; although it was unlikely that the lesson would do him any good.

All those thoughts rolled ponderously through the heads of the Shalupka brothers and Bernie Stoll during the brief time they were rising with the intention of killing the tall, menacing, yet empty-handed stranger.

Suddenly, miraculously it seemed to the trio, O'Day's hands were no longer empty. His elbows made pressing motions against his sides. Almost instantly two stubby Remington Double Deringers flashed from inside his shirt sleeves. Gripped in the jaws of a slender metal rod, which pushed it into exactly the right position, each weapon came to a halt where his fingers could enfold its butt. Without taking even the split-second which would have been required to turn the weapons from horizontal to vertical, O'Day thumbed back the hammers.

Flame spurted from the muzzle of the right hand weapons's upper superposed barrel. Its .41 calibre bullet drove a hole into Dick Shalupka's head. An instant later, the lower tube of the left hand Remington hurled its load into the centre of Bernie Stoll's chest. Both of the young men pitched backwards with their guns not clear of leather.

Although Henny Shalupka had been granted the opportunity to draw his Colt, the fate of his brother and Stoll caused him to freeze into immobility. That did not save him. Back clicked the two Deringers' hammers, the firing pins automatically rising or moving downwards so as to reach the edges of the unfired rimless cartridges when released to carry out their functions. O'Day turned his weapons to vertical. With his face looking even more devilish in the flickering red glow of the fire, he squeezed both triggers. The bullets took Henny in the left breast, ending unsaid the plea he had been about to make for his life.

Even as Henny followed his brother and Stoll to the ground, O'Day detected sounds which implied that he might have further need for weapons. A voice let out a startled yelp and then there was a crashing amongst the bushes to the south of the clearing as the speaker ran towards it.

Swiftly the man reached a decision. There would be no time to reload the little hide-out pistols. Nor, if the person making the noisy approach was who O'Day suspected, did he fancy using such short-ranged weapons. Throwing a disgusted glance at the three shapes that lay jerking spasmodically in death throes, O'Day swung on his heel. That was the worst of the Deringers, ideal as they might be as concealment armament. A man could not do fancy shooting with them. So O'Day had been compelled to shoot to kill instead of trying to wing one of the trio, keeping him alive and able to answer questions. However, if the sounds from the south meant anything, O'Day would soon have another – and probably better – source of information.

Dropping the left hand Deringer into his jacket pocket while striding across the clearing in the direction from which he had come, O'Day used his free palm to shove the other weapon into the shirt's cuff. Pressing it until the catch of the spring-holdout device attached to his forearm held it in place, he drew the Peacemaker. Taking cover behind the trunk of a tree, he raised the long barrelled revolver in both hands and squinted experimentally along the sights.

A stocky young man appeared in the other side of the clearing. He wore the same style of clothing and armament as O'Day's victims. Nor did the newcomer appear to exceed their intellect. Bounding in what should have been an agile manner on to the moss-covered trunk of a fallen tree, he slipped. With a yell of surprise, which turned to pain an instant later, he landed awkwardly. There was a dull crack and his left leg buckled under him. Going down, he lost his hold of the Army Colt he had drawn while running to investigate. Then he tried to reach and pick it up.

'Leave it be, young feller!' O'Day ordered, sighting the revolver without revealing himself. 'Then I'll come out and tend your hurts.'

Forgetting his desire to be armed, the newcomer clutched at his left leg.

'I don't know who you be, mister,' the man groaned. 'But I'm hurting bad and need help.'

'And I'll give it,' O'Day promised, walking forward with the Peacemaker dangling almost negligently in his right fist. 'Try to ease 'round and sit with your back to that deadfall.'

'Lord!' the injured man moaned as he obeyed. 'It hurts!'

'I'd say that's likely,' O'Day admitted. 'That was a nasty fall you took. Possibly I can do something to ease you, though. What do I call you?'

'Dipper Dixon,' the man answered.

'Then you just rest as easy as you can, Dipper,' O'Day instructed. 'I'm going to have to ruin your pants, but it's for your own good.'

'Wha – What happened to them?' Dixon inquired, indicating his companions.

'I don't know. Heard shooting as I was coming through the trees towards the fire. When I arrived, they were all down. Then I heard you coming and thought I'd better stay hidden until I could see who you might be. As soon as I saw your face, I knew I didn't need to worry. Anybody can see that you're a better class of man than those three.'

There were several inconsistencies about the story, but Dixon was in no condition to notice them. He had not cared greatly about his companions' fate. The only bond between himself, the Shalupka brothers and Stoll had died a week ago. It had only been a matter of time before they had separated for good.

Having satisfied the man's curiosity, O'Day took a Russel Barlow knife from his jacket's right pocket and opened its blade. Gently as if handling something fragile and priceless, he slit the seam of Dixon's trousers' left leg. After examining the injured limb, he collected two of the rifles from by the fire. Cutting strips from a blanket, he used it to hold the rifles as splints after he had drawn the leg back to its normal shape. Dixon fainted before he had finished working.

'You'll be all right in a few weeks,' O'Day promised, when the young man had recovered. Fetching him a cup of coffee from the fire, the dude continued, 'Now I'm going to help you some more.'

'How?' Dixon wanted to know.

'First you have to help me,' O'Day countered.

'If I can,' Dixon said warily.

'Tell me where I can find Joey Pinter.'

'Who'd he—'

'Friend, *friend*,' O'Day interrupted chidingly. 'Do you know why I'm taking all this time and trouble to help you?'

'Nope,' the young outlaw admitted.

'Because I believe that you're worth saving and giving a second chance. You're not like those three. They were bad all through, but you're not.'

'Who – Who are you, mister?'

'My name's O'Day. I'm Governor Stanton Howard's Chief Amnesty Inspector.'

'What's that?'

'You'll probably know that the Governor has promised to end the current wave of lawlessness in the Sovereign State of Texas?' O'Day asked.

'I've heard tell of it,' Dixon agreed bitterly.

Most outlaws in the Lone Star State grew bitter, or profane, when speaking of Governor Stanton Howard's vigorous policies regarding themselves. Unlike the Davis Reconstruction Administration, the present head of Texas' political affairs was pressing hard to contain the outlaw element's activities. Brought back to replace the corrupt, inefficient State Police, the Texas Rangers were running the various criminal bands ragged and generally making life unbearable for any man with a price on his head.

'The Governor is a humane man,' O'Day went on. 'He knows that a whole lot of young fellers were pushed into a life of crime through no fault of their own. He doesn't want them hounding down like the real bad *hombres*. So he's offering an amnesty and free pardon to those young men.'

'What's that mean?'

'The men he's after won't be outlaws any more. That's why I'm out here. It's my duty to find such men, interview them and decide on whether they are deserving of the amnesty.'

'And you're figuring on Joey Pinter as one of 'em?'

Dixon might lack intelligence, but he was smart enough to know that the brutal, murderous Joey Pinter would be an unlikely candidate for a pardon. Not even the most humane man in the world would risk his political career by publicly forgiving Joey Pinter's many crimes.

'Is that likely?' O'Day scoffed, reading the other's thoughts. 'But I know that you rode with him.' He waved a hand to silence Dixon's protest before it could be uttered. 'Don't try to shield him, which's what you planned to do.

I've read your character and you're not a liar. If I thought you was, I'd not offer to help you.'

'*You're* going to help *me*?' Dixon yelped.

'I am. But I must know where Pinter is, then I can arrange things so that he doesn't come and interfere with you in your new life.'

'He won't do that. He was killed by Ed Caxton up in Hell.'

'In—?' queried O'Day.

'Hell,' Dixon repeated. 'It's a town in the Palo Duro country.'

'I thought that the Indians still controlled that region,' O'Day remarked.

'They sure do. Hell's smack-dab in the middle of the *Kweharehnuh* Comanches' home-range.'

'And the Indians don't molest you?'

'Neither going there, nor coming back,' Dixon grinned. 'The mayor sees to that. Right smart feller he is for a dude. He's got them Antelopes eating out of his hand, thinking he's a mighty strong medicine man. What I heard, he does the damnedest thing to keep them that way. They say he saws his wife in half.'

'I've heard tell of it being done,' O'Day admitted, but there was a glow of interest in his eyes which did not match his casual tone. 'Did you see the mayor do it?'

'Nope,' Dixon replied, regretfully. 'Way I heard it, though, it's a sight to see. He's got this cute lil brown-haired woman all dressed in just about the shortest Injun gal's frock you ever did see—'

'You say that Pinter was killed there,' O'Day interrupted. 'By the law?'

'Naw. There's no law in Hell, 'cepting the mayor. It was Ed Caxton who made wolf-bait of Joey. Him's robbed the Yankee blue belly paymaster.'

'There's no sheriff, or town marshal in Hell?'

'Shucks, no. It's a town for owlhoots to go to when things get hot. All you have to do is give the mayor ten percent of your loot and you can stop on and have a good time for as long as your money lasts.'

'How is it that nobody's heard about Hell?' O'Day asked.

'It's been kept a secret,' Dixon explained. 'There's not many folks go into the Palo Duro and the mayor makes sure only real owlhoots get through to the town.'

'How does he do that?'

'He's got scouts up on the high points all 'round. They see somebody coming and light a fire. Ordinary folks see smoke up that ways, they steer well clear of it. Owlhoots, who know, head for it. Then one of the scouts meets you, takes all your guns and shows you the way in.'

'You mean that you fellers let him take *all* your weapons?' O'Day demanded.

'Them as didn't soon enough wished they had'd,' Dixon elaborated. 'If they didn't, the other scout signals and the Antelopes jumped em so fast they figured the hawgs'd come to feeding.'

'So all I need to do is ride towards the Palo Duro country,' O'Day commented, half to himself. 'Head for the smoke and get guided into Hell. That sounds easy enough.'

'It sure i—,' Dixon agreed, then stared as the dude started to walk away. 'Hey! Where're you headed?'

'To Hell,' O'Day replied.

'How's about me?' Dixon yelped. 'I've got this busted leg and can't travel on it.'

'That's right,' O'Day admitted. 'You're not wanted any place?'

'Nope.'

'And you don't have a price on your head?'

'Hell, no!'

'Then you're no use to me alive or dead,' O'Day said quietly.

Drawing and cocking his Colt, O'Day shot Dixon in the head.

CHAPTER TWO

THAT WAS ONE MEAN TOWN

'WHAT do you reckon's eating at Dusty, Lon?' Waco asked the Ysabel Kid as they stood clear of the laughing man and girls gathered around the camp fire. 'Something sure as hell is, and has been ever since we got clear of Hell.'

Tall, slim, yet conveying an impression of possessing whipcord, untiring strength, the Kid had hair as black as a raven's wing and a deeply tanned face with handsome, almost babyishly innocent lines. Except, that is, for its red-hazel eyes. They warned that beneath the exterior lay a wild, reckless spirit. Instead of his usual all black clothing, he wore a low crowned, wide brimmed J. B. Stetson hat of Texas style, fringed buckskin shirt and Levi's pants tucked into calf high Comanche legging-moccasins. About his middle hung a gunbelt, with a walnut handled Colt 1848 Dragoon revolver butt forward in a low cavalry-twist draw holster on the right and an ivory-hilted James Black bowie knife sheathed at the left.

There was something suggestive of the Indian about the Kid, which was hardly surprising. He had been born in the village of the *Pehnane* – Wasp, Raider, or Quick Stinger – Comanche band, maternal grandson of chief Long Walker and his French-Creole *pairaivo*.* His mother had died in childbirth and his father, a wild Irish-Kentuckian who had been adopted into the *Pehnane*, had often been away from the camp attending to the family businesses of mustanging and smuggling along the Rio Grande. So, in the traditional Comanche way, the Kid had been raised by his grandfather. That was no mean start in life. Long Walker was war leader of the Dog Soldier lodge and had been determined that his

* Pairaivo: chief and favourite wife.

grandson would be worthy of acceptance into the exclusive brotherhood.

So the Kid had received a thorough schooling in all those matters a successful Dog Soldier must know.* Skill with weapons rated high on the curriculum. He had acquired considerable proficiency with bow and arrows, war lance, tomahawk – and such expertise with a knife that he had earned the man-name *Cuchilo*. On obtaining the arms of his father's people, he had become adequate with the old Dragoon and almost unequalled in accurate shooting with a rifle. In the arts of horse-management, trick-riding, following tracks and hiding his own sign, locating hidden enemies or staying concealed when sought by keen-eyed hunters, he had graduated with honours.

It had not been an educational system calculated to endow its recipients with an exaggerated belief in the sanctity of human life. Nor had the Kid's formative years tended to increase his qualities in that field. When old enough, he had accompanied his father. By then Big Sam Ysabel had given up mustanging and was smuggling full time. So the youngster had been thrown into contact with some mighty tough, mean *hombres*, Texan and Mexican. The former had called him Sam Ysabel's kid at first, shortening it to the Ysabel Kid as he had come into greater prominence. Translating the name, the Mexicans had said *el Cabrito*. One thing all had been in agreement upon: kid or old as sin, that Indian-dark, soft-spoken youngster was equal to anybody in tough, salty courage, and deadlier than most.

The War Between The States had seen the Kid and his father employed as legal smugglers, delivering cargoes from Matamoros across the Rio Grande to the Confederate States' authorities. It had been tough and demanding work, carried out satisfactorily. With peace – or at least an end to open hostilities – the Ysabels had intended to go back to mustanging until more settled times made illegal smuggling profitable. Bushwhack lead had ended their hopes by cutting Big Sam down.

While hunting for his father's killers, the Kid had come to the turning point of his life. He had met and been helped by

* Told in: *Comanche*.

Dusty Fog, who was handling an assignment upon which the future peace of the United States had depended.* With both their missions concluded successfully, Dusty had offered to employ the Kid on the OD Connected ranch. Not as an ordinary hand, but to carry out scouting and similar duties as a member of the spread's floating outfit.

The great ranches often employed a floating outfit; half a dozen or so men who travelled the far ranges as a mobile crew, instead of being based at the main house. Ole Devil Hardin's floating outfit had also frequently found themselves dispatched to help their boss's friends out of difficulties and dangerous predicaments. In such tasks, the Kid's Comanche education had been of much use.

There were, the Kid had often mused, many points in common between himself and the youngster whose only name was Waco. And one difference. The Kid's life had been saved by Indians, Waco's parents had died by the same cause; although at the hands of the tribe from which he had taken his name. They were alike in that, but for meeting the Rio Hondo gun wizard, they might have now been riding the owlhoot trails with prices on their heads. Although the Kid had avoided it, there had always been the chance that he would run foul of the law when smuggling. Waco's fall from grace would probably have been that he had killed too often and without reason.

Raised by a North Texas rancher with a large family, Waco had drifted away from them. As a tough, proddy youngster with a brace of fast guns, he had drawn the attention of Clay Allison. Always on the look-out for such talent, the Washita curly wolf had hired Waco to ride with his wild onion crew. It was not company in which a mild-mannered introvert could have survived, and it had left its mark. The youngster had become sullen, watchful, quick to take offence, because that was a good way to avoid being put upon.

So things had stood that day up in the Texas Panhandle, when Dusty Fog had saved Waco's life at some danger to his own. From the moment he had been set down, after Dusty had snatched him clear of the stampeding CA herd,† Waco

* Told in *The Ysabel Kid*
† Told in: *Trigger Fast*

had begun his redemption. At Dusty's request, Allison had let the youngster become a member of Ole Devils' floating outfit. In the company of men who had treated him like a favourite younger brother and were willing to explain things – which Allison's crew would never do – he had lost his ready aggression and learned much which would be of use to him in later years.

Most important of all, Waco had learned *when* to add to his knowledge of *how* to shoot.

Slightly taller than the Kid, with wider shoulders and a frame that told of developing strength and muscular power, Waco was dressed in expensive cowhand clothing. A white Stetson perched on his blonde head at a jack-deuce angle over his right eye. Around his neck, a tight-rolled and knotted green silk bandana trailed its long ends down over a blue shirt. His Levi's cuffs hung outside high heeled, fancy stitched botts. Around his waist, a gunbelt of exceptionally fine workmanship supported matched staghorn handled 1860 Army Colts in contoured, tied-down holsters.

Concern showed on his tanned, handsome young face as he addressed the question to his older, more experienced companion.

'You reckon so?' countered the Kid.

'I *know* so, you slit-eyed *Pehnane*!' Waco growled.

'There's some's'd say ole Dusty'd've been right pleased to get out of it,' the Kid drawled. 'We had a good visit there, we're coming back alive.'

'Then what's—?'

'That was one mean town, boy, full of lousy folks.'

'Why sure,' Waco agreed, wondering if he could ever cease being 'boy' to the other members of the floating outfit. Not that he minded *them* calling him it, for their tones always implied that he would, eventually, grow up into a forty-four calibre man.* 'There wasn't a feller, nor woman, in it that hadn't done real bad meanness one time or another.'

'And we left them there,' the Kid pointed out. 'That's what's eating at Dusty, boy. He left those folks, men and *women,* in the Palo Duro, with the *Kweharehnuh* band all

* How the name came into being and what it implies is told in: *.44 Calibre Man.*

'round them. Comes time for the bucks to collect their bullets and the folks can't hand 'em out, all hell's going to bust loose in Hell.'

'And serve them right, the stinking bastards. There's murderers, cheats, thieves and worse, 'n' nothing else but there. They built the town, now let them pay for it.'

'Dusty don't see it that way, boy.'

'What we heard and saw of 'em,' Waco protested, 'they can take care of themselves.'

'Against things they know about, maybe,' drawled the Kid. 'Only they're most all of them dudes. They don't know sic 'em about Injuns and a whole heap less about riled-up Antelope Comanches toting repeating rifles—'

'Which they've give to 'em,' the blond pointed out.

'I'm not gainsaying it,' the Kid admitted. 'And when they handed those repeaters over, they made a promise. When it's not kept, which it won't be, there'll be a whole slew of riled up bucks wanting to know why. Them's're killed in the fighting'll be the lucky ones. And that goes double for their women-folk.'

'What'll Dusty do?' Waco inquired, having no need to be further enlightened upon the Comanches' treatment of white female prisoners.

'Likely he'll tell us when he decides,' the Kid replied. 'What do *you* reckon he'll do?'

'Go back to Hell and try to prize 'em loose,' Waco guessed. 'Just's soon's we've delivered the money in the wagon and seen the gals safe.'

'Talking about the gals,' the Kid said quietly, glancing at the group about the fire. 'How do you reckon they'll take it when they learn who we are and that they're not going to get any place close to as much of the money as they've been counting on?'

'I'd say that all depends on how Emma takes it,' Waco guessed. 'The rest'll go along with her. Happen they don't cotton to the notion, we can count on Belle to back our play. Anyways, once they learn we're not owlhoots, I reckon Hubert and the gals'll take what Dusty offers them. It'll be a fair offer.'

'Only not as much as they figured on getting,' the Kid reminded him.

'Things being how they are,' Waco replied. 'I'm betting they'll take it.'

Although the Kid would not have stated so audibly, he felt inclined to agree with his young *amigo*.

Despite what Dipper Dixon had told Break O'Day, the town of Hell had not remained a complete secret. Jules Murat, captain of Texas Rangers, had learned enough to make him suspect its existence. On being informed, the Governor had been faced with a problem. While determined to stamp out lawlessness, and wishing to destroy a safe haven for badly wanted men, Stanton Howard had no desire to provoke an Indian war. Any attempts at the former, unless carefully handled, could easily have resulted in the latter.

Unlike the other bands of the Comanche Nation, the *Kweharehnuh* had refused to come to terms at the Fort Sorrell peace treaty meeting.* Instead, they had retreated to their wild, practically unexplored Palo Duro and Tule country to follow the traditional *Nemenuh*† way of life. All the evidence had pointed to the citizens of Hell having obtained permission to make their homes in the Palo Duro and for immunity to outlaws who wished to visit or leave the town. Part of the payment for those privileges had been a repeating rifle and a regular supply of ammunition for every war leader, *tehnap* and *tuivitsi* in the band.‡

To send in the army would be inviting defeat, or an expensive, costly campaign against warriors fighting on their own terrain. Before victory could be obtained, restless, unsettled brave-hearts on the reservations would have learned what was happening and headed out to join the battle.

So Stanton Howard had decided that he must try to learn just how dangerous the situation would be. Sending in Rangers posing as outlaws had not been practical. With so many wanted men in the town, there would have been too great a danger of the spies being recognized and exposed. What had been needed were men of courage, initiative and ability, but who were not known to be connected with the forces of law and order. They would also need an

* Why they did not is told in: *Sidewinder*.
† Nemenuh: 'The People', the Comanches' name for their nation.
‡ Tehnap, an experienced warrior; tuivitsi, an adolescent, inexperienced warrior.

exceptional leader to steer them through such a dangerous assignment.

With that latter qualification in mind, Governor Howard had contacted Ole Devil Hardin and asked for the help of the man he believed to be most suited to fill his needs; the Rio Hondo gun wizard whose name was Dusty Fog.

People in Texas, never slow to praise their State's favourite sons, had often claimed that Dusty Fog was the fastest, most accurate gun-handler in the West. It was also said that few men could stand up against him in bare-handed fighting. Those were qualities which he would need to stay alive in Hell, but Howard had known there were others equally important. In the Governor's opinion, Dusty Fog had them all.

A captain in the Texas Light Cavalry at seventeen, Dusty Fog had built a reputation as a military raider equal to that of John Singleton Mosby or Turner Ashby. Ranging across the less-publicized Arkansas battlefront, Dusty Fog had played havoc with the Yankees.* It had been whispered how he had supprted Belle Boyd, the Rebel Spy,† on two of her missions.‡ Less well known was how he had prevented two fanatical Unionists from stirring up an Indian war which would have decimated much of Texas.§

With the War over, and his uncle crippled in a riding accident,‖ Dusty had become segundo of the great OD Connected ranch. He had earned a name as a tophand with cattle, a trail boss of considerable ability and – although not in Texas – had won acclaim as a capable town-taming peace officer.¶ Small wonder that Stanton Howard had felt confident that Dusty could take on the assignment.

In accordance with a carefully-formulated plan, Dusty the Kid and Waco had gone to Hell. Their pose of being wanted

---

* Told in: *Under the Stars and Bars* and *Kill Dusty Fog!*

† More of Belle Boyd's story is told in: *The Bloody Border, Back to the Bloody Border, The Hooded Riders, The Bad Bunch* and *The Whip and the War Lance.*

‡ Told in: *The Colt and the Sabre* and *The Rebel Spy.*

§ Told in: *The Devil Gun.*

‖ Told in 'The Paint' episode of *The Fastest Gun in Texas.*

¶ Told in: *Quiet Town, The Trouble Busters, The Making of a Lawman, The Town Tamers* and *The Small Texan.*

outlaws had been successful. So much so that they had completed their mission and, aided by Giselle Lampart, widow of the mayor and founder of the town, lady outlaw Belle Starr, Emma Nene and some of her saloon's employees, they had destroyed the *Kweharehnuh*'s next issue of ammunition and brought away much of the citizens' ill-gotten gains.

Up to that evening, only Belle Starr had known the trio's true identity and she had good reasons for not exposing them. However, after three days of hard, fast travelling – at a camp set up close to the Swisher Creek some five miles from its junction with the Red River's Prairiedog Fork – Dusty had decided that the time had come to let the others of the party know where they stood. They had been under the impression that the money in their wagon was to be divided equally amongst them, instead of being returned to the banks and stagecoach companies from which most of it had come.

'Well,' drawled the Kid, nodding towards the gloomy outlines of the trees which surrounded the camp. 'We'll right soon know what it's going to be.'

Following the direction of his Indian-dark companion's gaze, Waco watched three figures take form and advance into the circle of fire-light. Two were women with bodies and – in normal times – faces to catch the eye in any crowd. So far the various bruises gathered in the course of two long, gruelling fights with each other had not faded away; but both Belle Starr and Emma Nene still showed sufficient traces of their matching, yet different beauties.

Currently Belle Starr's hair was dyed black. In three days she had managed to clear up the tangle in which it had been left by Emma's clutching fingers, as they had fought and provided a diversion while the other members of the party had stolen Mayor Lampart's loot. She wore a dark blue shirt, black riding-breeches and high-heeled boots. A Manhattan Navy revolver swung in the fast-draw holster on her magnificently shaped right thigh. Her clothing showed off a body with rich, mature and eye-catching curves.

Although a riding habit, open-necked blouse and high-button shoes could not compete with Belle's attire for drawing male attention, Emma Nene had a figure every bit as voluptuous. She too had tidied up her blonde hair, for she had no desire to be seen at a disadvantage by the man who strolled between them.

Going by her expression, Emma had just received a shock. Waco and the Kid could have guessed at what it had been.

Silence fell at the fire as Emma's big, burly bartender, Hubert, Giselle Lampart and the six saloongirls stared in interest at the two women; but mainly at their escort. He was the man in whom Governor Stanton Howard had placed so much faith. A giant amongst his fellows as far as achievements were concerned.

From his low crowned, wide brimmed Texas-fashion Stetson to his high-heeled fancy stitched boots, Dusty Fog measured a mere five foot six. He had curly dusty blond hair and a fairly handsome face that was unnoticeable when in repose. Only when he was roused did its full magnetism, strength of will and the hint of intelligence beyond average make itself felt. Like his friends, he had played the part of an outlaw on a spree and purchased good clothes in Hell. He contrived to make them look like somebody's cast-offs. Nor did the excellent gunbelt and its twin bone-handled Colt Civilian Model Peacemakers in cross-draw holster appear to add anything to his stature.

In times of peace, Dusty Fog could have been overlooked as an insignificant nobody. That very rapidly changed when trouble reared its head.

'Dusty!' the Kid said quietly, forgetting for the first time since commencing with the deception to use the small Texan's assumed name. 'There's riders coming!'

CHAPTER THREE

WE'LL SHOOT YOU WHERE YOU STAND

'Who are they, Comanche?' Emma Nene asked, throwing a worried look around.

'Soldiers, sound of it,' the Kid replied. 'Ain't nobody else makes all that much clatter 'n' jingling.'

'How many of them?' Dusty demanded, for he could only just make out the faint sound of hooves.

'Four, five maybe,' estimated the Kid. 'No more'n that, anyways.'

'What colour hosses're they on?' Waco challenged cheerfully.

Having brought their assignment to a successful conclusion, the youngster could see nothing to be concerned about from the presence of the soldiers.

'Have they seen us?' Hubert wanted to know, not sharing Waco's feelings on the subject.

'I'd say "yes" to that,' the Kid drawled. 'Least-wise, they're headed right slap at us.'

'What're we going to do?' yelped the pretty red-haired girl who had been Waco's escort in Hell.

'How's about you-all taking them on tooth 'n' claw, Redgal,' Waco suggested. 'You can hold 'em off long enough for the rest of us to get away.'

'Like hell I will!' the girl snorted. 'Only I'd hate to have them find out what's in the wagon.'

'And me!' Hubert agreed. 'So how do we play it, Ed?'

'Make out you're a bunch of saloon-folk headed for work in Colorado,' Dusty decided. 'You'd best hide in the wagon, Belle. Matt, Comanch' and me, we're cowhands stopping by for the night. Play it that way and everything'll be fine.'

Even as he finished speaking, Dusty became aware of Emma Nene's eyes on him. There was more than a hint of suspicion in her scrutiny and he could guess at its cause. Whilst walking with her and Belle, he had disclosed his true identity and made her an offer. In return for their help in Hell, Emma, Belle and Giselle Lampart would each receive fifty thousand dollars. The rest of Emma's party were to be given ten thousand dollars apiece. That was less than any of them, with the exception of Belle, had anticipated; but it was backed by the small Texan's assurance that he would not mention their connection with the town. All in all, it was a generous offer.

Up to Dusty's speech, Emma had apparently been satisfied with the arrangement. Having seen the small Texan and his companions in action at Hell, she had known there was little her party could do other than accept. The three men and Belle Starr could nullify any protest. His words had created doubts. Instead of realizing that the subterfuge was for her and the other Hell's citizens's benefit, she had started to wonder if he really was Ed Caxton, wanted for murdering and robbing a U.S. Army paymaster.

There was no time for the small Texan to go into an explanation, even if – which he doubted – the blonde would be inclined to believe it. So he decided to say nothing further to Emma. In the interests of self-preservation, she would be unlikely to betray him.

Nearer came the sound of the hooves, mingled with the creaking of saddle leather and faint jingling of metal accoutrements which civilian travellers did not find necessary. Instinctively the Kid edged to where his Winchester Model 1866 rifle rested on the seat of the saddle he would be using as a pillow. Waco ambled across to stand alongside Dusty. Going to the wagon, Belle Starr swung herself on to its box and disappeared inside. The rest of the party remained around the fire.

'Hello, the camp!' bawled a voice. 'U.S. Cavalry here. Can we come in?'

'Answer him, Hubert!' Dusty growled when the bartender looked for guidance. 'It's you they'll expect it from.'

'C – Come ahead,' the bartender replied.

Led by a tall, broad-shouldered young 2nd Lieutenant, a sergeant and three troopers rode from amongst the trees. They drew rein by the line of horses picketed on the fringe of the firelight and swung from their saddles. While the enlisted men stood by their mounts, the officer crossed to the fire. As he walked, his eyes darted from side to side and he seemed to be examining his surroundings with some care.

'My names's Kitson, 4th Cavalry, ladies, gents,' the officer introduced. 'Is it all right if me and my men share your fire?'

'Feel free,' Hubert offered, darting another look in Dusty's direction. 'Coffee's on the boil and we're going to cook up supper.'

'Thanks,' Kitson answered, turning a quick glance in the direction the bartender had looked. 'We didn't expect to meet anybody out this way.'

'We've come up from Paducah,' Hubert explained, selecting the only town he knew to be roughly south of their position. 'Headed to work at the Bon Ton House in Denver.'

'*All* of you?' queried the officer.

'These three young fellers met up with us around sundown,' the bartender replied.

'We're on our way home from a trail drive, mister,' Dusty elaborated. 'The folks were good enough to let us stay on here for the night.'

'Huh huh!' Kitson grunted in a matter-of-fact manner, as if three cowhands were beneath his serious notice. 'I'll fetch my men along. I want to warn them about their behaviour.'

Swinging around, the officer strode away. Dusty watched him go, deciding that under the slightly pompous nature – which was only to be expected in a young 2nd Lieutenant – Kitson was most likely a capable soldier and popular leader. Certainly the enlisted men listened attentively to his low spoken words and showed no resentment, although they all had the appearance of long service.

After Kitson had finished speaking, each of the troopers unclipped his carbine from the leather sling draped diagonally over his left shoulder to the right hip. None of the Texans saw anything suspicious in the move. The carbine sling, a sixty inch long, three inch wide leather strap fitted with a polished steel ring and snap-hook, had become a standard issue to the U.S. Cavalry during the War Between The

States. That had been brought about by the tendency of Union commanding officers to make their mounted men fight on foot. A combination of the sling and carbine-ring had ensured that the weapon was always in its user's possession. However, the Springfield Model of 1870 carbine weighed seven pounds fifteen ounces – no mean burden to have dangling at one's side. Experienced men would not leave their carbines on the slings in a friendly camp, but would pile them in a neat, easily-separated pyramid close to the fire.

Fanning out in a casual-seeming manner, the soldiers walked towards the civilians. Suddenly, the troopers' carbines lifted and lined on the Texans. With fair speed, considering the awkward manner in which the United States' Army insisted that its personnel carried their revolvers, Kitson and his sergeant produced Colt Cavalry Peacemakers from their holsters.

'Don't move, or we'll shoot you where you stand!' Kitson snapped, thumbing back the Colt's hammer and lining its muzzle on Dusty's chest.

'What—?' Hubert croaked, starting to rise.

'Don't be alarmed, sir,' Kitson replied, without taking his attention from the small Texan. 'Your visitors are our concern. They're Ed and Matt Caxton and the other one's name is Comanche Blood.'

'Lands sakes a-mercy!' Emma gasped, right hand fluttering to her mouth. 'The men who robbed that paymaster and murdered all his men?'

'That's them, ma'am,' the sergeant confirmed and his revolver lined unerringly at the Kid. 'Paddy Magoon was a good friend of mine.'

Dusty could have cursed the unexpected turn of events. After leaving Hell, he and his *amigos* had shaved off the beards grown to lessen the chances of them being recognized. Unfortunately, the recognition had finally come from an entirely different source. That figured. Kitson had the look of a competent, efficient officer. So he would be unlikely to have forgotten the descriptions of the three men accused of robbing an Army paymaster and murdering his whole escort. What was more, he had been smart enough to plan the best way in which to arrest the trio. When the story came out, a number of Yankee officers who had served in Arkansas were going to have red faces. None of them had come anywhere near to capturing Captain Dustine Edward Marsden Fog.

Apart from the embarrassment which would be caused for various officers, there was another and more immediate point to consider. How could Dusty, the Kid and Waco evade capture without implicating Emma's party with the town of Hell? Or prevent Belle Starr from being arrested? Dusty had promised that his helpers would go free, without even being connected to the town, and he always believed in keeping his word.

One thing was for certain. Dusty knew that convincing Kitson of the truth would be anything but easy. The very nature of the deception had rendered impossible the carrying of written proof of the trio's true identity. Angered at the story which had been circulated, the soldiers would be unlikely to accept the mere word of men they believed had cold-bloodedly murdered several of their comrades in arms.

Unless, of course, they had no other choice but to accept.

Attaining that desirable situation would not be easy, if it was to be done without the help of Hubert and the women.

'Let your gunbelts fall,' Kitson ordered. 'Left-handed and real slow.'

'You've got us dead to rights, mister,' Dusty drawled. 'Best we do what he says, boys.'

'We can save a whole heap of fussing if we just shoot 'em now,' muttered the burly soldier covering Dusty.

'Shut off that kind of talk, Brill!' Kitson snapped. 'I'll have no more of it from you.'

That removed one worry from Dusty's mind. No matter what his personal feelings might be, the lieutenant did not intend to carry out any private revenge on his captives. Nor did he mean to let his escort do so. Although the other enlisted men showed their dislike of the trio, none of them appeared to be openly supporting Brill's point of view.

Studying Brill, with eyes which read his character as if it had been printed on his sullen face, Dusty decided that he would offer the best opportunity to turn the tables on their captors.

Freeing the pigging thongs which held the tips of the holsters to his thighs, Dusty unbuckled and lowered the gunbelt to his feet. All the time, he studied Brill with an infuriatingly mocking sneer. He could see the soldier's indignation rising. Which was just what the small Texan wanted to happen.

Waco and the Kid followed Dusty's example, satisfied that he had some plan for their salvation in mind.

'Back away from the belts,' Kitson commanded, as he continued to advance with Brill at his side.

'Could be you're making a mistake, mister,' Dusty remarked, standing his ground. 'We don't know anything about—'

'You heard the lieutenant!' Brill barked, delighted that the short-grown son-of-a-bitch had presented him with an opportunity. Striding ahead of Kitson, he directed the muzzle of his Springfield in a savage thrust towards Dusty's midsection. 'Move b—!'

Offered his chance, Dusty took it with devastating speed. In his eagerness to strike, Brill had inserted his big frame between the small Texan and the barrel of Kitson's revolver.

'Get out—!' the lieutenant bawled.

Like a flash, Dusty's right hand cupped under the Springfield's barrel and jerked it out of alignment. At the same moment, his left hand closed over the carbine's breech from above. Although Brill had involuntarily squeezed the trigger, the outside hammer was halted by the small Texan's hand before it could reach the head of the firing pin.

Finding his weapon grasped with surprising strength and turned from its target, Brill's first inclination was to reverse its direction. Instantly Dusty changed his twisting motion to the way in which the soldier intended it to go. Dusty's response took Brill by surprise. Pivoting slightly on his left foot, he plucked the carbine from the soldier's hands. Snapping it back, Dusty propelled the butt against the side of its owner's jaw and knocked him staggering.

Attracted by the commotion, the soldier covering Waco allowed his attention to wander. Watching the carbine swing towards Dusty, the youngster sprang forward. Taking his hold with both hands gripping from above, Waco felt the soldier trying to pull back from his grasp. Up swung the youngster's right foot to ram into the soldier's belly. Sinking into a sitting position, he dragged the trooper off balance. By rolling on to his back, pulling down with his hands and thrusting his foot upwards, Waco caused his assailant to turn a half somsersault through the air. With a startled yell, the trooper lost his hold on the carbine and landed upon his back beyond Waco's head.

Like Waco's watcher, the sergeant and third trooper heard the disturbance. They matched their companion's reaction in starting to turn away from their charge. Although the Kid immediately made his play, he was all too aware of the dangers doing so entailed. The non-com and the soldier were experienced fighting men. So they had halted well beyond the Kid's reach and sufficiently far apart for him to be unable to launch a simultaneous attack on them. Any other way he tried it would likely prove fatal for him.

However, the chance had to be taken. If not, either Dusty or Waco would die. While one of them kept the Kid covered, the other soldier would turn and shoot at their companions' attackers. Sure enough, the sergeant was already swinging his attention back to the Kid and the trooper made as if to throw up and sight his carbine towards Dusty.

Cutting loose with a ringing *Pehnane* scalp-yell, the Kid hurled himself into motion. He went forward in a swift dive, aiming for the sergeant's legs. So swiftly did he move that he passed under the barrel of the Colt as its wielder tried to throw down on him. Enfolding his arms about the yellow-striped blue breeches' knees, the Kid jerked them together and heaved. Thrown off balance, the non-com sent a bullet harmlessly into the air. Then his back smashed on to the ground with enough force to jolt all the air from his lungs. Wriggling forward with desperate speed, the Kid tried to drop alongside the dazed non-com and used his body as a shield. From the rapid way in which the third trooper was turning and handling the Springfield, the Kid would not be fast enough.

Having disposed of Brill, Dusty continued to move with planned alacrity. He put himself in Kitson's place and decided that the officer would expect him to keep the trooper between them. So he went the other way. That carried him in the direction of the fire. Dusty was gambling on Kitson being taken by surprise, but also that he would remain calm enough to think.

Baffled by Dusty's actions, Kitson attempted to change his point of aim. Instantly a difficulty arose. If he fired and missed, his bullet would fly towards the – as he assumed – innocent people around the fire. Rather than endanger the women, the lieutenant was determined to be certain of where his lead would end its flight.

With the Springfield lifting and lining at him, the Kid figured that his life expectancy was getting shorter by the second. The shot which cracked out did not come from any Army carbine. Struck on the foregrip by a bullet the Springfield spun unfired from the trooper's hands. He gave a yelp of surprise and spun around to see who had intervened. Although his right hand was clawing at the flap of his revolver's holster, he refrained from completing the motion.

Standing inside the wagon, left knee bent and its foot resting on the back of the driver's seat, Belle Starr cradled the butt of her Winchester Model of 1866 carbine in the firing position. Smoke curled from its muzzle, which did not mean that it was now harmless. Unlike the single-shot Springfield issued to the Cavalry, her weapon was a twelve shot repeater. Down and up flicked her right hand, operating the loading lever which automatically ejected the empty case, cocked the hammer and fed a live cartridge into the chamber. She made the movement with such deft ease that the Winchester ·44/28 calibre barrel never wavered in its alignment on the soldier's chest.

Belle had guessed at Dusty's predicament, and so had been prepared to lend a hand at the opportune moment. Collecting her carbine from the wagon, she had remained concealed and cut in most effectively to save the Kid's life.

Throwing a grateful glance at his rescuer, the Kid rolled from the sergeant and snatched up the other's discarded Peacemaker. Usually the Indian-dark Texan professed to despise the new metallic-cartridge Colt, but he admitted silently that one of them could feel right comforting to a man's hand given the correct conditions.

Advancing slightly to the right of Kitson, Dusty raised the borrowed carbine vertically and flung it at him. It struck the officer's gun-wrist with numbing force. Deflected aside and downwards, the Colt cracked. Dirt erupted a few feet from Kitson's feet as the bullet ploughed in. Giving the officer no time to recover, Dusty changed direction. Gliding in, he clamped both hands on to Kitson's right wrist. Carrying the trapped limb into the air, Dusty pivoted below it and snapped it downwards sharply. Unable to help himself, Kitson felt his feet leave the ground. Turning upside-down in mid-flight, he landed rump-first and lost his hold on the revolver. Releasing his grip, Dusty scooped up the Colt. Cocking its hammer, he turned to see if his *amigos* required assistance.

Going by all appearances, the Kid and Waco had contrived to deal with their share of the soldiers and were unharmed. The blond youngster was sitting up and lowering the carbine he had been lining on Kitson. Knowing Waco's sense of loyalty, Dusty figured that the lieutenant had come mighty close to being shot. Beyond a scared-looking trooper and recumbent sergeant, the Kid was rising. He looked a mite guilty as he noticed Dusty's pointed glance at the long barrelled Peacemaker in his hand.

'I figured it'd make a good club,' the Kid excused himself.

'Most times he wouldn't even say that,' grinned Waco, following the direction of Dusty's gaze and guessing what had prompted the Kid's comment.

From his companions, Dusty turned his attention to the rest of the camp. Giving a grateful nod to Belle in passing, he studied the people from Hell. Emma Nene's face showed a mixture of disappointment and relief. All the saloongirls had stood up and none hid her pleasure at seeing that the three Texans were back in control of the situation. Worry etched lines on Hubert's face as he waited to see how the 'Caxton brothers' and 'Comanche Blood' would deal with the soldiers. By all accounts, they had wiped out a colonel and his escort to steal a pay roll. So they would be unlikely to let the cavalrymen survive. Smarter than the girls, Hubert could foresee bad trouble ahead if the lieutenant and his men were murdered. Yet he knew of no way that he could prevent it happening.

Only Giselle Lampart appeared unmoved, either by the

Texans' escape or over the soldiers' possible fate. Small, brunette, with a beautiful, vivacious face, she wore a gingham dress that suggested her figure would have matched that of Belle or Emma if she had been their height. Her eyes darted around in an inquisitive manner and Dusty sensed that she was waiting eagerly for him to order the cavalrymen's deaths.

'Well!' Kitson gritted, rising to face Dusty. 'Get on with it, you murdering son-of-a-bitch.'

'Like I said,' the small Texan replied, accepting the insult as having been spoken by a man under great stress. 'Could be you've made a mistake.'

Shaking his head to clear it, Brill swung towards Dusty. Hate blazed on the soldier's face. Unmindful of the revolver in the small Texan's hand, the surly trooper clawed open his holster. Something hissed viciously through the air. A screech burst from Brill's lips and, forgetting the weapon he had meant to draw, his hands clutched wildly at the feathered shaft of an arrow which had penetrated his chest so deeply that its barbed head had emerged at the back.

War-whoops shattered the night and several *Kwehareh-nuh* Comanche warriors burst into the fire-light from all sides of the camp.

CHAPTER FOUR

GET THE WHITE WITCH!

THE attack was launched with typical *Nemenuh* speed, savagery and deadly intent. While there was not time for an accurate trail count, the Kid figured that at least two dozen assorted *tehnaps* and *tuivitsis* were boiling out from the places of concealment they had selected in a circle around the clearing. He noticed other things, his mind ticking them off automatically even as he prepared to defend himself.

Despite most of the Comanches' clothing having been made from the hides of pronghorn antelopes, which labelled them as *Kweharehnuh* to the Kid's eyes, only a few braves carried firearms. That fact gave the Kid less comfort or satisfaction than might have been expected. He knew that the people of Hell had presented every *Kweharehnuh* warrior with a repeating rifle or carbine and a regular supply of ammunition to go with it. If some of the attackers – the majority in fact – had elected to lay aside their Winchesters or Spencers, it was because they intended to count coup by personal contact. Doing so rated far higher in a Comanche's estimation than when one was claimed after standing back to take an enemy's life with a bullet or an arrow.

No matter what kind of weapons they were carrying, the braves displayed a mutually determined eagerness to come to grips with the hated white people around the camp-fire.

Screams of fright broke from the saloongirls. Instead of acting in a sensible manner, five of the six scattered wildly like chickens spooked by a diving Cooper's hawk. Acting in blind panic, the Mexican girl who had been assigned to keep the Kid company in Hell ran straight to her death. A grizzled *tehnap* rammed his war lance into her body and gutted her with casual, deft ease.

Clenching her fists like a male pugilist, Emma Nene stood

37

her ground. Letting out a screech, Giselle Lampart buckled at the knees and sank to crouch motionless. With his right hand fanning towards the butt of his holstered Colt, Hubert started to move in his employer's direction. While scared, Red showed a better grasp of the situation than her fellow workers. Instead of fleeing blindly, she darted rapidly in search of Waco's protection.

Lurching into a sitting position, the sergeant grabbed instinctively at his empty holster. An expression of horror creased his leathery face as he realized that he was unarmed. Deprived of his carbine by Belle's bullet, the second of the Kid's would-be captors tried to draw his revolver. Shooting on the run, one of the firearm-toting minority sent a Spencer bullet into the soldier's head.

Disturbed by the sudden commotion, the horses bucked, reared, snorted and generally displayed their disapproval. The animals owned by Dusty's party had been secured to a stout picket line and it held firm against their struggles. Having been eager to arrest the three 'outlaws', Kitson had ordered his men to leave their horses with the reins trailing. Normally that would have kept the well-trained remounts motionless. Fright overrode training and the cavalry horses went bounding into the darkness.

Not one of the braves gave the departing horses as much as a glance, although any of the animals would have been a valuable piece of booty.

Taking in the precarious nature of their situation with a swift glance, Dusty Fog responded with his usual speed. He held Lieutenant Kitson's revolver and so had the means to protect himself – but the officer was unarmed and would rate high on the attackers' list of victims.

'Here, mister!' Dusty snapped and tossed the long-barrelled Cavalry Model Peacemaker to Kitson.

Although startled and puzzled by such an action from a man he believed to be a cold-blooded killer, the officer grabbed for and caught the weapon around its frame. He transferred his right hand to the walnut handle and prepared to sell his life dearly.

Having provided the officer with the means of self-preservation, Dusty gave thought to obtaining the same for himself. Turning, he hurtled through the air in a rolling dive towards his own weapons. Even as he went down, he saw a wild-eyed *tuivitsi* rushing in his direction and holding a razor-sharp, spear-pointed war-lance ready to strike.

Hitting the ground on his left side and with his back to the lance carrier, Dusty closed his fingers around the matched Colts' bone grips. Rolling to face his assailant as the lance rose high to gain impetus for its thrust, Dusty flung aside the gunbelt and freed the four and three-quarter inch barrels from the holsters. Thumb-cocking the hammers while lying flat on his back, Dusty angled the guns upwards to where the brave was preparing to drive home the lance. Both revolvers spat at the same moment. Struck in the centre of the chest, the *tuivitsi* was flung backwards and down.

Hearing Red's scream as he bounded to his feet, Waco swung his gaze in search of her. What he saw brought an instant response. A pursuing warrior had caught up with the girl, gripped her by the hair and was dragging her backwards. Up swung the brave's tomahawk as the girl toppled to the rear. Waco flung the acquired Springfield to the aim and squeezed its trigger. With the back of his skull shattered where the bullet had burst out, the *Kweharehnuh* released the girl's hair and collapsed. Rolling on to her hands and knees with frantic haste, Red looked back at her attacker. Letting out a shriek, she flopped face forward in a faint.

There was no time for Waco to display concern over Red's indisposition. He held an empty weapon, for which he possessed no ammunition. *That* was not a good way to be situated under the circumstances. Tossing the Springfield aside, he darted to where he had laid down his gunbelt.

Believing that he had caused the blond ride-plenty's flight, a whooping young *tuivitsi* gave chase. Waco heard the rapidly approaching thud of feet and spun to face his pursuer. Around swung the *tuivitsi*'s tomahawk in a horizontal slash aimed at taking the blond's head from his shoulders. In his inexperience, the brave was over-confident. So he was taken by surprise by his would-be victim's rapid and unexpected response.

Instead of standing petrified until killed, Waco ducked under the blow. Still crouching, he lunged and butted his skull into the *tuivitsi*'s belly. As breath belched from the

Comanche's lungs, the blond wrapped both arms about his bare thighs. Straightening up suddenly, Waco raised the *tuivitsi* and released his hold at the height of the other's elevation. Expecting the Indian to crash helplessly, Waco once more turned and sprang towards his gunbelt.

Trained almost from birth to ride bucking horses, including numerous lessons in how to fall off without being injured, the *tuivitsi* contrived to light down on his feet. The impetus of the throw caused him to run forward several steps, but he retained his grip on the tomahawk's handle. Twirling around, he charged once more at the Texan.

Snatching out his right hand Colt in passing, Waco pivoted to meet the attack. The *tuivitsi* was closing fast and with a fanatical determination that would not be halted by less than death. There was neither the time nor the need for Waco to take a careful aim. Assuming a crouching posture, with his right elbow locked tight against his side, Waco flashed across his left hand to draw back and release the hammer. Three times, so fast that the shots could hardly be detected as separate sounds, Waco made the fanning motion. Each .44 bullet ploughed into the *tuivitsi*'s torso and turned his advance into a reeling, uncontrolled retreat.

Before Hubert could complete his draw, he was impaled by an arrow. Running past the front end of the wagon, a stocky war-bonnet chief nocked another arrow to the string of the bow he carried.

'Get the white witch!' he roared, starting to raise the arrow in Emma Nene's direction.

Hearing and understanding the words, taken with the sight of the chief's obvious interest in Emma, Belle lined her carbine. It barked and the flat-nosed bullet passed between the trailing ends of the head-dress to shatter the man's spinal column. He went down with his bow still undrawn.

'He's sure got old Emma's character off well,' Belle mused as she threw the carbine's lever through its reloading cycle.

A harsh ripping sound from behind caused Belle to spin around. Although the visibility inside the wagon was poor, she could make out that its closed, fastened rear flaps were shaking violently. Guessing that a Comanche was trying to gain access, she was faced with the problem of how to stop him. Then she saw a dull glitter as a knife's blade pierced the canvas. Four times, as fast as she could work the lever and squeeze the trigger, muzzle blasts illuminated the interior. Holes appeared in a vertical line across the flaps above the knife. A scream of pain followed the third shot. The knife was withdrawn suddenly. Its departure was followed by a thud and violent thrashing sound. Belle decided that these had been caused by the intruder falling and making violent, convulsive motions in his agony.

Satisfied that she had nothing further to fear from that direction, Belle swivelled once more to the open end of the canopy. Partially dazzled by the flashes of burning powder erupting from the carbine's muzzle, she saw a brave had caught Emma by the arm. Instead of striking the blonde down, he thrust her from him and sprang towards the crouching figure of Giselle Lampart.

Belle snapped off a shot which missed, due to the brave bending and taking hold of the brunette's left arm. Jerking down the lever, the lady outlaw felt something snap inside the carbine. Instead of completing its various reloading functions, the mechanism stayed stubbornly open. Having experienced such a sensation on another – although less demanding – occasion, Belle knew that one of the toggle-links had broken. It was a defect which plagued the earlier models of Winchester.*

Cursing furiously, Belle dropped the useless carbine. Down dipped her right hand and drew the Manhattan Navy revolver from its contoured holster. Then she prepared to spring from the wagon and move to a distance at which she might hope to hit something with the handgun.

Like Dusty, the Kid did not leave a soldier defenceless against the attackers. Dropping the revolver into the sergeant's lap, he leapt to retrieve his own rifle. A brave, taller and slimmer than most *Nemenuh*, came leaping to intercept the Kid with a tomahawk lifting ready to hurl into flesh.

Gathering up the Winchester, with his right hand grasping the foregrip, the Kid slid his left forefinger into the triggerguard and the other three through the lever's ring. Raising the rifle to waist level, he shot the brave with the

* A more detailed description of this defect is given in: *Calamity Spells Trouble.*

muzzle not three feet from the other's bare chest. Already the tomahawk had commenced its downwards swing. Sidestepping as soon as he had squeezed the trigger, the Kid heard the hiss as the blade passed his sleeve harmlessly. Then he saw something that demanded his immediate and undivided attention.

Grasping an arm each, two *Kweharehnuh tehnap* were dragging Giselle Lampart away from the camp fire. Even as the Kid snapped the Winchester's butt to his shoulder, knowing that shooting from the hip would not serve his needs, he felt puzzled. Not by the attempted abduction; a white woman made an acceptable piece of loot, almost as useful as a mule, but not so valuable as a horse or a gun. So he was not surprised to see the braves attempting to take the brunette with them.

What aroused the Kid's curiosity was their reason for having run straight past a saloongirl and for shoving Emma Nene aside when both were larger, stronger, and therefore more desirable as work-producing captives than the diminutive Giselle would be.

There was no time for the Kid to debate the problem. If he hoped to save Giselle from a fate worse than death, he had to concentrate. Sighting the Winchester, he shot the brave to the brunette's left in the head. Smoothly altering his point of aim as he flickered the lever up and down, he tumbled her second abductor in a lifeless heap. Shrieking hysterically, Giselle crumpled between the two dead *tehnap*.

Much to the Kid's further puzzlement, a leathery-faced *tehnap*, who had been bending to take Hubert's revolver from its holster, dropped the weapon. Yelling an order to the nearest *tuivitsi*, the old warrior discarded his trophy and ran to Giselle's side. Jerking his lance from the body of the saloongirl he had impaled, the *tuivitsi* darted to join the *tehnap*. Neither of them offered to use his weapon on the small woman, but bent to grab her by the ankles. With their holds obtained, they headed towards the trees.

The Kid shot the *tehnap* in the head, figuring him to have posed the greater threat to the brunette. Even as the Winchester started to turn, Dusty's, Waco's and Kitson's revolvers thundered and all three bullets found their mark in the *tuivitsi*'s vital areas. Spinning around, the dying brave crashed across Giselle's flaccid body.

Then, with the same abruptness that had marked their arrival, the remainder of the Comanches fled. They darted swiftly into the darkness from which they had erupted not five minutes earlier and were gone from sight. Four of the saloongirls, Hubert, two soldiers and ten Comanches lay dead or dying.

Screaming hysterically, Giselle Lampart was trying to wriggle from beneath the *tuivitsi*'s body. Having come within inches of being shoved into the fire, Emma Nene staggered clear of the flames. Covering her face with her hands, she sank to her knees and sobs shook her. Belle dropped from the wagon and moved cautiously towards the blonde. Regardless of the Manhattan in the lady outlaw's hand, the second living saloongirl dashed into her arms and clung on hysterically. On her hands and knees again, Red was shuddering and backing away from the body of her assailant.

At the first hint that the badly mauled *Kweharehnuh* were calling off their attack, the Kid had swivelled around and slanted his Winchester ready to cover the horses at the picket line. To his amazement, not one of the departing braves made any attempt to approach the restless animals. The omission merely added a further puzzling aspect to the various unusual actions of the attackers.

The Kid did not for a moment imagine that the *Kweharehnuh* braves were fleeing in panic. They had gone because they had seen that the attack was becoming a costly failure. Brave as they undoubtedly were, the Antelopes would not throw their lives away uselessly on a doomed project when they could escape. Nor would a *Nemenuh* brave-heart, forced to retreat, pass up an opportunity to regain something of his lost honour.

So why had the departing warriors ignored the line of horses?

Maybe the whole bunch could not be liberated simultaneously; but any *tuivitsi* old enough to follow his first war trail should have been able to cut loose, mount and ride away on one of the horses.

Yet none of them had offered to do so.

It was baffling behaviour, completely unlike anything the Kid would have expected from Comanches in general and *Kweharehnuh* – who he admitted to be near on as good warriors as the *Pehnane* – in particular. By birth, training and natural inclination, the Kid had developed a dislike for unsolved mysteries.

There could be an explanation to the departure without acquiring the horses. The braves might be planning to regroup and launch another attack. Not a likely contingency, but possible in view of so many departures from normal Comanche behaviour.

Usually night was a time for undetected travelling, raiding – called horsestealing by people who did not belong to the *Nemenuh* – but not for making war. Of course, presented with a suitable opportunity, the chance to count coups and gather loot would cause warriors to fight during the dark hours. After losing so many companions, that particular war party would be regretting its decision and were unlikely to return.

Or would be unlikely, *if* they were acting like typical members of the Comanche nation.

'Watch out in case they come back, Dusty!' called the Kid, lowering his rifle and bounding across the clearing. 'I'll see what they're doing.'

'*Bueno*,' the small Texan replied. 'Waco, tend to the horses before we lose some of them.'

'It's done,' the youngster answered, thrusting the Colt into his waistband and running to obey.

Lowering his smoking Peacemaker, Kitson turned slowly and looked around. His eyes flickered from Brill to the second dead soldier, then moved on to where Waco's 'watcher' was sitting up and shaking his head in a dazed manner. The sergeant was rising, also studying the situation.

'Are you all right, Tebs?' Kitson demanded.

'Huh?' grunted the soldier, gazing around with growing awareness of what he was seeing. 'What— What's happened?'

'He was down all through the fight, sir,' the sergeant commented, holstering his revolver. 'Come out of it better'n Chiano and Brill, they've both cashed in.'

'Did they get you, sergeant?' the lieutenant inquired.

'Nope,' admitted the non-com and nodded to one of the dead *Kweharehnuh*. 'He would've if that Blood feller hadn't given me back my gun.'

Hearing the words reminded the young officer that he too had been saved by the return of his revolver. They also brought back to him a recollection of why he had been pointing it at his rescuer. If that damned trouble-maker Brill had not acted in such a stupid manner, there would have been no need for Kitson to lose his Colt – or to be in debt to a man who he must now arrest, take in and most likely cause to be hanged.

Well, Brill was beyond any reproach for his actions. That left the small Texan. Kitson sucked in a breath, squared his shoulders and turned with the intention of doing his duty.

Two Civilian Model Peacemakers lined their .45 calibre muzzles directly at the lieutenant's stomach, hammers back at full cock and forefingers resting lightly on the triggers. Unnoticed, the small Texan had got up and was ready to resist being arrested.

'Just holster your gun, mister,' Dusty requested. 'Leave yours be, sergeant and have your trooper do the same.'

'Keep your hand offen it, Tebs!' growled the non-com as the soldier grabbed towards his holster. 'He could drop Mr. Kitson before you clear leather.'

'I can't let you ride off, even though you saved my life,' Kitson warned, showing no inclination to do as Dusty had suggested.

'All I'm wanting is a chance to talk,' the small Texan drawled. He twirled his Colts around, allowing the hammers to sink without setting off the waiting powder charges, and returned them to their holsters. 'Maybe this'll show you that I'm not asking for anything else.'

'You've got nothing to lose by listening, Mr. Kitson,' the sergeant remarked politely. 'They could've let us get killed, but they didn't.'

'They maybe figured we'd be more use alive than dead right then,' Kitson pointed out. 'Well, my grandfather always use to say that nobody was ever a loser by listening. Talk ahead, Mr. Caxton.'

'First off, mister,' Dusty said. 'I'd sooner you called me by my real name.'

'What would that be?' Kitson inquired.

'Dusty Fog,' the small Texan replied.

CHAPTER FIVE

THEY CAME TO TAKE GISELLE

'Dusty Fog!'

Two startled voices repeated the name as the officer and sergeant exchanged glances. Then they swung mutually disbelieving gazes in the small Texan's direction, subjecting him to a long, hard scrutiny.

'What I'd heard,' the sergeant declared, 'was that you was with Governor Howard meeting some other ranchers down to San Antone, *Cap'n Fog*.'

'That's just what the *Texas State Gazette* said,' Dusty admitted, feeling no annoyance at the soldiers' reactions. Few people could reconcile his appearance with his reputation, until they had come to know him. 'What the Ysabel Kid, Waco and I've been doing, it helped that everybody thought that's where we were at.'

To assist in the deception they had practised upon the citizens of Hell, Dusty had arranged for a story to appear in the *Texas State Gazette* and other newspapers. It had told of protests by various ranchers at a beef contract awarded to the OD Connected, and how the Governor had called the affected parties to a meeting in San Antonio de Bexar in the hope of averting a range war. He had sent Mark Counter,[*] another member of the floating outfit, to the town posing as himself. Six foot three in height, magnificently built, blond haired and exceptionally handsome, Mark had the kind of physical attributes most people expected of a man with Dusty Fog's reputation. The blond giant had been mistaken for Dusty enough times to give the subterfuge a chance of working.

'And where were you?' Kitson wanted to know.

[*] Mark Counter's history is told in other of the author's floating outfit novels.

'You said that Paddy Magoon's your friend, sergeant,' Dusty remarked, without answering the question.

'He was,' the non-com growled bitterly. 'I should have a hundred dollars for every drink we've took together.'

'Knowing him like you must,' Dusty went on. 'Do you think he'd sell out the Army and take up with a bunch of owlhoots who were fixing to kill and rob other soldiers?'

'I'd've staked my life he wouldn't,' the sergeant declared. 'Like I said, he was a damned good friend.'

'He won't be when he hears that you aim to toss me in the pokey for *not* having killed him,' Dusty grinned. 'Because that's just the kind of mean lie I aim to tell him.'

'Tell—?' repeated the sergeant. 'You mean he's still alive?'

'He is, unless he's been killed off by eating civilian cooking down to the OD Connected,' Dusty confirmed. 'Because that's where Paddy, Colonel Stegg and the rest of our "victims" are right now.'

'You're saying that there's no truth in the stories about y— the robbery and killings?' Kitson demanded.

'No more than in the ones about Wyatt Earp being a fine, honest, upstanding Kansas lawman,' Dusty agreed. 'It was all done for a purpose.'

'The editors of all those newspapers deliberately lied?'

'Most of them just copied what the editor of the *Texas State Gazette* printed, mister.'

'But he agreed to lie?' Kitson insisted.

'He was asked by the Governor if he'd do it,' Dusty explained and grinned. 'On top of which, he rode in my Company during the War and figured he'd best do me a lil favour.'

'And what was it all in aid of?' Kitson asked, but he still kept his Colt in his hand.

'To help us stay alive while we were carrying out a confidential assignment for Governor Howard *and* the United States Cavalry,' Dusty replied. 'I can't tell you more than it took us into the Palo Duro—'

'That's *Kweharehnuh* country!' the lieutenant ejaculated, looking at the body of the nearest Comanche.

'Like you say,' Dusty drawled. 'That's *Kweharehnuh* country. I can't tell you any more about what we were doing, though. And I can't come out with anything to prove I'm speaking the truth. We couldn't carry anything that might show who we really are.'

All the time they had been speaking, Kitson was studying Dusty carefully. The lieutenant had noticed that the small Texan's grey eyes met his without flinching and how he answered every question instantly. There was nothing evasive or furtive in his demeanour that hinted he might not be speaking the truth.

Yet could that short, insignificant-looking Texas cowhand really be the almost legendary Dusty Fog?

Kitson knew of Dusty's Civil War reputation, as a courageous, gallant and capable cavalry leader. There had been other stories told since peace had come, impressive enough individually or as a whole. They had not concerned the deeds of a small, almost inconspicuous man.

Fresher in the lieutenant's mind was the memory of how swiftly Dusty had moved when presented with the opportunity to evade arrest. Or of how the Texan had behaved following his taking of the chance. He had come into possession of a weapon with which to shoot Kitson if he had been so minded. Instead, at some considerable danger to himself, he had been content merely to disarm the officer. That had hardly been the act of a cold-blooded killer in a desperate bid for freedom.

During the conversation, Kitson had repeatedly found himself forgetting that he addressed a small, none-too-noticeable Texas cowhand. Instead he had begun to regard Dusty as a real big man with an air of command and leadership in his voice and attitude. The small Texan spoke with the accent of a well-educated Southerner; but that in itself was not a definite sign of innocence. Too many of them had been driven into a life of crime by the injustices of the Reconstruction period.

Kitson was a career officer and as such had developed the ability to judge men's characters with some accuracy. Continuing his scrutiny of the small Texan, he reached a conclusion. Unlikely as it seemed, he believed that he had been hearing the truth.

'It's a strange story,' Kitson declared, after a lengthy pause for thought. 'If you was "Ed Caxton", you'd have

49

thought up something a whole heap more likely than that.'

'Why didn't you tell us this from the start?' the sergeant wanted to know.

'Would you have listened if I'd tried right then?' Dusty countered.

'Probably we wouldn't,' Kitson conceded and finally replaced his Peacemaker in the high-riding cavalry twist-hand holster. 'I'll accept your story, Captain Fog, but I hope you'll not take offence if I talk to your two men?'

'Feel free,' Dusty offered. 'Only I reckon it can wait until we've got these folks settled down a mite.'

'Hey now!' the sergeant put in, ogling Belle Starr as she and Emma, having dragged aside the dead Comanche, tried to calm Giselle down. 'Who's she? That's no calico queen.'

'You're right, soldier,' Dusty agreed, then decided to become evasive. 'I reckon you've heard of Belle Boyd?'

'The Rebel Spy?' the non-com ejaculated. 'I'll say I have. Is that her?'

'Belle's been helping us on the assignment,' Dusty stated truthfully, without directly confirming or denying the sergeant's question. He saw a way out of a difficulty, providing the soldiers accepted the lady outlaw's borrowed identity. 'Only her part's not finished yet.'

'If there's anything I can do to help Miss Boyd—' Kitson began.

'There just might be at that,' Dusty drawled. 'Right now, though, those other folk could use our help.'

'They can,' the officer admitted and his eyes flickered to the dead soldiers. 'Damn it to hell! I've lost two of my men.'

'It happens, mister,' the small Texan replied gently. 'But a good officer never stops feeling bad when it does. If you want to tend to them, Waco and I'll do what we can for the women.'

In addition to wanting to help the lieutenant get over the loss of the two men, Dusty had no wish for him to make too close a scrutiny of the women. If he did, he might draw the correct conclusions from Belle's and Emma's bruised and fight-marked faces.

Leaving the soldiers, Dusty went to help Red rise. The girl

was shaking with mingled emotions, but calmed down when he assured her everything was going to be all right.

'Wh – What about them?' Red inquired in a whisper, nodding to Kitson and the sergeant. 'Aren't they going to arrest you?'

'Nope,' Dusty replied. 'I've got everything straightened out. Just keep quiet and Emma will tell you everything.'

Escorting the saloongirl to join the other women, Dusty had not time to do more than ask if anything could be done for Hubert and the other casualties when the Kid returned. The dark Texan led Kitson's and another of the cavalrymen's horses.

'They've gone, Dusty, and aren't likely to be coming back,' the Kid announced. 'How come the blue-bellies don't have you hawg-tied?'

'I've told them who we are,' Dusty replied.

'They believe it?'

'Sure, but they still wanted to jail *you* when I let on what your right name is.'

'I'm not surprised, company I keep,' the Kid sniffed and became serious. 'How much did you tell?'

'Who we are, where we've been, but nothing about Hell,' Dusty answered. 'I don't reckon you'll need to tell him more than that. Unless either of them asks who Belle is—'

'And then?' the Kid prompted.

'Make them think she's Belle Boyd.'

'You mean *lie* to 'em?'

'Let the white half do it, if the Comanche in you won't,' Dusty suggested. 'Or sort of make out she's the Rebel Spy without coming flat-footed and saying it's so. That should ease what passes for your conscience.'

'Count on it,' grinned the Kid, although he was not entirely sure what a conscience might be. 'I'll go give the shave-tail his hoss back. That ought to put me in good with him.'

'It's long gone time when you was in good with somebody,' Dusty grunted. 'Something bothering you, Lon?'

'Sure. I'm thinking about why those *Kweharehnuh* jumped us.'

'After loot, way you've always talked about things like this.'

'Not this time. They lit out without taking a hoss, and I saw one *tehnap* drop Hubert's handgun without being shot nor bothered by us.'

'So what do you reckon?' Dusty demanded.

'It's just a notion, mind,' the Kid replied quietly. 'But I think they came to take Giselle there back to Hell.'

'You've got more than a notion on it,' Dusty guessed.

'Plenty more,' the Kid confirmed. 'I saw enough— The shave-tail's headed this way.'

'Go and get in good with him,' Dusty ordered. 'And mind what I told you to tell him.'

Leaving the Kid to hand over the horses and answer Kitson's questions, Dusty turned his attention to the women. Belle and Emma had taken Giselle to sit by the wagon and left Red to care for her. They looked from Dusty to the soldiers and back.

'I was hoping to see you get arrested, Dusty,' Belle smiled. 'Isn't that shave-tail going to?'

'Nope,' Dusty answered. 'Neither you nor me, Miss Boyd.'

'*Boyd?*' Belle repeated, then a flicker of understanding crossed her face. 'You've told them that I'm the Rebel Spy?'

'Would I lie?' Dusty grinned. 'Let's just say that I've planted that same notion in his head.'

'And how about *us*, E ... Dus ... Captain Fog?' Emma demanded.

'Try saying "Dusty",' the small Texan suggested. 'You'll be all right. Maybe you won't be headed direct to Denver, but Lieutenant Kitson will see you safe to the nearest town.'

'What about you?' Emma asked and nodded to the wagon. 'And it?'

'I'll give you ladies your cut before we split up,' Dusty promised. 'And see that you get to wherever you want to go without anybody knowing you've come from Hell.'

'But where are *you* going?' Emma insisted

'Back there,' Dusty replied. 'If what Lon's told me is right, I have to get back to Hell as soon as I can.'

'Why, Dusty?' Belle gasped.

'They're not going to stand up and cheer when you get

there,' Emma warned, but there was a calculating glint in her eyes as she studied the small Texan.

'Maybe they will,' Dusty said quietly. 'For the same reason that Simmy Lampart liked having me around.'

'Because you're good with your guns,' Belle guessed, then stiffened slightly. 'Dusty! You think the *Kweharehnuh* are going to jump the town?'

'It's likely,' Dusty admitted.

'We all knew *that* would happen before we left,' Emma sniffed and there was a hint of suspicion in her tone for which neither Dusty nor Belle could account. 'Why're you bothered about it so suddenly?'

'Because I hoped we'd see you safe and get to Wichita Falls, then telegraph for the Army to move in before it happened,' Dusty explained. 'Only, if Lon's calling the play correct, things're due to pop wide open before they could get to Hell and fetch the folks out.'

'I *knew* something had been sticking in your craw ever since we pulled out,' Belle declared. 'And, if I'd been in better shape, I'd have seen what it was.'

'What?' Emma challenged.

'Leaving those folks behind at the mercy of the *Kweharehnuh*,' Belle told her. 'Dusty doesn't think he's done the right thing by them.'

'You're worried about the kind of folks there're in Hell?' the blonde asked, showing even more suspicion.

'Maybe you couldn't understand that—' Belle began.

'Lon figures the *Kweharehnuh* who hit us just now were trying to grab Giselle and take her back with them,' Dusty remarked, before Emma could make an angry response to the lady outlaw's words.

'Why Giselle?' Emma inquired, curious enough to forget her annoyance.

'Because she's the one who used to help Simmy make his "medicine" to guard the ammunition,' Dusty replied.

'Hey!' Belle ejaculated. 'That war-bonnet chief said something about grabbing the white witch, but I thought he meant—'

'Who did you think he meant?' the blonde bristled, having already formed her own conclusion.

'He said that, huh?' Dusty drawled, once more pouring oil

53

on troubled waters before anything could flare up between the women.

'Maybe not in those exact words, but close enough to them,' Belle answered. 'I understand enough Comanche to get his meaning. He said for his men to grab the white witch.'

'What use would Giselle be to them without Simmy to saw her in half?' Emma wanted to know.

A former stage magician, Mayor Simeon Lampart had made use of his talents to impress the Comanches. To prevent thefts of his reserve ammunition, he and Giselle had made 'medicine' before the assembled warriors and convinced them that any interference with the supply would have fatal results. The illusion of sawing his wife in half had been Lampart's main feature, baffling Chief Ten Bears and his medicine woman completely.

'Maybe the folks are running a bluff, pretending that Simmy and Giselle are still around ready to hand over the ammunition on the day,' Belle guessed. 'Only Ten Bears is figuring on calling them.'

'It could be,' Dusty admitted. 'One of the parties we saw after we pulled out could have recognized Giselle, told Ten Bears and he's trying to get her back. Or he may think that she's got the photographs Lampart took of him and the medicine woman.'

'They thought he'd captured their souls when he showed them the pictures,' Emma confirmed. 'But why go back, E ... Dusty?'

'Because those folks need me and the boys' guns,' the small Texan replied. 'Having us there could maybe help them hold out until the Army arrives.'

'I'll ride with you,' Belle offered without a moment's hesitation. 'You'll be able to use another gun.'

'We could use a battery of Williams rapid-fire cannon,' Dusty replied. 'But I'm not taking you along, Belle. Mark'd have my hide if I did and we all got killed.'

'Leave me to deal with Mark Counter,' Belle suggested, smiling a little at the small Texan's somewhat peculiar excuse. 'Even if we all do get wiped out by the *Kweharehnuh*.'

'I wouldn't want to put ole Mark to any trouble,' Dusty replied. 'Anyways, I need you to deliver the money to Governor Howard for me.'

'*Her?*' Emma snorted, suspicion right out in the open as she spoke the single, challenging word.

'Why not "*her*"?' Belle challenged.

'I can just see Belle Starr delivering close to half a million dollars to Governor Howard,' the blonde scoffed.

'Are you saying I wouldn't?' Belle hissed, fists clenching.

'With a price on your head—' Emma began in a milder tone, realizing that the time was anything but right for an open, head-on clash with the lady outlaw.

'There's no warrant out for me in Texas,' Belle declared. 'Or any other place, comes to that.'

'Innocence, Belle?' Dusty grinned.

'Lack of proof,' the lady outlaw smiled back.

'I know she'd do it for me, if she gives her word to,' Dusty told Emma. 'And you don't need to worry. Before I pull out, I'll give you girls your cut. Then you're free to go wherever you choose.'

'Even if I say that I want to go back to Hell with you?' Emma asked.

CHAPTER SIX

HE'LL BE BACK, WITH COMPANY

'WAS I a suspicious man, which nobody could right truthfully say I am,' announced the Ysabel Kid, holding his rangy, mean-looking blue roan gelding to a steady, but mile-devouring walk. 'I'd be asking myself just what did make those two gals conclude to come back to Hell with us.'

'I've been thinking long on that myself,' Waco drawled, keeping his black and white *tobiano* mount alongside the Kid's blue roan. 'And anybody's likes can say *I'm* a suspicious man; as long as they do it polite and not twice on the same Sunday.'

'Trouble being, you've got no pride,' grinned the Kid. 'Anyways, what's all this-here thinking got you?'

'Not a whole heap,' the blond youngster admitted. 'Was it just Emma, I'd say she's going and hoping Dusty'll take her to church 'n' make a honest woman of her when we get back.'

'Emma's smart enough to know it'll be more *if* than *when* we get back,' the Kid pointed out. 'Likewise, she's smart enough to know there's no chance of Dusty doing it.'

'They do tell me all women're a mite foolish and a whole heap hopeful when it comes to getting took to church and being made honest,' Waco answered. 'Could be Giselle's going back to hear the will read, her being a widow-lady and all.'

'She's a widow, for sure, you saw to that,' growled the Kid. 'But I wouldn't lay no "lady" brand on her.'

'You mean she's a *man*?' Waco demanded with carefully assumed interest.

'I don't know and I'm not caring,' the Kid replied. 'Was you wanting to find out, sneak off and look next time she goes. They do tell that women're different from us.'

'How, pappy?'

'They squat, 'stead of standing when they only want to pee— Or so I've allus heard tell.'

'Now why's they do that, would you say?' Waco wanted to know.

'You should've asked Red last night,' drawled the Kid. 'Likely she could've told you. I for sure don't know.'

Despite their casually cheerful discussion, the Kid and Waco never relaxed in their ceaseless vigilance. Always their eyes searched the surrounding terrain and they carried their rifles instead of leaving them in the saddleboots. With the sun sinking towards the western horizon, they had already covered almost thirty miles of the journey back to Hell. That put them on the fringes of the *Kweharehnuh*'s stamping grounds and, if the Kid's theory about Giselle Lampart should prove correct, moving deeper into danger with every sequence of their mounts' hoof-beats. A quarter of a mile behind, Dusty Fog escorted the two subjects of his companions' conversation.

The small Texan had not agreed to permit the women to accompany him without some argument, discussion and heart-searching. Nor was he yet convinced that he had acted for the best in concurring with Emma's and Giselle's demands to come along.

After the Kid had returned the previous night and said that the *Kweharehnuh* would be unlikely to come back, Dusty had organized things in a brisk, business-like manner which had won Lieutenant Kitson's approval. In fact, there had been moments when the young officer had found himself on the point of snapping into a brace and answering 'sir' as Dusty had rattled out some command or instruction. By the time the bodies had been buried and the camp generally settled down, Kitson had been convinced that Dusty was telling him the truth and was willing to carry out his request for further assistance.

Taking advantage of the soldiers accompanying the Kid to search for the rest of their stampeded horses, Dusty had talked with the women. Although Red and the other saloon-girl had not argued when they had been told they would each receive twenty thousand dollars – the increased amount having been granted as there was a smaller number to take shares – Giselle had sulked and pouted in her disappointment. She had been expecting a far greater sum than the fifty thousand dollars given to her and was inclined to be rebellious until Emma had intervened. Drawing the brunette aside, the blonde had talked quietly, but earnestly to her. At first Giselle had been in vehement disagreement with Emma's proposals, but had finally and grudgingly yielded to them. Much to Dusty's surprise, the blonde had then suggested that she and Giselle should return to Hell with the three Texans.

Dusty's first instinct had been to refuse, for he had not underestimated the dangers of going back. Slowly, but surely, Emma had won her point and was granted permission. She had repeated her statement that Dusty, the Kid and Waco would not be popular with the citizens of Hell and had suggested that her presence and that of Giselle might be in the trio's favour. On hearing why, Dusty had been compelled to admit that the blonde was making sense.

Before giving his permission, however, the small Texan had insisted on learning the real reason for the request. As he had suspected, Emma had financial rather than humanitarian motives. There was a fortune in jewellery at Hell and she hoped to lay hands upon some of it. Sufficient, in fact, to make up for the reduction in the sums she and Giselle had been forced to accept as their share of the mayor's ill-gotten gains. To prevent a similar happening, Emma had extracted Dusty's promise that any loot she and Giselle gathered would be their property and not handed over to the authorities.

Even with that much knowledge, Dusty might have refused; but Emma had pointed out that she might still have been able to ruin the good impression he had made on Kitson. There had also been the point of keeping Belle's true identity a secret for Dusty to consider. Emma had hinted that she would tell the officer the truth and dispel his belief – due to carefully-planted hints – that the lady outlaw was the Rebel Spy. There had been a heated scene between Belle and Emma which Dusty had ended by agreeing to the blonde's suggestion.

Belle had once more requested to accompany Dusty's

party, although on less mercenary grounds than those of the blonde. Not only had Dusty refused, but he had obtained her agreement to deliver the money for him. Neither the Kid nor Waco had been surprised by the trust Dusty placed in the lady outlaw. Apart from her close relationship with Mark Counter,* Belle had a strong sense of personal honour. Once she had given her word to carry out a project, she would do so without hesitation. The three Texans had been certain that when – or, as the Kid had said, *if* – they came back from Hell, they would learn that Belle had carried out her part in the assignment.

By the time the men had returned, everything had been settled. Each woman had collected her cut of the money and concealed it. Although Red and the other saloongirl had asked if they could ride with Dusty's party, they had been persuaded to accompany Belle and the soldiers. Kitson had shown no hesitation about escorting Belle and the two girls to Wichita Falls and acting as custodian of the wagon's load until such time as 'the Rebel Spy' could hand it over to Governor Howard. If he had been surprised by Dusty saying that Emma and Giselle would not be going with the other women, he had hidden it very well. That could have been due to the women's stories. While the blonde and brunette had insisted that they were going to their original destination, the girls had declared that they only wanted to reach civilization as quickly as possible.

So everything had been arranged. Waco and Red had spent the night together and had parted at dawn without too great regrets. Knowing that nothing could come of their association, the girl had accepted that it had been enjoyable and profitable but was now at an end. Red was to put her windfall to good use, returning to her home town, marrying well and settling down to a life of happiness and respectability. For his part, it would be a few more years before Waco met the girl who persuaded him to settle down in matrimony.†

---

* How that relationship began, developed and finally ended is told in the 'The Bounty On Belle Starr's Scalp' episode of *Troubled Range*, *The Bad Bunch*, *Rangeland Hercules*, the 'A Lady Known As Belle' *episode of The Hard Riders* and *Guns in the Night*.

† Told in: *The Drifters*.

No fool, Kitson had noticed certain inconsistencies in the story he had been told. The signs of physical strife on the lady outlaw's and Emma's faces, taken with the money being in the wagon which the saloonworkers had obviously been using, had pointed to the whole party travelling as a single unit. However he had been willing to accept that the blonde and her companions had helped Dusty and 'the Rebel Spy' to complete their assignment and asked no embarrassing questions. He had agreed to deliver a message to the Governor, requesting that the Army should move into the Palo Duro as soon as possible. Without mentioning the town, Dusty had given an accurate description of its location and asked that the soldiers be sent there.

Dusty, the Kid, Waco, Emma, Giselle and Belle had all offered up silent prayers that the Army would receive the news and reach the town in time to save it being wiped out by the *Kweharehnuh*.

Dawn had seen the two parties going their separate ways. After swinging to the north until hidden from Kitson's view, to keep from adding to any suspicions he might have been harbouring, Dusty and his companions had turned to the south west. By using the riding technique known as 'posting the trot',* they had made good time through the day. It had not been easy on the women, but, fortunately, both had done considerable riding in Hell and were fired by their eagerness to reach the safety of the town. 'Safety' would be a relative name for it, but at least they would have the buildings in which to shelter if they should be attacked by the Indians.

Unless, of course, the enraged citizens of Hell shot them on sight.

Their reception would depend upon the reaction to the story concocted by Emma and Dusty. If it was accepted, they might be spared by the citizens and would only need to worry about the *Kweharehnuhs'* retaliation when it became obvious that no ammunition was forthcoming.

Bearing in mind the possibility that Giselle might have been the target of the *Kweharehnuhs'* attack on the camp, Dusty had insisted upon taking precautions against ambush. The Kid and Waco had spent their time ranging ahead or on the flanks of the women's line of march. Although there had

* Described in detail in: *Under the Stars and Bars*.

been no sign of human life all day, the Texans did not regret having taken such preventive measures.

'What do you reckon those folks'll do when they see us riding in, Lon?' Waco inquired, becoming more serious.

'I'd say *if* they see us, it all depends on what *we* let 'em do,' the Kid replied. 'Or do you figure on Dusty taking us a-whooping and a-hollering, "Look, folks, we're back!" along the main street comes high noon?'

'I'll let you go in front if he does,' Waco promised. 'It's a pity you don't have your ole Nigger hoss along. He'd surely look elegant a-heading the parade.'

Due to the necessity for avoiding the drawing of attention to similarities between their real identities and those of the 'Caxton brothers' and 'Alvin "Comanche" Blood', the trio had not been able to use their favourite horses on the assignment. The big paint studs often ridden by Dusty and Waco bore, respectively, the brands of the OD Connected and Clay Allison's CA ranches.

Although it had never been branded, the Kid's magnificent white stallion was too large and distinctive to be overlooked. By leaving it in the care of the OD Connected's horse wrangler – one of the few people who could handle it in comparative safety – divesting himself of his usual all black clothing and refraining from demonstrating too much of his prowess with the Winchester or his bowie knife, the Kid had contrived to prevent the citizens and outlaws in Hell from suspecting whom he might be.

While speaking, Waco and the Kid had been climbing a ridge. They did not permit conversation to override caution. Instead of continuing over the rim, they halted below the sky-line. Elevating their heads, they peered at what lay on the other side.

'Now there's a feller who's just asking to get his-self scalped,' the Kid remarked.

Following the direction of his companion's gaze, Waco was inclined to agree with the cryptic comment. About a quarter of a mile away, a man was riding across their front. Holding his big blue-black horse to an ambling walk, he traversed the bush-scattered terrain as if he did not have a care in the world. Tall, well built, with darkish hair, the man wore the dress and rig of a cowhand. He had on a low-crowned, wide-brimmed Stetson hat, red shirt, dark blue Levi's pants which looked new and hung outside his high-heeled, spur-decorated brown boots. A brown gunbelt about his middle carried an ivory-handled Colt Cavalry Peacemaker in a contoured, fast-draw holster on his right thigh. For all his appearance, he did not sit his range saddle like a cowhand. He was leading a well-ladened pack horse at the end of a long line.

'Could be he's an owlhoot looking for Hell,' Waco suggested.

'Ways things are right now,' the Kid drawled, 'he's likely to find it a whole lot sooner than he'd figured on. Only it won't be the "Hell" he's hunting.'

'That's for sure!' Waco breathed, swinging his gaze from the rider. 'You see 'em, Lon?'

'Ten minutes back,' the Kid exaggerated and twisted in his saddle to wave for Dusty to keep the women away.

Even when he became aware of the half a dozen *Kweharehnuh* braves who had appeared and sat watching him, the rider displayed no great alarm. Instead, he merely lifted his right hand in a friendly greeting. His behaviour indicated that Waco had guessed correctly about his station in life. If he was an outlaw on his way to Hell and under the impression that he had nothing to fear from the *Kweharehnuh*, he received a rapid and unmistakable disillusionment. Instead of responding with an amiable gesture, one of the younger members of the Comanche group raised and fired a Spencer carbine.

As the bullet hissed by his head, the man gave a startled jerk and let go of the pack-horse's lead rope. He did not, however, take the appropriate and sensible course of trying to gallop to safety. Instead, he tilted to the left and his right hand wrapped around the wrist of a Winchester rifle's butt. Sliding the rifle from its boot, he straightened up on the saddle. Two more of the *tuivitsis* – there was only one warrior of *tehnap* status present – cut lose with their repeaters. Neither hit the man, but one's bullet spiked up an eruption of dirt to his horse's right. The other's lead rose in a vicious whining ricochet that passed within inches of the animal's right ear.

Giving his first hint that he had realized conditions had changed in the Palo Duro, the man attempted to rein around his mount. At that moment it was rearing its fore legs into the air and trying to back away on the hind limbs. It was moving to the left and its rider attempted to guide it in the opposite direction. His unequally distributed weight caused the horse's hind legs to slide to the left and its front hooves thrust forward in an unavailing bid to regain its equilibrium.

Despite his casual disregard for what the watching Texans regarded as essential precautions of Palo Duro life, the man proved himself capable of swift movement in an emergency. Almost before his mount's right rump had hit the ground, he had freed his feet from the stirrups irons and kicked his left leg forward across the animal's neck. Springing clear, he landed on slightly bent legs and the Winchester rifle's wooden foregrip slapped into his left palm.

Fast though the man had reacted, he had not done so a moment too soon. Letting out ringing war whoops, the braves jumped their mounts from stationary to a gallop almost in one motion. They fanned out, boiling down the slope at reckless speed and each with the same intention; to be the one who counted coup on the hated white brother and who, by doing so, would be entitled to the first pick at the victim's property.

Taking the brass butt of the Winchester to his shoulder, the man sighted and fired at the nearest of the warriors. Down went the *tuivitsi's* horse, head shot and buckling forward as its legs folded beneath it. With typical Comanche agility, the young brave not only quit the stricken animal's back and landed without injury, but he hit the ground running. Without a moment's hesitation after his narrow escape, he continued to bound onwards.

'We'd best go lend the feller a hand,' the Kid commented as the attack was launched, signalling with his heels for the blue roan to start moving.

'Be best,' Waco confirmed and his *tobiano* sprang forward alongside the dark Texan's mount.

Topping the rim, the Kid and Waco unshipped from their saddles. They released the split-ended reins, ground-hitching the horses as effectively as if they had knotted the leather straps to a saloon's hitching rail. Advancing a few strides, so that the noise of their shots would not be too close to the horses, the Texans prepared to help the stranger.

While his horse struggled to its feet and loped away, until stopped by its trailing reins, the man turned his rifle on the dismounted Indian. He himself was under fire from the rest of the braves, but he did not allow that to fluster him. Taking aim as the brave bounded on to a rock, he fired. Hit in the head, the *tuivitsi* threw aside his Winchester carbine and pitched over backwards. Lead hissed around the man, but none of it struck him. None of the *tuivitsis* had had sufficient experience to perform accurate shooting from the back of a war pony thundering at top speed over sloping, irregular ground.

Maybe the *tehnap* in the party would have had better success, but fate – in the shape of the Ysabel Kid – robbed him of the opportunity. Having decided that the experienced warrior posed the greatest threat to the man, the Kid had nullified it with his 'old yellowboy'* rifle. Standing erect, the dark Texan lined and fired with what barely seemed time to take aim. For all that, the *tehnap's* head snapped back sharply and he slid rearwards over his mount's rump.

Delaying only long enough to kneel and support his left elbow on his bent right knee, Waco blasted the *tuivitsi* who had started the shooting from his fast-moving bay pony.

Ignoring their companions, the remaining trio of *tuivitsi* kept shooting and advancing. Knowing that there was no other way to save the white man, the Kid turned his rifle on the centre rider. Through the swirl of powder smoke, he saw that he had made a hit; but the man had also selected that particular *tuivitsi* as his target. Waco's rifle had sent the right hand warrior sliding side-ways from his horse, but the last of the attackers was drawing closer. He was rapidly approaching a distance from which he would be unlikely to miss, even from a moving base.

The sound of hooves from behind reached the Kid's ears. More than one horse at that. Not that he felt alarmed, guessing correctly that Dusty had come up to lend a hand. Either with the small Texan's permission, or disobeying orders, the

* 'Old yellowboy'; name given to the brass-framed Winchester Model of 1866.

women had followed him. Emma and Giselle came over the rim just after the Kid and Waco fired their second shots.

Eager as he might be to count coup, the *tuivitsi* knew enough to watch more than his intended victim. He had detected the two ride-plenties on the other slope and noticed a third coming to join them. Then his eyes went to the women. Instantly all thought of killing and loot departed from his mind. There was something of greater importance on hand; a matter which could not even be delayed while he shot down the unhorsed white man.

'White witch!' the brave yelled, whirling his mount into a tight turn that saved his life.

Three bullets, any of which would have struck a vital region of his person went by the *tuivitsi's* body as he made the abrupt, violent change of direction. Guiding the pony in a weaving line, he flattened himself along its neck to offer a smaller, more elusive target. It said much for his early training that he escaped with his life. Four times the Kid's rifle cracked, but the flying lead narrowly missed its mark. Then the *tuivitsi* had rocketed over the rim and was gone from sight.

'Ole *Ka-Dih*'s* siding the *Kweharehnuh*, not the *Pehnane* today,' Waco commented, having watched the Kid's abortive attempts to hit the departing *tuivitsi*.

'Could be we'll come to regret it,' the dark-faced Texan replied grimly. 'He saw Giselle, yelled "White witch" and took off like the devil after a yearling. Likely he'll be back, with company.'

'Which case, I'll go catch that feller's hoss,' Waco drawled. 'This'll not be a good place to be when him and his company get here.'

While the young blond went to gather up the man's mount and pack horse, Dusty, the Kid and the two women rode down the slope. Resting the barrel of his rifle on the top of his shoulder, the man turned towards them. His eyes narrowed a little as they flickered from Emma to Giselle and back. However, he advanced with a friendly smile on his lips.

'I reckon I owe you gentlemen my thanks,' the man said. 'My name's O'day. My friends call me "Break".'

* Ka-Dih: the Great Spirit of the Comanches.

CHAPTER SEVEN

THEY WANT HER FOR SOMETHING

DUSTY FOG matched Waco's summation concerning Break O'Day's presence in their vicinity. So, without being too obvious about it, he studied every detail of the man's appearance.

First item of interest, the gunbelt was the rig of a fast man with a Colt. If O'Day could use it to its full potential, he would be a man to be reckoned with in a corpse-and-cartridge affair. Of good quality, his clothes and boots showed signs of hard-travelling; but they were otherwise newly purchased.

Turning his attention to O'Day's face, Dusty found it more interesting than his clothing or armament and rig. Good looking, tanned, it had an almost unnatural smoothness. Either he had shaved recently, or had a very slow beard, for his cheeks, top lip and chin were devoid of hair. His eyes looked strangely sunken for such a fresh, healthy face and their brows seemed almost artificially bristly. Deep brown in colour, the eyes were cold, yet strangely compelling in the intensity of their scrutiny. His voice had a slight, educated East Coast accent. It came out with a clarity that suggested it had been trained for being heard distinctly at a fair distance.

Having caught both O'Day's horses without any difficulty, Waco rejoined his companions. Dusty's quick examination of the animals told him that they were good stock, selected for their respective duties. Although somewhat older than the man's clothing, both riding and pack saddles had cost good money and were fairly new. From the look of it, the coiled rope strapped to the saddlehorn had never been used.

'We'd best get moving, Mr. O'Day,' Dusty suggested. 'That buck's likely gone to fetch help.'

'The way he was coming for me, I didn't think he'd need it,' O'Day replied cheerfully. 'I don't know what he shouted to you, but it sounded like one hell – if the ladies will pardon the term – of a mean cuss-word.'

'You could say that,' the small Texan drawled, seeing no point in enlightening the man as to what the brave had said. 'Let's move. Maybe you'd best stick with us for a spell, mister.'

'I'll be obliged for the opportunity of company,' the man declared. 'Unless my presence will discommode the ladies.'

'If that means do we mind having you along, the answer's no,' Emma put in, her eyes raking O'Day from head to toe in just as thorough but more noticeable scrutiny than Dusty had given the man. 'Say. Haven't I met you somewhere?'

'I would hardly have forgotten so charming and beautiful a lady as yourself, ma'am,' O'Day replied, with a flourishing bow, and turned to take his reins from Waco. 'My thanks to you, young feller.'

'Twarn't nothing,' Waco drawled. 'You-all wanting for me to take a point, Brother Matt?'

'Go to it,' the small Texan replied, pleased that the youngster had not forgotten to revert to using their assumed names. 'And don't you ride with your eyes closed, boy.'

'I only do that when I'm asleep,' Waco grinned. 'Look after my big brother, Miss Emma.'

The blonde made no reply, but sat her horse and continued to stare at O'Day with puzzled, suspicious wariness.

'This'll be your first trip to Hell, Mr. O'Day?' Emma inquired, after the man had mounted and the party started moving.

'Does my destination show so plainly?' the man countered.

'I'd say "yes" to that, way you took on when those *Kweharehnuh* bucks showed,' the Kid put in. 'Way you waved and all, you acted like they was your rich old uncles.'

'If I only had some,' O'Day sighed, then nodded to Emma. 'But you're right enough, dear lady. I'm going to

67

Hell for health reasons. A hanging always makes me feel ill, especially when it's to be my own. But my remark might shock you and your delightful companion.'

Although O'Day had aimed part of his speech in her direction, Giselle did not respond. Yet, like Emma, she had been paying a great deal of attention to the man's appearance, actions and words. A puzzled, almost nervous expression played across the little brunette's face. Seeing the man's eyes turning towards her, she deliberately swung her head away. It was left to Emma to answer O'Day's politely put comment.

'Neither of us've been shocked since we found out for the first time that boys have things that girls don't,' the blonde assured him. 'And there's a lot of folks in Hell feel like you do about hangings.'

'You know of Hell?' O'Day inquired.

'We live there,' Emma replied. 'Happen you're so minded, you can ride along with us, Mr.—'

'O'Day, but I hope that you will all call me "Break". It's a foolish name, but my father was something of a wit. He used to call himself "End".'

'That should have been a whole barrel-full of laughs,' Emma said dryly.

'You'd best go help Brother Matt, Comanch',' Dusty suggested.

'Yo!' assented the Kid and set the blue roan to travelling at a faster gait towards where Waco was riding ahead of the others.

'I was assured that the Indians could be trusted up this way,' O'Day commented as the Kid took his departure.

'They can, most times,' Dusty answered. 'Up closer to town, anyways.'

'Where the look-outs can see them?'

'Huh huh. I thought you'd not been to Hell before?'

'I haven't. But my informant was pretty thorough,' O'Day answered and looked at Dusty in a calculating manner. 'You may remember him. Dipper Dixon. One of Joey Pinter's gang.'

'I can't recall any such name,' Dusty stated.

'He wasn't in your class, Mr. Caxton,' O'Day praised. 'You are Ed Caxton, aren't you?'

'So they tell me,' Dusty admitted. 'But I don't mind this Dixon *hombre*.'

'He was a nothing,' O'Day sniffed. 'All he did was tell me about Hell and that you'd killed Joey Pinter.'

'Pinter had notions along that way about me,' Dusty explained. 'He died of a case of slow. Are his boys on the way back?'

'I shouldn't think so. They told me that Hell's an expensive town and none of them struck me as having enough brains to pull off a worth-while robbery,' O'Day replied, then he turned his gaze to Emma. 'Is there something wrong with me, Miss—?'

'Name's Emma Nene,' the blonde introduced. 'I don't know what it is, but there's something about you seems mighty familiar.'

'I've heard it said that everybody reminds somebody else of an old friend,' O'Day commented. 'Perhaps I look like a friend from your past?'

'No, you don't *look* like anybody I've ever known,' Emma declared. 'Who does he remind you of, Giselle?'

'N— Nobody!' the brunette answered, still avoiding meeting O'Day's eyes.

'Nobody, dear lady?' the man inquired, a faint hint of mockery in his soft and polite tone. 'I thought perhaps that I might recall some long-forgotten memory. A lover perhaps—?'

'N— No!' Giselle ejaculated and there was fear on her face. 'I— I'm a married woman.'

'Your husband is to be congratulated,' O'Day told her. 'But I'm crushed. I felt sure that I must remind you of somebody. Oh well. I must be wrong. Surely you ladies can't be going to Hell?'

'We live there, both of us,' Emma replied. 'I own the saloon and Giselle's husband's the mayor.'

'Then I could hardly be riding into town in better company,' O'Day answered, 'with you as my escort—'

'D— Ed!' Emma ejaculated. 'Look at Comanche and Matt!'

The two young Texans had turned their horses and were galloping back. Seeing that he had caught the others' attention, the Kid pointed towards their left. Swinging their gaze in the required direction, the women, Dusty and O'Day received a shock. Some twenty or more *Kweharehnuh* warriors sat their horses on a ridge slightly over a quarter of a mile away.

'Whee doggie!' Dusty breathed and hefted his Winchester carbine so that the Indians could see it. 'Show them your rifle, mister.'

'Shoot?' O'Day inquired as he did as Dusty had said.

'Just show them we've got repeaters, first off,' Dusty corrected.

'Now what?' Emma demanded, with surprising calm.

' 'Less we're lucky,' Dusty answered. 'Some of us are about to get killed.'

'Let's fight!' O'Day demanded.

'Only if they force us to it,' Dusty replied. 'We'll make a run for it. If that pack horse won't come along, turn it loose.'

'All I own in the world's on it!' O'Day protested.

'It'll not be a little mite of use to you after you're dead and scalped,' Emma pointed out. 'Say when you want us to run, D— Ed.'

'Leave us hear what ole Comanch' says first,' Dusty advised. 'Emma-gal, keep us between you and the Indians.'

'You can count on me for *that*!' the blonde declared.

'Well?' Dusty said as the Kid and Waco brought their horses to a rumpsliding halt. 'What's their play now, L— Comanch'?'

'I'm damned if I know,' the Kid admitted, knowing that the tension must really be hitting at Dusty for him almost to make a slip in the use of the name. 'I thought I knew all about Comanches, but this-here's got me licked to hell and back the long way.'

'How do you mean?' O'Day inquired, fingering his rifle nervously.

'It's what them bunch up there's doing,' the Kid answered.

'But they're not doing *anything*!' O'Day pointed out.

'*That*'s what's worrying me,' the Kid told him soberly. 'They've just been a-sitting and a-watching up there when they should've come down and at us so fast we'd've thought the hawgs'd jumped us.'

'Perhaps our having Winchesters scared them,' O'Day suggested. 'They'll have learned what repeaters can do, I'd say.'

'Should have, mister,' Waco drawled, watching the braves with undeviating attention, 'seeing's now how every last mother's son of 'em's toting either a Henry, Winchester or Spencer.'

'Know what I reckon, Ed?' asked the Kid, indicating the interest that the braves were displaying in one member of his party.

'Do tell,' Dusty requested.

'They're not fixing to jump us right now. Nor so long as it looks like we're taking Giselle back to Hell.'

'Could be, Comanch'. There's that *tuivitsi* who got away from us. He recognized her and that's him sitting next to the war bonnet chief.'

'Shows a man could allus learn given the right teacher,' grinned the Kid. 'You couldn't see that good when we first joined up together.'

'Why thank you 'most to death,' Dusty growled. 'Now tell me something that's going to help us out of this tight.'

'Keep your trust in the Lord, brother,' the Kid obliged raising his gaze piously in the manner of a hell-fire-and-damnation circuit-riding preacher. 'If he'd be willing to look favourable on a bunch of miserable sinners like us.' Red hazel eyes swung towards O'Day, who was displaying growing alarm. 'Leaving you out, friend. Happen you're not a miserable sinner like the rest of us.'

'Right now I'm wishing that I'd led a better, cleaner life,' the man answered. 'I want to go to the town of Hell, not the other one.'

'Given time, you'll likely make both of 'em,' the Kid remarked. 'Only not right now.'

'Why not, Lon?' Waco asked and could have cheerfully bitten off his tongue after his mistake on the last word.

''Less I miss my guess,' the Kid drawled and swung from his saddle. 'Those boys aren't looking for no war. They just want to see Giselle safe to home.'

'Why are they so interested in the lady's well-being?' O'Day wanted to know. 'Charming and gracious as she undoubtedly is, I'm sure that the Indians wouldn't appreciate her sterling qualities.'

'They want her for something or other,' the Kid answered, carefully easing a piece of his property from the folds of his bed roll. 'Question being, what'd it be they want her for?'

'Could go up and ask 'em,' Waco suggested, having identified the item in the dark Texan's hand.

'Happen I'd've figured *that* out in an hour or two,' drawled the Kid. 'But, seeing's how you licked me to it, I lose and'll have to be the one who does it.'

'You allus was a good loser, Comanch',' Waco praised.

'That's just another name for a dad-blasted fool,' answered the Kid.

With that, the Kid opened out the item. It proved to be a buckskin cylinder with a heavy fringe on its lower edge and covered with decorative symbols coloured red, white and blue. Sliding his Winchester into the mouth of the tube, he vaulted afork his saddle and looked at Dusty.

'Happen they're not in a talking mood, head out towards Hell. 'Bout a mile on, there's a buffalo wallow you can fort up in – if you can reach it.'

'What's that on Mr. Blood's rifle?' O'Day inquired as the Kid rode slowly towards the *Kweharehnuh*.

'It's the medicine boot of a *Pehnane* Comanche Dog Soldier,' Dusty explained. 'It's kind of a lodge symbol, like a wapiti's tooth is to the Elks. Boot the rifles.'

'Boot the rifles!' O'Day yelped. 'You mean put them away?'

'Do like Brother Ed says, *hombre*,' Waco ordered, as he obeyed. 'White folk aren't Injuns. They don't hold guns at a peace treaty meeting.'

'You mean—?' O'Day began, but did not comply with Dusty's demand.

'Matt means that Comanch's asking for a parlay and we've got to do things right if he's got "yes" for an answer,' Dusty elaborated, thrusting his carbine into its boot. 'So put up that Winchester.'

'You mean to trust a bunch of savages?' O'Day growled.

'We can't whip them in a fight, or run fast enough to

escape – especially with that important pack-horse of yours along,' Dusty drawled. 'So trusting them makes good sense to me. And I'm getting quite sick of seeing that rifle in your fist. Boot it, *pronto*.'

Any soldier who had served in the Texas Light Cavalry's hard-riding, harder-fighting Company 'C' during the War, or cowhand who had worked for the OD Connected, would have identified Dusty's tone of voice instantly. Gentle, almost caressing, it carried more menace and determination than a whole range of bellowed, blustering orders.

Suddenly, to O'Day's amazement, the small Texan was no more. He had been replaced with what appeared to be a man who towered over the others by the sheer driving force of his personality. There had been no suggestion of bombast or open threat in the quietly spoken words, just an assurance that the speaker intended to be obeyed.

'You're calling the play, Mr. Caxton,' O'Day stated and leaned over to replace his rifle in its boot. Straightening up, he managed a smile and went on, 'But if you're wrong and I get killed, I'll never forgive you.'

Halting a hundred yards from his companions, the Kid set about preparing the way for what he hoped would be a peaceful parlay. Cradling the rifle encased in the medicine boot on the crook of his left arm, he held his bent right arm in front of his chest with his palm open and downwards. By moving the raised arm from left to right with a wriggling motion, he announced that he too was a member of the *Nemenuh*.

At some time in the distant past, a party of the People had been making a long journey in search of fresh hunting grounds. There had been disagreement amongst the travellers as to which was the best course, to advance or return to the territory they had left. Those who wished to turn back had done so and the others had referred to them as resembling a snake going into reverse along its tracks. Since then, a Comanche – no matter to which band he belonged – always used the sign of 'the snake going backwards' when he wished to declare the identity of his tribe to other Indians.

Having stated his connections with the *Nemenuh*, the Kid continued to signal other information. Taking hold of the medicine boot at the wrist of the rifle's butt and muzzle, he raised it above his head so that the *Kweharehnuh* could identify its symbols. After raising and lowering the rifle three times, he removed his right hand and turned the butt forward with the barrel gripped in his left fist.

As clearly as if the Kid had shouted the words in his most fluent Comanche, the braves – or the *tehnaps* and the chief, for sure – had received his message.

'I am *Nemenuh*. A *Pehnane* Dog Soldier, and I want to talk in peace.'

'Looks like they aim to make talk,' Waco breathed as the chief answered the Kid's signal and the dark Texan started the blue roan moving up the slope. 'I came close to being scared they wouldn't.'

'I didn't come close,' O'Day commented. 'I *was* scared.'

Flickering a grin at the man, Waco noticed something so out of the ordinary that it intrigued him. The evening sun was still warm and O'Day was clearly feeling the strain of their situation as much as, or even more than, Dusty and the blond youngster. At least, they had the advantage of knowing that the Kid had been reasonably confident of success. Yet the man's face showed none of the sweat which dappled both Texans' features.

In later years, Waco would gain considerable acclaim as a very shrewd peace officer and, by his ability to observe and reason things out, be able to solve a number of puzzling crimes.* Even with deadly danger hovering so close, the youngster could still take an interest in the unusual. So O'Day's absence of perspiration was a source of speculation. Either the man was a whole heap cooler and less worried than he was acting, or he could control whatever internal function caused sweat to roll. Waco wondered which, or what other unforeseen circumstance, was responsible for the phenomenon.

Although satisfied that the danger of an immediate attack was over, Dusty did not allow himself to become complacent or incautious. So he turned to study the terrain behind them. As he had expected, the two women were holding weapons. Emma had taken out the nickel-plated, pearl-handled 1851 Model Navy Colt which had been thrust into the waist-band

*Told in: *Sagebrush Sleuth*, *Arizona Ranger*, *Waco Rides in* and *Hound Dog Man*.

of her divided skirt. Gripping a compact, equally fancy Colt 1871 House Pistol with a four-shot 'cloverleaf' cylinder, which she had carried in the pocket of her riding jacket, Giselle was pointing the .41 calibre muzzle of its one-and-a-half inch barrel at the centre of O'Day's back.

'Watch where you're pointing that gun, ma'am,' Dusty advised quickly, but gently.

Giselle's thumb was resting on the little revolver's hammer. If she drew it back, the unguarded trigger would emerge from its sheath ready to be pressed and make the weapon fire. Being aware of how light that particular model of Colt could be on the trigger, Dusty had felt that a warning was called for. At his words, the brunette snatched the revolver out of alignment. Her face showed guilt which appeared to go far beyond that caused by having been caught in a stupidly dangerous, but inadvertent act.

'I have never felt happy around ladies who hold guns,' O'Day commented, swinging around. 'So few of them take precautions with one in their dainty hands, I've always found.'

'Who are—?' Giselle began, in a strangled, frightened tone.

'Lon's coming back – Brother Ed,' Waco said and the brunette's question went unfinished.

'It's all right, Ed,' drawled the Kid, riding up. 'They'll not bother us— Just as long as we keep going towards Hell.'

'Why are they so friendly?' O'Day asked. 'The ones we met earlier weren't.'

'They was just a bunch of *tuivitsis*, young bucks, wanting to show what ornery, mean cusses they were,' the Kid replied. 'Seems like Doc Connolly, Happy Youseman and some of the others allowed that there'll be an ammunition hand-out same as always, Ed. Only Ten Bears'd heard about Giselle pulling out and didn't believe it. So he sent the braves to fetch her back. Now she's headed that way, they allow it's all right and we can go on.'

'May I ask why Giselle – if a chance-met stranger may be permitted to make use of your given name, ma'am – is so important to the allocation of the ammunition?' O'Day said, looking at Dusty.

'She used to help her husband trick the Comanches so

they wouldn't try to steal *our* ammunition,' Emma explained, for the brunette refused to answer.

'Now I see,' O'Day stated. 'You must be the lady who is sawn in half. Your husband must be a very competent illusionist, Mrs. Lampart.'

'He w—' Giselle commenced.

'A real good one, friend,' Dusty put in, before the brunette could announce her widowhood. 'They'll not fuss any with us, huh, Comanch'?'

'Not so long as we're taking Giselle back,' the Kid confirmed. 'Seems ole Ten Bears wants to see the whole ceremony when the ammunition's handed over.'

'But they can't!' Giselle croaked, realizing what was meant. 'With Simmy dead, nobody can work the sawing in half routine. I'm going back—'

'You try it and we're all dead,' warned the Kid. 'Ma'am, your only hope of staying alive is to make for Hell.'

'That's what we'll do,' Dusty declared. 'Once we're there, Giselle, we'll figure out some way of bluffing him. Find us a place to camp, Comanch'.'

'Keep riding a whiles, there's a stream up ahead,' the Kid replied. 'Have somebody on guard all night. You won't get attacked, but some of the *tuivitsi* might try their hand at raiding.'

'That's hoss-stealing to us civilized white folks, mister,' Waco informed O'Day. 'Way you talk, Comanch', anybody'd think you wouldn't be along with us.'

'They'd think right,' drawled the Kid. 'I won't. Wolf Runner, the chief up there, allows that I've got to ride with him and his boys. Just so's he can be sure the rest of you'll keep going to Hell.'

CHAPTER EIGHT

I DON'T WANT TO GO TO HELL

'Suppose we tell ole Wolf Runner we're right took with your company?' Waco demanded, scowling at the Comanches on the rim. 'And that he can go climb up his own butt end.'

'He wouldn't like that one lil bit, boy,' the Kid replied. 'And, seeing's how all the cards're stacked his way, we don't have a heap of choice but play 'em how he wants it.'

'We could show him that we mean business,' O'Day suggested.

'He'd right soon show *us* that *he* means it even bigger,' drawled the Kid.

'The odds wouldn't be much greater than against that bunch which attacked me,' O'Day pointed out. 'And they didn't impress me as being smart, or dangerous warriors.'

'You'd've likely learned different if we hadn't happened along,' the Kid warned quietly. 'See, they wasn't but *tuivitsis;* which-same's young hot-heads who don't know better'n charge in head down and horns a-hooking blind. Those fellers up there though, they're most of 'em *tehnaps*. Old, seasoned-on-red-meat brave-hearts, with hair hanging on their belts. Mister, even with us having happened along, you'd find them both smart and dangerous.'

'So you conclude to do like Wolf Runner wants, Comanch'?' Dusty asked.

'He done the concluding for me,' the Kid corrected. 'Only, just so long's you get Giselle back to Hell right-side-up and with all her buttons fastened, everything'll be fine. No ten-coup war leader's going to let hurt come to Long Walker's grandson, unless he can offer a real good reason for doing it.'

'You ride careful, mind, you blasted Comanche,' Dusty

ordered, with more concern than command in his tone. 'Is there anything you'll be needing?'

'Nary a thing,' grinned the Kid. 'Fact being, I'll likely be living better'n you white folks. Us Comanches know how to travel well-fed and comfortable.'

Although Dusty and Waco had serious misgivings, they raised no further objections to their *amigo* being held as a hostage. They had faith in his superior knowledge concerning the risks he was taking. All they could do would be to ensure that they carried out their side of the agreement.

'I don't want to go to Hell!' Giselle whined as the Kid rode back to join the waiting *Kweharehnuh*.

'Nobody does, but they go on sinning just the same,' Waco replied. 'And, even without Comanch' being held hostage, you'd get there, one or other of 'em, whichever way you headed.'

'We've no other choice but go on, Giselle,' Emma went on firmly. 'Don't fret yourself. Ed'll see that nothing bad happens to you.'

Although Giselle looked anything but convinced, she kept quiet and accompanied the rest of her party in the direction of the stream. If O'Day's behaviour was anything to go by, he shared with the brunette in feeling ill-at-ease. He constantly twisted in his saddle, searching the surrounding terrain with wary and worried glances. After a short time, however, he relaxed. All of the Indians had disappeared, taking the Kid with them, and the man could detect no sign of them. Neither could Dusty nor Waco. Their examination of the locality was less obvious, but possibly more thorough than O'Day's. The apparent dearth of watchers did not fool them. They both knew that keen-eyed wolf-scouts were keeping them under observation all the time.

In passing, Dusty nodded towards the buffalo wallow the Kid had mentioned as a place in which they might have been able to fort up and fight. It was about a hundred yards from the stream; a large depression worn by countless bison rolling on, pawing at and generally churning up the gound.

'That's where we'll bed down for the night. In the bottom. It won't be comfortable, but no raider can sneak in on us down there.'

'How about wood for a fire?' O'Day asked, looking around. 'We'll have to carry it from the trees by the stream.'

'*You* can go fetch some, if you're so minded,' Waco drawled. 'But me, I sure don't aim to chance it.'

'I thought that the Indians had given us a safe passage to Hell,' O'Day pointed out.

'They have,' Dusty agreed. 'Only they don't trust us a whole heap and're having us watched.'

'Where?' O'Day gasped, swivelling around and glaring about him. 'I don't see anybody!'

'They're wolf-scouts, trained to follow, watch and not be seen,' Dusty explained. 'It's work for *tuivitsis*, not *tehnaps*. Happen one of them should see you all alone in the woods, he might not be able to resist the temptation to count himself an easy coup.'

'They stop resisting *real* easy, friend,' Waco added. 'There's never enough coups to go 'round for all the young bucks who want 'em.'

By that time, the party had reached the edge of the stream. Dismounting, they removed the horses' bits and allowed them to drink. Giselle kept darting glances from O'Day to the range across which they had been travelling. She took her mount – one of the dead soldier's horses, borrowed by Dusty from Lieutenant Kitson – a short way down-stream of the others. Tired from the exertions of the day, Emma felt little desire to make conversation and paid no attention to the brunette. O'Day resumed his investigations into the habits of the Comanche, so Dusty and Waco did not notice Giselle's furtive actions.

'What is this "counting coup"?' the man inquired. 'Is it another name for taking a scalp?'

'Nope,' Dusty replied. 'It rates as more important than that, to the Comanches, anyways. They say that anybody can scalp a dead man, it proves nothing. But to count coup shows that the feller doing it has courage.'

'But how—?'

'The brave has to touch his enemy, either while killing

him, or soon after, and say, "*A:he!*", which means "I claim it". Once that's been done and said, he's counted coup.'

'Way ole Comanch' tells it,' Waco went on, 'there ain't nothing sets up a lusty young buck with those pretty lil Injun gals like having brought back plenty of loot and to've said "*A:he*" good and often. And the Comanches don't go for no taking seconds, thirds nor fourths.'

'That went right by me,' O'Day admitted.

'Some of the tribes let the second, third and fourth braves to touch an enemy count lesser shares in the coup,' Dusty elaborated.

'They do say Osages let 'most anybody who wants to share the coup, whether they was around to touch the body or not,' Waco grinned. 'Could be they just don't like Osages.'

'The Comanches figure that they've got so many enemies, they don't need to share coups,' Dusty drawled. 'All the other tribes called them the *Tshaoh*, the Enemy People and, most times, that's what they used to be.'

'You gentlemen appear to know a lot about Indians,' O'Day praised.

'All we know, Comanch' taught us,' Dusty answered. 'His mother was the daughter of a *Pehnane* Comanche war lodge's chief. Which's just about as high as a man can get in the tribe.'

'I thought your friend was a half—' O'Day began, then, as frowns came to the Texans' brows, revised his words. 'Part Indian.'

'He's all white to *us*, mister!' Waco growled.

'No offence intended and I hope none's been taken,' O'Day apologized and, with the air of wanting to change the subject, continued, 'Is a brave's statement that he has counted coup always accepted?'

'If there's any doubt on it and he's challenged, the band's medicine man or woman can have him swear to it on the sacred sun oath,' Dusty answered. 'No Comanche will dare to lie after he's taken it.'

'Do their medicine people have that much of a hold on them?'

'Their religion has, anyways. They take their beliefs a damned sight more serious than most white folks take God.'

'But they must believe in magic if Simm— Giselle's husband could take a hold of them with tricks.'

'Only if it's some kind of trick they've never seen and don't know how to pull,' Dusty corrected. 'Their medicine men and women have been pulling things out of the air and the like since afore Columbus landed. No sir, don't sell Simmy Lampart short. I didn't see him do it, but that sawing-his-wife-in-half trick must've been something special to fool the *Kweharehnuhs'* medicine woman.'

Something had been said which Waco instinctively knew had significance beyond the general trend of the conversation. He scowled and tried to recall just what it had been. Before he could do so, an interruption came which drove it temporarily out of his thoughts.

While the men had been talking, Giselle had allowed her mount to drink and had then led it away from the water. Emma was kneeling on the edge of the stream and bathing her face. Nobody was looking at the small brunette as she turned the animal's head to the south-east and swung into the saddle. If she had given more thought to her actions, she might have met with greater success in her desertion. Instead of walking slowly away, she gave her mount's ribs a sharp kick which made it grunt and bound forward.

'What the—?' Waco spat out, spinning around with hands fanning to the butts of his Army Colts.

Also alerted by the sudden thunder of hooves, Dusty and O'Day turned with equal speed. They too sent their hands towards weapons. Crossing his body, Dusty's palms enfolded the grips of his Peacemakers. All in a single, incredibly swift blur of movement, the matched Colts left their holsters and the hammers clicked to full cock. Although O'Day matched the small Texan's speed in turning, his long barrelled revolver had not cleared leather by the time Dusty was standing ready to shoot.

Shuffling hurriedly on her knees, Emma clawed to free the Navy Colt from her waist-band. Anger flickered across her face as she saw, not an attacking *Kweharehnuh* warrior, but Giselle Lampart galloping away as fast as the borrowed horse would carry her.

'Stop the crazy bitch!' Emma screeched, furious at the

thought of Giselle – who was vital to her plans for enrichment – behaving in such a stupid manner.

That proved to be a piece of needless advice. Waco reacted to the desertion without the need for prompting. Twirling the Colts on his trigger-fingers, he caused them to return to their holsters with the minimum of effort on his part. Then he caught hold of the *tobiano*'s saddlehorn and swung himself on to its back. Reaching forward, he jerked free and drew back the hackamore which was fixed to the bridle's *bosal*.

The horse Waco sat belonged to his work mount[*] when back at the ranch and it had been trained with careful patience. So it responded to his command of, 'Back', despite the lack of bit and reins to augment the single word. Instantly it started to retreat from the water's edge; chin tucked in, neck well flexed, hind legs moving in long, confident strides and fore feet taking deliberate steps. Waco sat with relaxed, easy balance, his vertebrae perpendicular for greater control of his horse's movements.

Once clear of the water, the blond struck the *tobiano*'s near shoulder with his right spur. At the signal, its forelegs left the ground and it pivoted fast on its rear hooves. With its head pointing after the departing brunette, it was urged into motion. Like the *tuivitsis* earlier, the youngster built his mount's pace up to a gallop in a very short time. Doing all he knew how to increase the speed, he guided it across the range.

'Shall we go after them?' O'Day asked, allowing his weapon to slide back into its holster.

'Likely Brother Matt can handle it,' Dusty answered and returned his guns to their holsters. 'What the hell's gotten into Giselle, Emma?'

'She's scared that the Indians will want her to be sawn in half when they come for their ammunition,' the blonde guessed, glaring after the riders and stabbing the Navy Colt into her waist-band. 'With Simmy dead, there'll be nobody who can handle the trick.'

'You say that Si— her husband is dead?' O'Day put in harshly.

[*] Texas' cowhands used the word 'mount', not 'string', for their work horses.

'He was shot by some of my people when they robbed him,' Emma explained, using the excuse she had arranged to make on her arrival in Hell. 'We're just on our way back after hunting them down.'

'Look there!' Dusty gritted, pointing towards the wooded land which fringed much of the stream's banks.

Having no wish to let the conversation continue on the subject of Mayor Lampart's death, the small Texan had been seeking a way to end it. Providence had presented him with the means to do so. Looking in the direction he was pointing, Emma and O'Day let out ejaculations of surprise and alarm. A stocky young Antelope brave stood on the edge of the trees, his repeater cradled on his left elbow and his whole attitude showing that he was watching the pursuit of Giselle.

'Like I said,' Dusty drawled. 'Wolf Runner's got us watched.'

'How long as he been there?' Emma breathed, hand creeping towards her revolver and voice showing tension.

'All the time,' Dusty answered.

'What shall we do?' O'Day demanded.

'Nothing we can do, except wait for Brother Matt to fetch her back safe and sound.'

'And if he doesn't?'

'Mister,' Dusty said quietly, '*if* he doesn't, we're in with the water over the willows and a fast stream running.'

'Huh?' O'Day grunted.

'It's what trail drivers say when they're in just about as bad trouble as they can find,' Dusty explained.

'You've been on trail drives then?' O'Day asked.

'Some,' Dusty admitted, wondering if apprehension over their danger or some other reason had prompted the question. 'You'll likely see what I meant, happen Matt doesn't bring her back.'

'So will Comanche, even worse than we do,' Emma put in bitterly. 'That stupid, no-account little tail-peddler.* She's got cow-droppings for brains. Damn it all, without her—'

---

* Tail-peddler: a prostitute, especially one of the cheaper kind.

The blonde stopped speaking, realizing that she had come close to saying too much about her plans and reasons for having persuaded Giselle to accompany her in the return to Hell.

'She's scared of something,' Dusty answered. 'Well, we'd best make out that we figure everything's all right. Let's take the horses back to the buffalo wallow and start making camp.'

'Your *brother* hasn't caught her yet,' O'Day commented, peering across the range and laying emphasis on the second word. 'But I'm sure he will. You are a remarkably competent family.'

At first, Giselle maintained her lead on Waco. That did not surprise the youngster as he had already analysed the situation and formed correct conclusions, based upon his practical knowledge of equestrian matters. Smaller and lighter than her pursuer, Giselle possessed no other advantages in her flight. She was neither such a good rider, nor so well-mounted. Kept short of cash by a Congress more concerned with winning votes than expending the tax-payers' money on defence projects, the United States' Cavalry could not afford to purchase high quality mounts for its enlisted men. On the other hand, Waco sat a horse belonging to a ranch which selected only the best for its riders and insisted that the animals be kept in the peak of condition.

So Waco realized that, barring accidents, it was inevitable he must overtake her.

On they raced through the gathering twilight – not an ideal time to be riding at a gallop over unfamiliar terrain. For all that, the woman encouraged her mount to greater efforts with cries, jabbing heels and slapping reins. Apart from an occasional soft word of praise, Waco rode in silence and concentrated on what he was doing. Controlling his speeding *tobiano*'s natural inclination to increase its speed until it was rocketing along blindly, he watched Giselle for any hint that she had become aware of his presence to her rear.

None came. What did show were growing symptoms that the brunette was rapidly losing control over her horse. By that stage of the flight, however, it was getting blown and its pace was starting to flag.

Nearer thundered Waco, edging the *tobiano* to the brunette's left. That had been done deliberately. It was unlikely that Giselle would show sufficient good sense to halt, so he intended to give her no choice in the matter. Having been trained in the typical white man's fashion, the cavalry horse had always had its rider climb on or off at the near side. If it felt its burden leaving over the right flank, its reactions might be unpredictable and dangerous to her or Waco.

Coming level with the woman, the youngster saw her head swing in his direction. Even as she opened her mouth to either speak or scream, at the same time attempting to rein her horse away, he leaned across and coiled his right arm about her waist. Giving her no time to resist, he cued the *tobiano* with knee pressure so that it veered away from the other animal. In her anxiety, Giselle had inadvertently helped Waco. The cavalry horse had shown little response to her manipulation of the reins, but it angled off slightly and furthered the blond's efforts at removing her from the saddle.

Giselle screeched, a mixture of fear and anger, as she felt herself being dragged sideways. Luckily for them both she had sufficient understanding of the position to kick her feet free from the stirrup irons – but she did not release her grasp on the reins.

Alarmed by the unexpected disturbance of the weight on its saddle, the cavalry horse started to shy even farther to the right. Giselle's rump and right leg slid across the seat until she was clear of it and hung suspended from Waco's encircling arm. Fright more than sense caused her to release the reins, but they had already snatched the horse's head around. Disrupted by the woman's actions, its head drawn abruptly in a new direction, the animal lost its footing. It went down and rolled over. Fortunately, the *tobiano* had turned just far enough to the left and galloped by without adding to the cavalry horse's troubles by trampling upon it.

Using what guidance he could exert with the hackamore,* Waco set about bringing the *tobiano* to a halt. Still

---

* The use of a hackamore and bosal is described in detail in: *A Horse Called Mogollon* and in *.44 Calibre Man*.

screeching, Giselle tried to reach his face with her fingernails. Spitting out a threat to drop her, he slackened his hold a little. That brought an end to her attempts to scratch her way free. Waco steered his horse in a wide curve which ate away its galloping momentum. On reaching a walking pace, he lowered the kicking, still protesting brunette to the ground. Then he rode to where her horse had regained its feet. Dropping from his saddle, he allowed the *tobiano*'s hackamore to dangle free and walked up to Giselle's mount. Although badly shaken by the fall, heavily lathered and winded, it did not appear to be seriously injured.

Pattering foot-falls came to the youngster's ears as he straightened up from examining the horse. Turning, he found a wild-faced Giselle bearing down furiously on him. Spitting out what he took to be obscenities in some foreign language, the brunette thrust her right hand into its jacket pocket. Seeing the Colt House Pistol emerging, he did not hesitate. For all that, she had moved with such speed that he was almost too late. Leaping towards the little woman, he watched the snub-nosed revolver come clear of the pocket and line in his direction. Its hammer went back under the pressure of her thumb, causing the trigger to click out its sheath to where her forefinger was waiting to press it.

Around lashed Waco's left hand. He struck Giselle's extended right wrist and deflected the House Pistol's muzzle. Flame spiked from the short tube and the bullet it propelled could not have missed the youngster by more than an inch. The narrow escape brought an instant reaction. Even before the incident, he had never liked Giselle's ways or morals. So he was less inclined to take her sex into consideration than he would have been with most women. Letting out a low, savage hiss, he drove his right hand in a slap which sent her spinning around and away from him. Dropping the House Pistol, she tumbled face down and lay sobbing, with both hands clutching at her cheek.

'Get up!' Waco ordered, retrieving the House Pistol and tucking it into his Levi's pocket.

Something in the youngster's tone caused Giselle to obey. Crawling to her feet, she turned a tear-stained face in what she hoped would be a pleading and pathetic manner to him.

'D... Don't take me b... back there!' Giselle pleaded. 'I ... I'll share my money with you ... you.'

'Like hell,' Waco replied. 'You start walking back where we come from. And, lady, if Lon gets killed through this, I'll do just the same to you.'

CHAPTER NINE

MEPHISTO'S BEEN DEAD FOR YEARS

'THIS'LL do us,' Dusty Fog declared, drawing rein and nodding to where a spring bubbled up through the floor of the valley the party was crossing. 'We'll make camp while there's still light to put on Scotch hobbles.'

'You're using them again?' O'Day inquired. 'They're hell to take off.'

'That's why we're doing it,' Waco drawled, throwing a pointed glance at the sullen, drooping Giselle Lampart as she sat her horse at Emma Nene's side.

'She won't run away again,' the blonde promised grimly.

'I thought you said we aren't far from Hell,' O'Day remarked as the Texans and women dismounted.

'It's maybe five miles from here,' Dusty answered. 'Happen you're that way inclined, Break, you can ride on and find it.'

'In the dark?' the man queried, glancing significantly to where the sun was sinking below the western rim of the valley.

'Should be able to *hear* what you can't see, you go on a ways,' Waco drawled. 'Hell comes alive after dark and sounds like Trail Street in Mulrooney when the drives are in.'

'Despite of which, you are staying here until morning,' O'Day pointed out. 'That means you have a very good reason, Ed.'

'Good enough,' Dusty confirmed as he loosened the girths and worked his saddle back and forwards to cool the horse's back. 'What with Simmy Lampart being dead, the ammunition supply destroyed and the *Kweharehnuh* acting sort of restless, there'll be guards out around town. They'll

88

be jumpy and won't shout, "Halt, who goes there, friend or foe?" until *after* they've thrown lead at whoever's coming to make sure they can't do anything but halt.'

'Even if they can't shoot good, they could get lucky,' Waco supplemented, scowling at Giselle as if wishing that he could send her to try out the sentries' skill or luck.

It was sun-down on the day after Giselle's attempted flight. Unencumbered by the wagon, Dusty and his companions had been able to travel faster than on the escape from Hell. So his estimation of the distance separating them from their destination was fairly accurate.

The day's journey had passed uneventfully, yet not without anxieties for Dusty and Waco. There had been no sign of the *Kweharehnuh* scouting party who were holding the Ysabel Kid as a hostage against Giselle's return to Hell. Shortly after the brunette had ridden away, a second wolf-scout had joined the first. They had talked, clearly discussing the situation, and the second *tuivitsi* had departed – presumably to take the news to Wolf Runner. Having waited until Waco returned with Giselle, the first wolf-scout had faded off. Since then, the small Texan and the young blond had been consumed with fears for the Kid's safety.

To take their thoughts from their *amigo*'s possible fate, Dusty and Waco had kept up a conversation with O'Day for much of the day's journey. On their side, they had tried to discover more about the mysterious man who had been thrown into their lives. O'Day had answered asked – and unasked – questions frankly and cheerfully. From what he had told them, he qualified for entrance to Hell and he had cleared up the matter of Eastern manners and western appearance to their satisfaction. When Waco had pointed out that he could not have purchased such a well-designed gunbelt at short notice, O'Day had laughingly reminded them that it was possible to purchase such an item in the civilized and peaceful East, provided one knew where to look and what to ask for.

For his part, O'Day had expressed a lively interest in all matters pertaining to the Comanches in general and Antelope band in particular. Although his questions had commenced on general topics, he had worked them around to the subject of the powers of the medicine men and women.

He had also been eager to hear how Lampart had won – or tricked – his way into the *Kweharehnuhs*' confidence and had obtained permission to build Hell in their domain.

Any details which the Texans had been unable to supply had come from Emma. It was the blonde who had told O'Day of another precaution Lampart had taken to protect his interests against the Indians. In addition to having convinced them that sudden death would come to any man who tried to steal his ammunition, or to molest legitimate visitors to the town, the mayor had had photographs taken of Ten Bears and the medicine woman. Believing that he had captured their souls, the spiritual and material heads of the band had been more amenable to his will and disinclined to make trouble for him.

No matter how amiable and pleasant O'Day had tried to be, Giselle had refused to have anything to do with him. She had lost some of the fear which had tinted her expression when being addressed by him the previous night, but made it plain that she wanted only to be left alone. After a succession of direct snubs and monosyllabic answers, O'Day had accepted defeat and concentrated his attention on Emma and the Texans. Dusty had noticed several times that Giselle was willing to observe O'Day, even if she refused to speak to him. Stealing surreptitious looks at the man, the brunette's face had shown mingled emotions. Interest, curiosity, alarm and disbelief played on her features, which would be swiftly turned aside if the object of her scrutiny looked at her.

Having sound reasons for wanting to arrive unnoticed in Hell and knowing that – as a result of precautions against accidental discovery taken by Lampart – the town came to life at night, Dusty had had no intention of making his entrance before dawn. Nor had he wished to let O'Day go in to spread the news of their coming. To prevent arousing the man's suspicions when he discovered how close to town they had halted, the small Texan had produced a valid and acceptable excuse for delaying their appearance until daylight.

'In which case, having as great an antipathy towards being shot as I felt regarding my being hung, I will bow to you gentlemen's superior wisdom,' O'Day declared cheerfully. Swinging down from his saddle, he went on, 'If the ladies can bear the proximity of my presence for another night, I will be honoured to spend it in their company.'

'I can never resist anybody who calls me a lady,' Emma smiled. 'Feel free to stay on with us, Break.'

'When you've off-saddled, Emma, you and Mrs. Lampart might's well go to the other side of the spring and pick the best bedding spots out,' Dusty suggested. 'We'll tend to the horses.'

Obtaining the added security offered by 'Scotch hobbling', as opposed to using the conventional leather cuffs and linking swivel-chain of double hobbles, was a time-consuming business. There was some need for haste as the sun, dipping below the rim of the western slope, threw dark shadows over the spring. Removing their saddles and leaving behind the ropes from the horns, Emma and Giselle carried out Dusty's instructions. They hauled their rigs around to the western edge of the water-hole, out of earshot of the men.

Making a large loop with Giselle's rope, Waco draped it around the cavalry horse's neck and tied a bowline knot behind the near shoulder. Then he took the longer end of the rope over and made a half-hitch about the right hind leg just above the ankle joint. Carrying the end of the rope forward and up, he secured it to the loop in such a manner that the trapped limb was raised and its hoof suspended about four inches above the ground. Held in that manner, the horse could neither stray far, nor move at speed. In addition, as O'Day had commented, removing the Scotch hobble was not easy – especially when attempted in darkness and with the need to avoid making any undue noise.

While Dusty did not believe that Giselle would try to escape again, he had no intention of presenting her with the opportunity. If he had been able to hear the conversation taking place between the two women, he would have felt less certain about the brunette's acceptance of the situation.

'Do you have your push-knife on you, Emma?' Giselle inquired with what she hoped sounded like casual interest, setting down her saddle.

'No!' the blonde answered and frowned at the brunette. 'If I did, I wouldn't let you have it.'

'I only wanted to—'

'I know what you want to do with it and the answer's still

"no". Hell, Ed won't let the folks do anything about us leaving them the way we did.'

'He's not your "Ed Caxton",' Giselle spat out. 'He's Dusty Fog!'

'Hold your voice down, damn you, or you'll be muttering through bloody gums!' the blonde hissed furiously. 'If O'Day hears—'

'All right, don't get mean!' the brunette whined, knowing that Emma's temper could be explosive on occasion.

'Anyways, seeing that he is Dusty Fog, you should be even more sure that he'll look after you. A feller like "Ed Caxton" might have said the hell with you and let the folks do what they want. Dusty won't.'

'It's not what the people will do that bothers me. Or having to do the trick. We both know you can handle Simmy's part easily enough as long as the box hasn't been damaged.'

'Then what is it?' Emma demanded.

'Who does that feller O'Day put you in mind of?'

'Nobody that I can remember. His face isn't familiar.'

'Not the face,' Giselle corrected. 'His voice.'

'His voice—?' the blonde repeated. 'Yes, it does sound kind of familiar.'

'He talks just like Mephisto used to,' Giselle said, dropping her tone almost to a whisper and throwing a frightened glance in O'Day's direction.

'*Mephisto!*' Emma gasped and, for a moment, she looked nearly as frightened as the little brunette. Then she mastered her emotions and gave a shrug. 'Aw, go on. Mephisto's been dead for years.'

'We don't know that for sure!' Giselle pointed out. 'His body was never found and—'

'Take a hold of yourself, you little fool!' the blonde interrupted in a savage manner. 'There were a dozen or more people saw him rush out of the hotel and jump into the East River—'

'But his body wasn't found!' the brunette protested.

'If it had've been, you and Simmy would most likely have wound up in jail,' Emma said coldly. 'That feller's not Mephisto. After what you pair did, his face wouldn't look like that.'

'D... Don't...!'

'And don't you come the harmless little angel with me. I know you, Giselle Lampart and know how much that's worth. So O'Day talks a mite pompous, like Mephisto used to. I've heard plenty of fellers, actors, magicians, confidence tricksters and the like, who did. Hell! Look at his face. It's not had vitriol thrown into it. Or do you think he looks like it might have?'

'N... No, it doesn't,' Giselle admitted with a shudder. 'Emma, I didn't thr—?'

'I don't care who threw it!' the blonde snapped. 'Mephisto's dead. Only your guilty conscience makes you think O'Day is him. So forget any fool notions of running away again. We've too much at stake to have you hurt.'

'Yes, *we* have,' the brunette agreed and her fears appeared to flicker away. 'And I'm the only one of *us* who can open the locks and safe doors.'

'Don't get smart, little half-sister,' Emma warned. 'If you double-cross me, I'll show you that I can be as mean as Mephisto would be if he was still alive and caught up with you.'

'D... Don't even think things like that, Emma!' Giselle pleaded.

Seeing the men approaching, the women allowed their conversation to lapse. Darkness had come down by the time Dusty, Waco and O'Day had spread their bed rolls and the women had made ready for the night.

'I could drink a whole gallon of coffee,' Emma remarked, looking at Dusty.

'Why not light a fire and make some?' asked a familiar voice, drifting from the blackness of the western slope.

At the first word, the blonde let out a startled yelp, which mingled with Giselle's squeal of alarm. Instinctively Dusty, Waco and O'Day reached for their guns. Only the Easterner completed his draw and even he did not fire. Coming on foot out of the gloomy shadows, the Kid grinned cheerfully at the various signs of alarm caused by his unheralded arrival.

'You folks're sure jumpy,' the dark Texan commented, halting with his Winchester's barrel resting on his right shoulder.

'Blasted Injun!' Waco snorted disgustedly, hiding his

relief at seeing his *amigo* was unharmed. Letting the Colts sink back into their holsters, he went on, 'I was like to blow windows in your fool head, thinking you was some other kind of varmint.'

'Could you hit me, that is,' countered the Kid. 'Howdy, Miss Emma, Mrs. Lampart, friend. See this pair of buzzards didn't manage to get you lost.'

'Them *Kweharehnuhs* now, they've got right good sense,' Waco declared. 'They soon enough give you back to us.'

That seemed obvious. The Kid might be afoot, but he was in possession of all of his weapons. His attitude of cheerful ease suggested that he had not escaped and was expecting to be pursued. Staring through the darkness, Emma sought for hints that he had arrived in time to overhear her conversation with Giselle. Nothing about his voice or attitude suggested that he might have.

'Wolf Runner figured's how you could use some food, seeing you didn't cook any last night or this morning,' the Kid drawled. 'So he sent me over to fetch you some.'

'He's surely generous and free-handed with his giving,' Waco commented, staring from the Kid's empty left hand to the rifle-filled right.

'I've got it, and enough wood to make a fire, on a pack hoss up there,' the Kid answered. 'Left it on the hoss so I could sneak down quiet-like, 'case you wasn't saying what a real nice young feller I be.'

'Why'd we talk different about you than other folks?' Waco wanted to know.

'You're just natural mean, boy. Why'n't you 'n' Ed help me tote it down?'

'I'll come, if you need me,' O'Day offered.

'Might be best if one of us stayed on here,' Dusty replied, throwing a meaning nod towards Giselle.

'I only asked hoping you'd say "no",' O'Day answered.

'How're things, Lon?' Dusty inquired as they walked up the slope.

'Easy enough,' the Kid replied. 'I thought they might get rough when that wolf-scout come to say Giselle'd lit out. Then the other brought word that the boy'd fetched her back.'

'I'm damned if I know why I bothered,' Waco injected.

'Then tonight Wolf Runner was asking why you'd stopped instead of going on to bed down in Hell,' the Kid continued. 'I 'minded him that you're only *white* folks 'n' likely didn't know for sure where the town's at. Then it figured to him.'

'And he let you-all come back seeing's we're this close,' Dusty guessed.

'Said I could come—'

'Likely got tired of feeding you,' Waco interrupted.

'So's I could tell you I'm fixing to go with him to the village, so's I can say "howdy" to Ten Bears for Grandpappy Long Walker,' the Kid concluded as if the youngster had never spoken. 'And he allowed he'd be right honoured to have me along.'

'I thought you allus reckoned Comanches don't tell lies?' Waco remarked.

'And they don't,' confirmed the Kid.

'Then why don't you say truthful that you had to threaten to bust both his legs and make him herd sheep afore he'd agree to be seen in your company?' the youngster demanded. 'That's the only way you'd get *me* to agree to take you anyplace. *And* I wouldn't be right honoured about it.'

'You know how to handle the blister end of a shovel, boy?' Dusty growled, eyeing the blond menacingly.

'I can't right and truthful claim I do,' Waco admitted proudly.

'Keep flapping your lip and, comes us getting back to home, I'm going to improve your education on them lines,' Dusty threatened. 'You got something special in mind, Lon?'

'Why sure. I aim to find out just why they was so all-fired set on having Giselle come back.'

'You don't reckon it's just to see her dance in that fancy lil costume and be sawn in half?'

'There's a mite more to it than that, I'd say. The braves aren't saying much, but, what I can make out, the medicine woman, *Pohawe*, 's been getting hoorawed bad over not knowing how Lampart's tricks was pulled. That's not good for her business.'

'Could be she reckons she could work out how it's done was she to see it done again,' Waco suggested.

'Or she's maybe counting on the folks not being able to do it, with Lampart dead,' Dusty went on. 'If they can't, their medicine's gone sour and they can be treated like other pale-faces.'

'That could be,' admitted the Kid. 'Anyways, I'll see what I can learn. Say, I'm right pleased you didn't have that O'Day *hombre* come with us.'

'I concluded you didn't want him along,' Dusty drawled.

'You was right. What do you make of him?'

'I don't know, Lon. He's amiable enough to talk to. Way he tells it, he's bad-wanted in a few places and figured to lay low in Hell for a spell. Says he bought all his gear new afore setting off, so he'd be less noticeable than in city duds. Which's true enough. But I don't know what it is, I'm uneasy having him around.'

'Could be you're jealous of him being so clean-shaven,' Waco put in.

'Huh?' Dusty grunted, laying a hand on his stubble-coated face.

'Yes, sir,' the youngster said, delighted at having noticed something that had slipped the small Texan's notice. 'He's either shaved when we wasn't looking, or got a face as bald's a girl's.'

'I've known fellers who didn't need to shave, even when full grown,' the Kid announced. 'Maybe you pair've been too busy to notice, but the folks in Hell're still keeping to that no fires in the daytime ruling.'

'We'd noticed,' Dusty assured him. 'Are the *Kwehareh-nuh* still letting folk in and out of town?'

'Sure,' the Kid confirmed. 'Likely Ten Bears's waiting to see whether he gets his ammunition afore he stops it. Anyways, I'll learn all I can at the camp, then come in and let you know how things stand.'

CHAPTER TEN

THE REST OF THE MONEY'S HIDDEN

WALKING along Hell's main street, Emma Nene, Giselle Lampart, Dusty Fog and Break O'Day went by Doctor Connolly's home and office building towards the front door of the Honest Man saloon. Largest building in the town, the saloon alone had two floors. On the upper's verandah rail was nailed a large wooden sign bearing the name of the establishment, but no painting to illustrate the title as was common in such premises elsewhere.

'How could an artist paint something that doesn't exist?' Emma countered when O'Day mentioned the discrepancy.

It was noon and, apart from themselves, the street was deserted; which did not surprise the women or Dusty. In fact, they had been banking on finding such a condition.

During their approach from the tree-lined top of the hollow in which the town had been erected, they had seen no sign of human life. For all appearances, the entire population might have been laid to rest in the large graveyard. A few horses were hitched outside the various adobe *jacales* which sprouted irregularly beyond the business premises flanking the main street and more occupied the livery barn's corrals. The barn's staff had not been present, so the newcomers had tended to their horses unaided and left the animals in previously untenanted stalls. Having been presented with ownership of the barn, for his part in removing the original proprietor, Dusty had the keys to its side rooms in his possession. Unlocking the office, he had allowed the others to leave their saddles and portable property until it could be more suitably cared for.

After the Kid's departure the night before, Dusty had told O'Day the story concocted by Emma and secured the man's

97

offer of assistance if it should be needed. So O'Day accompanied the women and the small Texan, while Waco went off to attend to another matter.

To an unknowing observer, Hell would have looked like any other small, sunbaked range country town. A mite more prosperous in its appointments than most, maybe, but with nothing to hint at its true nature and purpose. Most of the conventional business and social amenities could be located; with the notable exceptions of a bank, jail or stagecoach depot. There was neither school nor church, but other small towns also lacked them.

Facing the Honest Man stood the lengthy, well-appointed 'Youseman's Funeral Parlour'; which probably had a sobering effect upon revellers who were all too aware that capture by the law would mean death on a hangman's rope. Beyond the saloon and on the same side was Giselle's home which also combined with the mayor's office and what had passed for a bank.

On stepping through the batwing doors into the large barroom, Dusty, the women and O'Day found that they could no longer remain unobserved. Although the majority of the room was unoccupied, the stairs and balcony empty of people, six men and a big, buxom, garishly-dressed woman sat around what had been Emma's private table. Startled exclamations burst from them as they looked towards the main entrance. An angry hiss broke from the blonde, for the red-haired, good looking brothel-keeper Rosie Wilson was sitting in her chair at the head of the table.

Dusty recognized four of the men. Tall, gaunt, miserable of features, Doctor Connolly might have been the undertaker and the big, burly, jovial-looking Emmet 'Happy' Youseman, in his check suit and diamond stick-in, the town's surgeon. Fat, pompous as when he had attended board meetings in the East, the hotel's owner, Emanuel Goldberg, turned red and spluttered incoherently. His partner in many a crooked deal, now acting as jeweller and pawnbroker, Sylvester Crouch, muttered something to the nearer of the two strangers.

Although Dusty did not know the pair, he could guess at what they were. Tall, lean and wearing low-tied guns, they had a matching wolf-cautious alertness. One had black hair and a walrus moustache that did nothing to conceal a hard, cruel mouth. The other was going bald, needed a shave and had a patch over his left eye. Dressed cowhand fashion, they neither of them struck Dusty as having any legitimate connections with ranching.

'Easy, all of you!' Dusty ordered as the townsmen made as if to rise.

Soft-spoken the words might have been, but they caused the quartet to halt their intentions. The other two male occupants of the table exchanged glances, but made no hostile moves.

'Well well, Emma-gal,' Rosie Wilson boomed, swinging to face the blonde. 'I never thought to see *you* back here.'

'That figures, way you're making free with my place and my stock,' Emma replied, indicating the bottles and glasses on the table, then the cigars which the bunch around it – including the woman – were smoking.

'We didn't think you'd da – be coming back,' Crouch insisted, altering his words half-way through.

'I can see that,' the blonde snorted, swinging a gaze around the room. 'I don't think the floor's been cleaned and washed since I left.' She turned cold eyes in Rosie's direction. 'You're in my chair, *Mrs.* Wilson.'

'There's some might say different,' the brothel-keeper answered.

'I had my fill of rolling on the floor and hair-yanking with Belle Starr,' Emma warned, right hand resting on the butt of the Navy Colt. 'So if you want *my* chair that badly, get up and tell me – with a gun in your hand.'

'Who're these bunch?' the one-eyed man demanded, his voice showing that he had done more than his share in making free with Emma's stock.

'The folks we told you about, Alec,' Goldberg answered. 'Emma Nene, Mrs. Lampart and Ed Caxton. I don't know their companion.'

'I'm just a man they met on the trail,' O'Day announced.

'Then bill out of things that're none of your concern,' the one-eyed man ordered and swung cold, challenging eyes to Dusty. 'You're the yahoo who gunned down Ben Columbo 'n' Joey Pinter, huh?'

'Seemed like a good thing to do at the time,' the small Texan replied. 'Who're your friends, Happy?'

'Visitors like yourself, Ed,' Youseman answered. 'Alec Lovey and Jack Messnick. They came in last night.'

'See they pay for their drinks before they go to bed,' Dusty ordered. 'And they look tired enough to go right now.'

'You telling us to get out of here?' Lovey demanded, lurching to his feet.

'What we've got to say's for the Civic Regulators' ears, *hombre*,' Dusty replied. 'And I figure it'd be easier for you two to go than all of us.'

'That's big talk for a small man,' Messnick stated, also rising. He had taken less to drink than his companion and looked the more dangerous.

'I can back it, if I have to,' Dusty assured him.

'Against all of us here?' Lovey challenged, jerking his left thumb around the table.

'There's not but the two of you'll take cards,' Dusty pointed out. 'The rest of them know us – and want to find a few things out.'

'So two of us's all,' Lovey sneered, listening to the confirmatory mutters which had followed the small Texan's statement. 'That still puts the odds in our favour at two to one.'

'Only it's more like one to one,' commented a voice from the rear of the barroom.

Turning their heads, the party around the table saw Waco standing at the doorway which led to the rear of the building. With his left shoulder leaning on the door's jamb and hands thumb-hooked into his gunbelt, he contrived to present an impression of deadly readiness.

'Maybe we'll just try taking those odds,' Lovey announced, his one eye glinting dangerously.

'Then you just go to doing it, *hombre*,' Dusty offered.

Less drunk than Lovey, Messnick could read the danger signs better. Like other men before him, the outlaw suddenly became aware of Dusty's personality and forgot about him in mere feet and inches. There stood a *big* and very capable man, full able to hold up his end in a shooting fuss. Taking him on in a fair fight would be fraught with peril.

'Aw hell, Alec,' Messnick said in a mild tone. 'We're here

to have fun, not to make trouble. If these folks want to talk private, we should be gentlemen and leave them do it.'

'You mean eat crow to this—?' Lovey blazed.

'I mean let's go and grab some sleep,' Messnick interrupted, before some unpardonable insult was made and needed to be accounted for. 'Come on. Maybe tonight we'll get lucky just like we did that time in Fort Worth.'

'Huh?' grunted Lovey, then his puzzled expression turned into a knowing and sly grin. 'Sure. Just like in Fort Worth.'

If the words carried any special meaning to the other participants in the scene, they failed to make the fact known. Break O'Day looked from the two outlaws to Dusty Fog and then at Emma. The latter couple were apparently giving all their attention to the townspeople. Disappointment showed briefly on the faces of the brothel-keeper and four members of the Civic Regulators. However, they made no attempt to address the outlaws. Lurching away from the table, Lovey accompanied Messnick across the room in the direction of the main entrance. O'Day sensed that the quartet at the table had expected a more aggressive response to the small Texan's challenge.

Walking slowly, the men exchanged quick glances and nods. Their hands had stolen surreptitiously to the butts of their holstered weapons. Suddenly they sprang away from each other, turning and jerking out their weapons. On another occasion, they had employed a similar strategy and escaped arrest at the hands of three lawmen. Neither expected too much difficulty in dealing with two young cowhands.

Just an instant too late, Lovey and Messnick discovered that their strategy had failed to take their proposed victims by surprise. Instead of giving his undivided attention to the Civic Regulators, that *big* Texan was watching *them*. His young companion – kid brother, by all accounts – no longer lounged against the door, but was standing erect and looking even more ready for trouble.

Knowing that his companion would take 'Ed Caxton' as his target, Messnick devoted attention to handling the 'younger brother'. The outlaw was the fastest man Waco had ever faced. So fast in fact, that he could have completed his draw and put a bullet into the youngster before Waco's lead struck home and prevented him. In fact, under the circumstances, Messnick's gun cracked ahead of Waco's Army Colt going off.

With his revolver lifting into line, Lovey saw the *big* blond Texan's hands crossing. The outlaw's last living impression was of flame erupting from the centre of his opponent's body. Before his mind could register the fact that Dusty had drawn and fired with both hands, two bullets sped his way. One passed through his good eye, the second puncturing the patch over his other eye and driving onwards into his head. So close had the shots been together that they formed into a single sound. Firing once as he pitched backwards, the bullet ending its flight harmlessly in the front of the bar, Lovey's body crashed through the batwing doors and on to the sidewalk beyond its portals.

Where Messnick set his faith in firing from waist high and by instinctive alignment, Waco had decided that the range was too great for accuracy by such a method. So the youngster had taken the necessary split-second to raise his Colt to shoulder level and use its sights. Messnick missed his only chance of survival. On the heels of his shot, the long barrelled Army Colt barked wickedly. Like Dusty, Waco shot for an instantaneous kill. His bullet centred neatly in the middle of the outlaw's forehead. Dropping his gun, Messnick twirled on his toes almost like a ballet dancer. He sprawled face down on the floor as his companion passed lifeless through the batwing doors.

'Sit still, gentlemen!' O'Day said, but the Cavalry Peacemaker that came into his hand and slanted towards the table made it more of an order than a polite request.

'That goes double for you, Rosie!' Emma warned, producing her revolver. 'You're so big I couldn't miss you.'

'Easy there!' Goldberg put in, sounding alarmed. 'We didn't know what they planned to do.'

That was true as far as it went. While the party at the table had not encouraged the outlaws in their actions, the subject for discussion had been that Messnick and Lovey should accompany a group of Hell citizens in an attempt to locate Emma's party. Having arrived without much money, the pair had been willing to go along. The return of the blonde and her friends had removed the need for the posse, which probably had been the cause of the two men's actions.

'How many *amigos* do they have?' Dusty demanded, holstering his Colts.

'N . . . None,' Goldberg answered. 'They came in alone.'

'Mister,' Dusty growled, adopting the character of Ed Caxton once more. 'Happen anybody takes up for them, I'll figure I've been lied to—'

'I assure you that they're not with any other visitors,' Goldberg declared pompously. 'We were surprised to see you back, Emma.'

'You mean you figured that Emma, Matt, Comanch' and me'd robbed Simmy's office and lit out?' Dusty challenged, nodding his approval as Waco crossed to check up on Messnick and look along the street.

'That was never suggested,' Youseman said, in a tone which implied it had been and believed.

'May I ask where you have been since it happened, Emma?' Connolly put in.

'Hunting for the money Hubert, Belle Starr and some of my gals stole,' the blonde replied, so sincerely that she might have been speaking the truth. 'Him and the girls grabbed Giselle while everybody was watching Starr and me tangling in the duelling basin. They made her open the boxes and cleared off with her and the money the gang leaders had left in Simmy's care.'

'The hostlers at the barn said you told them to have a wagon ready that morning, Ed,' Youseman remarked, almost apologetically.

'Sure I did,' Dusty agreed. 'Hubert had seen me, saying Emma wanted him to collect some supplies. I knew she used the wagon, so I told them to have it waiting for him.'

'How did you know about the robbery?' Goldberg inquired.

'Let's sit down and we'll explain everything,' Emma countered, going towards her usual chair.

For a moment Rosie Wilson remained seated. Then she shrugged and rose to select another place. Youseman joined Waco at the front doors and told the men, who had been attracted by the shooting, something of what had happened.

Having arranged for the bodies to be taken to his place, the undertaker returned to the table with Waco.

'You can thank Brother Matt here for what's happened,' Dusty commenced. 'He got to thinking why that explosion might have happened and headed for the barn—'

'I didn't want any of the gang leaders to guess what was up, so I made out's I was running afore the *Kweharehnuh* come, all riled over losing their bullets,' Waco interrupted, covering a point that Goldberg might have raised if he had recalled their conversation shortly before the youngster had taken his departure. 'When I saw the wagon'd gone, I headed after Brother Matt 'n' Comanch' 'n' told them what I reckoned'd happened.'

'We got the whole story out of Belle Starr,' Dusty continued. 'Hubert'd brought her in to help rob the mayor. That's why she'd started those two fights with Emma—'

'And, like a sucker, I let her!' the blonde put in, sounding convincingly angry. 'Still, I paid her back good before she died. Say. It's a pity we couldn't fetch her in for you and Doc, Happy. There was a good bounty on her head.'

'Did you catch up with Hubert?' Youseman inquired hurriedly, desirous of changing the subject and wondering if the blonde knew their secret or had only been guessing.

'We got him,' Dusty confirmed.

'Where is he?' Goldberg demanded.

'Dead, along with all the bitches who helped him!' Emma spat savagely. 'There's wasn't a bounty on them, so it wasn't any use us fetching them back.'

'There's fifty thousand dollars here,' Dusty went on, tapping the bulging left side of his shirt. 'The rest of the money's hidden—'

'It's what?' Youseman growled and his companions showed their indignation.

'Stashed away safe, friend,' Dusty repeated. 'We didn't know how you'd act when we came back, although we guessed what you'd have been thinking. So we concluded to make sure we got a hearing.'

'It's our money!' Goldberg spluttered.

'What didn't belong to the gang leaders was the Civic Improvement Fund,' Dusty corrected. 'Which last's no more *yours* than it was Simmy Lampart's.'

'That's true enough,' Goldberg admitted. 'But as a committee appointed to run Hell until a new mayor can be elected—'

'That's one problem you don't have any more,' Dusty interrupted. 'Mrs. Lampart's taking over as mayor, with Emma to help her.'

'Why should she!' Rosie Wilson yelled, starting to rise.

Emma scooped up the revolver which lay on the table before her and lined it at the bulky brothel-keeper. Looking from the muzzle to the blonde's face, Rosie sank down on to her chair again.

'Ben Columbo, Joey Pinter, the Smith boys and those two yacks who just got toted out of here're right good answers to *that*, ma'am,' Waco drawled. 'We sided Mayor Lampart against Basmanov's bunch and we'll stand by his widow.'

'Matt's put it as well as I could have,' Emma went on, laying down the Colt. 'Anything Giselle doesn't already know about the town, me, Ed or the boys can tell her.'

'Well—' Connolly began.

'What does exhumation mean, Doc?' Dusty asked quietly.

'Digging up a body for—' the doctor commenced.

'I thought it was something like that,' the small Texan admitted. 'They do say a whole heap of strange things've come to light through exhumations.'

'I've heard tell of graves being found empty when they was opened up,' Waco continued. ''Course, that wouldn't happen in our boothill, now would it?'

Worried glances passed between Connolly and Youseman. They had once been surgeons, experimenting in longevity. Needing human bodies upon which to work, they had begun by robbing graves. Requiring fresh blood and tissues to further their studies, they had solved their problem by murdering healthy patients. When news of their actions had leaked out, they had escaped on a wagon train of assorted fugitives gathered by Simeon Lampart.

The party's original intention had been to reach Mexico. Circumstances had permitted them to settle in the Palo Duro and make Hell a profitable proposition. Connolly and Youseman had developed a process for embalming the corpses of outlaws killed in the town. With the aid of

Lampart's contacts, the corpses had been taken to legitimate towns and the bounties collected on them.

Connolly and Youseman had believed that their secret was known to only four men. From what they had just heard, Emma, possibly Giselle and certainly the two Texans were a party to it. The pair were all too aware of what their fate would be if news of their activities should reach the outlaws in town.

'I think that Giselle would be an excellent mayor!' Youseman declared. 'And it'll save unpleasantness all round if we accept her.'

'That's true enough, Happy,' Crouch enthused. 'I'm for it.'

'So am I!' Goldberg hastened to declare.

Glancing around, Dusty held down a grin. After Lampart's body had been discovered, there had clearly been controversy over who should replace him as mayor. Unless Dusty missed his guess, two sets of former business associates were divided on the issue. He was also willing to bet that Goldberg's response, having come so quickly after Crouch's acceptance, stemmed from a desire to ingratiate himself with what would become a powerful faction in the town's affairs.

'What happened when the Indians learned that the ammunition shack had blown up?' the small Texan inquired, keeping his thoughts to himself.

'Ten Bears came to see us the next day,' Youseman replied. 'We tried to convince him that everything is still all right, but he's given us a warning. Either the next issue's made, or he'll run us out of the Palo Duro.'

'How long do we have?' Waco asked.

'They're coming for it tomorrow,' Goldberg replied. 'It's all right, we can make the issue. A few of us didn't think it was advisable for Lam – Simmy to hold the only supply. So we laid in a stock of our own.'

'So everything *is* all right,' Emma remarked.

'It is *now*,' Rosie Wilson answered, with a malicious grin. 'You see, Ten Bears wants the *full* handing-out ceremony. And that means he's expecting to see Giselle do her dance – then get sawn in half.'

CHAPTER ELEVEN

IT IS THEIR RIGHT TO KILL YOU

WALKING through the darkness, accompanied by Wolf Runner, the Kid looked at the large, open square of ground illuminated by four huge fires. Just as he had suspected on receiving an invitation to eat with Chief Ten Bears, the affair was not a small, informal family gathering, but a meeting with all the prominent members of the band.

The Kid had felt a pleasurable sense of nostalgia as he had accompanied Wolf Runner's party into the *Kweharehnuh* village shortly before sundown. Apart from the different medicine symbols on the panels of the conical, buffalo-hide *tipis* – the emphasis being on sketches of pronghorn antelope rather than bison – they might have been those of the *Pehnane* Comanche in whose care he had been raised and educated.

Warring against the nostalgia had been a growing sense of concern for the welfare of his *amigos*. There were aspects of *Nemenuh* life going on all around which had been cause for alarm to a man schooled in the ways of the People.

Women and *naivis*, girls of marriageable age, had gathered in laughing, chattering groups to make or mend clothing, repair sections of *tipi* walls, or prepare food. Several of the groups had been engaged in putting up supplies of jerked meat and pemmican – traditional rations for warriors, being nutritious and easily transported when away from the village on scouting, raiding, or fighting missions. Particularly the latter, when there would be little time to spare in hunting for fresh food.

There had been other, allied preparations being made, the Kid had observed. Despite Lampart's gift of repeating rifles and ammunition, the *Kweharehnuh* warriors clearly had no intention of allowing themselves to become completely dependent upon his bounty. Under the guidance of *tehnaps*, *tuivitis* had been sharpening the blades of knives and tomahawks. Two old men and a trio of Mexican boy-captives had sat before a *tipi*, busily fletching arrows to be added to a large number they had already equipped for use. The Kid had noticed that the barbed heads would be horizontal, instead of vertical, when fitted to the string of a bow. That meant they had been intended for use against a creature which stood erect on its hind legs, so that its rib cage was parallel to the ground. Such arrows were not designed to be discharged at whitetail deer, wapiti, buffalo nor pronghorn antelope.

Outside another *tipi* a *tehnap* had worked with unwavering attention. He had been packing pages ripped from a thick, looted Montgomery-Ward catalogue into the saucer-shaped interior of a round shield. Beyond the circle of dwellings, *tuivitsis* and *tuineps* – boys not yet old enough to be classed as warriors – practised with weapons, or at riding. They had been concentrating the latter on handling a bow from horseback and towards picking up a dismounted or injured companion at full gallop.

Taken individually, the various activities might have been harmless. Put together, they suggested that the bravehearts were planning a foray in strength. It might be launched against the white settlements beyond the Tule and Palo Duro country. Or the expedition could be aimed at an objective much closer to hand.

There was only one place in the latter category. The town of Hell.

While the rest of the party had headed for their respective *tipis*, or to leave their mounts with the horse-herders beyond the camp, Wolf Runner had escorted the Kid to the home of the *paria:vo*; the senior, or 'peace' chief of the band. The Texan's presence in the camp had attracted some attention, but none of the people had shown more than a casual interest in him. Certainly they had not displayed open hostility at the sight of a white man in their midst. Ten Bears had been courteous and had offered the visitor hospitality. As the grandson of a famous war leader, and a name warrior in his own right, *Cuchilo* rated a dance in his honour. So the invitation had been made and accepted.

Studying the scene before him, the Kid wondered if maybe he was making a mistake in trusting the *Kwehareh-nuh*. The faces of the onlookers showed no emotion as he passed through their ranks. Yet he sensed an undercurrent of restlessness which was not entirely caused by the prospect of a celebration. On the surface, however, everything seemed normal. Twelve chiefs and war leaders, all wearing their finest clothes, formed a semicircle around Ten Bears. The woman standing at the right of the *paria:vo* could only be *Pohawe*.

Although Ten Bears was nominally a 'peace' chief, responsible for the administration of the band's domestic and social affairs rather than being a leader in battle, he gave evidence of his earlier martial prowess. In his right hand, he held a seven foot long *bois d'arc* war lance with a spear-pointed, razor-sharp head and a cluster of eagle's feathers at its butt. Only the bravest of the *Nemenuh* carried a lance. Ten Bears, as the Kid knew, was one of the very few warriors to have been permitted the honour of retaining his weapon after his retirement from active, fighting life.

Thickset, though running a little to fat, the *paria:vo* was an impressive figure. There was nothing in his appearance to suggest that he might be a drunken degenerate, sucked into an alliance with the white man by a craving for whiskey. He was a tough old Comanche who had never seen the boundaries of a reservation. In his attire, only the gunbelt about his middle, with its holstered Army Colt and sheathed Green River fighting knife, was of paleface origin.

From the *paria:vo*, the Kid turned his eyes to the medicine woman. Tall and slim for a *Nemenuh*, *Pohawe* had short-cropped curly black hair with the part-line, trimmed down the middle, accentuated by vermilion. Her features looked more mulatto or quadroon than Comanche, for all their traditional adornment. Red lines ran above and below her eyelids, crossing at the corners. The insides of her ears were coloured bright red and a red-orange crescent had been carefully marked upon each cheek. Numerous bracelets and necklaces attested to her wealth as did the rest of her clothing. She wore a soft, pliable, muted-yellow buckskin blouse and skirt, covered with intricate beading designs and carrying luxurious fringes on the elbow-long sleeves and calf level hem. The joining of the blouse and skirt was concealed beneath a coyote-skin peplum bearing several geometric medallions of silver and trimmed with numerous bead-covered leather thongs. The moccasins on her feet had cost somebody much time and labour, being well-made and intricately decorated with still more beads.

Going closer, the Kid was conscious of the medicine woman's eyes raking him from head to toe. He was bareheaded and had donned a clean shirt and Levi's for the occasion. Carrying his Winchester in its boot across his left arm, he had his gunbelt buckled on. As a *Nemenuh*, he could – and was expected to – be armed when attending such a function. His saddle, bridle, bed roll and Stetson had been left in Wolf Runner's *tipi*, as he was classed as the chief's guest.

Pohawe's eyes left the Kid. Following the direction in which they gazed, he saw two *tehnap* in the forefront of the onlookers. They had buffalo-hide robes draped across their shoulders, but underneath wore nothing except their breechclouts and moccasins. Each held a tomahawk and a round shield. More significantly, they had war paint on their faces and torsos.

To the Kid, it seemed as if a message passed between *Pohawe* and the pair of braves; although no words had actually been spoken. However, the social courtesies had to be carried out. He came to a halt and raised his right hand in the palm forward salute which was also a sign of peace. As a guest, it was his place to speak first – especially in the presence of older, respected members of his host's band.

'Greetings, medicine woman; *Paruwa Semenho*, friend of my grandfather, Long Walker of the Quick Stingers; and chiefs of the *Kweharehnuh*,' the Kid said, in the slow-tongued accent of a *Pehnane*. 'I come in peace to your camp.'

Apart from the speaker being dressed and armed like a white man, there was nothing unusual in his arrival. Any Comanche warrior could expect to be made welcome in the village of another band. A noted war leader like Long Walker would assume that his only grandson was obliged to pay a courtesy visit to the chief of the *Kweharehnuh* while in the Palo Duro.

'Greetings to you, *Cuchilo*, grandson of my old friend,' Ten Bears answered. 'You will sit with us and eat?'

'My thanks to you, *paria:vo*,' the Kid assented, adopting the half-mocking, half-respectful tone with which a lusty, active young *tehnap* addressed a person who might rank high in social prominence, but who was – in the warrior's opinion – no longer of great importance.

A grin twisted at Ten Bears' lips as he caught the inflexion in the Kid's voice. *Cuchilo* might now live with the white people, but he still thought, spoke and acted like a Comanche.

'Did you also come in peace when you fought with the blue-coat soldiers against Kills Something and braves from this band?' *Pohawe* demanded, speaking loudly enough for her words to reach the ears of the assembled people.

'I did,' the Kid confirmed. 'They were my friends and I was riding with them. So I fought.'

There would have been no point in the Kid trying to conceal the part he had played during the fighting in which the war leader, Kills Something, had died. The survivors of the affray – which had been a prelude to the floating outfit's assignment in Hell – were certain to have told the story of their defeat. It was inconceivable that they would have omitted to mention the man who had played a major role in their downfall. The Comanche had admiration for a shrewd, brave and capable fighting man; but nothing except contempt for a liar.

'You say you are *Nemenuh*,' *Pohawe* went on, clearly directing her words to the crowd as much as to the Kid. 'And yet you helped the soldier-coats to kill our braves.'

'I am a man of two people,' the Kid countered. 'And, as I was riding a war trail with white men, I fought alongside them.'

'No man can be loyal to two peoples, *Cuchilo*,' *Pohawe* warned.

'Who are *you* loyal to, medicine woman?' the Kid challenged.

From the expression on *Pohawe*'s face, the barb had gone home. The Kid felt that he had scored a point of dubious value. As the daughter of an unimportant, not-too-successful warrior and his mulatto captive-wife, she had risen high in the band's society. There were many who resented her position of influence. So she objected to any drawing of attention to her mixed blood. Even if she had not been the Texan's enemy before, she was now.

'Some of our brave-hearts were killed!' *Pohawe* gritted.

'And some of the men I rode with,' the Kid reminded her. 'They all died with honour and as true warriors.'

This time the Kid knew that he had made a telling point. Like all Indians, the Comanches set great store by a man dying well and with honour.

'My son died in that fight, *Cuchilo*,' one of the 'old man' chiefs remarked. 'You had dealt with him as a *tehnap* with a *tuivitsi* earlier.'

'I remember him,' the Kid admitted, thinking of the young warrior whom he had taught a lesson in manners. 'He died well, attacking us and helped others to escape without hurt.'

That was not entirely the truth, the *tuivitsi* having been stupidly reckless before meeting his end. However, it helped an old warrior's grief to hear such words. The Kid had made a friend.

'Those two men, Charging Wapiti and Came With The Thunder, had a brother at the fight,' *Pohawe* announced, indicating the pair of warriors to whom she had signalled on the Kid's arrival. 'They claim you for his death. It is their right to kill you.'

'It is *my* right to die fighting,' the Kid pointed out. 'I am a *Pehnane* Dog Soldier and I have never gone against my oath to my war lodge. I am sworn to die with a weapon in my hand.'

'A fair fight, Ten Bears!' boomed Wolf Runner, who had stood at the Kid's side through the conversation. '*Cuchilo* came here as my guest. If Charging Wapiti and Came With The Thunder want blood, let them come singly.'

Going by the low rumble of approval which rose from the onlookers, the war leader's words had their support. A *paria:vo* was always a shrewd politician and, as such, Ten Bears knew better than to fly in the face of public opinion.

'A fair fight it will be,' the 'peace' chief declared. 'What weapons will you use, Charging Wapiti?'

Shrugging off his robe, the taller, heavier of the pair stalked forward. He raised the shield and tomahawk into the air.

'These!'

That was caution, for the brothers had heard of *Cuchilo*'s deadly skill with a rifle.

'I'm sorry for your brother's death, *tehnap*,' the Kid declared, handing his rifle to Wolf Runner. 'You have no guns, so neither will I.'

With that, the Texan unfastened and removed his shirt. Passing it to the war leader, he untied the pigging thongs holding the tip of his holster to his thigh and unbuckled the gunbelt. Sliding out the bowie knife, he let Wolf Runner take the belt. As the Kid was about to move forward, the 'old man' chief who had asked for information rose. Advancing, he offered the shield which had been resting on his knees.

'Take this, *Cuchilo*,' the chief suggested, ignoring the disapproving scowl which *Pohawe* directed at him.

'My thanks,' answered the Kid, conscious that he had been paid a great honour. 'May it serve me as well as it always served you.'

Made from the shoulder hide of an old bull buffalo, heated and steamed until contracted to the required thickness, then pounded and rubbed with a smooth stone to remove every wrinkle, the shield was about two feet in diameter. The space between the separate layers of hide had been packed tight with feathers, hair, or possibly paper, which would deaden the impact from arrows or blows by other weapons. A pliant buckskin cover had been stretched over the convex outer face and laced into position by thongs which passed through holes around the edges. A dozen or so long, flowing feathers were secured to the rim of the outer sheath; and not merely for decoration. Also affixed were the teeth from a Texas flat-headed grizzly bear, indicating that its owner was a mighty hunter. The painted scalps below them told that he was also a famous warrior.

While the chief was making his loan to the Kid, Came With The Thunder discarded his robe and joined his elder brother. The *tuivitsi* whispered in the *tehnap*'s ear, glancing towards the Texan. At first Charging Wapiti appeared to disagree with what was said, then he nodded and gave some advice. Having done so, the *tehnap* advanced a few strides as if eagerly waiting for the duel to commence.

'I don't want this fight, *Paruwa Semenho*, chiefs and people of the *Kweharehnuh*,' the Kid announced, as the chief returned to his place in the semicircle. 'But it has been forced on me and I will do all I can to win.'

With that, the Texan slipped his left arm through the two stout rawhide loops fixed to the concave inner side of the shield and drew them to either side of his elbow. Moving his arm a few times, he tested the weight and balance of the shield. He gripped the bowie knife in the fashion of a white man, or a Mexican, with the blade extended ahead of his thumb and forefinger.

Experienced eyes took in the way the concave swoop of the false edge met the convex curve of the cutting surface, exactly in the centre of the eleven and a half inch long, two and a half inch wide clip-pointed blade. That was a fighting knife second to none and its owner handled it like a master.

One question was in every warrior's mind. Would the unfamiliar shield be a liability or an asset to *Cuchilo*?

'You insist on your right, Charging Wapiti?' Ten Bears asked formally.

'We do,' the *tehnap* agreed. 'While that one lives, our brother cannot rest easily in the Land Of The Good Hunting.'

'You hear, *Cuchilo*?' the *paria:vo* inquired.

'I hear, *Paruwa Semenho*,' the Kid answered. 'And I say to all who can hear, Ten Bears is not to blame whichever way this fight comes out.'

While speaking, the Kid had turned to the chiefs. He saw Ten Bears give a nod of satisfaction and approval. The fight that was to come might be justified under Comanche law, but it was well that there could be no cause for complaint from Long Walker. Maybe the *Pehnane* were eating the white brother's beef on the reservation, but the Dog Soldiers had long since established a reputation for being quick to avenge any insult or injury to other members of their lodge. The Kid had absolved Ten Bears of all blame in the affair.

Swinging to meet the first of his attackers, the Kid saw that they had separated. Charging Wapiti crouched slightly, as if preparing to attack. Loud into the silence that had fallen rang a *Kweharehnuh* scalp-yell. It did not come from the *tehnap*'s lips. Instead, the younger brother sprang forward from the Kid's right side.

Although Came With The Thunder had been supposed to be launching an unsuspected, surprise attack, he had committed an error in tactics. Young and inexperienced, he could not resist the temptation to give his war cry before charging at his enemy.

There was no time for the Kid to gain the feel of the shield. Fortunately it was of the same general size, shape and weight as those he had been trained to use and with which he had practised when visiting his grandfather. Pure fighting instinct triggered off an almost automatic response to the assault.

Pivoting to meet the charge, the Kid saw the *tuivitsi*'s tomahawk hissing towards his head. Throwing up the shield, he realized that it had gone too high and was too perpendicular to cause the blow to strike at an angle and glance off. There was no time to make alterations – and no need. The sharp cutting edge of the war axe thudded against the centre of the shield. Meeting the flint-hard, yet resilient cover, it rebounded harmlessly.

Like a flash, the Kid swooped his knife around for a low thrust at Came With The Thunder's body. The *tuivitsi* dropped his shield deftly, deflecting the bowie knife downwards and to its user's left. Allowing the bottom edge of the shield to slide along the back of the blade, until halted by the outwards turn of the guard's recurved quillon, the Kid angled his weapon upwards. Doing so locked the shield between the back of the blade and the quillon. Helped by the leverage of the quillon's inwards bend against the lower phalenge of his forefinger, the Kid raised the blade and shield.

A sudden reversal of direction drew the bowie knife free when it was level with the *tuivitsi*'s shoulder. Shock twisted momentarily at Came With The Thunder's face as realization of his predicament struck him. Nor, if the exclamations which arose on all sides were anything to go on, had the precariousness of his situation escaped the onlookers' attention.

Down and to the left flashed the bowie knife, its cutting

edge tearing a shallow gash across the *tuivitsi*'s exposed chest. Gasping in pain, Came With The Thunder fell back a pace and left himself wide open. Even if doing so would have availed him anything – for the youngster was pledged to kill him and would have continued with the attempts to carry out the oath – the Kid could not have halted his movements. Inherited, age-old instincts guided what was practically a subconsciously directed reflex action. At the lowest point of its stroke, the bowie knife altered its course. Coming up, it raked the false edge – honed as sharp as the cutting surface itself – to its target. Blood burst from the terrible wound as the bowie knife laid the *tuivitsi*'s throat open to the bone.

Spinning around, dropping his tomahawk and allowing the shield to slip unheeded from his left arm, Came With The Thunder sprawled face down on the ground in front of the chiefs. Even with his blood racing in the savage exultation of having emerged victorious from a primitive conflict, the Kid did not growl out the coup claim, '*A:he!*' No Comanche would think of counting coup if circumstances forced him to strike down another member of the *Nemenuh*.

Having watched his brother tumble, spewing out life's blood on to the turf underfoot, Charging Wapiti attacked. There was no warning this time. He moved in silence, but was not entirely unexpected. The *tuivitsi*'s trick had warned the Kid what to expect. From delivering his killing stroke, the Texan whirled to face his second assailant. One glance told him that he would be meeting a far different, more dangerous antagonist. Instead of duplicating his brother's wild, announced rush, the *tehnap* glided forward in the manner of an experienced warrior. He would not allow anger, or over-confidence, to lure him into rashness.

For a few seconds, the Kid and Charging Wapiti circled and studied each other. They held their shields before them at chest level, ready to be raised or lowered as the need arose. Each carried his assault weapon in the manner suited to its specialized requirements. While the *tehnap* held his tomahawk's head upwards and out to the right, to be used for sideways or downwards chopping blows, the Kid kept his knife so that he could aim for the torso with a thrust, cut, or the savage hacking slash for which the James Black bowie was perfectly adapted.

Although the *tehnap* was slightly heavier, there would be little difference in their weights. Any advantage that the Kid gained from his height and greater reach was to some extent nullified by the tomahawk's sixteen inch long, tapering from one-and-a-half to one inch diameter shaft.

While watching for the opportunity to attack, Charging Wapiti made circling motions with his left arm. That set the feathers fringing his shield rippling and ruffling in a manner calculated to bewilder the Kid's eyes and conceal its wielder's purpose. For his part, the Kid knew that he could not hope to match Charging Wapiti's skill in manipulating a shield. So he contented himself with watching and waiting. If he hoped to escape with his life, he must fight on the defensive until presented with a chance to change things.

With a yell, the *tehnap* bounded forward. He swung his shield to the left, striking at the Kid's in the hope of knocking it aside. Just in time, the Texan turned his arm, so that the shields met face to face instead of his being struck on the side.

Leaning on the *tehnap*, the Kid tried to keep them close. In that way, he would be inside the swing of the tomahawk, but could use the point of his knife. Even as the great blade drove upwards and under the shields, Charging Wapiti sensed the danger and flung himself away. As he went, he swung his tomahawk towards the Kid's head. Thwarted in his intentions, the Texan protected himself. Feathers flew as the Kid's shield rose and halted the war-axe.

Around the two men circled, with Charging Wapiti initiating further attacks and the Kid defending. Such was each's speed of reactions and body movements, as well as with the shields, that neither could blood his weapon on the other. Yet both of them had narrow escapes. Once the Kid mistimed a block with his shield. Twisting his body like an eel in a trap, he carried himself clear of the tomahawk's downwards chop. A few seconds later, having had a side cut parried, the *tehnap* found his belly once more in peril from the Kid's hook upwards with the clip-pointed knife. He was saved by a rapid jump to the rear.

Soon after, with the breath hissing through his parted lips, the Kid was granted a desperate chance. Also showing signs of the strain, Charging Wapiti had kept up a continuous, yet unavailing attack. Drawing away slightly, the *tehnap* flung himself bodily at the Texan. The shields met face to face with a solid crack. To the *tehnap* and the onlookers, it seemed that the impact had knocked the Kid staggering.

Letting out his scalp-yell, Charging Wapiti followed up his advantage and put all he had into a roundhouse swing aimed at the side of his enemy's neck. The Kid extended his left foot as far to the rear as he could take it, bending his right knee and resting the shield on the ground for added support. That carried him under the arc of the other's blow. Instantly, the Kid struck in the manner of an *epee* fencer delivering a low lunge. Carried forward by his impetus, the *tehnap* met the bowie knife's point. Charging Wapiti's weight combined with the Kid's thrust to sink the blade hilt deep in his belly. Forcing himself erect, the Kid tore his knife free and the *tehnap* went down.

CHAPTER TWELVE

YOU WON'T SHOOT ME, MADAM

ALTHOUGH Emma Nene knew that her stay in the town would be limited, she felt completely at home in the barroom of her saloon. With Dusty Fog and Waco to her right and left, she sat on the chair she had always occupied at her private table. The half a dozen gang leaders currently visiting Hell, together with Crouch, Goldberg and Connolly were the blonde's guests. All things considered, the slight air of tension was understandable.

There had been a lengthy, although on the whole amicable discussion that afternoon. All the town's major citizens had assembled and the same gang leaders had arrived on hearing of Emma's party's return. Once again the blonde had told her story, being ably backed by Giselle. The little brunette had confirmed the details and added others which only she, as the 'victim' of a kidnapping plot, could have known.

Maybe the story would not have received credence but for two factors. If the women and the Texans had stolen money for their own ends, they would have been unlikely to return. That aspect had been mentioned and accepted. The second item went unsaid; but nobody wanted to cast doubts with 'Ed Caxton' and his 'brother Matt', hovering close at hand. None of the audience had even offered to inquire why the two Texans had taken the trouble to shave off their beards during the time spent away from Hell.

Of course, things might not have gone so smoothly if the various gang leaders and other depositors in Lampart's 'bank' had been the losers out of the robbery. Faced with the threat of the outlaws going on the rampage, to recoup their looted money, the people of the town had formed a pot and paid them off in full. So what would have been the most

119

dangerous element of opposition, the visiting fugitives from justice, had seen no reason to cross trails or lock horns with a pair of deadly efficient gun-fighters like the 'Caxtons'.

Having accepted that any hostile moves would have to be carried out by themselves, the townspeople had been inclined to accept Emma's story. With that decision made, the two factions had vied with each other for gaining the support of the blonde's party. All had given their agreement to Giselle assuming her dead husband's duties, with the proviso that she allowed the committee to audit and have access to the Civic Improvement Fund on its return. Dusty and the women had agreed, promising that they would collect the 'buried money' on the morning after the allocation of the ammunition to the *Kweharehnuh*.

Eventually the meeting had broken up, with everybody apparently on the best of terms. One jarring note, soon ended, had come when Emma had ordered Rosie Wilson to quit the saloon and take her employees along. However, finding that she no longer commanded support in her claims to ownership, the brothel-keeper had yielded to the inevitable and obeyed.

The saloon's original staff had shown their delight at finding Emma re-established as their boss. Setting to work willingly, they had given the building a thorough cleaning. By sundown, the Honest Man had once more become the elegant, well-run place it had always been under the blonde's guidance.

To prevent the chance of smoke rising and giving away the location of the town, there was a strictly-enforced ruling that no fires could be lit in the daytime. So Hell did not come to full life until after darkness had made possible the cooking of food. Several outlaws had pulled out following the destruction of the ammunition, to avoid the wrath of the *Kweharehnuh* which they had felt was sure to come. There were still a number of visitors and business at the saloon was satisfactory.

'Will Giselle be joining us?' Goldberg inquired, glancing at the stairs which led to the first floor.

'I don't think so,' Emma replied. 'She said that she intended to take a bath and grab some sleep.'

Although the mayor's home had been ransacked after the

discovery of Lampart's body, it had still been habitable. However, the little brunette had been vehement in her refusal to stay there. In the interests of peace and quiet, Emma had agreed to let Giselle share her quarters above the Honest Man's barroom. The blonde had felt that she was acting for the best. Knowing her half-sister very well, Emma did not trust her and preferred to have her under observation.

'We'll be able to put on the usual show for Ten Bears tomorrow?' Crouch asked after a moment.

'Well, Giselle says that the box's all right as far as she can tell,' the blonde answered. 'The trouble is that she's got nobody to help her. She says that it needs somebody who knows the trick.'

'And none of us knows it!' Connolly breathed, darting a nervous glance around the table. 'Damn it! I always knew somebody should have learned how to do it from Simmy.'

'They did,' Emma announced calmly.

'Who?' demanded the three townsmen, all in the same breath.

'Me,' the blonde told them and sat back, enjoying the sensation she had created. 'Simmy taught me how and we had something rigged between us in case he wasn't able to do it for any reason.'

'None of us knew that,' Crouch said in an aggrieved tone.

'We never needed for me to do it before,' Emma pointed out. 'Hey. Where's Happy? Don't tell me that he's embalming those two yahoos Ed and Matt killed?'

'Embalming?' Goldberg put in, throwing a puzzled look from the blonde to Connolly.

'Isn't that what an undertaker does when he's getting a body ready to be buried?' Emma asked, oozing innocence. 'You boys'll never believe it, but I had one as an admirer back East. I didn't know how he earned his living, mind, and when I found out, I dropped him fast.'

'He's probably at Rosie's,' Crouch commented. 'Happy, I mean, not your undertaker friend from the East, Emma.'

'She can probably use the business,' the blonde smiled, hoping that the dangerous subject would drop. 'The damned nerve of that woman, trying to take over my place.'

'There were some who agreed that she should,' Crouch replied.

'Are you hinting at something?' Goldberg demanded indignantly, seeing the jeweller's words as an attempt to undermine himself with the blonde's faction. 'I didn't hear *you* objecting to it.'

'Shucks, you boys weren't to know what had happened,' Emma smiled, satisfied that her slip of the tongue had been laid aside, if not forgotten. 'Rosie always was a pushy woman. Let's have a drink to the future prosperity of Hell. And this one's on me.'

Wearing nothing but a pair of long john underpants, Emmet Youseman sat nursing a naked, pretty brunette employee of Rosie Wilson's brothel. There was a partially filled glass in his hand and an almost empty bottle of whiskey on the dressing-table, which along with the bed and a chair, formed the small room's furnishings. Male and female clothes lay in an untidy pile on the floor, discarded by the couple on their arrival earlier in the evening.

The girl had long since become adept at persuading her customers to drink more than was good for them, while remaining sober herself. That night she had paid an even greater attention to her task, for she had been given orders by her employer. However, despite being very far gone in liquor, Youseman still showed no inclination of giving her the required information.

'You've got a fine mammary protuberance there, Peggy,' the undertaker announced with drunken gravity, his free hand jiggling one of her jutting breasts. 'Let'sh go 'n' lie down so I can examine it some more.'

'Aw, Happy,' the girl protested. 'You was telling me how you and Doc Connolly took care of them dead fellers. What'd you need Doc there for, seeing's they was both of 'em dead?'

'Huh?' grunted Youseman and finished his drink with a single gulp. 'Why, that'sh a she ... she-cret, Peggy.'

'Gee, Happy,' the girl protested, knowing that he was fast approaching the point where he would collapse in a drunken stupor. 'It's not right that you keep secrets from lil ole me.'

'I shuppose-sh not,' Youseman muttered, still fondling the breast. 'You ... a good girl, Peggy. Only that miserable old bash ... my esteemed and respected partner ... Isn't he the most mish-erable old bash-tard you've ever met?'

'Sure he is,' Peggy agreed. 'And he's not worth keeping any ole secret for, is he?'

'No, shiree,' the undertaker mumbled, lurching to his feet and letting the girl slide from his lap. 'Le'sh go bed 'n' I tell.'

An angry curse broke from Peggy's lips as she watched the burly undertaker staggering unevenly across the room. All too well she recognized the symptoms and knew that her boss would gain no further information that night. Falling heavily on to the bed, Youseman lay snorting like a pig as he dropped into an unassailable drunken sleep. Obviously Rosie Wilson had been eavesdropping at the door. Its drapes jerked open and the woman entered.

'The drunken, useless pig!' the big woman snarled, crossing to the bed and delivering a stinging slap to Youseman's face.

'It wasn't my fault!' Peggy yelped, wishing to exculpate herself. 'You know he never talks about anything important until he's nearly ready to go under from the drink.'

'I know,' Rosie confirmed. 'Get dressed and go out front. There're some fellers wanting company and a roll in the hay. What you make, you can keep.'

'Gee, thanks, Rosie!' the girl enthused and started to sort out her clothes.

While the girl dressed, not a lengthy affair, Rosie searched the undertaker's pockets. The woman let out a low hiss of excitement as she produced two door-keys.

'Leave him sleep here,' Rosie commanded, not troubling to hide her excitement at the find. 'Maybe you'd better stay with him and make sure he doesn't leave if he wakes.'

'Aw, Rosie—!' Peggy began, seeing her chance of a fee slipping away.

'I'll cover what you'd've made from those fellers,' the brothel-keeper promised. 'And mind you keep your mouth shut about this.'

'You can count on it,' the girl assured her employer's departing back.

Going through the customer's lounge at the front of the building, Rosie entered and locked the connecting door of her private office. At her desk, she produced a Smith & Wesson No. 3 American revolver and bull's-eye lantern. Setting them down with the two keys, she collected and donned the long black cloak which hung on a hook behind the parlour's door. After lighting the lantern, but covering its lens, she left by the side entrance. Peering cautiously around, she made her way between the *jacales* and towards the rear of the undertaker's place of business.

Rosie had often suspected that Youseman and Connolly were involved in clandestine activities outside, yet in some way connected with, their respective lines of employment. Previously, when very drunk, the undertaker had hinted as much; but had always avoided saying exactly what they might be. Having noticed how the pair had reacted that afternoon to the comments of Emma Nene and the Caxton brothers about exhumations, her suspicions had grown even stronger.

Actually, the two men's behaviour had merely strengthened the brothel-keeper's theory of what their activities might be. One earlier attempt to unearth it — literally as well as figuratively — had come to nothing. The man she had sent — an impoverished outlaw — to open up a grave had been shot by somebody who had seen him about to commence his work. While Rosie's part in the affair had not been detected, she had come no closer to solving the mystery.

Still trying to obtain knowledge which might have proven profitable, the woman had ordered Peggy to try to worm it from Youseman. On every occasion, he had fallen into a drunken sleep without yielding his secret. While he had always carried the key to his premises' rear door, it had availed Rosie nothing. It had given her access only to his living quarters. Her searches of them had not produced the means of entering the building's business section. With the second key in her possession, she hoped to be able to carry her investigations into the previously protected regions.

If the secret had been sufficiently important — or potentially dangerous — to make Connolly and Youseman instantly compliant with the demands of the saloon-keeper and the Texans, it ought to be worth the effort taken to learn it. Rosie had never rated high on the town's social scale. The other citizens, no matter how loathsome the crimes which had driven them to Hell, had always tended to look down on her. Having access to information that would put the two men under her domination would go far towards changing the situation.

Entering Youseman's establishment, the woman tried the second key in the lock on the inner door. It worked and she passed through into the laying-out room.

Earlier that day, the bodies of the Texans' victims had been displayed there in their coffins for anybody who wished to come and pay their last respects. Rosie had been one of the few to attend and had watched the lids of the coffins screwed firmly into place. Although Youseman had ushered her and a couple more mourners out into the waiting carriage, he would not have had time to unscrew the lids and remove the bodies before the coffins were carried from the room and into the hearse.

Frowning, Rosie directed the beam of her lantern on to the sturdy bench upon which the coffins were always placed for the last visits. She saw nothing at first and its stout wooden front prevented her from looking underneath. Then her attention was attracted by a slightly protruding knot in the timber. She pressed and felt it give, but nothing else happened. Still certain that she was on the verge of making a discovery, she began to press the top of the bench where one of the coffins had been resting. Silently, but smoothly, an oblong section of the top hinged down from its further narrow end. It was only down for a few seconds and rose again of its own volition.

Pressing again, Rosie directed the beam of her lantern into the cavity. It illuminated a section of the building's basement and another bench immediately below her. Hardened as she might be, Rosie could not hold back a startled gasp; nor resist withdrawing hurriedly. The trapdoor closed automatically.

But not before Rosie had seen the two vaguely human forms, swathed in tarpaulin, which lay on the basement's bench.

'So that's what your game is, huh!' Rosie breathed. 'Now we'll see who's so high and mighty.'

Making sure that she left no traces of her visit, the woman walked from the laying-out room. Having locked both doors behind her, she stepped warily away from the building. Give them their due, Youseman and Connolly had come up with a real smart way of retaining possession of bodies. Nobody who had seen the coffin's lid secured would have suspected that its bottom opened and deposited the corpse into the basement. Those Chinese labourers brought in by Li Chin of the Oriental Laundry – and once a prominent Tong leader, who had been put on the run after a race war – would have built the basement. Probably Simeon Lampart was the designer of the trap-doors. A scheme such as the two men were carrying out could only have succeeded with the mayor's assistance and authority.

Rosie could not decide just to what purpose she could put her knowledge. Yet she felt certain that she could reap some advantage from it. Even if the two men were of no use, the outlaw leaders might find the information interesting.

Wanting time to think out a line of action, she strolled along the rear of the buildings flanking the main street. She continued to move cautiously, keeping to the shadows. Hinges squeaked and a cloaked and hooded figure emerged furtively from the back door of the combined barber's shop and bath-house. Beyond guessing that the shape was feminine and small, Rosie could gain no clue to its identity.

Giving a shrug, Rosie walked slowly on. Since the death of its owner, the barber's shop had been kept in operation by his assistant. The brothel-keeper had never considered that the young man would make a worth-while ally. So she felt little interest in his private affairs. She would have strolled straight by the open door, but a male voice from the darkened interior reached her ears.

'You acted in a stupid manner, my gauche young friend. Only a fool would have believed the story she told to you and trusted her. I'll admit that she is very easy to believe and trust. I did so once myself. Well, you are dead. But the price you have paid for your folly was, I think, less than mine.'

Hearing footsteps approaching the door, Rosie looked around. The female visitor had already gone from sight and there did not appear to be any other witnesses in the vicinity. If murder had been done, which seemed likely going by what she had heard, she might be able to turn a profit out of it. The voice had been that of an educated man, an Easterner, yet not one she recognized. If it should be one of the citizens, the possibilities of blackmail were worth Rosie taking a few chances.

Raising and cocking her Smith & Wesson, she pointed it at the doorway. At the same time she levelled the bull's-eye lantern ready for use. A tall shape materialized before her, coming to a halt on catching sight of the woman.

'Don't move, feller!' Rosie commanded, flicking open the front of the lantern. 'I'll shoot if you do.'

As far as the brothel-keeper could discern, the shape in the doorway was male. He had on a top hat, from beneath which long, reddish hair flowed to disappear beneath the black cloak which his left arm held up in front of his face.

'Good evening,' the man greeted politely, without offering to lower the cloak. 'And a pleasant one—'

'Put your arm down so I can see your face,' Rosie interrupted.

'I would rather you didn't see it,' answered the man.

'That's likely, but I aim to,' Rosie replied, a little scared by his attitude and the glint in the hollow eyes which showed between the top of the cloak and the brim of the high hat. 'Damn you, I'll sh . . .'

'You won't shoot me, madam,' the man declared and carried out her order.

Instantly Rosie stiffened and her face showed horror at what had been exposed to the lantern's light. The man's right hand emerged from the folds of the cloak. It held a Remington Double Deringer. Even as Rosie's mouth opened to let out a shriek of terror, flame blossomed from the little gun's uppermost barrel. Hit below the left breast by the .41 calibre bullet, the woman reeled and the lantern's glow flickered away from the man's face. Rosie fired once, the revolver sounding loudly and driving its load into the side of the building harmlessly. Again the man's pistol spat and the second ball ploughed its way into the staggering woman's body. She dropped the lantern and the Smith & Wesson, crumpling down herself. From the street, shouts sounded and feet thudded as people came to investigate the shooting.

'I said I'd rather not show you my face,' the man commented and turned to stride away into the darkness.

Five minutes later, Dusty Fog knelt at the stricken woman's side. Connolly had done what little he could to save her, but he had warned the small Texan that she would not last much longer.

On his arrival, accompanied by members of the Civic Regulators, Dusty had taken charge of the affair. Leaving Connolly to attend to the woman, the small Texan, Waco, Goldberg and Crouch had entered the barber's shop. They found its new owner sprawled face down on the floor in the living quarters. He was dead, knifed through the heart. There had been no signs of a struggle, nor anything to suggest why he had been killed.

From his examination of the outside, Dusty had concluded that Rosie surprised the killer rather than being the guilty party herself. She had no knife on her, nor had one been found in the vicinity. The lantern and the Smith & Wesson revolver with one chamber discharged had given strength to his theory. So he wanted, if possible, to learn what the woman had seen.

'Did you know the man who shot you, ma'am?' Dusty asked gently.

'M...Man...!' Rosie answered, turning agony-distorted features to the small Texan. 'H...His...f...face...'

'What about it?' Dusty prompted in the same quiet tone.

'H...He...didn't...have...a...face...!' the woman almost shrieked. Blood burst from her mouth, her body was convulsed briefly and then went limp.

CHAPTER THIRTEEN

MY MEDICINE WILL STRIKE YOU DOWN

SPREAD-EAGLED back downwards, with wrists and ankles secured to stakes driven firmly into the ground, the Ysabel Kid peered through the gloom towards the conical roof of the tipi above him. He was forced to admit that he could only blame himself for his present predicament. Which did not make him feel any better about being in it.

Having ended the second duel, he had known that he could not stay longer in the *Kweharehnuhs'* village. Not only did convention demand that he should leave, but he had felt sure that *Pohawe* would make other attempts to remove him if he stayed. For some reason or other, the woman wanted him dead. So, having no wish to be forced into more duels or to be poisoned by *Pohawe* if she could not find further challengers, he had announced his departure.

Understanding at least part of the Kid's motives, and approving of them, Ten Bears had given his consent for the Texan to leave. However, the dance had not been cancelled. It was to continue, even though its guest-of-honour would no longer be present. From comments the Kid had heard passed during the afternoon, the allocation of ammunition was to take place the following day. That too had been an inducement to continue with the celebrations.

While collecting his property from Wolf Runner's *tipi*, the Kid had heard enough to warn him that the allocation might not be peaceful. The braves started chanting the words of the *Kweharehnuh* war song, then a warrior had interrupted the singing to recount the story of his greatest, bravest deed. Taken with all he had seen earlier, the Kid had known that he must not delay in taking a warning to Dusty. Unless the allocation went off without a hitch, the braves would commence an attack.

The Kid had been struck down and captured on the outskirts of the village. Hurtling from a *tipi*'s entrance, an all-but naked brave had tackled him around the knees. Before he could resist, three more had pounced upon him. The back of a tomahawk's head had collided with his skull and he had known no more until recovering in what his nose had warned was the *tipi* of the medicine woman.

Going by the reduced volume of noise from the dance, the *tipi* was situated some distance from the village. That figured. A medicine man or woman often set up an establishment well clear of other human habitations, to permit a greater secrecy and increased freedom to carry out his, or her, duties.

The Kid was alone in the *tipi*, but he knew that it did not greatly enhance his chances of escape. Having already tested the strength and security of his bonds, he knew that he could achieve little or nothing against them. A slow and painful death lay ahead for him – and for many of the people at Hell – if he could not regain his freedom.

A memory stirred at the back of the Kid's mind, prodded into life by his realization of where he was being held prisoner. On the night before he had ridden away on his first war trail – to join the Confederate States' Army – he had been visited by the *Pehnanes*' respected senior medicine woman. She had been the midwife who had attended his birth and had subsequently taken a great interest in his welfare and career.

'If you are ever in medicine trouble, *Cuchilo*,' she had said. 'Call on me no matter where you are and I will help you.'

Well, the Kid figured that he could say he was in medicine trouble. Just about as deep and dangerous as a *Pehnane tehnap* could get. Relaxing as much as his bonds would permit, he turned his eyes towards the apex of the *tipi*.

'Raccoon Talker!' he gritted, from deep down in his chest. '*Cuchilo* needs your help!'

Again and again he repeated the words, while sweat bathed his face and soaked his clothes. If there had been a witness present and able to see, he would have been amazed at the strain of concentration showing on the babyishly innocent dark brown face.

Close to four hundred miles away, at the reservation agent's home on the lower slopes of Mount Scott in the Indian Nations, two thrilled, middle-aged white women were having their fortunes told by a genuine Comanche medicine woman.

Carefully selected for his post, liked, respected and trusted by the Comanche bands under his care, Agent Stanley Beckers was not the kind of man to allow exploitation of his charges. That he had given permission for Raccoon Talker to see the women was a tribute on his part to the man who had made the request. Few white men could have persuaded Long Walker, now *paria:vo* of the *Pehnane* band, to ask such a favour of the medicine woman. Stocky, bearded, almost Comanche in build, the rancher, who wore a vest made from the hide of a cattle-killing jaguar that had raided his herds, was such a man. His name was Charles Goodnight.

In addition to showing a pair of influential Eastern cattle-buyers some excellent sport and hunting, Goodnight had found himself faced with the task of entertaining their wives. Being close to the Comanche reservation, he had visited his old friend Long Walker and had been given the answer to his dilemma. The wives had been delighted for the opportunity to meet an Indian medicine woman and it had been a rather amused Raccoon Talker who suggested that she should tell their fortunes.

Suddenly Raccoon Talker stopped speaking. She broke off her conventional phrases – which had been basically the same as those employed by fortune tellers of every nation, creed or cult – abruptly and without apparent reason. Stiffening on her seat, she stared with fixed intensity across the room. Her face set into lines of intense concentration and she showed signs of being under a tremendous mental strain.

'Wha ... What's wrong with her, Charles?' gasped one of the white women, rising hurriedly and displaying alarm.

'I don't know,' Goodnight admitted, looking at the buxom, white-haired, yet impressive figure in the spotlessly clean doe skin clothes and the finery of her profession. In fluent Comanche, employing the accent of the *Tanima*, Liver

Eater, band, he went on, 'Is all well with Raccoon Talker, brother?'

'Keep quiet, *Chaqueta Tigre*,' Long Walker requested politely. 'Tell your women not to be alarmed. There is medicine power here and it is no longer a foolish game for the squaws.'

Goodnight nodded and passed on the information. To give them their due, the plump Eastern matrons fell silent. Each of them realized that she was participating in something of more importance than a mere fortune telling exercise such as they could have received from a gypsy pedlar back home in New Jersey. For his part, the rancher knew they were witnessing something unique.

During the War Between The States, while riding with Captain Jack Cureton's company of Texas Rangers, Goodnight had learned much about the Comanches and something of their religious beliefs. So he had a slight inkling of what might be happening. It had been during that same period he had won his *Nemenuh* man-name, *Chaqueta Tigre*, Jaguar Coat, by his courage and his always wearing that distinctive vest.

For almost three minutes Racoon Talker sat as if turned to stone. Only the increased rate at which her bosom rose and fell, in sympathy with her deep breathing, showed that she was still alive. No sound came from her and a deep silence dropped over the room. Then the glazed expression left her face and her eyes took on a new light of animation. Coming to her feet, she inclined her head in response to the white women's exclamations of concern.

'I must go,' Raccoon Talker declared. '*Cuchilo* has need of my help, Long Walker, and I cannot give it in this place.'

'Give the paleface chiefs' squaws our apologies, *Chaqueta Tigre*, as you white men do such foolish things,' the stocky, grey-haired *paria:vo* of the *Pehnane* requested, showing none of the anxiety that had been caused by the medicine woman's words. 'But we must leave this place.'

'We need no apologies, brother,' Goodnight replied. 'Is there anything I can do to help? As you know, I owe your tawk* a debt and he is my friend.'

---

* Tawk: Commanche word meaning both grandfather and grandson.

Colonel Goodnight – the military title was honorary, granted by virtue of his courage, reliability and powers of leadership – had never been a man to ignore a friend in trouble, nor to forget to repay a debt. All too well he knew just how much the success of his first big cattle drive across the *Llano Estacado* – which had helped pave the way for the economic recovery of Texas – had been due to the Kid's knowledge and assistance.*

'Yes,' Raccoon Talker put in. 'Send word over the singing wires to the *paria:vo* of the Texans. *Cuchilo* says the time has come. The blue coats must ride to the Palo Duro.'

'That I will do,' Goodnight confirmed. 'Is there anything more?'

'I think not,' the woman answered and turned from the table. 'The rest is medicine, *Chaqueta Tigre*.'

'That I understand,' agreed the rancher and crossed to open the door with all the gallantry he would have displayed to the Governor's wife or a saloongirl.

'We will make medicine this night, Agent Beckers,' Long Walker announced, as Raccoon Talker left the room. 'Tell the soldier coats at the fort there is nothing to fear from our drumming.'

'I will tell them,' the agent promised. 'I know your heart is strong for peace, my brother.'

'What's happening?' asked the wife of the senior cattle-buyer, after the Comanches had taken their departure and the rapid drumming of horses' hooves had faded away.

'It's a personal matter, ma'am,' Goodnight explained. 'Long Walker told me to express his apologies for them having to leave so abruptly.'

'But why did they have to leave?' the second woman inquired.

'Raccoon Talker heard that a young friend of ours needs help,' the rancher replied. 'She's gone to give it.'

'I didn't hear anything,' the first wife protested.

'Neither did I, ma'am,' Goodnight assured her. 'The Comanche medicine people have powers which no white person can understand. If you will accept Mr. Becker's hospitality for a short time longer. I have business to which I must attend. Stanley, I'll deliver the message to the Fort.'

* Told in: *Goodnight's Dream* and *From Hide and Horn*.

'Sure, Charlie,' Beckers agreed. 'I don't know what's going on, but I *do* know we'd better do what Raccoon Talker said we should.'

Despite having been born and raised amongst the *Pehnane*, the Kid had little actual knowledge of medicine powers. They were the prerogative of the elite few, mostly older men or women. If a young person showed the correct gifts, he or she would be chosen for training and introduction to the medicine arts. Mostly the male candidate would be of a mild, dreamy nature and unlikely ever to gain acclaim in the martial subjects. From his youngest days, the Kid had been marked down as a warrior. So he had learned of medicine as an outsider, knowing only what it was claimed those in the inner circle could do.

How it had happened, the Kid could not say; but he knew that Raccoon Talker had 'heard' his message. More than that, he was certain that she had promised him her assistance and protection. Settling himself as comfortably as possible under the circumstances, he waited for the next development.

A lantern glowed and footsteps approached the *tipi*. Its door flaps were opened to let in a flood of light. Followed by a trio of war-painted *tehnaps*, *Pohawe* strode into the Kid's presence. Having looked at the newcomers, the Kid devoted his attention to his surroundings. In addition to the usual paraphernalia of a medicine *tipi* he saw all his portable property had been brought in. The rifle, still in its medicine boot, leaned against his saddle and his gunbelt, carrying its usual armament, lay across its seat. At the opposite side of the *tipi*, encased in a medicine boot, leaned a long Sharps Model of 1859 rifle.

The latter weapon must be in the *tipi* so that it could absorb medicine power. Yet a rifle rarely received such treatment. Obviously it must be required for some special purpose.

'What evil is this, witch-woman?' the Kid demanded, swinging coldly contemptuous eyes towards *Pohawe*.

Anger showed on the woman's face, brought there by the name that the Kid had applied to her. While a medicine woman was a person to be respected, a witch – who used her powers for evil – was regarded with revulsion.

'You die, *Cuchilo*,' *Pohawe* promised. 'Not this night, but after the sun has gone down tomorrow, you will go to join your white father. There will be no living palefaces in the Palo Duro. I will not have them here.'

'Does a woman lead the *Kweharehnuh*?' the Kid mocked, looking at the braves. 'Are the Antelopes like the foolish men in the Land Of The Grandmother,* waiting to be led by a warrior maid with a war lance?'†

'He talks well, *Pohawe*,' snorted the biggest of the *tehnaps*. When he moved forward, he exhibited a very bad limp to his left leg. 'We will see if he dies well—'

'Not this night, Kills From Far Off,' the medicine woman barked.

'Why wait, witch woman?' challenged the Kid. 'Are you afraid that my medicine will strike you down?'

'What dog of a half-breed ever had medicine?' *Pohawe* snorted.

'I know a half-breed *bitch* who *thinks* she has,' replied the Kid.

For a moment, the Texan thought that he had pushed *Pohawe* too far. Rage twisted her features into almost bestial lines. Her hand reached towards the knife at a *tehnap*'s waist. Then, with a visible effort of will, she relaxed.

'It is well for you that I have chosen the time and how you are to die, half-breed. I want you alive to hear of the great thing I have done and will do.'

'Then kill me now, witch woman,' challenged the Kid. 'Your words tire me and you will do no deeds worth listening to.'

'You think not?' *Pohawe* screeched. 'I am the one who will guide the *Nemenuh* as they drive the palefaces from Comancheria.'

'The *Kweharehnuh* are good warriors, those who are not led by a witch woman,' the Kid told her. 'But I don't think they can drive out the white people.'

'The other bands will ride with us,' the medicine woman stated.

'You couldn't have been at the Fort Sorrel peace meeting,'

---

* Land of the Grandmother, Canada during the reign of Queen Victoria.

† More details of this legend are given in: *The Whip and the War Lance*.

drawled the Kid. 'The chiefs of the other bands were wise enough to know that not even the *Nemenuh* could win victory against the wheel-guns of the soldier-coats. So they made an honourable peace and will keep it.'

'They were old fools and cowards, all of them!' *Pohawe* snapped. 'And their braves did not have many rifles. Every *Kweharehnuh* warrior carries a repeater and has bullets for it. Tomorrow we will have many more bullets. With them, we can fight and beat the soldier-coats. As for their slow wheel-guns, they are only good for shooting from far away at the *tipis* standing still in a village.'

'When the news goes out that the *Kweharehnuh* are counting many coups and bringing in much loot,' Kills From Far Off continued, 'the brave-hearts eating the white man's beef on the reservations will ride swiftly to join us.'

Looking from the *tehnap* to the woman, the Kid managed to school his expression into one of amused disbelief. Yet, in his heart, he knew that they had been speaking the truth. Armed with repeaters against the Springfield single-shot rifles and carbines with which the U.S. Army was equipped, the *Kweharehnuhs* would have a decided advantage in firepower. Nor would batteries of cannon be of any great use against a highly mobile force of attacking braves who, knowing every inch of the terrain, would select with care the places from which they launched their assaults.

What was more, the couple had been correct in their summation of how the news would be received by the restless young braves on the reservation. They would be determined to share in the *Kweharehnuh*'s glory. So the very thing that Governor Howard had feared – and which the floating outfit had come to Hell to try to avert – a bloody, costly Indian war would have to be fought. Certainly many people of both races would be slaughtered if *Pohawe* had her way.

Ever since the challenges by the two brothers had been issued, the Kid had sensed that they were instigated by *Pohawe*. At last he could see possible motives for her wishing to have him killed. On learning of his arrival in the village, she must have come to the wrong conclusions concerning the reason for his visit. She could have believed that some hint of her plans had leaked out and he had been sent in an attempt to persuade Ten Bears to stay at peace – if only nominally –

with the white people. Or she had suspected that the Kid was connected with Hell and had not wanted word of the preparations being made for war to be carried to the citizens.

In either case, she would have wanted him out of the way and the brothers' hatred had offered her the means. Maybe she had talked them into the belief that they must avenge their brother. The plan had gone wrong for her, but she clearly did not intend to let things go at that.

There was only one hope for the Kid. That his faith in Raccoon Talker's medicine powers would be justified.

'The brave-hearts on the reservations won't follow you,' the Kid warned, trying to sound a whole heap more confident than he felt. 'Not when you, like them, depend on the white men for weapons and ammunition.'

'That will not be so after tomorrow,' *Pohawe* replied and the other three *tehnaps* directed knowing grins at Kills From Far Off.

'*Paruwa Semenho* is a man of honour,' the Kid stated. 'If the white people keep their bargain, so will he.'

'They will not keep *all* of their bargain,' the woman countered. 'There will be no pretended making of medicine tomorrow.'

'*Pretended*?' queried the Kid. 'I have heard it said that the great witch woman of the *Kweharehnuh* does not know how such medicine is made.'

'It is false medicine,' declared the youngest *tehnap*.

'So the witch woman tells you,' answered the Kid. 'But that is because she doesn't understand it. Perhaps *she* does not have true medicine power herself.'

'You are asking to die, *Cuchilo*!' *Pohawe* hissed, playing into his hands.

'Then have me killed,' the Kid suggested. 'I say you can't, because I am protected by a greater power than you know. Try to kill me, witch woman, and see if I speak with a crooked tongue.'

'Kill him, One Arrow!' the woman spat at the youngest *tehnap*.

'Try it if you dare, *namae'enuh*,*' jeered the Kid, using the most insulting term in the Comanches' vocabulary as he saw the brave hesitate.

* Namae'enuh: put politely, he who has had incestuous intercourse.

There ought to have been sufficient time for Raccoon Talker to have made her medicine. If not, going by One Arrow's response to the deadly insult, the Kid could count himself lucky if he stayed alive long enough to come under her promised protection.

Spitting out a curse, the young *tehnap* snatched his knife from its sheath. Watched by his companions and the medicine woman, he took two strides in the Texan's direction. Then he stopped as if he had run into an invisible wall. Fright and shock contorted his face and he collapsed in what looked like a fit.

Startled ejaculations burst from the other men and they backed away involuntarily. Brave enough in the face of mortal dangers, they were unnerved by the manifestation of powers beyond their understanding. One Arrow was known to suffer from such seizures, but the attack had come on just too conveniently for it to be discounted on natural grounds.

'Kill him, Small Post Oak!' *Pohawe* screeched, sounding frightened.

'Not me!' the brave addressed by the woman replied. 'Come, brothers. We leave this place.'

Snatching up the Sharps rifle, Kills From Far Off followed his companions as they dragged One Arrow from the *tipi*. *Pohawe* watched them go, seething with fury, yet shivering with fear.

'*Cuchilo*!' the woman hissed, glaring her hatred but keeping her distance. 'If those men won't follow me tomorrow, I will return and kill you slowly. And if I come, no medicine power will save you.'

CHAPTER FOURTEEN

MY NAME *IS* DUSTY FOG

'YOUNG Duprez had been knifed,' Dusty Fog told Emma Nene as they stood away from other ears in the Honest Man saloon. 'Rosie Wilson had been shot outside the back door, but I think she'd run into the killer not that she killed him.'

'Had he been robbed?' the blonde inquired, glancing at the ceiling.

'There wasn't any sign of it,' Dusty admitted. 'Why'd you think he might have been?'

'There doesn't seem to be any other reason for him to be killed,' Emma answered, just a shade too emphatically. 'He wasn't a prominent citizen, or an important asset to any of the cliques. Nobody else, that I know of, can handle the barbering. So he wasn't killed to let somebody else take over the business. That doesn't leave much else but robbery, does it?'

'Was he a ladies' man? They do say those French fellers mostly are.'

'I don't think Paul Duprez could even speak French. His folks were born in Brooklyn. Anyways, when he used to come in here, I've never seen any of the girls trampling over each other to get to him. I'll ask around for you.'

'*Gracias*,' Dusty drawled.

'*Es nada*,' Emma answered, forcing a smile to her lips. 'It could have been one of Rosie's girls, though. Her being outside and all.'

'Like you say,' Dusty replied. 'It could be.'

Watching the blonde, the small Texan could sense that she was deeply disturbed by the news. Her eyes repeatedly flickered towards the first floor and, in a controlled way, she was agitated by what she had just heard.

Then Dusty remembered something which he had been told about Duprez's late employer. Jean le Blanc had been a society barber in the East, until he had been persuaded by a woman he had thought loved him to murder her millionaire husband. Too late, he had learned that she was merely using him to open the way for herself and her real lover. He had killed the couple and carried off a large sum of money and a valuable collection of jewellery they had been meaning to use in their life together.

Emma Nene and Giselle Lampart had known le Blanc's life story – and the reason for their return to Hell had been to lay hands on a fortune in jewellery.

'Where's Giselle?' Dusty asked, watching carefully for reactions.

'Upstairs, of course,' the blonde replied, a hint of alarm dancing in eyes which were a whole heap more expressive than she imagined. 'Why?'

'She went to the bath-house. Maybe she saw or heard something.'

'It's not likely. She was there as soon as the baths were ready.'

'Did you see her come back?'

'Yes,' Emma lied. 'When I went out to check on the liquor supply. She came in the back way and went straight upstairs.'

'Huh huh!' Dusty grunted non-committally.

'Where's Wa . . . Matt?' the blonde inquired in an obvious attempt to change the subject.

'He went with Goldberg and Connolly to the cat-house.'

'I didn't think Manny or the esteemed doctor went in for *that* kind of entertainment.'

'I wouldn't know,' Dusty admitted. 'We found a couple of keys in Rosie's pocket and I want to know what locks they fit. She was away from her place and I don't see her as the kind who'd take a walk just for the good of her complexion.'

'I suppose not,' the blonde smiled.

'Maybe I'd best go and talk to Giselle, anyways,' Dusty remarked.

'You're the boss,' Emma declared, hoping that the sinking

sensation in her stomach was not openly obvious. 'But I don't think you'll learn anything from her.'

At the brothel, Waco, Goldberg and Connolly were being confronted by the big, brawny bouncer. Half a dozen Chinese, Mexican and white girls hovered nervously in the background. One of the latter was staring at the blond youngster with a puzzled expression on her face.

'Where's Mr. Youseman?' Goldberg demanded pompously.

'Who says he's here?' countered the bouncer.

'We *know* he is,' the hotel-keeper declared. 'And we want to see him immediately.'

'Rosie said that she don't take to the marks being disturbed,' the bouncer answered. 'It's bad for the girls, getting stopped half-way through. So you can't go and see him.'

'Now me,' Waco drawled. 'I don't rightly see any way you-all can stop us. These gents're mighty important citizens and members of the Civic Regulators and, top of that, there's me—'

'You?' the bouncer said, showing his puzzlement.

'Me,' confirmed Waco, right hand Colt flashing from its holster and its hammer going back to full cock. 'And this.'

The instantaneous response robbed the bouncer of any further inclination to resist. Not only — as the blond Texan had pointed out — was he dealing with two mighty influential members of the community, but he was facing 'Matt Caxton'; younger brother of the most deadly *pistolero* ever to arrive in Hell and no slouch with a gun on his own account. With Rosie absent — the man still did not know of her death — he lacked guidance and figured that he had better co-operate. If only to save his own life.

'Aw, I didn't mean nothing!' the bouncer stated, with an ingratiating grin. 'You'll find him in the third back room. Only, way he is, he'll not be any use for undertaking tonight.'

Going to the third of the rooms used by the girls and their clients, Waco's party discovered the truth of the bouncer's words. Youseman lay in his drunken stupor, but Peggy was awake and talkative. On learning the reason for the visit, she admitted that her late employer had taken Youseman's keys with the intention of visiting and searching his premises.

Waco had already guessed that the doctor had recognized the keys. Anger showed on Connolly's miserable face, mingled with considerable alarm. Going by the other's reactions, Waco figured that he had made a smart and correct guess.

'Why would Rosie want to search the funeral parlour?' Goldberg demanded.

'I dunno,' Peggy lied, holding back the full extent of her knowledge in the hope that it might later be turned to her advantage. 'She just wanted to is all she told me. You don't argue with Rosie when she tells you to do something.'

'What did she tell you to do?' Connolly gritted.

'Get him drunk, is all,' Peggy replied.

Watching the girl, Waco sensed that she was not speaking the whole truth. He also decided that he would let her reasons for lying go unquestioned for the moment. Dusty's purposes were better served right then by preventing an exposure of the undertaker's and doctor's second line of business.

'Yousemen always had plenty of money around the place,' Connolly remarked, as Goldberg seemed to be on the verge of asking another question. He had no desire for the investigation to dig further into the brothel-keeper's motives. 'She probably planned to rob him.'

'By cracky, doc,' Waco enthused. 'I reckon you've hit it. We'd best go see if she got in and took anything.'

'I'll attend to that, Manny!' Connolly declared hastily. 'There's no need for us all to go.'

'I think it would be better if we all went,' Goldberg answered. 'Let's get going now. There's nothing more to be learned here.'

'It'd be best if we all went, doc,' Waco agreed, knowing that a refusal would increase any suspicions Goldberg might be harbouring.

Although agreement entailed some risk, Waco felt that they were justified in taking it. Rosie Wilson had been a shrewd, smart woman. She would have removed all the evidence of her visit to the funeral parlour. She had not made it in the interests of public duty and would not wish for a prior exposure of her knowledge. So it was unlikely that the hotel-keeper would see anything that might tell of the undertaker's and doctor's dealings in human bodies.

'I think that we should send for Crouch to come and help us,' Goldberg stated, as the trio left the brothel.

Since their clash of interests over who should run the town, a distinct coldness had risen between the former partners. So the words had been provoked by nothing more than Goldberg's objections to having to work while Crouch was doing nothing.

'There's no call for that,' Connolly replied hurriedly. 'We three ought to be able to handle things.'

'Why sure,' Waco agreed.

'Huh!' Goldberg sniffed. 'I dare say *my* wife was alarmed by the shooting. But *I* didn't have to dash off and comfort her while other people do the work. Some of us have a sense of duty.'

'He's got him a right pretty lil wife,' Waco commented soothingly, but without displaying too much tact.

'*Wife!*' Goldberg snorted. 'I'd like to see the synagogue *they* were married in—'

Anything more the hotel-keeper might have felt like saying was stopped by the sight of a man running towards them. Coming up, he proved to be one of Emma's waiters and in a state of considerable excitement.

'*Senor* Caxton says come *pronto*,' the man gasped. '*Senor* and *Senora* Crouch have been attacked and murdered.'

Having reached his decision to visit Giselle, Dusty turned towards the stairs. Before he could leave Emma's side, there was an interruption. The bat-wing doors burst open and Crouch staggered in. Agony contorted his face and blood smeared his hands as they clasped on the gore-saturated front of his shirt at belly level. Reeling forward a few steps, he stood swaying and glaring around.

Racing across the barroom, Dusty caught Crouch as his legs buckled and he started to collapse. Gently easing the man into a sitting position, Dusty supported him against his bent knee. Pain-glazed eyes stared at the small Texan and he knew there would not be much time in which he could gather information.

'What happened?' Dusty inquired, then scowled at the people as they came crowding around. 'Back off, some of you damn it! Emma. Get them back to what they were doing, *pronto*. And send a man to fetch Doc Connolly.'

It said much for the strength of the big Texan's personality that the onlookers drew away without Emma needing to do much prompting. Satisfied that his demands were being respected, Dusty raised no objections to the gang leaders and a couple of citizens hovering close by.

'B ... Betty ...!' Crouch gasped, clutching at Dusty's right arm. 'Be ... Bet ... I found her d ... dead. M ... Mur ... murdered!'

'How?' Dusty asked, conscious of the mutters which arose from all around.

'W ... With ... knife ... j ... just ... like ... Duprez. M ... Man did ... it.'

'Which man?'

'Str ... Stranger t ... to me. Ne ... Never seen him be ... fore. He ... knifed me as I turned to come ... help.'

'What did he look like?'

'Tall,' Crouch croaked, clearly making every effort to think straight and give helpful facts. 'He wore ... top hat ... had long hair. Had an ... opera cloak on, couldn't see his other clothes.'

'How about his face?' Dusty inquired gently.

'I ... I ... don't know,' Crouch admitted. 'L ... Light was behind him. Don't think he was anybody I know.'

At that moment, Dusty saw O'Day come in through a side door. The man had not offered to continue the acquaintanceship they had struck up on the way to town. In fact, he had explained that he did not wish to become associated with any particular faction of Hell's society. In view of Giselle's obvious dislike of the Easterner, along with his own inclination, Dusty had not forced himself into O'Day's company. With the situation so unsettled, O'Day had not yet been required to make his contribution to the Civic Improvement Fund. Although he had taken a room at the hotel, he apparently had not followed the usual outlaw trend of purchasing fancy 'go-to-town' clothes. Bare headed, showing short brown hair that was going thin on top, he was dressed as when the floating outfit had saved his life.

'Did he say anything?' Dusty asked, turning his attention back to Crouch.

'N ... He ... didn't spe ...!' the jeweller began, then a fit of coughing sprayed blood from his mouth and he sagged limply against the small Texan's supporting arm.

Gently laying Crouch on his back, Dusty rose and looked around. While the crowd had withdrawn in accordance with his demands, they watched with interest and muttered amongst themselves.

'What happed, Ed?' O'Day inquired, strolling up.

'Crouch and his wife have been attacked,' Dusty explained, eyes on the other's smooth, hairless face. 'He allows he'd know the man who did it.'

'May I ask who it is?'

'*That* he didn't get around to telling me,' Dusty admitted, alert for any hint of emotion. He had seen no sign of alarm at his first statement, nor did O'Day display relief over the second. 'Maybe he will when he recovers. Until then, how about you coming with a few more of us to see what we can learn at his place?'

'Why me?' O'Day wanted to know.

'Why not you?' Dusty countered. 'You're as good as a gang leader and you're intelligent enough to use your eyes and your head.'

'After praise like that, how can I refuse?' O'Day conceded with a smile.

'Which of you gents wants to come?' Dusty asked, looking at the nearest members of the crowd.

Before any volunteers could step forward, running footsteps pounded across the sidewalk. Followed by the two panting townsmen and the waiter Emma had sent to collect them, Waco entered. They listened as Dusty told them what had happened. Then, while Connolly went to attend to the jeweller, Goldberg stared at O'Day.

The hotel-keeper was a badly frightened man who did not care to contemplate the implications of the night's happenings. Except for the combatants who had fallen during the recent struggle to determine which faction would control Hell, and Lampart's demise, death had always steered clear of the citizens. Outlaws had been killed in quarrels, or while being robbed by others of their kind, but none of the town's people had come to harm.

And now, in the course of a single evening three – probably four – of the citizens had met untimely, mysterious deaths.

While not concerned too much with who might have committed the crimes, Goldberg had no desire to become another victim. So he searched for a possible culprit. Every gang leader present was making a return visit. There did not appear to be any reason for one of the town's inhabitants suddenly to go on the rampage. All had warrants out for them and would be arrested if they left the security of the Palo Duro. There was only one stranger in their midst.

'Nothing like this ever happened before *you* came here!' Goldberg shouted, pointing his right forefinger at O'Day.

An excited rumble of comment rose from the occupants of the room. The sound had an ominous, menacing ring to it. By nature the citizens and visitors were suspicious-minded. Most of the crowd, particularly the regular inhabitants, had been thinking along the same general lines as Goldberg. However, it had been left to the hotel-keeper to supply a suspect.

'Just who *are* you, feller?' demanded a burly gang leader, hand hovering over the butt of his low-tied Colt.

'My name is O'Day,' the Easterner replied. 'And, like yourselves – or most of you—,' his eyes flickered towards Waco and Dusty, 'I am a fugitive from justice who fled here for safety.'

'I've never heard tell of you,' the gang leader declared. 'Has anybody here heard his name?'

Negative answers came from all sides. From his experiences as a peace officer, Dusty could see all the symptoms of a lynch mob. Alarmed by the murders, the customers and employees were wide open for suggestions of who the killer might be. Given just a hint, as they had been, they would strike blindly. Darting a glance at Waco, the small Texan prepared to intervene. O'Day beat him to it. Showing no sign of concern, the man looked around the circle of threatening people.

'None of you had heard another name, either,' O'Day pointed out. 'Yet you accept the man who bears it.'

'Who'd that be?' Goldberg barked suspiciously, yet impressed by the man's demeanour.

'Ed Caxton,' O'Day replied.

'*Ed*—!' the hotel-keeper yelped, then snorted. 'Huh! We all know what he did so that he had to come to Hell.'

'You know what you read in a newspaper,' O'Day corrected. 'And what he himself told you.'

'Mister,' Waco drawled, moving to Dusty's side. 'You're asking to find all kinds of trouble.'

'Ah! The younger of the "Caxton brothers",' O'Day answered. 'I cast no aspersions on your mother's reputation, but she did not throw a very good family likeness between her sons. You are remarkably unalike in other ways, too. "Ed" speaks like a man with education and breeding. "Matt" sounds like a common trail hand—'

'Keep talking,' Waco interrupted, wondering when Dusty would take cards. 'And I'm going to—'

'People are strange,' O'Day went on and something about him held the attention of the whole room. 'They have preconceived ideas about how others should look. Take Dusty Fog for example. Everybody assumes that he must be a veritable giant. Yet I have heard on very good authority that he is a small man, not more than five foot six in height. Yet, when trouble threatens, he seems taller than his fellows. He has companions, too. One is part *Comanche,* his name is the Ysabel Kid. Another is a man of gigantic stature and handsome to boot, who might be taken by the unknowing for Dusty Fog himself. Suppose, for example, it was wanted to appear that Dusty Fog was in – say San Antonio – instead of – say here in Hell – Mark Counter could go there and pretend to be him.'

'What Mr. O'Day's trying to get across to you,' the small Texan drawled, 'is that I'm Dusty Fog.'

'He's *loco*!' Emma snapped, standing to one side of Dusty and with her right hand rested upon the butt of her Navy Colt. She had donned her working clothes, but wore the gun in a holster belted about her waist.

'Am I, Ed?' O'Day challenged. 'Will you give me your word of honour that you are not who I say?'

'No,' Dusty answered, in a quiet voice that still reached every pair of ears. 'My name *is* Dusty Fog.'

Half a second later, almost before the shock of the announcement had died away, before the exclamations of surprise, amazement and anger commenced, the *big* Texan held a cocked Colt in each hand.

Knowing his *amigo*, Waco had expected such a line of action. So, an instant behind the appearance of Dusty's revolvers, the youngster's Army Colts cleared leather to throw down on a section of the crowd.

'Scatterguns!' Emma yelled at her bartenders, almost as quickly as the Texans made their draws. Then she produced and aimed her Navy Colt.

Grabbing the twin barrelled, sawed-off shotguns which lay beneath the counter readily available for use, the two drink dispensers lined them and drew back the exposed double hammers.

Long before any of the room's occupants could think of making physical resistance, the chance to do so with any hope of success had departed. Under the threat of the assorted firearms, to have tried to fetch out a weapon would have been suicidal.

'What do you want here, Fog?' demanded one of the gang leaders, as the general conversation died away.

'Do you reckon you can take us all in?' another leader went on.

'I don't aim to try,' Dusty replied. 'My work here is done, but I've come back to help you save your scalps.'

'I'd listen if I was you,' Emma advised. 'Because if you don't, by this time tomorrow the whole bunch of you'll be dead.'

CHAPTER FIFTEEN

MAKE YOUR MEDICINE, WHITE MAN

'WELL,' said Emma Nene, turning slowly on her toes in front of Dusty Fog and Waco. 'How do I look?'

'Like I'm seeing a ghost,' the blond youngster declared. 'Miss Emma, you handed me one hell of a scare when I first walked in.'

'You didn't even look at Giselle, so I must have,' Emma smiled.

There was justification for Waco's comment. The blonde wore a man's evening clothes, top hat and opera cape. Not only that, but with her hair hidden beneath the hat, she had contrived to look almost exactly like the late mayor of Hell.

Coming on such a startling resemblance to the man he killed had been a real surprise to the youngster, but not enough to make him ignore the brunette. Giselle wore a brief, almost minute, white doeskin version of an Indian girl's dress. With a décolleté more daring than would have been permitted even in the most wide open of trail end towns, the midriff bare and the skirt extending just below her buttocks, it showed off her figure to its best advantage. The clothes and moccasins were the garments she wore when performing her 'medicine dance' and being sawn in half to entertain the *Kweharehnuhs*.

'I can understand the clothes,' Dusty remarked. 'But the face has me beat.'

'It's a rubber mask,' Emma explained. 'I doubt if a dozen people, other than professional magicians know where to lay hands on them.'

'Let's hope it stays that way,' Waco drawled. 'It surely fooled me.'

'What's happening in town?' the blonde inquired, taking

both Texans' attention from the uses to which such rubber masks might be put.

'All the owlhoots have pulled out,' Dusty replied. 'Your scouts, the Chinese and the Mexicans you folks had from the *Kweharehnuh*'ve all gone. There's only the folks from the original wagon train left.'

'At least, you made sure that the owlhoots left without robbing us,' Emma reminded him. 'If you hadn't been here, they'd've taken everything they could tote off.'

Backed by the menace of the lined guns, Dusty had been allowed to say his piece downstairs in the barroom the previous night. He had begun by pointing out that Hell's days as an outlaws' refuge were numbered. The town was no longer a carefully kept secret, for the Texas Rangers, the United States' Army and the authorities in Austin had learned of its existence. By that time, they would also be aware of its location, Dusty had warned. The soldiers who had helped fight off the kidnap attempt on Giselle would have delivered their report. Probably an expedition was already on its way. When it came, Dusty had gone on, it would be in sufficient strength to fight its way through the whole of the *Kweharehnuh* band.

That was, of course, Waco had reminded the audience, unless the Antelope Comanches had not decided to take matters into their own hands. Then Dusty had predicted that the latter contingency might become a fact. He had elaborated upon the significance of the attempt to capture Giselle, then on the unrestricted passage which had been granted to his party when it had become obvious that they were returning to Hell.

Everybody had accepted that the Indians must have had a good reason for wanting the brunette back in time for the allocation of the ammunition. They had also agreed that it might be to do with an attempt to break Lampart's 'medicine' hold over the band. In that case, the braves would come prepared to deal with the white interlopers on their domain.

Such had been the power of Dusty's eloquence that he had persuaded his audience that he and the others had returned with the best of motives. The citizens had not been able to forget that the small Texan and his party had brought about much of their present predicament. However, with the fear of exposure hanging over him, Doctor Connolly had done much to keep the other inhabitants from making their annoyance more active. Once again, the outlaws had no reason to back up the town's people. In fact, some of the visitors had seemed to find the situation amusing. With the lawbreakers disinclined to take up the issue, the citizens had lacked the courage to do so.

O'Day had improved Dusty's chances of avoiding a clash, by stating that he was not going to stay on and be massacred. That had brought similar comments from various outlaws. The general consensus of opinion amongst them had been that it would be safer to take one's chances against the forces of white law and order than to lock horns with the rampaging *Kweharehnuh*.

Satisfied that the danger of trouble was shelved, if not entirely finished, Dusty had suggested that they should resume their investigations into the killings of the evening. An examination of Crouch's safe, opened with the keys found in his pocket, proved that robbery had been the motive for the couple's murders. Although there had been no evidence, Dusty had assumed that the same cause had resulted in Duprez's and Rosie Wilson's deaths.

Explaining that he had exposed the small Texan merely as a means to avoid being lynched for a crime of which he was innocent, O'Day had insisted that his property be searched. On the way to do it, he had told Dusty how he had formed the correct conclusions on remembering what he had heard about the descriptions of the small Texan and of Mark Counter, and aided by the story he had read in the *Texas State Gazette*. It had been a piece of quick thinking on the Easterner's part, Dusty had admitted.

The examination of the man's belongings had apparently established his innocence. While his packs had held a number of clothes, they did not include a top hat or an opera cloak. Nor did he have the quantity of jewellery that had been taken from the Crouch family's safe. O'Day had no support for his story that he had not left the hotel room until going to the Honest Man, but his word had been accepted.

Later, Dusty had searched Giselle's room and questioned

her without coming any closer to the solution. The saloon had closed early, but there had been considerable activity around town. Throughout the night, men and some women had been taking their departure. With the time approaching noon – the hour at which the allocation was due to take place – Dusty and Waco had just returned from making their rounds. Everything was ready for the meeting with the *Kweharehnuh*, but Hell had lost more than half of its population.

'The Rangers have got Sheriff Butterfield and your man Hatchet,' Dusty remarked, referring to a crooked lawman they had met and the town's main contact with the outside world. 'One of Butterfield's pigeons had come in with a message about it.'

'Butterfield sent a warning?' Emma asked. 'I'd've thought all he'd think about was saving his own neck.'

'The message was for me,' Dusty explained. 'It said, "Uncle Jules is here, has met sheriff and seen goods delivered by Mr. Hatchet."'

'Who's "Uncle Jules"?' Giselle asked as she draped a cloak about her shoulders.

'Captain Jules Murat of the Texas Rangers,' Waco grinned. 'The gent who first learned about Hell and got us sent here.'

'So it's all over, E— Dusty?' Emma said quietly.

'Near enough,' Dusty admitted. 'Depending on today, that is. I've got a feeling something just might be about to go wrong.'

'How?' Giselle demanded worriedly.

'I don't know, ma'am,' Dusty answered.

'If there's any danger, I'm not getting into that box!' the brunette stated.

'Could be that'd be the biggest danger of all, ma'am,' Waco warned. 'Happen you don't, they'll say our medicine's gone back on us. Only this time, they'll not be caring about keeping you alive.'

'Oh lord!' Giselle wailed. 'Why did I let you talk me into coming back, Emma Nene?'

'Because you're a money-hungry little bitch with no more morals than an alley-cat,' the blonde told her bluntly. 'You came back to pick the locks and open the safe so that we could steal all the jewellery Crouch had gathered in his place. Only somebody beat us to it.'

'And to Jean le Blanc's?' Dusty commented.

'It's possible that Jean had already got rid of it,' Emma pointed out. 'It wasn't anywhere in his place when we searched last night. He used to play a lot of poker and wasn't especially good at it.'

When questioned privately by the blonde, Giselle had sworn that she was innocent of Duprez's murder. An even more thorough search than Dusty had been able to give her had also failed to produce the barber's loot. So, although still suspicious and determined to keep a close eye on her half-sister, Emma had been compelled to accept the other's story that she had done no more than go to the barber's shop, take a hot bath and return to her room.

'Time we was headed out to see Ten Bears,' Waco remarked.

'The Kid hasn't come back?' Emma asked.

'Likely he's getting all them fancy Comanche foods he's always telling us about,' Waco answered. 'Raw, fresh killed liver dipped in gall and such. Or they give their makings away easier not knowing him.'

'I hope he's all right,' the blonde breathed, noting the undertones of anxiety in the youngster's voice.

'Trust Lon to be that,' Dusty answered. 'If anything had been bad wrong, he'd've been out of there faster than a greased weasel. What now, Emma?'

'Giselle goes down there and starts doing her dance,' the blonde explained. 'Simmy follows. You'd best go with her, Ma— Waco.'

'I'll do that,' the youngster promised. 'Let's go, ma'am.'

'How about those pictures of Ten Bears and the medicine woman?' Dusty asked and the blonde produced them from a drawer in her dressing-table. Taking them, Dusty tucked them into the front of his shirt. 'They might come in useful.'

'What happens to us after this, Ed?' Emma inquired, as the door closed behind Waco and Giselle.

'You go your way, like before,' Dusty replied. 'With your fifty thousand dollars, you've a better than fair start someplace.'

'Do you know something,' the blonde smiled. 'I think I'd've come back, even without wanting Crouch's jewellery, just to see how things turned out. You're a real nice man, Ed Cax ... Dusty Fog.'

'And you're a real smart, nice gal, Emma Nene,' Dusty countered.

'You'll be wanting to kiss me next,' the blonde smiled.

'I've never kissed a man,' Dusty grinned.

'At least, this man hasn't any stubble on his face,' Emma remarked, running her left forefinger over the mask. 'I never liked your bristly old beard.'

'Hell's fire, that's it!' Dusty snapped. 'Now I know what's been eating at me. Emma, who did you and Giselle think O'Day was?'

'She said he reminded her of Mephisto,' the blonde replied. Then her hand once more felt at the mask. 'Oh god! No. It couldn't be!'

'Who was he?'

'Simmy's partner. On the stage and in crimes. It was Mephisto who taught Giselle all she knows about picking locks and opening safes. Simmy and Mephisto organized and financed the wagon train that brought us here.'

'Only Mephisto didn't make it,' Dusty guessed.

'That stupid little bitch!' Emma snapped bitterly. 'She had to get them both in love with her. There was an argument a few days before we left, in a hotel room. I wasn't there and don't know just what did happen. But either Simmy or Giselle threw vitriol into Mephisto's face. He ran out of the place, screaming in torment, and flung himself off a bridge into a river. His body was never recovered. There was a fast current running and everybody assumed he was dead.' A shudder ran through her, but she mastered it with an effort. 'Where's O'Day now?'

'Gone with the others, it looks like. All his gear's been taken from the hotel and his horses aren't in the livery barn. Would he know how to get hold of those masks, this Mephisto *hombre*, I mean?'

'Yes. Part of their act used to be a transformation trick. They'd go into boxes at opposite sides of the stage, change their clothes around and put on the masks and make it look like they'd switched boxes. Do you think O'Day is Mephisto, Dusty?'

'I don't know,' the small Texan admitted. 'Anyways, it looks like he's gone. And we'd best get going to make our play for the *Kweharehnuh*.'

'I'll have to come out of Simmy's back door,' Emma remarked as they went downstairs. 'He always did it that way. I'm scared, Dusty!'

'Lady,' Dusty drawled and kissed her. 'So am I.'

There was, Dusty admitted to himself, plenty to be scared about. Leaving Emma to go to Lampart's house, so that she could make the expected kind of appearance, he walked by the crater formed when the ammunition shack had exploded and through the town. On the open ground beyond the last of the *jacales*, the other participants of what might develop into a bloody massacre had assembled.

All the remaining citizens of Hell formed a nervous, worried group on the side nearest to the town. In front of them, the garishly painted wooden box had been set up ready to be used in the illusion. A gleaming, obviously sharp saw was laid on its top. In front of the box, Giselle gyrated and twisted her magnificent little body in a musicless, abandoned and sensual dance that held the eyes of every white man present despite their anxieties. Yet, voluptuous as she looked, the mass of *Kweharehnuh* warriors behind the semi-circle of chiefs and the medicine woman showed no sign of being interested.

Studying the Comanches' ranks, Dusty noticed that only a small proportion of the braves were wearing war paint. There was no sign of the Kid. That most likely meant he was—

Dusty fought down the thought. If he and the people of Hell were to survive, he must keep a very clear head.

'Where's Lon?' Waco gritted irritably as Dusty joined him.

'Around, likely,' Dusty replied. 'I'm going to talk to Ten Bears.'

'I'll do more'n talk if Lon's been—!' the youngster blazed.

'You'll stay put and keep your mouth shut, boy!' Dusty

commanded grimly. Walking forward, he raised his right hand in a peace salute to Ten Bears. In Spanish, which he hoped would be understood by the chief, he said, 'Greetings, *Paruwa Semenho*.'

'You I know,' the *paria:vo* replied in the same language. 'It was you who broke the medicine of the Devil Gun and who stood by *Cuchilo* when he spoke to the chiefs of the *Nemenuh* at Fort Sorrel. You are the one called Magic Hands by my people.'

'I am the one,' Dusty confirmed, knowing that to lie would be futile.

'Why are you here?' Ten Bears inquired.

'To keep the peace between the *Kweharehnuh* and my people.'

'*Those* are your people?'

'They are white,' Dusty pointed out, amused by the note of contempt in Ten Bear's comment as he had indicated the citizens of Hell. 'The *paria:vo* of my people thinks they are such poor trophies that it would disgrace his *Kweharehnuh* brothers to count coup on them. So he has sent me, *Cuchilo* and the young, brave one there to fetch them out of the Palo Duro.'

'Where is *Cuchilo*?' asked the old man chief who had loaned the Kid his shield, looking around.

Dusty did not know whether he should be pleased and relieved or even more concerned by the question. From all appearances, the Kid had left the *Kweharehnuh*'s village and was expected to be present at the allocation.

'Make your medicine, white man!' *Pohawe* screeched, having no desire to let the chiefs learn of the Kid's absence.

'I make no medicine,' Dusty replied, wondering if the woman knew why his *amigo* had not returned. 'I am a warrior. The one who makes it comes.'

'I do not see him,' the medicine woman declared, looking towards the town. 'It is in my thoughts that he is dead.'

'Then you have wrong thoughts,' Dusty told her. 'He will come.' To himself, he growled silently. 'Come on, Emmagal. Show yourself.'

Almost as if receiving Dusty's thought-message, the cloaked, top hatted figure made its appearance. Despite the warning of what to expect given by Waco, the citizens let out a concerted gasp at the sight. It might have been Lampart himself stalking majestically towards the box. Emma was no longer moving with her customary hip-swaying glide, but stepped out like a man.

On reaching the box, the substitute illusionist removed the saw and raised the lid. At a signal from the gloved, extended hand, Giselle moved forward. She hesitated for a moment, glancing around at the watching *Kweharehnuhs*. A slight shudder ran through her, but she allowed her 'husband' to help her into the box. Resting her neck, wrists and ankles in the holes carved to receive them, she made no protest as the lid was lowered into position.

As Lampart had been unable to speak Comanche or Spanish, his man, Orville Hatchet had acted as interpreter. Dusty assumed Hatchet's role, addressing the *Kweharehnuhs* in the latter language. Reminding the visitors of how effective the white man's 'medicine' had proved to be, he said that the demonstration of 'Lampart's' powers would commence. Those of the braves who could not understand Spanish had his words translated for them by their more fortunate companions.

'And while the white witch is in the box, she can feel no pain?' asked *Pohawe* in a carrying voice. 'Even while she is being cut in half?'

'The saw cannot harm her,' Dusty replied. 'She is protected by the medicine which protects all the white people of this town.'

'Then make this great medicine,' the woman ordered. 'If it is as good as you claim, no harm will come to her or the people of your town.'

Watching *Pohawe*, Dusty felt a growing sense of perturbation. He felt certain that the woman had something tricky up her sleeve. For her part, the medicine woman was conscious of Dusty's scrutiny and guessed that he was alert for possible trouble.

Small good that would do the *big Tejano* ride-plenty, she mused as the illusionist picked up the saw. Soon the palefaces' medicine would be broken and the way opened for her to carry out the great scheme.

CHAPTER SIXTEEN

I HOLD YOUR SPIRIT, *POHAWE*

THE Ysabel Kid twisted his head around to see who had lifted the door flap of the medicine *tipi*. It was well past sun-up and he had not been disturbed since *Pohawe* had followed her companions into the darkness. However, the rawhide thongs still held him securely in their clutches and he could not do anything to escape. His eyes rested upon a bent, white haired old *Kweharehnuh* man who stepped inside and stared in a puzzled manner at him.

'What is this?' demanded the old man.

'Set me free, *naravuh*,' the Kid requested, using the word which meant respect when addressed to an old timer. 'Much death comes to the *Kweharehnuh* if you don't.'

Instead of replying, the newcomer lifted his eyes and gazed with fixed intensity at the opposite wall of the *tipi*.

'I am close to the Land Of the Good Hunting, Raccoon Talker, medicine woman of the *Pehnane*,' the old man announced, drawing the knife from his belt's decorative sheath. 'That is why I came to this place. Speak well of me to *Ka-Dih*, for I will do as you ask.'

Moving around, the man severed the Kid's bonds. While the pain caused by restored circulation beat at him, the Texan satisfied some of his curiosity.

'Where are the men of the village, *naravuh*?'

'They have ridden to the white men's wooden *tipis*. Only the old ones, women and children are left.'

'Did *Pohawe* go with the men?'

'This is the day when she breaks the palefaces' medicine,' the old man replied. 'It is my thought that evil will come if she does, *Cuchilo*.'

'I am honoured to think as you do, *naravuh*,' the Kid replied. 'Now I must ride to my friends.'

'Let me saddle your horse,' requested the old man. 'It is outside and I think I will never handle such a fine animal again.'

'You have my thanks,' the Kid said with quiet sincerity. Five minutes later, wearing his hat and in possession of his full armament, he crossed to the *tipi*'s door. Before he left, he faced the interior and went on, 'And my thanks to you, Raccoon Talker.'

Tired and showing signs of the great strain to which she had been subjected, Raccoon Talker emerged from her secret medicine *tipi* high on the slopes of Mount Scott. She found Long Walker waiting.

'*Cuchilo* is free,' she announced. 'I can help him no more this day.'

'Count coup for me, *Cuchilo*!' called the old man as the Kid galloped away. 'This day I die.'

By riding in the direction from which he had heard the sounds of celebration the previous night, the Kid soon located the *Kweharehnuhs*' village. From there, he knew that he could easily find his way to Hell. Even if he had not been sure, the massed tracks of the warriors' horses would have served as an excellent guide. Circling the village beyond its occupants' range of vision, he urged the blue roan between his legs to a better speed.

Pausing only to slake his thirst from a stream he had to ford, the Kid travelled as a *Pehnane tehnap* on an urgent mission. He did not follow along the line of tracks, but kept off to one side of them. That was a precaution taken in case the party should have scouts watching their rear. It paid off in another way as he approached the trees which surrounded the great basin that held Hell. Four riders had quit the main body, heading at a tangent towards the wooded land.

Dismounting at the fringe of the tree-line, the Kid slid free his Winchester and tucked its medicine boot under the bed roll. Swiftly he catered for the lathered, leg-weary horse. With that done, he glanced at the midday sun as it approached its zenith. The preliminaries to the allocation of the ammunition would have commenced. If anything was going to happen, it would be during that part of the ceremony.

Darting through the trees on foot, his rifle held ready for use, the Kid moved in as near silence as he could manage. How well he succeeded showed in that his presence was undetected by the four war ponies which stood grazing under a large old flowering dogwood tree. One of the horses had a long rifle's medicine boot draped across its blanket-covered saddle. The last time the Kid had seen that boot, it had been covering a Sharps owned by—

In that moment, the Kid saw through *Pohawe*'s plan to break Lampart's medicine. Springing to his mind, the name of the limping *tehnap* had furnished the Indian-dark Texan with the vital clue.

Kills From Far Off!

Because of his infirmity, the brave must have developed exceptional ability in using a rifle; especially at long ranges. The powerful Sharps rifle, even a model handling paper cartridges and with percussion cap priming, was a weapon noted for its extreme accuracy. A bullet fired by it would carry from the trees to the town, retaining sufficient energy on its arrival to pass through the walls of any building – or to burrow into the occupant of the box used for the medicine illusion.

Keeping down wind and taking ever greater care with his movements, the Kid continued his advance. He did not expect that he would have to go far. With the prospect of coups to be counted and loot to be gathered, no Comanche *tehnap* worthy of the name would put too much distance between himself and his mount. Once Kills From Far Off had carried out his assignment, the quartet would waste no time in boarding their horses and heading to the centre of the action.

Sure enough, the Kid had barely covered thirty yards before he found the four braves. And not a moment too soon by all appearances. Already Kills From Far Off was cradling the Sharps at his shoulder, with its barrel supported by a forked stick that he had thrust into the ground. Holding their Winchester carbines, the other three braves stood watching with rapt attention. There was no way in which the Kid could move closer without being instantly detected. Nor could he bring himself to open fire without giving the quartet a chance to defend themselves.

'*Namae'enuh!*' the Kid called, snapping the Winchester's butt plate against his right collar-bone.

The word brought an instant response. Spinning around, the three *tehnaps* with the repeaters gave startled exclamations and raised the weapons. On the point of pulling the Sharps' trigger, Kills From Far Off jumped slightly. In doing so, he tilted the barrel out of line at the moment of the detonation.

Flame belched from the Kid's Winchester and One Arrow died with a bullet in his head. Spinning around, he dropped his 'yellow boy' carbine close to Kills From Far Off and tumbled lifeless in the other direction.

Right hand moving like a blur, so that an almost continuous flow of empty cartridge cases spun through the ejection slot, the Kid demonstrated how to attain the three-shots-in-two-seconds rate of fire promised by Mr. Oliver Fisher Winchester's advertisements. He moved the barrel in a horizontal arc as he fired, throwing the shots like the spreading spokes of a wheel.

Small Post Oak was torn from his feet by the impacts of three bullets in rapid succession, before he could raise and use his rifle. Although the third brave got off a shot, he missed. He was not granted an opportunity to correct his aim. The invisible fan of flying lead encompassed him. Four of the deadly, speeding missiles found their marks in his head and chest. He died as he would have wished; facing a name warrior and with a weapon in his hands.

Throwing aside his empty Sharps, Kills From Far Off made a twisting, rolling dive that carried him to One Arrow's discarded carbine. Snatching it up as he landed facing the Kid, he fired. As if jerked by an invisible hand, the black Stetson spun from the Texan's head. Inclining the rifle downwards, the Kid responded. Struck in the forehead, Kills From Far Off made the journey to the Land Of Good Hunting.

Ceasing his operation of the Winchester's mechanism, the Kid ran by the four dead *tehnaps*. This was not the time for him to count coup in honour of the *tsukup** who had set him free. That ancient warrior would not expect such an act to

---

* Tsukup: another name for an old man.

be committed against another *Nemenuh*. Striding through the trees, the Kid came into sight of the town. Everybody was turning his way. So far there had been no hostile response to the sound of the shooting. He wondered how long the condition of peace – or surprise – would continue to hold the two parties in check.

Everything seemed to be going satisfactorily, Dusty had been telling himself when the shooting had started. Even knowing that some trickery was involved, it had been a fascinating experience watching the saw biting through the side of the box and, apparently, cutting into the little brunette's body. He still had no idea how it was done, for the women had refused to explain. Certainly the Comanches had been suitably impressed. *Pohawe* had moved in as close as she dared, staring with great interest and clearly trying to decide how the trick was done.

Suddenly the shots had rang out; the deep boom of a Sharps, followed by the rapid crackle of Winchesters. Coming from the tree-line on the rim, the lead screamed by unpleasantly close to the illusionist's top hat. Although nobody took much notice at that moment, the sound brought a very masculine ejaculation of surprise in its wake.

'What the—?' Waco demanded, moving to Dusty's side. Then he stared to where the shot had come from. 'Look! It's Lon!'

Every eye had already been directed in that direction. Much to the two Texans' relief, their *amigo* made his appearance and loped swiftly towards them.

'It's a trick!' *Pohawe* screamed, speaking Spanish in the hope of provoking a hostile gesture by one of the white men.

'Not on our part, Ten Bears!' Dusty countered. 'If there is treachery, you can blame it on your medicine woman.'

'Keep your weapons down!' the *paria:vo* ordered his braves. 'We will hear what *Cuchilo* has to tell us.'

'I tell you their medicine is bad!' *Pohawe* screeched, but this time she spoke in Comanche.

With that, the medicine woman snatched a double-action Starr Navy Model revolver from under her peplum. Three times she fired, driving the bullets into the box's side level with Giselle's shoulders. The brunette screamed and started to struggle convulsively.

'She can be hurt in the box!' *Pohawe* shrieked. 'I told you—'

As surprised as everybody else by the medicine woman's actions, Dusty Fog responded fast. Even in his haste, he used his head and did not act blindly. He remembered that the photograph of *Pohawe* had been in the outer position when he had placed them inside his shirt. So he extracted the correct picture and left that of Ten Bears concealed. Gripping the top corners between his thumbs and forefingers, he held it so that the woman could identify it.

'I hold your spirit, *Pohawe*!' Dusty warned. 'If you—'

'I fear no white man's medicine!' the woman interrupted, turning her revolver in Dusty's direction.

Instantly, the small Texan ripped the photograph down the middle. Even as the fragments fluttered from his hands, *Pohawe*'s body jerked violently, The top of her skull seemed to burst open and she crumpled lifeless to the ground.

On the slope, the Kid had read the implications behind Dusty's and *Pohawe*'s actions. Knowing that his *amigo* would hesitate before shooting a woman – even one as evil as her – the Kid had removed the need from him to do so. Skidding to a halt and whipping up his rifle, he had driven a bullet through the back of the medicine woman's head. By doing so, he had demonstrated in a satisfactory manner that some aspects of a white man's 'medicine' could be deadly effective.

Half a dozen braves, those most deeply involved in *Pohawe*'s scheme for the reconquest of Comancheria, bounded from the crowd. The woman had planned badly, for her faction had been gathered in one place instead of scattered amongst the other braves. It proved to have been a costly error.

Two died almost immediately, their rifles still not at shoulder level, for Dusty did not hesitate to defend himself against armed, desperate men. Showing the devastating speed and ambidextrous control of his weapons for which he was famous, he drew and fired the twin Colts simultaneously. Those of the *Kweharehnuh* who had not seen him confront the two Unionist fanatics and their Agar Coffee Mill 'devil' gun learned how he had gained the name 'Magic Hands'.

Slightly less rapidly, Waco tumbled the third and fourth of the braves from their feet. The fifth fell to the last bullet held by the Kid's Winchester. Screaming out his war cry, the sixth leapt to wreak his vengeance upon the white 'medicine man'.

With a heave, the illusionist overturned the box and dropped behind it. Its lid burst open as it struck the ground, allowing Giselle's bloody, lifeless body to roll out. In the dive for cover, the cloaked figure lost its top hat. Although the attacking brave sent a bullet into the box, he missed his intended target. While he was still working the repeater's lever, four Colts and Ten Bears' rifle spat at him. Any one of their bullets would have been fatal.

'I'll kill any brave who raises a weapon against the white people!' Ten Bears announced.

There was no need for the *paria:vo*'s warning. Obviously *Pohawe*'s medicine had gone very bad, so those who had considered following her lead now changed their minds. Not another weapon was lifted and the warriors stood impassively awaiting the next developments.

'My thanks, *Paruwa Semenho*,' Dusty said, holstering his guns on becoming satisfied that there would be no further need for them where the *Kweharehnuhs* were concerned. 'I regret having to kill your men.'

'They would have killed you,' Ten Bears pointed out. 'And the white medicine man.'

'Are you all right, Em—?' Dusty began, turning towards the overturned box. 'What the ... Where's Emma, O'Day—'

The figure which had risen still had the face of Simeon Lampart, but it was not topped by feminine blonde hair. Instead, the skull was completely bald. For the first time Dusty and Waco realized that the illusionist was taller than Emma; and noticed the deep-set, glowing eyes.

'In Simmy's house,' the man answered in O'Day's voice.

'If she's dead—!' Dusty growled.

'She's not,' O'Day interrupted. 'She'll have a sore head, but nothing more. I'm like you, I respect and admire Emma. So I contented myself with clubbing her insensible. I had to do it. She would never have willingly let me step in as her understudy.'

'My apologies, Ten Bears,' Dusty said in Spanish, turning his eyes towards the *paria:vo*. 'I must talk to this man.'

'We will wait until you are finished,' Ten Bears promised.

'Why'd you do it, O'Day?' Dusty inquired, giving his attention to the man once more.

'So that I could become the next medicine man of Hell,' the illusionist replied. 'It struck me as a most lucrative proposition.'

'It might be,' Dusty admitted, 'if the town wasn't closing down.'

'Why should it close down?' O'Day demanded. 'The ammunition is waiting to be handed over—'

'Only the medicine's been spoiled,' Dusty replied, indicating the box and the motionless woman on the ground beyond it. 'The town's done, *hombre*.'

'Perhaps not,' O'Day purred. 'I think that I might yet save the situation.'

'Not while Dusty and me can stop you,' Waco growled.

'I know it wouldn't be any use offering you shares in the concern,' the man declared, left hand rising as if to rub at his forehead. 'So I must make certain that you cannot interfere with my arrangements.'

While he was speaking, O'Day extended his open, upturned right palm and rested its elbow against his side. It was an innocent-seeming movement and had met with success when used against the three outlaws in Baylor County. Yet he realized that he now faced a vastly different proposition. The two Texans were not slow-witted yokels, but intelligent and lightning fast gun fighters. Even with the surprise element of the Deringer in its sleeve-holdout rig, he would be unlikely to drop them both quickly enough to save his life.

He did, however, have an ace in the hole. Something that had saved his life on at least two occasions; once during his quest for Simeon Lampart's whereabouts* and last night while confronted by Rosie Wilson. Once Dusty Fog and Waco saw what lay under the mask, they would be frozen into immobility long enough to give him his chance.

* Told in: *To Arms! To Arms In Dixie*.

'Just how do you figure on doing it, *hombre*?' Waco inquired, eyeing the wide shirt cuff above the extended, empty hand.

'Like this!' O'Day spat and tugged downwards with his left hand.

Doing so peeled off the mask and left his features exposed. There was no face as such, only a cratered, seamed, hideous mass of dirty grey flesh without a real nose or much by the way of lips. As the mask was removed, O'Day pressed his right elbow against his ribs and set the Remington Double Deringer free. It was propelled forward towards the palm that was waiting to close upon its bird's-head grip.

O'Day was only partially successful in his assumption of the Texans' reactions to the sight of his face. What he had not known was that Dusty Fog was aware of the vitriol attack and could guess at something of the horror which must lie behind the mask.

Like Dusty, the blond youngster had suspected that O'Day carried a hide-out pistol up his sleeve and was ready to counter its threat. The sight of the man's ruined features prevented Waco from responding with his usual speed. Letting out of gasp of horror, the blond kept his hands motionless.

Fortunately for Waco, Dusty was not so badly affected. On learning about the incident which had ruined O'Day's face, the small Texan had reached an accurate estimation of how Rosie Wilson had been killed. From his memory of the sequence in which the shots had been fired and after examining the rear of the barber's shop, Dusty had concluded that the woman had surprised her killer as he was leaving. Obviously she had been holding her revolver and the bull's eye lantern. According to Emma, Rosie had known how to handle the gun. So something must have diverted her, giving the person she had confronted time to shoot. Seen in the lantern's light, that hideously-marked face would have had such an effect.

So Dusty had been prepared. Yet he knew that Waco might not be so ready. Throwing himself sideways, Dusty sent his hands towards their respective weapons. He charged into Waco, knocking the youngster staggering. Even as he moved, the Remington appeared and barked. Something like a red-hot iron gouged across his right shoulder, but he knew that he had been lucky. If he had remained motionless, he would have caught the .41 ball in the torso. Pain halted his right hand, but the left completed its draw. Crashing, once, the Colt from the off side holster sent its bullet into O'Day's left breast. The man reeled, spun around and landed face down on the ground.

Dusty lowered his smoking Colt and let out a long, low sigh. The assignment was over. All he now had to do was get the remaining citizens of Hell out of the Palo Duro alive.

CHAPTER SEVENTEEN

LET THEM LEAVE IN PEACE

MORTALLY wounded, Mephisto O'Day lay on top of the box, which had been set up again, and allowed Doctor Connolly to do what little he could to treat the wound. Having had his shoulder bandaged, Dusty Fog stood with the Ysabel Kid and Waco in front of the *Kweharehnuh* chiefs.

'What now, Magic Hands?' Ten Bears asked and pointed to Giselle's body. 'The medicine is broken—'

'I only said that the saw couldn't hurt her,' the small Texan pointed out. '*Pohawe* shot her.'

'The witch woman has told you many times that the white man's medicine was a trick,' the Kid went on. 'Yet she could not understand how it was done. So she killed the woman in anger and paid the price. She had no medicine power, or if she had, it left her for her badness.'

'*Cuchilo* speaks with a straight tongue,' declared the 'old man' chief who had loaned him the shield. 'All along I said that she was no true medicine woman.'

'This I give to you, *Paruwa Semenho*,' Dusty said and drew the photograph from his shirt.

Watching, the Kid gave a silent whoop of delight and approval. Trust old Dusty to do just the right thing. Returning the photograph, without being asked or using it as a bargaining point, had been a masterly stroke.

'My thanks to you, Magic Hands,' the *paria:vo* replied and his deep sense of gratitude showed plainly. 'What now?'

'You will be given your ammunition,' Dusty answered. 'The people have it. In return, I say let them leave in peace.'

'They wish to leave?' Ten Bears inquired.

'Maybe they don't, but they will. You have the word of

Magic Hands on that. Let them go and have your bravehearts give the sun-oath that they will not harm them as long as they leave the Palo Duro.'

'The *paria:vo* of the Texans is right,' Ten Bears admitted, throwing a disgusted glare at the bunch of citizens huddled in the background. 'They would be coups only for *tuineps* just becoming *tuivitsi*. It will be done, Magic Hands.'

'Captain Fog,' Connolly said. 'This man wants to speak to you.'

'I'll come right now,' Dusty promised, having translated the request and received Ten Bears' permission to finish the conversation. 'Make the allocation, you folks.'

'Then we can stay here?' Youseman asked.

'Nope,' Dusty replied. 'But you're getting out alive with anything you can tote with you.'

'But—!' the undertaker began.

'Can we leave in safety?' Goldberg interrupted.

'No *Kweharehnuh*'ll harm you, I'll have their word on that,' Dusty assured the citizens. 'They'll let you out of the Palo Duro. So start handing out that ammunition.'

Leaving Waco and the Kid to attend to the allocation, Dusty walked over to the box. Holding her head, Emma came up with the men Dusty had dispatched to make sure that she was all right. Ordering everybody else to keep away, Dusty stood with the blonde alongside the hideously disfigured man.

'Have you ever seen a death scene in a drama, Captain Fog?' O'Day asked. 'If not, you are now. I am going to play my death scene, using breath some might say would be better employed in confessing my sins.'

'Don't talk, Mephisto—,' Emma began.

'Talk is all I have left, my pet,' the man answered. 'So let me have my grand dying scene. I am sorry for striking you down—'

'That's all right,' the blonde replied. 'I've always taken lumps from one man or another.'

'You're not the delicate flower you would have us believe, Emma,' O'Day chided. 'But it is a good role and you can play it well. You'll find the jewellery from Crouch's safe, with that which Giselle stole from Duprez, in the left-hand drawer of Simmy's desk.'

'*You* killed Duprez?' Dusty put in. 'I didn't suspect you of doing it.'

'Why not?' O'Day inquired. 'Did I impress you to such an extent with my glowing honesty?'

'Nope. I just couldn't see Duprez showing you where the jewellery was hidden. I figured that it'd take a pretty woman to get that. On top of which, I *knew* that Emma and Giselle had come back to lay hands on the jewellery.'

'You thought that *I'd* sent Giselle to do it?' Emma demanded angrily.

'Nope,' Dusty replied. 'I reckoned that was her idea. You'd've been planning to get it without fuss and killing.'

'That's what I planned,' the blonde confirmed. 'I kept warning her that you'd only stand by your word as long as nobody got hurt. Only she had to do it her own way.'

'Come now, no further recriminations,' O'Day put in weakly. 'This is *my* death scene and I should hold the stage, not the supporting players.'

'Go to it,' Dusty requested, unable to hold down his admiration for the dying man. 'There's nothing anybody can do to save you.'

'I don't think I wanted saving,' O'Day countered. 'With a face like mine, there is nothing to live for except revenge. And even that is no longer with me.'

'Simmy and Giselle were always afraid that you hadn't drowned,' Emma remarked. 'They knew that you'd be looking for them if you hadn't.'

'And they were right. After Simmy had thrown the vitriol into my face, I dashed from the hotel and flung myself into the river. I almost drowned, but the water saved at least some of my face. Don't ask me how I got out of the river. Luck, maybe. I was always a strong swimmer. Or determination not to die until I had been avenged on Simmy and Giselle. So I lived – if you could call it living – but by the time I had recovered sufficiently, they were gone. I headed for Mexico, only to discover that they had not reached the original destination. So I wondered if something had gone wrong. I returned to the United States and began to haunt the theatres. If Simmy needed money, that is where he would turn. I had all my props, wigs, masks, everything. Few people ever saw my real face and none who did lived. Yet there was no word of Simmy. Until at last I picked up a hint about Hell. It was enough to set me to trying to find it.'

'You got here in the end,' Dusty drawled.

'And found that I had arrived too late,' O'Day pointed out. 'I could hardly believe the luck which threw me in with Giselle and Emma. It gave me a chance to see how well my disguise would stand up to old friends' scrutiny.'

'It worked real good,' Emma praised. 'But Giselle thought she recognized your voice.'

'And put it down to the workings of her conscience, I'll bet,' the man grinned. 'What a blow to be told that Simmy was dead. I had planned a different end for him. However, I decided to have my vengeance upon Giselle. And then I saw what a good proposition the town was. It would be a sop for my loss if I could take it over and run it in Simmy's place. First, of course, I would have to eliminate you and your companions, Captain Fog. No. Don't interrupt. I was seeking ways of doing it, when I followed Giselle to the bathhouse. I broke into the living quarters and hid in the bedroom. I saw her entice Duprez into producing le Blanc's loot. Then she killed him and carried it off with her. I wasted some time commiserating with her victim and was confronted by the Wilson woman as I left. I don't think she liked my face.'

'It would have worked again, except that Emma had told me about you,' Dusty commented. 'So I was expecting something like it when you pulled the mask off.'

'So *that's* how I failed. No matter now. Slipping away from the barber's shop, I decided to make some trouble for your party. I went to the jewellers and was opening his safe when his wife came in. I killed her to silence her, then I'm damned if her husband didn't arrive. I knifed him, but he managed to run away. So I changed wigs and left the long one with the jewellery, my cloak and top hat hidden behind the hotel's back-house, then came to the saloon. It was my intention to incriminate Giselle, knowing that you would protect her and, given good luck, be killed. Instead, I found myself accused and in danger of being lynched. So I exposed your identities to divert attention from myself. May I say that you handled the situation in a masterly and efficient manner?'

'Thank you'most to death,' Dusty answered dryly. 'Why did you come back to town? I thought that you'd figured the *Kweharehnuh*'d settle your score with Giselle and'd lit out.'

'That's what I wanted you to think,' O'Day admitted. 'My real intention by that time was to become the ruler of Hell. I left my horses and property in the woods, returned before daylight and concealed myself in Simmy's house. That was how I came to find le Blanc's loot. I knew that Giselle was too smart to have kept it on her person.'

'How did you know that I'd come and give you a chance to take over from me?' Emma wanted to know.

'Ah. That, I admit, was fortunate rather than planned. I had learned how the allocation was always made and knew that, apart from myself, only you in Hell knew how to handle the trick. I had come prepared, in the hope that an opportunity might arise. It did and I took my chance.'

'And near on bust my head!' the blonde stated indignantly.

'Pure necessity, my dear Emma,' O'Day apologized. 'I assure you that I struck as gently as I could. It was my hope to perform the trick, then amaze the Indians by a transformation to my real self. Then I would have persuaded them to kill you and your men, Captain Fog. What I didn't count on was that somebody would have plans of their own. What caused the shooting?'

'*Pohawe* the witch woman, was fixing to bust your medicine by having Giselle shot from the rim,' Dusty explained. 'Only Lon happened along and cut in.'

'A woman again,' O'Day sighed. 'All my troubles have stemmed from women. Poor, treacherous, vicious little Giselle. I might have forgiven her for the betrayal if it had left me dead. But not for this—' He indicated his face. 'Oh well, it's all over now. Maybe I'll meet her and Simmy in the other Hell.'

Looking around, Dusty found that the ammunition had been handed out. He heard the words of the sun oath rumbling out as the braves agreed that they would allow the citizens to leave unharmed and unhindered.

'Sun, father, hear my words. Earth, mother, hear my words. Do not let me live for another season if I do not keep this promise.'

The small Texan nodded in silent satisfaction. No warrior would go against the sacred sun oath. The people could leave in safety. The town of Hell would no longer offer its citizens a refuge, but they would escape with their lives and such of their property as they could take with them. When he left this time, Dusty Fog would have no conscience troubles to worry him.

THE SOUTH WILL RISE AGAIN

For my bueno amigo Louis Masterson in the hope that he will give Morgan Kane a decent gun.

AUTHOR'S NOTE

The events in the earlier chapters of this book run concurrently with those recorded in HELL IN THE PALO DURO and GO BACK TO HELL. While complete in itself, the story concludes Belle Boyd's search for the Frenchman, which commenced in TO ARMS! TO ARMS, IN DIXIE!

CHAPTER ONE

DEATH TO ALL TRAITORS

The sign at the side of the stage read, 'MELANIE BEAUCHAMPAINE & TEXAS, Cowgirl Magic'.

There were few male members of the audience who would have objected to sharing their camp-fires with such 'cowgirls'. Each wore a skin-tight, sleeveless, black satin blouse of *extremely* extreme décolleté, ending short enough to leave its wearer's midriff exposed. The riding breeches, of the same glossy material, clung so snugly that every curve, depression and movement of the hips, buttocks, thighs and calves showed tantalizingly. They had black Stetsons set at jaunty angles on their heads. Hessian riding boots graced their feet. Each had on a gunbelt, with a revolver in its holster.

Of equal height, Melanie Beauchampaine was a tall, slender girl; although anything but flat-chested, skinny or boyish in appearance. For all that, she was out-done in the matter of a figure by the rich, voluptuous curves of her beautiful assistant. A close observer might have noticed that Texas's left eye was blackened and Melanie had a thickened top lip, hinting possibly at a disagreement between them over some matter.

Whatever the cause of controversy had been, the girls displayed no sign of it. They were a trifle nervous, but that might have been on account of the quality of certain members of their audience. The Variety Theatre in San Antonio de Bexar was that night acting as host to the Governor of Texas, Stanton Howard, and several prominent figures in the State's all-important cattle industry.

Nervous or not, the girls had given a good performance of magical tricks. They had been a fitting climax to a pleasant show. Clearly, however, they were coming to the end of their act.

'And now I would like the assistance of a few gentlemen,' Melanie announced. Seeing several male members of the audience rise hurriedly, she went on, 'With so many handsome volunteers to choose from, I do declare I don't know who to take.'

'We'd best pick them quickly, Melanie,' Texas suggested, speaking in a similar Southern drawl to that of her companion. 'If we don't, they'll stompede all over us.'

'Why sure,' Melanie agreed. 'Let's be tactful for once, shall we? I think all you boys had better sit down and we'll get somebody a bit further away. They won't be coming on the stage, anyways.' Waiting until the men had returned to their seats, she waved a hand towards the guests-of-honour's box. 'Perhaps his Honour, the Governor, will oblige?'

'I wish I was the Governor,' yelled one of the disappointed candidates.

'The job has to have *some* consolations,' Governor Howard pointed out, standing up.

'May I ask Captain Dusty Fog to take part,' Melanie called, 'without being thought to be making favourites?'

'Go on, Dusty,' the burly rancher known as Shangai Pierce suggested. 'It'll make up for you losing out on that beef contract.'

'We haven't lost it yet,' the well-dressed young man whom the rancher had addressed replied and came to his feet.

'No bickering, boys!' Melanie warned. 'This is a peace conference you're all here for.' Swinging towards the box on the opposite side of the theatre, in which were seated the same ranchers' foremen, she said, 'Now let me see, how about you, Mr. Figert?'

'Which shows you've got right good taste as well as beauty, ma'am,' drawled Miffin Kennedy's segundo as he stood up.

'If I get something like that said to me, I'm picking the next one,' Texas declared. 'Mr. Counter, will you make our other assistant?'

'Why I'd admire to assist you, most any old time, ma'am,' declared the handsome blond giant to whom the words had been directed.

Going by the glance Melanie threw at her assitant, she had not expected the interruption. However, she made no comment on it.

'Now Texas will go into the magic box,' Melanie announced, indicating the large, gaily-painted but as yet unused structure standing in the centre of the stage. 'We will see what happens next.'

'Mind you-all drop me on top of the handsomest of them, Melanie,' Texas requested, opening the door and showing the empty interior of the box, then entering.

'Why I'd do that, honey,' Melanie answered, closing the door. 'But I doubt if Governor Stanton's wife would approve.'

There was a laugh from the audience, wiped away by the orchestra in the pit commencing a long roll of the drums.

Every eye was on the slender, beautiful girl as she reached for and jerked open the door of the box.

It was not empty!

Two male figures in range clothes sprang out, holding revolvers.

'Death to all traitors!' bellowed the smaller, swinging his weapon into alignment.

Shots thundered from both the newcomers' revolvers, their barrels pointing towards the guests-of-honour's box. Clapping his hands to his forehead, Governor Howard spun around and tumbled to the floor. Clutching at his left breast, Captain Dusty Fog was pitched backwards and landed across the knees of Pierce and the third rancher, Richard King.

Instantly wild confusion reigned in the building. Due to the delicate nature of the situation—the Governor was trying to avert a range war between his companions—the San Antonio town marshal had caused every visitor to the theatre to be disarmed on arrival. Voices raised in shouts. Women screamed. Men rose, grabbing at empty holsters and blocking the lines of fire of the peace officers who were standing guard at the exits.

The moment the two men had made their appearance, Melanie stepped into the back of the box. She pressed herself to the rear, for there was little enough room inside.

Having fired at and sent the Governor down, the smaller of the pair leapt to Melanie's side. Instead of following them immediately, the taller, younger man—a boy in his late teens—swivelled in the direction of the foremen's box. Left, right, left, the long-barrelled 1860 Army Colts in his hands boomed out. Mark Counter's giant frame rocked under the impact. Before the big blond had pitched headlong out of sight, the youngster was joining his companion and the girl. The bottom of the box sank rapidly downwards and carried them from view.

CHAPTER TWO

YOU'RE NOT LONG OUT OF JAIL

A few weeks before the incident at the Variety Theatre.

Strolling slowly along the sidewalk in the direction of the German's Hotel at Mooringsport, Sabot the Mysterious displayed the attitude of a man engrossed in his problems. He was so preoccupied with his thoughts that he ignored the scrutiny of the slender, beautiful young woman who was standing outside Klein's General Store. Somewhat overpainted and dressed in the kind of clothes poorer actresses, or saloongirls, wore when travelling between jobs or walking the streets, she held the inevitable parasol and vanity bag in her left hand.

Going closer, Sabot became *very* aware of the girl. Advancing in a casual-appearing manner, she bumped into him. The collision was anything but accidental. As soon as their bodies came into contact, her right hand slipped under his jacket towards the wallet in its inside pocket.

Sabot had just concluded a most satisfactory interview with the town's marshal and was returning to his hotel feeling, for the first time in days, a sense of relief. The state of nervous tension under which he had been living since arriving in Shreveport, to fulfil an engagement at the Grand Palace Theatre, was ebbing away.

Give de Richelieu his due, Sabot mused before coming into contact with the girl, he had been correct in his assessment of how the military and civil authorities would react if their enterprise had not reached its ultimate aims. For all that, being aware that things *had* gone wrong, the business in which they had been engaged was of such a serious nature Sabot had hardly been left feeling comfortable, or easy in his mind.

Nobody could have been relaxed and free from care when trying to stir up an open rebellion against the United States' Congress. Which is what Sabot the Mysterious and the other members of the Brotherhood For Southron Freedom had been hoping to do in Shreveport.

When the Brotherhood had got into their stride, with a campaign of agitation that was calculated to provoke the Southern States into a second attempt to secede from the Union, they had met with little success. By 1874, the worst elements and excesses of Reconstruction had been eliminated. Prosperity was returning to the lands south of the Mason-Dixon line and the white population had no desire for a resumption of the hardships of war, nor to sample again the bitter consequences of defeat.

There had been some response to the Brotherhood's rallying cries; 'Give money to buy arms!'; 'Make ready for the day of reckoning with the Yankees!'; 'THE SOUTH WILL RISE AGAIN!'. Not enough, however, to have made the dreams of secession become a reality. The men behind the conspiracy had realized that some dramatic proof of the Union's perfidy and hatred of the South was needed. So a devilish plot had been hatched to bring this about.

All that had been achieved so far was to obtain sufficient money to buy a hundred obsolete Henry repeating rifles and ten thousand rounds of .44/28 Tyler B. Henry ammunition. The chief satisfaction from the purchase had been that the arms—and some military uniforms and accoutrements taken as an excuse for making it—had originally been destined to equip a Kansas volunteer Dragoon regiment that was being raised to fight the Confederate States. So far, the weapons had not been put to use in the cause of Southern freedom.

They would have been, if everything had gone according to plan in Shreveport.

Althought friendly relations had been resumed between the United States' Army and the Southern civilian population through much of Dixie, that happy state had not existed in Shreveport. Brevet Lieutenant Colonel Szigo, in command of the local Army Post, was an embittered man who had been passed over for promotion or even elevation from his substantive rank of captian. Blaming the South, which had given up the fight before his brevet rank could be made substantive, he had allowed—even overtly encouraged—his men to behave as if they were still a garrison force of the Reconstruction Period. So there had been little love lost between the soldiers and the citizens.

Knowing of the hostility which existed in Shreveport, the leaders of the Brotherhood had selected it as the ideal area for their demonstration. Having thrown the United States' Secret Service off the trail of the arms,* they had made ready for action.

Throughout his engagement at the Grand Palace Theatre, Sabot had worked to win the confidence of the Army officers at the post and certain influential members of Shreveport society. He had succeeded to such an extent that Szigo not only permitted him to give a benefit performance free to ex-members of the Confederate States' Army and Navy—he had already done the same for the soldiers—but had agreed, in the interests of avoiding possible clashes, to place the town off limits to his own troops on the evening of the show.

That latter, engineered by Sabot, had been very necessary to the success of the scheme.

Towards the end of the benefit, masked members of the Brotherhood had 'invaded' the stage and 'interrupted' Sabot's display of magical illusions. They had made inflammatory speeches, then taken certain precautions to ensure that nobody interfered with their escape.

Present in the audience had been Colonel Alburgh Winslow, a member of the Louisiana State Legislature and owner of the *Shreveport Herald-Times*, and other prominent citizens noted for their moderate opinions and their efforts to prevent open conflict between the town's people and the soldiers. It had been planned that, later in the evening—disguised in the Dragoons' uniforms†—Victor Brandt would take an 'escort' and 'arrest' Winslow's party on charges of organizing a treasonable assembly. Any who had resisted were to be shot on the spot. Those who had gone quietly would have been murdered and their bodies—

* Told in: *TO ARMS! TO ARMS, IN DIXIE!*
† By 1863, the Dragoons had begun to wear the standard U.S. Cavalry uniform.

decorated with boards inscribed, 'So perish all traitors to the Union'—left hanging in the city's main square.

Unfortunately, Sabot's assistant, Princess Selima Baba, had not been convincing in her behaviour during the 'invasion' of the stage. In fact, her attitude had threatened to spoil the whole effect. So, in the dressing-rooms after changing into his uniform, Brandt—an arrogant, bad-tempered and vicious young man—had beaten her with his fists. Furious at the punishment, Selima had fled. Suspecting that she might warn the authorities of what was planned, Sabot had suggested that the scheme be delayed until she had been captured. Taking two of his men, Brandt had set off to fetch the girl back. One of his escort had returned to say that she was trying to reach Colonel Szigo, but that the others were on her trail and hoped to prevent her visiting the Army post. Brandt had also warned that the 'arrests' must not be attempted until he had given the word. As he alone wore an officer's uniform, that had been sound advice. The party would have lacked credibility if it had arrived to make the arrests comprising only enlisted men.

When Brandt and his companion had not returned in a reasonable time, Sabot had taken it upon himself to call off the whole affair. Dismissing the men, he had sent a warning to de Richelieu—who had left the theatre to supervise the delivery of the arms from their hiding place five miles away—that something was wrong. After that, Sabot had continued with his pre-arranged intention of leaving Shreveport on the *Texarkana Belle* and travelling to Mooringsport. From that town, he was to commence an itinerary of Texas engagements. During it, he was to spread the word of the 'Yankees'' dastardly deed and to help arouse enmity in the Lone Star State.

On his arrival in Mooringsport, shortly before noon, Sabot had immediately visited the town's marshal. He had told the peace officer a story that would, all being well, hold water when compared with the recollections of the audience concerning what had happened on the stage.

To hear Sabot tell it, he had been attacked and, along with Selima, driven to his dressing-room by the masked agitators. After they had completed their treasonable activities, he had been compelled to return to the stage and satisfy the audience that he had not been harmed. Then his assailants had departed, taking Selima as a hostage against his behaviour. They had also warned that he would be kept under observation and killed, along with the girl, if he should attempt to consult the authorities.

Fearing for his assistant's life, despite the men's promise that she would be allowed to join him aboard the *Texarkana Belle*, Sabot had complied with their demands. However, the girl had not made her appearance at sailing time and he had left without her. In exculpation for his desertion, he had claimed that, on thinking the matter over, he had reached the conclusion that Selina had been an active participant in the plot. That, he had told the marshal, explained how the masked men had known the trick with which he planned to end his show; and had been able to substitute their treasonable portraits—which portrayed Union generals in an uncomplimentary light and showed an unsavoury aspect of life under Reconstruction—for the harmless illustrations which he would have used.

Although the marshal had apparently been satisfied with Sabot's story, he had insisted that the magician remained in Mooringsport until after he had telegraphed the Shreveport authorities. Stating that he had intended staying over to give a few performances, Sabot had acceded to the request. He had been allowed to go about his business and was promised that he would be kept informed of any future developments.

At four o'clock in the afternoon, a deputy had arrived at the hotel and asked the magician to accompany him to the marshal's office. Managing to conceal his anxiety, Sabot had obeyed. He had spent the hours in trepidation, wondering what the answer from Shreveport would be. Flight had been impossible, for it would have been construed as evidence of guilt. The marshal's kindly, sympathetic attitude had hinted that he had nothing to fear.

There had been answers from the Shreveport Police Department and the commanding officer of the Army post. The former had merely stated that the incident at the theatre was being investigated, but everything pointed to Sabot being a victim rather than a participant. Numerous witnesses had seen him struck down and had testified to the interruption to his performance.

The latter message had been both puzzling and a source

of relief. Apparently Selima had 'escaped from her captors', but was killed before she could reach the gates of the post. Opening fire, the guard had shot down her murderers—there was no mention of them having been in uniform—before they could flee from the scene of the crime.

The puzzling aspect had been that the message was signed, 'Manderley' and not 'Szigo'.

With something like satisfaction, the marshal had said that the intruders had slipped through the Shreveport police's and the Army's fingers. Sabot was free to go. The meeting had ended amicably with the magician handing out free tickets to his first performance.

Sabot had quit the marshal's office with a lighter heart than when he had entered. Despite the failure to carry out de Richelieu's scheme, the affair had not ended too badly for him. He had emerged without being suspected of complicity in the plot. With Brandt dead, he stood a chance of stepping into the 'captain's'—Brandt's rank for the deception—shoes as second-in command of the Brotherhood. Not that he gave a damn for the ideals which guided de Richelieu's actions. He merely wanted to gain a larger proportion of the financial benefits he felt sure would accrue as a result of the organization's activities.

Thinking of the future had brought another aspect to Sabot's attention. He would be continuing to produce his show, which allowed members of the Brotherhood to visit, or meet in, different towns without raising questions concerning their presence. So he would require a replacement for Selima. Only this time he must be more selective in his choice. His rivals for Brandt's position might use Selima's inadequacies as a tool against him, blaming him for the failure of the Shreveport affair.

What Sabot needed was a pretty, shapely, fairly intelligent girl who was not overburdened by scruples. There had not seemed much chance of him finding such a person in the small Lake Caddo town of Mooringsport.

Having just reched that conclusion, Sabot collided with the girl and felt her fingers reaching into his jacket. He grinned internally at her mistake. Of course, if he had been wearing his stage make-up and clothes, instead of being clean-shaven and clad in a snappy grey suit of the latest Eastern sport's fashion, she might have known better than to make the attempt at picking his pocket.

Catching hold of the girl's wrist, before she could completely withdraw the wallet from his pocket, the magician plucked her hand from beneath his jacket. They had that particular length of the sidewalk to themselves and he realized how nobody could see what was happening between them.

'Let me go!' the girl hissed, trying to snatch her wrist from his grasp. 'What do you-all think you're doing?'

Sabot was on the point of shouting for somebody to fetch the marshal. Hearing the girl speak, he hurriedly revised his opinion and studied her. The ribbons of a grubby white spoon bonnet were fastened in a bow under the chin of a beautiful face. The hat effectively covered her hair, but Sabot sensed that it had been cut almost boyishly short. Taken with the tanned texture of her skin, the hair's length was significant. She had on a basque jacket, but did not wear the socially-required blouse underneath it, and a shiny black skirt which emphasized the shape of her slender hips before ending short enough to expose an indecorous amount of her cheap high-buttoned shoes.

While her appearance had intimated that she was a not-too-prominent actress or a saloongirl, she had spoken in the accent of a well-raised Southron lady. Except that her tones had been hardened and harshened by life and unpleasant experiences. Such a combination suggested possibilities to the magician.

'Shall we call the marshal so that you can complain?' Sabot inquired, holding the girl close to him with his left hand while the right moved swiftly on a mission which she failed to detect. 'I'll do it, if you're so inclined.'

'So call him and we'll see whose word he'll take,' challenged the girl, drawing back but still held by the wrist.

For all her brash answer, she looked decidedly uneasy.

'Very well,' countered the magician and turned his head as if to do so.

'This is all a misunderstanding,' the girl put in hurriedly. 'I don't want to be involved in a public spectacle. So I'll overlook your behaviour.'

Retaining his grip on her wrist, Sabot moved back to arm's length and gave her another scrutiny. While slender and willowy, she was anything but scraggy. Dressed in a suitable manner, she would be worth looking at. Despite her obvious poverty, she carried herself with an air of breeding and refinement. That was possible. Reconstruction had seen many formerly well-to-do and respectable Southron girls driven on to the stage, or into even less savoury occupations. Most of the unfortunates blamed the Yankees bitterly for their downfalls and had no love for supporters of the Union. Some could not adjust to their lowered status. Those who did, in Sabot's experience, became tough, hard and unscrupulous.

Unless the magician missed his guess, the would-be pickpocket fell into that category.

Moreover, there were certain indications about her as to where she had spent time recently.

'Don't try and run away!' the magician warned, releasing her. 'If you do, I'll have you arrested. You wouldn't like that. You're not long out of jail, are you?'

'How dare you?' the girl spat, with well-simulated indignation. 'Just what do you mean by——'

'That spoon bonnet looks like hell on you, but you have to wear it to hide your hair,' Sabot interrupted and grinned as her right hand fluttered nervously towards her head. 'They cut women prisoner's hair short at the State Penitentiary. Your clothing suggests that you're an actress, or a calico cat. But you've got a tan that says you've spent more time out of doors than you would in either job. It all adds up to you just having been released from prison.'

'Smart, aren't you?' the girl demanded bitterly.

'Shrewd—and correct.'

'All right, mister. So I've only been out for a few days. What's that got to do with you?'

'I could have you send back,' Sabot warned her.

'For what?'

'Stealing my wallet.'

'Try proving that n——' grinned the girl.

'Before you make me do that,' Sabot answered, 'take a look in your vanity bag.'

Jerking open the mouth of the bag, the girl glanced inside with an attitude of disbelief. Then she stiffened and stared harder. Raising her eyes, she glared at Sabot in open-mouthed amazement.

'I-It's there!' the girl croaked, looking frightened. 'What

—How——?'

'The next time you try to pick a pocket, make sure it's not a magician's,' Sabot advised. 'Like I said, I could send you back to jail.'

'But you won't if I'm nice to you, huh?' the girl guessed.

'Not entirely. I assume that you're short of money.'

'Mister, that's a mighty shrewd assumption.'

'Could you use a meal?'

'I aimed to buy one with whatever I found in your wallet,' the girl admitted. 'The food at those stagecoach way stations isn't fit for a hawg, or a Yankee. In that order.'

'If you'll be my guest,' the magician said, delighted that he had summed up another aspect of her character so well. She had no love for 'Yankees'. 'I'll stand treat for a meal.'

'As a reward for me trying to lift your leather?' the girl said dryly.

'Do you want the meal, or don't you?'

'I want it. But I was wondering why you're being so all-fired nice to me.'

'Why do you think I am?'

'If it's for the reason I suspect, you're wasting your time,' the girl declared. 'One of the reasons I'm so short of money is that I don't.'

'I'll remember that, if I get inclined to want it,' Sabot promised. 'My last assistant quit and I need a good-looking, shapely girl to replace her. While we're eating, I'll decide whether to offer you the job or not.'

'Why, thank you "most to death,"' replied the girl, taking the wallet from her bag and handing it back to its owner. 'And I'll decide whether I want to take it.'

CHAPTER THREE

STOMP THE BASTARD GOOD

Although Sabot the Mysterious did not realize it, he had played into the hands of the Brotherhood For Southron Freedom's most implacable and deadly enemy.

Yet, taking her early life into consideration, Belle Boyd

might have seemed ideally suited to become a leading light in an attempt to secede from the Union.

Born the only child of a wealthy Baton Royale plantation owner, Belle had been given a most unconventional upbringing. In addition to receiving the normal instruction in the social- and lady-like graces, she had been taught to ride astride, fence with sabre or epee, handle every type of firearm and perform skilfully at *savate*, the foot and fist boxing practiced by the French Creoles. Her father had always wanted a son and, by teaching her the martial arts, had given her an excellent education for what had lay ahead.

Shortly before the War Between The States had commenced, a drunken mob of pro-Unionists fanatics—led by a pair of liberal-intellectuals called Tollinger and Barmain—had raided the Boyds' plantation. By the time the family's 'downtrodden and abused' slaves had driven off the attackers, Belle was wounded, her parents dead, and the fine old Boyd mansion had been reduced to a blazing ruin.

On her recovery, Belle had sworn to take revenge on Tollinger and Barmain. They had fled to Union territory and were said to be members of the United States' Secret Service. As an aid to hunting them, Belle had joined a Confederate spy ring organized by her cousin, Rose Greenhow. Acting as a courier, the girl had specialized in delivering messages and other information through the enemy's lines. Gaining fame for such work, she had graduated to handling assignments of a difficult, dangerous nature.[*] To the Yankees, for whom she had become a thorn in the flesh, she had earned the title, the Rebel Spy.

Not until the War was over had Belle's path crossed that of her quarry. In pursuing and settling her account with them, she had paved the way for a change in her employers, if not in her way of life.[†] She had sworn the oath of allegiance to the Union and accepted General Handiman's offer to become a member of the United States' Secret Service.

Called in by the head of her organization to help prevent the Henry rifles from being delivered, Belle might have been faced by a clash of loyalties when she had learned of the

[*] Told in: *THE COLT AND THE SABRE*, *THE REBEL SPY* and *THE BLOODY BORDER*.
[†] Told in: *BACK TO THE BLOODY BORDER*.

Brotherhood For Southron Freedom. It did not arise. One of the organization's leaders, whom she knew only as 'the Frenchman' had been responsible for the death of two of her friends. He had tortured and brutally killed Madame Lucienne with his own hands. So Belle had sworn that she would take revenge on him, even if she had to smash the Brotherhood to do it.

It had been chiefly due to Belle Boyd's efforts that the Shreveport affair had failed. Arriving in that city, with information that something special was planned at the theatre, she had been a member of the audience. In fact, disguised as an elderly woman, she had been on the stage as part of Sabot's committee.

A variety of circumstances had led her to deduce the nature of the plan's second phase. Brandt and his companion had died at her hand, inside the Army post, after they had murdered Selima.

Unknown to the Brotherhood, there had been a change of command at the camp. Stories of Szigo's treatment of the Shreveport citizens had reached Washington. To avoid trouble, a more moderate commanding officer had been dispatched secretly to take sharge and bring an improvement in the relations between the soldiers and the town's people.

Having failed to arrest any of the Brotherhood, Colonel Manderley and Belle had debated their next line of action. One point had been decided upon. Under no circumstances must the full implications of the plot be made public. To have done so would have come close to achieving the Brotherhood's ends for them.

Naturally the incident at the theatre could not be overlooked. However, Colonel Winslow was Belle's uncle and he had agreed that his newspaper would treat the affair as nothing more than a stupid, ill-advised piece of foolishness. Shown in such a light, it would soon be forgotten. Winslow had also arranged for a story which would explain away Selima's murder and the deaths of the two conspirators.

Writing a report of her activities, Belle had arranged for it to be delivered at all speed to her superiors in New Orleans. Then she had made her preparations for resuming her pursuit of the Frenchman. Having arrived in Shreveport expecting trouble, she had brought in her trunk a number of items which she had felt might be of use. Selecting clothing that she believed would suit the situation, she had asked her uncle to hold the rest of her property until she could let him know where to send it. Then she had organized transport for the journey.

It had been decided that Sabot offered the best means of locating the rest of the Brotherhood. Following him had proved to be the easiest part of the affair. To help police the Red River, the U.S. Navy had placed two of its fast steam launches at the Army's disposal. So Belle had not needed to wait for a regular passenger boat, but had travelled from Shreveport in a launch. In that way, she had arrived in Mooringsport at three o'clock in the afternoon. She had taken a room in the town's cheapest hotel, then set off to locate the magician. Finding his place of residence had not been difficult. Having learnt that he was paying a visit to the marshal's office, she had waited with the intention of scraping up an acquaintance.

After the trouble Selima had caused, Belle had suspected that the magician might be looking for a more reliable type of assistant. She had settled upon a character which she believed would satisfy his requirements and had made the correct decision.

Over a meal at the German's Hotel, Belle had told Sabot how she had been put in jail for helping to swindle 'a fat Yankee pig who deserved it'. She had also admitted that the Pinkerton National Detective Agency were looking for her. Not for any serious crime, or with extra persistence, but merely because they liked to solve their cases and she could help with one. She had declared that, having made alterations to her appearance, they would be unlikely to recognize her. All in all, she had left the magician with the impression that she was a tough, unscrupulous girl, with a deep, lasting hatred for anybody who lived north of the Mason-Dixon line. He had accepted that she had once been rich, but was left a pauper by the War and had lived a hard life since its end.

Satisfied that he had found a suitable candidate for the post, Sabot had offered to make her his assistant. After haggling over pay, Belle had accepted. She had said that her name was 'Melanie Beauchampaine', but would not object to being known as Princess Selima Baba.

The rest of the day, Belle had never been out of Sabot's sight for more than a few minutes. She had tried on the garments which she would wear on the stage. Flimsy, scanty and revealing, they were what people expected of a girl who had been 'rescued from a life of sin in the Sultan of Tripoli's harem'. They had required some alterations, for the previous Selima had been a more buxom girl. That had been done and Belle had spent the evening learning her duties.

While Sabot had apparently trusted her, he had pumped her for more details about her past. She had told him plenty, hinting that she had double-crossed confederates and generally conveying the impression that she would not be troubled by scruples.

One factor more than any other had helped Belle to gain acceptance and avoid arousing suspicion. Mooringsport lay on the shore of Lake Caddo. To reach it, one had to branch away from the Red River along the Caddo River. Only one boat made regular runs between the town and Shreveport. As the girl had not been on the *Texarkana Belle*, Sabot accepted that she must have either come in on a stagecoach from the west, or had been in Mooringsport before he had arrived. He did not suspect that she had found another means of traversing the distance.

Belle had learned her duties well enough to help in Sabot's first performance. It had been a novel, not entirely pleasant, sensation, appearing on the stage clad in the flimsy, revealing 'harem girl's' costume; but she had forced herself to go through with the act. She had known that she would soon become accustomed to the situation.

One thing Belle had established quickly was that she wanted no amatory relationships with her fellow performers. Sabot, the five members of the orchestra and the two cross-talk comedians had accepted her decision without question. Not so the show's baritone, who fancied himself as being something of a lady-killer. It had taken Belle's knee, delivered hard into his groin, to convince him that when she said 'no', that was exactly what she meant. Sensing that he had found an ideal assistant, Sabot had backed up Belle in her treatment of the singer. The magician had issued a warning to all his employees, after the incident, that 'Melanie's' wishes must be respected.

Being only a small town, Mooringsport could not support a theatre. So the show had taken place on an improvised stage in the biggest saloon. While they had had a good reception each night, Belle wondered how Sabot was able to afford to play to such a restricted audience. He seemed content to do so and she did not ask questions.

Four days went by and on the fifth evening, Belle was presented with an opportunity to impress Sabot.

During the magician's performance, the girl had seen what she suspected was an exchange of signals between the magician and a big, burly, red-haired man in the audience. Although the latter was dressed differently, Belle had recognized him as 'Mick', a member of the Brotherhood whom she had seen in Memphis. Apart from the brief byplay, Sabot gave no further sign of interest in Mick.

After the show was over, and the girl had donned her street clothes in the small store-room which had been converted into her dressing-room, she went to find her employer. All the rest of the cast had already gone, but the door of the men's dressing-room was open. Seated at the table, with his 'jewel'-emblazoned turban, black opera cloak and frock coat removed, the magician was peeling off his false moustachios and sharp-pointed chin beard. At his side, the owner of the saloon had just finished counting out a pile of money.

'I'm sorry it's not more, Sabot,' the owner was saying. 'You've given me a full house and good bar sales every night. I'm sorry to see you go.'

'I've other commitments, unfortunately,' Sabot answered, his sallow face almost looking as if it was unfortunate. 'And this's enough. We couldn't move on until the *Belle* came back and doing the shows has helped me to teach Melanie her duties.'

'Say!' the owner ejaculated, indicating the newspaper which lay on the dressing-table. 'It was a bad thing, your other gal getting killed that way.'

'Tragic,' Sabot intoned soberly. 'It seems I misjudged her and she wasn't in cahoots with those men. She escaped and was trying to notify the authorities. If she had only come to me, things would have been different.'

'Maybe she didn't get away from the bastards until after the *Belle*'d pulled out,' the owner consoled. 'Anyways, it's not *you* us folks blames for her getting killed.'

There had been considerable discussion caused by the reports of the 'mysterious doings' in Shreveport. Some of the *Texarkana Belle*'s officers had been at the show. They, and the marshal, had told enough of Sabot's part in the affair for a garbled version of it to have made the rounds. Belle had watched and listened, hoping to learn in which direction public sentiment was swinging. From her findings, she had concluded that the officially-sponsored version of Selima's murder had swung public sympathy away from the Brotherhood. If the people of Mooringsport reflected the trend throughout the South, Sabot and his companions would be unable to benefit in any way from the incident.

'She was a good girl,' Sabot sighed, 'but always chasing after men. That's one problem I don't have to worry about now. Not chasing after m——.'

'Hey, Selima!' called the owner, becoming aware of Belle's presence and wanting to warn the magician before he made an indiscreet statement concerning his assistant's sexual behaviour.

'Changed and ready already, heh?' Sabot went on, turning to look at the girl. 'Come in. I'll not be long. Then we'll go back to the hotel and it'll be pay-day.'

'There's a word I love to hear,' Belle smiled, advancing. Then the newspaper's headlines caught her eye. 'Hey! Do you know her? Of course you do. I'm sorry, Sabby.'

Acting contrite and flustered, as a person would after making such a mistake, Belle picked up the paper. To the men, it seemed that she was merely covering her embarrassment; or motivated by morbid curiosity concerning her predecessor's death.

Under the headline, 'MAGICIAN'S ASSISTANT MURDERED', the *Shreveport Herald-Times* had done a fine job in covering the true facts of Selima's death. Her uncle had used it in a masterly fashion to condemn the Brotherhood's activities. Dismissing the incident at the theatre as he had promised, he had also commented that what had probably begun as a practical joke misfired badly when Selima had escaped. Being a courageous young lady with a strong sense of public spirit, she must have intended to report the incident to the authorities. Rather than allow it, the men had pursued her and killed her within sight of the post's main entrance. Unfortunately for the murderers, the guards had been on the alert and both men had been shot down while resisting arrest. There was no mention, once more, of Brandt and his companion having been dressed in U.S. Army uniforms.

A second headline announced Lieutenant Colonel Szigo's departure 'for a command on the Western frontier'. As the new commanding officer, Colonel Manderley wished to improve relations between the citizens and his soldiers. With that in mind, he, Winslow and the mayor of Shreveport—who would have been one of the victims in the plot—had come together and organized a 'Friendship Week'. During the seven days, there would be a variety of sporting, entertainment and social events, culminating with a Grand Ball on the Saturday.

'You wily old bas—gentleman—Uncle Alburgh,' Belle thought as she finished reading. 'With all that to look forward to, nobody will spare a thought for the speeches they heard. Nor about Selima's death. Not enough to query it deeply, anyway.'

Packing the money into his wallet, Sabot completed his change of clothing. Then he and Belle passed through the saloon's bar-room towards its main entrance. Avoiding the various offers to stop and take a drink, by pointing out that the show was moving on early the following morning and so he and Selima wished to grab some sleep, he escorted the girl from the building.

There had been no sign of Mick in the bar-room, but Belle soon detected him standing in the shadows across the street. Clearly he did not want his connection with the magician to be known. Instead of coming straight over, he waited until the couple hd moved away from the saloon before starting to cross the street. Belle became aware of certain possibilities opened up by Mick's actions. If he only would hold off from joining them for a little while——

Obligingly, Mick did as Belle wished.

'Sabby!' the girl whispered, after they had covered about a hundred yards along the practically empty street. 'There's a man coming——.'

'So?'

'He's following us. He was lurking outside the saloon and's been dogging our tracks ever since.'

'Why'd he do that, do you reckon?' Sabot inquired.

'It's our last night here. He'd know that you'd be getting paid off and he's fixing to rob you.'

'It could be,' the magician admitted soberly, hiding the amusement he felt. 'Shall I yell for the marshal?'

'That one-horse town knobhead!' Belle scoffed. 'He couldn't catch a blown-off hat with three extra hands. Anyway, I don't like turning anybody in to the john-laws.'

'So what do we do?' Sabot challenged.

'Let's teach the bastard a lesson,' Belle suggested. 'I think I know how we can do it.'

'All right,' the magician agreed, having heard the girl's plan. 'We'll play it your way.'

Continuing to the end of the building they were passing, Belle and Sabot turned into the alley. In the shadows, they waited and listened to the sound of Mick's feet drawing nearer. Whispering for Sabot to get ready, the girl returned to the street. She timed her arrival so that she walked straight into the burly man's arms.

'What's the hurry, darlin'?' Mick demanded, dropping his hands to rest on Belle's hips, 'Did old——?'

'My, you're a big one,' Belle purred, not wanting a premature exposure of Mick's connection with the magician.

'If that's the way you like them, darlin',' Mick grinned, feeling her body moving invitingly under his palms. 'Then 'tis what I am.'

'I'll just bet you are,' Belle enthused, turning as if to walk away.

'Seeing's we're going the same way, darlin',' Mick commented, following and curling his right arm about her waist. 'Let's go together.'

Advancing a couple of steps side by side, Belle contrived to angle them so that their backs were to the mouth of the alley. Her right hand rose to rest on his, its thumb pressing against the rear-centre of his knuckles. Curling her fingers under, she gently and provocatively tickled his palm as an aid in lulling him further into a sense of false security.

'Perhaps not all the way,' Belle drawled.

Tightening her grip on his hand, she stepped sideways with her right foot. Before he realized her intentions, she had hooked her left leg behind his right knee. Bending her knees slightly, to get below his centre of gravity, she completed her escape. Working in smooth coordination, she propelled her left elbow rearwards against his solar plexus, kept her left leg rigid and thrust her body into his. Taken by surprise and off balance, Mick let out a startled curse. Belle released his hand, the arm flew from about her middle and he stumbled backwards into the alley. Unable to regain his equilibrium, he sat down hard.

'Stomp the bastard good, Sabby!' Belle hissed, spinning around around. 'Teach him a lesson——!'

Instead of following the girl's excited advice, Sabot was laughing. So Belle reacted as she could be expected to have done if she had been genuine. Letting her words trail off, she displayed bewilderment at his lack of activity.

'Are you all right, Mick?' the magician inquired, moving forward.

'Wha——What——?' muttered the burly Irishman, shaking his head in a dazed and winded fashion. Then a dull, angry flush crept across his face and he started to lurch erect. 'Why you——!'

Watching Mick rise and look menacingly in her direction, Belle prepared to take measures for her protection. However, Sabot stepped between them. Flicking from inside his right sleeve, a shiny nickel-plated Remington Double Derringer settled its 'bird's head' butt in his waiting palm.

'Easy, Mick,' the magician ordered. 'She thought you was following to rob us and reckoned she could handle you. I see now that she could.'

Mumbling under his breath, Mick allowed his eyes to drop to the Remington. Although it dangled negligently at the magician's side, the Irishman was under no delusions as to its deadly qualities. Nor did he doubt that Sabot would use it if necessary.

'She near on bust my back!' Mick growled. 'I'll——'

'Do nothing,' Sabot finished for him.

'Just what the hell's going on?' Belle demanded, as she felt would be expected of her.

'It's all right, my dear,' Sabot replied, keeping his eyes on the other man and speaking over his shoulder. 'Mick's a friend of mine. We do business together. I should have told you, but I wanted to see how you'd make out.'

'Sure and it's slick the way you did it, darlin',' Mick went on, starting to grin. 'You wouldn't have Irish blood, would

27

you?'

'You'd better come to the hotel with us, Mick,' Sabot suggested, giving Belle no chance to reply. 'We'll talk there.'

'That I'll do,' the Irishman agreed, looking at Belle. 'Can I take hold again without getting throwed over your head?'

'I wouldn't count on it,' Sabot warned and moved closer to whisper something in Mick's ear.

'If he's telling you I like girls, not fellers, he's right, Mick,' Belle said calmly. 'I'm not ashamed of it and your knowing will save us both time and inconvenience.'

'So that's the way of it?' Mick grunted, sounding disappointed. 'Well, 'tis everybody to their own tastes, I always say. Is she in it with us, Sabot?'

'I haven't asked,' the magician admitted. 'But I hope she will be.'

CHAPTER FOUR

U.S. ARMY PAYMASTER ROBBED

Dressed in her 'harem girl' attire, Belle Boyd was seated in Sabot's dressing-room sharing a pot of coffee and doughnuts with the magician. They were waiting to start their first performance in Fort Worth, Texas, three weeks after their departure from Mooringsport.

Belle's time in Sabot's employment had not been wasted. Having been accepted at face value by her travelling companions, she had learned plenty about the Brotherhood For Southron Freedom. On first being told of its aims, she had displayed such enthusiasm that the magician had been convinced of her sincerity. So much so that he had not hesitated to speak freely with Mick in her presence.

According to the Irishman, with four exceptions, the Brotherhood had made good their escape from Shreveport. Brandt and his companion's fate was known; but nobody could discover what had happened to the two men who had followed Winslow from the theatre, and should have watched his house until the arrival of the 'arrest detail'.

Sabot had guessed that they had taken alarm and fled when they realized the 'detail' was not coming; and Mick agreed that it was possible. Belle could have enlightened them on the matter, having dealt with the men in question, but felt disinclined to do so.

Continuing his report, Mick had said that de Richelieu—who appeared to be the supreme head of the Brotherhood—was taking the rifles and ammunition to a ranch in Texas. As Sabot had apparently known the ranch's location, Belle had not heard it mentioned. She had not pressed the point, for to do so might have aroused the magician's suspicion. Instead, she had listened to the orders for their future activities. They were to follow the original itinerary, but to act in a different manner than had been arranged. Instead of spreading the news about the Shreveport incident, they were merely to pass out pro-Secession propaganda and select supporters for the movement.

In addition to improving her abilities as Sabot's assistant, Belle had been required to help further the Brotherhood's cause. The show had played one-night stands at various towns since leaving Mooringsport. In each, Sabot had given an informal dinner to carefully selected members of the community. The selection had been carried out by another member of the Brotherhood, whom Belle had not yet met. Travelling ahead of the show, he decided who would be the most likely candidates and left a list of their names for Sabot to collect at the towns' best hotels. After the third of the dinners, at which she was required to act as hostess, Belle had concluded that the unknown man was highly competent in his duty.

At each dinner, the main topic of conversation had been the evils of living under Yankee domination. Belle had identified the guests as malcontents, trouble-causers and rabid Secessionists of the kind she had always mistrusted as much as violently pro-Unionists. Fanatics of any kind had always been dangerous.

Once the magician had felt sure of his audience, he had told them of the forces at work to 'liberate' the suffering Southern States. When that happened, he had gone on, there would be positions of power, influence, importance—and wealth—in store for the men who had played an active part during the early days of the struggle. Men like themselves, in fact, if they had the courage, and sufficient loyalty to the Confederate cause, to lend a hand in the work that lay ahead. The arguments being presented had been calculated to appeal to the guests' patriotism, personal ego, avarice and other basic human emotions. Always the message had been there.

Give money to purchase arms!
Make ready for the day of reckoning with the Yankees!
THE SOUTH WILL RISE AGAIN!

There had been oaths of allegiance and secrecy sworn at the dinners. Arrangements had been discussed for the collection of the donations contributed, or gathered from others, by the guests and turned over to the Brotherhood's funds.

Always when that point had been reached, the listeners had grown cagey and unresponsive. While willing to support another attempt at Secession, and to donate—or at least collect—the money, none of them had been willing to hand it over without some convincing proof that the Brotherhood's intentions were honourable. Waving aside as unimportant, or as evidence of his guests' sound business sense, the comments about not doubting his word, Sabot had promised that a sign would be forthcoming in the near future. He had never offered to name a date, but had insisted that no donations would be accepted until the proof had been forthcoming. That had always impressed the listeners. It had also produced replies that he, or some other member of the Brotherhood, could contact their supporters *after* the promised sign had become a proven and established fact.

To help her play her part the more successfully, Sabot had purchased Belle a more presentable wardrobe. He had insisted that she toned down her facial makeup and generally improved her appearance. Dressed in stylish clothes and displaying a gracious, yet somewhat condescending manner which had been highly impressive—especially in the small towns where such sophistication was rarely seen—it had been her duty to pave the way for the real purpose of the dinners. Her shame-faced admissions of how she had been driven on to the stage—breaking her dear mama's heart in the process— through Yankee oppression had invariably won her much sympathy and guided the conversation along the required lines.

Belle had had some heart-searchings before she had decided to play her part so well. After serious consideration, she had concluded that the end justified the means. By presenting an image of complete loyalty and proving herself to be a capable ally, she would be all the more likely to be taken into the confidence of the Brotherhood's leaders.

The trend of the meetings had confirmed that her decision was a reasonably safe one. Until the promised sign was given, there was little danger of the guests carrying out their duties. Once it happened, if the need to take action arose, Belle knew the men in each town. They could be arrested before they did any harm.

Despite her growing knowledge of the Brotherhood, Belle had not yet managed to learn the identity of 'the Frenchman'. Although she had never heard of him mentioned in such a manner, de Richelieu had seemed the most likely candidate by virtue of his name. She had decided to leave positive identification until a more convenient date. There were other matters, of greater importance than personal vengeance, to occupy her.

Belle had heard enough to know that the Brotherhood was a large and growing organization. From what Sabot, Mick—who acted as liaison between the magician and the mysterious selector—and the other men in the show had told her, de Richelieu had assembled a fighting force. Men, wanted by the law in their own States, or willing to fight if necessary, had been dispatched to the ranch. So far, she had been unable to discover its location. In fact, she had reached the conclusion that none of her companions were better informed as to its whereabouts. Avoiding displaying undue, possibly suspicious, interest, she remained alert for any hint concerning it. She was also on watch constantly for the promised sign.

Belle's arrival at Fort Worth had, in one respect, strengthened her chances of survival.

Having won Sabot's trust, the girl had learned the names of the towns where they would be performing. Her reason had been, she had claimed, to warn him of any in which the law might take an unwanted interest in her arrival. Wanting to avoid such an eventuality, the magician had supplied the required details. Later, before leaving Mooringsport, she had contrived to send a telegraph message secretly to Winslow and requested that he should forward her property to Fort Worth.

That afternoon, Belle had visited the Overland Stage Line's depot and was told that her trunk had arrived. Without revealing her true identity, she had persuaded the agent to let her open it in the privacy of a rear room. Taking out her Hessian boots, black riding breeches, dark-blue shirt, Western-style gunbelt and ivory-handled Dance Bros. Navy revolver, she had locked the trunk again. Then she had arranged for it, and a written report of her activities, to be shipped to the wife of the Secret Service's Texan-based coordinator. Mrs. Edge would know what to do with Belle's property.

Since Belle was satisfied that Sabot and his men trusted her, she did not worry about the clothing being found in her possession. They accepted her pretence of being a lesbian and she felt sure that she could explain away the garments, gunbelt and Dance. However, she had not taken chances of being seen with them. Selecting a time when she had known that the others would be at the theatre, she had taken her property to the hotel. Concealing it under the other garments in the trunk which Sabot had purchased for her to use, she had locked it and joined the men.

Belle was comforted by the knowledge that she had the clothing and revolver in case of strenuous activity or the need to escape.

The door of the dressing-room flew open. Waving a copy of the *Fort Worth Globe*, the baritone entered followed by the two comedians. All of them showed considerable excitement.

'Is this it, Sabot?' demanded the singer, holding the newspaper so that Belle and the magician could see its front page.

The headlines, large—and seeming larger—sprang out to attract Belle's attention. A cold, anxious sensation bit at her.

U.S. PAYMASTER ROBBED!
$10,000.00 HAUL FOR GANG.

Was the robbery the promised incident that might trigger off and embroil the Unionist and Confederate States in another war?

'Let me see it,' Sabot commanded, sounding genuinely surprised and hopeful.

With an effort, Belle concealed her impatience. She waited until Sabot had read the story, then asked if she could take a look. Grinning, he handed it over.

'Is it?' the singer, Stapler by name, repeated.

'I don't know,' Sabot admitted. 'Mick hasn't said that anything was planned, and there isn't anything in the instructions.'

While the men talked, Belle began to read. Nothing in the story intimated that the incident had been organized for propaganda, or financial gain, by the Brotherhood.

In the first place, the robbery had taken place over two weeks earlier. It seemed unlikely that the organization would have kept quiet about their participation if they had been involved.

Secondly, the descriptions of the three men who had committed the crime struck the girl as being vaguely familiar.

Apparently the trio had learned that the Paymaster would be transporting the money from a Sergeant Magoon of the 8th Cavalry. With his connivance, they had planned the robbery. He had then been shot by them, along with the Paymaster and the rest of the small escort. News of the theft had not been released sooner to increase the chances of apprehending the culprits. A reward of ten thousand dollars was offered for the arrest of each of the trio. According to the newspaper, the Texas Rangers and Colonel Edge, of the Army's Adjutant General's Department, held high hopes of making an early arrest.*

No mention of the Cause. Not the slightest suggestion that the robbery had been perpetrated to help the Confederate States regain their liberty. Yet there was something in the story which perturbed the girl. Just what, she found herself unable to decide.

Certainly it was not the fact that the Adjutant General's Department was involved which aroused her interest. In addition to his military duties, Colonel Edge acted as co-ordinator for the Secret Service in Texas. Both his capaci-

* The full newspaper story is given in: *HELL IN THE PALO DURO.*

ties would lead him to be deeply concerned by the robbery. Probably it had been by his orders that news of it was suppressed for so long.

Another, small, headline on the front page caught Belle's attention as she stood turning the matter over in her mind.

GOVERNOR ACTS TO STOP RANGE WAR.

If Belle had not glimpsed one of the names in that item, she might have dismissed it as unimportant to her assignment. On the face of it, there was no possible connection between the robbery and the second story. Nor, unless there was much more to it, could the Governor of Texas' intervention be regarded as forming a part of the Brotherhood's promised sign.

Ranchers Shangai Pierce, Miffin Kennedy and Richard King were protesting about a beef contract which had been awarded by the U.S. Army to General Ole Devil Hardin's OD Connected ranch. All the men concerned, particularly the latter, had been loyal to the South in the War. So de Richelieu would not be able to make propaganda profit from the selection.

According to the stories, tempers were high amongst the ranchers. To prevent a range war erupting, Governor Stanton Howard had asked the protesting trio and the OD Connected's segundo—since his injury while riding a bad horse had left him crippled,* General Hardin was unavailable—to join him at the end of the month in San Antonio de Bexar. It was hoped that an amicable solution could be reached at the gathering. The first shipment of cattle—which were going by sea from Brownsville to New Orleans—would be dispatched as arranged, under the care of several well-known members of the OD Connected's work force.

Frowning in concentration and oblivious of the men's conversation, Belle returned her gaze to the coverage of the robbery. She read the descriptions of the Caxton brothers, Edward Jason and Matthew 'Boy', and of their companion-in-crime, Alvin 'Comanche' Blood, noting the tribe of Indians mentioned and paying especial care to scrutinize

* Told in the 'The Paint' episode of: *THE FASTEST GUN IN TEXAS.*

the weapons they were alleged to carry. From there, her eyes took in once more the name of the disloyal, betrayed and murdered non-commissioned officer.

'Poor Sergeant Magoon,' Belle mused, thoughts racing through her head and a theory forming. 'He had so many friends at the OD Connected. If Dusty wasn't going to attend this peace conference, and Mark or Lon weren't on their way to New Orleans with the cattle, I just bet they'd all be out hunting down his killers.'

'What do you make of it, Selima?' asked Hugh Downend, the straight man of the cross-talk duo, cutting in on the girl's theorizing and bringing her back to reality with a jolt.

'Of what?' Belle asked, hardly able to remember anything of the conversation that she had only half heard between the men.

'You looked like you're giving this affair some thought,' Miller Dunco, the comic of the pair told her.

'I was,' the girl admitted. 'Boy! What I'd give to meet those Caxton brothers and "Comanche" Blood. Anybody who'd do that to the Yankees is all right from where I sit—Hey though! Are they in the Brotherhood?'

Belle felt that she had covered her obvious preoccupation in an adequate manner. Certainly the men appeared to be satisfied with her explanation. While her final words had raised a point in which the men were interested, the baritone eyed her in a speculative manner.

'Do you know them?' Stapler asked.

Ever since the singer had taken her knee in the groin, he had been faintly but definitely hostile. He was a compulsive womanizer, who tried to make a conquest in every town they visited. While he was frequently successful, his failure with the slender, beautiful girl had rankled. Her presence with the show had been a constant reminder of the incident; nor had the other men allowed him to forget that there was one girl who would not respond to his charms. In view of Sabot's orders, Stapler had kept his distance; but he had always made it clear that he disliked 'Selima'.

'Why should I know them, *Mr.* Stapler?' Belle countered, laying emphasis on the honorific in a way which expressed a mutual dislike.

'I thought you're the biggest lady bandit since Belle

Starr,' Stapler answered, referring to her frequent hints concerning her 'criminal activities'.

'I've heard it said that *you're* God's own gift to womanhood,' Belle countered viciously. 'But that doesn't mean you've laid every woman West of the Big Muddy. Some of them have better ta——'

'Let it ride, both of you!' Sabot snapped, being desirous of averting an open clash with its danger of one or the other performer quitting his show.

'These mixed marriages never work out,' Dunco went on, rolling his eyes at his partner and winking.

'I'm with Dick, though,' Downend remarked. 'Not about you, Selima. But how do we answer if we're asked at the dinner?'

'Say "yes",' Dunco suggested, his smooth, fat face a-glow with excitement.

'I don't agree,' Belle put in, aware of what might happen if they followed the comic's advice and were believed. 'If we say "yes" and it comes out that they weren't doing it for the Brotherhood, we'll be discredited and mistrusted. Everybody will think we're just trying to slicker them out of their money.'

'That's true enough,' Sabot conceded. 'Look, Mick's due here any day with our pay from de Richelieu——'

'*Pay?*' Belle put in.

'Just a little added inducement for us to continue with the good work,' Dunco smirked. 'Didn't Sabby mention it?'

'I wanted it as a surprise for you,' the magician apologized and, seeing that Belle did not look impressed with the explanation, changed the subject. 'If de Richelieu has seen this story and they're not part of the Brotherhood, he'll have sent us orders on how to act. So we'll wait until Mick arrives before we decide what to say.'

'About this pay, Sabby?' Belle queried, figuring that a real 'Melanie Beauchampaine' would do so.

'It's a bonus for our work,' the magician elaborated. 'I wasn't trying to cheat you, Selima.'

'Why not, I'd do it to you,' Belle smiled. 'Whooee! This Brotherhood's bigger and richer than I imagined.'

'They've got some powerful foreign backing, from what we've been told,' Dunco commented.

Belle had already heard, during Sabot's interrupted

Shreveport show, that the Brotherhood was being sponsored by an undisclosed European country. That was one of the details she must check out, discovering if she could which nation was involved.

'Come on, fellers,' Sabot said, preventing Belle from probing deeper into the subject. 'We're on soon.'

The meeting broke up on that note.

Mick arrived the next evening. Meeting with Sabot and the other performers in the magician's dressing-room, he confirmed that the Brotherhood had not been involved in the robbery. Belle's stock as a shrewd judge of a situation was enhanced by his next piece of information. De Richelieu had sent word for them to disclaim all responsibility and had given an identical reason to the girl's for having reached the decision.

'On top of which,' Mick went on, 'he says he doesn't want folks thinking we're a bunch of thieves, murderers and such like.'

'Very wise,' Sabot confirmed, hoping that the Irishman would remember to mention his support to their leader. 'It might scare off the more respectable candidates.'

'You've been to the ranch, huh Mick?' Belle remarked casually, in the pause which followed Sabot's words, acting as if she was making casual conversation.

'I sure have,' the Irishman enthused, showing that his first visit had left a deep impression. 'There's well over a hundred men there already, trained, armed with Henry repeaters and r'aring to lay into the Yankees.'

'Good for them!' Belle whooped, sounding genuinely delighted. 'I can't wait to meet them.'

' 'Tis likely you will, darlin',' Mick assured her.

'Come on, Selima,' Sabot put in amiably, eyeing her street clothes. 'Nobody will believe I rescued you from "a life of sin in the Sultan of Tripoli's harem" if you go on dressed like this.'

Accepting the obvious dismissal, Belle left the room. She hoped that she might be able to pump Mick for further information after the performance. However, he had departed before she was free to do so.

That night, in the privacy of her hotel room, Belle wrote a report for Colonel Edge. In it, she gave the latest information and mentioned how serious she believed the situation to be. An armed force of over a hundred desperate, ruthless men would be a formidable weapon in the Brotherhood's hands. So she warned that she would require assistance to deal with the meance. To show that she had noticed a possible connection between the stories in the *Fort Worth Globe*, she concluded her request for reinforcements by saying:

'Send me three regiments of cavalry—or Dusty Fog.'

CHAPTER FIVE

MY NAME IS BELLE BOYD

'Selima darling,' Dunco said, walking into Belle's room without knocking, as she was packing to leave Fort Worth. 'Can you lend me——?'

The words trailed off as he stared at the riding boots and black breeches which lay on the bed. Having intended to hide them more thoroughly amongst her conventional clothing, the girl had unpacked them. She had forgotten to lock her door and was caught out.

'I bought them and these with my bonus,' Belle explained, thinking fast and producing the gunbelt with the Dance in its holster.

An understanding expression flickered on to Dunco's face. Being a homosexual who enjoyed wearing women's clothing, he appreciated the reason for 'Selima' making such unusual purchases. Many of the bull-dykes* he had met donned male attire to emphasize their 'masculinity'.

'Very fashionable, I'm sure,' Dunco simpered. 'Can you loan me a needle and some thread, dear, I've a button to sew on and I can't find mine.'

Belle obligingly produced the required items. Watching the man leave, she gave a wry smile. Forgetting to turn the key had been a dangerous oversight which she would have to avoid in the future. However, no real harm—in fact, possibly some good—had been done. She did not doubt that

* Bull-dyke: dominant, 'masculine' partner in a lesbian relationship.

Dunco would tell the other members of the show of what he had seen. In which case, having accepted her sexual aberration, they would regard the purchase in the same manner as Dunco. So it no longer mattered if they should see the garments and weapon. The fact that the Dance was a cap-and-ball revolver from a defunct Confederate firearm's manufacturing company would aid the deception. It would be regarded as nothing more than an added prop in her pretence of being a man.

At the dinner the previous evening, the usual discussion had run its almost predictable course. When the subject of the robbery had been introduced, Belle had seen that de Richelieu's conclusions were correct. At least three of the guests, respectable businessmen with real or imagined grudges against the Federal Congress, had shown relief on being told that the Brotherhood would not stoop to robbery and murder—even of Yankee soldiers—to achieve their aims.

Moving on to Dallas, the show played a week there. No more reports of the robbery appeared in the newspapers and the proposed peace conference was also forgotten. Nothing out of the ordinary happened until the last night. Then Stapler's dislike for Belle took a more active form. It had come about because she had accidentally knocked over a piece of scenery, which had fallen with a clatter and ruined the finale of his act. In the wings, he had accused Belle of doing it deliberately and a heated scene was averted only by Sabot's intervention.

The dinner was to be held in the banqueting room of the Cattlemen's Hotel. As had become the usual procedure, Belle and Sabot had arrived before the others to supervise the seating arrangements. They were alone in the room when the doors were thrust open and Stapler entered. Hanging on to his arm was a buxom, good-looking redhead. From the cut of her clothes and general appearance, the baritone's companion did not come into the socially-acceptable 'good woman' class. On top of that, both she and her escort looked to have taken just a little too much to drink. Shoving the doors together behind them, the couple made their way towards Belle. They halted, arm in arm, before the girl and were obviously looking for trouble.

'My my, look at our little Selima,' Stapler mocked, run

ning his eyes up and down Belle's elegant ball gown in derision. 'She looks almost like a woman, don't she, Bertha?'

'You're drunk!' Sabot growled, turning from the table at which he was standing.

'I've had a few, but not enough to make me like her,' growled the baritone. 'What do you make of her, Bertha?'

'Dykes of any kind turn my guts,' the redhead answered. 'And bull——'

'Hold your voices down, blast you!' the magician hissed, walking forward. 'And, if this's the best you can do, you'd better stay away from the dinner.'

'What's up, Sabby?' Stapler demanded. 'Ain't Bertha good enough to meet your friends. If a dirty little dy——'

Gliding forward a pace, Belle caused the baritone to chop off his words abruptly. She was responding as 'Melanie Beauchampaine' would have done. However, her dislike for the singer—and a subconscious detestation of being regarded as a lesbian, no matter how much the untrue supposition assisted her work—helped to bring the reaction.

Belle's right hand lashed towards the singer's face. Not as a slap, but in a well-aimed, skilfully delivered punch. Pivoting from the waist, she put her full weight behind the swing of the blow. Her knuckles arrived against the edge of his jaw hard enough to snap his head sideways and send him staggering.

Taken by surprise at the speed and force of Belle's response, Stapler did not find time to release Bertha's arm before he was hit. So he dragged the redhead with him as he made his involuntary retreat. Snatching her arm free, Bertha let out a furious screech. Then she hurled herself towards the slender girl with crooked, long-nailed fingers reaching out to take hold.

Spitting blood and mumbling obscenities, Stapler caught his balance with an effort. He retained his footing and made as if to follow Bertha. Darting forward, sallow features contorted by rage, Sabot intervened. Catching the singer by the shoulder, the magician jerked him around and followed Belle's original means of dealing with him. Caught between the thighs by Sabot's knee, the baritone gave vent to a croaking, tormented moan. If the anguish on his face, as he doubled over, was anything to go by, Stapler would not be much of a bed-mate for Bertha that night.

Nor, in view of what was happening, would the buxom redhead be harbouring many romantic notions.

Having expected a similar response from Bertha, Belle was prepared to meet it. However, she had no intention of becoming involved in a prolonged hair-tearing brawl if she could avoid it. So she figured out a way which would settle their differences quickly and with a reasonable chance of permanency.

Snatching up the hem of her gown to leave her legs unencumbered, Belle allowed Bertha's claw-like hands almost to reach her head. Then she side-stepped to the left, twisting and inclining her body at the hips in the same direction. Missing her target, but unable to halt her forward momentum, Bertha continued to advance. Like a flash, Belle turned her body, standing on her left leg, and swung her right knee as hard as she could into the redhead's belly.

Bertha's whalebone corsets were no protection against such an attack. In fact, their constriction tended to magnify its effect. Feeling as if her stomach was being thrust back into her spine, she let out an agonizing croak. With hands clutching at the point of impact, she doubled over and stumbled on a couple of paces.

Spinning around, Belle grabbed hold of the redhead's bustle in both hands. With a sudden, jerking upwards heave, she snatched Bertha's feet from the floor. The woman turned a somersault and landed with a crash on her back.

Knowing that 'Melanie Beauchampaine' would not be likely to let her assailant off so lightly, Belle acted in the manner of her assumed identity. Turning she moved around and stood astride the winded, helpless woman's body. Sinking to her knees and straddling Bertha's ample bosom, Belle settled her weight on it. Grabbing a healthy double handful of the red hair, the girl raised and thumped the woman's head on the floor.

The doors were thrown open and, followed by a couple of waiters, the other members of the show flooded in. Glancing at them, Sabot indicated Stapler as he crouching moaning and retching on his knees.

'Get that bastard out of here,' the magician ordered. 'And

pull Selima off of that tail-peddler* before she caves her skull in.'

Hurrying across the room, the cross-talk duo grabbed Belle by the armpits and lifted her erect. Although she made a token resistance, she was pleased that there had been such a prompt intervention. Bertha was lying limp and unconscious, so the girl had wanted an excuse to end her attack. However, she must play her part out thoroughly.

'Lemme go!' Belle demanded, struggling in the two men's grasp. 'Lemme get at her——'

'That wouldn't be fair,' Dunco pointed out. 'Not unless we brought her round first. She's out colder than last week's pot-roast.'

'But not near on so attractive to look at,' Belle admitted, grinning and ceasing her 'attempts' at regaining her freedom. Then she frowned and snapped. 'Where's that no-good, screeching, off-key lantern†?'

'He's not feeling too good,' Dunco grinned as he and his companion released the girl's arms. 'In fact, I bet he feels more like a gelatine‡ than a baritone right now.'

Turning, Belle saw that two of the musicians were hoisting Stapler to his feet. Beyond them, Sabot was apologizing to the hotel's employees for the disturbance.

'He's had too much to drink, gentlemen,' the magician announced. 'I assure you that there won't be a repetition of his disgraceful behaviour.'

'He sure looks like he's learned his lesson,' the senior of the waiters drawled, studying the baritone's agonized expression and general symptoms of suffering. 'You want for us to give him the old heave-ho?'

'We'll attend to him, and her,' Sabot promised and, continuing his platitudes, he edged the men from the room. Closing the door behind them, he swung towards Stapler. 'You stupid, no-good, drunken son-of-a-bitch!'

'Y-Y-Y-F—bast—!' the baritone moaned.

Advancing, Sabot lashed the back of his right hand across the man's face. Then he grabbed hold of Stapler's lapels and wrenched him bodily from the musicians' grasp. With a surging heave, the magician propelled the baritone

---

* Tail-peddler: a prostitute of the cheapest variety.
† Lantern: derogatory name for an inferior baritone.
‡ Gelatine: a tenor with a high, tremolo tone.

across the room to collide with the wall back first. Looking even more demoniac because he had followed his usual habit of retaining his stage make-up and clothing, Sabot rushed after the man.

Nauseated, suffering agonies, and with his mind befuddled by Sabot's rough handling, Stapler could still think well enough to realize his danger. He had seen enough examples of Sabot's evil side to believe that his good looks—perhaps his very life—might be in jeopardy.

'N—No!' Stapler croaked, throwing up his hands to shield his face from the expected attack.

Sabot made a disgusted sound deep in his throat, surveying the cowering singer with deep contempt. Then he took hold of the other's wrists and wrenched them away, glaring into the sweat-soddened, pain-filled and frightened face.

'You no-account, useless, womanizing bastard!' the magician snarled. 'I ought to cripple you so's you'd lose this craving to lay every she-male you set eyes on. Or alter your face so thay won't look twice your way, except to retch——.'

'D—Don't!' the baritone moaned.

'I won't, this time,' Sabot promised, stepping away. 'But only because you're useful in the show. The next time you make a fool play like this, I'll make you wish you'd never been born.' Having delivered the warning, he turned to the other men and continued, 'See that he gets back to the hotel. And take that tail-peddling whore away from here. Make sure she doesn't come back.'

'Sure, Sabby,' replied the orchestra's leader. 'Do you reckon he'll be—all right—left alone, after what's happened?'

'If you mean, do I think he'll run out on us, or lay information with the town clowns, the answer's "no",' the magician stated confidently. 'They couldn't prove anything against us, without catching us in the act. And, anyways, I know about a girl in Vicksburg whose folks'd just love to hear where he's at.'

'Y—You wouldn't tell them?' Stapler gasped, showing that he understood the full implications behind the comment. 'If they laid hands on me——.'

'That's what I mean,' Sabot purred. 'You're safer working with me—as long as *I* want it that way!'

'S—Sure, Sabby!' the singer whined. 'I—I wouldn't cross you——.'

'It's nice to know *that*,' Sabot sneered. 'Get going.'

After the singer and the unconscious woman had been removed, the dinner went by uneventfully.

Meeting Belle and Sabot at breakfast the following morning, Stapler made no reference to the events of the previous evening. If Bertha harboured any ill-feelings towards the girl who had mishandled her so effectively, which she probably did, she had sufficient prudence not to come and make them known. In fact, Belle never saw her again.

Coming out of the post office later that afternoon, having mailed her latest report to Colonel Edge, Belle noticed Stapler was across the street. However, the singer did not look in her direction and strolled into a saloon without displaying any awareness of her presence. She concluded that he had not seen her and carried on with her intention of going to the theatre.

In addition to developing her competence as Sabot's assistant, Belle had taken a genuine interest in his work. Soon after their first meeting in Mooringsport, flattered by her obvious appreciation and admiration for his talents, he had started to teach her how to do some of his illusions. Always a quick learner, and being an exceptionally intelligent, nimble-fingered girl, she had made rapid progress in acquiring the basic sleight-of-hand moves that formed the essence of a stage magician's act. It had been far easier for her to gain proficiency in the more spectacular mechanical illusions with which Sabot climaxed his performance. Taking an active part in them, and helping to set them up, had made her wise to how they were carried out. By the time the show had reached Dallas, the rest of the performers had begun to warn Sabot jokingly that 'Selima' was likely to take over the act.

Leaving Dallas, the party travelled on the Overland stagecoaches as they continued with the tour. Still the mysterious selector roamed ahead of them, leaving letters of guidance for Sabot in every town they visited.

Waxahachie, Martin, Cameron and Temple fell behind them as one-night stands. Although each was its respective County's seat, none had been of sufficient size to sustain the show for a longer stay. The party were moving roughly south-west, in the direction of Austin.

With a week to go before the end of the month, Belle still had not received replies to her reports. Having mail addressed to her, even in her assumed name, would have been more dangerous than dispatching an occasional letter, so she had not been expecting any. She was looking forward to playing at the State's Capital. Once there, she would be able to arrange a meeting with Colonel Edge and exchange verbal information. Perhaps too her request for assistance would be given its answer by Dusty Fog being in the city

Before her arrival, she hoped to learn the location of de Richelieu's ranch.

While Belle found herself in a position to acquire the desired information, concerning the ranch, the chance to hand it over was not presented to her.

On reading his instructions at Temple, in Bell County, Sabot had informed the others that their visit to Austin had been cancelled. Instead, they would make their way to San Antonio de Bexar. They had moved on to play one night in Blanco County's Johnson City. From there, they had travelled farther south-west to what they had assumed would be the scene of their next engagement.

Climbing out of the stagecoach at sundown, the entertainers looked with considerable disfavour at the straggling main—almost only—street of Los Cabestrillo. The usual variety of business, social and professional buildings were scattered haphazardly along its length. They were a mixture of heat-baked adobe and sun-warped planks, pointing to a fusion of Mexican and Anglo-Saxon architecture that was functional if not artistic or aesthetically pleasing to the eye.

'Lordy lord!' Belle groaned. 'If anybody gave me a necklace like this, I'd ram it down their throats.'

'How's that?' Dunco inquired.

'*Cabestrillo*,' Belle elaborated. 'It's Spanish for "necklace". Only I wouldn't use that in your act. The citizens might not like it.'

'This's a hell of a looking town,' Stapler complained. 'It's the worst since Mooringsport.'

'Why worry?' grinned Downend. 'We'll get paid whether we play to a handful of rubes or a full theatre.'

'Isn't that Mick across the street?' Belle inquired, pointing to the front of the imposing—a full *two* stories high—Longhorn Hotel.

'Yes,' Sabot agreed, looking puzzled. 'I wonder what he wants?'

'Here he comes,' Dunco commented needlessly.

Dressed like a cowhand, with an Army Colt holstered at his right thigh, the Irishman slouched over. He offered to help tote the party's baggage, acting as if they were strangers. Then, after the coach had moved off and the agent's crew had dispersed, he looked around to make sure that they were not likely to be overheard.

'I've got a wagon at the livery barn,' Mick announced.

'What for?' Sabot demanded.

'To take you out to the ranch,' Mick explained and was pleased by the reaction to his words. 'There's something big coming off and Colonel de Richelieu wants you to know about it. Besides, he doesn't want you doing the show and giving the dinner here. Foks in town don't know what's going on at the ranch and he doesn't want anybody starting to think things.'

'That's reasonable,' Sabot admitted. 'Let's get the gear down to the wagon and ready to move.'

'Aw, Sabby,' Belle protested. 'I'm hungry. Can't we eat before we leave?'

'It might be as well,' Mick agreed. 'We've a fair ride ahead of us.'

'All right,' the magician confirmed. much to Belle's delight. 'We'll load up, grab a meal, then go.'

While working, Belle felt a surge of excitement. At last she had some definite information. The ranch was within fairly easy distance of Los Cabestrillo. Close enough to make the town a useful point from which to start a search. Most likely the local marshal could be of help in deciding which property was being used by the Brotherhood.

One thing was for sure. No matter how great the risk, Belle must pass on the news to Colonel Edge. Then, if she should be recognized or suspected, the Secret Service would have been warned.

The question was, how could she send her message?

Mick's comments about the people of the town supplied Belle with a possible answer. Telegraph wires glinted in the last, dying rays of the sun, stretching from the Overland

Stage Depot out across the range. There was her means of communication, if only she could reach it without arousing suspicion.

'Phew!' the girl ejaculated, looking with distaste at the wagon. 'Riding in that will play hell with my good clothes.'

'Change into your old things,' Mick suggested.

'I don't have them any more,' Belle pointed out. 'I burned them as soon as I got something decent.'

'You could always put your riding breeches on,' Dunco remarked, just as Belle had hoped somebody would.

'Hey!' she grinned. 'That's an idea. I'll do it.'

'Not until after we've fed,' Sabot protested. 'You can do it while us fellers sink a couple of drinks.'

Belle concealed her elation, knowing that the magician had once more played into her hands.

After a decent meal at the hotel, Belle returned to the livery barn. It was deserted, which was just how she wanted it to be. Working swiftly, she boarded the wagon and unlocked her trunk. Changing into her masculine attire and buckling on her gunbelt, she decided against placing percussion caps on the Dance's nipples. To do so would consume valuable seconds; and she did not expect to need the weapon. So she placed it in her holster, packed away her discarded clothing and walked from the building. Her appearance would help to convince the telegraph operator of her *bona fides* when she made her request for assistance.

Although Belle kept alert as she made her way to the Overland Stage Depot, she saw nothing to alarm her. Reaching the building, she found it deserted except for an elderly man who was about to go out through the side door. He wore the dress of a clerk and sported a green eye-shield, implying that he was of a higher grade than a mere hostler.

'Excuse me, sir,' Belle said, hurrying around the corner and meeting the man in the alley. 'Are you the telegraphist?'

'I am, young lady,' the man admitted, after giving her a long, appraising scrutiny. 'Can I do anything for you?'

'Yes. My name is Belle Boyd——'

Just an instant too late Belle realized that the man was staring too intently at something beyond her.

Or *somebody*!

'So you're *Belle Boyd*!' said Stapler's voice from behind

the girl and it throbed with gloating triumph.

Spinning around, Belle twisted her right hand palm outwards to the ivory butt of the Dance. While the revolver was empty, she could use it to bluff the baritone; or pistol whip him.

Neither chance was permitted!

To her horror, Belle completed her turn to find herself face to face with Stapler *and* Dunco. The comic looked bewildered, but the baritone clearly had no doubts about what action he should take.

Gliding in fast, Stapler sank his right fist savagely into Belle's stomach. Winded and gagging for breath, she still had the wits to try to draw away as she folded over. The attempt was only partially successful. Instead of taking her in the centre of the face, Stapler's rising left knuckles met her forehead and lifted her erect. With everything spinning crazily around before her eyes, Belle was helpless and defenceless. Across hurled the baritone's right hand, smashing against her jaw. Flung sideways, her limp body measured its length on the ground. She did not feel the impact.

CHAPTER SIX

ISN'T THAT CAPTAIN FOG?

'Captain *Fog*!' ejaculated the desk clerk at the Longhorn Hotel in Los Cabestrillo, jerking his gaze from the register to study the man who had just inscribed the name he read out with such interest. 'Are you Captain Dusty Fog, sir?'

There was frank and open admiration in the clerk's voice and manner, for the newly arrived guest bore a name that was honoured, respected and revered throughout the length and breadth of Texas.

At a mere seventeen years of age, Dustine Edward Marsden Fog had been promoted in the field to captain and given command of the Texas Light Cavalry's hard-riding, harder-fighting Company 'C'. From then until the end of the War, he had built up a reputation as a military raider equalling that of Dixie's other maestros, Turner Ashby and the 'Grey Ghost', John Singleton Mosby. Ranging over the less-publicized Arkansas battle-front, he had matched their efforts in making life unbearable for the Yankees.* Rumour claimed that he had supported Belle Boyd, the Rebel Spy, on two of her missions. Less public knowledge was that he had also prevented two pro-Unionist fanatics from stirring up the Texas' Indian tribes into a rampage that would have decimated much of the Lone Star State.† Also to his credit had been his capture and eventual destruction of a great cannon with which the Union's Army of Arkansas had hoped to swing the balance of power into their favour.‡

With the War over and his uncle crippled and confined to a wheelchair, Dusty had taken on the responsibility of being segundo of the great OD Connected ranch. He had gained the name as cowhand, trail driver and trail boss par excellence,§ as well as being a town-taming peace officer of considerable ability.¶

Never slow to give credit to their favourite sons' good qualities, Texans also claimed that Dusty Fog was the fastest, most accurate and efficient handler of two Colts ever to draw breath; also that there were few men who could come close to matching his skill in a bare-handed brawl.

From where he was standing, the desk clerk admitted mentally that Captain Dusty Fog looked just as he had always imagined.

Six foot three in height, with a tremendous spread of shoulders and tapering to a lean waist and long, powerful legs, the man had curly, golden blond hair and a strong, tanned, almost classically handsome face. Encircled by a black leather band, sporting decorative silver conchas, a white J.B. Stetson hat of Texas style sat jauntily on the back of his head. Its fancy, thin plaited leather *barbiquejo* chin strap dangled loosely under his jaw. Around his throat, a scarlet silk bandana trailed long ends over a tan-coloured shirt that had obviously been tailored to fit his

* Told in: *UNDER THE STARS AND BARS* and *KILL DUSTY FOG!*
† Told in: *THE DEVIL GUN.*
‡ Told in: *THE BIG GUN.*
§ Told in: *GOODNIGHT'S DREAM, FROM HIDE AND HORN* and *TRAIL BOSS.*
¶ Told in: *QUIET TOWN, THE TROUBLE BUSTERS, THE MAKING OF A LAWMAN, THE TOWN TAMERS* and *THE SMALL TEXAN.*

giant-muscled frame. His Levi's trousers were of an equally excellent fit, their cuffs were turned back and hanging outside high-heeled, spur-bearing, fancy stitched boots.

While the clerk studied the big blond's clothing, his main attention was on the other's armament.

Around the blond's waist was cinched a brown, hand-carved *buscadero* gunbelt made by a master craftsman. In its contoured, carefully-designed holsters—the bottoms of which were secured to his thighs by pigging thongs—rode a brace of ivory-handled Colt Cavalry Peacemakers. Their metal work showed the deep rich blue of the manufacturers' Best Citizens' Finish, but they were functional and effective fighting weapons for all of that.

'That's what the book says,' the blond giant answered, his voice deep, amiable and that of a well-educated Texan. 'Room Twenty-One, huh?'

'Yes, sir,' the clerk confirmed and indicated a boy who was hovering near by, taking everything in with eager eyes and ears. 'I'll have the bell-hop help you with your things, Captain Fog.'

'Shucks, I'll tote my own gear,' the blond countered, holding the heavy low-horned, double-girthed* range saddle—which had a Winchester rifle in its boot, a long rope coiled at its horn and a bulky bed roll lashed to its cantle—without apparent effort. 'Maybe you'll fetch along the key, *amigo*?'

'Yes sir, Cap'n Fog!' the youngster replied, displaying an unusual zeal in the performance of his duties. Taking the key, he escorted the giant to the stairs. As they started to ascend, he indicated the gunbelt and went on, 'Is them the new-fangled Colts you used when you floating outfit fellers whipped the whole blasted Mexican Army last year?'

Emerging from the bar-room, on the left of the entrance lobby, two men stopped in their tracks as they heard the name spoken by the boy. Tall, slender, with swarthy, Gallic features, they wore white planter's hats, cutaway coats, white shirts, cravats fastened bow-tie fashion, fancy vests, Eastern riding breeches and Wellington-leg boots. Each had a Western gunbelt on, the older carrying a short barrelled British Webley Bulldog revolver in a cross-draw holster at his left side. The younger man's weapon was an

* Texans did not use the term 'cinch'.

Army Colt, in a low cavalry-twist rig.

First staring at the big blond, they exchanged glances and the younger opened his mouth. Before he could speak, his companion gave a vehement head-shake and strolled, with all too plainly assumed nonchalance to the desk.

'Isn't that Captain Fog going upstairs?' the man asked, holding his voice to a level which would not reach the blond giant's ears.

'It certainly is, Mr. Corbeau,' the clerk agreed warily, watching the second of the men in case he made a hostile movement. There was something furtive about the pair's attitude which—along with them being 'scent-smelling Creole frogs'—caused him to mistrust them. 'Do you know him?'

'Not personally, although I saw him several times during the War,' the man called Corbeau replied. 'Perhaps I will pay my respects to him later.'

'I reckon he'll enjoy that,' the clerk said dryly, but Corbeau was already turning away.

Rejoining his companion, Corbeau nodded in reply to his unasked question. Then they strolled—trying to act leisurely, but with obvious haste—out of the hotel.

Watching them go, the clerk gave a disapproving sniff. From the way they had acted, Corbeau and Petain were might interested—and considerably put out—by seeing Captain Dusty Fog. Maybe they had locked horns with him in the War. Sure, they had most likely worn the Grey; but those Creoles had, by all accounts done as much fighting amongst themselves as with the Yankees. Perhaps Captain Fog had had to make wolf bait of one of their kin in a duel.

Whatever the cause, Corbeau and Petain had not lingered long after seeing Captain Fog. They might, of course, be planning to come back later. The clerk wondered if he should convey a warning to the blond giant. Then he grinned and told himself that such an action would be unnecessary. Captain Fog could chill the milk of a couple of fancy-smelling Louisiana dudes, happen they got feisty, one-handed; and left handed at that.

Unaware of the interest he had aroused in two of Los Cabestrillo's visitors, the big blond continued to climb the stairs and answered the boy's question.

'The very ones,' he confirmed, thinking with some amusement how the incident to which the boy referred had become enlarged upon and distorted.* 'Only it wasn't the *whole* Mexican Army. I heard tell that at least ten of them were on furlough at the time.'

'Folks do say that you, Mark Counter, the Ysabel Kid 'n' Waco stopped us needing to go to war 'n' whip the Greasers,' the boy went on.

'That's what they say,' the blond admitted, for the boy's words had been close to the truth.

'Who-all's the strongest, you or Mark?' asked the bell-hop, studying the man's magnificent physique and recollecting various stories he had heard concerning Mark Counter's physical prowess.

'It's about even.'

'Did he for real heft ole Calamity Jane's wagon out of a gopher hole?'†

'Yep.'

'And yank the whole danged window, bars 'n' all out of the wall of the Tennyson jail, one-handed, so's he could get out secret 'n' lick the whole blasted Cousins' gang?'‡

'He always told me he used both hands to do it,' the blond corrected.

'*You* could've done it *one*-handed,' the boy praised.

'Not *left*-handed,' the blond objected modestly. 'What's doing in town?'

'Same's every danged night,' the boy replied disgustedly. 'Nothing. You on your way to San Antone to face down Shangai Pierce and them other fellers?'

'I'm going to talk peace with 'em,' answered the blond.

'Happen they've got a lick of good sense 'tween 'em, they'll listen good,' the bell-hop declared. 'Meeting's not for two weeks or so, is it?'

'Nope. Only I've got to visit some kin and do things before I get there.'

By that time, they had reached the door of Room Twenty-One. Showing his disappointment at having arrived so quickly, the boy unlocked and opened the door. Entering,

* Told in: THE PEACEMAKERS.
† Told in the 'The Bounty On Belle Starr's Scalp' episode of: *TROUBLED RANGE*.
‡ Told in the 'Better Than Calamity' episode of: *THE WILDCATS*.

he hurried across and turned up the light of the lamp on the dressing-table. The room was small, but neatly and cleanly furnished.

'Hope it's all right, Cap'n,' he said anxiously.

'Best I've seen this side of Mulrooney, Kansas,' the blond giant assured the boy, setting his saddle down carefully on its right side by the wall. Taking a silver dollar from his pocket, he flipped it through the air. 'Here. Don't you go spending it all on the one woman, mind.'

'*Woman!*' the boy spat disgustedly. 'You don't catch Waxahachie Smith wasting money on no woman. I'm going to put it to good use 'n' buy some powder, balls and caps for my Navy Colt.'

Having delivered the sentiment, the boy left the room. Whether the blond's tip was spent on ammunition or not, Waxahachie Smith would one day become almost as well known in gun-fighting circles as was the man who had given it to him.*

'Somebody should ought to have a long talk to that boy,' the big Texan thought, grinning, as he watched the door close behind the bell-hop. 'Still, time was when I'd've figured the same way.'

Having delivered the sentiment, he removed his hat. He ran his fingers along the fancy barbiquejo and the sardonic grin changed to a gentle smile. Hanging the hat on the bed post, he sat down and took a letter from a pocket built into the inside of his shirt. The envelope had seen frequent handling; which might have been due to the fact that the address was written in a neat, feminine hand.

It said:

> *MARK COUNTER,*
> *c/o Duke Bent,*
> *Bent's Ford,*
> *Indian Nations.*

Taking out the letter, the man who had signed the register as 'Captain D.E.M. Fog' read it with every evidence of pleasure.

If the clerk had been in a position to witness the scene, he might have been deeply disappointed. Apparently the man

---

* How Waxahachie Smith gained and earned his fame is told in: *SLIP GUN, NO FINGER ON THE TRIGGER* and *CURE THE TEXAS FEVER.*

he had so admired for years, one of Texas's most honoured and respected sons, was stooping to read a good friend's private and *very* personal mail.

Appearances are frequently deceptive.

There was a simple explanation to why the blond giant should be reading mail addressed to 'Mark Counter'.

That was his name.

He was not Dusty Fog!

When the Governor of Texas had been informed that a town was acting as a safe refuge for wanted men, he had sworn that he would cause it to be closed down. Stanton Howard had been brought in to clean up the mess left by Davis's corrupt, inefficient Reconstruction Administration and the return to law and order stood high on his list of priorities.

How to bring an end to the town—which went by the dramatic name of Hell—had posed a problem. Even if a Company of Texas Rangers might not have been capable of handling the situation, Howard could have called upon the services of the United States' Army and sent a regiment or more of cavalry to the town.

Except for one *very* significant objection.

The town was situated deep in the Palo Duro country and that was the undisputed domain of the *Kweharehnuh* Comanches. Unlike the other bands of the *Nemenuh** at the Fort Sorrel Peace Treaty meeting, the Antelopes had refused to come in to the reservation.† Retreating to their wild Palo Duro and Tule terrain, they had expressed their determination to continue living in their traditional manner.

The full story of how Mayor Lampart had obtained permission to set up his town for outlaws, and had won the active co-operation of the *Kweharehnuh* has been told elsewhere.

Briefly: one of the prices he had paid for the privilege had been to give every Antelope brave-heart a repeating rifle and a regular, but not excessive, supply of ammunition.

To send in soldiers armed with single-shot Springfield carbines—even if they were given the backing of artillery—

* Nemenuh: 'The People', the Comanches' name for their nation.
† The reason that the Kweharehnuh did not come in is told in: *SIDEWINDER.*

would have meant a long, hard, campaign and a high cost in lives. Fighting over terrain which they knew as well as the backs of their hands, all the advantages would have been with the Comanches. What was more, once the fighting started, it might spread to and involve the warriors living restlessly at peace on the reservations.

Howard had decided to dispatch a small party to scout out the situation. Using members of the Texas Rangers had been considered unwise, if not downright precarious. With wanted men from all over Texas likely to be in town, the risk of the peace officers being recognized as such could not be ignored. What had been needed were men with courage, gun skill, initiative and intelligence; but who were less likely to be known by outlaws.

That had been where Dusty Fog had come in. His experience as a peace officer had been in Kansas, or Montana, and he had all the other qualities. Enough, at any rate, to give him an even chance of survival. However, before he would agree to take in his companions, the Ysabel Kid and Waco, Dusty had insisted that they were given an elaborate, but thorough cover-story. At his instigation, the stories of the Paymaster's robbery and the Governor's arbitration for the quarrelling ranchers had been circulated.*

Instead of accompanying his *amigos*, Mark Counter had been given an equally important—if more passive—role. That did not imply a lack of faith in his courage, intelligence, initiative or abilities.

The youngest son of a wealthy Big Bend rancher, Mark had accepted Dusty's offer of employment as being more likely to lead to adventure, excitement and fun than working on his father's spread. Master of every branch of the cowhand's trade, famous for his prowess in a roughouse brawl and by virtue of his enormous physical strength, he was known as Dusty Fog's right bower. Living as he did in the shadow of the Rio Hondo gun wizard, Mark's true potential as a gun fighter had received small acclaim. People in the position to make a judgement declared that

---

* While Belle Boyd had drawn the correct conclusions from the two stories, that the 'Caxton brothers' and 'Comanche Blood' were Dusty Fog and his amigos, she had misinterpreted the nature of their mission. They were not hunting for the Brotherhood For Southron Freedom.

he was second only to Dusty Fog in the matter of speed and accuracy.

Mark's role in the deception had stemmed from the fact that he looked like most people imagined a man of Dusty Fog's legendary reputation would be. So he was travelling by an indirect route to San Antonio de Bexar, where he would pose as the OD Connected's segundo when the Governor held the peace-keeping talks.

From information he had received, Howard had warned that the town's people of Hell had reliable sources of information and effective means of obtaining news from more civilized areas. So it had been decided, with the ranchers in question's co-operation, that the meeting must take place as announced. Nobody could have been sure how long Dusty's mission would take. The Governor had been determined to do everything in his power to keep up the pretence which might save the three young Texans' lives.

Taking the letter from its envelope, Mark smoothed and read it familiar words. It was written by lady outlaw Belle Starr, with whom he was on close—and occasionally intimate—terms.* She had sent it to Bent's Ford, knowing that Mark would be coming by the place on his way home from a trial drive. In addition to a warm, tender message, she had enclosed the plaited leather *barbiquejo*.

'That Belle sure is a loving gal,' Mark told himself, having re-read and returned the letter to his shirt's pocket. 'A man could do worse than marry her. Trouble being, I'm not the marrying kind—and neither is she.'

CHAPTER SEVEN

I DON'T LIKE STINKING REBS!

Mark Counter's arrival in the bar-room of the Longhorn Hotel attracted considerable attention. Having found the dining-room empty, he was meaning to do no more than

* How Mark's association with Belle Starr began, developed and finally ended is told in: *TROUBLED RANGE, RANGELAND HERCULES*, the 'A Lady Known As Belle' episode of *THE TEXAN*, *THE BAD BUNCH* and *GUNS IN THE NIGHT*.

inquire if he could be served with a meal. Finding so many of the local citizens present, he decided that he might as well establish the fact that 'Captain Dusty Fog' was in Los Cabestrillo. Gathered in by the reports which the desk clerk and the bell-hop had spread, almost every male member of the community sat or stood in the room. There was an anticipatory hush as the blond giant made his way to the counter.

'Good evening, Captain Fog,' the bartender greeted, loud enough to ensure that none of his customers would be left in doubt as to the giant Texan's identity. 'What can I get you?'

'A meal would go down right well,' Mark replied. 'My cooking's not what it used to be. It's got a whole lot worse.'

'I'll have the cook make you up a meal,' the bartender offered, after having laughed immoderately at the comment. 'Dining-room's closed by rights, but I figure we can do something for *you*. Is there anything else I can get for you while you're waiting?'

'Whiskey, four fingers for me and set up drinks for these gents,' Mark answered. To himself, silently, he went on, 'I sure hope Governor Howard can explain away all the money I've spent like this, making folks remember ole Dusty's been to town.'

There was a modest swarm for the bar. Nobody wished to appear greedy, but had an equal objection to allowing others a better chance of making the acquaintance of their illustrious visitor. However, they soon found that 'Cap'n Fog's' desire for hard liquor was not extensive. Finishing his drink and another set up by the bartender, the blond giant announced that he would not be drinking any more.

'Not on an empty stomach, gents,' Mark apologized. 'Anyways, I've been in the saddle since sun-up and I'm fixing to make an early start comes morning. So I'll say, "Thank you, but no more." And we'll let it go at that.'

Even if they felt disappointed at losing the opportunity of a lengthy drinking and yarning session with 'Dusty Fog', nobody displayed an inclination to dispute his right to decline further hospitality.

Strolling out of the bar-room, Mark crossed the hall. A smiling Mexican waiter stood by a table in the otherwise deserted dining-room and indicated the place which he had just set.

'The food won't be long, *senor*,' the waiter declared as Mark sat down.

Mark still had the room to himself when he reached the coffee stage of his meal. Nor did he feel any particular need for company. Especially of the kind which arrived.

Barged in would have been a better term.

Stamping truculently with their heavy, Wellington-leg Jefferson boots, two big, brawny soldiers came into the dining-room. They wore the usual Burnside campaign hats, blue tunics, riding breeches with yellow stripes along the outside seams, and accoutrements of the United States' Cavalry. The brass buttons were dulled, the clothing and leather work dirty. One was a corporal, with a tawny stubble of whiskers on his surly face. The other, an enlisted man, was also unshaven and his features had a slightly Mongoloid look. Neither was sober, and they gave the impression of having taken enough to drink to make them dangerous.

'It's too late to get a meal, *senores*,' the waiter warned politely.

'Like hell it is!' growled the corporal. 'Me 'n' Jan here've rid a long ways and wants feeding.'

'We being here to protect you lousy Rebs from Injuns, and all, you owe us that,' Jan went on, his accent indicative of Mid-European upbringing. 'So you just get to it.'

While talking, the two slouched towards Mark's table. He watched them with no great interest and concern. Dirty, drunken soldiers were not sufficient of a novelty to warrant his attention. Unless, of course, their behaviour provided him with a reason.

'The cook's gone home——,' the waiter began.

'You've fed the beef-head here,' the corporal pointed out, jerking a thumb in the big blond's direction. 'So now you can feed us.'

No Texan took to being called a beef-head, which was the derogatory name applied to them by Kansans who wished to be insulting. So the man's behaviour looked like causing Mark to take an interest in him.

'I don't like stinking Rebs!' Jan declared, standing slightly to one side and behind the non-com, as he thumbed open the flap of his holster.

Taken with the comment, the soldier's action drew Mark's eyes in his direction. Almost as if following a preconceived plan, the corporal took a step closer. His big hands hooked up under the edge of Mark's table and started to lift.

Realizing his mistake, the big blond tried to thrust back his chair and rise. Under the corporal's propulsion, the table elevated and tilted. The coffee cup slid from it, followed by the cruet and sugar-bowl, cascading into Mark's lap. Coming downwards, the nearest edge of the table caught him on the thighs before he could get clear. Pain caused him to jerk rearwards, slamming his rump on to the chair's seat. Unable to take the strain, the rear legs snapped and precipitated him backwards.

Watching Mark going down, Jan grinned and lunged forward. The soldier planned to stamp on the centre of the Texan's chest as soon as he hit the floor. An attack of that kind would render him practically helpless and wide open to anything further the two men wished to do.

Years of horse-riding experience had taught Mark how to fall, even unexpectedly and backwards, with the best chance of alighting safely. So, although he could not prevent himself going down, he managed to break his fall with his hands on arrival.

Looming over what he assumed was a winded, incapacitated victim, Jan put his plan into action. Balancing on his left foot, he raised and bent the right leg. Down it drove, but did not reach its target. Two hands, which felt more like the crushing jaws of a bear-trap, clamped hold of the descending boot and halted it.

Having made his catch, Mark proceeded to make the most of it. Thrusting himself into the sitting position, he gave a twisting heave at the trapped boot. Jan felt as if his leg was being turned into a corkscrew. Then he was thrust with irresistable force and sent sprawling wildly across the room.

After tipping over the table, the corporal made as if to advance and join Jan in assaulting the big blond. Showing courage, the little waiter yelped a protest and grabbed the non-com's arms. Small and slight of build, the Mexican lacked the strength to do more than delay the burly two-bar. However, by doing so, he gave Mark the opportunity to attend to the trooper's attack.

And caused the corporal to make a hurried revision of his plans.

With a snarl, the bulky non-com wrenched himself free and sent the waiter staggering. At which instant, he observed Jan going away helplessly from Mark's counter to the attack.

Swiftly the non-com reviewed the situation and formed his conclusions.

Sure, he almost equalled the blond giant in height. Being more thick-set, he probably had an edge in weight. He had the benefit of being on his feet, against a seated opponent.

All good, sound, advantages which boded well for a successful assault.

Ecept when the opponent in question was 'Dusty Fog'!

There were far too many stories told, concerning the Rio Hondo gun wizard's equally magical ability to protect himself with his bare hands, for the corporal to be enamoured with the idea of fighting in that fashion.

Most men, treated as 'Fog' had been, would have been winded and helpless after such a fall. That big, blond bastard had not only broken the force of the impact, he had done it quickly enough to let him stave off Jan's attempt at caving in his chest.

A man with such ability would be anything but easy meat in a brawl.

So, no matter how *they* wanted things playing, the plan must be changed.

No matter that he had shown considerable sympathy for the Yankees since the end of the War, 'Fog' would not let their blue uniforms stop him taking severe measures to protect himself. He looked strong enough to have duplicated Mark Counter's trick of ripping out the bars at the Tennyson jail; and doing it one-handed.

Bearing that in mind, displaying a speed which implied long experience with the awkward rig United States—and many Johnny Reb's—soldiers were compelled to use, the corporal thumbed free the flap of his holster. His right hand twisted, grasping the butt and snaking the revolver from leather. Cocking back the hammer, he turned the muzzle in Mark's direction.

Seeing his danger, the blond giant realized its full, deadly potential. Joe Gaylin, the El Paso leather worker, had designed Mark's holsters for security of their weapons, comfort during hours of wear and ease in allowing the Colts to be drawn. However, the seven-and-a-half inch lengths of the Cavalry Model Peacemakers did not lend themselves to a fast draw when seated.

Even as Mark's right fingers enfolded the ivory butt, he knew that he would be too late. Maybe he could throw himself aside and avoid the corporal's first shot, but a second must surely find his body before he could make a positive response. As if that was not enough, Jan had collided with the wall rump-to-timber. He was glaring in Mark's direction and duplicating the non-com's actions with regard to continuing the fight.

Even as death stared Mark in the face, a shot rang out. It was the deep, distinctive sound of a heavy calibre, short-barrelled revolver. Fired from the doorway, the bullet took the corporal in the head. He was twirled around by the impact and the revolver tumbled from his lifeless hand.

Wanting to discover who had saved his life, Mark flickered a glance across the room. Guns in hand, the two Creole dudes he had noticed earlier had rushed from the hall. Smoke curled from the Webley Bulldog in the hands of the elder. Gripping his cocked Army Colt, the younger man swung immediately in Jan's direction. It was almost as if he had known just where to look for the trooper.

Although Jan had completed his draw, he ignored the new arrivals in his determination to be avenged upon Mark. Then he seemed to become aware that one of the pair was forming a threat to his well-being.

Skidding to a halt, the younger Creole started to raise his weapons to shoulder-height. Extending the revolver at arm's length, as leisurely as if he was taking part in a formal duel with no especial need for haste, he took careful and deliberate aim.

As if suddenly becoming aware of Petain's actions, Jan swung his head around. He stared, almost registering disbelief at what he saw, and his revolver wavered instead of aligning itself on Mark. The trooper opened his mouth, but was not granted the opportunity to speak.

Having made certain of his aim—in a way which would have proved fatal under Western gun fight conditions—

Petain squeezed the Colt's trigger. Flame lashed from the muzzle and powder smoke swirled briefly. A .44 of an inch hole appeared just over Jan's left eyebrow. Then blood, brains and slivers of shattered bone sprayed on to the wall as the bullet burst out of his skull. Down Jan slid, as if he had been boned, the revolver clattering by his side.

'Are you all right, Captain Fog?' Corbeau asked solicitiously, walking forward with the revolver dangling in his hand.

'I am now,' Mark admitted, standing up. 'Thanks, mister.'

'No thanks are necessary, sir,' Corbeau declared. 'We Southrons should stick together and be willing to help each other.'

Before any more could be said, there was a commotion in the hall. Attracted by the disturbance, the occupants of the bar-room came streaming in. Crowding forward, they stared about them and all seemed to be speaking at the same time.

'What happened?'

'Why'd they jump you, Cap'n Fog?'

'Where's the marshal?'

'It must be some of them blue-bellies who've been causing all the fuss around 'n' about!'

'Where the hell did them two come from?'

'Gentlemen! Please!' Corbeau shouted, facing the thickest portion of the crowd and waving his left hand in a signal for silence. 'Can we please have a little order?'

Slowly the chatter died away and the new arrivals waited expectantly for the next development.

'Somebody'd best go and fetch the marshal,' Mark suggested, having failed to locate that official amongst the town's men. 'And I'd be obliged if most of you'll go back to the bar until we've talked this thing out.'

Glaring coldly about him, as he had seen Dusty do when determined to enforce an unpopular decision or command, Mark brought about the desired effect. Slowly, with every evidence of reluctance, the citizens retreated into the entrance lobby. There, they asserted their independence by hovering around and straining their ears to hear what was being said in the dining-room.

'You gents came just in time,' Mark drawled, after his request had been fulfilled. 'I'm obliged.'

'It was our pleasure to help, sir,' Corbeau insisted, returning the Webley to its holster. 'We were just passing when we heard them abusing you. Knowing how Yankees stand by their own, we thought that you might care for witnesses who could testify that the provocation was on their part.'

'When we saw your danger,' Petain went on, sliding away his Colt. 'We knew that we would have to take more positive steps to help.'

'I wouldn't have said "no" if you'd asked before cutting in,' Mark stated. 'But I didn't know that there was a military post near here.'

'There's a detachment, about a company, not far away,' Corbeau replied. 'Or so I've been told. Apparently its commanding officer doesn't take to having Southron visitors.'

'His men have been getting into fights and generally raising hell in the surrounding counties,' Petain enlarged. 'So far, though, they've left Los Cabestrillo alone.'

Mark was puzzled by the words. News travelled fast, surprisingly so, across the Texas range country. Yet he could not recollect having heard of trouble being caused by soldiers. Not recently, at any rate. Shortly after the War, there had been incidents in plenty. With the passing of time, however, reasonably friendly relations had returned.

There were, of course, soldiers—and civilians—who refused to accept that the War had ended. Mark's late assailants had looked like the kind of men who would fall into that category.

Further conversation was ended by the arrival of the town marshal. Looking at him, Mark decided that Los Cabestrillo's city fathers went in for economy rather than efficiency in their law enforcement. Big, pot-bellied, clad in old town clothes, Marshal Flatter—a remarkably inappropriate name—looked, moved and spoke in a legarthic manner.

Staring around him myopically, Flatter asked to be told what had 'come off in here?'

While Corbeau started to give the Creoles' version, Mark found his attention straying to the corporal's body. The blond giant wondered why the two men had made their unprovoked attack. Hatred for Johnny Rebs might have accounted for it, yet that seemed a mighty flimsy reason for trying to kill him. If the two dudes had not intervened, it might easily have come to that.

One thing was for sure. No matter how great his antipathy towards Southrons, the soldiers' commanding officer could hardly substantiate a claim that they had been killed without good reason. Each had drawn his revolver with the intention of using it. The weapons lay by their sides——

Walking to the corporal's body, Mark bent to take up the revolver. At first glance, it looked like an 1851 Navy Colt. That was unusual. Not because the weapon in question was cap-and-ball fired; the Army had not yet equipped every regiment with metallic cartridge revolvers. The U.S. Cavalry had, however, standardized its armament by supplying the *1860 Army* Colt.

Occasionally men purchased their own sidearms, but the pair did not strike Mark as being so keen that they would have done so. And even if they had——

The revolver's frame was brass, instead of the usual steel!

No Colt had ever been manufactured in such a fashion!

Frowning, Mark lifted the weapon and read the inscription along the top of the octagonal barrel.

'SCHNEIDER & GLASSWICK, MEMPHIS, TENN.'

'Do you-all know why they jumped you, Cap'n Fog?'

Although Mark heard the words, they did not register immediately as having been addressed to him.

'Do you know them from somewhere?' Petain supplemented, when the big Texan did not answer Flatter's question.

'I can't place them,' Mark admitted, putting the revolver down and turning to face the men. 'Anyways, I don't think that they jumped me because of who I am——.'

'Just because you are a Southron,' Corbeau finished for Mark, speaking in a louder voice than was necessary.

The words clearly had carried to the listening men in the hall, for a low rumble of talk rose in their wake. Indignation filled the voices of the eavesdropping citizens, at the attempt by Yankee soldiers upon the life of the town's distinguished visitor—perhaps merely because he was a Southron.

'They were drunk,' Mark began. 'Likely just mean and looking for a fight.'

'More'n that, I'd say,' Flatter injected, trying to look wise. 'If these gents hadn't cut in, they'd've gunned you down without a chance.'

'Somebody ought to do something about it!' Petain growled angrily. 'These damned Yankees think that they can come rampaging through Southron towns, terrorizing the women and endangering lives with impunity.'

'What're you fixing to do about it, Flattie?' demanded an indignant voice from the hall.

'Well now,' the marshal answered, scratching his head. 'I don't rightly see's how I can do anything. Can't arrest 'em, for sure, them being dead 'n' all.'

'Their blasted officer ain't dead!' the speaker from the hall pointed out.

'And he ain't in town, neither, so far's I knows,' Flatter countered. 'Nor camped in Kendal County. Which means he ain't in my juri—jurification.'

'You'll have to make sure that he knows you hold him responsible for what happened, marshal,' Corbeau warned. '*That* is in your jurisdiction.'

'I ain't rightly sure I knows where to look for him,' Flatter complained.

'Maybe they're carrying something that'll tell us where they're from,' Mark suggested, kneeling and reaching towards the pocket of the corporal's tunic.

The tarnished brass buttons differed in two respects from those normally worn by members of the United States' Army. Firstly, they bore a letter 'D' and not the 'A', 'I' or 'C'—Artillery, Infantry, Cavalry—by which the wearer's arm of the service could be recognized. Secondly, encircling the embossed spread-eagle on a three-pointed shield device, were the words, '*AD ASTRA PER ASPERA*'.

Mark knew that the words were the motto of the Sovereign State of Kansas.

At one time, the 'D' would have announced that the man sporting the button so inscribed was a Dragoon.

Although in the early days of the War the Yankees had permitted the various States, and other patriotic bodies, to arm and equip volunteer regiments in any way they had chosen, Congress had eventually insisted upon standardization of uniforms. At about the same time, the terms like 'Dragoon', 'Lancer', 'Hussar' and '*Chasseurs*'—which had graced the volunteer regiments—had been superceded by the more prosaic 'Cavalry', regardless of the outfit's composition and characteristics.

So why was a cavalryman, in 1874, still wearing the buttons of what must have been a Kansas volunteer regiment of Dragoons?

Perhaps he had been so proud of his home State, and old outfit, that he was willing to flout *Dress Regulations* and wear the means of displaying his loyalty to both.

Even if that should have been the case, it did not explain why he was armed with a revolver which had been manufactured in a Confederate States' firearms' factory.

CHAPTER EIGHT

THAT'S MARK COUNTER

Holding their horses to a steady trot, Mark Counter, Louis Corbeau and Paul Petain rode through the star-lit darkness towards where, half a mile away, the lights of a building flickered intermittently through gaps in a large clump of post oaks.

'You understand, of course, Captain Fog, that I'm telling you this in all confidence.' Corbeau warned solemnly. 'And that I expect you, as an officer of the Confederate States' Army, and a Southron gentleman, to respect this confidence.'

'I understand,' Mark answered.

'And that, whatever action General Hardin decides upon,' Corbeau continued 'he will be discreet.'

'O—Uncle Devil's always discreet,' Mark declared. 'And, like I said, it's his decision on what we do. I'll go along with him. It may take him some hard thinking, but he'll send you an answer, count on it.'

Some instinct, for which he had subsequently been grateful, had warned the blond giant against commenting upon the dead corporal's buttons and weapon. To add to his puzzlement, Mark had found that Jan sported similar buttons and carried a Confederate Leech & Rigdon Army revolver.

Although the task should have been performed by the

marshal, Mark had taken it upon himself to search both bodies. He had found neither document nor clue to their identity, nor anything to suggest to which regiment they belonged. Even more surprising, if they should have been visiting the town for recreational purposes, their pockets had been equally devoid of money.

On the latter point, Petain had stated—speaking in tones loud enough to reach the listening men in the hall—that the pair had probably believed their blue Yankee uniforms were all the currency they would need when dealing with Southron businessmen. At the time, Mark had put the comment down to having come from an embittered young hot-head who refused to accept that the War had ended in 'Sixty-Five.

If Flatter had seen and drawn any conclusions from the puzzling aspects, he had successfully kept them to himself. Mark was inclined to believe that the marshal had not noticed either factor; but was taking everything at its face value, to make sure that he did not embarrass his town's distinguished visitor.

Pressed for a comment on what he was planning to do next, Flatter had declared that it was his intention to telegraph the County Sheriff in Boerne and turn the matter over to that official. When Mark had asked if he would be required for a hearing into the incident, Flatter had grown even more vague. Finally, the blond giant had taken pity on the peace officer and had promised that he would remain in Los Cabestrillo until the sheriff arrived from the County seat.

Compassion for the bumbling, incompetent marshal had not been Mark's sole motive. The big blond had sensed that some connection might exist between his attackers and the men whose timely arrival had saved his life.

There had been at least two pointers in that direction. While the soldiers had been drinking and had certainly been on the prod, they had seemed to be making a predetermined rather than a spontaneous attack. When the Creoles had made their presence known, Jan had not reacted in the manner which Mark would have expected. Instead of turning immediately, to discover who had shot his companion, the trooper had continued to devote his attention to the giant Texan.

It had almost been as if Jan believed there was nothing to fear from the newcomers. Not until Petain had taken a deliberate aim at him had Jan shown any realization of his peril; and then it had been too late.

If the Creoles were connected in some way with the soldiers, why had they saved Mark's life?'

Could it have been because they had very strong reasons for wishing to place 'Dusty Fog'—for it was he whom they had assumed Mark to be—into their debt?

That was possible.

The Rio Hondo gun wizard was famous for standing by his friends and always repaying favours. Without a doubt, he would have been grateful to men who had saved his life and willing to help them in return.

If Mark's theory should have been correct, it had implied that the Creoles had most likely arranged for the soldiers to attack him. They must have had a mighty powerful reason for taking such a dangerous and desperate step. Sufficiently so for Mark to have decided that he wanted to know what it might be.

Arranging the means by which he could satisfy his curiosity had not been difficult. In fact, doing it had been taken out of his hands completely.

After the marshal had concluded what had satisfied *him* as a detailed and instructive inquiry into the affair, he had allowed the three men concerned to go about their business. Knowing that he would learn nothing more from that source, Mark had left Flatter to dispose of the bodies. At Corbeau's invitation, he had accompanied the Creoles into the bar-room and had done the honours at the counter.

Once they had obtained their drinks, Corbeau had left Petain to divert the other occupants of the room by a description of the fight with the *Yankee* soldiers. Mark had noticed how the young dude had laid great emphasis on the word 'Yankee', but had put it down to the same motives as had inspired his comment on the dead men's lack of money.

Taking Mark aside, Corbeau had asked if he would accompany them—Petain and himself—to the ranch of a friend which lay some five miles outside the town. Mark had discarded the idea that they might be planning to lure him away and kill him. If they had merely wanted him killed, they would have allowed the soldiers to do the job, shooting the pair down in such a way that it would have seemed they were just too late to prevent 'Captain Fog's' death.

Robbery might have been their motive, but Mark doubted it. While it might have been assumed that the segundo of the OD Connected would not be travelling with empty pockets, he also would not be likely to carry sufficient money to make such an elaborate plot worth trying.

Concluding that he would lose nothing by going along, Mark had given his consent. He had pointed out that his trousers were soaked with coffee and had gone to his room to change them for a dry pair. Collecting his hat and saddle, leaving the bed roll behind, he had returned to the barroom. On entering, he had found the crowd in a kind of mood such as he had not seen since the earliest and worst days of Reconstruction.

Curses were being directed from all sides at the United States and men had been recounting tales of Yankee atrocities, before, during and since the War. Mark had hoped that no more soldiers would arrive. The sight of a blue uniform might easily have led to a lynching, or open conflict, and Marshal Flatter was not the kind of peace officer who would control such a situation.

Sensing that the Creoles, particularly Petain, had been responsible for the crowd's mood, Mark had been grateful for his decision to accompany them to their friends' ranch. He had wasted no time in getting them out of the hotel.

Collecting their horses from the livery barn, the two men had guided Mark from the town and across the range. At no time did either of them act in a manner which suggested that they might have been contemplating a robbery. Within five minutes, Mark had lost all apprehensions on that account; and had known, or detected what might have been, a reason for his 'rescue'.

Corbeau had done most of the talking. First he had reminded Mark of the worst attributes of Reconstruction; including how his—Dusty Fog's—cousin, John Wesley Hardin, had been turned from a happy-go-lucky cowhand into a wanted killer through the oppression of Yankee carpetbagger officials.* Then he had told how the Brotherhood For Southron Freedom had been formed and planned to

* Told in: *THE HOODED RIDERS*.

bring an end to the Union's tyranny. When the time was right, the South would rise again.

Until then, there were preparations to be made.

What the Brotherhood needed was men—and leaders. Already Colonel Anton de Richelieu was gathering the nucleus of a new Confederate States' Army. When the day of reckoning came, a European country—Corbeau had tactfully refused to say which one—would pour arms, supplies and money into the South.

Would Captain Fog be interested in taking his place amongst the ranks of the Confederate States' liberators.

Could the Brotherhood For Southern Freedom count upon General Ole Devil Hardin's support and blessing?

If the answer to both the questions should be in the affirmative, Corbeau had claimed—and Mark had known it to be true—that most of Texas would flock to the Stars and Bars battle flag of the reborn Confederate States.

Revising his first inclination to refuse, Mark had decided to make a pretence of interest and possible acquiesence. He had wanted to know more about the Brotherhood and felt certain that his boss would be most interested; although probably not in a manner that would meet with its members' approval.

So Mark had stated that, while he could not answer for his 'Uncle Devil's' sentiments, he felt sure that they would be suitable. He had also warned that his own participation would depend upon how Ole Devil decided to act.

Although that had apparently satisfied Corbeau and brought a warning of the need for discretion, Petain showed how he believed a more positive response should have been forthcoming.

'I can't see why there should be any hesitation,' the young Creole growled. 'You *are* Southrons——.'

'And damned proud of it,' Mark interrupted. 'But this isn't a small thing, *mister*. Uncle Devil will need time to consider it.'

Apparently Petain had learned that if a Texan said 'mister' after being introduced, it implied he did not like the person to whom he addressed the word. An angry scowl flickered across his handsome features as Mark said it.

'Some would say it should need no consideration,' the young Creole snapped.

'*Some* would say that a Spanish ring bit's damned cruel and unnecessary, happen a man can handle his horse,' Mark countered.

Nothing the blond giant had seen of Petain had led him to form a liking for the other. There was an air of superior, condescending, arrogant snobbishness about the Creole which ruffled the Texan's normally even temper. At the livery barn, Petain had been far rougher than was necessary in his handling and saddling of the horse. Since then, he had ridden with a strict control over the animal's movements; backing his imperious will with spurs and the use of the big, fancy Spanish ring bit. The latter device, with a metal circle that slipped over the horse's lower jaw, had always been regarded as unduly severe by Texas cowhands. In skilled hands, it could be comparatively harmless and effective; or punishing and cruel. From what Mark had seen, the Creole lacked the necessary ability to render the bit harmless. Nor would he, the big blond suspected, have been inclined to use it in a harmless manner.

'Just what are you implying?' Petain spat out, a dull red flush creeping into his cheeks.

'I figured I was just making talk,' Mark replied. 'The same as you.'

'I take your remark as a personal affront——,' Petain began heatedly.

'Take it any way you want, *mister*,' Mark drawled. 'Only you'd best mind one thing. This isn't Louisiana. In Texas, we settle our affairs-of-honour differently. There's no waiting until dawn. It's finished right then, on the spot, fast and permanently.'

'*Gentlemen!*' Corbeau barked, reining his mount around and forcing it between the other two animals. 'Our Cause is too important for us to let private differences come between us. Captain Fog meant no offence, *Captain* Petain.'

'With respect to the major,' Petain answered, bristling with indignation. 'I don't see it in that light.'

Suddenly Mark saw the reason for the young Creole's animosity. Clearly Petain took the Brotherhood For Southron Freedom's military status very seriously. He was proud to hold officer's rank in the proposed new Army of the Confederate States. So he had taken exception to Mark's use of the word 'mister'. In the Army, that was the term applied to 1st or 2nd lieutenants. A captain was accorded his corect title.

Knowing that the affair was being caused by a misunderstanding did not make the blond giant like Petain any better. However, Mark figured that he had best avoid locking horns head on with the young Creole at that time. To kill one of its senior members would not make the Brotherhood feel inclined to show him their secrets.

'My apologies for saying *'mister'*, Captain Petain,' Mark said formally. 'I didn't know.'

'Well, Captain Petain?' Corbeau challenged, when the young Creole did not make a reply.

'You cast doubts as to my ability as a horseman, Captain Fog,' Petain complained, unwilling to let the affair slide by without a further gesture.

'I didn't care for your remarks concerning General Hardin's and my loyalty to the South,' Mark pointed out. 'However, if you'll withdraw your comment, I'll take mine back.'

'All right!' Petain growled grudgingly, after a pause in which Corbeau had glared angrily at him. 'I withdraw it.'

'So do I,' Mark drawled.

Although the big blond had averted a clash with the Creole, he also knew that he had made an unforgiving enemy. Reared in the school of the *code duello*, Petain would never forget that he had been forced to back down and deprived of an opportunity to demand satisfaction for a grievance.

Having continued to ride as they talked, the men were approaching the edge of the post oaks. Mark could see that Petain was darting glances around as if expecting something, or somebody. Whatever, or whoever, it was did not materialize. An angry snorting snarl broke from the younger Creole as they emerged beyond the clump and into their first clear sight of the ranch's headquarters.

Lights showed at the windows of the big, plank-built, two storey main house, through the open double doors of the barn and outside the three-holer back-house. The long one-floor adobe cabin which most likely served as a combined cook- and bunk-house was unilluminated, as were the three pole corrals and other structures.

'Where're all your men?' Mark inquired, for the premises

before him could hardly have housed over a hundred would-be soldiers.

'A few use the bunkhouse,' Corbeau answered. 'But the main body are camped in a valley beyond the post oaks.'

'We don't want anybody to see them,' Petain went on. 'So we keep them away from the ranch-house. There are pickets and vedettes all round. It's impossible for any unauthorized person to get near the camp by day, or night.'

'We've done it,' the big blond pointed out.

'Only because we were expected,' Petain answered, looking uneasy.

'*Three* of us?' Mark queried.

'The vedette recognized Major Corbeau and I,' Petain growled.

'Or he was asleep,' Mark suggested.

'By God!' Petain snarled, glaring behind him. 'I'd——.'

'He probably recognized us,' Corbeau said soothingly.

Leading the way to the barn, Corbeau told Mark that he could make use of an empty stall. The men cared for their horses, with Petain muttering and glowering repeatedly into the darkness of the post oaks. At last, with the work done, the young Creole set his hat on firmly and stalked towards the door.

'I'll just take a stroll,' Petain announced, trying to sound casual, and swaggered nonchalantly from the building.

'I hope that vedette isn't asleep,' Corbeau remarked to the big blond. 'If Petain catches him, he'll wish he'd never been born. He's a mean, evil-tempered young hot-head.'

'He sounds that way,' Mark said dryly. 'Happen it'll kill him one of these days, he keeps it going.'

Taking Mark across to the main house, Corbeau opened the front foor and escorted him into the hall. Voices sounded from one of the rooms which led off from the hallway and Corbeau looked at it.

'Will you wait here for a moment, please, Captain Fog?'

'Why sure,' Mark agreed.

Striding to the door, Corbeau pased out of the big blond's sight. Mark tried to see into the room, but failed. He was not kept in suspense for long. Returning to the hall, Corbeau signalled for him to come forward. Clearly the Creole intended to make as big an impression as possible and show off his find in an impressive manner.

'Gentlemen,' Corbeau announced, standing aside for the blond giant to precede him. 'May I present Captain Dustine Edward Marsden Fog, Company 'C', Texas Light Cavalry.'

Strolling into the large, comfortable, if functionally, furnished combination library-study, Mark was confronted by half a dozen men gathered at a polish-topped table. Four of them wore the uniforms of Confederate States' Army Officers and were, the blond noticed with relief, strangers.

Unfortunately, that happy state did not apply to the other two.

Dressed in range clothing belting low-tied Army Colts, they were all too familiar to Mark; despite the fact that they had not met for several years.

One thing was for certain sure.

Maybe the four officers would accept Mark as the genuine article. But Cal Roxby and Saul Brown had good cause to know that he was not Dusty Fog.

While handling an assignment unaccompanied by the other members of the floating outfit,* Mark had locked horns with the two men. A pair of hired gun fighters, they had been in the process of bullying a rancher and his wife when the big blond had intervened. Disarming them, he had handed the woman his own weapons and delivered a beating which neither would be likely to have forgotten. Then he had turned them over to the local sheriff and had last seen them, screaming threats of vengeance against him, on their way to the State's Penitentiary.

Apparently they had served their sentences and been released. Mark doubted if that would have made them feel any better disposed towards him.

'You stupid bastards!' yelled Roxby, as he and his companion sprang from the table with hands diving towards guns. 'That's Mark Counter, Not Dusty Fog!'

Having expected such a reaction, Mark dipped his right hand in a sight-defying motion. The off-side long-barrelled Peacemaker flowed from its holster, lined and fired. Before Roxby's revolver had cleared leather, the blond giant's bullet was tearing into his chest. Cocking the Colt

---

* Floating outfit: four to six cowhands employed by a large ranch to work its more distant ranges independently, instead of being based at the main house. Ole Devil Hardin's floating outfit also acted as trouble-shooters for any of his friends who required their services.

on its recoil, Mark turned it and cut loose at the second outlaw. Already the man's weapon was lifted into alignment. Struck by the flying lead, his body jerked violently and his own load winged harmlessly into the door.

Although he had taken the two men out of the deal, Mark knew that he was a long ways from being out of the tall timber. Every other man in the room was rising and commencing his draw. The blond giant knew that he could not hope to stop them all.

CHAPTER NINE

WHIP MY SOLDIERS INTO SHAPE

Even when Mark Counter prepared to sell his life dearly, and brought out his left hand Colt to make the price still higher, he heard the room's second door being thrown open.

'Attention!' barked a crisp, authoritative voice which sounded vaguely, yet positively, familiar to the blond giant's ears.

While the four confronting Mark did not go to the extent of assuming correct military braces, they at least refrained from completing their draws. For his part, the big Texan kept the matched Colts lined. Their hammers were held at full cock by his thumbs, and his forefingers depressed the triggers. Instead of taking any further action, he turned to gaze at another figure from his past.

Tall, lean as a steer raised in the greasewood thickets, the man in the doorway looked little different to when Mark had last seen him. He still wore an immaculately-fitting Confederate States Cavalry officer's undress uniform. But, where there had only been a single major's insignia on his stand-up collar, he now sported the three gold stars of a full colonel.

Maybe the face was more lined than in the days when Major Byron Aspley had commanded Mark's Company of Bushrod Sheldon's 18th Cavalry Regiment. It was still the same hard, tanned, expressionless mask, with cold brown eyes, a straight nose and tight, thin lips that never seemed to smile. Bare-headed, he had a mass of long black hair, carefully combed to conceal his ears.

Except that Mark knew there was no ear on the left side. It had been lost, during the War, while Aspley had been saving the big blond's life.

'What's all this, Major Corbeau?' the man Mark had known as Byron Aspley demanded, striding forward as stiff-backed and smart as if he had been approaching General Robert E. Lee.

'This—He told me he was Captain Fog, Colonel,' Corbeau spluttered, standing slightly behind and to Mark's rear. 'Roxby and Brown said he was Mark Counter, then tried to kill him.'

'It seems you haven't lost your dexterity with your hand-guns, Mr. Counter,' Aspley commented. 'You can holster them now.'

'Could be I might need them again, Maj—Colonel Aspley,' Mark drawled.

'Not "Aspley"!' the lean man snapped. 'I renounced my birthright after the shameful surrender at the Appomattox Courthouse. Until the South regains its freedom, I will go by the name "de Richelieu".'

'I see, sir,' Mark drawled, and meant what he said.

'De Richelieu's' home, the magnificent Aspley Manor, had been one of the properties to suffer from the ravages of Sherman's 'March To The Sea'. It had been reduced to ashes and, attempting to save something from the burning rooms, his parents had died in the conflagration. Learning of this, Aspley had become obsessed with a deep, bitter hatred for the Yankees. He had raged furiously over General Lee's surrender; and was a prime mover in the scheme to offer Sheldon's Regiment to the French's self-appointed ruler of Mexico. Aspley alone had elected to remain in Maximilian's service when Dusty Fog had delivered President U.S. Grant's message requesting that the Regiment returned to their homes.*

Having helped Dusty—it had been then that they had had their first meeting—Mark had sometimes wondered how his old commanding officer had fared and what had become of him after the French's defeat and flight from

* Told in: *THE YSABEL KID*.

Mexico. Apparently he had come through safely and had made some useful, lucrative contacts.

'While I have a good reason for becoming Colonel Anton de Richelieu,' the man continued. 'I am puzzled why you should claim to be Captain Fog.'

'I've my reasons,' Mark admitted and edged around until he could see Corbeau as well as keeping the other men covered.

'What reasons?' demanded the Creole indignantly, his face working angrily and fingers going closer to the Webley's butt.

'Private ones,' Mark replied. Almost casually, his left hand Colt swung its muzzle to point at Corbeau's chest. 'Don't try it, major. *I'm* not expecting *you* to side me against anybody.'

'That's no answer,' growled one of the men at the table; before Corbeau could comment, although he showed that he understood Mark's meaning.

'It's all the answer I aim to give, asked this way,' the blond declared.

'The odds are against you,' warned the captain who was kneeling alongside Roxby's body. 'We could enforce our demands for an answer.'

'You could *try*,' Mark drawled, making a slight gesture with his Colts. 'But the Brotherhood will be shy at least two of its officers before I go under.'

'You've not changed, Mr. Counter,' de Richelieu commented and his voice seemed to hint at approval. 'Will you tell me your reasons, in private?'

There was only one reply that Mark could give. 'Yes, sir. I'll tell you, in private.'

'You won't need your guns. So put them up and come with me.'

'Roxby's dead and Brown soon will be,' the kneeling captain remarked.

'I'll accept that you had good reasons for killing them, Mr. Counter,' de Richelieu told Mark.

'May I go on record as saying that they drew first on Capt—Mr. Counter, sir?' a third officer inquired, darting an accusative glance at Corbeau. 'Even if their deaths have deprived us of the services of two useful men.'

'Useful!' Corbeau spat back. 'Cheap hireling killers——.'

'Who were, at least, what they pretended to be,' the third officer, a surly-featured, paunchy major, pointed out.

'And what does that mean, Kincaid?' Corbeau demanded hotly.

'*Gentlemen!*' de Richelieu snapped, bringing both men's eyes in his direction. 'If you have nothing better to do than stand bickering, I would suggest that you take yourselves to bed.'

'Brown's gone,' remarked the captain who had been examining the strickenen men. 'I'll fetch a detail and have them removed.'

'Perhaps you'll attend to that, Major Kincaid?' de Richelieu ordered, for the officer and Corbeau were still glaring at each other. 'Major Corbeau. Would you be good enough to go to the camp and inform the sergeant of the guard that there is no reason for him to come and investigate the shooting?'

'Yo!' Corbeau assented and stamped from the room.

'Come with me, Mr. Counter,' de Richelieu commanded and walked back into the room from which he had emerged.

Following his old commanding officer, Mark found himself in a small, snug den. De Richelieu waved him into the chair at the front of the desk and took a seat on the other side.

'It's been a long time, Maj—Colonel,' Mark commented, declining the offer of a cigar.

'I wouldn't come back until I was in a position to help the South,' de Richelieu answered. 'But I'm interested to hear why you claimed to be Captain Fog.'

At that moment, footsteps pattered in the hall. Lighter steps than would have been made by male footwear, they came to a halt outside the den. Its second door opened and a tall, shapely, beautiful woman walked in. Taken with the long white robe she wore, the pumps on her feet and her somewhat dishevelled shortish auburn hair suggested that she had only recently left her bed.

'I heard shots, Anton,' the woman stated in a deep, husky contralto voice. Cold, appraising eyes flickered to Mark as he, like de Richelieu, came to his feet. 'So *this* is the famous Captain Fog?'

'No, Virginie,' de Richelieu contradicted. 'This is not Captain Fog.'

'Did Corbeau's men have to kill him?' the woman asked brutally.

'It was all a misunderstanding,' de Richelieu replied, scowling. 'Mr. Counter, may I present the Baroness de Vautour. Baroness, this is Mr. Counter, he was a first lieutenant under my command. Corbeau mistook him for Captain Fog.'

'Mr. Counter,' the woman greeted, advancing and extending her right hand. Her grip was strong, cool and impersonal as she shook hands.

'Ma'am,' the big blond acknowledged.

'Please be seated, gentlemen,' Virginie commanded regally and, after they had obeyed, went on, 'Which of those fools was it this time?'

'Mr. Counter——,' de Richelieu began.

'Not another noble exponent of the *code duello*, surely,' Virginie interrupted, eyeing the blond giant with cold, barely hidden contempt.

'I don't go around looking for reasons to slap another feller's face and call him to meet me at dawn,' Mark told her calmly. 'But, happens somebody concludes to shoot me, I figure I've a right to stop him.'

'I suppose Roxby and Brown had some grudge against you, Mr. Counter?' de Richelieu asked.

'*They* figured they had,' Mark drawled and told why the pair had hated him.

'What a remarkable judge of character Major Kincaid is,' Virginie purred. 'But where is Captain Fog? Corbeau's message said——.'

'That Captain Fog was in town and he intended to either get "me" to join the Brotherhood, or have me killed in a way that would rile up the town's folk against the Yankees.'

'A shrewd assumption, Mr. Counter,' Virginie praised, eyeing him with added interest.

'It cost you two more *good* men,' Mark warned. 'Corbeau and Petain killed the "soldiers".'

'They were expendable,' Virginie answered, clearly dismissing Jan and the corporal as of no importance.

'A pair of drunken, sullen malcontents, who were spreading ill-feeling amongst our soldiers,' de Richelieu elaborated.

'So you sent them in to Los Cabestrillo to get them

killed,' Mark guessed. 'To have them make fuss with the folks and wind up wolf-bait. Only Corbeau saw a better way of using them.'

'That doesn't tell us why you pretended to be Captain Fog,' Virginie put in, before de Richelieu could confirm or deny the blond giant's comment.

Something about the woman's attitude annoyed Mark. So he decided that he would try to ruin her cool, slightly mocking and detached poise.

'I never said that I'd tell "*us*",' the blond said to de Richelieu. 'What I have to say is private, Colonel.'

Mark had achieved his end. Letting out an angry cluck, Virginie went to the third chair and sat deliberately on it.

Since her arrival, the big Texan had been studying Virginie with considerable interest. Beautiful, beyond any question, she had a magnificent, full bosomed, slender waisted figure which the flimsy robe emphasized to its best. If her title was genuine, she must have married a foreigner. Her accent was American, well-educated and Northern in its origin. There was an air of standing no nonsense about her and more than a hint of temper in the set of her full lips.

However, Baroness or plain Mrs., if she wanted a clash of wills, Mark was willing to accommodate her.

Not only that. The blond giant could see that his next actions might be of tremendous importance.

From the start, Mark had known that General Hardin would not support a movement that might once again plunge the United States into the bloody hell of a civil war. In fact, loyal as he undoubtedly was to the South, Ole Devil would take steps to have such an attempt suppressed. To do so would require information concerning the people involved and the means by which they hoped to achieve their ends.

If the Brotherhood For Southron Freedom had been comprised solely of men like Corbeau, Petain and the 'soldiers', Mark would have dismissed them as all puff, blow and bellow; nothing more than a noisy nuisance. With Byron Aspley—or *Colonel* Anton de Richelieu—in command, especially if the stories of his powerful European backing should be true, the organization was a horse of a very different, vastly more dangerous colour.

Knowing that the question of his assumed identity could

not be shelved and forgotten, the big blond had been wondering how he might best explain it. At first, he had considered saying that he was merely making the most of the benefits which accrued from being 'Captain Dusty Fog' instead of plain Mark Counter. It would be logical and easily understandable—but would not show his own character in a creditable light.

Far better, Mark concluded, to devise a stronger reason. One that would bring him favourably to the Baroness's and de Richelieu's attention. First, however, he had to put them in the correct frame of mind. Allowing himself to be browbeaten by a woman was not the way to do that.

'How have things been with you since Mexico, Colonel?' Mark inquired, in the manner of making idle conversation, and hooked his right foot up on to his left knee.

'The Baroness has my full confidence, Mr. Counter,' de Richelieu growled; but the big Texan sensed that he was not entirely opposed to the way things were going.

'That doesn't mean she has mine,' Mark pointed out and felt sure that he saw a flicker of approval on the other man's lean face.

'Suppose that *we* insist upon you answering, Mr. Counter?' Virginie challenged, studying his giant frame with cold eyes.

'Roxby and Brown're good reasons for *you* not to have it *tried*, ma'am,' the Texan answered.

'You might not find others of our men so easy to handle,' Virginie warned.

'Maybe not, ma'am,' Mark drawled, knowing instinctively that he was handling her in the best possible manner. 'But it'll cost you a few more of them, trying to show me how good they are.'

'He's speaking the truth, Virginie,' de Richelieu put in quietly. 'Unless he's lost his ability—and the two men suggest that he hasn't—we don't have a man who is his equal with a revolver.'

The Baroness did not answer for several seconds. Flickering her gaze from one man to the other, she seemed to be trying to bring them under the influence of her will. At last she conceded that she could not and gave a shrug.

'Then we'd be advised to let him tell us in his own way,' Virginie said and made as if to rise.

'I'd be honoured if you'd stay and listen, ma'am,' Mark declared, having made his point and certain that such permission would further suit his needs. He carried on as if satisfied that his offer would be accepted. 'Tempers are a mite high over that Army beef contract. Shangai Pierce and the others figure that, us having helped the Yankees a few times since the War——.'

'You have,' Virginie agreed thoughtfully.

'We'd good enough reasons, ma'am. Anyways, Shangai's bunch figured Ole Devil's got enough pull to swing the contract our way no matter what they say. So they're not fixing to do any saying.'

'I don't follow you,' de Richelieu stated.

'They reckon that, happen the OD Connected doesn't send a representative to that old meeting, the Army will have to find against us.'

'So Captain Fog has kept you back from that shipment and is using you as a lure to draw Pierce and the others off the track.'

'Yes, ma'am. Only I was never on to the ship. That was to keep them from figuring there's too many "Dusty Fogs" around and about.'

'And where is Captain Fog now?' de Richelieu demanded.

'Back home on the spread,' Mark lied. 'We don't want it running over with hired guns. So I've been roaming around, telling folks I'm Dusty and hoping to draw off any who've been hired.'

'Don't you mind being used that way?' Virginie asked, frowning.

'Shucks, no,' the blond giant grinned. 'It beats plain old working on the spread. And folks're sure accommodating to "Captain Dusty Fog". More than they'd be to plain ole "Mark Counter".'

Watching an exchange of glances between Virginie and de Richelieu, Mark guessed that his story had been accepted and that he had achieved his intention. They were impressed by his loyalty to the OD Connected and his casual acceptance of a dangerous assignment.

'Why did General Hardin send Captain Fog to Sheldon?' de Richelieu inquired.

'Because he figured that our men could do more for the South back home,' Mark answered. 'And he was satisfied that we'd get better treatment from the Yankees for coming back when *they* wanted us to.'

'Shrewd thinking,' Virginie praised.

'He's a mighty shrewd man, ma'am,' Mark replied. 'He saw early that the only way of getting Texas over the effects of losing the War was to play along with the Yankees.'

'How do *you* feel about it?' de Richelieu challenged.

'Things were bad, Colonel. I figured we should take any means to make them better. And, down in Mexico, it wouldn't have been long before our men had insisted on coming home. They didn't like the French in any shape or form.'

Watching the couple, Mark discovered that the woman did not appear to be annoyed at the remark. Possibly her marriage had not given her any respect, love or pride in France.

'It's a pity you aren't Captain Fog,' Virginie remarked. 'We could do with a man like him here.'

'How's that, ma'am?' Mark inquired.

'You've seen Corbeau, Kincaid and the others?' Virginie answered.

'Yes. 'm'.'

'What do you think of them?'

'I haven't known them long enough——'

'Which means that you think as I do,' the woman guessed. 'That not one of them is worth a damn as an officer.'

'Corbeau's a good administrator,' de Richelieu put in.

'When we need one, he'll be a blessing,' Virginie answered. 'The others are all right in their fields—But their fields aren't much use to us right now.'

'Why's that, ma'am?' Mark wanted to know.

'Because not one of them has the qualities it takes to weld a bunch of men into a fighting regiment,' the Baroness explained. 'Especially when they don't have the weight of a formal Army's disciplinary machine behind them.'

'How about Petain?' Mark asked.

'An arrogant bully, with a mean, vicious streak,' Virginie stated. 'He would make a fine commandant for a penal colony, or chief torturer for a mediaeval court.'

'He isn't a leader,' de Richelieu agreed. 'And it's a leader I need to whip my men into shape.'

'You could do it, Colonel,' Mark said and was sincere.

'Thank you,' de Richelieu answered. 'But I have other things to do. What we need, if all I've heard of him is true, is a man like Captain Fog.'

'As Anton says,' Virginie went on, eyeing Mark in an appraising manner. 'A man *like* Captain Fog.'

'So you've got "Captain Fog" here right now,' the big blond drawled, grabbing his chance in both hands.

'You mean——?' the Baroness prompted.

'Have you many Texas boys around?' Mark asked.

'None. Anton sent men from east of the Mississippi out here. It was easier in the South to select those we could be reasonably sure of trusting.'

'Being the kind of outfit we are, we thought it advisable on another score,' de Richelieu took up where the woman had finished. 'Even in the Army, Texans were notorious for not being amenable to discipline when it was applied by what they chose to regard as dudes.'

'I saw some of it,' Mark admitted with a grin. 'Are there any of them likely to know Dusty?'

'It's not likely,' de Richelieu claimed.

'Then, providing your officers haven't been flapping their lips too much about what's gone on,' Mark drawled, 'you-all can do like I've been doing—and getting away with. Pass me off as Dusty Fog.'

'It could work, Anton!' Virginie ejaculated.

'It could,' de Richelieu agreed. 'Mr. Counter was a promising young officer and I wouldn't be surprised if he hasn't learned some of Captain Fog's tricks. If only they haven't blabbed—— I'll go and see. Virginie, just in case we need them, could you go and wake up Pieber and his assistant?'

'Who are they?' Mark asked.

'Our tailors,' Virginie answered. 'By morning, I want to see you in a Cavalry captain's uniform.'

CHAPTER TEN

YOU TRIED TO GET ME KILLED

'This is the best we could do in the time, Captain Fog,' apologized the plump, red-faced Albert Pieber—in the mock deprecatory tone of one who knew that he had done an excellent piece of work—as he watched the blond giant draw on the tunic which had had made during what remained of the night.

'Happen it fits as comfortable as the breeches,' Mark Counter answered, 'it'll be real fine.'

Having accepted the idea that they might be able to pass off Mark as Dusty Fog, Baroness Virginie and de Richelieu had wasted no time in implementing the scheme. De Richelieu's questioning had satisfied him that his 'officers' had not told the 'enlisted men' of Corbeau's mistake. Probably the Creole had had something to do with their reticence, for he had been furious over his error and in a dangerous mood. Or their silence may have stemmed from another source. Being aware of how slender a hold they had over the lower ranks of the Brotherhood, they had hesitated to let it become known that two of the 'officers' had been hoodwinked.

So excellent had the web of secrecy been that even Petain did not know of Mark's true identity. Inadvertently, the young Creole had helped to divert the 'enlisted men's' interest from the shooting of Roxby and Brown. As Mark and Corbeau had suspected, the young man had gone in search of the vedette who had neglected to challenge them on their arrival. After a search, Petain had located the man asleep uncer a tree. Going up quietly, he had taken the vedette's rifle. Kicking the man awake, he had smashed the butt of the rifle on to his head as he rose still half-asleep. Then, leaving his victim sprawled on the ground with a fractured skull, Petain had gone to send the sergeant of the guard to collect him. The Creole's action had been sufficient to lessen the speculation that might have otherwise been felt over the two men's deaths.

On returning to the main house, full of his importance

and efficiency, Petain had not been pleased to hear that 'Captain Fog, was to assume command of the training schedule. However, the Creole had kept his thoughts to himself and stalked angrily off to his room.

For his part, Mark had spent a most useful and instructive couple of hours before going to the quarters which were assigned to him. He had seen something of the extent to which the Brotherhood's preparations had advanced. Even if he had doubted it before, he had then realized just how serious a threat they might easily become.

Not only had de Richelieu been able to produce sufficient cadet-grey cloth, brass buttons, gold braid and other items to create a uniform, he had had located a weapon belt and a pair of Hessian boots for Mark to wear. Pieber and his assistant, fetched from their quarters by the Baroness, had taken their measurements and worked without stopping until they had delivered the first outfit.

So Mark had found himself donning the yellow-striped breeches of a Cavalryman once more. Like the breeches, the tunic proved to be an excellent fit. It had a formal stand-up collar, although bearing a captain's three gold bars and not the two of a first lieutenant. The sleeves, with the two strands of gold braid twisted into the 'chicken-guts' Austrian knots on each of them, and the double-breasted front, bearing two rows of seven brass buttons, were of formal, correct pattern. There was, however, one innovation which Mark had insisted upon. He had caused the tunic's skirt 'extending halfway between his hip and knee', as the *Manual of Dress Regulations* prescribed, to be omitted.

Although it had been Mark himself who had first done this—incurring the displeasure of numerous hide-bound senior officers—he had explained that Dusty Fog was one of the many young Southron bloods who had followed his lead in flouting the Regulations.

On another matter Mark had been equally adamant. Again he was helped by well-known facts. The Texas Light Cavalry had been noted for wearing western-style gunbelts. So Mark could continue to use his *buscadero* rig without losing credibility.

That had been a relief to the blond giant. Knowing the desperate nature of the men with whom he was dealing, he wanted his weapons to be a damned sight more easily available than in a close-topped, high riding, twist-hand draw holster.

'We have made you a cravat, sir,' Pieber hinted, as Mark left the collar open sufficiently for him to fasten on his bandana.

'I only wear one in full dress,' the blond answered, secure in the knowledge that it was another detail he and Dusty had had in common. 'You've done a real fine job, *monsieur*.'

'*Danke schön!*' the tailor answered; his pleasure at the praise was tinged with annoyance and irritation for some reason.

Mark was not given the opportunity to ponder on the man's contradictory attitudes. At that moment there was a knock at the room's door. It was not the sound of a person giving notice of wishing to come in, but a demand to enter.

'Who is it?' Mark called.

'Baroness de Vautour,' came back the answer in Virginie's voice. 'May I come in?'

The polite words sounded more like, 'Open the door, I insist on coming in.'

Darting an apologetic glance at the blond giant, but without permitting him to make known his sentiments on the matter, Pieber scuttled hurriedly to the door. The tailor jerked it open. Then he and his assistant slammed into rigid postures of attention. Watching them, Mark could not remember ever having seen Maximilian's French troops display such a high standard of military smartness.

Wearing a neat, plain, figure-concealing, yet expensive grey serge two piece travelling costume, the Baroness swept regally into the room. She had taken her hair back tightly, concealing it under a grey Baden hat that resembled a narrow-brimmed, low-crowned Stetson which had been decorated with a wide black lace band and a cluster of white ibis feathers.

Clearly she did not consider the tailors as being of sufficient importance to warrant a glance. Advancing across the room in what—if it had been done by another women with her physical attributes—would have been a sensual glide, she contrived to look as if she was marching in a military review.

'Good morning, Mis——,' Virginie began, chopping off her words angrily as she realized what she had been on the point of saying.

'*Captain* Fog, ma'am,' Mark supplied, being unable to resist the temptation to try and break down her composure.

'Good morning, *Captain* Fog!' Virginie spat out viciously, cheeks reddening.

Holding her temper with an effort, the Baroness stalked around the big blond. She studied him with the air of a rancher examining an animal before deciding to purchase it. Off to one side, still rigidly at attention, the tailors displayed a wooden apprehension as they watched her making the inspection.

'I hope it meets with your approval, ma'am,' Mark drawled, his whole attitude suggesting that he did not care a damn one way or the other about her opinion. Taking up his gunbelt, he buckled it on.

'It will do,' Virginie said off-handedly and the tailors beamed as if they had received a hearty vote of thanks for their efforts. 'Have you had breakfast?'

'Not yet,' Mark admitted.

'Then I would suggest that you do so. After you've finished, we'll take you to meet your troops.'

'I was just going to say that's what I aimed to do.'

Sucking in a deep breath, Virginie spun on her heels and almost stamped her way across the room towards the door. The Texan's hateful voice followed her.

'I'd already thanked these gentlemen for doing such good work. But I reckon they're pleased that *you* approve.'

Pieber had bounded to the door and jerked it open, without appearing to have lost his rigid brace. There was an expression of awe on his face as he watched Mark stroll out after the Baroness. Clearly the tailor had never expected to see anybody treat her with other than slavish, abject respect.

'You'll try my patience once too often, *Mister* Counter!' Virginie hissed furiously as she and the big Texan started to descend to the ground floor.

'Just so *you* don't try *mine* too far, Baroness,' Mark answered, with no display of alarm over the threat. 'And the name is *Captain Dustine Edward Marsden Fog*. Remember?'

If looks could have killed, Mark Counter would not have lived long enough to become the great-grandfather of a jet-age peace officer who would handle a handgun with as much skill as shown by any of the legendary Old West *pistoleros*.*

Having tried, and failed, to quell the Texan with a cold, icy glare, Virginie almost ran down the stairs. In the hall, she led the way to he dining-room which faced the study. Going in, Mark found all but Petain of the officers present. The blond was conscious of the other men's scrutiny and wondered how many of them would have bitterly opposed his wearing the skirtless tunic if he had been under their command during the War.

'Good morning, sir, gentlemen,' Mark greeted formally as he went to the table.

A Mexican waiter drew out a chair for the Baroness and another prepared a place for Mark.

'Are you staying with us for long this time, Baroness?' Corbeau inquired.

'No,' Virginie replied. 'I want to make sure things are ready in Austin for the magician's arrival.'

'Sabot won't be going to Austin,' de Richelieu remarked and something in his voice brought immediate silence to the men and woman around the table. Their attention went to him. 'When you've finished breakfast, Captain Fog, I want you to accompany the Baroness and myself to the camp.'

'Yo!' Mark affirmed.

'The rest of you gentlemen have your duties,' de Richelieu went on, his manner indicating that the subject was closed.

'Talking of duties,' Kincaid remarked. 'Young Petain's starting to take his real seriously. Here it is not yet ten o'clock and he's up and gone to the camp.'

'Maybe he's gone to apologize to the man whose head he busted,' Captain Raphael—the man who had examined Mark's victims—commented. 'That was a damned stupid thing to do. We're not an Army—Yet.'

The last word had clearly come as an after-thought, brought about by the cold glare which de Richelieu had directed at the speaker. Lowering his gaze to his plate, Raphael went on with his breakfast.

* Mark Counter's great-grandson, Bradford, appears in the author's Rockabye County stories.

Half an hour later, Mark rode with Virginie and de Richelieu towards the Brotherhood's camp. It was set up in a wide, but well-sheltered and hidden valley. Again the blond giant was impressed by the standard of the equipment. Even from the rim, he could see that the rows of Sibley, 'umbrella', wall and wedge tents were new and in excellent condition. Horses stood along picket lines at the far side of the valley. Down at the foot of the slope, ahead of Mark's party, Petain stood watching over a hundred men in cadet-grey cavalry uniforms forming—ambling and slouching being more descriptive—into three solvenly, crooked ranks.

'You see what we're up against, Mr. Counter?' de Richelieu demanded, reining his mount to a stop and indicating the assembled men. 'They're still no better than a disorganized rabble.'

'Looks that way,' Mark conceded.

'I was in Europe in '70 and '71,' de Richelieu continued. 'And I saw what happened to badly, or wrongly, disciplined troops.'

'That was when the French and Prussians were fussing, huh?'

'Yes. The French had their *Chassepot* breech-loading rifles and the new *Mitrailleuse* machine guns that are a vast improvement over the Gatling, against the Prussians' needle-guns. Yet they were still defeated. Discipline is what brought it about, Mr. Counter. The Prussians had it. The French didn't.'

'That's true,' Virginie confirmed, concealing any bitterness she might have felt over her husband's country having met a crushing defeat.

'I'll see if I can lick 'em into shape,' Mark promised. ''Least, I know how Dusty would go about it; and I reckon his way's good enough for me. Let's go and make a stab at it.' As the horses started moving, he went on, 'Who-all's the worst trouble-maker?'

'Cyrus Purge——,' de Richelieu began without hesitation.

'The same Cyrus Purge who took that Yankee Napoleon single-handed at Spotsylvania, then turned it on the other guns in the battery?'

'The very same,' de Richelieu agreed.

'He's that big, dirty, hulking brute in the centre of the

front rank,' Virginie elaborated.

'The rest follow him, huh Colonel?' Mark drawled, finding no difficulty in picking out the man in question.

Massively built, Cyrus Purge stood in the position which Virginie had mentioned. He had his hands thrust insolently into his pockets and was clearly enjoying being the centre of attention. Grinning men nudged each other in the ribs and nodded towards the approaching trio, then at Purge.

'He has a lot of influence,' de Richelieu admitted.

'Shoot the mutinous son-of-a-bitch!' Virginie advised savagely, jerking a contemptuous thumb towards the young Creole captain. 'Petain should have done it the first time Purge showed signs of disobedience. I'm surprised he didn't.'

'Maybe *he's* smart enough to know that doing it would lose the Brotherhood more than it would gain,' Mark drawled. 'The French were all for shooting fellers, but it didn't do them much good in Mexico. Nor against the Prussians, way the Colonel tells it.' Ignoring the glare of hatred the Baroness threw at him, he continued, 'Reckon he'd made a good man, Colonel?'

'He *could* be a power of good, if he'd take discipline,' de Richelieu declared. 'But, so far, I've not had a man capable of winning his respect and making him accept it.'

'But Mr. Counter thinks he can!' Virginie spat out.

'If you can't remember I'm "Captain Fog", ma'am,' Mark growled. 'I'd sooner say the hell with this whole idea. It won't work.'

'Remember what I said to you earlier this morning, *Captain Fog*!' Virginie hissed, her right hand tightening on the grip of the heavy quirt she carried until the knuckles showed pallid white through the tight-stretched skin.

'And you keep on minding the answer, ma'am,' Mark warned. 'Anybody who tried to lay a quirt on me—Well, I might not let whoever *tried* being a woman stop me stopping them.'

'Anton!' Virginie shrilled, but let the quirt drop to dangle by its wrist strap. 'Are you going to allow——.'

'The Colonel knows I'm right about the name, ma'am,' Mark drawled. 'If somebody calls me the wrong name, it could blow the whole Brotherhood to pieces. Men don't take kindly to thinking somebody's been trying to hoodwink them.'

'*Captain Fog* is right about that,' de Richelieu confirmed, laying great emphasis on the first two words. 'We mustn't make mistakes. There's too much at stake for that.'

'On the other thing, ma'am,' Mark went on. 'The Colonel likely thinks it's a personal matter between you and me.'

By that time, they had reached the foot of the slope. Still the 'soldiers' made little more than a token attempt to form their ranks. Watching them, Mark sensed an air of expectancy in the way their eyes remained upon him. He knew instinctively that it was connected in some way with the big, heavily built Purge.

Urging his mount forward at a slightly faster pace, Mark swung from its saddle in front of Purge's position in the ranks. He allowed the split-end reins to drop from his fingers, 'ground hitching' the animal as effectively as if it had been tied to a snubbing post. Then he strolled, smartly yet nonchalantly, towards the 'soldiers'. Behind him, Virginie and de Richelieu halted their horses. They remained in their saddles, watching his every move.

'This is Captain Fog,' Petain commented, throwing a meaningful glance at Purge.

'He the feller's you-all allows going to make us toe the line like we'n's's regular Army?' Purge inquired.

A dull red flush crept over the Creole's handsome features. It was clear that the comment had displeased him. However, Mark gave no sign of having understood the enormous man's meaning.

'If I didn't see the uniforms,' Mark said to Petain, making sure that his words could be heard by the assembled men but never as much as glancing in Purge's direction. 'I'd swear they were *Yankees*. Don't you see to it that they wash, shave and tidy themselves up for Colonel's muster, Captain Petain?'

'I thought I'd leave that to you!' the Creole gritted, almost quivering with rage at the rebuke.

'I'm right pleased you did,' Mark declared, advancing but avoiding any obvious scrutiny of Purge. In fact, he seemed to be looking everywhere except at the brawny man. 'You damned, hawg-filthy——.'

Conscious that every 'soldier's' eyes were on him, Purge decided that he must assert himself. He equalled the blond giant in height and, with his barrel-like belly, was far heavier. Long brown hair covered his ears and caused the kepi to perch like a bump on a log. Blowing out his cheeks, he started to step from the ranks.

'Can't say's I take kind——!' Purge began.

He advanced only one pace.

Like a flash, Mark pivoted at the hips and threw the full power of his two hundred and eighteen pound frame behind a back-hand slap to the side of Purge's head. Taken by surprise, with his right leg in the air for his second step, the burly man was twirled around. He lost his kepi as he blundered into and brought down four other men with the force of the collision. Yells and curses rose on all sides.

Down flipped Mark's right hand, joining the left as it swept the near side Peacemaker from leather. Both guns lifted, swinging their muzzles in an arc which encompassed the men who had been closest to Purge and who were, Mark assumed, his special cronies.

Sitting up and rubbing the back of his right hand against his right cheek, Purge shook his head. Then he lurched erect and glared at the blond Texan beyond the two Peacemakers.

'Now that's a whole heap of dee-fence, even for an officer ag'in an 'listed man,' Purge growled.

'If those things are worrying you,' Mark drawled, gesturing with the Colts. 'I'll have Captain Petain hold 'em.'

With that, the big blond lowered the hammers and tossed the revolvers to the Creole.

Immediately, letting out a whoop, Purge charged forward. He believed that he was going to take Mark as unawares as he had been. Always a plain rough-house brawler, willing to take all his opponent could give and confident that he could more than repay it, the soldier expected Mark to duplicate his style of fighting.

That was where Purge made another mistake. Mark had learned the art of self defence from a man who had known the value of protective methods. So he knew just how to deal with a blind, bull-like charge.

Side-stepping Purge's clumsy rush, Mark hurled his left hand into the pit of the other's belly. The impact halted the huge man, causing him to feel that the rock-hard fist was shoving his guts into his backbone. Watching Purge fold over, the blond giant stepped behind him. Up swung

Mark's right boot, laying its sole on the man's pants' seat and pushing. Sent forward, Purge lit down on his face almost at Petain's feet.

Acting as if startled, the Creole jumped away and dropped Mark's Colts in front of Purge. Gasping for breath, the big soldier hunched himself on to his knees. Scrabbling for support, his right hand came to rest on the butt of Mark's left hand Colt. Before Purge's mind could take in what the thing under his palm might be, Mark was already moving towards him. Bending, the Texan hooked both hands into Purge's tunic's collar. Then Mark exerted all his enormous strength in a lifting heave. Purge rose from the ground like a pheasant rocketing out of cover. Witnesses later claimed that his feet were elevated some six inches above the grass. Hurled away by his captor, Purge went spinning and teetering. This time the crowd scattered hurriedly in all directions and he did not have other bodies to cushion his fall.

Silence fell over the soldiers and they stared in awe from Purge to the big Texan who had handled him with such ease. Slowly, painfully, Purge eased himself into a sitting position. Once more he shook his head. Admiration showed on his face as he saw the blond looming menacingly in his direction.

'You feel that strong about it, Cap'n Fog,' Purge said, grinning amiably. 'I'll go 'n' wash 'n' shave right now.'

'You do that,' Mark agreed, offering his hand and helping Purge rise. 'And the rest of you hear this. In one hour, I'm coming to make inspection. By then, I'll expect to see you looking like soldiers of the Confederate States' Army. Dismiss!'

Watching the hurried disintegration of the crowd, the big blond knew that he had achieved one thing. He would now have no trouble in controlling the men. There was, however, another matter to take up. Returning, he picked up and holstered his Colts. Then he strode over and confronted the Creole.

'You lousy Cree-owl pelican!' Mark growled. 'You tried to get me killed.'

'I don't know what——,' Petain began, throwing a look to where Virginie and de Richelieu had started to ride forward.

'You dropped my guns purposely, so that Purge would

pick one up and turn it on me,' Mark elaborated. 'That way, you'd be rid of both of us. The Colonel would have had him shot for doing it.'

'I won't even trouble to deny it,' Petain declared haughtily. 'My seconds will call on you.'

With that, the Creole turned and stalked away. He went at such an angle that his right side and hand were hidden from Mark's view. Carefully, he eased out the Army Colt from its twist-draw holster. With the weapon in his hand, he swung fully sideways on and began to elevate the weapon to shoulder height.

In the process of adopting his duellist's stance, Petain learned the basic and very deadly difference between his style of fighting and that of his proposed victim.

Looking along the barrel to align his sights, he watched the blond giant crouch slightly. Mark's hands whipped hip-wards. Before Petain's brain could assimilate what was happening, he saw the two Peacemakers appear from their holsters and point his way. Flame and smoke gushed from their muzzles.

That was the last living memory of Paul Petain.

Passing under the Creole's raised right arm, two .45 bullets crashed between his ribs and tore his heart to pieces. He was snapped backwards, firing a shot involuntarily. Its bullet went into the air and he was dead before his body struck the ground.

CHAPTER ELEVEN

GET INTO MY BED

'May I come in, Captain Fog?' Virginie de Vautour asked, as Mark opened the door of his room to her knock.

It was night and the woman stood in the lamp light, dressed as she had been when he had first seen her; except that her hair was tidy. In her right hand, she grasped the neck of a wine bottle and her left fingers held the stems of two glasses. The robe hung open, exposing a diaphonous nightdress which made her look more naked than she would have been if she had been completely unclothed.

'I'm not dressed for having callers,' the big blond warned.

Which was true enough. Having been undressed ready to go to bed, Mark was wearing only his riding breeches. He had not recognized Virginie's knock, for it had a less commanding sound, and so he had opened up without troubling to don other garments.

After killing Petain, Mark had spent a very busy day.

Virginie and de Richelieu had stated that they could hardly blame Mark for defending himself, even to the extent of shooting the Creole. On hearing of the incident, the other officers had failed to display concern over Petain's death. All had seemed relieved, at least, to know that the hot-tempered, always quarrelsome Petain would no longer be around looking for ways to issue a challenge to a duel.

Giving the men the hour he had promised, and not a second longer, Mark had had 'Assembly' blown by the bugler. While they were still far from being perfect, the improvement in their appearance and decorum had been very marked. So much so that de Richelieu had stated his satisfaction.

At the same time, de Richelieu had also explained why there were no men from Sheldon's Regiment amongst the Brotherhood. Recalling with deep bitterness how they had accepted Grant's offer to return to their homes, he had been disinclined to turn to his old comrades-in-arms for support. Having now seen how effective one of them could be, he was contemplating changing his mind. Wishing to avoid bringing men who had been his friends into the affair, Mark had pointed out that doing so would increase the danger of somebody letting slip his true identity.

Mark had given the men little rest all that day. Pushing them hard, he had caused the tent lines to be straightened, the area policed until there was not so much as a cigarette butt in the living area or the horse lines. There had been a longer grooming session than any of the animals had ever suffered before, examinations of their condition and exercise periods. Weapons had had to be produced and put through a rigorous scrutiny. Finally, Mark had made certain that the members of the Brotherhood would have plenty to occupy their time until 'lights out' was blown.

Mark had been pleased with his work. While he was

welding the Brotherhood into an efficient fighting unit, he had felt sure that the majority of them would soon give him their loyalty. There were, however, a hard core of Secessionist fanatics who would remain true to de Richelieu. They—most of them were non-commissioned officers—were the real danger and had, in Mark's opinion, a far greater potential than Corbeau or the other 'officers'.

Stepping in as the big blond withdrew, Virginie kicked the door closed with her heel. Then she held out the bottle and glasses.

'Was I a suspicious sort of feller,' Mark drawled, without taking them. 'I'd be wondering why you've come.'

'How do you mean?' the Baroness inquired.

'Seems like every time we've met today, I've raked you with my spurs.'

'Or I've raked you,' Virginie pointed out. 'So I think it's time we called a truce, don't you?'

'Why the change of heart?'

'Why do you think?'

'Lady, I don't know—but I aim to find out.'

'I consider that you are the best man here,' Virginie assured him, still holding her smile even if it ended clear of her eyes. There was something cold and wary in them. 'None of the others, even de Richelieu, could have done what you accomplished today. So I've decided that we must end our differences.'

'How'd your husband feel about that, ma'am?' Mark asked.

'He's dead.'

'Do I say I'm sorry?'

'It's a matter of indifference. Raoul and I weren't the same age and had little in common. For one thing, he chose the wrong side in the Franco–Prussian War. That was a fatal choice for a man with all his estates and assets tied up in the Alsace. Well, do we drink and become friends?'

'I'm all for friendship,' Mark declared and relieved her of her burdens.

'Do you have to drink—*first*?' Virginie purred as Mark stood at the side-piece pouring wine into the glasses.

Looking around, Mark found that the Baroness had slipped off her robe. It lay on the floor and she was walking towards him. He set down the bottle and glass, swinging to face her. The nightdress had a slit from hem almost to its waist. As she advanced, first one, then the other shapely leg came into view.

The big blond concluded that she did not really need *that* effect.

Reaching out, Mark prepared to scoop her into his arms. For all that, he could not shake off an uneasy feeling that all was far from being well. He had had a fair amount of experience with women and success in attracting them. Without being unduly immodest, he was aware that he had physical attributes which the opposite sex found most attractive. Accepting that a woman might take such steps to improve their relationship, he was still puzzled at why that particular one would do so. It was, he felt, completely out of character for Virginie de Vautour to come—cap-in-hand, as it were—to beg forgiveness from a man who had repeatedly antagonized her.

With that in mind, while willing to accept the olive branch Virginie had offered, Mark wondered what had caused her to come to his room.

He learned the reason quickly enough!

Even as he touched the warm, smooth flesh of her shoulders, an alarm bell triggered off a warning in his mind. Her skin felt warm, yet he could sense that tension and not eager response lay beneath it. Added to that, he saw all the seductive expression leave her face. It was replaced by a glow of growing triumph. Instead of a potential lover, Virginie resembled a poker-playing bull about to bring off a master-stroke that would completely defeat an opponent.

Up hurled the Baroness's left leg, aiming its knee towards Mark's groin. It failed to reach its target, but not by any great margin. Alert for the possibility of treachery, the blond giant had turned the pull which would have brought her up close into a puch. At the same instant, he swivelled his body away. Instead of impacting against the ultra-sensitive region, her knee caught him on the thigh. It arrived hard enough to warn him of what would have happened had it reached its intended target.

'You bitch!' Mark growled, thrusting her from him.

'You bastard!' Virginie shrilled, catching her balance, coming to a halt and returning to throw a punch at the Texan's head.

Rising swiftly, Mark's right hand intercepted the blow in mid-flight. His fingers closed around her wrist, grasping it savagely. Retreating, towing her after him effortlessly, he sat on the bed. While she must have known what he was intending, she could not prevent it happening. A quick jerk hauled her belly-down across his knees.

'This's what somebody should've done to you a long time ago!' Mark gritted.

Up and down rose his left hand, while the right transferred itself to the back of her neck and held her as helpless as a butterfly pinned to a collector's display card. His flat palm descended hard on her barely protected rump. Slap after slap rang out, while she struggled futilely, squealed in pain or yelped out curses in English and French.

After administering the spanking—which would have gladdened the hearts of numerous people, including the late Baron de Vautour, if they had been privileged to witness it—Mark rolled the woman from his knees. Turning over twice on the floor, Virginie landed supine. Tears streamed down her face as she sat up. Glaring at the big Texan, she was stopped speaking by a realization that *sitting* was painful. So she rose, delicate fingers going to the fiery source of her discomfort and gently rubbing it.

'All right,' Mark drawled, standing up but not approaching her. 'Your little notion for showing me who's boss didn't work.'

'Wh—What are you going to do to me?' Virginie sniffed.

'That's up to you,' the blond replied. 'You can get into my bed, or you can get the hell back to your own room. Me, I'm going to finish undressing and put weight on the mattress.'

Turning and walking painfully, still rubbing at where her buttocks showed redder than the white of her skin under the nightdress, Virginie went to the door. Her fingers were on the knob when she spun around.

'You big, handsome bastard!' the Baroness gasped and ran towards the blond giant.

This time there was no pretence, nor ulterior motive, in how she acted.

If any of the other men had heard the spanking, or otherwise been disturbed, they gave no hint of it at breakfast the following morning. Nor did the Baroness when she entered and gingerly took her seat at the table. The incident of the previous night might never have happened, but for a slight wince, which Mark alone observed, as she moved incautiously on her chair. She was still the same cool, distant, imperious Virginie de Vautour to everybody but the big blond. Him she ignored except for addressing the usual commonplaces.

'Will you come with the Baroness and me to my office, before you go to your duties, Captain Fog?' de Richelieu inquired as the meal ended.

'Yo!' Mark replied.

Having dismissed the others to their duties, de Richelieu escorted the woman and Mark into his small den. The Texan noted, without showing his amusement, that Virginie selected the softer of the guests' chairs and lowered herself on to it carefully.

'How will General Hardin react to our plans?' de Richelieu commenced, without preliminary formalities.

'He'll do whatever's best for the South,' Mark replied, evasively.

'And Captain Fog?'

'Him too.'

'Will they support us?' de Richelieu insisted.

'I wouldn't want to answer that "yes", or "no", in case I'm wrong,' Mark drawled. 'But I know they'll do the best for the South.'

'Which means they'll join us,' de Richelieu declared. 'Especially if——.'

'If——?' Virginie prompted.

'I would imagine that there will be considerable entertaining during the peace meeting with the ranchers, Mr. Counter?' de Richelieu said.

'You can count on it,' Mark agreed. 'Governor Howard will want to keep everything friendly, and that's a right good way of doing it.'

'Including a visit to the theatre, if a suitable show was playing there,' Virginie said, face showing understanding. 'What do you intend to do, Anton?'

'It's what Mr. Counter is going to do, my dear,' de Richelieu answered. 'He's going to persuade the Governor and the ranchers to attend a performance by Sabot the

Mysterious——.'

'And?' the Baroness demanded eagerly.

'I haven't decided quite what we'll do yet,' de Richelieu admitted. 'But I've an idea that we can do what we planned to do in Shreveport. Only this time we'll make certain there are no mistakes.'

Although Mark hoped that he might gain a better idea of what de Richelieu was considering, the opportunity to do so was not presented. Instead, the leader of the Brotherhood came to his feet and intimated that the meeting was at an end. Politely, but in a manner which showed that he wanted no further discussion, he ushered Virginie and Mark from his den. In the hall, Virginie did not address a word to the blond giant, but strolled away in a preoccupied manner.

Collecting and saddling his horse, Mark rode to the camp. He too was preoccupied and deeply perturbed. Whatever de Richelieu was planning must be important, maybe even very dangerous for Dusty and the other ranchers. So Mark knew that he must discover what the scheme was going to be. The reference to Shreveport could possibly offer a clue.

Virginie had left the ranch when Mark returned that evening after putting his 'Company' through a gruelling day they would be unlikely to forget for a long time. From what the blond was able to gather, the Baroness and Kincaid travelled from town to town—posing as man and wife—selecting potential supporters for the Cause. Having done so, they left written instructions—using a harmless-seeming but complex code—for use by the stage magician whom de Richelieu had mentioned. Apparently the Baroness and her 'husband' did not let themselves be known as part of the organization. It was Sabot the Mysterious who entertained the possible candidates, checked their loyalties, and spread the first seeds of the Brotherhood's propaganda.

In the days that followed Virginie's departure, Mark tried several times to gain some inkling of what de Richelieu was planning for the Governor's visit to San Antonio de Bexar. On each occasion the big blond had tried to raise the matter, the Colonel had grown evasive. De Richelieu merely stated that he had not yet formulated his plan, but when he did he would tell Mark everything.

Nor did the Texan have any greater luck in discovering what had happened in Shreveport. So well had Colonel Winslow done his work, that the story had not been printed in Texas' newspapers. None of the men at the ranch appeared to know anything about the incident.

For his part, Mark went ahead with training the company. In that, he had practical experience as his guide and also the lessons in man-management which he had acquired from Dusty Fog. It was his intention to so sicken the men with their present life that they would desert and break away from the Brotherhood. So he drove them as hard as he could; which ought to have been a wole heap harder than they could take.

Each day, Mark held inspections of clothing, arms, equipment, horses, living accommodation. Not only that, but he filled their hours with drills, weapon training and a sequence of hard riding marches which reduced the participants to cursing, complaining masses of bruises.

To Mark, there were times when he felt that the clock had been turned back. He would ride at the head of his grey-clad company, with the Stars and Bars flag fluttering overhead, covering rough terrain at speed by the system known as 'posting the trot'.* That was a hard, gruelling and wearing method, until a man's muscles grew accustomed to it. However, any of the 'soldiers' who failed to do so found Mark at his side and roaring invective into his ears.

On the second day, three men 'deserted', but where caught by the fanatical non-coms. What happened to the trio caused all the others to reconsider if they had nourished plans of a similar nature.

Not only did the non-coms hold the men in check, Purge did more than his share. Filled with admiration for the blond giant who had defeated him, the burly man used his influence—which was still considerable—to keep others loyal to 'Captain Fog'.

The Baroness and her party returned, having left instructions for Sabot the Mysterious at Temple, in Bell County. When he received them, he would come to Los Cabestrillo and be delivered to the ranch. Virginie had called at the

* Posting the trot is described in detail in: *UNDER THE STARS AND BARS.*

town on her return and brought Mark news from Marshal Flatter. Apparently the Kendal County sheriff had reached a decision concerning the deaths of the soldiers. No Army post admitted to having lost two of its men, so they were assumed to be deserters heading for the Mexican border. In which case, the sheriff considered that it would be sufficient if Captain Fog merely wrote and had witnessed a statement of what had happened.

Would Captain Fog go into Los Cabestrillo the following day and do it?

Accompanied by de Richelieu and Corbeau, all of them dressed in civilian clothing, Mark rode into the town shortly after noon on the appointed day. They were leaving their horses at the livery barn when Flatter arrived.

'Colonel!' the marshal said, mopping his face with a bandana.

'I thought I told you never to let on you knew me!' de Richelieu snarled.

'It's important!' Flatter protested. 'Them fellers who robbed the Yankee paymaster and killed all them bluebellies——.'

'The Caxtons and Comanche Blood?' Corbeau put in.

'That's them!' Flatter agreed, delighted with the impression he was making on the three men.

'What about them?' de Richelieu demanded.

'They're up to the hotel now,' Flatter replied. 'In the dining-room, having a meal.'

'Are they?' de Richelieu said quietly. 'Come along, gentlemen. I'm looking forward to meeting them.'

CHAPTER TWELVE

HANDS FLAT ON THE TABLE

When Dusty Fog announced his identity, unless there was trouble or danger threatening, he frequently took the chance of being disbelieved. Many people found it impossible to reconcile his appearance with his legendary reputation.

That only applied in times of peace.

Such a period existed in the dining-room of the Longhorn Hotel in Los Cabestrillo. While the waiter had studied Dusty's two companions with interest, and a few misgivings, he had barely afforded the Rio Hondo gun wizard a second glance.

Seated at the centre table, with his black Stetson dangling by its *barbiquejo* on the back of his chair, Dusty Fog looked like a small, insignificant cowhand; or horse-wrangler, which was even lower down the social scale.

Yes, *small*!'

Dusty Fog stood a mere five foot six inches in his high-heeled, fancy stitched boots. While he possessed an exceptional muscular development, it did not show to any advantage under his expensive clothing. In fact, he contrived to make the garments look like somebody's cast-offs. About his waist was strapped a gunbelt made by Joe Gaylin. Neither it, nor the matched bone handled Colt Civilian Model Peacemakers in the cross draw holsters, added anything to make him more noticeable. He had curly dusty-blond hair. In repose, as at that moment, his face was tanned, fairly handsome, but showed nothing of his true potential.

Each of the men with whom Dusty was sitting caught the eye far more than the small Texan.

Take Waco, at Dusty's left, who had passed himself as 'Matthew "Boy" Caxton' during the visits to Hell.

Something over six foot in height, blond haired and handsome, he had a powerful young body broadening and strengthening towards full manhood. He had on somewhat dandified cowhand's clothing, purchased in Hell to help his role of an irresponsible outlaw on a spree. There had been men in that town—and other places—who could testify to how well the youngster handled the brace of staghorn handled 1860 Army Colts which rode his *buscadero* gunbelt.

That Waco was highly skilled in all matters *pistolero* was not surprising. Left an orphan almost from birth in an Indian raid, he had been raised by a rancher with a large family. Leaving his adopted home early, he had drifted the range country; a silent, morose boy with sufficient dexterity in gun-toting to prevent himself from being bullied. He had been working for Clay Allison's wild onion crew when he had first met Dusty Fog, Ever since the small Texan had saved his life, by snatching him from under the CA's stampeding herd,* Waco had changed for the better. Previously he had been proddy, quick to take offence, always too ready, willing and able to protect himself. Treated as a favourite younger brother by the other members of the floating outfit, he had been given an education in many subjects. One of the most important lessons he had learned had been *when*, to add to his knowledge of *how*, to draw and shoot.

Dangerous as Waco had been, and, under the right conditions, still could be, there were many who would have accorded him second place in that to the tall, black haired, Indian-dark, almost babyishly-innocent featured man called the Ysabel Kid.

Born and raised amongst the Comanche Indians' *Pehnane*—Wasp, Quick Stingers or Raiders—band, of which his grandfather was a war leader of the Dog Soldier lodge, the Kid might have made a famous Indian brave-heart.† However, he had been taken by his father on mustanging, or smuggling, missions along the Rio Grande. There he had acquired a reputation for being a bad *hombre* to cross. In the War Between The States, the Kid and his father, Big Sam Ysabel, had spent much of their time delivering goods —which had been slipped through the Yankee blockade into Mexico—across the international border to the Confederate authorities in Texas. They had also aided Belle Boyd on two of her assignments, including the hunt for Tollinger and Barmain. Bushwhack lead had cut Sam Ysabel down soon after. Hunting for the killers, the Kid had joined Dusty Fog and helped him to deliver Grant's message to Bushrod Sheldon. Then he had agreed to join the OD Connected's floating outfit. His duties were less of cowhand than scout. By birth and training, he was ideally suited for the work.

Not quite as tall as Waco, the Kid was slimmer; but gave the impression of whipcord, tireless strength. He had left off his usual all-black clothing, so that nobody would connect 'Alvin "Comanche" Blood' with Loncey Dalton Ysabel, also known as the Ysabel Kid. Instead, he wore a fringed buckskin shirt, Levi's pants and calf-high Comanche moc-

* Told in: *TRIGGER FAST*.
† Told in: *COMANCHE*.

casins. He had, however, retained his usual armament; in the use of which he was accounted very expert. So his walnut-handled old Dragoon Colt hung in the twist-hand draw holster at the right of his belt and an ivory hilted James Black bowie knife was sheathed on the left.

The trio had the room to themselves. After delivering their food, the waiter had—although they did not know this—slipped away to inform the marshal of their presence.

Having completed their assignment and ensured that the town of Hell would no longer be available for use by outlaws,* Dusty's party were relaxed. So they paid little attention to the sound of feet approaching the main entrance of the dining-room. Even the fact that the town's marshal entered, accompanied by three more men, caused them no alarm. Two of the newcomers looked like prosperous Southron gentlemen.

The third was the trio's *amigo*, Mark Counter.

Good old Mark would be able to clear up any misunderstandings which the local peace officer might be experiencing.

'Stay put, you *Caxtons*, *Blood*!' Mark snapped, flashing out, cocking and lining his Colts at the trio. 'Hands flat on the table.'

On the point of speaking, Waco left the words unsaid.

Just as Mark had anticipated, when deciding upon how to handle the new development, his *amigos* responded perfectly. Even the boy, who had been set to give the whole snap away, played along exactly as the blond giant wished. Showing alarm, anger, yet a realization that resistance at that point would be futile or fatal, Dusty, the Kid and Waco kept in their seats and slapped their hands, palms down, on the top of the table.

All of them had noticed the emphasis which Mark had laid upon the use of their assumed names. Knowing him, they had read the correct implications from the words—and even more from his actions. While Mark might have been playing a joke on them, or upon the fat, slothful peace officer, before revealing their true identities, there were limits to how far he would take it. A man of his great experience, for example, might have even drawn his guns; but he would never have cocked the hammers—and be

* How this was achieved is told in: *GO BACK TO HELL*.

holding back the triggers!—in the course of a joke.

Having taken note of the big blond's words and actions, especially with regard to the triggers of the Colts, the three cowhands concluded, correctly, that he wanted them to continue being the 'Caxton brothers' and 'Comanche Blood'.

'What's the idea, *hombre*?' Dusty growled, darting glances around as if in search of an avenue of escape.

'You're under arrest, is what!' Flatter announced, suddenly catching up with the rapid turn of events and starting to haul his revolver from its holster.

'Now, now, marshal,' de Richelieu put in. 'Don't let's be hasty.'

'Wha——?' Flatter gurgled, looking baffled.

'You don't know for sure that these young men are the Caxtons and Comanche Blood,' de Richelieu pointed out, shoving the barrel of the marshal's revolver down out of alignment. 'Do you?'

'But, I thought—You mean——!' Flatter spluttered, visions of the reward money floating away from his grasp. 'Cap'n Fog here——.'

'Me?' Mark put in, allowing the triggers to return to a more harmless position. 'I was going on what you told us, marshal. If they should have been those owlhoots, I figure the best way to mention it would be after they couldn't do any arguing.'

'We ain't those fellers you reckon we are!' Waco complained, stirring with an all too casual motion.

'You stay put!' Mark ordered, gesturing at the youngster with his right hand Colt. 'The other two've likely got sense enough to know better.'

'The marshal tells us you're wanted men,' de Richelieu remarked, as Waco settled into surly immobility. 'Now I've always prided myself on being a good judge of human nature. And I believe that you are nothing more than three young cowboys, out of work and looking for employment.'

'*Work!*' Waco jeered, perfect in his response and part. 'We don't take to——?'

'Choke off, *half*-brother!' Dusty commanded angrily, then looked at de Richelieu. 'Yes, sir. That's just what we are.'

'Then you'll be willing to come with me to my ranch?'

'Well——,' Dusty began, fingers moving restlessly.

'Keep your hands still!' Mark snapped. 'It's one thing or

the other, *hombre*. You come to work for Colonel de Richelieu. Or the marshal holds you until the Rangers come and say who you really are.'

'You've just hired three men, Colonel,' Dusty drawled. 'Hasn't he, Comanch', half-brother?'

'Me, I'd sooner work cattle'n be locked indoors,' agreed the Kid.

'Matt?' Dusty challenged.

'You're running things, big brother,' Waco submitted sullenly.

'We'll start by having you get up one at a time, shed your gunbelts and move away from the table,' Mark suggested.

'Like hell!' Waco spat.

'Do it, damn you, boy!' Dusty barked.

'I for sure ain't fixing to argue with you, Cap'n Fog,' the Kid went on and stood up, keeping his hands in sight.

'Left handed and real easy!' Mark warned.

Obeying, the Kid left his gunbelt on the table and moved away from his place. Dusty repeated the dark Texan's actions, picking up and donning his hat in passing.

'Now you,' Mark told Waco.

'Suppose I tell you to go crawl up your butt-end?' the youngster challenged.

'If I do it,' Mark replied, 'you'll be a heap too dead to know.'

'You do like the man says!' Dusty raged. 'Damn it! Don't you have enough sense to know when to yell "calf-rope"?'

'I never took to eating crow!' Waco answered. 'So——.'

'So do like the man says!' Dusty snarled. 'I figure this's for the best.'

'You always figured good enough for us so far, Ed,' drawled the Kid.

'All right, all right!' Waco muttered. 'Happen doing it gets us hung, I'll never talk to neither of you again.'

Glowering furiously at Mark, the youngster obeyed. Waco did not know what was happening, or greatly care, such was his supreme faith that his *amigos* would be a match for it. So he played along in a manner which was clearly convincing the dudes about his character. They would never guess that he, Dusty and the Kid knew Mark, after the display he was putting on. Waco considered that such a condition might be important.

With the three belts on the table, and their owners standing some feet away, Mark holstered his Colts and walked to hook his rump on the back of what had been Dusty's chair. He sat in a position which would prevent the 'Caxtons' and 'Comanche Blood' regaining possession of their weapons.

'I don't think we need you any more, marshal,' de Richelieu drawled, turning to Flatter.

'Huh?' gulped the peace officer.

'I'd say your boss's saying for you to get the hell out of here,' Waco explained with a grin.

'And I'd say it's easy to see who's the *younger* brother,' Mark drawled. 'The one with the biggest mouth.'

'Yeah?' Waco growled. 'Well I don't——.'

'Shut your hay-hole!' Dusty interrupted viciously. 'Leave him be, Cap'n Fog. He's young——'

'That's been saving him,' Mark answered, 'so far.'

'You'd better explain to the citizens that it's all a mistake and these aren't the outlaws,' de Richelieu told the marshal.

'I'll do that,' Flatter agreed and slouched disconsolately from the room.

'Mind if I ask what your notion is, Colonel?' Dusty inquired. 'You *know* who we are.'

'If it's the Army's reward you're after——,' Waco began.

'I could have had it by saying nothing,' de Richelieu pointed out. 'Or shared it with Captain Fog, Major Corbeau and the marshal.'

'Could be you're figuring on the loot,' the Kid pointed out. 'Which being, you've come *way* too late. We spent it all down in Hell.'

'If you're broke, so much the better,' de Richelieu smiled.

'I've never found being broke better'n anything,' Waco complained.

'In this case, it is. If only for me,' de Richelieu answered. 'You'll be the more likely to take my offer of work. It will give you a safe hiding place from the Army.'

'We've done all right dodging 'em so far,' Waco scoffed, playing the irresponsible, hot-headed hard-case to the hilt. 'Hell, we ain't seed hide nor hair of a stinking blue-belly patrol in weeks. Last 'n's we met up with wound up awful dead.'

'And you think that the Army have forgotten you?' de Richelieu asked. 'They never will.'

'Colonel's right, boy,' Dusty confirmed. 'So we need some place safe to hole up for a spell.'

'Let them have their gunbelts back, Captain Fog,' de Richelieu ordered. 'I think we can trust Mr. Caxton, his brother and Mr. Blood to accompany us.'

'We'll need the belts when we go out of here,' Dusty pointed out, as Mark displayed reluctance. 'And I'll promise you the boy'll behave.'

Leaving the hotel, the party found that a crowd had gathered. Various citizens were still hovering around, hoping for some kind of action. However, the fact that the men emerged in apparent friendliness and with the three cowhands still wearing their guns, implied that the marshal had been telling the truth.

Collecting the horses at the livery barn, the men were about to mount when de Richelieu reminded Mark that he had not completed his business in town.

'Go and do it, Captain Fog,' the Colonel went on. 'You can catch up with us on the trail.'

'But——' Mark began, darting a meaning look at the three cowhands.

'You can trust them,' de Richelieu assured the big blond. 'That small one might look like a nobody, but I sense that he's shrewd enough to know when he's well off. And he can keep the other two under control.'

'It's your horse, Colonel, ride it any way you see fit,' Mark drawled. 'Only, was I you, I'd make sure they knew I'm not toting any money on me.'

'I'll do that,' de Richelieu promised.

Leaving Mark and Corbeau behind, de Richelieu accompanied the three Texans across the range. At the man's suggestion, Dusty signalled to his companions to drop behind. Falling a few yards to the rear, the Kid and Waco started up a conversation calculated to further their deception.

'Tell me a little about yourself, Mr. Caxton,' de Richelieu suggested.

'There's not a whole heap to tell,' Dusty replied, wanting a lead as to how he should answer.

'Were you driven to becoming outlaws by Reconstruction?'

'Yankee carpetbaggers took our ranch,' Dusty admitted,

using a reason why more than one Texan had been sent on the outlaw trail. 'There wasn't much else a feller could do down here after the War.'

'Why did you decide to rob that Paymaster?'

'He was carrying enough money to make it worth while.'

'Knowing that by doing it, you'd have the whole U.S. Army after you?'

'Something told me they'd not like us doing it,' Dusty admitted cheerfully.

'But you went right ahead.'

'Why sure.'

'Because you hate blue-bellies?' de Richelieu inquired.

Something in the man's voice supplied Dusty with the required clue on how he should continue.

'I hate their guts. They killed my mother, in a raid early in the War, down to Brownsville. Pa married again. A widow-woman who wasn't our class——.'

'That explains the differences between yourself and your brother.'

'Sure,' Dusty agreed. 'But he's useful to have around and, second to me, he's the fastest I've ever seen with a gun. Anyways, we'd started up ranching on the Panhandle range when peace came. While we was away, carpetbaggers run the boy's maw off, she was killed. We came back from that trail drive and found her grave. Paw went after the carpetbaggers. The State Police got him. Boy 'n' me, we escaped and've been on the dodge ever since.'

'So you've no love for the Yankees?' de Richelieu inquired.

'Colonel,' Dusty replied vehemently. 'I'd kill every blasted one of 'em, given but just a chance.'

'Including Governor Howard?'

'Him more than anybody! It's him who's got the Rangers raising such hell that a wanted man don't hardly dare to go to bed at nights, even in places that used to be safe.'

Instead of commenting, de Richelieu rode on for a time in silence. Dusty also did not speak, but sat as if waiting for the other to continue. The small Texan guessed that the man at his side was debating whether to say anything more. So he decided to prod de Richelieu along.

'These questions about my past're taking us some place,

I'd say,' Dusty drawled.

'They are,' de Richelieu agreed. 'Have you ever heard of the Brotherhood For Southron Freedom?'

'Nope,' Dusty confessed. 'I can't rightly say I have.'

Speaking quickly and with growing excitement, de Richelieu described his organization and its aims. At Dusty's signal. Waco and the Kid ceased their chattering and closed the distance so that they could listen. All of them could now understand why Mark had gone to such lengths to present them as a trio of badly wanted outlaws.

'Just where do we fit in this idea?' asked Waco.

'Would you kill an enemy of the South?' de Richelieu challenged.

'We'd kill *anybody*,' drawled Waco. 'Just so the price's right.'

'Who is it you want killing, Colonel?' Dusty inquired.

'Governor Stanton Howard,' de Richelieu replied. 'With him dead, we'll have the South preparing for war with the Yankees. And this time we'll not be beaten.'

CHAPTER THIRTEEN

KNOW HER? SHE'S MY WIFE

'Get down, Miss Boyd, or whoever you are!' Stapler commanded, glaring up as she climbed tiredly from inside the wagon on to the box.

By the time Belle had recovered consciousness, the wagon had been on its way out of Los Cabestrillo. She was in its body, not tied up in any way but guarded by Dunco. Although he had not been hostile, the comic had stated that he would take no chances until the matter of her behaviour was settled one way or the other. He had made her remain where she was, but had also told her what had happened after Stapler had knocked her down.

With the connivance of the town's marshal, Stapler had convinced the old telegraphist that Belle was a desperate murderess, badly wanted by the law. Satisfied that the baritone was a Texas Ranger ordered to capture her, the telegraphist had gone about his business. Then Belle had been taken to the barn.

According to Dunco, there had been a heated scene between Sabot the Mysterious and Stapler. The magician had been inclined to discount the baritone's story as no more than jealousy. However, the other men had insisted that Belle must be delivered to the ranch as a prisoner and Colonel de Richelieu informed. Knowing what his fate might be if he refused, the magician had yielded to their demands.

Satisfied that she could not hope to escape in her present weakened condition, Belle had remained passive during the journey. She had spent her time in throwing off the effects, or as much as possible, of the attack she had suffered. She had also tried to think up an explanation for her actions. There had seemed only one course left open to her. That Sabot would support her against Stapler. It was not much comfort, but at least it might produce a respite for her.

Dropping down, Belle tried to read some expression on Sabot's sallow face. She failed and turned her gaze to the other men. Something white showed at Downend's waist. Looking at it, the girl recognized the butt of her Dance. Clearly Sabot had won one point, refusing to allow Stapler to keep hold of the weapon. She darted glances about her, but could see no way in which she might escape if she made a bid for freedom.

'Let's go see the Colonel,' Mick ordered.

With Stapler gripping her arm, and showing his determination to prevent her from fleeing, Belle allowed herself to be escorted to the big main house. Mick opened its front door and they entered the hall. Several people were already present. A beautiful, elegantly-attired woman, men in the uniforms of Confederate States' officers and three cowhands.

'What's all this about, sergeant?' de Richelieu demanded, seeing from the attitudes of the new arrivals that something was wrong.

'I don't know, sir,' Mick admitted.

Before any more could be said, Stapler thrust his way to the front of his party. He shoved Belle ahead of him and pointed an accusing finger her way.

'This here's Belle Boyd, Colonel,' the baritone declared. 'I caught her trying to send off a telegraph message.'

Looking around, Belle felt her heart leap with joy. Somehow, her request for assistance had been answered even better than she could have wished it might be. Not only was Dusty Fog present, but he had his three loyal, very capable *amigos* available to back his play. They would make a fighting force to be reckoned with——

Certain facts began to leap through Belle's mind.

Mark Counter was wearing an officer's—a *captain's*—uniform.

Dusty Fog, the Ysabel Kid and Waco had on clothing similar to that described in the newspaper's story. That was made more obvious by the fact that the Kid was not attired in the all black clothing which Belle had been the cause of his first acquiring.

If Belle read the situation correctly, Mark was pretending to be Dusty, while the small Texan and the other two must still be acting as the wanted men.

So how could Belle make herself known to them without admitting her true identity, or spoiling their deceptions?

That problem was taken out of her hands in no uncertain manner.

'You stupid whore!' Dusty roared, leaping towards the girl.

Before Belle, or any of the others, realized what the small Texan was planning, he had lashed the palm of his hand savagely across her face. The slap was not a light one, for Dusty did not dare try to fake his actions. It staggered the girl. Following her, Dusty swung another blow which sent her reeling to fall almost at de Richelieu's feet. Although the attack had hurt, Belle still retained sufficient conscious thought to know what she must do.

'No—No—Ed!' she screetched, watching Dusty stalking in her direction.

'Take it——!' Mark began, when nobody else offered to speak.

'Stand there, big man!' Waco snarled, flashing out his right hand Colt. 'Brother Ed's got the right to beat up on his woman, happen he's so minded.'

Bending, Dusty took hold and almost tore the shirt from Belle's back as he wrenched her to her feet. Shaking her savagely, he shouted furiously into her tear-smeared, scared face.

'How many times did I tell you about not saying you're somebody famous?' Dusty roared, thrusting her from him. 'Last time it was Belle Starr.'

'Ole Belle whomped her better'n you're doing when she heard about it.' Waco grinned.

'I—I—I——!' Belle whined, stumbling against the wall and huddling herself protectively with both arms covering her head. 'D—Don't beat m—me—u—, Ed!'

Nobody in the hall made a move to interfere. While Waco kept his Colt lined on Mark, as if determined that he should not, the others showed no inclination to do other than watch and listen. As Belle sobbed her plea, de Richelieu advanced a couple of paces.

'It seems you know her, Mr. Caxton!'

Spinning on his heel, grateful for the excuse to take no further action, Dusty growled, '*Know* her? She's my wife!'

'*Wife!*' Stapler spat out, sensing that things might turn out badly for him. 'Damn it! She's a dyke.'

'I didn't hear you right, *hombre*,' Dusty said, almost mildly, swinging towards the baritone. 'Now did I?'

Suddenly Stapler found that he was no longer confronted by a small, insignificant cowhand. To him, it seemed that Belle's assailant had taken on size and weight until looking larger than the blond giant in the captain's uniform.

It was one of the moments when Dusty Fog could not be measured in mere feet and inches.

'She—That's what——!' Stapler spluttered, drawing away a pace. 'She told us she was!'

'I—I did it to stop him mauling and chasing me, Ed!' Belle explained.

'I—I wasn't meaning anything by it, Selima!' Stapler apologized. 'Honest, feller, I never went near——.'

'None of them did, Ed!' Belle hastened to assure Dusty. 'I wouldn't let them come hear me.'

'That's real lucky for you,' Dusty drawled and the words sounded far more menacing than any amount of a lesser man's bawled out threats.

'And even luckier for the man's'd tried it,' Waco grinned, holstering his Colt. 'Brother Ed's sure particul——.'

'Boy!' Mark barked, joining the youngster in the good work of diverting attention from Belle's admission of her true identity. 'Happen you ever pull down on me again, drop the hammer. Because I'll kill you if you don't.'

'You wanting your chance now?' the youngster challenged, with such ferocity that Belle was almost taken in.

'Would your brother and Mr. Blood help the sergeant with the wagon's team, Mr. Caxton?' de Richelieu put in.

'Go do it, boy!' Dusty commanded.

'Come on, paleface brother,' the Kid went on, advancing and gripping Waco by the arm.

'All right, all right!' Waco spat, wrenching himself free. Continuing with the line he and Mark had followed since their arrival, he went on, 'One day you 'n' me's going to meet and nobody step 'tween us, Captain Fog.'

'That's the day they'll bury you,' Mark answered.

'Hey, how's about coming and giving your husband a loving kiss?' Dusty demanded of Belle, drawing attention from Mark and Waco so that they could let the matter lapse.

Scrubbing her face with her hands, the girl scuttled forward. Once in Dusty's arms, she continued to act perfectly. Although she started by delivering a frightened peck, she changed it into a passionate embrace. Mark studied the by-play and decided, whatever else they might believe, nobody in the hall would accept that Belle had lesbian tendencies.

'I—I didn't know where you'd be at when I came out of the State Penitentiary, Ed!' Belle said hurriedly, but distinctly, wanting Dusty to know something of her 'history'. 'So I've sent a couple of letters—in our code—to the old hide-outs.'

'*That's* what you were doing!' Sabot put in, throwing a vicious, hate-filled glare at the baritone.

'Y—Yes, Sabby,' Belle confessed, having been told by Dunco that Stapler had seen her mailing a letter. She continued with the correct reaction. 'But—But how did you——?'

'Our good friend here told me.' Sabot answered coldly.

'I just figured that Ed and the boys would be useful for the Brotherhood,' Belle explained. 'But I didn't want Stapler a-chasing me again if he heard I wasn't a dyke. So I sent them off without saying anything.'

'So you've been making fuss for my wife, huh?' Dusty said to the baritone.

'Let *me* take care of this, friend,' Sabot suggested, reaching to pluck the Dance from Downend's belt.

'Sabby!' Belle yelled as the magician turned the barrel in Stapler's direction and thumbed back the hammer. 'It's not capped!'

The warning came too late.

Having realized that his plans for humiliating Sabot had failed, Stapler had not been unaware of his own position. The magician would never forgive him and had a vile temper when roused. So the baritone had taken precautions. Ever since the night of the fight in Dallas, he had carried a Colt 'Cloverleaf' House Pistol* in his jacket's right-hand pocket. At the first hint that things were going wrong, he had slipped his fingers around its butt. Jerking it out as Sabot turned the Dance towards him, the baritone aimed from waist level and fired.

Although Sabot heard Belle's warning, its full import did not register until the hammer fell. Nothing but a dull, dry click came to his ears. Evan as shock twisted at this sallow face, he saw Stapler's revolver belch flame. Numbing agony tore briefly into the magician as the .41 calibre bullet ripped through his left breast.

'Now for you, you whore!' Stapler screamed, starting to swing the weapon in Belle's direction.

Thrusting the girl away from him, Dusty flung his left hand across to the right side Colt. Waco and Mark also commenced their draws, determined to protect the girl. Stapler had less than a minute left to live.

Three heavy calibre revolver shots crashed in a rapid, ragged volley. Each bullet found its mark in the baritone. Any one of them would have been fatal. The combined force of the impacts hurled Stapler backwards. Colliding with the wall, he bounced lifeless to the floor.

'Sabby!' Belle gasped.

'He's done for,' Captain Raphael declared, kneeling and making an examination of the motionless figure of the magician.

'Damn it!' de Richelieu bellowed, face turning almost white in rage. 'Why didn't you shoot him more quickly, Mis—Captain Fog?'

* Despite its name, the Colt Model of 1871 'Cloverleaf' House Pistol is a revolver.

'How was I to know what he aimed to do?' Mark countered.

'You knew how much our plans depended on Sabot!' Virginie snapped, glaring furiously at the blond giant. 'So you ought——.'

'It's too late now, Virginie!' de Richelieu said, making a visible effort to regain control of his emotions. He looked around for a moment, then shrugged. 'Will you gentlemen from the show go and unpack your wagon. You could probably use a meal, too.'

'Shouldn't we learn more about—— Mrs. Caxton—first?' Virginie asked.

'Do any of you know anything more about her?' de Richelieu inquired.

'She's always done real good for the Brotherhood,' the orchestra's leader stated. 'Stapler never liked her, after she put the knee into his ba—Sorry, lady.'

'But he claimed that she said she was Belle Boyd,' Virginie remarked, ignoring the apology which had been thrown her way.

'I heard her,' Dunco said. 'I'm sorry, Selim—Mrs. Caxton, but you did.'

'That's right, I did,' Belle admitted, having concocted an acceptable excuse. 'Like I said, I wanted to bring Ed and the boys into the Brotherhood. So I aimed to get word to them by telegraph. Only they won't send messages in code for ordinary folks. I figured on claiming I was Belle Boyd, working for the Pink-Eyes*, and that way he'd be likely to do it.'

'It worked last time she did it, Brother Ed,' Waco commented.

'Did you hear any of this?' Virginie asked the comic.

'She'd no sooner said she was Belle Boyd than Stapler jumped her,' Dunco replied.

'Are you calling me a lair?' Belle demanded, glaring at the other woman.

'I see you've lost your wedding ring,' Virginie purred.

'Not lost it, sold it,' Belle corrected. 'To get money for travelling while I was looking for Ed. Maybe *you*'d've found another way to do it, but I stop way short of *that*.'

---

* Pink-Eye: derogatory name for a member of Pinkerton's National Detective Agency.

'How dare you!' Virginie hissed.

'How dare you go hinting I'm not Ed's real wife?' Belle blazed back.

'Ladies!' de Richelieu barked. 'Mr. Caxton, please bring your wife into the study. Captain Fog, come with us. Major Corbeau, take the performers to the bunkhouse and settle them in. Major Kincaid, have the bodies removed.'

'Where will Mrs. Caxton sleep?' Virginie purred.

'With my man, of course,' Belle flashed back.

'And his brother and the hal—Mr. Blood?' the Baroness asked.

'Maybe you'd like my knuckles in your mouth!' Belle raged, starting to cock her right fist and move forward.

'Easy, gal!' Dusty ordered, catching her arm and holding her. 'The Baroness didn't mean it that way. Me and the boys've been bunking in the same room upstairs.'

'Maybe your men could sleep at the bunkhouse?' Mark suggested, seeing that Virginie had inadvertently given the solution to one problem.

'Or in the hay loft at the barn,' the Kid offered. 'I don't take to bedding down among too many folks.'

'Make your own arrangements, gentlemen,' de Richelieu advised. 'Come this way, Mr., Mrs. Caxton.'

Going into the study, Dusty was satisfied by what had happened so far. Not only had he saved Belle, but the way was paved for his companions to obtain a greater freedom of movement. Although they had been treated as guests, de Richelieu had insisted that the trio should occupy a room in the house. Having no wish to arouse even slight doubts, they had concurred. However, having Waco and the Kid at liberty and away from the main building might prove advantageous.

Inside the study, de Richelieu seated Belle and Virginie well clear of each other. With the blond giant and the small Texan supplied with chairs, the Colonel brought the meeting to order and commenced:

'Will you please tell us everything, Mrs. Caxton?'

'*Everything?*' Belle countered, throwing a glance at Dusty as if seeking permission.

'Have you something to hide?' Virginie asked, glaring bitter animosity at the slender girl.

'No more than you have, likely,' Belle replied.

'I'd quit riding her, was I you, ma'am,' Dusty advised. 'She might have been born a lady, but she's been mixing in rough company long enough to have forgotten how to make polite cat-talk. Now she goes to scratching, biting and clawing real easy.'

'Belle Starr didn't get it all her own way,' Belle went on. 'She won't have forgotten some of ole Melanie's slaps, I'll bet.'

'We'd like to know more about how you came to be with Sabot,' de Richelieu interrupted firmly.

'It was like I said, I met him while I was looking for Ed, after I'd come out of the State Penetentiary,' Belle replied and continued with a verion of how she had become the magician's assistant so as to travel without paying and to have an excuse for moving from town to town.

'We rigged a code between us before Mellie-gal got arrested,' Dusty elaborated, when Belle reached the point where she had been caught trying to send the message. 'Knowing how me and the boys feel about the Yankees, she'd figure we'd want to get into the Brotherhood and try to let us know where to come. Looks like I owe you a forgiveness, Mellie-gal. I thought at first you was just trying to pull a confidence trick on that ole feller in Los Cabestrillo.'

'Aw, that's all right, Ed,' Belle answered, gazing at him with starry-eyed love. 'You wasn't to know.'

'There'd been bad blood between the magician and that damned singer, you say?' de Richelieu asked, for Belle had established that in her story.

'Sure,' the girl agreed and turned a suddenly frightened face to Dusty. 'It wasn't because of me, Ed-Honey!'

'Professional jealousy, I'm sure,' Virginie purred.

'Some of us're choosey who we bed with,' Belle slashed back, swinging her gaze pointedly between Mark and the Baroness.

For a shot in the dark, the words brought a not unexpected response. Belle saw the anger glow in Virginie's eyes and knew that she had called the play just right. However, although she was seething with a barely controllable rage, Virginie remained in her seat. Once again it fell upon de Richelieu to pour oil on troubled waters.

'Perhaps you would care to retire, Baroness?' he inquired

and continued tactfully, 'With the magician dead, we can't make our arrangements.'

'Surely we could put a show on?' Virginie answered.

'Without its star performer?' de Richelieu snorted. 'It was the magician who would have drawn Howard's party to the theatre.'

'I know how to do most of Sabby's tricks,' Belle put in, knowing that one of the other performers might mention her newly-acquired ability.

'*You* do?' Virginie ejaculated.

'Maybe not as well as he did them, but good enough,' Belle replied.

'And the novelty of *you* doing them would cover any slight inadequacies,' de Richelieu breathed. 'Can I see you perform?'

'Tonight?' Belle wailed.

'In the morning will do.'

'I'd need an assistant—a girl——.'

'Perhaps you would do it, Virginie?' de Richelieu suggested.

'*Me?*'

'*Her?*'

Two feminine voices raised at the same instant. Virginie's registered shock and Belle put a load of contempt into her response.

'You reckon the Baroness couldn't learn how to do it, Mellie-gal?' Dusty drawled, grinning.

'Well——,' the girl began, with well-simulated mock hesitancy and contempt.

'I will do it!' Virginie shouted, rising angrily.

'You'd have to dress right for the part,' Belle warned and judged, by the flush which came to the other's cheeks, that Virginie had seen the act.

'If I could get a suitable costume——' Virginie began, accepting the challenge she was sure had been thrown her way by the girl.

'There's one the girl before me left when she quit,' Belle answered. 'It should fit. She was on the over-stuffed side— My, what have I just said!'

'I will try it on in the morning!' Virginie snapped and stalked out of the study.

'You sure put a burr under her saddle, Mellie-gal,' Dusty

grinned. 'Come on, let's us go to bed.'

'Those are the loveliest words I've heard in years,' Belle purred.

'If your husband has no objections, we will see your performance in the morning,' de Richelieu stated, in a manner that implied the meeting was over.

'I'd admire to see her do it,' Dusty admitted, knowing that they would learn nothing more from the Colonel that night.

'You'll be real proud of me, Ed-honey,' Belle purred, eager to discuss the situation in private with Dusty. 'And I'm sure tired.'

While going upstairs, after the Kid and Waco had collected their bed rolls from the room, Belle continued to act like an amorous wife eagerly awaiting her reunion with a very satisfactory husband. She crawled as close as she could to Dusty, nuzzling his cheek and her hands explored his body in a way which drew a cold, disapproving glare from de Richelieu. She carried on in the same manner until they were inside the room. Allowing Dusty to move away, Belle closed the door and turned towards him. Her fingers touched her cheeks where his slaps had landed.

'Ed-honey,' the girl cooed.

Turning without any inkling of his danger, Dusty found her actions at variance with the tone of voice. Taking aim, she whipped a right swing that connected with the side of his jaw. Such was its force that he shot across the room and went headlong over the bed.

'Ow!' Belle screeched as the crack of her knuckles, arriving against Dusty's jaw, rang out. Timing the rest of her words perfectly, she went on, 'No! Ed! I didn't make sheep's eyes at Captain Fog—Ooof!'

Crossing to the bed, Belle grinned down at the small Texan. Looking dazed, Dusty sat up. He shook his head and gently worked his jaw.

'I never could let anybody slap me without wanting to hit back,' the girl remarked, helping Dusty to rise. 'Perhaps I swung a bit too hard.'

'That depends on whether you wanted to kill me, or just bust my jaw a mite,' Dusty replied. 'Let's talk.'

'We'd best do it in bed,' Belle advised. 'I've an idea we haven't seen the last of her highness tonight.'

As usual, Belle proved to be a good judge of the situation. Insisting that they made everything look right, she and Dusty undressed and climbed into bed. With the lamp out, they lay in each other's arms and talked. Before they could go far in their conversation, the door was opened and light flooded in from the passage. Jerking into sitting positions, they allowed the covers to fall away.

'I'm sorry!' Virginie said, standing in the doorway. 'I've come to the wrong room. How foolish of me. Please forgive me.'

'Just so long as it is the wrong *room*, and not the wrong *night, dear*,' Belle replied, bare torso entwined with Dusty's in the lamp-light. 'Good night.'

CHAPTER FOURTEEN

I'LL SCRATCH HER EYES OUT!

'Whee-Doggie!' Waco enthused, coming to a halt inside the barn and staring in an approving manner at the Baroness de Vautour. 'Now aren't you a fetching picture, ma'am?'

Although Virginie's eyes glowed with annoyance at the youngster's easy familiarity, she forced herself to smile.

It was the fourth day after Belle Boyd's arrival and the Baroness was waiting to commence a further lesson in her duties as magician's assistant. Dressed in the 'harem girl's' costume which had been discarded by the original 'Selima', Virginie filled it even better than had its previous owner. Her rich, sensual body left nothing to the imagination about its shape.

While the Baroness had hated to play a subordinate role, especially to 'Melanie Beauchampaine'—or 'Mrs. Caxton'—had been compelled to do so. On seeing Belle demonstrate her ability, de Richelieu had expressed his belief that she could do all that was needed. Without explaining more of his scheme, he had dispatched Corbeau and Kincaid to organize a performance for the Governor in San Antonio de Bexar's Variety Theatre. Then he had requested Belle to instruct Virginie in her duties and to re-arrange the show to suit its changed status.

Stapler's death had been turned to Belle's advantage. Being short of a singer, and knowing that the Kid had a fine tenor voice, she had persuaded him to replace the dead baritone. That would ensure that Belle had a loyal friend and a capable fighting man at her disposal, even if the other members of the floating outfit were not on hand.

Since that first performance, things had progressed smoothly. Belle and the Texans had continued to play their parts as if their lives depended on doing it; which they did.

Keeping up their pretence of being a devoted, if occasionally violent, couple, Belle and Dusty had slept together every night. That had allowed them to discuss the situation and formulate their plans without fear of being overheard. Apparently the Baroness's first visit had satisfied her, for she did not intrude upon their privacy again.

Dusty and Belle had decided that they must go along with de Richelieu, at least until they had discovered what his plans for dealing with the Governor would be. Having been told of the incident at the Shreveport theatre, Dusty had suggested a line de Richelieu might be contemplating. What they would do if the theory should prove correct had been discussed, without their reaching any firm conclusions.

Belle had achieved little on another matter. When she had discussed 'the Frenchman' with Dusty, he had proposed de Richelieu as the most likely candidate. However, taking advantage of accompanying Mark to the camp, he had obtained the big blond's views. Mark had suggested that Petain, whom he had killed, would have been even more qualified by virtue of his temper and behaviour. Even Virginie had been mentioned, by Waco, as a possibility. The Baroness's visit to Mark's room had been cited as an example of her vindictive and ruthless nature. However, Belle had pointed out that Madame Lucienne would have been sure to mention it if her torturer had been a woman.

Much as Belle wanted to solve the mystery, she had refused to allow it to interfere with her main assignment. So she had made no great efforts to learn who was, or had been, called 'the Frenchman'. Possibly, as the name was no longer mentioned, he was already dead. Certainly Waco and the Kid, who mingled freely with the enlisted men, could gain no clue concerning him.

There were, moreover, other things to hold the girl's and the Texan's attention.

In addition to continuing with his training programme for the soldiers, Mark kept up his 'feud' with Waco. With each clash of their temperaments, Virginie had displayed a growing interest in the youngster. She had never been near the blond giant's room since that night when she had come and indulged in passionate love-making. Nor had she shown the slightest hint that it had happened. Learning of the incident, through Dusty, Belle had passed a warning to Mark that the woman probably regretted her actions and hated him more for having caused them. Wanting to know what was on Virginie's mind, Dusty had told Waco to play along with her and see what he could discover.

So far, the youngster had been unable to learn anything. In the hope of getting him better acquainted, Mark had provoked an argument with Virginie at breakfast that morning. It was hoped that she might become more amenable to Waco as a result of the heated scene. Meeting her in the barn was, however, an accident. While Waco and the Kid bedded down in the hay loft, they had been asked to stay away from the building during the day and leave it for the women to use in their rehearsals. The youngster had returned to collect a bandana he had forgotten. Finding Virginie there, he had decided to make the most of his opportunity and try to get better acquainted.

It seemed that the Baroness had notions along the same lines.

'I'm so pleased that you approve,' Virginie smiled, walking forward.

'Can't see anybody's wouldn't, ma'am,' the youngster declared. 'Now me, I don't cotton none to skinny gals like Mellie.'

'Your brother seems to like her.'

'Ed's got a whole slew of foolish notions. Me, when I take to a gal, I want her with more meat to lay hold of, and less temper.'

'You're very discerning,' Virginie smiled, extending her right hand. 'May I use your shoulder for support, my shoe needs adjusting.'

'Feel free any ole time,' Waco offered eagerly, placing his hand under her arm-pit. 'Yes sir. Give me a gal like you any old time. A for-real lady and all.'

'That's not how Captain Fog thinks of me,' Virginie pointed out, leaning closer until her hips rubbed against the front of his body.

'*Him?*' Waco jeered, sliding the arm to her waist. 'He doesn't mean nothing, one way or t'other.'

'They say he's the fastest gun in Texas.'

'*They* say!'

'You don't think so?' Virginie inquired, turning so that her flimsily-concealed bosom rubbed against the youngster's shirt and her arms slid about him.

'I'm game to go and prove it!' Waco boasted. 'Happen *you* was to give the word.'

'You'd be my champion?' the Baroness whispered.

'Try me,' Waco offered and an instant later they were kissing.

And Belle walked in, tossing aside the robe which she had worn from the house to conceal her 'harem' costume.

If the girl had realized what was going on, she would have delayed her entrance and left Waco with a clear field. Before she could withdraw, Virginie had seen her and pulled away from the youngster's arms. So Belle decided that she must act as the woman would be expecting of her.

'My my!' Belle drawled, sauntering forward in a gait that was redolent with mocking offence. 'How romantic.'

'This here's none of your concern, Mellie!' Waco growled.

'You're right,' the girl admitted, but knew that she could not let the incident slip by so casually. 'But I'd've thought you'd go for somebody a heap closer to your own age—or is she *mothering* you?'

'Why you dirty little whore!' Virginie ejaculated, jumping away from Waco and slapping Belle's face hard.

If the Baroness had expected the affair to end with her slap, she was to be rapidly disillusioned. Not only did Belle object to being struck and not giving anything in return, she had her character to consider. A girl like 'Melanie Beauchampaine' would not have permitted such a liberty to be taken and go unpunished.

Catching her balance, Belle whipped around her left arm. With an explosive 'whack!', her hand imprinted finger marks on the Baroness's right cheek. Although the blow snapped her head aside and caused her to reel a couple of steps, Virginie showed no inclination to withdraw from the fray.

Letting out a screech, the Baroness lunged at Belle. Sidestepping, the girl allowed her to rush by. Pivoting smoothly, Belle delivered a kick to the woman's shapely rump, sending her sprawling belly down across a bale of hay.

'You wait until I tell Ed what's happened, Matt Caxton!' Belle yelled, turning as if she meant to go and do it.

Rising from the bale, face wild with anger and humiliation, Virginie hurled herself forward. She went after Belle like a football player making a tackle. Locking her arms around the girl's slender waist, she used her superior weight to sweep Belle from her feet. They hit the floor together, hands diving into hair. Screaming, squealing curses, shedding strips of their flimsy garments, they rolled over and over in an inextricable tangle of waving arms and legs.

About to intervene, Waco realized that doing so would be out of character for 'Matt Caxton'. A youngster with 'Matt's' irresponsible outlook would never think of interrupting what he would regard as an enjoyable spectacle. If there had been any real danger to Belle, Waco would not have hesitated. Figuring that that girl could more than hold her own, he stood back. The noise they were making, especially if he helped out a mite, would soon enough attract attention and bring other men on the run. Sure enough, he could hear startled yells from off by the house.

'Go to it, ma'am!' Waco whooped. 'Give her more than Belle Starr did.'

At that moment, Virginie appeared ideally situated to follow the advice. In the upper position, with Belle's hips straddled between her shapely thighs, she had her fingers knotted into the girl's shortish hair. Bracing her neck desperately, the girl struggled to reduce the force with which her attacker was trying to pound her head on the floor. Groping wildly, Belle scrabled with her fingers at the Baroness's back. While the girl's nails were neither long nor sharp, they hurt and ripped apart the upper section of Virginie's 'harem' outfit.

Bracing her feet and shoulders on the floor, Belle arched her body upwards in an attempt to displace Virginie. It was a mistake. Slipping sideways, the woman slid her left leg under the girl's body. Instinct might be guiding Virginie's response, but it did so in an effective manner. With the girl's slender midsection clamped between her legs, she crossed her ankles and started to apply a crushing, savage leverage.

Belle croaked in agony, grasping at Virginie's columnar thighs with both hands as she tried to relieve the constricting pressure. Realizing that she could not, the girl changed her point of attack. Both hands flew to Virginie's scantily protected bosom, thumbs and fingers hooking deep into the mounds of flesh. The Baroness let out a screech of torment. Numbing agony ripped through her, causing her to untangle her legs hurriedly. Still retaining her grips, Belle writhed free. Turning the frantically struggling woman over, Belle crawled to pin her down with a knee jammed against her pelvic region.

Watching Virginie's desperate struggles, Waco knew that she was as good as beaten. He wondered if he should intervene, before Belle's anger made her go too far.

Dusty, de Richelieu, the Kid, Corbeau and Kincaid burst into the barn. Skidding to a halt, they stared at the embattled women for a moment. The small Texan recovered first. Hurrying forward, he hooked his hands under Belle's arm-pits and dragged her backwards from her victim. In doing so, he completed the ruin of half of the Baroness's costume. As Belle's fingers were dragged from their grip, they brought the upper section away with them. Sitting up, Virginie tried to grab her departing assailant. Before she could do so, Waco and Corbeau had caught her by the biceps and hauled her to her feet.

'Let me at her!' Belle screamed, struggling to get free.

'I'll kill her!' Virginie shrieked, trying to shake off the man. She was oblivious of her naked bosom, barely concealed lower limbs, or anything but the equally dishevelled and bedraggled girl.

Throwing Belle from him, Dusty propelled her into a hay-filled but otherwise unoccupied stall. Following her, he hoped that she was not in such a state of fury that she would be unaware of her actions. Anger glared in her eyes as she rose and moved towards the small Texan. Then it cleared. Yet, to all other appearances, she was still in a raging temper.

'I'll scratch her eyes out!' Belle screamed, darting forward.

'Get her to hell out of here!' Dusty roared, restraining Belle who was continuing to act in a convincing manner. 'Throw her into the horse-trough to cool her off. I'll do the same with Mellie.'

Suddenly Virginie became aware of just how little clothing remained. With a shriek of mortification, she stopped struggling and clutched both hands to her bosom. Shaking herself free from the men's grasp, she fled out of the barn.

Left in possession of the battle-field, as it were, Belle allowed Dusty to shake her out of her 'anger'.

'Don't hit me, Ed!' the girl wailed. 'She started it!'

'And if we didn't need you both all pretty and not marked up, I'd have let you settle it all the way,' Dusty answered.

'God!' de Richelieu raged. 'The stupid bitches! Now what the hell do we do?'

'About what?' Belle gasped.

'The idea,' Dusty answered savagely. 'These gents have just got back from San Antone and the theatre's ready.'

'She started it!' Belle insisted. 'She hit me first!'

'By God, I know who'll hit you *next*, happen you don't shut up!' Dusty warned. 'Colonel. Happen you can make the Baroness go through with it, Mellie here'll do her part.'

'I wo——!' Belle began.

'Oh yes you will!' Dusty snarled, swinging to face her. 'Or I'll beat you black and blue. Now get going to the house and clean yourself up. Once she's done it, Colonel, we'll meet you in the study and talk this thing out.'

Two hours later, washed, hair combed neatly, wearing a dress and with only a swollen top lip to show that she had been in a fight, Belle went with Dusty into de Richelieu's study. While she had been bathing and changing, they had decided that they must go along with de Richelieu's plan, learn what it was, then figure out how to counter it. They found Corbeau, Kincaid, the Kid and Waco present. The youngster stood protectively beside Virginie's chair and scowled at Belle. The Baroness looked the same as she usually did, except for her blackened left eye.

'Go on!' Dusty growled, nudging Belle with his elbow.

'Do I have to?' the girl demanded, then showed alarm. 'All right! All right, if that's how you want it, Ed.' She crossed the room to halt in front of Virginie. 'I'm sorry for whip—for what happened, Baroness.'

'So am I!' the woman gritted.

'And I'd admire for you to help me in the show,' the girl continued, after a pleading glance in her 'husband's' direction and receiving a warning glare in return.

'Very well, I'll do it,' Virginie promised, almost duplicating Belle's actions in her hurried gaze at de Richelieu. 'We'll forget our differences for the good of the Cause.'

'And now you wish to know what this is all about, ladies and gentlemen,' de Richelieu guessed, as Belle rejoined Dusty and they sat down.

'I for sure do,' Waco drawled eagerly. 'Virginie here couldn't tell me no more than it was important and we'd set a burr under the Yankees' sadles.'

'Matthew was good enough to come and offer his apologies for what happened at the barn!' the Baroness put in, darting a worried glance at de Richelieu. 'I told him a little.'

'And I'll tell him more,' de Richelieu promised. 'At the performance your wife and her people will put on for the Governor, Mr. Caxton, we intend to create an incident that will bring the people of Texas flocking to our side. Not just Texas. Once the word is spread of what is happening, the whole of the South will rise again.'

'How'll that happen?' asked Dusty.

'I've seen both you and your brother hit a small target at long range with your handguns,' de Richelieu replied, referring to a display of fast drawing and accurate shooting which Dusty and Waco had given on their way out to the ranch. 'Could you do the same on a man?'

'Even easier,' Waco stated. 'He'd be a bigger mark.'

'I want him killing,' de Richelieu pointed out.

'One or more .44 balls anywhere between the neck and knee-bone'll do that,' Waco declared. 'Who's the man?'

'Governor Stanton Howard,' de Richelieu replied. 'Mrs. Caxton and the Baroness will do the disappearing lady trick. But when your wife opens the box's door to show it's empty, you and your brother will leap out and start shooting.'

'At the Governor, in his box,' Dusty drawled.

'Of course,' de Richelieu confirmed.

'Where he'll be with Cap'n Fog and them other ranchers,' Waco went on. 'Any one of them's fast enough to make blue windows in us as soon as we pop a cap.'

'They won't be armed,' de Richelieu replied. ' "Captain Fog" will see to that.'

'What do we gain by doing it, even counting we get away alive?' Dusty asked. 'Howard's a right popular man. Killing him won't make folks in Texas feel friendly towards the Brotherhood.'

'That's true,' de Richelieu conceded. 'But they won't be blaming the Brotherhood. All their blame will go to the Yankees.'

'How'd you make that out?' Dusty asked.

'Because of the soldiers who will appear and arrest the ranchers straight after the shooting,' de Richelieu replied. 'When it's learned that they've shot Pierce and the others "trying to escape", everybody will believe that the Yankees were behind the killing of Howard——.'

'Because he's doing such a good chore of setting Texas back on its feet,' Dusty finished for de Richelieu and, sounding far more enthusiastic than he felt, he continued. 'By cracky, Colonel, I do believe it could work.'

CHAPTER FIFTEEN

SHE WANTS ME TO KILL YOU, MARK

'Lordy-lord, Dusty!' Belle breathed, lying alongside the small Texan in bed. 'Did you ever hear such a cold-blooded plot?'

'It's a dilly for sure,' Dusty agreed, thinking of the discussion and consultation which had been carried out in the study as de Richelieu had enlarged on his plan to plunge the United States into a second civil war. 'What do we do about it, Mellie-gal.'

'I hate that name,' Belle said tartly, then became serious. 'Get out, fetch back a regiment of cavalry and break up the Brotherhood seems the obvious answer.'

'Trouble being, it's too damned obvious,' Dusty pointed out. 'There's no garrison closer than a three day ride; and that's even after we've got to town, or over to San Antonio to send a telegraph message.'

'How long would it take us to reach San Antonio?'

'Half a day with the wagon, less just on horses.'

'How *quickly* could it be done?'

'Riding Comanche-style, Lon could make it there and back in a night,' Dusty answered. 'But, good as you are, Melliegal, you couldn't do that. In fact, I'm willing to bet Mark, Waco and I couldn't either.'

'But Lon could,' Belle breathed.

'Given just half a chance, and two good horses to ride relay. Do you see this the same way I see it, Mel—Belle?'

The changing of the girl's name came as she registered her disapproval in a painfully effective manner.

'Such as, *Ed-honey*?' Belle purred.

'Hey! No fair grabbing me like that, I can't do it back,' Dusty protested. 'And stop fooling around, lil wife.'

'How *do* you see it, Dusty?'

'We have to let it go through, de Richelieu's notion. I mean. And stomp on it away from here.'

'That would be terribly risky,' Belle pointed out.

'So would handling it any other way,' Dusty countered. 'If we let Lon go and send the message, de Richelieu's smart enough to figure out what's happened. In which case, I don't reckon we'll leave here alive. Even if he doesn't cotton on to us, just one slip on the Army's part, one tiny little word that they're coming, and there'll be a battle here that could do all he wants.'

'We could save ourselves by all slipping away.'

'"Mellie Caxton" might think that's the answer, but Belle Boyd knows it's not,' Dusty drawled. 'As soon as they found we'd gone, the leaders of the Brotherhood would figure out where and why. Then they'd have their men scatter and be over the border into Mexico before the Army laid hands on them.'

'And leave them free to try other, even worse, schemes,' Belle breathed. 'I wish I wasn't smart like that girl you mentioned. Then maybe I'd not be afraid.'

'There's not many——.'

'Don't stay saying, "many women", Dusty Fog!' Belle interrupted furiously. 'Not in that smug, superior male tone.'

'I'm right sorry, ma'am,' Dusty apologized. 'So get your cotton-picking hands off!'

Only by the lighter exchanges could the girl and the small Texan relieve the tension that was rising inside them. Both had seen the worst effects of the War Between The States and its aftermath. So they knew the full deadly peril of their present situation.

'Have you any ideas how we do it, Dusty?' Belle wanted to know.

'Some. It'll take planning, be risky as hell, but it could work.'

'Thank God you're here!' the girl whispered, moving closer to Dusty as he completed a recital of his plan. 'It has to work and I'm praying it will. If I'd been alone——.'

'Would you rather've had the three regiments of cavalry?' Dusty inquired, recollecting the message which Belle had mentioned sending.

'I don't think I would, *right now*,' Belle replied.

'They'd sure crowd the bed a mite,' Dusty grinned and kissed the girl. 'I like this man's Army. In the Texas Light Cavalry I never got to sleep with a full colonel.'

In both the Confederate and U.S. Secret Service, Belle had been awarded the rank of colonel to help her deal with military personnel on her assignments.

'Well, I was always for democracy,' Belle replied. 'But I never carried associating with my inferiors *this* far, Captain Fog.'

'What about when this is over, Belle?' Dusty asked as her mouth found his.

'You'll go your way and I'll go mine,' the girl answered. 'I'm not cut out to make anybody, especially a nice feller like you, an ever-loving wife.'

'Lady,' Dusty breathed, after their long embrace. 'You could've fooled me on that score.'

Next morning, after breakfast, Mark Counter entered the centre cubicle of the three-holer back-house. While Waco and the Kid occupied the end compartments, Dusty had just quit the one in the middle. Closing its door, Mark picked up the sheet of paper which Dusty had left on the floor. There was sufficient light let in by the decorative ventilation holes for him to read the message on the paper.

'Whooee!' Mark breathed. 'So that's the notion, huh?'

'Didn't the Colonel tell you?' asked the Kid.

'Only that they're planning to stop the show and make a patriotic speech,' Mark replied. 'Counting on Stanton Howard showing how loyal he is to the Yankees by ordering them to stop, or trying to have them arrested.'

'They figure you believe it?' Waco inquired.

'De Richelieu put up a mighty convincing argument,' Mark answered. 'In the end, I let on like I believed it—So they're going to have you and "Brother Ed" pop up on the stage, gun down the Governor and "Captain Fog", huh, boy?'

'Why sure,' Waco agreed. 'Figuring that, by doing it and laying all the blame on the Yankee's, Ole Devil'll be riled and state out loud and clear he's backing the Brotherhood For Southron Freedom up to the Green River and on to the hilt.'

'And I'm supposed to set them up for the kill?' Mark growled.

'That's just what you're going to do,' the Kid agreed.

'Found something out last night about Virginie,' Waco remarked, sounding just a mite too casual.

'She don't have any hair on her chest,' suggested the Kid, referring to a discovery the youngster claimed to have made about a young lady of his acquaintance in Mulrooney, Kansas, on their first visit.

'That too. She sure is one demanding woman, I tell you. But she's took quite a shine to me——.'

'Now *there's* a gal with what I'd call real good taste,' Mark said dryly, knowing there must be more to Waco's story.

'Better'n you figure,' Waco drawled. 'She wants me to kill you, Mark.'

'Somebody's coming!' warned the Kid, then raised his voice. 'Hey, Matt, is there any paper in your place?'

'You want for me to fetch it with my pants round my knees?' Waco bellowed back. 'Let me get through and I'll fetch you a page from the dream book* that's got pictures of gals in things us boys never see 'em wearing.'

Reading through Dusty's instructions, after the Kid and Waco had taken their noisy departure, Mark completed his other reason for paying the visit. He wondered how the small Texan would cope with the latest developments. The scheme Dusty had laid out was risky, dangerous, but could work.

If it failed——

Mark did not care to contemplate the results of failure.

Making use of the sheet of paper, so that nobody would be likely to retrieve and decipher it, he let it flutter into the hole. Hitching up his riding breeches, he adjusted his clothing and stepped from the cubicle.

After Mark had left to carry out a final day's training, before he set off to join the Governor's party at San Antonio de Bexar, de Richelieu took Dusty, the Kid, Waco and Belle into the house's cellar. It was their first visit, for the entrances had always been kept locked, and it handed them quite a surprise. The big room held several boxes, with the Henry rifles which had brought Belle on to the Brotherhood's trail. French *Chassepots* and a plentiful supply of ammunition for both types of weapon.

The rifles alone did not create the biggest shock. That came from the sight of a strange-looking, wheel-mounted, multi-barrelled gun.

'What is it, a Gatling?' asked Waco, moving forward.

'A Montigny *Mitrailleuse*,' de Richelieu corrected. 'The weapon which, had it been used correctly, would have defeated the Prussians despite their discipline.'

'Looks lighter than any Gatling I ever saw,' Dusty commented. 'I've seen a few, around Army posts.'

'It is,' de Richeliue enthused. 'On this carriage, one man can traverse it.'

'Which, way you're talking, didn't do the Frogs no good at all,' commented the Kid.

'That was because they didn't appreciate how it should have been used,' de Richelieu replied. 'They insisted on using them as artillery pieces, even this light model, instead

---

* Dream-book: mail order catalogue; old issues were used in place of toilet rolls.

of using them as infantry support arms.'

'That's how you'd've done it, huh, Colonel?' Dusty inquired.

'That's how I wanted to do it,' de Richelieu agreed. 'But I was overruled by the short-sighted High Command. And so they lost the War. If I'd had my way, gentlemen—— Well, that's in the past. When we declare Secession, the Armies of the Confederate States will use their *Mitrailleuses* correctly, allowing our infantry to lay down such a volume of fire that no foot or cavalry assault can penetrate it in an attack.'

A far-sighted professional soldier, de Richelieu had assessed correctly the manner in which a machine gun should be used. He was many years ahead of his time.

'You mean you've got more of these guns?' Dusty inquired, indicating the *Mitrailleuse*.

'They'll be made available when we need them,' de Richelieu replied. 'And how is your problem coming along, Mrs. Caxton?'

'Both our outfits are ruined,' Belle replied, jerking her gaze from the machine gun's protective shield. 'They weren't meant for anything so strenuous as we went at it.'

'Can't Pieber do anything?' de Richelieu growled.

'It would take a real magician to do anything with what's left,' Belle replied. 'Your man doesn't have any suitable material, for one thing.'

'By God?' de Richelieu blazed. 'If you two——'

'I've come up with an idea——' Belle began hurriedly.

'It was *Virginie*'s notion,' Waco interrupted indignantly.

'All right, all right!' Belle yelped, glaring at her "brother-in-law". '*We* got to talking it out after breakfast and she came up with this notion. See, neither of us were too happy about wearing those flimsy "harem" outfits on the stage. They'd be hell to ride in if things go wrong and we have to light out in a hurry.'

'That's something we never took into account, Colonel,' Dusty remarked.

'It's not a thing *men* would take into account,' Belle declared. 'So we—all right, she figured we should wear something that we *could* ride in.'

'You'll need something fancy, to hold the crowd's attention, Mrs. Caxton,' de Richelieu warned. 'Good as you are——'

'Hell! I know I'm not set to make a steady living out of being a stage magician,' Belle put in. 'So *we*——,' she glared defiantly at Waco, who let the word go by unchallenged, 'figured out our costumes. We're going to be two cowgirls.'

'In Stetsons, Levi's pants and all?' Dusty drawled.

'Stetsons, sure,' Belle confirmed. 'But we picked something a mite more eye-catching for the rest of it. We've got the tailors cutting up one of the "Duchess's" black satin frocks, to make us a pair of blouses that will knock your eyes out, and *real* tight riding breeches. Then we'll have riding boots and gunbelts, so everybody will know we're cowgirls.'

'I see,' de Richelieu drawled. 'But how about your billing?'

'Mr. Corbeau just said I was a lady magician, he told us when we asked,' Belle replied. 'So we'll have it announced that it's my first performance and the beginning of a new act. That ought to do it.'

'Virginie's sure one smart gal!' Waco praised. 'She come up with most of the answers——'

'It's still me who has to do the tricks!' Belle snapped and stormed out of the cellar.

'You and your big mouth!' Dusty growled at his "brother". 'If you rile Mellie so she busts up this deal, I'll fix your wagon for good.'

'I'll mind it,' Waco promised sullenly and followed the girl.

Locking up the cellar, after the girl's and the Texans' departure, de Richelieu frowned. Clearly Virginie had been working on the susceptibilities of young 'Caxton'. De Richelieu wondered why. Completely ruthless and immoral, she was never promiscuous. As long as he had known her, she had never sought men out merely to satisfy her lust; but only to serve more material ends.

The daughter of a once wealthy Yankee businessman—of Germanic origin—who had been arrested and ruined for trading with the Confederate States during the War, Virginie had fled to Europe. She had married the aged, very rich Baron de Vautour. Although his estates were situated on the German border of the Alsace, the Baron had been violently pro-French. Despite Virginie's warnings and suggestions, the Baron had refused to change his allegiance to the Prussians when the clouds of war had gathered. His stubborness had cost him his life and threatened to lose something which Virginie had held even more dear. As part of the consequences of defeat, France had ceded control of the Alsace to Germany and the de Vautour lands were to have been confiscated.

Hearing of this, Virginie had made an arrangement with the Prussians. For permission to retain her lands, and a suitable salary, she would become a spy. Showing more imagination than might have been expected, they had agreed.

It had been Virginie who had located de Richelieu and offered aid. He had been unable to learn from whom she had heard of him and his ambitions. Nor did he yet know if she was working for the Prussian Government, or upon the behalf of wealthy speculators. Whoever held the purse strings, they had been lavish in their payments. That was one of the reasons why de Richelieu had not delved more deeply into their identities. As long as they helped with his dreams of liberating the South, he did not care where the money came from.

Whatever Virginie might have in mind for young 'Caxton', de Richelieu figured she was cold-bloodedly calculating enough to avoid it interfering with their grand plan.

'Well,' Waco drawled, lounging at ease on the bed in Belle's and Dusty's room. 'Now we know who's behind the Brotherhood.'

'Who'd that be?' the girl inquired innocently, darting a glance from the youngster to Dusty and the Kid.

'There's some, being *real* smart, "sister-in-law", who might figure French *Chassepot* rifles and the *Mitrailleuse* gun add up to them coming from England or maybe Mexico——.'

'Or even Prussia?' Dusty put in.

'So you-all saw it too, Ed-honey?' Belle asked. 'I didn't know that you understood German.'

'I don't——!' Dusty began.

'Way he cusses a man out, he doesn't need but good old U.S.,' Waco growled.

'Admit it, boy,' suggested the Kid. 'You've missed something and your "kinfolks" haven't.'

'All right,' the youngster sighed. 'What was it?'

'If you hadn't been so busy siding with your rich sweetie against your loving kin,' Belle answered. 'You might have seen the writing on the gun's shield. I don't read much German, but I made it out as, "Property of the King of Prussia".'

'Not being smart, like the rest of my kin,' Waco drawled, rising and crossing the room. 'I don't even know where Prussia is. Maybe Virginie'll tell me. Hey. What do you call a feller who marries a Baroness?'

'A stupid knobhead is one name,' Belle answered. 'I could think of worse.'

'Brother Ed,' Waco drawled, making sure that he had the handle turned and the door on the point of being opened. 'You sure married beneath yourself with that gal.'

With that, the youngster beat a hasty retreat. Belle lowered Dusty's hat, having snatched it up to throw, watched the door close and chuckled.

'That Waco!' she ejaculated. 'What a boy!'

'He'll likely make a hand,' the Kid drawled, delivering the cowboy's supreme accolade, but with reservations. 'Happen he lives that long. Company he keeps, he could get lucky and be hung young.'

'I don't want to be the kind of wife who complains about her loving husband's friends, Ed,' Belle said, eyeing the Kid pointedly.

'Humour him, Mellie-gal,' Dusty advised, safe in the knowledge that the girl would not show her disapproval of the name in the same way she had the previous night. At least, not while the Kid was present. 'He's got to take a long ride tonight.'

'Can you make San Antonio and back before morning, Lon?' Belle inquired.

'Why sure,' replied the Kid. 'There're three hosses at the corral's'll do it easy.'

'You won't be using your own mount?' the girl asked.

'No ma'am,' the Kid declared. 'For one thing, it'd be a sure give-away.'

'What's the other reason?' Belle wanted to know.

'The hosses I use won't be fit for work for days,' the Indian-dark Texan explained. 'If at all.'

'You're sure that Counter will go through with his part in it?'

Hearing Virginie's words, Waco decided against knocking at her door and announcing his presence. The passage was deserted, so he knew that he could listen to the conversation without being interrupted or detected.

'Yes,' came de Richelieu's hard tones in reply. 'I don't think he was so favourably disposed towards acting as Fog's decoy as he pretended.'

'That's what I thought,' Virginie admitted, having the type of mentality which refused to accept somebody else could reach a conclusion that she had not already formed. 'It must be galling to a man like him to have to pretend he's somebody else.'

'Yes. And it must have been even more galling to know that all the good work he is doing with the enlisted men is being credited to Captain Fog.'

'Does Counter know what we're planning—All of it, I mean?'

'Only that we'll interrupt the meeting. But he's smart enough to have figured it's something bigger than that. Perhaps he even guesses correctly.'

'It could even be that he's looking forward to continuing being "Captain Fog",' Virginie purred. 'He's often commented how he never gets such good treatment as himself.'

'That's why I trust him,' de Richelieu admitted.

'Where will he be at the theatre?' Virginie inquired, just a shade too casually.

'In the box with the other ranchers' foremen, so that he can make sure none of them are armed,' de Richelieu answered. 'Why are you so interested in him? I thought your tastes went to *younger* men.'

'Young Caxton will be useful——.'

'To the Brotherhood—or to you, Virginie?'

Hearing footsteps on the stairs, Waco concluded that he would be unable to continue eavesdropping. Which was a pity, as he had hoped that he might discover why the Countess had formed her attachment to him. While he had a good idea of one reason, she could have had others. Knocking at the door, as if he had just arrived, he turned its handle and strolled in without waiting for an invitation.

'Why Matthew,' Virginie greeted, lips smiling but eyes

showing her irritation at his behaviour. She darted a glance at de Richelieu. 'The Colonel and I were just talking about the plan.'

'Why sure, Virginie-gal,' the youngster drawled cheerfully, his whole attitude hinting that he doubted if anybody could replace him as the centre of her affections. 'I was wondering if you'd care to come riding—or something?'

Virginie was saved the trouble of making excuses to evade the issue. There was a knock at the door and Pieber entered, carrying her stage costume.

CHAPTER SIXTEEN

SHE TRIED TO KILL ME!

With a few slight, but necessary, changes, de Richelieu's plan went off practically exactly as scheduled.

No matter who had devised them, Belle Boyd's and Virginie de Vautour's costumes had carried out their functions in a most satisfactory manner. Or so Mark Counter had concluded as he watched the performance from the box which held the other ranchers' foremen. Belle's Dance rode in the holster of her gunbelt. Improvised from a military weapon belt, Virginie's rig carried a fancy-looking, pearl handled Lefauchex pinfire revolver in its now flap-less holster.

That everything went as smoothly as it did, right up to the 'deaths' of Governor Howard, the member of his staff who had dressed in range clothes and posed as Dusty Fog, and Mark, was a tribute to the small Texan's organizing ability—and the part played by the Ysabel Kid.

Few, if any, white men could have done what the Kid had achieved.

Extracting the three selected horses from the corral, at night and so quietly that the occupants of the near by buildings had not been disturbed, was quite a feat in itself. The fact that the Kid had already spent time in gaining the animals' confidence did little to diminish the praise he had deserved for his efforts.

Having passed through the ring of vedettes without being detected, the Kid had set off on his assignment. Riding as only a Comanche *tehnap** could, he had made very excellent time in covering the forty-odd miles to San Antonio de Bexar. On his arrival, he had located and obtained an interview with the Governor. Delivering Dusty's message and suggestions, he had received Howard's promise that everything would be done as the small Texan requested. With that assurance, the Kid had made the return journey to the ranch before daybreak. He had ridden six horses—three borrowed from the Governor's party—into the ground, but he had done his share in averting the peril of another civil war.

Although de Richelieu had cursed when the loss of the three horses had been reported, he did not even come close to suspecting what had happened. The Kid had given a convincing display of tracking the 'thieves', finally losing the 'trail' on some hard, stony ground. Having nobody else who could handle the sign-reading, de Richelieu had accepted the Kid's excuse without question. He had vetoed a more lengthy search on the grounds that there would be insufficient time before the show left for its engagement in San Antonio de Bexar's Variety Theatre.

The conspirators' journey to San Antonio had been uneventful. Leaving the others about a mile clear of the outskirts, Mark had ridden on alone. Meeting the Governor, he had been pleased to discover that all of Dusty's arrangements were being respected. Not only had Shangai Pierce, Miffin Kennedy and Richard King willingly given their co-operation, but the town marshal had placed his entire department at the small Texan's disposal.

De Richelieu had not accompanied the party. There had been considerable discontent amongst the men at the camp. Already many of them were becoming disenchanted by Mark's strenuous training programme. So they had been ripe to accept a rumour—started by the Kid and Waco at Belle's suggestion—that the Brotherhood was to be disbanded. So cleverly had the Texans done their work that a furious de Richelieu had been unable to track down the source of the fabrication.

---

* Tehnap: an experienced warrior.

As he would be using his most fanatical followers as the 'soldiers' who were to 'arrest' and murder the ranchers, de Richelieu had known that his chief support in the camp would temporarily be absent. If the restless, disgruntled men saw that all the leaders had gone, they might conclude that the rumour was true and desert *en masse*. So de Richelieu had reluctantly decided that he must remain at the ranch. That would offer a convincing argument against the Brotherhood disbanding. He would leave the 'arrests' to Corbeau, Kincaid and Raphael.

On the evening of the show, all had been made ready. Not only on the Brotherhood's side. Dusty had suggested certain precautions in his message to Governor Howard and they had been implemented. Every patron entering the theatre had been disarmed and searched for concealed weapons by the marshal and his deputies; ostensibly as a measure against interference with the smooth running of the conference. That had only applied to the people who used the main entrance. Going in by the stage door, Dusty and Waco were still in possession of their Colts.

To cover Dusty's absence, Howard had selected one of his most trusted secretaries. An accomplished performer in amateur theatricals, the young man had thrown himself whole-heartedly into the role. Dressed in a suitable manner, he had played his part admirably and had given a stirring display of getting 'shot'.

All had gone without a hitch. The cross-talk duo had been well received, garnering laughter and applause by their rapid flow of patter. Looking more worried and frightened than when he had set off to 'borrow' the three horses—or handle even riskier chores—the Kid had sung his songs to an appreciative audience. He had left the stage, swearing in three languages, and stating that he would never again allow himself to be talked into such a nerve-wracking position.

If Belle and Virginie had been anxious, or concerned by performing before an audience, it had not shown. Although there had been a couple of slight fumbles, the women had covered them up in a professional manner. Certainly, in view of Belle's and the Baroness's appearances in the 'cow-girl' outfits, the primarily male audience had not been inclined to be over-critical.

Inside the box, as soon as the door had closed, Virginie stamped twice on its floor. Instantly the section had slid down silently and swiftly through the open trapdoor over which the structure had been positioned. On reaching the floor of the basement, the woman jumped out of the open-sided framework. She made way for Dusty and Waco to enter, directing a pointed, conspiratorial glance at the youngster as he went by. Having delivered what she hoped would be a reminder to Waco of his added duty, she withdrew.

As soon as the Texans were aboard, the Kid, Dunco, Downend and the man who usually conducted the show's orchestra—they were using the Variety Theatre's regular musicians that night—manipulated the ropes to send the platform shooting upwards again.

Backing away slightly, Virginie watched them go. Hatred drove any semblance of beauty from her face. It would have given warning that she planned something evil, if any of the men had happened to look around. Drawing the Lefauchex, she stared with fixed intensity at where the platform was once more forming the floor of the magic box.

Shots roared overhead!

Almost before they had received the foot-stamping signal, Dunco, Downend and the musician started the platform on its return journey. With a yell, the Kid tightened his grip on the ropes. So did the others, but the over-loaded elevator was descending somewhat faster than had been anticipated. It landed with a crash and precipitated its occupants into the basement.

'Get the hell out of here!' Dusty roared, striving to retain his footing and acting as if the deed had been in earnest.

Stumbling in the opposite direction to Dusty and Waco, Belle saw something that handed her one hell of a shock!

Not far away, Virginie stood looking as mean as all hell!

Raising the Lefauchex, the Baroness aimed it at the girl!

Instead of trying to halt her stumbling steps, Belle threw herself forward even faster. Her right hand turned palm-outwards as she went, curling around the Dance's ivory handle and twisting the weapon from its holster.

Cracking viciously in the confines of the basement, Virginie's Lefauchex vomited its bullet while she was still trying to correct her aim.

Lead made an eerie 'splat!' sound as it whipped by Belle's head; so close that she felt its wind stir her hair. Refusing to be thrown into panic, she skidded to a halt and swivelled to face the peril. Already drawn, the Dance was thrust into instinctive alignment at waist-level. Belle adopted the gun fighter's crouch which she had learned from Dusty Fog and it served her as well as it had him on numerous occasions.

Down flashed the Dance's hammer. Its .36 calibre ball took Virginie in the left breast as the Baroness tried to improve on her first effort. She reeled, tottered in a circle, dropping the Lefauchex, and went face-foremost to the basement's floor.

'She tried to kill me!' Belle gasped, standing with the smoking Dance dangling at her side.

'That's what she must've been getting at when she kept asking me if I'd side her against everybody, even you, "Brother Ed",' Waco growled. 'She aimed to do it all along.'

'Looks that way,' Dusty answered. 'Only this's one hell of a time to discuss it. Let's go. That crowd will be so riled they'll not stop to ask us what's happened, or why we did it.'

Holstering her Dance, Belle joined the men in the rush to the stairs and out of the building. They ran to the waiting horses, set free the reins and swung into the saddles.

'What do we do?' yelped Dunco, looking thoroughly shaken and scared.

'Scatter and ride like hell!' Dusty advised. 'Go in twos at the most. Come on, Mellie-gal!'

'Which's the way to the ranch?' Downend demanded.

'Out to the north-west, happen that's where you want to go,' Dusty answered. 'We aim to head *anyplace* except there.'

'He's right, Miller!' Dunco stated, watching Dusty and Belle send their horses in a different direction to that selected by the Kid and Waco. 'Let's go south to Mexico. This deal's gone way too far for safety.'

Walking towards the theatre, Corbeau, Kincaid, Raphael,

Mick and the other nine men looked every inch a U.S. Cavalry captain, his sergeant and troopers. A closer examination would have revealed that their tunics bore the buttons of a long defunct Kansas regiment of Dragoons. Under the circumstances, however, nobody would be likely to have been so observant. Corbeau's party would have been larger, but there were neither extra uniforms, nor more men sufficiently fanatical to the Cause to be entrusted with such a delicate mission.

Everything was still highly chaotic outside the building, although not so bad as it had been a few minutes earlier. Already the marshal had departed, taking the majority of the audience's male members to form a posse and 'hunt down' the assassins. Claiming—loudly so as to be heard by as many people as possible—that he intended to bring in living prisoners, the peace officer had declined the ranchers' and foremen's offers of assistance.

Pierce and the other 'survivors' stood in an apparently disconsolate group, clear of the remnants of the audience. Not far away, a Rocker ambulance* was parked before the theatre's main entrance, its rear doors thrown open. Dripping blood in a convincing manner—from bottles they held beneath the blankets which concealed them—three motionless shapes on stretchers were carried out of the building. Low mutters of sympathy, or deep anger, rose at the sight. Hats were swept from heads and anger showed on many faces.

Watching the crowd's reaction, Corbeau felt certain that de Richelieu's scheme would be successful. Even if open war with the Yankees did not immediately result, the flames they had kindled that night in San Antonio de Bexar would smoulder and grow until the South rose again.

The appearance of the 'soldiers' created something of a stir, drawing attention from the departing ambulance. Stalking forward, sabre held in the regulation manner as it dangled sheathed on his weapon belt's slings. Corbeau halted his men. Apart from the buttons, everything looked just right. Kincaid, with a sergeant's chevrons on his sleeves, toted a revolver in the traditional close-topped Cavalry holster. Although the rest of the party also dis-

* A description of a Rocker ambulance is given in: *HOUND DOG MAN*.

played holstered sidearms they each had a Springfield single-shot carbine hanging by its sling at their right sides.* While the men had wished to carry either *Chassepot* or Henry rifles, Dusty Fog had pointed out that they would lose credibility by doing so. Having a few Springfield carbines, de Richelieu had overruled their objections and insisted that the single-shot weapons were taken.

The small Texan had tried to visualize every eventuality and eliminate, as far as possible, the danger to his friends. While not gun-fighters in the accepted sense of the word, Shangai Pierce, Miffin Kennedy and Richard King could take care of themselves in a dangerous situation. Knowing that they would most probably be outnumbered, Dusty had tried to even out the odds.

'Gentlemen,' Corbeau greeted, addressing the ranchers in a well-simulated Northern accent.

'What the——?' Shangai Pierce growled, looking startled. 'Where did you blue bellies come from?'

'We learned of a plot to assassinate the Governor and the members of the peace conference,' Corbeau explained. 'So I was ordered to come here and protect——.'

'You left it a mite late for that,' slim, wiry, Richard King declared, sounding genuinely bitter.

'Y—You mean——?' Corbeau gasped, acting just as well as any of the ranchers' party, as he swung and stared after the departing Rocker ambulance.

'You didn't come fast enough,' the tall, tanned, well-built Miffin Kennedy pointed out.

'No, sir, but we tried,' Corbeau answered. 'My orders were to take everybody concerned with the conference under my protection.'

'*Protection!*' Kennedy barked, slapping at where his revolver should have been hanging at his right thigh. 'My old hawg-leg's the only protection I——.'

The words trailed off as the rancher's face registered his realization that he was unarmed. Fortunately all three men, while not actors, were skilled in the business of horse-trading. So they possessed sufficient histrionic ability to fool their opponents in the deadly game.

'You said, Mr. Kennedy?' Corbeau challenged; a typical

* A description of the functions of a carbine-sling is given in: *GO BACK TO HELL.*

rank-conscious senior officer who had made his point with an influential citizen and placed the other at a disadvantage.

'All right, so none of us are dressed,' Kennedy growled, glancing at the unadorned thighs of his companions. 'Maybe we'd best do what the captain says.'

Corbeau also raked the party with his eyes. For such an important social engagement, they had donned their best town clothes and none sported the gunbelt with which he normally counted himself as being fully dressed. Young Counter had achieved that most important part of the plan.

Thinking of the blond giant's success brought another point to Corbeau's attention.

'Who were the victims, gentlemen?'

'The Governor, Dusty Fog and Mark Counter,' Pierce replied. 'Hey! It wasn't me who hired those two yahoos who killed them.'

'Or me!' Kennedy asserted.

'I'm damned if *I* did!' King went on heatedly. 'I figured we'd won——.'

Suddenly Corbeau realized in which direction the conversation was drifting. He had only half heard the first two protestations of innocence, being engrossed in his own thoughts. Learning that Mark Counter had been a 'victim' had momentarily thrown him off balance. Then he had understood. That was why the Baroness de Vautour had been cultivating the acquaintance of young 'Caxton'. She had always hated the blond giant, for some reason, and had taken her revenge regardless of how doing it might affect the rest of their plans.

'Who was responsible isn't our concern at the moment, gentlemen,' Corbeau interrupted, not wanting the crowd to think too closely upon that aspect. 'Our informant said that you are all to be killed. So I intend to escort you to a place of safety.'

'What if we allow we're safe enough, way we are?' Pierce inquired.

'I have my orders, sir,' Corbeau replied, pleased that the opportunity to do so had arisen. 'I have to take you, regardless of how you feel on it.'

'And if we don't go?' Kennedy asked.

'I *have* my orders, gentlemen,' Corbeau insisted, 'Under

the circumstances, I would be compelled to enforce them.'

'You mean take us against our will?' King wanted to know.

'If I have to,' Corbeau agreed. 'My orders come from the highest authority.'

'Best do like he says, boys,' Pierce advised. 'Damn it all. I feel right naked without my plough-handle.'

'We have horses at the Charro livery barn,' Corbeau announced. 'Mounts for you gentlemen are available there. It will save us time in getting you to a place of safety.'

'You're bossing this trail drive,' King declared and the others gave their muttered agreement.

Already the crowd was scattering. The few who had shown signs of being interested in the ranchers and soldiers were persuaded to go about their business. That had been handled by Kincaid, acting in a tough, bullying manner calculated to arouse bitterness and remain in the recipients' minds. Without actually using violence, as he had urged the onlookers to get the hell to their homes, he had conveyed a suggestion that he would very much like to. Certainly there had been many hostile glances and muttered comments about 'damned Yankee blue-bellies' by the time he had completed his work.

There was little conversation as the men walked through the streets. As they passed along an alley towards the Charro livery barn, the soldiers slipped the rings of their carbines free from the slings' clips. They held the weapons in both hands before them, but did not yet elevate the barrels into a firing position.

Although the barn's main doors were wide open, and its interior illuminated by lamps, there was no sign of its owner and his employees. The latter had been sent to a saloon and given sufficient money by Corbeau to ensure that they did not return in a hurry, while the former had been a guest at the theatre. Corbeau's party had left their horses, ready for a hurried departure, fastened to the top rail of the nearest corral.

'Your mounts are inside, gentlemen,' Corbeau remarked, his voice showing a tinge of tension. 'If you'll collect them, we'll move out.'

Allowing the reanchers' party to draw ahead, the 'soldiers' followed them into the barn. It had been decided that the shooting should be done where there would be no chance or survivors escaping into the darkness. If Corbeau and his men had been less confident and more observant, they might have seen that their victims were striding out at a faster pace and putting distance between them.

On entering the building, the 'soldiers' fanned out to form a line. In its centre, Corbeau and Kincaid started to draw their revolvers. The former had changed his weapon, producing an 1860 Army Colt instead of the Webley with which he had saved Mark Counter's life.

Something moved in a shadowy corner at the right side and rear of the barn, taking shape as a giant of a man.

Another, smaller figure emerged from the unlit proprietor's office to the left of the room.

Up in the hay-loft, a female and two male figures rose from places of concealment behind the bales of hay.

Flickering his gaze around, Corbeau felt as if an icy finger had rubbed itself along his spine.

Mark Counter moved into the lighted area, uninjured, with his jacket removed and the *buscadero* gunbelt strapped on.

Stepping forward, 'Ed Caxton' halted with hands raised ready to go into sudden, devastating action.

Up in the loft, 'Matt Caxton' stood, with his hands thumb-hooked into his gunbelt, at 'Melanie Beauchampaine's' right side. Winchester rifle dangling with deceptive negligence in his grasp, and his face the cold, savage mask of a *Pehnane* Dog Soldier, 'Alvin "Comanche" Blood' conveyed the impression of a mountain lion crouching to spring from the girl's left.

Shaken by the sudden interruption to their arrangements, Corbeau's party froze into immobility.

Turning fast, the ranchers and their foremen sent hands dipping inside jackets to the weapons they had carried concealed but ready for use.

'Get them!' Corbeau screamed, lifting his Colt.

All hell tore loose in the barn!

Out flickered Dusty's, Mark's and Waco's Colts; in that order. Three double crashes shattered the brief hush which had followed Corbeau's words, being echoed by the rapid blasting of the Winchester which had flowed lightning fast to the Kid's shoulder. Then a variety of short-barrelled, easily-hidden revolvers banged, cracked, or spat, in the hands of the would-be victims.

Faced with the threat of certain death for their friends—or themselves—the Texans threw lead in the only way they dared under the circumstances.

To kill!

Corbeau went down, with Dusty Fog's first two bullets smashing apart his skull. Taking Mark's twin loads in the chest, Kincaid died an instant later. A split-second after that, Raphael fell to the long barrelled Colts in Waco's hands. This time the 'Caxton brothers' had something more lethal than wads of paper ahead of the powder charges in their revolvers' chambers.

First of his party to recover from the shock, Mick had managed to bring his carbine almost to his shoulder, before a flat-nosed Winchester bullet impaled his brain and crumpled him as limp as a disembowelled rag doll.

A veritable tempest of lead slashed its way into the ranks of the Brotherhood. Yet not one of them tried to surrender. Even when stricken, the blue-clad figures attempted to continue the fight. Before the Texans dare cease firing, every member of Corbeau's party lay dead.

The price of the slaughter, and for preventing the possibility of another civil war, had been a bloody furrow carved across Figert's side.

If it had not been for the courage of Belle Boyd, the planning ability of Dusty Fog, the horse-savvy of the Ysabel Kid and the faith of the other men in the small Texan, the cost would have been far dearer.

CHAPTER SEVENTEEN

I OWE HIM MY LIFE, BELLE

Colonel Anton de Richelieu, or Major Byron Aspley, looked up as the door of his study opened.

It was mid-afternoon on the day after the incident in San Antonio de Bexar. He was expecting a messenger from Corbeau; bringing word of how things had gone. Instead of returning immediately to the ranch, Corbeau's party were to head north-west into the direction of New Braunfels, as if making for the nearest Yankee army post. On reaching the Marion River, they would enter and either go up or downstream until locating a place at which they could emerge without leaving tracks. With that done, they would make a long circle back to the Brotherhood's headquarters.

At first glance, de Richelieu assumed that the show's party had made better time than Corbeau's messenger, or were dispensing with his services and delivering the news themselves.

Then certain worrying and contradictory factors started to imprint themselves upon de Richelieu's mind.

The 'Caxton' family came in first, the 'brothers' flanking 'Ed's wife'.

However Virginie de Vautour did not follow them.

That alone was a puzzling development. Knowing the Baroness, de Richelieu would have expected her to be in the forefront of the party; eager to claim all the credit that was to be awarded. She most certainly would not have permitted the 'Caxtons'—whom she hated as a bunch of inferior beings that refused to recognize and respect her superior status in life—to precede her.

'Melanie Beauchampaine', or 'Mrs. Caxton', was wearing a dark blue shirt, riding breeches and Hessian boots, but they were not the sensually-revealing garments in which she was to have appeared on the Variety Theatre's stage. That was not too significant a point. Knowing that they would need to travel fast after they had done their work, she could have carried more suitable attire along and changed at the first opportunity.

None of which explained Virginie's absence.

Nor suggested why Mark Counter should be bringing up the rear of the newly arrived party. The blond giant should have remained in San Antonio, learning how public sentiment was reacting and steering it along the required lines.

On top of everything, the expressions on the 'Caxtons'' and young Counter's faces warned de Richelieu that all was far from well.

'What happened?' de Richelieu demanded, coming to his feet. 'Where's the Baroness?'

'She tried to kill me at the theatre, so I shot her,' the girl he knew as 'Melanie Beauchampaine' replied.

'She's dead?' de Richelieu asked.

'Yes,' the girl replied. 'Your scheme's finished, Colonel de Richelieu. My name is Belle Boyd. I'm a member of the U.S. Secret Service.'

'*Belle Boyd!*' the man repeated the name incredulously.

'I would like you to meet Captain Dusty Fog,' Belle went on, indicating the small Texan and moving her finger to point to 'Matt Caxton'. 'And Waco, of the OD Connected.'

Black rage distorted de Richelieu's face as his eyes ran from one to the other of the young people before him. Then the expression faded and the old, disciplined mask returned.

'I see,' de Richelieu growled. 'And you're in it too, Mr. Counter?'

'I'm in it, Major Aspley,' the blond giant agreed.

'Where are my men?' de Richelieu wanted to know.

'Dead,' Dusty answered. 'Not one of them would surrender, they fought to the last man.'

'God rest their souls!' de Richelieu barked, stiffening to a brace and raising his hand in a salute. 'They died for their beliefs.'

'That's one way of looking at it,' Dusty drawled. 'But there'll be no war between the North and South.'

'Won't there?' de Richelieu challenged. 'Once word of what happened gets out, the radicals and liberals up North will use it against the South. My people here will lay the blame on the Yankees——.'

'I doubt it, Colonel,' Belle said, reaching behind her. She plucked out a newspaper and tossed it on to the desk. 'This is the story that will go out.'

Even before he picked up the paper, de Richelieu saw its headlines.

OUTLAWS STRIKE AT GOVERNOR!

Murderous Attempt At Variety Theatre Frustrated

Reading the story, he saw that there was no hope of turning the affair into propaganda for his cause.

First came the story of the town of Hell's existence, with

hints of the control it wielded over the State's outlaw population. Its organizers, fearing Governor Stanton Howard's strong-minded campaign against the lawless elements, had tried to remove him from office. Fortunately, a warning of the proposed assassination had reached the Governor. Displaying his usual courage, he had volunteered to act as bait for the trap. Apparently some hint of his future intentions—sending Ole Devil Hardin's floating outfit to Hell to reconnoitre and prepare the way for the U.S. Cavalry to bring the nefarious community to an end—had reached the town. So Captain Fog and Mark Counter had also been targets for the assassins. Being forewarned, they had all escaped injury. The men responsible—badly wanted outlaws—the 'Caxton brothers',' 'Comanche Blood' and their two female accomplices had been killed resisting arrest. The same fate had been meted out to a further bunch of owlhoots who, dressed as members of the U.S. Cavalry, had been meaning to murder the other members of the Governor's peace conference, to divert attention from the real reason for the killings at the theatre. The plot had been foiled and the Governor promised an early end would be brought to the activities of the town called Hell.

No mention of the Brotherhood For Southron Freedom. Not a hint that could be turned into a means to arouse animosity between the North and the South.

'Your idea, Captain Fog?' de Richelieu inquired, laying down the newspaper.

'Mine, and Colonel Boyd's,' Dusty agreed.

'Ah, yes. *Colonel* Boyd,' de Richelieu drawled, turning his cold eyes to the girl. 'I could expect such brilliance from the Rebel Spy—But not that she would turn traitress to the South.'

Belle winced as if she had been lashed across the face with a riding quirt. Then her features hardened into a mask as impassive as de Richelieu's.

'I swore the oath of allegiance to the Union, Colonel. And if I'd had any respect for the Brotherhood For Southron Freedom, after you caused the destruction of the *Prairie Belle* and Jim Bludso's death, the Frenchman would have driven it out.'

'The *Frenchman*?' de Richelieu said, frowning. 'What did Victor Brandt do—Of course! Madame Lucienne must have been your friend.'

'A damned good one!' Belle confirmed. 'You say Victor *Brandt* was "the *Frenchman*"?'

That was the man she had killed in the headquarters of the Shreveport military post. An ex-officer in the United States' Army, who had been dismissed the service for mistreating the enlisted men.

'That was a private name and joke, known only to a few of us,' de Richelieu explained. 'He came from the Alsace and was of Germanic origin. So he would never admit to being French. Some of the Brotherhood called him "the Frenchman" to annoy him. He was killed by the Army in Shreveport——.'

'I killed him, as I swore I would when I saw poor Lucienne,' Belle corrected. 'No human being could have treated another as he did her.'

'I'm not excusing him, or trying to apologize for what's been done,' de Richelieu declared. 'It was the fortunes of war. And now, Colonel Boyd, what do you plan to do with me?'

All through the conversation, Mark Counter had remained silent. In his mind's eye, he could see that day during the War when Major Aspley had saved his life. Mark's horse had been shot from under him and he lay stunned by the fall. Leaping from his mount, Aspley had held back the sabre-armed Yankee cavalrymen who had rushed the blond giant. Before they had been driven off, Aspley had lost an ear and received another wound.

'I can't let you take him in,' Mark declared. 'I owe him my life, Belle.'

'What do you suggest we do, Mark?' Belle asked.

'Let him go,' answered the big blond. 'Ask him to give his word that he'll leave the country, never return or try to make more trouble for the United States. Then Lon'll guide him across the border into Mexico.'

'Very well,' Belle said. 'That's what we'll do.'

'How about my men at the camp?' de Richelieu put in. 'I'll not leave them to face the consequences.'

'They won't suffer from it,' Mark promised. 'I'll go over and tell them that the Botherhood's disbanded and send them to their homes.'

'Some of them won't be sorry to go, the way you've been

driving them,' de Richelieu drawled. 'You've done a real fine job, Mr. Counter.'

'My thanks, sir,' Mark said, flushing a little with delight at the praise.

'The keys to my safe are in the desk's drawer,' de Richelieu went on. 'In it, you'll find the Brotherhood's funds. Use them to pay off the men.'

'We'll do that,' Dusty assured the man. 'Now, sir, about Mark's suggestion. Will you give us your word?'

'Would Colonel Boyd accept it?' de Richelieu challenged.

'Of course, because I know that you will keep it,' the girl replied. 'And apart from that, I can't have you arrested and brought to trail without the whole story coming out. *That* would never do.'

'Making such an admission to me could be a mistake, Colonel Boyd,' de Richelieu pointed out.

'You've already thought of it—And know that we, the Secret Service, daren't let you go to trial.'

'What do I do if I accept your offer?'

'Go back to Europe. A soldier of your ability can always find employment.'

'And if I decide to stay and go to trial?'

'Don't, Major Aspley, *please*,' Belle begged. 'If you try, you'll never see the inside of a court. *I'd* have to see to that.'

'You'd kill me?' de Richelieu inquired.

'I would,' the girl confirmed, scarcely louder than a whisper. 'I'd even do that, before I'd see our country plunged into another civil war.'

'I wouldn't want a lady—and a loyal Southron—to have that on her conscience,' de Richelieu declared. 'And I give you my apologies, ma'am, for calling you a traitress. I wish I'd had a dozen like you on my side.'

'My thanks, sir,' Belle said stiffly.

'Do I have *your* word, *Colonel* Boyd,' de Richelieu continued, 'that my men will not be arrested or in any way punished? None of them at the camp have taken part in our operations.'

'You have it, sir,' Belle replied. 'They are free to go.'

'Then I give you mine,' de Richelieu barked. 'May I leave now?'

'The Ysabel Kid's got horses waiting, Major,' Dusty

drawled. 'If you'll come with us?'

'Very well,' de Richelieu agreed. 'But I don't need an escort. You can rely on me to waste no time in leaving.'

'It's your choice, sir,' Dusty answered.

Making way for de Richelieu to pass, the girl and the Texans followed him from the building. The Kid was waiting outside, with two saddled horses.

'The Colonel's leaving alone, Lon,' Dusty drawled.

'Why sure,' the Indian dark Texan replied and handed over the reins of de Richelieu's mount.

Swinging into the saddle, de Richelieu gravely saluted Belle. Then he turned the animal and started it moving. Nobody spoke as he rode away.

Fifty yards from the building, de Richelieu dropped his right hand and thumbed open the flap of his holster. Drawing the revolver, he reined the horse around.

'The South will rise again!' he roared and set his spurs to work.

Bounding forward, the horse carried its rider back in the direction from which it had come. De Richelieu fired once, his bullet splitting the air close to Mark Counter's head.

Sliding the Winchester from its saddle boot, the Kid pivoted and flung its butt to his collarbone. He squinted along the barrel and squeezed the trigger. Smoke wafted briefly between his and the onrushing figure, but his rifleman's instincts told him that he had made a hit.

Sure enough, when the smoke cleared, the Kid saw de Richelieu sliding from the saddle.

Guns in hand, Belle and the Texans ran forward. De Richelieu sprawled on his back, mortally wounded but still alive and conscious, when they reached him.

'Why'd you do it, Major?' Mark asked, kneeling by the stricken, dying man. 'We'd have let you go, knowing you'd keep your word.'

'I saved your life because it was my duty as your commanding officer,' de Richelieu replied.

'And I saved yours for doing it,' Mark pointed out.

'You owed me nothing, I merely did my duty,' de Richelieu corrected. 'If I'd taken your offer, I'd have been beholden to you, Mr. Counter. No major wants to be that to a 1st lieutenant.'

Two minutes later, de Richelieu was dead.

Leaving Mark to visit the camp and send the men home, Belle and Dusty watched Waco and the Kid take shovels to dig a grave.

'It's over, Belle,' Dusty said.

'Will it *ever* really be over?' the girl countered. 'Lord, I hope so. And I hope the day never comes when the South has to rise again.'